A serial killer stalks the city streets. To private eye, Brett Grant, things are seldom what they seem.

When he starts asking questions, the action hots up. The Angels, who run a funny kind of religious cult, prove to be anything but . . . and they don't take kindly to intruders who take an interest.

Not one to be put off by mere terror, the more Grant gets to know, the less he likes. A gripping struggle to the end in the underbelly of city life and organised crime.

Angels of Death

Howard Wilson

ANGELS OF DEATH

HOWARD WILSON

Argyll
publishing

© Howard Wilson

First published 1994
Argyll Publishing
Glendaruel
Argyll PA22 3AE
Scotland

British Library Cataloguing-in-Publication Data.
A catalogue record for this book is available from
the British Library.

ISBN 1 874640 95 5

Cover design
Typeset and *origination*
Cordfall Ltd, Civic Street Glasgow G4 9RH
Printing
HarperCollins, Glasgow G64 2QT

All characters and organisations
named in this book
are entirely fictional.

Contents

PART I
KILLER

1

AS NIGHT FELL, A DENSE NOVEMBER FOG CREPT IN from the Atlantic. Slowly gathering the skyscrapers of New York into its smothering embrace, it choked the great metropolis into a state of catalepsy. The normal night sounds of the city were muted to near silence by the chill grey shroud. Street lights and neon signs were dimmed to isolated pools of phosphorescence glowing eerily in the murk, and the city's life-blood of traffic slowed to a blind crawl through the clogged arteries of its streets.

The fog lay thickest on the waterfront areas, swirling sluggishly along the courses of the mighty Hudson and its twin tributaries, the East and Harlem Rivers. The foul conditions had driven most of the law-abiding citizens from the streets, or prevented them from venturing abroad in the first place. It was an evil night – and a night when evil stalked the streets.

Around midnight, Mary-Lou Evans emerged from the swing-doors of a sleazy waterfront bar on Manhattan's Lower East Side and weaved her way unsteadily out onto the sidewalk. She staggered along for a few uncertain paces before coming to a halt, blinking owlishly around her in a vain attempt to clear her vision. It took her a few seconds to realise, with a sense of relief, that her alarming loss of sight was due to the dense fog and not to the cargo of cheap wine she had taken on board.

Despite being three parts drunk, she shivered as the billowing grey murk closed in around her, enveloping her in its icy embrace and piercing the false warmth of the alcoholic glow which suffused her body. Tugging her thin wrap-around coat tighter about her, she gathered her collar lapels over her nose and mouth with one hand, in an attempt to prevent at least some of the throat-stinging filth from invading her lungs. Now she understood why business had been so slow for the past couple of hours and potential customers so few for her special talents.

"Bloody fawg," she mumbled drunkenly to herself. "Ain' much point hangin' roun' hereabouts, Mary-Lou. Might as well git yo' ass off home t'bed. One thing's f'sure, ain' nobody gonna buy th'goods when they cain' even see what's on offer!"

And she reckoned she still had the goods to offer anyone interested in buying. She'd kept herself in pretty good shape for a twenty-eight year old black hooker working the waterfront bars. It was a hard life but she came from a hard background. She had learned her trade on the streets and back-alleys of the ghetto. She could handle it.

Mary-Lou looked around her, trying to get her bearings for the long cold haul to the nearest subway station. From there she could get transport to within easy walking distance of her East Harlem apartment. Fat chance of a cab tonight, she told herself, so the sooner she got started the better.

The swirling fog was so thick, it seemed to be pressing physically in on her as she peered into it. For one panicky moment she felt that the claustrophobic grey blankness was wrapping her in a suffocating cocoon, cutting her off from all contact with the rest of humanity. A sudden illogical premonition of impending danger brushed her spine with an icy finger, urging her to return to the comfort and safety of the almost deserted bar. Its warmth and light was still only a few yards away from where she stood, undecided and swaying drunkenly, on the sidewalk. Then her natural self-reliance reasserted itself and she fought down the strange unsettling feeling.

"Git a grip on y'self, y'dumb bitch," she muttered irritably. "Damn fawg ain' goin' nowhere t'night. You neither, if y'don' git y'ass outa heah."

She decided to make for the subway station at the junction of East Broadway and Canal. It was the nearest one she could think of, but even so it was several blocks away. She encouraged herself with the thought that once she reached the distant station, she might even get the chance to pick up a late-night customer and so prevent the night from being a complete loss.

Her mind made up, she began walking in the general direction she had chosen. Weaving slightly as the cold night air hit her, she kept to the inside of the sidewalk, groping her way blindly along the frontage of the buildings. Her visibility limited to no more than four feet by the impenetrable grey-black night surrounding her, she progressed slowly from one comparatively lighter patch to the next as she passed under the hazy blur of unseen street lamps high above. Occasionally as she stumbled forward she sensed, rather than saw, other figures passing by in the murk. Shuffling indistinct forms, they drifted past like phantoms of the fog, their footfalls so muffled it lent strength to the illusion, increasing Mary Lou's unease.

Half an hour later she was hopelessly lost. She had tried to hold to her intended route by keeping count of the blocks and turnings but it was no use. The trouble was everything looked the same to her in the fog. In fact, she was certain she had travelled in a complete circle at one point, when she passed a couple of suspiciously familiar shopfronts. To make matters worse, for at least ten minutes she hadn't passed another living soul from whom she could ask directions and this complete lack of even fleeting human contact was increasing her sense of isolation and unease.

Finally she decided to allow herself a few minutes rest to steady her fraying nerves and ease her aching feet, which were beginning to signal their throbbing discomfort at being trapped in stiletto heeled shoes a size too small and an inch too high. Leaning back gratefully against the reassuring solidity of the nearest wall, she pulled a crumpled pack of cigarettes from her shoulder-bag and shook one loose with clumsy, drink-fuddled movements. She stuck the filter tip in the pink lipsticked gash of her mouth, cursing thickly as drops of condensation fell from her soaking wet Afro hairdo and landed on the drooping cigarette. Dropping the pack back into her bag, she rummaged around in its depths for her lighter.

So intent was she on her search for the elusive lighter, she did not see the tall figure loom silently out of the fog and stand watching her from only a few feet away. Dressed entirely in black the man was wearing a Homburg hat which threw the upper half of his face into deep shadow. The overall impression of dark menace was relieved only by the startling contrast of the white silk scarf which covered his nose and mouth. While the scarf no doubt afforded the stranger's lungs some protection against the fog, it also lent him a decidedly sinister appearance. His tall black form was starkly outlined against the faint glow of a hidden street lamp.

Mary-Lou's first indication that she was no longer alone in the night was when she heard a deep voice say, "Allow me ..." and simultaneously a black-gloved hand appeared from nowhere, only inches from her face and flicked a gas lighter into sudden flame.

Nerves already frayed by her eerie feeling of isolation in the thick fog, Mary-Lou's surprise was complete. With a shriek of terror, she shrank back against the unyielding stonework of the wall, clutching her bag defensively in front of her. The sodden cigarette fell from the startled gape of her mouth as she stared, round-eyed with fear, at the menacing black figure which seemed to have materialised from her over-heated imagination, so silently had he appeared before her in the fog-shrouded night. Nor was her fright at his sudden presence helped by her first glimpse of his masked features. Then the man spoke again and broke the spell.

"I'm sorry. Did I startle you? Please, allow me ..."

Snapping off the lighter flame, he produced a slim gold cigarette case from an inside pocket, flipped it open and extended it towards her. As he spoke, his voice seemed to register amusement, rather than concern at her reaction to his sudden alarming appearance beside her.

Indignation at the impression she was being laughed at helped Mary-Lou to recover some composure. She hitched the strap of her bag back onto her shoulder and reached for the proffered cigarette case with an unsteady hand.

"Startle me? Oh my, you sho' did." Her speech was thick from the combined effects of drink and relief. "Lawd, but I thought ... well, I don' 'zackly know what I thought, t'tell th'truth. I bin imaginin' all kindsa creepy things. This lousy weather, y'know?" She waved a clumsy hand at the surrounding fog.

It now occurred to her that this chance meeting might just prove to be her night's meal-ticket and this was helping to dispel the last vestiges of the alarm she had felt. Trying to look coy, she added suggestively, "I mean lotsa things c'd happen to a pore defenceless gal on a night like this ... thank you ..." She leaned forward and accepted a light for the cigarette she had fumbled from the expensive gold case.

The man had stepped closer to her and as she leaned forward she noticed in the brief flare that the hand which offered it was clad in a thin black leather glove, obviously expensive, like the thick black material of the coat. In fact everything about this cat smelled of money – and men with money were Mary-Lou's special interest in life.

Play yore cards right here, Mary-Lou baby, she thought to herself, an' it sho' looks like you jes' might catch y'self a rich fat chicken t'pluck.

She inhaled deeply, savouring the taste of the smoke as she drew it down into her lungs. Then expelling it slowly, she glanced up at the man from under her lowered false eyelashes, trying for a look of smouldering seduction.

The man's narrowed eyes gleamed momentarily and she took this for a sign of sexual arousal. She was considering which of her wide range of verbal come-ons to employ to fan the ember of his interest into a flame of passion, when he spoke again. "Tell me, are you available for hire? If so, I should like to engage your services." His inquiry was so casual, so matter-of-fact, for one startled moment it occurred to Mary-Lou that he might have been addressing a cab driver, rather than herself.

In the course of her career as a well-patronised hooker, Mary-Lou had been picked up oftener than a nun's rosary. She thought she had heard every possible variant of the "pick-up" routine from men wanting to lay her. But this one was so novel it threw her momentarily. She gaped up at him.

"Huh? Come again?"

"I asked if you were available for hire?" he replied evenly. "If you are, then I would be interested in engaging your services."

She nodded dumbly at him. "Yeah, I thought that's what y'said," she replied weakly. Then her sense of humour kicked in and she grinned up at him and added, "Okay, you silver-tongued devil. You jes' talked me into it!"

"Good." He seemed not to have noticed her gentle sarcasm. "How much do you charge for what I think you term 'a short time'?"

"Thirty dollars," she answered automatically. Then, mentally kicking herself for not upping her price by another ten-spot, she hurried on, "But fer a hundred, we c'd go back to yore place an' I'd show you a real good time, know what I mean? After all ..." she waved a hand at the surrounding fog, "this ain' 'zackly romantic weather, is it?"

When he didn't answer immediately but stood gazing down at her, she pressed home her argument. "Truth is, I don' usually op'rate outside when it's as bad as this," she said.

Her sales pitch delivered, she eyed him hopefully. But he shook his head. "No ... my place is out of the question," he replied.

Yeah, I bet it is! The cynical thought flashed into her drink-blurred mind with surprising clarity. Nigger meat's okay fer fuckin' in a dark alley but it wouldn' do fer mister fancy coat'n'silk scarf whitey t'be seen takin' a piece o' black tail back to his nice clean pad! But she let none of this show on her face.

"Okay." She shrugged her acceptance. "You th'pitcher, you call th'shots." She took a last pull at her cigarette then crushed it out underfoot.

He glanced around them. "Do you know of anywhere suitably ... ah ... private around here where we could go?" He drew back the cuff of his coat and glanced at a slim gold wristwatch. "I don't have too much time to spare ..."

"Oh yeah, sure," she nodded. "These streets got lotsa alleys runnin' offa them. We c'd find us a nice deep doorway in one, if y'like?"

He gazed at her for a long moment, shadowed eyes gleaming under the brim of his hat. Then he nodded, offered his arm with old fashioned courtesy and said, "Well then, shall we? ..."

Mary-Lou took his arm, giggling as she did so. Adopting a mock Southern drawl, she said, "Oh my, thank yuh kindly, suh. Y'all makin' me feel like a real ol' Southern Belle, ah do declare."

Without breaking stride, her escort glanced sideways at her and this time she was certain there was real withering scorn in the hooded eyes. Suddenly, for no apparent reason, she felt uneasy in his company. She decided there and then to give him what he wanted, get her money and be rid of this rich white mother as quickly as possible.

They walked on in silence for a few minutes, the echoes of their muffled footsteps fading each time they passed a fog-shrouded doorway. Suddenly a yawning black gap loomed on their right, announcing they had reached the entrance to one of the numerous alleyways which intersected the streets, allowing access to service entrances for delivery vans and garbage trucks. They stopped at the kerb.

Nodding towards the dark, uninviting opening, her companion asked, "Is this what you had in mind?"

"I ... I guess so," she answered hesitantly.

Mary-Lou still couldn't put a finger on the cause of her unease. She frequently used places such as this, in the course of plying her trade, so it couldn't be that. Her companion, then? Compared to her usual standard of client he was a prime trick – but for some reason his cultured speech and polite manner was doing nothing to dispel her sense of disquiet. Her drink-dulled mind couldn't grasp why this should be, although the answer seemed to be hovering just out of reach of her groping mental fingers.

"Very well then, let's go." Her escort's voice broke into her thoughts and she found herself being steered into the shadowed opening.

They had walked only a few paces into the darkness of the alley, when her companion stopped. With a brief "Excuse me a moment," he stepped a pace away and drew a small package from his coat pocket. She watched bemused as, with a flick of his wrist, he unrolled the object into a long strip, which he then unfolded into a black plastic mack.

"Keeps my outer garments clean and dry," he said in answer to her unspoken question. Then, glancing at the luminous dial of his watch, he added briskly, "Right, let's go. Time is pressing."

As they began walking slowly forward, Mary-Lou's companion snapped on a slim pencil torch. Although its narrow beam was almost swallowed up by the fog, it was still sufficient to guide them past the piled-up garbage outside each rear entrance.

Mary-Lou's unease was increased sharply when a sudden burst of scrabbling, squealing activity among a tumbled stack of shop litter by her feet jerked her to a trembling stop with a stifled shriek of terror. In the same instant, the fright served to focus her mind sharply on the sobering little thought which had earlier been trying to attract her wine-befuddled attention.

This cat was too well dressed, too well-spoken, to be the type who went in for a quick uncomfortable fuck in the icy dark of a garbage-strewn alley. Money and breeding always demanded comfort with their clandestine sex. Not cold, filth and rats. There was something wrong here!

This sudden revelation rooted her to the spot, despite the pressure from the strong hand which had gripped her upper arm tightly and was urging her forward again.

To gain time, she quickly blurted out, "Hold on a minute. I ain' bin paid … an' … I like t'be paid in advance."

Her reasoning was that if he responded by paying her the agreed price of thirty dollars, then her nameless fears would be proved groundless. It could turn out that he was just another high-class honky out for cheap thrills and another dirty story to amuse the boys in the golf club locker-room. But his response did nothing to dispel the unease in her mind. On the contrary, she felt the first trickle of real fear coursing through her still sluggish brain cells, as the pressure on her arm became insistent and his curt reply whipped back at her.

"Not now. But never fear, you will be paid … in full." Then his voice hardened to match the pressure on her arm as he added, "Now, let's go. We are wasting time."

As she was forced into reluctant forward motion again, Mary-Lou stole a sideways glance at him. In the dim light reflected back by the fog from the torch beam, she saw his eyes clearly for the first time since she had met him. They were looking straight into her own from under the shadow of his hat-brim. They seemed to be glowing as though lit from within in some strange way and they had the same sort of fixed stare she had always imagined crazy people to have. She decided there and then, no way was she going anywhere with this man. Not for a million and thirty dollars!

She tried to resist the pressure on her arm and another burst of squealing and scrabbling nearby lent her instant inspiration for an excuse to get out of the alley and back to the relative safety of the streets. Once there, she would then be better able to get away from this man whom she now instinctively knew to be dangerous.

Desperately she blurted out, "Wait ... couldn' we go someplace else? I don' like it here. It's the rats ... I cain' stand rats."

Instantly the grip on her arm tightened into a painful vice. Her whimper of protest was ignored. Then the trickle of fear in her mind burst into a torrent of numbing terror as her escort's voice sounded close to her ear in a malevolent snarl. "Why should you fear them, whore? They are vermin ... just like you. Now, move!"

A violent thrust on her trapped arm forced her forward into the dark depths of the alley, her stumbling feet ploughing through the scattered garbage of a toppled pile. The torch light had disappeared, adding to her fear and confusion. But her captor did not seem to need it as he propelled her roughly ahead of him. She moved unresistingly, her legs turned to rubber by the appearance of another terrifying thought which, like a shooting star of ill omen, had just scorched a path through her brain.

From time to time over the past few years she'd read lurid press reports and heard the gossip of her fellow hookers, concerning a number of unsolved sex murders in various parts of the city. True, there hadn't been any of these mutilation-murders reported for some months now but it just could be that the crazed killer – if indeed there was only one – had decided to strike again. And it just could be that a cruel fate had singled her out as the latest victim. This sudden thought forced a moan of terror from her fear constricted throat.

"Oh Lawd ... not that ... not me ... please Lawd ..."

Her strangled plea rose hysterically as she stumbled along but was silenced by the snarling tirade which hissed savagely in her ear.

"Shut up, whore!" His hot breath fanned her cheek. "How dare a pestilence like you defile the name of the Lord in your leprous mouth. Your foul life has condemned you to the abyss, you unclean slut. You have the gall to ask for payment for your filthy fornication? Oh, you will be paid, whore ... oh yes ... you will be paid in full. You will be paid the wages of sin!"

The hissing hate-filled words seared across the swirling chaos of Mary-Lou's terror-stricken thoughts. In their wake, like a comet's tail, came a flash of memory from her childhood. It was of a little Bible tract, which appeared in her mind's eye with startling clarity, the sort of thing they used to hand out at the old John the Baptist Mission she had attended as a kid. It read: THE WAGES OF SIN IS DEATH!

Frantic with terror now, she made a last desperate effort to pull free of her assailant. But to no avail. It felt as though she was being gripped by five bands of steel instead of human fingers.

Suddenly she was thrust roughly into a deep doorway, the imprisoning grip released so unexpectedly that she collapsed in a sobbing, petrified heap in the dark. Her head struck sickeningly, but almost unfelt, against a metal door as she went down.

Frantically she tried to struggle to her feet but her trembling legs refused to obey the commands being screamed at them by her brain. She fell back into a crouching position against the metal surface of the door. Raising her hands defensively before her, she sobbed hysterically in her terror, hot tears coursing down her cheeks, painting blue streaks of eye-shadow down to her jaw-line.

"Please don' hurt me ... I'll do anythin' you want ... you don' have to ..."

Her terrified pleading was suddenly cut off by the black gloved fist which smashed brutally into her mouth, splitting her lips and breaking several teeth under its impact. Her head spun crazily. Then as it cleared she realised she was standing upright again, held in position against the steel door by the choking grip clamped round her throat.

All she could see of her assailant was his dark outline towering over her. A menacing black form, relieved only by the pale blur of the silk scarf covering his mouth – and by those terrible glowing eyes. As she stared into their depths, she could read no hope of pity in the smouldering hellfires burning there. Only her imminent death!

"Oh Lawd, help me ..." she choked out against the strangling pressure of the grip round her throat, her hands clawing feebly at the slick surface of the leather-gloved hand.

"Shut your mouth, slut!" The cruel grip tightened momentarily, then she was jerked forward and slammed back into the door with stunning force. Her senses reeled again and her throat filled with the salt taste of blood from her injured mouth, forcing her to swallow past the constricting hand in order to breathe. She gagged as she felt pieces of broken teeth catch in her throat.

"You dare to call on His holy name, whore!" His voice rose to a quivering snarl of hatred – but the hatred was now overlaid with a mounting excitement. "You cheap gutter trash! I will cleanse that organ which He gave you for procreation and which you have contaminated by fornication."

As these words fell on her throbbing eardrums, Mary-Lou became aware of another sensation. Something was sliding slowly up the inside of her right thigh. Something smooth. Something cool. Wild irrational hope flooded her frantic brain. Maybe he was after all, just some Bible freak into violence for his sexual kicks. Maybe he was even now groping his way up her leg, working himself up for a good fuck. Desperately she hoped for this to be case and not the unthinkable alternative.

Then the smooth-cool something touched the tender lips of her vulva and slid inexorably between them – and the first sharp sensation of agony lanced upwards from her crotch. Only then did she realise what it was that had crept up her leg and was now pushing slowly into the entrance of her vagina. It was a blade!

Horror seared across her consciousness along with the pain. She opened her mouth to scream her terror into the night. But the black-gloved vice round her neck clamped tight, crushing her shrieks to choking gurgles in her throat. Simultaneously, an unbearable white-hot agony erupted from her groin as the pitiless blade inched its way bloodily up ... up ... up into her lower body.

Her whole world exploded into pain beyond endurance. She barely felt the liquid warmth coursing down her legs, as her life-blood mingled with the urine from her punctured bladder and poured unchecked from the terrible wound inflicted by the razor-sharp blade, now hilt-deep in her lower body. Her last fading impressions were of the virulent snarling hatred in her executioner's voice and the molten column of white-hot agony erupting from the volcano of her groin. Then her tortured consciousness finally gave up its tenuous hold on life and she plunged into welcome oblivion.

Mary-Lou's dying body sagged limply at the knees, dropping its full weight onto the hand which was gripping her by the throat. The killer flexed his arm and rammed his elbow into her chest, jamming her inert form against the metal door. Still mouthing his insane fury into her uncomprehending face, he withdrew the knife from her vagina with a quick downward jerk and immediately plunged it deep into her lower abdomen instead.

Snarling, "Whore! Whore! Whore!" in time with his efforts, he savagely wrenched and sawed the blade upwards through flesh and clothing, until its bloody progress was halted by her breastbone. Then as he continued to heave and jerk the blade against the obstruction of her ribcage, the killer's head snapped back. His mouth opened wide, teeth bared, under the silk scarf and he groaned deep in the back of his throat as a great shuddering orgasm shook his rigid body.

Long seconds passed. Then he slowly relaxed with a hoarse sigh, as his raging climax abated. The insane glow was less evident in his eyes, which were now dull with sated passion ... although not as dull as the eyes of his victim, only inches away from his own. Blankly, he stared into them. Uncaring. Emotionally spent.

He was abruptly jerked back to full awareness when a low

bubbling moan came from Mary-Lou's slack, gaping mouth along with a trickle of blood, as she died. Quickly he stepped back, released his grip on her throat and allowed her lifeless corpse to slump heavily to the ground at his feet.

For the next few minutes he stood motionless in the swirling fog, regaining control of his breathing and listening intently into the night. When he was satisfied that no-one had come to investigate any sounds they may have heard from the street, he moved into action again.

Reaching down with his left hand, he gripped the collar of the dead woman's coat and with a powerful jerk pulled her limp body from its slumped posture, to lie face downwards at his feet. Crouching over the corpse, he wiped his hand clean of blood on her clothing, plucked the pencil torch from his pocket again and snapped it alight. The reflected glow from its thin beam showed his face above the silk scarf to be covered with a film of sweat, the pupils of his eyes still dilated from the effects of his sexual frenzy of a few moments before.

Wielding the knife again, he slit open the back of Mary-Lou's coat from hem to collar, with one smooth sweep of its razor-sharp edge. Then, slicing through her figure-hugging white woollen jumper, he pushed the cut garments away to either side and exposed the smooth brown skin of her back.

Working quickly now, with the expertise of long practice, he deftly slashed a series of short cuts into the unresisting flesh along the length of her spine. Very little blood oozed from these fresh wounds as he inflicted them, mute testimony to the fact that his victim was dead.

When he had completed his ghoulish task to his satisfaction, the killer wiped the knife clean on Mary-Lou's shredded clothing and rose to his feet. For a long silent moment, he surveyed the results of his handiwork by the narrow beam of his torch then switched it off.

Moving a few paces away, he stooped and laid the torch and knife on the ground at his feet. Straightening up, he quickly unbuttoned his blood-streaked plastic mack, and shrugged it off. Spreading the coat on the ground, soiled side up, he carefully peeled off the thin leather gloves and dropped them in its centre.

Unbuttoning his heavy overcoat, he next removed and stepped out of a pair of plastic leggings, which he folded and dropped on top of the gloves. Lastly he stooped and unzipped a pair of clear plastic overshoes from his footwear and these joined the other articles in the centre of the mack. He neatly folded and rolled the garment and its blood-spattered contents into a tight compact package, which he slipped into one of his overcoat pockets. The torch went into the other pocket.

Stooping, he retrieved the knife from the ground at his feet. For a long moment he stood, lightly stroking the smooth steel of its blade with his fingertips. The gesture was curiously tender, almost as though he were caressing the body of a lover. The dull sheen of its lethal edge was mirrored for a fleeting instant by an answering gleam of unnameable emotion in his hooded eyes.

Suddenly he snapped out of his trance-like state, shook his head as though clearing it and slid the blade under the cuff of his coat into the sheath strapped to his left forearm. Then, without so much as a glance at the butchered corpse sprawled a few feet away, that minutes before had been an attractive, fun-loving young woman, the killer turned away and walked noiselessly back to the alley entrance.

Stopping briefly in the deep shadow just short of the street, he checked once more that no-one in the vicinity was showing any undue interest. Then he slipped from the alley, turned right and strode quickly away. He turned left at the first intersection he reached, then left at the next, before he encountered another human presence in the fog-bound night, a staggering old wino who shrank away in alarm from his looming black presence and whom he ignored as he hurried past.

Maintaining his brisk pace, he turned into several streets in succession, putting distance between himself and the scene of his kill. When he had mentally counted off ten blocks, he paused briefly to drop the tightly packaged evidence of his crime into a trashcan. Then he walked away, his pace more relaxed now, and his tall black form was silently swallowed up by the swirling fog.

2

IN THE FOG-SHROUDED DEPTHS OF THE ALLEY, THE first to discover Mary-Lou's butchered corpse were the rats who nightly took possession of the place. These needle-toothed denizens of the dark had crouched, silent and wary in their shadowed hiding places, while Death in human form savagely struck down another victim.

Then they had waited, until long after the sound of receding footsteps had informed them of the departure of the dangerous human creature who had invaded their domain.

When their acute hearing registered no further intrusion into their night-world, another sense took over then – smell – as the rank odour of newly-spilled blood and intestines permeated the foul atmosphere. After a time, the boldest of them crept from concealment, nose twitching, whiskers quivering, red eyes afire in the dark like glowing coals. Soon others joined him. The feasting began.

Some thirty minutes later, as the fog was thinning before a rising breeze, the feeding rats fled with squeals of alarm before the coughing, shuffling approach of another fellow-scavenger of the night hours. The thinning fog was allowing more light from the street lamps to filter into the alley and it dimly showed a shambling old down-and-out poking about amongst the piles of garbage.

Grey bearded and unkempt, he was wearing an old army greatcoat. Most of its buttons missing, epaulettes dangling loose at the shoulders, it was held shut by a length of twine knotted round his waist. His hands were partly covered by grubby, fingerless mittens and his shuffling feet were wrapped in newspaper and stuffed into down-at-heel boots a size too large for him. The whole apparition was topped by an ancient flop-brimmed felt hat.

Old Wally the Wino earned himself a few cents, the odd hamburger or two and loads of free drinks by sweeping out some of the seamier waterfront bars. Then, fortified by his bellyful of cheap booze and pockets filled with the contents of the ashtrays, he headed for his main occupation – scavenging trashcans and the piles of garbage dumped in the alleys by the stores at closing time.

Soiled stock, slightly damaged goods – anything useful – was reclaimed by Old Wally. What he gathered, he cleaned and repaired to be hawked round the bars or bartered for free drinks. During the daylight hours he snatched a few hours sleep in a dingy basement squat piled with partly fixed items like a junkyard, in a crumbling abandoned brownstone tenement. One of the countless pieces of pathetic human flotsam bobbing in the wake of the luxury liner that was the SS Great American Dream, he was like the rats, a creature of the night. And here he was now, searching and picking his way through the previous day's crop of garbage in the alley.

Hearing the squealing retreat of the rats, Old Wally cursed loudly and clumsily hurled in their general direction a shoe he had just picked up. During the course of his years of garbage-raking, he had been bitten on more than one occasion by these rivals in the scavenging business and consequently had a healthy respect for them.

He peered short-sightedly into the gloom up ahead, searching for what had attracted the gathering of so many rodents to the one spot. He shuffled a few steps forward, then he made out the motionless shape on the ground. A spilled garbage bag? A pile of trash? A few more hesitant steps – and the object took on a familiar form, even to his watery old drink weakened eyes.

He stopped a few feet away and stared hard. Yes, it was a sprawled figure. Someone was lying drunk, or stoned, by the looks of it – and a woman at that! His bloodshot eyes gleamed as they crawled lecherously over the bare legs and disarranged clothing. Slipping a hand inside his coat front, he absently scratched at a flea-bite on his stomach as he licked his parched lips and pondered his good luck.

Wally had come across drunk females before this, in the course of his nocturnal prowling. Usually they were prostitutes who'd had one too many, or who'd got themselves smashed out of their skulls on drugs. Not only were they easy pickings for him, a windfall for his thieving old fingers, but also – and he felt a faint stirring in his groin as the thought occurred to him – it gave him the rare and welcome opportunity of a sly grope at their defenceless, soft female bodies.

With a wheezing chuckle of delighted lust, he shuffled forward and lowered himself stiffly onto his creaking knee joints beside the prostrate form, failing to notice that he was kneeling in a pool of congealed blood. He reached out to touch her – and froze in shock!

He was momentarily incapable of any physical movement. For the space of two thunderous heartbeats, his outstretched hand hung suspended in mid-air before he jerked it back as though scalded, emitting a strangled yelp of fright as he did so. He stared, numb with shock, at the exposed skin of Mary-Lou's mutilated back and the cruel, bone-deep cuts the killer had incised in it. Suddenly, the full impact of the sight hit him and he gagged, fighting to stem the rising tide of sickness which was clutching at the back of his throat. But he lost the battle as the sour stink of congealed blood and spilled intestines filled his nostrils and he vomited violently and repeatedly over his nightmare discovery.

Then, choking and gibbering incoherently in mindless terror, he scrambled frantically to his feet and broke into a shambling run – a pace he hadn't attained in years – to get away from the butchered horror in the alley and back to the relative safety of the street.

3

AT THE VERY MOMENT OLD WALLY WAS MAKING his gruesome find, a police prowl car eased its way slowly into the street and began to cruise slowly along the kerbside. The two cops who crewed the car were tired after a long hard night.

Since taking up duty at 10 p.m. the previous evening, they had spent a seemingly endless four hours answering a constant stream of radio calls. They had been sent to deal with incident after incident, all caused in varying degrees by the arrival of the fog.

In the early part of the night, they had dealt with traffic pile-ups, as normally sane drivers lost their vision, their common sense and their no-claims bonuses in short order. Later, they had attended the scenes of hold-ups and smashed plate-glass windows, as the street hoods and smash-and-grab artists took full advantage of the ideal conditions and moved into action.

These street cowboys knew full well that on a night like this, even the mob-protected stores were fair game – not even the all-powerful Luciano himself had ever claimed to have the X-ray vision of Superman. And of course, there had been the usual crop of muggings, although these particular victims received scant sympathy from the overworked cops – their opinion being that anyone crazy enough to venture out in conditions like these deserved to be mugged! And so it had gone on …

Now, as the fog was lifting, things at last seemed to have settled down into the usual boring routine of cruising the silent streets and counting off the long dragging minutes till their shift finished. The driver, Patrolman James Cassidy, the older of the two and senior crewman with twelve years service behind him, was taking his spell at the wheel. He was leaning back in the driving seat, hands resting lightly on the bottom of the steering-wheel, his foot barely pressuring the gas pedal, allowing the car to cruise along in second gear at a steady 20 m.p.h.

His colleague, Patrolman Thomas Martin, was a young keen rookie of only twenty months service. He hadn't yet had time to become completely soured and disillusioned by the monotonous grind of police work. This was his second week of a two-week relief tour of duty, in which he had been assigned to cover for Cassidy's regular partner who was on leave. He was still fresh enough to the job to be affected by the comparatively glamorous image lent by TV and movies to the squad car cop, as compared to his lowlier foot-slogging colleague on the beat. But for now, he too was slumped tired in his seat, struggling to keep his heavy eyelids from closing as he squinted glassy-eyed out into the night streets.

By this half way stage of their night shift, neither man could be bothered with the effort of making conversation with the other. Occasionally, over the low purring of the engine, the car radio muttered statically to itself, as though disapproving of the lack of action. But thankfully it too remained inactive, allowing the crew of Delta-Tango-Six to enjoy thoughts of warm beds and steaming mugs of chocolate, only a few hours away.

Suddenly both men were jerked rudely out of their mood of peaceful torpor, as an arm-waving apparition charged straight out of a side alley and skidded to a petrified halt right in front of them.

"Jeezus!" Cassidy's reflexes averted a certain catastrophe as he stamped on the brake pedal, almost standing the car on its nose as it skidded to a halt, the locked wheels etching white lines on the frosty road surface as they fought for grip. Only a few inches from the dipping front fender, Old Wally stood paralysed, mouth open in a soundless yelp of fright, arms thrown defensively out in front of him, his bleary eyes screwed shut against the glare of the head lamps.

Alerted by Cassidy's shout, in the instant before the car jerked to a halt with its engine stalled, Martin had instinctively shot out a hand against the dash and braced his legs. Shocked wide awake, he reacted angrily.

"Fuckin' stupid ol' prick! I'll fix his ass!" Martin elbowed the door open as he spoke. Grabbing his flashlight from the seat beside him, he ducked his way out of the car.

"Cool it, Tom," Cassidy called after him. "Don' go beatin' up on the ol' soak. It's only ol' Wally Cairns. Prob'ly loaded t'the gills. He usually is." Then more to himself he added, "Lucky ol' bastard."

Martin flipped the passenger door shut, then paused and leaned down to speak through the open window. "You wan' I should book 'im for vagrancy? Or do we jes' take 'im to the drunk tank to dry out?"

"Nah." The senior man shook his head. "Jes' kick his ass onto the sidewalk, so's the ol' fart don' git hisself run down. I don' wan' the ol' bum in the car. He'd prob'ly throw up. Besides,"

Cassidy added warningly, "we'd hafta git the car deloused into the bargain. He's a walkin' flophouse fer lice'n'fleas."

Martin had no sooner digested this last item of disturbing information from his more experienced partner, than he felt a hand pawing at his arm. He turned his head and found himself looking straight into the grimy, bearded visage of the old wino only a few inches away. The combined stench of stale wine and tobacco, body odour and fresh vomit blasted full into his nostrils. He recoiled with a yelp of alarm and disgust, shaking his arm free from the clutching mittened fingers.

"Don' touch me, ya fuckin' ol' louse bag!" he bawled angrily, brushing frantically at his sleeve as though he could already feel the tramp of hundreds of tiny feet marching hungrily up his arm.

He pointed the flashlight warningly at Old Wally. "You stand right there, you hear me? Don' move one step nearer or I'll fuckin' stiffen you! Now, whaddaya want that's so damn important it's worth gittin' y'self run down fer, huh?"

For a few seconds Martin listened with barely concealed impatience to the almost incoherent babbling of the old derelict. Then he caught the gist of what he was trying to tell him. He cut across the torrent of words sharply.

"Hold it ... hold it ... what did you say? A stiff? You puttin' me on, ya ol' fucker?" He looked hard at Old Wally's staring eyes and trembling mouth. He saw shock there, fear too. "No ... no you ain't, are you?" He spoke musingly, half to himself.

"Okay, this stiff you say you've found, where is it?" Wordlessly the old wino pointed and Martin's eyes followed the trembling, pointing finger to the black, uninviting gap of the alley entrance. He looked back at Old Wally. Then almost as an afterthought, he switched on his flashlight and played its beam up and down the oldster's figure. Suddenly his eyes narrowed.

He steadied the beam of light on the skirts of Old Wally's coat and stooped forward for a closer look. Abruptly he straightened with a sharp intake of breath and called into the open car window by his side.

"Hey Jim, c'mon out here, willya? Come an' have a look at this. I think maybe we got trouble!"

Cassidy had been enjoying a quiet smoke, lost in his own thoughts and not really paying much attention to the events outside the car. As the sound of his partner's summons broke into his reverie, he sighed in exasperation, grabbed his flashlight and climbed grudgingly from the warmth of the vehicle. He listened, sceptically at first but then with quickening interest as Martin repeated Old Wally's tale. Then he followed Martin's pointing finger down the torch beam.

With a muttered, "What th'fuck ..." Cassidy crouched down for a closer look. For a long moment he stared at the unmistakable smears of congealed blood on the loose skirts of the old wino's coat. Then he straightened slowly and raised his eyebrows expressively at his partner. Both men turned their attention back to Old Wally. The oldster was standing silent and shivering in the cold night with an air of puzzlement about him, as the cops first inspected his coat skirts, then stood staring at him as though he'd just sprouted horns.

Cassidy broke the silence. "Wally," he started carefully, not wanting to frighten the old guy into clamming up on him. "You say you've jes' found a stiff in the alley over there, right?"

The old man nodded jerkily. "Okay ... so tell me about it. Exactly how'd ya come t'find it, huh?"

"Well ... Mister Cassidy sir ... I wuz jes' havin' a look roun', see, fer anythin' useful ... y'know ... an' there she wuz ... jes' layin' there. It's ... it's a female wummin' ... an' she's cut up sump'n awful ... cut all over, she is. I got an awful scare, I kin tell ya. It's da wust thing I've ever seen, an' I've seen plen'y in my time ..." The words tumbled out in fits and starts at first then began to speed up as relief loosened his tongue from the aftermath of shock.

"Okay Wally, take it easy." Cassidy spoke reassuringly then continued in the same even tone, "How'd ya git the blood on your coat, Wally?" He pointed downwards.

"Huh?" The oldster looked down, gaping blankly at his blood-smeared coat front. Then his head jerked up again. He looked wildly from one cop to the other, blinking rapidly, watery-eyed in the strong reflected light of the flash lamp. Then his face cleared as he remembered.

"Oh ... that musta happened when I knelt down aside 'er ... ah ... t'see if she wuz hurt ... or anythin' ..." he tailed off weakly.

"Yeah sure," Martin sneered in disbelief. "T'see if she'd anythin' worth rollin' 'er for, you mean!"

Cassidy ignored his partner's comment and gestured towards the alley. "Okay Wally, let's go see this stiff you've found us."

Old Wally realised he was being asked to go back into the menacing black gap from which he had just fled. His mouth began to tremble with sudden alarm and he spread his hands in a gesture of appeal.

"Please, Mister Cassidy sir, I didn' do nuthin', so help me," he whined. "You ain' got no call t'make me go back in there. I never done 'er no harm ... honest t'Gawd."

"Hey Wally, take it easy, willya," Cassidy interrupted him. He kept his tone reasonable, trying to calm the old fellow down. "No one's accusin' you of anythin'." Ignoring Martin's muttered "... yet!" he continued, "But you found 'er, see? An' now all I want you to do is show me where she is. That's all. Okay?"

Somewhat reassured both by Cassidy's manner and by the presence of the two cops, Old Wally turned and reluctantly led the way back into the alley, his path lit this time by the brilliant beams of the powerful flashlights. The bobbing cone of combined light from the two lamps cut through the last traces of fog, turning the garbage-strewn alley into a stark contrast of glaring brightness and dancing black shadows as the little party advanced. But as soon as the moving swathe of light touched the outstretched form up ahead, Old Wally stopped dead in his tracks.

"There she is, Mister Cassidy. Please ... I don' wanna see it again. Don' make me. It made me sick to my stummick the fust time I seen 'er ... It's real bad."

Cassidy eyed him levelly for a moment, then made his mind up. "Okay Wally. But you stay right here till I git back to you. You'll hafta give a statement to the Homicide boys, tellin' 'em how you found the body. You're a material witness now. So, stay put, okay?" he ordered firmly.

"Sure thing, Mister Cassidy. I'll be right here when y'want me," the old wino replied, obviously relieved. He lowered himself stiffly onto a trashcan and began rummaging in his pockets for the makings.

Leaving Old Wally sitting there, the two cops picked their way gingerly forward, taking care not to disturb anything, over the last few yards to where the corpse lay sprawled in undignified death. They came to a halt a couple of feet away, just beyond the pool of congealed blood which had spread from the underside of the mutilated body. The twin beams of their flashlights showed up the details of the carnage in all their horrific clarity. Cassidy stared, speechless. He felt the hairs rise on the back of his neck. Then, realising he was holding his breath, he let it out through his clenched teeth with a little hissing sound. He had seen some gruesome sights in his twelve years of service. But this one was bad.

He became aware of Martin's harsh breathing by his side, then the younger cop's voice, strangely tight, grated out, "Oh Jeezus! What kinda sick fucker coulda done this?"

There was a pause before Martin asked in the same tight voice, "Hey Jim, what's that kinda bluish-pink stuff beside 'er? ... It's not? ..." His question hung unfinished on the night air with the last drifting wisps of fog.

Cassidy leaned forward for a closer look then straightened up. "Guts," he confirmed tersely. "Tell you one thing," he added partly to himself, "they ain' gonna hafta do much cuttin' at the autopsy. Looks t'me like the fucker's already done most of it for 'em. Fact is, they'll hafta do the autopsy in reverse ... they'll hafta stuff 'er guts back in, insteada takin' 'em out!"

Suddenly and without warning, Martin threw up. A stream of vomit, bright and steaming in the flashlight beams, splattered neatly across the corpse to join Old Wally's earlier contribution.

"Fuck sake!" snarled Cassidy thickly, fighting down a similar urge. "Homicide'll jes' love that. Why don'chya have a fuckin' crap on it while you're at it?"

Ashen-faced, Martin turned away, retching uncontrollably. Cassidy shoved him towards the alley wall, with the unsympathetic comment, "If you're gonna throw up, go do it over there."

Forcing himself to assume a detached coolness he didn't feel,

Cassidy swept the immediate area with his flashlight beam, satisfying himself there was no weapon lying around. He then stepped carefully round the corpse and walked the length of the alley, flashing his light into every doorway. As he did so he kept his free hand on the butt of his holstered gun. He experienced a feeling of relief when the last recessed opening revealed nothing – or no-one – to his probing light. Cassidy felt that the maniac who'd butchered the girl back there was someone he'd prefer not to have to confront.

Spinning on his heel, he retraced his steps. As he passed his colleague, who was leaning weakly against the far wall, he called out, "Stay here with the stiff, Tom. I'll go call Homicide an' git the show on the road."

He didn't wait for a reply – nor was there any forthcoming. Making his way back to the parked car, Cassidy passed Old Wally and signed for him to follow. As he walked on, he lifted his uniform cap from his greying hair and mopped the cold sweat from his forehead with the back of his hand. He made himself take deep breaths of the cold pre-dawn air to calm his heaving stomach. The sound of dry retching followed him faintly along the alley and back to the street.

4

THE BRIGHT OVERHEAD LIGHTS REFLECTED COLDLY back from the white tiled walls of the city morgue. It gleamed on the stainless steel surfaces of the refrigerated pull-out drawers which lined the body-storage area four rows high. One of these was open and fully extended into the room, its silent occupant covered by a sheet, an indication that the body was about to be viewed by someone other than morgue staff or medical personnel.

On the front of the drawer, a small white card headed by a date of admission and serial number, gave brief known particulars of the deceased. Under the name, EVANS Mary Louise, were listed her date of birth and an East 106th Street address in the Harlem ghetto. Under this was stamped in red – SUBJECT OF HOMICIDE INVESTIGATION – STRICTLY NO DISPOSAL WITHOUT SIGNED AUTHORISATION OF DISTRICT ATTORNEY.

Standing alongside the shrouded form was a young black doctor wearing a white lab coat. A pair of gold-rimmed glasses lent him a mature and somewhat studious air. He was holding a clipboard, on which he was adding a few final notes to the record of his recent examination of the body. As he wrote, his smooth features were drawn into a frown of concentration.

Hearing the sound of approaching voices, he looked up as the double doors were pushed open on their pneumatic hinges and two men entered the room. Both were wearing overcoats which were unbuttoned and hanging open. The older of the two was carrying a soft hat in one hand and doing most of the talking. A burly six-footer somewhere in his late forties, this individual broke off in mid-sentence when he spotted the white-coated doctor over by the body. A smile of recognition lit up his craggy features, completely altering his habitually sour expression.

"Hi Jim," he greeted the doctor with easy familiarity. "Thought we'd find you here." He gestured round the otherwise empty room and continued, "I take it my tame cowboy sidekick hasn't put in an appearance yet?"

"Hi Ben, I've been expecting you." The young doctor returned the greeting affably. "No, Tex hasn't arrived yet. I imagine he won't be far behind you though. I told Homicide to call him out along with you, just as soon as I saw the …" He hesitated, his eyes flicking momentarily in the direction of the third man, then finished guardedly, "the … ah … case was one of yours."

Detective Lieutenant Bernard Curtis caught the look the doctor had aimed at the younger man by his side.

"It's okay Jim," he reassured the doctor, "you can speak freely in front of Brett. He's an old friend of mine. Ex-colleague, actually." Indicating his companion with a flap of his hat he continued, "Like you t'meet Brett Grant. He's gone private now. One of the glamour boys y'see on TV. Y'know the sorta thing … us dumb cops do all th'leg work, an' then he steps in at the last moment, tells us where we've fucked up, solves the crime in five minutes flat, an' leaves with the good-lookin' dame."

Curtis then turned to his companion, who was grinning good naturedly at this description. This time the hat flapped in the doctor's direction. "Brett, like you t'meet Doctor James Easton. Unlike the rest of the sawbones from the Medical Examiner's Office, he actually describes things to us ordinary mortals in plain language, insteada goin' on like a walkin' medical textbook an' spoutin' Latin at us."

As Easton and Grant shook hands, the doctor nodded in Curtis's direction and commented smilingly, "Get him! The truth is he's attended so many autopsies he could lecture the M.E.O.'s staff on pathology!"

Introductions over, Curtis once again addressed himself to the doctor. "Brett an' me were havin' us a little reunion at my place with our womenfolk, when I got your call. So I took the opportunity t'bring 'im along. He used t'be my Squad partner some five years back but he left the force jes' before these killin's started. In his line of work he picks up a lotta information from people who wouldn' be seen dead talkin' to a cop – a real cop, that is. So, with a bitta luck, he might jes' pick up somethin' we'd miss. It's worth a try." He paused, then added bitterly, "Y'see, I'd sure like to nail the bastard who's doin' this …" he nodded at the sheeted form.

The doctor nodded his agreement and Curtis concluded, "So I'd appreciate it if you'd give us a quick run-down on what you've found so far, Jim. For Brett's benefit, as well as my own. I want 'im to see first hand what we're up against here."

"No problem, Ben …" Easton began, but before he could continue, the double doors swung open again and their heads turned as a tall young man hurried into the room. Two inches taller than Grant's six feet two, the newcomer was fair-haired and clean shaven and looked to be in his late twenties. He covered the distance to the others in a few long-legged strides. Joining the group, he nodded affably and greeted them in a slow drawl that was pure east Texas.

"Howdy y'all." Then to Curtis he added, "Sorry I'm late, Chief. Got m'self lost in th'damn fawg. It's still layin' purty thick out Brooklyn way. I did me a complete circle at one point, an' found m'self headin' fer Staten Island."

"Typical!" grunted Curtis. "I'd be willin' t'bet that's how your folks wound up in Texas in th'first place. They wuz prob'ly headin' fer the California gold-fields in their covered wagon, an' took a left at Nebraska by mistake."

Turning to Grant, Curtis continued without a break, "Brett, this is our tame cowboy cop all th'way from the Lone Star State. Detective Robert Edward Lee Turner, would y'believe? 'Tex' to you." Then to Turner he said, "Tex, like you t'meet Brett Grant, my ex-partner."

Turner stepped forward and with an affable grin engulfed Grant's hand in a strong grip. "Pleased t'make yore acquaintance, Brett. Heard a deal about yuh from the Chief here. You've gone private now, aint'ya? Heck, I've never met me a real live private eye till now. Only seen 'em on TV. D'you prefer it to workin' on the Force?"

Grant rescued his hand before its circulation got cut off entirely. He shrugged. "Well ... yes and no. It has its good points, like being your own boss, an' makin' your own hours. The money's better too, I must admit. But despite what Ben here'd have you believe, it ain't much like what you see on TV. Fact is, most of the work's pretty damn boring."

"So what's new?" growled Curtis sourly. He went on, "Anyhow, excuse me interruptin' jes' when you two wuz gittin' on so well, but we got us some more urgent matters to attend to fer now. Okay Jim, go ahead. Whenever you're ready."

Grant and Turner grinned self-consciously at each other like two school kids caught talking in class and moved to join Curtis and the doctor in a group around the open body-drawer. Easton glanced round the group.

"I'll run you through my preliminary findings, gentlemen. But you must bear in mind that these are only my opinions for the moment, based only on a superficial examination of the corpse. I won't be able to reach any definite conclusions until after the autopsy later today." The others nodded their understanding.

Consulting his clipboard, Easton cleared his throat and began briskly. "Right ... the body is that of a twenty-eight year old negress, identified from police records as one Mary Louise Evans."

Curtis met Grant's eye and in answer to his unspoken question, grunted, "Hooker ... ten cons."

The young doctor's voice picked up smoothly from where he had left off. "The deceased was generally in good physical condition, if a little under-nourished. No track marks anywhere to indicate intravenous injection of drugs, but slight deterioration of the lining of the nasal passages suggests a habit of some kind, which she satisfied by snorting, rather than mainlining, to use the current jargon. Traces of alcohol in the mouth suggests that she had been drinking not long before her death. Analysis of the blood samples I've taken will confirm the presence and levels of any alcohol or drugs in her system.

"Now, as to the probable time of death. Allowing for a slightly more rapid rate of cooling, due to the low atmospheric temperature at the locus, I'd estimate death occurred some two to three hours before the body was discovered. That would place the time of death somewhere around midnight, by my initial reckoning."

Easton paused and laid the clipboard on a nearby trolley. Grant's eyes followed the doctor's slim fingers as they reached for the edge of the sheet covering the body, and he resisted a feeling of apprehension. He always felt slightly squeamish when confronted by corpses. It was something he'd never been able to overcome during the ten years he'd spent as a cop – a period of his life when he'd been faced with the mangled and mutilated results of violent death more times than he cared to recall. Unconsciously, he clenched his jaw muscles as he steeled himself against showing any reaction. Even so, he was still totally unprepared for what was to come.

"Now, as to the probable cause of death ..." As he spoke, Easton drew the sheet downwards to the foot of the drawer, exposing the mutilated horror underneath to their full view.

In death, Mary-Lou's black skin had taken on a greyish pallor. Her mouth stretched wide in a soundless scream of agony, displaying broken front teeth and split, blood-encrusted lips. The swollen protruding tongue and bulging eyes added to the horrific appearance of her once attractive features.

But the distorted face was nothing compared to the sight of her mutilated body. It gaped obscenely open down its entire length, exposing glistening intestines which had been rudely stuffed back in by the paramedics at the murder scene. The great ragged wound ran from a point midway between the flattened breasts, down as far as the dark triangle of pubic hair.

"Jeezus!" The involuntary exclamation hissed from between Grant's clenched teeth.

Grant's shock was mirrored in Turner's face. The tall detective paled visibly beneath his tan and he looked up at Curtis. "This 'un's the worst yet, Chief," he said hoarsely.

To Grant he added, "Like I told you on the way here Brett, all the previous fourteen victims of this particular screwball have suffered multiple stab wounds. Some he's mutilated in various ways. An' each case has gotten progressively worse than the ones before. Last one had a hundred an' twenty holes in 'er, an' both tits cut off. But this is the first one he's gutted!"

With an effort, Grant tore his fascinated gaze from the mute evidence of the killer's savage butchery and looked up. He blinked as though clearing his vision and licked dry lips before speaking. "How d'you know they've all been the work of one killer? You said something to me about some … common factors or other, if I remember correctly?"

"That's right," replied Curtis. "An' I'll show you inna coupla minutes. But first I'll let the doc' here take us up to that point."

The lieutenant turned to Easton with a wry grin. "Sorry Jim. We must sound like a buncha nuns who've jes' found a used rubber in th'Convent can. Go ahead with your report an' don' mind us – if it gits too heavy, we'll jes' pass out an' lie quiet till you've finished."

Easton smiled. "That's okay, Ben. Your reactions are perfectly normal. For the record, it would have been more disturbing if any of you had shown no reaction at all. Now, where was I …

ah yes, the probable cause of death ... this would appear to have been due to extensive abdominal injuries." He indicated the mutilated corpse with a sweep of his hand. "These have obviously been inflicted by an extremely sharp instrument. In this case, I'd say a knife with a blade of not less than four inches in length ... probably more, I'd guess at something nearer six. It was inserted here, in the lower abdomen ..." he pointed, "and then drawn with considerable force up to the sternum here ..." his hovering finger traced the path of the gaping wound as far as the ribcage, "causing extensive loss of blood and massive damage to the internal organs, during its passage."

Here Easton paused and met Curtis's eye significantly, before continuing, "My initial examination has also revealed one other severe internal injury inflicted by the weapon. Because of the nature of this injury, it is not visible, but it is undoubtedly one of your ... ah ... common factors, Ben." As he spoke, his free hand indicated the region of the corpse's groin.

Curtis's eyes narrowed in understanding. His mouth tightened but otherwise his craggy face remained expressionless. When he spoke, his voice betrayed his anger and disgust.

"He stuck it up 'er! Right?" The words fell harshly into the silence of the white tiled room. The young doctor nodded silently in return.

Turning to Grant, Curtis explained, "He does it to 'em all. Knife up the cunt. It's one of his trademarks you might say ... one of the common factors." He emphasised the words bitterly.

One of them? What are the others?" Grant asked. He didn't feel all that keen on learning the answer to his question, even as he asked it.

Instead of answering him, Curtis turned to Easton. "You ready to turn 'er over yet, Jim?" He indicated the body with a jerk of his head.

"In a moment, Ben. There's just one other thing I'd like to show you before that," replied Easton. "Look here ... and here ... at these bruises. Familiar pattern?" As he spoke he pointed out the areas of the corpse's throat and upper chest. "Once again, as on previous victims, we have here pretty conclusive evidence that our killer is someone possessed of considerable physical strength. As before in those cases, he has been able to pin a live victim upright – either struggling or unconscious, it hardly matters which – with one hand, while wielding the murder weapon with the other. He is also right-handed, because in all cases he has used the left hand to grip the victim and the right hand to wield the weapon. So, I would surmise from all that we know so far, that we are looking for a tall man, say at least six feet tall, well built, with powerful hands and arms."

"You say he, Doc'?" queried Grant. "I agree the evidence seems to support your theory of a physically powerful male killer. But have you considered the possibility that your killer might be a female? I've come across some pretty powerful bulldykes in my time."

Before Easton could comment on this, Curtis replied for him. "If that were th'case, then this fuckin' dyke must be built like Godzilla," he growled. "Cuz she wears size eleven in male shoes. We've found footprints at some of the murder scenes. But havin' said that," he added sourly, "with my luck, the killer's prob'ly an insane midget with long arms an' big feet!"

The others chuckled at his cynicism, Grant and Turner in particular, glad of anything which distracted them, even momentarily, from the gruesome human remains in their midst. Their relief was only temporary however, as they now found themselves watching Easton close the gaping wound in the corpse's abdomen, by deftly criss-crossing broad strips of adhesive medical tape along its length. He finished and straightened up.

"Now, if you'd give me a hand to turn her over please, gentlemen ..."

The others moved to help, each one suppressing a natural reluctance to touch the cold, stiffening flesh. When the body was manhandled over into position, Grant stared at the newly revealed line of cuts which ran the entire length of the back. They began between the shoulder blades and ended just above the swell of the buttocks.

"Take a good look, Brett." Curtis's rasping voice broke the sudden stillness which had fallen over the room. "This the main common factor that confirms every one of these killin's as the work of one man. He's done the same to 'em all. First the knife up the snatch. Then he stabs 'em to death. Then this ..." He gestured at the body.

"And you say he's done fifteen, including this one?" asked Grant numbly. Curtis nodded and Grant continued, "Then, how have you managed to keep the press off the scent all this time?"

"Only cuz no-one's made the connection yet," Curtis replied. "An' Christ help us if they do – we'd be crow meat! The only thing savin' our asses right now is the fact that our man operates right across the whole city, an' he don' seem to follow any pattern of movement either. At least, none we've bin able to work out."

"How about the intervals between his attacks?" asked Grant.

Curtis pursed his lips and shook his head. "Irregular," he grunted. "Same as the locus of each killin'. That's also helpin' t'keep the news hounds off the scent. Y'know how these pricks love slappin' horror-movie labels on killers, an' the gorier the better. Nothin' like a little sensation fer sellin' papers. Well, so far they've helped throw themselves off the scent by callin' the guy 'The Brooklyn Butcher', 'The Central Park Slasher', an' 'The Richmond Ripper', over the past five years. That last one had us sweatin' fer a bit, cuz we thought some smartass crime writer would make the connection from that."

"What connection?" asked Grant.

"That every victim's bin a hooker – same as the original Jack The Ripper. Luckily some of 'em hadn't bin long enough on th'game to become well known, so we were able to hide the fact in those cases. But the fact remains they were all peddlin' ass, an' sooner or later someone's bound t'make the connection, an' then ..." He drew a finger across his throat.

Turner nodded in agreement and put in, "Yeah, an' the only good thing t'come out of it would be that the Mayor, the Commissioner, an' Deppity Commissioner Elrick c'd all kiss their chances of re-election good-bye next Fall ... that is, if they lasted that long."

"Yeah, they might even git lynched ... with a bitta luck,"

commented Curtis acidly. "Only thing is, if that happened they'd do their best t'shift the blame first, an' a few other necks'd git stretched along with theirs. Includin' mine, seein' as how I've bin put in charge of th'case.

"Right now, Elrick an' the D.A.'ll be havin kittens over at the murder scene, watchin' the forensic boys siftin' their way through a coupla tons of garbage, lookin' fer evidence. An' if our man runs true to form, they won't find anythin' worth a wooden dime. He's never left us anythin' ... apart from his trademark on the bodies, that is.

"The press'll be there by now too, lookin' to interview anyone who'll give 'em a quote. But I've got ol' Wally Cairns under wraps till the official press conference later today. By then I'll have 'im sobered up an' well coached in what to say ... an', more important, what not to say. These fuckin' vultures kin smell a story faster'n a blow fly kin smell shit."

Curtis finished his spiel and stared morosely at the corpse for a long moment. His broad shoulders were hunched in what was almost an attitude of defeat. Then his face cleared and turning to Grant, he cocked a challenging eyebrow at him.

"Okay Shamus, here's where y'git t'do your Sherlock Holmes bit an' astound us all with yer powers of deduction. I wanna hear what y'make of these cuts. "He nodded down at the body. "You'll notice they form a kinda rough pattern. Do they suggest anythin' to you ... anythin' familiar in th'way they're arranged, I mean?"

Thoughtfully, Grant examined the line of cruel slashes along the middle of Mary-Lou's back. Each cut was a few inches in length, some of them sliced so deeply into the flesh that the white gleam of exposed rib-bone was visible underneath. At first glance the line of slashes seemed to have been randomly inflicted, some vertical and some meeting in rough V shapes. It was the V shapes which gave him the clue. The pattern suddenly became clear, revealing itself like the hidden figure in a child's puzzle picture. He looked up and met Curtis's eye.

"Roman numerals," he said.

"Right on!" Curtis sounded pleased. Jerking a thumb at Grant, he added jokingly to Turner, "See how well I trained 'im."

Serious again, he turned back to Grant. "That wuz pretty sharp, ol' buddy, I gotta admit. I wuzn't sure they were Roman numerals until I saw 'em on the second victim. In this case, as y'kin see, we have two vertical lines, then a V, two more vertical lines, an' finally two more V's." His blunt nicotine finger jabbed at the cuts in question as he spoke. "So, the whole sequence seems t'read 'one, five, one, one, five, five'. Right?" As he spoke, his blunt nicotine stained finger jabbed downwards, pointing out each incised numeral as he identified it."

Grant nodded, his brow furrowed in thought. "That's how it looks to me too," he agreed. He waited for Curtis to continue, but when no further explanation seemed to be forthcoming, he asked, "Okay, I'll buy it. So what does it mean?"

Curtis scrubbed a hand over his craggy features and sighed tiredly before replying, "Now, that's the sixty-four thousand dollar question. Only thing is, we can't come up with an answer worth a bent nickel.

"We thought at first it might be some weird kinda cult sign. Y'know, Charlie Manson stuff? But then the number sequences began t'change. Not every time, though. So far the killer's used three different sequences, all at various times, with no apparent reason for the changes. For example, this is the sixth time he's used this particular one. He's used the other two sequences six times an' three times each.

"It's got us beat, I kin tell you. We can't figger the crazy bastard. We reckon he c'd be leavin' us a message of some kind. Y'know how some killers like t'prove how much smarter than us they are? Who knows? But there's one thing we are sure of. We reckon he uses Roman numerals on accounta they're formed by straight lines – they're easier t'make with a blade!"

The lieutenant repeated his tired gesture, rubbing his hand over his face, before concluding grimly, "An' that's another good reason fer keepin' th'press outa this ... or every fuckin' screwball in th'country'd be doin' it." He turned to Easton. "Well Jim, guess we'll call it a night an' let you git cleared up here. Thanks fer your time. Lemme have your autopsy report as soon as possible."

"You'll have it by this afternoon at the latest, Ben," responded

Easton.

"Thanks Jim, see y'later." Turning away, Curtis made for the door. "Okay guys," he jerked his head towards the exit. "Let's go grab a coupla hours shut-eye before anythin' else happens."

Taking their collective leave of Easton, the other two followed him from the room. They left the young doctor staring thoughtfully down at the line of numerals carved into the corpse's back.

5

LEAVING THE MORGUE, THE THREE MEN MADE their way to where Curtis and Turner had parked their cars. Turner pulled out his pack of Lucky Strikes and offered them round. He and Curtis lit up but Grant declined saying, "Never use 'em Tex, thanks all th'same. I don' wanna wind up like him …" he jerked a thumb at Curtis who at that moment was coughing up a lung.

Turner eyed his breathless, red-faced boss with mock concern as the latter recovered his composure and answered gravely, "Hell, if that's what they do to a man, I might even give 'em up m'self."

They laughed as Curtis cleared his throat and replied sourly, "Very funny. If th'smokin' don' kill me, I might die laughin' at you two comedians. If I have th'choice, I'll choose th'smokin'."

They had reached the parked cars by this time and Turner took his leave of the other two. Assuring Curtis he'd be in sharp at eight – just over four hours away – he climbed into his car, a slightly worn looking five-year-old Chevvy, and drove off trailing exhaust smoke.

Grant settled himself comfortably in the front passenger seat of Curtis's Lincoln. Through the windscreen he watched Turner's car turn left at the next intersection and disappear from view, leaving a faint blue cloud hanging on the air like an after-image.

"He's burnin' oil," he commented, nodding up ahead at the blue haze which was mingling with the departing fog. "Must be needin' a re-bore." Then he went on, "Seems a nice guy. Friendly too. What's he like to work with?"

"He's okay," Curtis replied, squinting his eyes against the smoke curling up from the cigarette between his lips. "I know I kid 'im 'bout bein' a big country hick, but he's pretty sharp when he needs t'be. Reliable too, when th'goin' gits tough. He stays cool an' he's some shot too ... on th'range an' off it ... a real dead-eye dick, y'c'd say. Hah!" He chortled at his own pun while Grant pulled an agonised face.

Then Curtis shot a sidelong glance at his companion. "Only cloud on th'horizon is he's another Mister Clean ..." He let the remark hang on the air between them for a moment, before adding meaningfully, "So, I hope I don' lose 'im, like I already lost another partner I once had ..."

Grant recognised the dangled bait in the comment but chose to nibble at it rather than bite. "See," he responded, "I told you you'd eventually knock someone else into shape – someone who'd fit into your way of working, didn't I? An' after you givin' me all that big daddy shit about what a mistake I was makin' leavin' the force, an' how I was breakin' up the best damn team in Homicide."

Now it was Curtis's turn to pull a sour face. But Grant grinned at his friend to take any sting out his remark and added, "An' all the time, all you were really bothered about was whether you'd find someone else who'd be able to put up with you."

But Curtis wasn't to be side-tracked. "Nah, I meant it when I said it, an' I ain't changed my mind on that score," he replied seriously. "Even after all this time – what is it, nearly six years now? – I still think y'did th'wrong thing, leavin' the job like y'did. Like I've always said Brett, principles're fine t'have, but y'gotta make allowances fer th'fact that other people think an' act different from you. An' it don' necessarily mean t'say they ain't good at their work neither."

The good humour had drained from Grant's face while Curtis was speaking and his jaw had set stubbornly. "Aw, come on Ben. That's crap an' you know it," he replied impatiently. "We've had this out dozens of times an' I still can't get you to admit that cops who're on the take – who accept Mob money – can't possibly do their jobs with one hundred per cent impartiality. No, let me finish …"

Grant held up a hand to stop Curtis from interrupting and went on, "Ben, ol' buddy, you know I think the world of you, both as a friend and as a cop. But I'll never understand how you can turn a blind eye to all the graft. What gets me is the fact that you don't even touch it yourself for Chrissake! Yet you're quite content to be a member of a force where every goddam station house has its fuckin' bagman!" He spat the last word out and fell silent, moodily staring ahead through the windscreen.

Curtis shrugged his broad shoulders. "I wouldn' say I'm content exactly. I jes' happen t'think that it takes all kinds … y'know, live an' let live, so t'speak. I don' like it any more'n you, but graft an' corruption an' bent cops're facts of life, an' y'gotta learn t'live with 'em, whether y'like it or not."

But Grant was on his favourite hobby-horse now and wasn't going to be put off so easily. "Ben, it goes deeper than that. Much deeper. It's not just a case of live an' let live, as you put it. We're talkin' about cops on the take … acceptin' money from the Mob, from organised crime, for fuck sake! Dirty money. The profits from drugs, from vice, extortion, numbers rackets, loan-sharkin' … Christ, you name it, an' if it's dirty enough, the Mob's into it. An' the dirtier it is, the better they like it!" he finished heatedly.

"Okay, okay … keep y'hair on. I know how y'feel about it. But I still say there're some things y'jes' gotta learn t'live with," Curtis reasoned. "Some things y'can't change overnight. No matter how much y'd like to. An' no one-man crusade's gonna do it neither. Remember what happened t'Serpico? An' right now, as I think even you'd agree, graft is so widespread that if it wuz possible t'sack every cop tomorrow who's on the take … fuck sake, you'd hafta call out the fuckin' National Guard. You wouldn' have a police force worth th'name by lunch time the same day!"

"While half your colleagues are on the Mob payroll, you don't have a force worth the name," Grant shot back.

"Yeah, well, that's a matter of opinion," argued Curtis. "I still say there are some things in this life y'gotta ignore, if y'wanna live with the resta the human race, that is ..."

"Ignore? Ignore? Hah! That's rich, that is," cut in Grant heatedly. "As I recall, it was me that got ignored – an' by a buncha pricks that should've been in the fuckin' State Pen for corrupt practices." He lapsed into a resentful silence.

"Only because you insisted on shootin' off your mouth about bent cops on th'take, in fronta the whole fuckin' shift in the muster room, fer Chrissake! An' then, jes' t'put the lid on it, you hadda go an' hang one on Pat Mulligan's chin." Curtis retorted.

Grant gave a snort of disgust. "Yeah, Sergeant Pat Mulligan." He spat the name out as though it left a bad taste in his mouth. "The Precinct bagman. Your friendly dispenser of Mob money."

Then his mood lightened suddenly as he recalled the incident Curtis had referred to and he chuckled as he added, "I sure put his lights out, didn't I?" He mimed throwing a short jab at the windscreen with his right fist.

Curtis grinned at the memory and nodded. "You sure did. An' it wuz long overdue, I admit. In fact, I shoulda done it myself long before you did. But seriously, I still think you shoulda ridden out th'storm, insteada chuckin' your shield in so soon afterwards. That stupid boycott nonsense woulda soon died away. See, th'thing is, it sounded like you were accusin' th'whole shift that day. So it wuzn't jes' th'pricks who were on th'take who were mad at you fer tellin' 'em th'truth about themselves ... all th'guys who weren't were sore as hell at bein' included along with th'rest, as they thought at th'time. But these guys – th'clean ones – they'd soona come round."

"Fuck 'em all! Who needs 'em?" Grant replied dismissively. Then he reached out and dug Curtis lightly on the shoulder. "At least you still spoke to me, ol' buddy. That was the main thing."

"I had t'speak to you ... I wuz workin' with you, remember?" Curtis growled. They both laughed, the tension broken, the old recurring argument shelved again – till the next time.

Curtis drove in silence for a bit, then said, "Well Brett, whaddaya think of tonight's business?"

"Pretty grim," commented Grant. "I reckon you got yourself

a class-one psycho on the loose. I don't envy you the job you're gonna have nailin' this one down."

"That makes two of us. I don' envy me neither," grunted Curtis. "I jes' wishta fuck I c'd crack these numbers. Whether or not th'bastard's leavin' 'em as some sorta message, I got th'feelin' they're th'key that'll unlock th'snakepit he has for a brain. Once I kin establish some kinda motive, at least I'll have somethin' t'go on."

"How about that new computer they installed at HQ a few months back?" asked Grant. "Have you tried feedin' the numbers sequences into that, to see what it comes up with?"

"New computer!" Curtis snorted disgustedly. "Oh yeah, I gave it a try. That wuz somethin' else! You'da thought I wuz tryin' t'break into the Pentagon, fer fuck sake! I even had t'git security clearance, before they allowed me in. No kiddin', I felt like a fuckin' KGB spy tryin' t'gatecrash the CIA Christmas party at Langley. An' after all that, y'wanna know what our multi-million dollar Star Wars kit came up with? Zilch! A big fat zero, that's what. An' that's about the same worth as the useless cunt whose baby it is – namely Deputy Commissioner Jason T. Elrick – another big fat zero."

He drew deeply on his cigarette, the tip glowing redly in the dark interior of the car, then continued, "Then, jes' t'make my day, this smooth-talkin', four-eyed prick in charge of th'place tells me I've 'provided insufficient data for an in-depth analysis of the problem'. I told him if I'da had more fuckin' data, I coulda solved the problem myself, without wastin' my time on his heapa expensive electronic crap. Y'shoulda seen 'is face. Asshole!"

Grant laughed at Curtis's account of his abortive encounter with modern police technology, then asked, "What's with this Elrick character? That's twice you've mentioned him tonight."

Curtis paused while he negotiated a left-hand turn at a junction, then glanced at Grant. "Elrick's new to you – after your time. He came into office last election. Him, th' Commissioner an' th'Mayor, on a Law 'an Order ticket. He's always beefin' about how he'll resign if he don' make the streets safer fer th'citizens t'walk on – that sorta crap.

"Only last month he had me an' th'Captain on the mat. He demanded t'know how come we ain't nailed anybody yet, despite th'fact that th'Captain put me in charge of a special Homicide team investigatin' these killin's. Devlin let 'im run off at the mouth for a bit, then made th'point that even supposin' we had the entire fuckin' NYPD on th'case, we still wouldn' be able t'make an arrest without any hard evidence pointin' us to a suspect.

"But Elrick wasn't prepared t'listen. He's terrified of any bad publicity breakin' on th'case. All he's interested in is savin' his greasy political hide. Know what he says to Devlin? He says it won' look good if we ain't had a breakthrough in th'case by next Fall. See, that's when him an' the other two're up on th'same ticket, facin' the voters again. He's runnin' scared th'press'll git an angle on th'case before then, cuz they'd gut 'im cleaner than that poor bitch back there in th'morgue. He'd have t'kiss his political career good-bye an' start workin' fer a livin', like th'rest of us."

Curtis crushed out the remains of his cigarette and lit a fresh one. He sucked in a deep lungful of smoke, which prompted another coughing fit. Recovering his breath, he hawked noisily and spat out of the window. Grant regarded his friend with concern. "You're smokin' too much, ol' buddy," he remarked pointedly.

"Ah … you talk too much … do I complain?" retorted Curtis and adroitly changed the subject. "Anyhow, what the hell're we doin' talkin' shop? This wuz supposed t'be a social evenin' … Christ, look at th'time!" he exclaimed, glancing at his watch. "Hey, how about you an' Pam bunkin' down in th'spare room? It's far too late t'drive home now. Ruth won' mind, in fact it'll give her someone t'talk to over breakfast. That way, I kin read th'papers an' catch up with th'news, without her bellyachin' at me."

"I might've known there'd be some ulterior motive behind the offer," Grant replied with a grin. Then he added, "Okay Ben, thanks. I reckon we will stop over if it's okay with you an' Ruth. As for our visit, I've enjoyed it an' I know Pam did too … up until you decided to get called out on duty in the middle of the night, that is."

"Ah, gimme a break, willya," protested Curtis half-heartedly. "You're startin' t'sound like Ruth. The way she tells it, you'd think I arranged fer folks t'git themselves wasted, jes' so I kin spend half my fuckin' life on extra duty, livin' off stale sandwiches an' cold coffee ... or in th'morgue, lookin' at things like we got tonight," he concluded grimly.

"Anyhow," he caught himself, "like I said ... no more shoptalk. We don' see enougha you an' Pam these days, buddy. An' this visit's bin cut short by the business tonight. So, how about we git together again soon ... an' a lot oftener in future, okay?"

"Sure thing, Ben," Grant agreed. "I'd be all for that an' I know that goes for Pam too. She's taken a real likin' to you an' Ruth. Tell you what, how about I give you a ring, say ... sometime next week ... an' we can arrange a night over at our place next time?"

"You're on." Curtis accepted with alacrity. Then his face creased into a grin as he added, "I'll look forward to that ... 'specially as it'll be your turn to lay in th'booze." They drove on into the night, chatting amiably in the easy manner of old friends. Neither of them knew it but their mutual wish to see each other oftener was going to be granted over the next few days – though not exactly for reasons either of them would have chosen.

PART II
BETHLEHEM

6

DEEP IN THE UNTAMED FOREST COUNTRY OF THE state hinterland, some ninety-five miles north of New York, was located the headquarters of the exclusive quasi-religious sect calling itself The Children of Bethlehem. A rambling four-storey colonial mansion, it stood black and forbidding in the fitful moonlight, surrounded by a vast, densely wooded private estate. On the same night that Mary-Lou Evans met her death in the distant city, another life-or-death drama had begun unfolding a couple of hours earlier in the grounds of the big house.

The leading edge of a moving cloud crept stealthily across the face of the moon, leaving the darkness of the night relieved only by the dim light of a few stars. In the same instant that the moonlight was extinguished, two figures detached themselves from the ink-black shadow of the building, ran swiftly across thirty yards of lawn and plunged into the cover of a wide belt of dense shrubbery.

The figures were those of two long-haired youths of about 17 or 18 years of age. What was remarkable about them was the manner of their dress. Each was clad in a short-sleeved scarlet cotton robe, reaching from neck to mid-calf. On their feet they wore grubby, rubber-soled sneakers.

The youths crouched low in the cover of the chest-high shrubbery bordering the broad expanse of lawn over which they had just sprinted, their panting breath misting the cold night air about their heads. For long, tense seconds they stared back towards the dark brooding bulk of the big house, etched black against the night sky. Nerves taut, they searched the darkness for any signs of pursuit, their ears straining to catch any sounds of alarm, which would announce the discovery of their escape.

Dangling down the side of the building from the roof, they could just faintly make out the pale line of the knotted sheets down which they had descended to the ground. But apart from that there was nothing out of place. Nothing stirred. It seemed their luck was holding.

As they crouched in the temporary concealment of the bushes, the moon broke momentarily free of the ragged cloud cover. Its ghostly radiance made the looming black presence of the house seem even more menacing. Not a glimmer of light showed from any of the blank, dead eyes of the heavily shuttered windows. Yet, it almost seemed to be watching them like some gigantic primeval beast of prey – waiting for them to make a move before it pounced.

Despite the fact that they were breathing hard from their recent exertions, both boys were shivering visibly – but this was not altogether due to the icy night wind. Fear was the main reason. Fear of what would happen to them if they were captured – and fear of what lay ahead of them out there in the dark woods before they could bring their escape attempt to a successful conclusion.

During the preceding days of careful planning, the whole thing had taken on the aspect of some kind of exciting adventure. Now that they had taken the first steps of putting their plans into effect, the reality was proving to be alarmingly different. The black-shadowed night surrounding them was filled with menace – with real and deadly danger.

Beyond the belt of shrubbery where they were concealed, stretched another thirty yards of manicured lawn. They would have to cross this in full view of any watching eyes from within the house, before gaining the shelter of the woods – the dense, untamed woods which filled the vast estate. Then fully half a mile of hard going lay between them and the final obstacle to freedom – the sixteen foot high chain-link fence which encircled the entire perimeter of the grounds.

That was the final obstacle. But their mounting fear was caused by what stood between them and that fence. The Hellhounds. A killer pack of ten half-wild Doberman pinschers, set loose to prowl the grounds every night after evening curfew. Sleek, ferocious man-killers, these razor-fanged sentinels of the night were employed on dual-purpose guard duty – to keep unauthorised intruders out of the grounds, and to keep unauthorised departers in! And the ten-dog killer pack was somewhere out there in the menacing darkness – now!

As an intended defence against an encounter with these feral beasts, each youth clutched a small paper bag filled with pepper. This they had managed to steal while on kitchen duties, after making their joint decision to escape from the weird sect, run by its megalomaniac creator and leader, the self-styled Prophet.

Since joining as Initiates some six months before, they had discovered to their cost that no-one was permitted to leave the sect of their own free will. Membership was for life. It had also been made very clear to them that any attempt to escape would be doomed to failure and subsequent punishment.

Even if any would-be escapees were fortunate enough to evade the killer pack, they had been told the alarmed perimeter fence would trigger automatically if climbed or cut. Immediate pursuit, aided by the remoteness of Bethlehem House from the nearest population centre, would ensure speedy re-capture.

Neither boy was under any delusion as to what fate awaited them should their escape bid end in failure. The initial punishment meted out to other recaptured runaways had been a vicious public flogging, carried out before the assembled sect members. The agonised victims had then been dragged away and had never been seen or heard of again. It was as though they had simply never existed. No-one amongst the rank-and-file membership could tell what had happened to them. That these unfortunates had been put to death in some way was certain – it was only the method of their execution that was left to the imagination. This was deliberate policy on the part of the sect leadership. They knew only too well that rumour and speculation spread fear more effectively than known facts could ever do.

In the case of the two would-be escapees now crouched

shivering in the bushes, once the initial attraction and novelty of joining and belonging to the seemingly esoteric and exciting sect had worn off, they had soon begun to realise that there was something very wrong with the whole set-up. The cumulation of all they had experienced in their first few months of membership had convinced them there was something more to the sect than merely an extremely exclusive religious organisation. Tightly run by a leadership which was suspicious of interference from the outside world, to the point of paranoia, total and unquestioning obedience was demanded. To achieve this, Initiates like them were allowed virtually unrestricted access to drugs of all kinds, especially heroin. This was supposedly 'to heighten religious experiences', or so they were told. In reality, it was to encourage addiction, thus ensuring dependence on the sect for continued supplies.

Up till now, both youths had separately resisted the temptation, backed up by subtle persuasion, to try anything heavier than smoking hash or dropping speed, and so had managed to avoid getting hooked on any of the harder drugs available. However, this unintentional resistance to the sect's primary control method had only resulted in their being subjected to the sect's alternative method of crushing individuality and ensuring total submission to the leadership – violence. They had increasingly found themselves the targets for physical abuse from the sect heavies who were responsible for keeping the ordinary members in line.

Drawn together by their mutual desire to leave the sect and by their increasing alienation from the other members, the two had become friends and started planning their escape. So far, everything had gone as planned. The break-out through a skylight window of the attic sleeping quarters, followed by the descent to the ground had been the easy part. The alarmed fence would present the problem of immediate pursuit as soon as they triggered it – but right now they faced the greatest danger in the shape of the killer pack out there prowling the woods for prey.

The paper bags full of pepper they clutched so trustingly as they crouched in the rustling dark of the bushes, resulted from one of them having read somewhere that an effective defence against an attacking dog would be to fling pepper into its eyes and muzzle. However, what had seemed possible during the optimism and excitement of the planning phase, had now taken on a very different aspect in the cold, threatening darkness. They both seemed to realise the fact, without putting the disquieting thought into words, that their pathetic little bags of pepper had no more chance of stopping the ten savage Dobermans, if they were attacked by them, than would a lion-tamer's chair a raging lion. It did nothing for their confidence or peace of mind.

The moon slid once more into hiding behind a bank of cloud and the woods beyond the last stretch of grass merged into the starlit darkness. Having reached the bushes without being seen, the boys now faced another sprint across open ground to gain the cover of the trees, before they would finally be safely out of sight from the windows of the house.

One of the youths stirred. "C'mon Tom," he hissed, tapping his companion on the shoulder. "We'll need t'git movin' before they find we've split. Let's go …"

The other youth nodded with an odd, jerky movement of his head. "Okay Jim. You go first." His fear was evident in the tightness of his voice.

Jim realised that his fellow escapee was feeling the strain even more than he was himself and decided to take the lead. He reached out and squeezed Tom's arm reassuringly, at the same time using the gesture to tug him into motion behind him as they ducked their way through the thick bushes. Seconds later, they had reached the edge of the last thirty yard expanse of exposed grass, which lay between them and the dubious sanctuary of the woods beyond.

The black outline of the waiting trees marched off into the distance in either direction as far as they were able to see. The trees – somewhere amongst whose untamed depths prowled the Hellhounds.

Jim glanced back at the black bulk of the big house. Still no lights showing. No undue activity. So far, so good. Facing to his front once more, he raked the dark treeline with his eyes, searching for signs of movement – but this time for animal movement. Still nothing.

"Okay Tom ... you ready?" he whispered.

There was no reply from the figure crouched by his side. Puzzled, he glanced to his right. Tom was trembling violently, seemingly oblivious of Jim's presence as he stared, wild-eyed and white-faced, out across the gap at the trees. Rigid with terror as he was, Tom's fear was infectious and Jim felt its chilling aura reaching out to envelop him too.

With an effort, he recovered himself and shook Tom fiercely by the arm. "Hey man, snap out of it," he hissed urgently. "Don't freak out on me now, fer fuck sake, or you'll blow everythin'!"

Something in the urgency of Jim's voice seemed to loosen the numbing grip of Tom's fear. His eyes cleared and he turned to look at Jim as though noticing him for the first time. His bloodless lips moved stiffly as he tried to speak and failed. He tried again. This time the words tumbled out haltingly from between his clenched jaws, as he fought to prevent his teeth from chattering.

"I'm okay ... sorry, Jim ... it's ... it's th'dogs ... you've seen 'em ... same as me ... in th'kennels ... they fuckin' terrify me ... I can't help it ..." His voice cracked and rose slightly, hysteria riding on the flood-tide of his panic.

"Easy man, keep your voice down," Jim hissed warningly. Then he continued in a more soothing vein, "Don't worry, they won't catch us. We'd hear 'em comin' long before they got near us. Dogs always start yowlin' when they pick up a scent, right? Well, we'll have plenty of time to scatter the pepper on our tracks an' shin up a tree outa their way, till they've lost our trail an' fucked off."

The thought flashed through Jim's mind that he wasn't even convincing himself. But he continued his attempt to talk down Tom's near phobic terror of the dogs, which was threatening to blow everything. Jim, like all the other sect members, had heard the rumours and purportedly 'true' stories concerning the night-time activities of the killer pack. It was even said that the reason recaptured escapees were never seen again after being flogged, was because they were put out into the grounds at night to be hunted down and torn to pieces by the dogs. If even half what he'd heard was based on fact, then as far as Jim was concerned, they were aptly named the Hellhounds – and Tom's fears were more than justified.

Like Tom said, he had seen the dogs. They all had. Every sect member had to take a turn on the work party attending to the vegetable gardens. These were laid out around the area of the kennel compound at the rear of the house, where the pack lay up during the daylight hours. As a result, the work entailed being in close proximity to the tall chain-link fence enclosing the compound with its ten dark-mouthed dens.

It was an unpopular work detail with all sect personnel. No-one liked being too near the big ferocious beasts, who unblinkingly watched everyone with their cold, amber eyes. What was equally unnerving was the fact that they never barked. They just fixed you with that disturbingly intense canine gaze, as though marking you down for their future attention. Their only reaction being bared fangs and menacing snarls, if anyone dared to approach too close to the fence.

Jim decided the best thing would be to get moving. Activity might help to distract Tom from his fear, or at least keep it to manageable proportions. Raising his eyes cautiously above the level of the bushes, Jim quickly re-checked to the rear. All quiet. He sank back into a crouch beside the other boy. One last time he swept the tree-line out front with his eyes, at the same time whispering to Tom by his side.

"Okay buddy? You ready?" He glanced to his right.

"Yeah." The terse reply was accompanied by a jerky nod. Tom was still shivering visibly, his face tight and strained.

Jim decided to delay no longer in case Tom froze up completely on him. With a sharp, "Okay … go!" he grabbed Tom by the upper arm and thrust him bodily into motion as they burst from the bushes and sprinted flat-out for the trees. Fear lent them speed as their racing feet flew over the short grass. Seconds later they were standing a few paces into the edge of the woods, panting for breath.

For a full minute they stood anxiously watching the house, while they recovered their breathing again. There were still no signs of lights or activity to announce they had been spotted. It looked like they had successfully completed the first part of their escape plan. Now they had to avoid the lethal hazard of the fearsome killer pack as they made their way to the perimeter fence. This Jim reckoned they could do by employing stealth and by keeping their senses on full alert as they moved.

Once they reached the fence, they would follow it to a point about two hundred yards south of the main gates. There, while on a firewood-cutting detail earlier that day, Jim had managed to saw part-way through the slender trunk of a young tree, ideally situated to be toppled against the fence. This would serve them as a means of surmounting this final 16 foot high obstacle to their freedom.

They had waited for weeks for the opportunity to complete this last part of their preparations. The chance had finally presented itself that very morning, when the brown track-suited Disciple in charge of their work-party, one of a number of minor-rank heavies responsible for sect discipline, had been temporarily distracted when one of the woodcutters had gashed himself badly with a deflected axe-blow.

Leaving Tom to keep watch, and further distract the Disciple if necessary, Jim had slipped away unseen through the trees till he had reached the nearby boundary fence. There he had hastily selected the tree and prepared it with several rapid strokes of his saw. Then, taking a calculated risk on its discovery, he had tied his handkerchief to a twig projecting at head height from the partly sawn-through trunk. This was to act as a marker to make the tree easier to find again in the dark.

He had swiftly re-joined the others before his absence was noticed, although he had barely made it in time. The Disciple, a shaven-headed, mean-looking black, had just finished binding the injured boy's leg with a temporary dressing, and was about to muster the work-party for a head count, before escorting them back for the midday meal break. The two plotters had then spent the rest of the day in a state of nerves, for fear the doctored tree should be discovered by one of the roving security patrols. But their luck had held.

Now the tree was waiting for them, roughly half a mile from where they stood. All they had to do when they reached it was to shove it over against the chain-link fence, and they had a ready-made ladder to freedom.

Jim turned to his friend with an encouraging grin. "Okay Geronimo, let's make like injuns," he said, assuming an air of flippancy he certainly did not feel. Tom's answering grin was a little lopsided, but he looked less tense than he had done only minutes previously in the bushes.

They about-turned and started to thread their way cautiously through the dense trees. Moving through virgin forest as they were, and with their visibility restricted to a few feet in the darkness of the night, it was rough going. Avoiding the thick tangles of underbrush wherever possible, they tried to pick a path through the few relatively clear spaces, where carpets of leaf-mould lay thickly and helped to muffle their soft footfalls.

After a few minutes, they found the going a little easier when their night vision adjusted itself. They were further aided by the moon's infrequent appearances amongst the scudding clouds, when its pale beams filtered down through gaps in the tree canopy and lit their way. But most of the time, they had to grope their way slowly and carefully from tree to tree, hands outstretched before them like ghost walkers.

Complete silence was, of course, impossible to achieve, hard though they tried. Small twigs snapped underfoot every now and then as they crept forward. Each tiny report sounded like a gunshot to their straining ears, and the sudden rustlings of nocturnal animals in the surrounding undergrowth set their hearts pounding in their chests, in terrified anticipation of an imminent attack by the Hellhounds.

However, despite all their fears and unavoidable lack of speed, they made steady progress until Jim reckoned they must be almost half way to the perimeter fence. His confidence was beginning to increase with every stealthy pace, although his mind was a turmoil of conflicting emotions, as hope and fear in equal parts strove to gain the upper hand.

To reassure himself, and Tom, he glanced over his shoulder as they crossed a patch of moonlit clearing, grinned and made a circle of his thumb and forefinger to indicate things were going well. He was encouraged to see Tom grin back and return his sign, although plainly still nervous.

It was at that precise moment that they passed between two hidden photo-electric cells set at chest height in the dense thickets on either side of the clearing, breaking the invisible beam connecting them. They were quite unaware of having done so. Neither were they aware, above the constant rustling of leaves in the night wind, of the sibilant hiss of the activated ultra-sonic whistle attached to a branch high overhead, as it broadcast its silent message out into the night, summoning the dogs ...

7

SATAN, SHIVA, MOLOCH, BAAL, HADES, LOKI, Nemesis, Kali, Ahriman and Set, each aptly named after an age-old deity of destruction and death – were at that very moment padding silent-footed through the dank woods. They were some three hundred yards downwind of the boys, but moving in their general direction.

They were hungry. Ravenously hungry. But for them this was quite normal. Their keepers fed them sparingly each dawn with only the barest minimum of food required to sustain them, but never enough to dull the edge of their hunger. This meant they were forced to live on whatever prey they hunted down and ate during their nightly freedom.

Hunger breeds good hunters – especially when they have developed a taste for the warm flesh and blood of a fresh kill. Into the bargain, careful selective breeding had ensured that each of the ten brutes was physically bigger and more powerful than the average Doberman. The final factor was that the natural ferocity of the breed had been developed to lethal proportions too.

They hunted rabbits, chipmunks, rats, mice – anything, in fact, that moved and was edible. Occasionally they ran down and killed a deer which had been set loose by their keepers to keep their hunting instincts for larger prey honed, but this was not often. And from time to time, at even more irregular intervals, they received the ultimate treat – human flesh. So the pack had been conditioned to accept that life for them during the night hours was a constant search for food to fill the aching void of their lean bellies.

This particular night was little different from most others. Prey had been scarce. Only a few night-feeding rabbits, swiftly killed, ravenously torn apart and devoured. When the boys triggered the hidden intruder-detection device, the pack was on the move again, the dogs arranged in a loose diamond formation, with the pack leader Satan out in front. Spread out some five to ten yards apart, they were loping through the darkness, noses, ears and eyes questing constantly for prey.

They moved with the silent easy grace of their kind, hard muscles rippling powerfully under their glossy black hides, tongues lolling out from between their slightly parted jaws. The gleam of white fangs could be glimpsed whenever a faint moonbeam pierced the tree cover, eerily lighting small patches of the forest floor, through which the dark forms of the hunting pack ghosted like black phantoms.

Suddenly, the lead dog Satan stopped. Immediately, as though a silent command had been flashed to the others, they all instantly froze into amber-eyed statues. Satan beamed his keen canine senses out into the darkness ahead. Pointed ears erect, he strained to catch again the faint sound which had alerted him. And there it was again … borne faintly on the gusting night breeze came the distant wavering scream of the ultra-sonic whistle, inaudible to human ears at that frequency on the sonic scale but not to the incredibly sensitive canine hearing of the fearsome brute who now stood motionless, body quivering with rising excitement. He used his erect pointed ears like scanning radar antennae, probing the night ahead of him.

The others heard it too, as was evidenced by the low growl which rumbled deep in the throat of Shiva, the second dog in the pack hierarchy. Satan growled sharply in reply and Shiva subsided into obedient silence. Motionless, their dark forms discernible only by the faint gleam of fang and eye, and the misting of their panting breath on the chill night air, the pack waited for Satan to lead.

The big Doberman stood, snout pointing upwind, questing for some more specific information to be carried to him on the night breeze. Training and experience told him the shrill whistling sound would last only for a short period of time. In fact, the device, one of many situated at random in the dense woods of the estate, was timed to operate for only five minutes before cutting off – long enough to attract the attention of the pack and guide them close enough to pick up the quarry.

Suddenly, under the thin ultra-sonic scream came the faint snap of a breaking twig … a pause … another distant snap … then another. Something sizeable was moving in the distance. A deer? Nostrils flaring, Satan waited for confirmation to be carried to him on the night wind. And then – there it was! Wafting into his sensitive snout, with its sense of smell a thousand times more powerful than a human being's, came the tantalising fear-scent of the best prey of all, the tenderest, most succulent flesh of all – the two-legged man-creature.

Hopefully it wouldn't be covered, like the man-things who fed them meagre scraps in the dawn and confined them to their day-quarters, in thick coarse skins, impervious to fangs. Nor armed, as they were, with the long metal rods which delivered burning jolts of pain. But in Satan's experience, any man-creatures which roamed the woods at night were always soft-skinned, defenceless and good eating.

Excitement coursed through the quivering sinews of the pack. They were all tasting the delicious scent on the breeze now. Satan's canine brain speedily processed the wind-borne data feeding into it, and instantly computed the quarry's estimated distance and line of movement. With a low growl, he moved off swiftly on a converging course calculated to bring them into close contact with the quarry. Like a single living entity the pack moved with him, still instinctively maintaining their hunting formation.

As they bounded forward, the scent, at first faint, grew stronger with each eddy of wind drifting through the trees. The provocative scream of the whistle and the snapping of distant twigs grew louder, clearer. Saliva glands, activated by anticipation of food to assuage their gnawing hunger, poured their juices over glistening fangs and lolling tongues.

Suddenly the whistle malfunctioned and cut off prematurely, but in the same instant Satan sighted what, up till then, he had only heard and scented. A reflection of moonlight on white limbs amongst the trees up ahead. There were two of the man-creatures. Rich feeding tonight!

With a snarl of excited fury, he hurled himself flat out in close pursuit. The others likewise gave tongue to their eagerness with sharp growls as they bounded after him, joining in the final chase like a ten-fold messenger of death. And only death itself could stop them now as the kill-fever seized them, coursing through mind and body like electrifying fire. Nothing mattered now but the primitive lust for blood raging in them.

The excited growls of the dogs as they moved swiftly in for the kill, were the first and only warning the boys got that the menace they had feared so much was upon them. As one, they whirled round, caught a brief terrifying glimpse of amber eyes and gleaming fangs in the dark forms bearing down on them, then they both screamed, turned, and ran for their lives.

Mindless with terror, they pounded through the night, Jim a few strides in the lead. But as they sprinted forward their courses began to diverge, as they frantically tried to avoid the looming black trees which leapt at them out of the darkness. They cannoned off them, unheedingly grazing shoulders and arms in their panic-stricken flight from the terrible slavering jaws, now only scant yards behind them and gaining fast. Then fate intervened in a series of split-second events.

Jim's flying feet had led him, quite by chance, along a line of retreat reasonably clear of impeding trees for a short distance. This had opened up a lead of some ten to fifteen yards on his luckless companion, who was racing along behind him and somewhere off to his left. Stricken with terror as he was, the fingers of his left hand closed convulsively on the forgotten paper bag full of pepper. It burst open, allowing its contents to pour out behind him in a spreading cloud.

Then, in a heart-stopping instant, he trod air as he ran over the edge of a sharp drop in the forest floor, and pitched headlong with a despairing yell. His head slammed into a rock with sickening force, and as he lost consciousness he was vaguely aware of feeling cold water running over his arms and against his face. Blackness engulfed him....

In the same instant that Jim fell, Tom, running for his very life only a few feet in front of the fast-gaining Satan, ran smack into the trunk of a tree, unseen by him in the inky darkness. The impact broke his nose and front teeth, stunning him and causing him to stagger blindly off to his left, taking him even further away from Jim's line of flight.

The pack had split into two uneven groups as they followed the diverging courses of the fleeing boys. The larger group of six, led by Satan, had gone after Tom – the other four dogs chasing Jim. Tom's catastrophic collision with the tree caused Satan to overshoot him, and the big Doberman skidded round in a tight circling turn a few yards further on, claws scrabbling for purchase in a spray of dirt.

Baal, coming up fast on Satan's left rear, leapt straight for the disoriented boy's midriff as he stumbled dazedly round to face the oncoming dogs. The hound's outstretched forepaws hit Tom squarely in the chest, sending him crashing onto his back. As Baal's momentum carried him on over the falling boy, he chopped viciously at Tom's face, his fangs ripping away half the upper lip and part of the right cheek.

Shocked back to full consciousness by the searing pain, Tom screamed and his hand flew to his maimed face. His fingers met teeth and gums where his upper lip should have been. He screamed again in horror and tried to struggle to his feet just as Satan returned to the attack. In the same instant, the four rearmost dogs of the group of six arrived and struck simultaneously. Tom went down again helplessly under the force of their combined attack.

Satan went for the throat. But the boy's frantic attempt to regain his feet caused the pack leader's powerful jaws to close instead on the neck muscle, just above the shoulder. With a savage sideways jerk, he tore out a sizeable chunk of flesh and bolted it down, all in one swift movement. But the pain of Tom's torn face and neck was nothing compared to what he suffered as the terrible fangs of the Hellhounds slashed and tore at his agonised body.

Mercifully the boy's death struggles were brought to a swift end when Satan's ravening jaws this time found his throat and ripped it open. As the last vestiges of awareness fled from Tom's dying brain, he seemed to float free of the pain. His fading vision fell on one of the dogs as it lunged backwards from him, jerking free something red and dripping in its bloody jaws, which it instantly gulped down. His final fleeting thought, quite detached, registered the fact that the dogs were not just killing him – they were eating him, as they tore at his mangled body.

Off to the right, the smaller group comprising Shiva, Kali, Nemesis and Set, had followed Jim's line of flight. Suddenly, just as the flying figure ahead of them had fallen and disappeared from sight, the dogs pulled up sharply, claws scoring deep gouges in the leaf-mould, as though they had run into an invisible wall. They backed off, snorting and sneezing violently, as the accidentally scattered pepper seared their ultra-sensitive canine noses and stung their eyes.

Their sense of smell was temporarily lost to them. After a couple of minutes sneezing and pawing at their muzzles, in an attempt to ease the terrible burning sensation, Shiva and the others became aware of the commotion of the kill off to their left. They also became aware of a far more compelling thing, as their noses cleared of pain and their smell-sense returned – the scent of fresh blood.

Immediately, their ravenous hunger drove them to join the others at the scene of the kill and they lunged off to their left to claim their communal share, as was their right according to the ageless pack law handed down from the mists of pre-history. Within seconds they were re-united with the others, and the entire pack were gorging themselves on the still twitching corpse.

For the moment, as they satisfied their raging hunger, they forgot that there had been two man-creatures in the original chase. The other one even then lying unconscious and utterly helpless, face downward in the icy water of a shallow stream.

Its course ran along the bottom of the natural dip in the ground into which he had fallen.

8

AS JIM STRUGGLED BACK TO FULL CONSCIOUSNESS, he became aware of two things – the icy caress of the stream washing against his face, and the sensation of choking. Paradoxically, he was being revived by the invigorating effect of the same water which was also threatening to drown him. Instinctively realising his survival depended on his silence, he quickly smothered his spluttering attempts to clear his air passages and breathed through the side of his mouth which was clear of the water.

Fortunately his shocked brain recovered quickly enough to provide him with instant recall of the events immediately prior to his plunge into oblivion. The memory of the nightmare race for his life from the bounding black shapes with their amber eyes and gleaming fangs, froze him rigid with terror again. He hardly dared breathe, let alone move, for fear his terrible pursuers were nearby, perhaps even standing over his prostrate body. He had no way of knowing how long he had lain unconscious but guessed, accurately as it happened, that it could only have been a few minutes.

With the left side of his face partly submerged he concentrated to hear over the chuckling and gurgling of the water. He strained his ears in an attempt to pick up and locate any sounds of animal presence in the vicinity – either the panting of canine breathing or the soft padding of paws on the stream bank. He could hear nothing.

His right eye was above the level of the water and he now opened it a fraction. Peering out under the slitted lid, he examined as much of his immediate surroundings as he could, before opening it further. No dark animal forms impinged on his limited field of vision.

Despite this encouraging evidence he had to summon all his courage in order to raise his head clear of the water and check the surrounding area properly for any sign of the dogs. His relief knew no bounds when he found they were nowhere in sight. He was alone in the night, as far as he could tell.

He couldn't believe his luck. How the pursuing dogs lost track of him, he couldn't imagine. He was only thankful that they had. Unknown to him, his luck had saved him twice that night so far. The first time when the bag of pepper had burst and distracted the killers from their purpose. The second time when he had regained consciousness the commotion made by the feeding dogs themselves as they ripped and tore at the carcass of their kill, had covered the first faint sounds of his muffled coughing as he fought to bring his breathing under control.

Cautiously he raised himself till he was kneeling in the shallow icy water of the stream. The front of his loose robe was soaking wet and clung to his shivering chest. The moment he sat up, his injured head began to ache. Trying to ignore the throbbing pain, he concentrated again on listening for any noises he could pick up over the running water which would indicate the whereabouts of the killer pack.

Just then, he thought he heard sounds of activity amongst the trees off to his rear and he went rigid with fear. In that same instant, he remembered Tom. Where was Tom? Was he still running from the pack – or had they caught him? If they had caught him, shouldn't he then be hearing sounds of a struggle, or at least of Tom screaming with fear or pain? He strained his ears to catch again what he had heard. There it was again … indistinct and muffled by the intervening trees … unidentifiable, yet somehow disturbing …

Suddenly shocked realisation of what the sounds were exploded in his brain. The low growls, the wet snapping and tearing noises of the pack feeding. Feeding? Feeding on what? The horror of the truth hit him like a physical blow in his midriff, almost making him throw up on the spot. He pressed both hands over his mouth and fought down the rising bile which was scalding the back of his throat.

Shaking with terror, he tried to calm himself and think rationally. He had to get away from his present dangerous location – to put as much distance as possible between himself and these fearsome brutes. He looked around trying to get his bearings. Even that small amount of movement caused his aching head to swim dizzily, making concentration difficult. But he saw that his fall had fortunately placed him out of sight and downwind of the dogs. So, for the time being, he was safe from their sighting or scenting him. It was noise he would have to avoid if he wanted to stay alive. He forced himself to think clearly. The rushing water of the stream intruded on his thoughts and gave him the solution to his problem. The water ... that was the answer ... use the noise of the running water to cover any sounds of movement, until he was safely out of hearing range.

Climbing unsteadily to his feet, he swayed dizzily for a moment as the pounding in his head increased and his eyes blurred with pain and vertigo. Then his vision cleared and he willed himself to start moving. Crouching low, he began to wade slowly along the stream bed, carefully testing each foothold on the rounded stones underfoot, before committing his full weight to them. In this manner, he followed the meandering course of the stream for about five minutes, until he estimated he had put almost a hundred yards between himself and the feeding pack.

The cold night wind plastered the freezing wet robe to the front of his body and his feet had gone numb from immersion in the icy water. Thankfully though, the throbbing pain of his injured head had eased slightly. But he bore the twin discomforts of cold and pain stoically. He knew these were nothing compared to what he would suffer, should he alert the feeding dogs to his presence.

Suddenly the stream changed course, curving away sharply to the left, in the opposite direction from his intended route to the partly sawn tree, which was to be his bridge to safety and freedom. Jim knew this part of the woods reasonably well, having reconnoitred it as best he could while on firewood gathering details. He reckoned he was roughly three hundred yards from his objective as the crow flies, so he decided to head straight for it to save time, instead of making for the fence first and following it along to the tree, as had been his original intention.

With a last fearful glance over his shoulder, he quickly scrambled up the four foot bank of the stream and struck out, treading carefully, in the direction of the cut tree. With each stealthy pace, he fervently prayed that he had weakened the trunk sufficiently to enable him to topple it onto the fence, given his own weakened state. Always assuming he found the tree before the dogs found him!

Now that he was on his own in the night, and with the terrifying knowledge of Tom's fate as an added mental burden, Jim's imagination began to work overtime. Several times the sounds of small nocturnal animals in the nearby undergrowth made him catch his breath in terrified anticipation of another appearance of the Hellhounds. Even the gusting night wind rustling the trees was beginning to spook him.

Despite his growing terror, he managed to cover about a hundred and fifty yards, roughly half the distance to his waiting bridge to life and freedom, when it happened. A night roosting bird, startled by his stealthy passage, suddenly clattered off noisily through the branches of a nearby tree. It was the last straw. His young nerve snapped under the accumulated strain of the night's events. He broke into a trot which got faster and faster, all thoughts of caution swamped by his rising panic, and then he was running flat out.

Whimpering with fear, he raced through the night, wildly dodging the looming trees and crashing through patches of brush, heedless of the noise he was making. As he ran, his mind – his entire being – screamed out the silent words in time with his pounding feet and pumping arms – The tree ... the tree ... the tree ...

Satan, Nemesis and Set had detached themselves from the feeding group around the kill and were thirstily lapping water from the stream, washing down the rich, salty blood-taste. The spot at which they were drinking was a few yards downstream from where Jim had lain, only a short time previously. His lingering scent-trace had puzzled the three dogs at first, but the combination of the cloying blood odour on their own gory muzzles, added to their desire to slake their thirst, had overcome their curiosity for the moment.

Suddenly their heads snapped up, trails of bloody saliva and water drooling from their slightly parted jaws, as the first faint sounds of Jim's panic-induced flight reached them. Their long muzzles pointed into the darkness, ears stiffly erect, canine brains instantly processing the information being fed into them. Movement ... large object ... direction ... line ... man-scent! ... Interpretation – prey ... Decision – kill!

Summoning the others with a sharp growl, Satan cleared the shallow stream in one easy bound, closely attended by Nemesis and Set. Within seconds they were followed by the rest of the pack as the kill-fever gripped them all again.

The fierce excitement of the chase spurred them on as they sped through the night. They weaved effortlessly through the impeding trees, swiftly closing the distance between themselves and their unseen quarry. Then, moments later, for the second time that night they sighted the flash of pale limbs racing through patches of moonlight up ahead. The sighting of the quarry raised their blood-lust to fever pitch, and hurled them forward like ten black thunderbolts as they redoubled their speed to run him down.

Without looking round, Jim knew the dogs were onto him again. Some primitive instinct, an echo from a distant era when man the hunter was himself constantly hunted by fang and claw, informed him of the fact without the need of visual confirmation. The terrifying knowledge hit him at the same moment his frantically searching eyes spotted the white flash of the marker he had placed a few hours earlier. Throwing back his head, he ran as he had never run before – racing for the tiny scrap of white which represented his last and only hope of avoiding an unthinkable death.

Now he could hear the sounds of pursuit as the pack gained on him, and terror lent him strength for a last despairing burst of speed over the remaining yards to the partly-sawn tree. Sobbing for breath, he threw himself bodily against it and felt it give under his thrusting weight. Even while it was still toppling, Jim leapt for his life up the rough trunk, grasping at small protruding twigs and branches in a desperate attempt to claw himself upward, his loose robe flapping around him as he did so.

Satan, closing fast, saw the quarry reach the tree and start to scramble up its sloping trunk. Enraged at the imminent escape of his prey, he hurtled forward and launched himself upward in a powerful flying leap. He struck viciously at the man-thing's bulky shape as it scrambled upwards ... and his fangs closed on cloth!

There was a sharp tearing sound and Satan sailed on past, to land several yards further on, a ragged scrap of scarlet cotton clamped in his slavering jaws. Angrily he shook it free and joined the others in trying to run up the sloping trunk in pursuit of the climbing figure above them.

But the steep angle of the leaning tree defied their attempts to get any higher than about eight feet from the ground before they fell back. In their fury at being thwarted of another easy kill, they began to give tongue, bellowing their savage rage to the night sky, as they milled around the foot of the tree.

Once realisation dawned that he was safe from the baying killers below, suddenly weak with relief, Jim slowed his frantic ascent. He clung to the trunk for a few seconds while he regained his breath, his face pressed thankfully against the rough friendly bark. Then aware of the need for speed, now that he had doubtless triggered the fence alarm with the tree, he roused himself to action again. He eased his way quickly through the branches until he was able to step onto the top of the chain-link fence.

Stooping, he grasped a branch which protruded at right angles over the fence top, and lowered himself till he was hanging full-length on the other side. Letting go, he dropped to the ground, reflexively jumping back as the nearest dogs hurled themselves snarling against the fence, their fangs rasping on the metal links in their savage determination to reach him.

But he had made it – he was free! He drew in a lungful of the cold night air. It tasted good. Clean and refreshing, as though the very air itself was free and untainted this side of the fence. Suddenly he became aware that it had gone quiet. The dogs had stopped their row. After their initial furious attempt to get at him when he dropped down close to the fence, they had retreated a few yards to the edge of the trees and were now standing silent watching him. It was as though they had been switched off – except for their eyes, which glowed malignantly at him from the dark like amber coals.

Swiftly he took stock of his position. He had landed on the verge of a four-lane highway. The verge was several yards wide and heavily overgrown with tall grasses, weeds and scattered scrub. He searched the gaps in the cloudy night sky for a sight of the Great Bear constellation. His luck was holding for he found it in one of the clear patches, and from it he found the Pole Star to give him his bearings. From that, he reckoned the highway was running roughly north to south.

He waded through the waist-high weeds to the roadside. When a quick check revealed no sign of approaching vehicle lights in either direction, therefore no chance of hitching a lift, he immediately turned and began trotting at a steady pace towards the south. Towards the Big Apple. New York – and home. It was imperative now that he put as much distance between himself and Bethlehem House as possible, before his escape was discovered and the inevitable pursuit began.

As he moved off, the dogs paced him on the other side of the fence, until he passed the southern limit of its perimeter. Then they turned and melted silently into the darkness of the woods. Satisfied that the man-thing did not intend to re-enter their domain, they lost interest in him. Besides, they had an interrupted meal to finish...

9

DEEP IN THE BOWELS OF BETHLEHEM HOUSE, ONE of the basement rooms had been converted into a sophisticated security control centre. It commanded a level of security set-up far in excess of that required by a religious community – no matter how exclusive that community desired to remain.

One entire wall of the room was covered by an impressive array of electronic equipment. The upper level was taken up by a double bank of closed-circuit TV monitor screens. Each was linked to a remote-controlled camera of the surveillance system which covered strategic points of the house's interior. Below the glowing TV screens the wall was divided into several panels, on which were arrayed orderly ranks of numbered and colour-coded warning lights connected to the various sections of the surveillance network.

One panel of these lights was allocated to the alarm system installed within the house itself. This guarded all external means of entry and exit, as well as certain prohibited areas within the building – such as the control centre – to which access was forbidden to rank and file sect members without special permission. The remainder of the panels were allocated to the front gates and perimeter fence. The latter was alarmed in fifty yard sections, each linked to its own indicator light on the display.

In the centre of the room, facing this wall, stood a large semi-circular control console, its surface studded with rows of variously coloured push-buttons and switches. Seated on a padded leather swivel chair within the curve of the console was a young oriental male, dressed in a close-fitting black tracksuit.

Jim, the lone survivor of the two escapees, would have recognised him instantly under his sect identity of Angel Two – one of four Orientals in overall charge of discipline and security. They also acted as official bodyguards to the Prophet, one or more accompanying him at all times on his religious 'crusades' in and around New York. The Prophet had flamboyantly styled them his four 'Archangels' – Michael, Gabriel, Uriel and

Raphael – and from this they had adopted amongst themselves the shorter code names of Angels One, Two, Three and Four respectively. This was also how they were generally referred to among the sect members, their full titles only being used when addressing any of them directly.

One of the Orientals' main concerns was apparently to ensure that no member was allowed to leave, once he or she had joined. From what he had seen, Jim had come to realise that the four sinister Angels were the real power behind the running of the sect, despite the Prophet being its creator and nominal leader. The four were feared by the ordinary sect members for their brutality, and for the utter ruthlessness they displayed when dealing with those who dared to step out of line.

Angel Two was sitting motionless at the control console, hands resting lightly on his thighs, his eyes fixed unblinkingly straight ahead. Though still outwardly conscious of his physical surroundings, he had placed his mind on a second level Tai Chi meditation discipline. Like his three fellow Orientals, Angel Two was not only proficient in Karate, but was also a master of Tai Chi – The Way Of The Peaceful Warrior – one of the most lethal of the martial arts of ancient China, incorporating strict disciplines of mind and body.

The instant Jim pushed the tree onto the fence, he triggered a section of the alarm system. A millisecond later, a red light flashed into life on one of the panels on the control room wall. Simultaneously a high-pitched buzzer began sounding urgently, synchronised with the pulsing ruby glow of the warning light.

As the light and buzzer activated, the Oriental's mind snapped back to full awareness. The slanted eyes narrowed as they fastened on the flashing light, and he swiftly reached out and jabbed one of the buttons on the sloping surface of the control console before him. The button he selected was black – the same colour as his tracksuit.

Immediately, in various other parts of the house, three pencil shaped portable alarms set up an insistent bleeping in the breast pockets of three other identical black tracksuits. The Orientals wearing the suits each stopped what he was doing, slipped a small flat transceiver from a pocket and keyed the 'receive' button. Motionless, they stood awaiting the message to follow. Within seconds the pocket alarms fell silent and Angel Two's voice sounded flatly from the slim two-way radios in their hands.

"Control to Angels One, Three and Four. Please acknowledge in turn. Angel One? Over."

One of the motionless black-clad figures stirred. Slim and smooth shaven with close-cropped black hair, this individual was at first glance unremarkable. However, on closer inspection his slight figure, allied to a certain hardness of features suggested an indefinable quality of strength and danger. He lifted his hand and spoke into his set. His voice was harsh, overlaid with a nasal Cantonese accent.

"Angel One receiving. Over."

The other two were then called and acknowledged in turn. Then the disembodied voice issued from the miniature speakers again.

"Control to all Angels. We have a Code Red in Sector Alpha-Zero-Five of outer perimeter. Report to Control immediately for briefing. Out."

Angel Two finished speaking into the mike on the control console, reached out and this time punched the yellow master button which connected him to the speakers of the P.A. system installed throughout the house. He paused for ten seconds to allow the soft chimes to sound over the system, which announced that a general message was to follow. Leaning forward, he spoke into the mike in his heavily accented English.

"Control to Apostles ... report to Assembly Room immediately. Control to Disciples on Monitor Duty ... take up Supervision Posts immediately. Control to Disciples on Roll-call duty ... begin immediate head count ... report results to Control soonest. Control to all other sect members ... go to your Assembly Points for Roll-call procedure immediately. Out."

Within the many rooms and corridors throughout the big house, the terse orders resulted in a sudden flurry of movement, as every sect member immediately ceased whatever they had been doing and began to head for their specified destinations. Twelve in particular, all dressed in close fitting grey tracksuits, began to converge swiftly on a large room situated on the ground floor. They moved with single-minded purpose, passing among the many other hurrying figures in the corridors, most of whom were dressed as the two escapees had been, in loose calf-length cotton robes, but of varying colours. Some wore the same scarlet as Jim and Tom, a greater number wore green, but the majority wore pale blue. Several others were evident, clad in brown tracksuits, and these were now seen to be directing the robed figures and hurrying them along to the various assembly points within the house for the head count.

The whole scene was a kaleidoscope of movement and colour. But there was no accompanying mood of light-heartedness to match the carnival-like scene. The brown tracksuited figures were arrogant in their manner and curt in their issue of commands, while the robed figures obeyed meekly.

All gave way to the hurrying grey figures. No-one greeted them or even looked directly at them as they strode past. If any attitude at all was displayed towards them, it was one of fear, from those members who shrank aside to allow them right of passage. As these twelve gathered in the large Assembly Room, they seated themselves in a loose semi-circular group in the curving tiers of seats facing the raised platform at one end of the room. Strangely, no-one spoke – not one of the twelve acknowledged any of his companions with so much as a nod.

All were young, in their late teens or early twenties, well muscled and superbly fit. Whether by chance or design, the group was divided into equal parts in its racial composition. Four were Caucasians, one Nordic type with hair so blond it was almost white; four were Negroes, all shaven-headed, their oiled brown scalps gleaming dully in the overhead lighting; the last four members of the group were young Hispanics, one of these sporting an old knife scar down one side of his face. With the exception of the shaven-headed blacks, the others all wore their hair close-cropped.

Apart from their unnatural silence and lack of human response to one another's presence, each one of the grey-clad group possessed another disquieting common feature. The eyes – they were flat, expressionless and cold. The empty, emotionless eyes of the psychotic killer. These were the Prophet's Twelve Apostles.

Despite the esoteric nature of their title – like the four oriental 'Archangels' who had selected and trained them – their function was decidedly unbiblical. Lethally proficient in karate, each Apostle was a brutally efficient weapon in the sect's security force, who would unquestioningly obey any order from the Four. They in turn commanded the numerous brown-clad lesser heavies, the so-called Disciples. From the very existence of such an emphasis on surveillance and discipline, it would soon have become apparent to an outside observer that the sect took its security and exclusiveness very seriously indeed.

A few minutes after the last of the Apostles had entered the Assembly Room, the brooding silence was broken by the arrival of the three Orientals from their emergency briefing at Control. Their movements fluid and athletic, they mounted the side steps to the platform, walked forward and stood facing the twelve.

Angel One was flanked by his two colleagues, his dominant status evident from the way they remained a respectful half-pace to the rear. But even without this mark of deference, there was something about the commanding presence of the man which would have marked him out as leader.

It was nothing physical. A slim, compact, five foot eight, he actually gave the impression of being less muscular than his two stockier companions. But there was a self-assurance bordering on arrogance in his bearing, the air of one used to total command and instant obedience. It was as though some indefinable force of will, as powerful as it was subtle, radiated out from the man to impose his authority on the other occupants of the room.

His fathomless black eyes swept over the silent figures in the seats below him, checking all twelve were present. Then he spoke, his harsh voice cutting loudly into the stillness, his speech clipped and thickly accented. "We have a suspected breach of perimeter security. While the head-count is being completed, you will carry out a House Security Check. I will check the perimeter fence personally. Angel Three will assign you to your posts." He paused, eyed the seated figures for a moment, then shot out a blunt forefinger to point at one of the white youths.

"You ..." he barked. "Come with me!"

With this curt command, Angel One spun on his heel, left the platform and strode swiftly from the room followed by the chosen Apostle. None of his companions displayed the slightest flicker of interest in his going. They sat on impassively. Machines waiting to be activated.

Angel Three now stepped forward and, without preamble, began issuing orders to the remaining eleven Apostles. Like his leader before him, his speech was clipped and thickly accented, although less harsh in tone. "For the House Security Check, each of us will command a search party of six Disciples. The four levels of the house will be allocated as follows. Angel Four and myself will divide the basement between us. You four …" he pointed at the Apostles in question, "divide the ground floor between you. You four …" the finger stabbed out again at those selected, "take the second floor. You three …" he indicated the last members of the group, "top floor sleeping quarters. Check all doors and windows thoroughly. Report results to Control. As soon as you have finished, report back here for further orders. Go!"

His command emptied the room in a flurry of rapid movement, each group dispersing swiftly to its designated search area. Within minutes the entire house was a hive of activity as its interior was thoroughly searched for any signs of a breach in its security. At the same time, a complete head-count of the ordinary members was being carried out with equal efficiency by those Disciples on Roll-call duty.

Even as the security check of the house and its occupants was swinging into action, Angel One was speeding for the main gates of the estate in one of the sect's vehicles. A squat, powerful Dodge van, its dark blue paintwork was relieved only by the sect logo of a small gold cross stencilled on each side panel.

The young white Apostle was driving. Expertly he eased the van through the sweeping curves of the S-bend near the end of the main drive. This was designed to shield the house and its grounds from the highway with a screen of intervening trees. Emerging from the last bend, the driveway ran straight for a further fifty yards through the overhanging trees, before terminating at the inner pair of a double set of tall, metal-barred gates.

The van braked to a smooth halt only inches from the first set of gates. These were sited thirty feet from the outer set, and linked to them on either side by an extension of the high perimeter fence, effectively forming an oblong enclosure. Electronically controlled, the gates could only be negotiated one set at a time, this preventing any would-be escapees – human or animal – from slipping out while vehicles were entering or leaving.

The van engine idled quietly while Angel One and the driver checked from the windows and in the mirrors for any sign of the dogs. Once satisfied the pack was nowhere in the vicinity, Angel One nodded to the driver, who pressed a button on the dash. Immediately, the tall gates swung silently open, receding away to either side in the headlight beams. The driver rolled the van forward to the centre of the enclosure and pressed the button again to close the inner gates behind them. Another quick check confirmed that no unwanted canine company had slipped through with them. Angel One nodded again and the driver pressed a second button, this time to activate the outer gates, which swung silently inwards towards them. While they were still in motion, he eased the van through the widening gap and signalled them to close again.

Turning sharp right, they drove slowly along the edge of the highway until they reached the relevant section of the fence which had been indicated by the alarm system in Control. Leaving the van parked on the verge, they removed two powerful flashlights from under the seat and began walking slowly along the fence, playing the beams on it and checking it carefully for any signs of interference or damage.

Suddenly Angel One halted and swore softly in Cantonese, as the beam of his flashlight speared the fallen tree leaning on the fence. He ran the shaft of light down the slope of the trunk, until it unwaveringly spotlighted the tell-tale fresh wood of the sawn stump. A quick sweep of the surrounding area with the powerful lights revealed the mute evidence of trampled grasses, clearly indicating the fugitive's pathway to the roadside. The oriental eyed this for a few seconds, his eyes thoughtful. He glanced in both directions along the empty moonlit highway but his field of vision was restricted from their position close to the fence, so he ordered his companion to advance to the roadside where he would be able to see further. Then, plucking the personal radio from his breast pocket, he thumbed the switch to extend the small aerial, and spoke into the mike in rapid-fire Cantonese. "Angel One to Control. Code Red is caused by tree leaning on fence. Tree has been cut down. It would appear we have a break-out. What are the results of the head-count? Over."

"Control to Angel One. Break-out confirmed," came the swift response in the same language. "Two ... repeat ... two Initiates are missing. Both male. Their identities are being checked by roll-call. What are your orders? Over."

Before replying, Angel One glanced round and raised an eyebrow at the Apostle, who was wading back towards him through the waist-high grass after making his check of the moonlit road. His unspoken question was answered by a negative shake of the head.

His eyes bleak, the oriental thumbed the transmit button. "Angel One to Control. We will carry out External Search Procedure. As soon as roll-call is complete, send me three more vans and sufficient personnel to conduct a four-vehicle search pattern. Out."

Barely fifteen minutes had elapsed since Angel One's message, before the other three vans had arrived and the search parties assembled at the roadside. Two of the vans were commanded by Angel One's fellow Orientals, each accompanied by a grey-clad Apostle acting as driver. The third vehicle was crewed by two of the shaven-headed black Apostles, one of whom was appointed to command that particular search party. The bulk of the assembled searchers was made up of twenty-four brown tracksuited Disciples, each one provided with a powerful flashlight and carrying a long stick for probing undergrowth.

Angel Three briefed his leader, informing him of the identities of the missing boys and the method of their escape. He described how they had apparently climbed out onto the roof of the house, having broken through the glass of a skylight window. By doing so, they had exploited an unforeseen weakness in the alarm system, because only the window catch had been wired up. They had then lowered themselves to the ground using an improvised rope made of torn-up and knotted sheets.

Angel One heard out the report in brooding silence, then without further comment began to issue orders for the manhunt. The Disciples were split up six to a vehicle. They would be used, if necessary, for search or pursuit on foot. He directed the two vans commanded by Angel Four and the black Apostle to search to the north – the direction seemingly indicated by the evidence of the trodden grass of the verge. Meanwhile, the parties commanded by himself and Angel Three would search in what he still considered to be the more likely direction of south, towards New York.

The road on which they were standing was an offshoot of the main Inter-State highway, and ran for several miles in either direction with no turn-offs, through hundreds of square miles of densely forested wilderness. So it was considered most unlikely that the escaping youths would have left the highway and headed off into the trackless forests, unprovisioned, unarmed and poorly clad as they were assumed to be.

The north-bound search parties set off first. Angel One stood beside his vehicle and watched their tail lights dwindling in the distance for a couple of silent minutes. Then he addressed Angel Three by his side. "Usual first-phase procedure. You go on ahead and flush the quarry. I will follow and spring the trap. Carry on."

Angel Three nodded in acknowledgement and climbed quickly into his vehicle, which started up and pulled slowly away. It was running on sidelights only. Angel One waited in his own van till his colleague's tail lights had disappeared from view round a bend in the road a few hundred yards further on. Then he ordered his driver to follow, keeping their speed to a minimum and displaying no lights at all.

The van's highly tuned engine purred into life and they moved off. Running without lights as they were, they relied solely on the faint starlight and sporadic moonlight to guide them, as the van whispered along the edge of the road. Each time they came to a slope the driver switched off the engine, allowing the vehicle to coast along in almost total silence.

This initial phase of the search procedure was an attempt to trap the fugitives between the two vans, should they detect the approach of the lead van and take cover, only to resume moving again once it was safely past. It was simple, but had proved effective time and again in the past. Angel One settled back, relaxed but alert, his eyes scanning the road ahead and probing the verge as they crept along. He was fully confident they would soon run down and re-capture the two fugitives, if not by this method, then by another. They had never yet failed to do so. The hunt was on!

10

THE HIGHWAY WOUND ITS WAY SOUTH THROUGH the wild upstate forest country. Like any other backwoods highway, it seemed in no great hurry to arrive anywhere in particular. The tall trees pressed densely in on either side, dark and impenetrable, leaving only a few yards of scrub and tangled weed for a roadside verge. Eerily lit by the fitful moonlight, the dusty blacktop surface stretched out ahead of him like a pale river snaking through the whispering black canyon of the seemingly endless forest.

Jim had settled into an easy pace and was jogging steadily along, frequently checking the road behind him. In this way he had managed to cover a little over three miles when he caught the faint sound of a vehicle approaching from the rear. He glanced back but found that it was hidden from view by a slight rise in the road not far behind him. However, its low engine note, carried clearly to him on the chill night air, made him instantly suspicious. It was travelling too slowly on an empty road in ideal driving conditions and miles from the nearest possible destination!

Quickly he dived to his right into a thick patch of tall grass and weeds, and dropped to his hands and knees facing back the way he had just come. Keeping his head below the tops of the swaying weeds, he watched through their lacy screen just as the oncoming vehicle crested the brow of the rise. Instantly he dropped flat on his stomach, a thrill of fear running through him. It was one of theirs. He had recognised the familiar squat silhouette of a sect van, but what had provided confirmation was the fact that it was showing only sidelights. No normal drivers ran on sidelights on unlit public roads at dead of night.

He lay pressed tightly against the unyielding ground, his eyes squeezed shut, waiting in dread for the screech of brakes to tell him he had been spotted. His heart pounded against his ribs and he felt its racing pulse throbbing painfully in his injured temple. But the vehicle didn't stop. The engine note faded steadily into the night.

Gradually he relaxed. Suddenly he felt as though he were suffocating, and only then did he realise that he had been holding his breath. He released the pent-up air in his lungs in a long sigh and lay still while his pulse rate and breathing returned to near normal. By which time he could no longer hear any sound of the van that had passed his hiding place.

Now another subtler danger began to assert itself. Now that he had stopped moving, a sort of delayed-shock reaction to the night's events set in. A feeling of mental and physical lassitude began to creep over him, lulling him into inactivity. Suddenly he was reluctant to move. He felt he just wanted to lie there in hiding, like the hunted animal he felt himself to be.

Why risk moving again? He was safe here. The treacherous thought wormed its way insidiously into his mind. Surely to move meant taking the chance of being sighted? Wouldn't it be more sensible just to lie here in hiding, safe and secure, while the hunters scoured the road ahead searching for him in vain? Then, when daylight came, he'd be able to hitch a lift to safety. That made sense. So, why not? ...

With a start, Jim rejected this dangerous line of thinking. He had to keep moving or he was lost. He had no other choice. Now that the hunt was on, they would search unceasingly for him throughout the night. And once their initial efforts had failed to net him, they would redouble their efforts and begin to comb the immediate area more thoroughly – using extra personnel if necessary. Then, when he was recaptured, he would be taken back to face the wrath of Angel One ...

This thought galvanised him back into a mood of action and he was about to force his reluctant body into motion again, when an idea struck him. If he were to take full advantage of the dark, it would help if he blackened his face, arms and legs. This would make him less visible to his hunters, and might prevent his being spotted at a distance from a moving sect vehicle before he could take cover.

He rolled over and sat up, his head level with the tops of the wind-stirred weeds and grass. Grasping a fistful of stems, he uprooted a sizeable bunch and dug his fingers into the damp black soil he had exposed. Spitting on the handful of earth to moisten it still further, he liberally smeared his face and neck with it, careful to avoid the crusting scab of his aching head wound. Then he repeated the process with his arms and lower legs, where these showed beyond his robe.

So preoccupied was he in camouflaging his person with the mud, he was completely unaware of the approach of the second van. Its engine switched off, it came ghosting silently down the slight incline towards him, creeping out of the darkness like some animate mechanical beast. Jim became aware of the imminent danger only when his ears picked up the soft hiss of its tyres on the road surface. By then, it was almost on top of him.

He looked up – and froze! Through the swaying tops of the tangle of weeds and grass he stared straight at the blank Cyclops eye of the van windscreen. For a heart-stopping instant his shocked mind refused to accept the terrifying image being fed into it. Then suddenly it registered. Fear gripped his insides in an invisible fist and set his heart hammering in his chest again. He was seized by a sudden wild impulse to leap to his feet and run, but his legs refused to respond, his fear-induced paralysis thus saving him from certain disaster.

As the van glided level with him, Jim seemed to look straight into the probing eyes of the pale featureless face of the figure in the passenger seat. The eerie silence of the vehicle's progress seemed to increase its aura of menace. Time hung suspended. The van filled his vision, the dull gleam of the gold cross on its side panel catching his eye as it slid past. Then it was gone.

He didn't know it, but his freshly blackened face had prevented his discovery and capture. Angel One's keenly searching eyes had failed to notice him, blending as he did into the general darkness of the overgrown verge.

Jim felt a great tide of relief tinged with exhilaration wash over him, as the unlit black shape of the van receded into the night. Seconds later he heard its engine restart as it reached the bottom of the slope and soon the soft mutter of its exhaust grew fainter and fainter, until it faded into silence.

Paradoxically, this unnerving experience had a beneficial side-effect on him. The adrenalin was now pumping round his body, toning up his muscles for action and dispelling the strength-sapping lethargy of a few minutes before. He took stock quickly. He had no idea how many vehicles they would employ in the hunt, but decided on impulse to cross to the other side of the road, a thing he should have done from the start. That way, not only would he be facing any oncoming traffic, but more importantly he would not be so vulnerable to being spotted by any of his hunters overtaking him from behind.

Checking that the road was clear of enemy eyes in both directions, he sprinted across. Then glancing back frequently, he settled once more into a steady, distance-eating trot. On the move again, he began to benefit from the exercise as it heated him up, despite the sharp bite of the rising wind. Also, his torn wet robe had begun to dry out as he ran and provide a little more protection against the cold.

Keeping up a steady pace, he had covered perhaps another mile when he heard again the sound of vehicle engines in the distance behind him. Immediately he swerved into the roadside jungle to his left and stood still, looking back along the road to the north.

In the distance Jim saw four sets of lights approaching. Not only headlights, but also smaller riding lights high above these. This, in addition to the growing rumble of heavy diesel power, told him that whatever vehicles were coming were far larger than anything the sect possessed. Within seconds it became clear that he was looking at a convoy of four big long-distance trucks, eighteen wheelers from the size and sound of them. As they bore down on him, he glanced quickly in the opposite direction for any sign of the hunters. Clear. With a sudden surge of hope, he decided to take the chance of trying to hitch a lift.

Jim waited until the four big rigs were about a hundred yards from him, then he stepped out onto the road. Standing in the increasing glow of the swiftly oncoming headlights, he extended his arm and stuck out his thumb in the universal signal of the hitch-hiker.

The rising growl of the onrushing rigs swelled to a full-throated roar. Jim screwed up his eyes against the blinding glare of the double-banked head lamps, and began waving his free arm over his head in an effort to draw attention to his plight. Suddenly he was deafened by the strident blare of the lead truck's horn, as it drowned out even the bellow of the powerful engines. Then the towering eighteen wheelers were thundering past him in quick succession, each passing monster buffeting him with a warm blast of oil-laden slipstream. The ground shook under him and his mind was temporarily numbed by the noise and glare. But they didn't stop. The horn blared once more, fainter now, sounding a derisive farewell as the trucks roared off into the night.

Jim stared despairingly after the swiftly receding tail lights of the end vehicle in the small convoy. Subconsciously, in the couple of minutes it had taken for the trucks to reach him, he had pinned all his hopes on being able to thumb a lift to safety. Hot tears of disappointment stung his eyes, and in a surge of impotent rage he screamed after them, "You bastards! You dirty fuckin' BASTA-A-ARDS!!" He held the last word, emptying his lungs on it. His throat ached from the violence of his emotions.

Choking back a sob of disappointed fury, he walked dejectedly back to the side of the road again. With grim determination he started jogging along in the wake of the fast decreasing rumble of the convoy. The lights of the trucks dwindled to pinpoints and were suddenly cut off completely by a distant bend. Once again he was alone in the night at the mercy of the hunters.

Several times during the next half hour he had to take evasive action as the vans passed him, heading back in the opposite direction, only to overtake him again later, running silently in the dark. Pursuing – hunting – relentlessly. Then the search pattern suddenly changed.

Jim hadn't long resumed moving after being overtaken yet again by the vans, but had covered no more than another mile, when he saw a flicker of light up ahead – then another – then several. He slowed to a walk, ready to slip into cover. He peered intently into the night, trying to identify the source of the moving lights. Even as he watched, they split into two separate groups, weaving and bobbing about, some on his side of the highway, the others moving across to the opposite side. Flashlights – at least a dozen of them, he decided. His hunters were obviously beginning to carry out a more thorough search of the roadside verges.

Jim sank down into the waist-high weeds at his side. From a safe distance he watched the vans ranging up and down the road flanking the searchers on foot, who advanced steadily towards him, working six-abreast on either verge. His nervousness increased the nearer they came. When the searchers reached a point about hundred yards from his position, he reluctantly eyed the uninviting blackness of the forest edge, looming a few paces away to his left. It was as he turned his head to do this that he caught another flicker of light on his peripheral vision – this time from behind him! Startled, his sharply indrawn breath hissed through his clenched teeth as he spun round on his haunches and stared wide-eyed at this new threat. Far off in the distance to his rear, two more lines of bobbing lights were steadily approaching. It seemed Angel One had called up reinforcements to form a pincer movement. He was trapped!

He knew he was left with only one option – he would have to enter the forbidding dark of the forest in order to outflank the advancing searchers. After his earlier encounter with the Hellhounds, the mere thought of doing this filled him with dread, even though he knew they could no longer reach him. But he had no other choice. So gathering all his courage, he moved quietly to his left and slipped deep amongst the trees.

His fear of being captured was greater even than his dread of the unknown dangers of the rustling dark of the forest, and drove him to penetrate further into its depths than he had at first intended. When he eventually stopped, he set his back firmly against the security of a thick trunk and stood still, watching back towards the highway. Within minutes he was rewarded by a brief glimpse through the intervening trees of the search cordon's flashlights, as they flickered past from left to right.

Despite being sheltered from the wind's bite by the dense trees, Jim was starting to feel cold again now that he had stopped moving. But he knew he had to wait until the searchers had moved well away before he risked retracing his steps to the verge, so he mentally counted off five minutes.

He had just decided it was safe to move, when suddenly he sensed he was not alone in the night. A shiver ran up his spine quite unrelated to the cold and he felt the hairs stir on the nape of his neck. Obeying his instincts, he remained motionless, senses straining into the dark around him in an effort to locate the unknown danger. Long seconds crawled past and he was on the point of dismissing the feeling, putting it down to an understandable over-reaction to his earlier encounter with the dogs, when something moved in the dark a few yards to his front.

His night vision had adjusted to the stygian dark of the forest and he stood rooted to the spot, hardly daring to breathe, as his keen young eyes followed what seemed to be a flitting black shadow gliding stealthily across his front through the ebony columns of the trees. Jim didn't need to be able to see the menacing figure clearly to identify him – he knew who it was! Only Angel One would have the cunning to anticipate his move to escape the cordon, and then stalk him single-handedly among the sheltering trees. Once again Jim had cause to thank his foresight in camouflaging his person with mud, that and the initial caution which had prompted him to seek safety so deep within the forest edge.

After a wait of a few more minutes to allow the brutal oriental to move well out of earshot, Jim made his way quietly back to the verge. Off to his right he could see the far-off lights of the search cordons as they approached one another, closing the jaws of their now empty trap. He waited till the moon went in again, plunging the night into darkness, then slipped back onto the road and resumed his steady jog to the south and freedom.

A few minutes later the road took a slight bend and Jim lost sight of his hunters, but at the same moment he caught sight of more lights in the distance ahead of him. His heart sank. Surely not another search cordon? They must be bloody desperate to re-capture him, if it was. He dropped his pace again and studied the lights. But he quickly decided that these were not flashlights – they were too steady and too bright at that distance. What then? So intent was he on trying to identify the source of the lights, he almost trotted straight past the roadside signpost without seeing it.

He drew up sharply, breathing hard from his run, and stared at it uncomprehendingly for a second. Then he felt a surge of elation. The sign read, TRUCK STOP AHEAD – 1 MILE. Below that were the words, GAS – EATS – OPEN 24 HOURS.

All his strain and fatigue seemed to melt away. He felt this could be his first real break of the night in his bid to escape the evil clutches of the sect. Now he would stand a much better chance of hitching a lift and failing that, he'd have access to a phone to contact his folks for help as a last resort.

The night was still moonless and the distant lights beckoned welcomingly. He was about to launch himself forward with renewed energy when something made him pause. What if Angel One had also anticipated that he might evade the search cordons, wouldn't he then have taken the added precaution of covering this last stretch of road leading to the truck stop?

Crouching at the foot of the signpost, Jim carefully scanned the darkness up ahead for signs of an enemy presence. Long seconds passed with nothing to alert him. And then his caution paid off. Not far ahead, between his position and the lights of the distant gas station, his eye caught the momentary glow of another light off to the left in the darkness – tiny, red and quickly extinguished. Someone was lurking at the edge of the tree-line, keeping watch on the road.

His assumption had been proved correct. It seemed that Angel One had indeed posted a sentry to prevent his reaching the haven of the gas station, while the search teams carried on the hunt for him further back. It had almost worked too. In fact, hadn't it been for the sentry sneaking a smoke, no doubt strictly against orders, he would have blundered straight into the trap.

Just then the moon came out again and put paid to any idea of crossing to the opposite verge and crawling past the watcher's position. In any case, Jim reasoned, there was every possibility that there might be a second sentry posted there too. There was nothing else for it – he reckoned he would have to use the cover of the trees again.

This time, however, his reluctance to enter the forbidding dark of the forest was much less. In fact, his main concern was to keep down the noise of his passage amongst the trees and underbrush, rather than who or what might ambush him there. Nevertheless, he spent a nerve-wracking fifteen minutes stealing through the looming trunks, trying to avoid the densest patches of undergrowth as he went, in order not to alert the sentry to his presence.

In this manner, he kept going until he reckoned he was well past the enemy outpost, then carefully made his way back to the edge of the treeline. Glancing to his left, he was relieved to see the lights of the gas station were a lot closer. It was now or never. One final time he waited for the moon to hide itself behind a substantial bank of cloud, plunging the night into darkness again. When this happened, he darted quickly back to the deserted highway, lowered his head and sprinted forward flat-out to gain the safety of normal human company.

11

JIM DROPPED TO A WALK A SHORT DISTANCE FROM the brightly lit forecourt of the gas station and approached it cautiously. He paused in the shadows at the limit of the oasis of light created by the combination of neon signs and arc-lamps and examined the place and its surroundings thoroughly. Then he quickly re-checked the highway in both directions. He could see no sign of his pursuers.

Satisfied, he padded softly along the last few yards of roadway and turned into the curving driveway leading to the double-ranked pumps. A brightly lit kiosk sat behind them, nestling among display racks holding new tyres and cans of oil. Through the large windows, he could see the pump attendant, a thin-faced elderly man, sitting with head bowed as he concentrated with narrowed eyes and moving lips on the paperback book he was reading.

Jim was about to approach the man, with the intention of begging a couple of coins to use in the phone booths he could see at the far end of the forecourt, when he suddenly stopped short. Just in time he had remembered his mud-blackened face, arms and legs and imagined the reception he'd be liable to get if he confronted anyone in that state, not to mention his outlandish mode of dress.

He looked for and spotted the TOILETS sign at one end of the main building, a long single storey construction at the rear of the forecourt, with a huge neon TRUCK STOP sign on its roof. Keeping behind the bowed head of the pump attendant, he quickly crossed the floodlit forecourt and tried the door marked GENTS. To his relief it was unlocked, and he slipped inside. Out of the biting wind, he suddenly felt warm, though the room itself was unheated.

Glancing round, Jim found the toilet to be empty as he had hoped. The place was surprisingly clean and smelled faintly of disinfectant. A row of six wash-hand basins lined one wall, toilet cubicles and urinals occupied the one opposite. He relieved himself at one of the urinals, then went to a wash-hand basin and examined himself in the mirror above it.

He hardly recognised himself. His long hair, blown into wild disarray by the wind, framed a black, mud-caked face. The whites of his eyes staring back at him from his reflection made him look like a badly made-up performer from some amateur minstrel show. He grinned at himself in the mirror and the startling whiteness of his reflection's teeth grinning back at him served only to heighten the image.

He turned on the taps and after some metallic grumbling, water spurted reluctantly from them into the basin. Finding a thin dry bar of soap, he worked up a lather and spent the next few minutes vigorously washing the dried mud from his face, arms and legs. Then, having carefully bathed his injured forehead, he dried himself using the rough paper towels from the wall-dispenser. He completed his tidying-up operation by combing his fingers through his long hair, until he had restored some semblance of order and neatness to it.

When he was satisfied that he looked a little more presentable, he went to the door and after first taking the precaution of switching off the light, eased it open. A quick check of the forecourt revealed no signs of the enemy.

He stepped outside and looked around. He was at the far end of the long single storey building. Behind and off to his right was the parking lot and only now did he take note of the four big rigs sitting back there. He suspected that they were probably the same four that had refused to stop for him earlier, which wasn't exactly encouraging. But it couldn't be helped – he'd have to try to bum a few coins from someone for the phone.

Briefly he considered trying to phone home 'collect', but just as quickly dismissed the idea. His martinet father would probably refuse point-blank to accept the call from him, he thought. He recalled the final blazing row they'd had, the last in a long series of similar verbal battles since Jim had started to assert his independence from the strict paternal authority his father had imposed on him from early childhood.

This final blow-up had been brought about by Jim's informing his parents of his decision to cut college and leave the family home in order to join the sect. His old man had ranted and raved for an hour, finishing up with the ultimatum, over the futile tears and pleadings of his mother, that if he dared to do such a thing he need never darken the parental door again, as he'd be disowned, disinherited, cut off without a red cent – and much more in the same vein.

His father was a strong-willed man, used to getting his own way both at home and in the office, where he was managing director of the family firm of accountants. But he had reckoned without the fact that the son had inherited his father's stubbornness in the face of opposition to his will. Jim had stormed out, cut college and gone to 'commit his life to Christ' under the benevolent guidance of the Prophet – or so he'd thought then. But the dream had quickly turned into a nightmare – a nightmare that was for real. It wasn't the kind you could escape from by waking up. And what's more, it was here with him now – all around him in the night – and he was the central figure in it.

He didn't even dare to consider phoning the police. Such an action would only result in bringing down a terrible retribution on his defenceless parents. All sect members were well warned on this point. Police investigation, they had been told, would be effectively neutralised by the counter-claim of a sick runaway patient from a private mental home, which was the official front for Bethlehem House. Thereafter, following a suitable time-lapse to allay suspicion, parents and families would become the targets of unexplained attacks on person and property by unknown perpetrators. No way could he expose his parents to that.

No, his only hope lay in somehow persuading his father to listen long enough to let him explain the facts about his dire situation. Then, if he succeeded in making peace with his old man, he could then ask him to come and pick him up, bringing clothes and money. His father could then drop him off at a Greyhound depot, where he'd catch the early morning bus for Pittsburgh Once there, he'd arrange to stay a while with his maternal grandparents until the heat had died down. That way, his parents would be able to plead ignorance of his whereabouts,

99

should they be accosted and questioned by Angel One or any of his sect thugs.

Angel One ... with a start Jim realised he was standing in full view of his pursuers, should they pass by or enter the gas station. He looked to his left. Light was spilling onto the forecourt from two long, frosted glass windows, flanking a door about half way along the building. A faint aroma of cooking reached him on the night breeze.

He moved quickly along to the door. Its frosted glass panel bore a hand-printed sign which announced, WE DO THE BEST DAMN BEEFBURGERS IN THE STATE! TRY ONE – AND IF YOU AIN'T SATISFIED, WE PROMISE NOT TO SELL YOU ANOTHER!

Jim turned the handle and stepped inside. Warm air engulfed him, thick with the competing smells of cooked food, hot coffee, tobacco smoke and sweat. He found himself looking across a few rows of empty formica-topped tables, some of which had chairs upended on their surfaces, to a long snack-bar which ran the entire width of the place. A row of high, swivel-topped stools on shiny steel poles fronted the long counter, on the far end of which sat six big chrome-plated urns, each emitting wisps of steam and the tantalising odours of coffee and hot soups into the warm atmosphere. A big multi-coloured juke box glowed in benign silence over by the far wall.

The place had five occupants – one behind the counter, the other four perched on alternate stools in front of it. From the litter of dirty plates before them and the mugs of coffee they were hunched over, it was apparent the four were relaxing after a meal. There was a buzz of conversation competing with a background of rock music blaring from a transistor radio behind the bar.

As Jim entered, the counterhand glanced up automatically to inspect the new customer. He was a stout, moon-faced man, wearing a soiled white apron over a check shirt, the sleeves of which were rolled up to his elbows. A crumpled white cap was perched low on his forehead, the pasty face below it glistening with a permanent sheen of sweat. A wet cigar butt protruded from one side of his slack mouth. His piggy eyes narrowed in hostility at Jim's appearance. Resting his hands on the cluttered counter, he leaned forward aggressively and snapped in a high-pitched bullying tone, "Git yore fuckin' ass outa here, bum! Yore sort ain't welcome hereabouts."

All conversation ceased instantly. The ensuing silence being filled only by the sounds of the late night radio station. The four drivers had been casually pumping the fat counterhand for information on the potential of the local area for spot of illegal weekend deer-hunting, when his attention had been diverted by Jim's entry. As one, they glanced round to see whom he was addressing with such hostility. Their reactions varied. The two individuals on either end of the group merely raised their eyebrows at his outlandish appearance, then faced their front again, minding their own business. But the two in the centre of the group took a more immediate interest.

One swung himself right round to face Jim, straddling his stool and leaning his elbows on the counter behind him. A tall lean character, his receding chin made his large upper teeth more prominent in his thin-lipped mouth. A baseball cap was pushed to the back of his head and he wore jeans and a sweat stained T-shirt, across the front of which was the message, SOLVE WORLD OVER-POPULATION – START WORLD WAR III NOW!!! He eyed Jim insolently up and down and sniggered. Then he addressed the company at large in a nasal Southern drawl.

"Waal, fuck me! Lookit what the wind's jes' blew in."

Stretching out a hand he nudged the shoulder of the trucker next to him in the centre of the group, a thick-set figure wearing a fur-collared mackinaw in a faded red and black check.

"Hey Red, git y'self an eyefulla this. Ah do believe we got us a real live fairy heah. An' after ma ol' pappy tellin' me never t'believe in 'em, cuz there wuzn't no sech things."

Red, whose nickname obviously derived from his fiery ginger hair and ruddy complexion, was a tough looking individual. He swung half way round on his stool, leaned an elbow on the counter, and surveyed Jim with undisguised contempt. When he spoke, his scathing tone matched his look.

"Looks like a fuckin' AIDS dispenser t'me," he sneered.

"Wanna know somethin' else, Jube?" he continued, "I think that's the same long-haired cunt we almos' ran down tonight, back up the road a piece."

"Yep, ah sho' do believe yo're right at that," agreed Jube, adding, "Pity we missed, ain't it?" Then he switched suddenly to address Jim directly for the first time. "Lookin' fo' th'powder room, Missy? Or y'all jes' lookin' t'sell some ass?"

This taunt really broke up the two tormentors and they roared with laughter, slapping their thighs and digging each other in the ribs. Jim felt his face flushing as scarlet as his robe, under the scathing remarks and sneering scrutiny. The thin one called Jube seized on this, leaning over to nudge the black leather jacketed figure hunched over his coffee on the other side of him.

"Hey there, Chuck, where's yore manners? Ain'tcha gonna offer the lady a seat? Aw … ah do believe she's blushin'. Now, ain't that real fetchin', an all?"

A fresh outburst of laughter greeted this sally, the fat counterhand joining in now, content for the moment to allow his customers to amuse themselves at the wierdo's expense, before he threw him out.

The one addressed as Chuck glanced round briefly. He was wearing black jeans under the leather jacket, and a black peaked cap sat squarely on his shock of dark hair. His lean, sallow face sported a Burt Reynolds moustache, and a thin cheroot was gripped between his clenched teeth. He stared at Jim for a moment, his face expressionless, but said nothing. Then he shrugged and turned back to lean over the mug of coffee on the counter before him, seeming to want no part in the baiting. Undismayed, Jube addressed Jim again in his sneering Southern drawl, apparently content to play to a reduced audience.

"Waal now, what kin we do fo' sech a ravishin' creature? Y'all lookin' fo' some han'some prince t'take yuh t'the ball, or' yuh jes' lookin' fo' yore glass slipper, Cinders?" He grinned mirthlessly at Jim, his large front teeth emphasising his undershot jaw.

The one called Red guffawed with laughter, then spluttered, "Nah, I think y'got it right the first time, Jube. He ain't Cinderella – he's the fuckin' fairy!"

This broke the two of them up again and fatso behind the counter cackled along with them. As their laughter died away, Jim grabbed the opportunity to speak. He advanced a hesitant pace and licked his dry lips nervously. "Look, I ... uh ... I need help ... I'm in bad trouble ... there's some real mean people after me out there ... I wonder if ..."

He got no further before the buzz-saw drawl interrupted him. "Aw, now ain't that a cryin' shame. An' you in that condition too! Some fella done git y'all in trouble, did he? An' ah bet he jes' fucked off an lef' yuh, after he'd had his wicked way. Aw shucks, an' yore purty dress is all tore too. Now, ain't that jes' too much! Whatever happened to y'all anyway?" Suddenly the bantering tone sharpened into malice as he continued, "D'yuh git gang-banged by some bikers – or jes' by the resta yore fuckin' faggot hippie friends?"

This last jibe was greeted by appreciative sniggers from his two supporters but something in the atmosphere had changed. The black-clad, saturnine Chuck shifted restlessly on his seat and shot a quizzical glance at Jube from under a raised eyebrow. Jim's embarrassment was giving way to anger at the verbal baiting from this chinless Southern redneck and the charged atmosphere had reached that stage of subtle balance where it was at the point of turning into something ugly.

It was abundantly clear to Jim that he could expect no help here – quite the reverse, in fact. And there was nothing to be gained in getting himself beaten up and thrown out, which was just where this was leading. He had just decided to leave and take his chances outside again, when the fourth man in the group stirred. He had sat quietly all this time. Now he looked round over a massive hunched shoulder and spoke. His voice was deep, his accent nasal and pure Bronx.

"Okay Jube, knock it off. Give da kid a break."

"Aw heck Rocky," responded Jube in an aggrieved tone. "He don' deserve no better. I mean – goin' roun' dressed like some kinda weirdo fairy, an' all. Fuck sake man, look at 'im!"

"I said knock it off, an' dat's what I meant," the big man growled back menacingly, swinging half round on his stool. "He jes' said he's in some kinda trouble, didn't he? I gotta kid his age. If he wuz in trouble, I'd wan' fer someone t'help 'im. Not fer some smartass t'bad mouth 'im."

The latest raucous offering from some obscure rock group filled the heavy silence that followed Rocky's gruff voice.

Jube held up his hands in a gesture of appeasement and said in placatory tones, "Okay Rocky. Don' git sore, man. Ah wuz only foolin' anyhow."

Jim looked gratefully at the man called Rocky, the one who seemed to be sympathetic to his plight. He saw a middle-aged, greying haired individual with a deeply tanned, square-jawed face set over a massive spread of shoulders and chest. He had the misshapen nose, thickened ears and slightly flattened features of an ex-boxer. The nasal tone of his gravel voice fitted that image too.

He was obviously regarded with a certain amount of respect by the others. The taunting stopped dead and the two tormentors turned back to the counter, raising their eyebrows at each other like two kids who'd been caught tying a can to the cat's tail.

Rocky turned to the now silent counterhand. "Hey mister, gimme a mugga soup over here," he ordered.

The man hesitated, spat out his cigar butt and ground it out underfoot. When he spoke, his voice was truculent. "I ain't servin' that fuckin' hippie bum in here. I don' want his sort comin' …" He got no further.

"You ain't servin' him, punk. You're servin' me!" Rocky's deep voice rasped out angrily, cutting off the complaint in mid sentence. "An' I don' give a fuck what you want. What you'll git's a smack inna mouth, if I don' git what I want. Right?"

Fatso tried one more time to assert his authority. He cleared his throat and said nervously, "Now listen friend, I don' want no trouble …"

"An' you won' git any … if I git served," interrupted Rocky bluntly. As he spoke, he raised his massive frame from the stool and leant forward threateningly to emphasise his point. He fixed the sweating moon face behind the counter with a pair of smouldering blue eyes, daring him to answer back.

"Another mugga soup, I said. Pronto!" So saying, he withdrew a ham-sized fist from the pocket of his thick blue reefer jacket where he'd been fumbling and slammed a crumpled bill onto the counter top, flat-handed. The dishes rattled along its length. The fat counterhand flinched, stepped back a pace and licked his loose lips. He glanced quickly at Jube and Red, his erstwhile allies, for support.

Jube shrugged eloquently. "Ah'd do like the man says, if ah wuz you," he advised quietly. Red for his part, stared wordlessly straight ahead, studiously avoiding fatso's eyes.

The counterhand got the message. Sullenly he moved to the far end of the bar and filled a large plastic mug with hot soup from one of the urns. Returning, he placed it gingerly on the counter before the glowering Rocky, and reached out a tentative hand towards the bill lying there.

"Fix da kid a 'burger." Rocky's sudden growl startled the counterman. He snatched his hand away as though he had been stung, and almost fell over his feet in his haste to comply.

The black-clad Chuck laughed quietly into his coffee.

"An' turn dat fuckin' noise down!" Rocky ordered, pointing at the blaring radio. "I kin hardly hear myself thinkin'."

The fat counterhand did as he was told and the rock music faded to an acceptable level to permit conversation.

Rocky swung round from the counter and held out the mug to Jim. "Here kid, git y'self outsida dat. You look like you c'd use it. Grab y'self a seat."

Jim had followed the interplay and exchanges between the five men in surprised silence, after his unexpected ally had intervened on his behalf. Now as he advanced to accept the proffered cup, a sudden surge of emotion, part relief and part gratitude, momentarily tightened his throat and stung his eyes. For one embarrassing instant he thought he was going to burst into tears like some snivelling first-grader, earning the further contempt of the assholes who'd been baiting him. But he swallowed hard, flashed the big man an uncertain smile and mumbled, "Thanks sir."

To cover his confusion and give himself time to regain his composure, he busied himself lifting down one of the stacked chairs from a nearby table and sat on it. He took a few sips of the hot soup, and felt its liquid warmth coursing down through him, driving out the bone deep cold of his night on the run.

"Catch ..." Rocky tossed him a dry roll. "Have a dip."

Jim thanked him again and Rocky watched him silently for a minute or two as he tucked hungrily into the rolls and hot soup. The 'burger arrived, and the big man leaned over and deposited it on the table.

"Wanna coffee, kid?" he asked.

Jim shook his head, and swallowed to clear his mouth before replying. "No thanks, sir. This is just great. I guess I was as much cold as hungry."

The 'burger soon followed the rolls, washed down in its turn by mouthfuls of hot soup. Rocky let him finish eating before speaking again.

"Feel better now?" When Jim grinned and nodded, he went on, "As a matter of interest, wuz dat you we passed on da road back there earlier?"

Jim said it had been and Rocky continued, "See, it's like dis, no-one's gonna stop fer someone dressed like you are ..." he nodded at Jim's torn and stained robe. "It wouldn' be da fust trucker's got hisself mugged by a gang an' had his load hijacked, after stoppin' t'pick up what he thinks is a lone hitch-hiker. Da rest of 'em hide by da roadside till da driver stops, then jump 'im. So now company policy says, 'lose y'load – lose y'job', see?"

Jim nodded and Rocky went on, "Anyway, you wuz sayin' you're in some kinda trouble, kid? Looks t'me like y'bin leadin' with y'face, too!" He nodded towards Jim's head wound. "What's y'handle, by the way?"

"Jim Miller, sir," he answered. "I'm tryin' t'contact my folks in New York. I wanna call 'em an' ask 'em t'come an' pick me up. Y'see I was in a kinda religious sect ... which accounts for this ..." Self-consciously he indicated his torn robe. "But after a while I found I didn' like it ... fact is, there's some real mean people in charge ... I told 'em I wanted out ... but they run it like a prison camp ... y'can't leave or nothin' without permission ... when y'join, you're in for keeps ... but they don' tell you that at the start ... an' if y'try t'leave ..."

"Sorta like dem Moonies, y'mean?" Rocky commented.

Jim blinked as the big man interrupted him. He hadn't been aware of the fact, but his voice had been rising and his speech becoming jerky, disjointed, and Rocky had been watching him closely, a frown of concern clouding his craggy features.

"Yeah," Jim agreed, "Sorta like them ... only worse! I've read that the Moonies use brainwashing to control their members ... well, the sect uses drugs ... anythin' you want, you kin get ... it ain't just religion they're peddlin' ... they're into a heavy drugs scene ... an' even heavier violence ... so I'm splittin' ... gettin' out ... if my folks'll help me ... but like I said ... they don' allow anyone t'leave ... they come after you ... if the dogs don' git you first ..."

By now, the other three drivers had half turned on their stools to watch and listen to the boy with growing interest. Even the fat counterhand had stopped clearing away the dishes to stand and listen. They had all heard of such things through the occasional sensational reports in the press or on TV. Like the extensive media coverage of some years before on the weird religious community who ran a Nazi-style concentration camp in a South American jungle clearing and forced their entire membership to commit mass suicide by drinking cyanide, rather than face outside investigation. But these things were only lurid stories and gruesome pictures that were barely credible to ordinary folk like them. Here was someone in the flesh who was their first personal contact with that twilight world – a young kid who had experienced the grim reality behind the headlines.

"Y'mean they're afraid if y'leave you'll blow da whistle on 'em, dat it?" deliberately Rocky interrupted him again, keeping his voice carefully neutral to calm the boy's obvious agitation.

Jim nodded jerkily, his face drawn and strained. "I guess that's it ... they warn you about goin' to the cops ... they've bin chasin' me all night ... they're out there now ..." he nodded towards the door, "... lookin' for me ... an' they've got these dogs ... Dobermans ... the Hellhounds ... out in the woods every night ... I got away from 'em ... but they ... they got my pal Tom ... it was awful ..."

Without realising it, he had begun to tremble, his eyes wild

107

and staring as the events of the night began to catch up with him.

Rocky, sensing the boy's rising hysteria, though without fully understanding the reason for it, broke in with, "Hey, ease off on the gas pedal there! Not so fast. You're leavin' me way behind."

The torrent of disjointed words was cut off by the sound of Rocky's soothing voice. Jim stood blinking at him as the big man continued cheerily, "Tell y'what, y'kin fill me in on all da details on da way back to da city. How does that grab ya?"

He grinned at the look of surprise on Jim's face. "You still wanna call y'folks an' tell 'em you're on y'way back t'the Big Apple?"

Speechless, Jim nodded. Then he found his voice.

"Yessir. Gee thanks, that's terrific. But ... I've no money on me for the phone. Y'see, we weren't allowed to have any ..."

"Ah, no problem kid." Rocky produced another crumpled bill from his pocket. He grinned at Jim. "Y'sure y'don' wanna coffee fer da road?"

Jim grinned back. "Okay," he accepted.

Rocky flipped the bill onto the counter. "Coffee. White an' sweet," he ordered. "An' gimme some quarters fer da phone."

The coffee and change arrived quickly and Rocky handed Jim the cup and a handful of coins.

"Here y'go Jim. Phone booths're outside on y'left. Tell yer old man he kin pick y'up at ..." he glanced at his watch, "say ... oh-six-hundred outsida da Long Island Haulage Company's Bronx depot. It's on East 163rd, tell 'im. Y'got dat?" Jim repeated the instructions, thanked him and headed joyfully for the door, clutching his coffee in one hand and the fistful of coins in the other. Rocky called after him.

"After you've called y'folks, climb into my rig. It's da one nearest da buildin', other end from da phone booths, okay? I'll see ya dere in a few minutes, after I've used da john."

Thanking Rocky again, Jim shot out of the door and headed for the phone booths. He felt safe now, for the first time in that long terrifying night, confident that the sect wouldn't dare attempt a snatch in the presence of so many witnesses, shunning publicity as they did. He scarcely noticed the cold night wind now, as he trotted along the path to the phone booths, filled as he was with a heady mixture of elation and hot food.

He pulled open the folding door of the first of the four booths, slipped inside, and drew it shut behind him. When he'd picked up the receiver, he had to pause for a moment to recall his home phone number. It seemed so long since he'd used a phone. He had to concentrate hard to recall it – a number he'd been familiar with for years, too! Then memory flooded back, and he fed coins into the slot and dialled.

The ringing tone started at the other end and butterflies of anticipation began to flutter their soft wings against his stomach lining, as he wondered what sort of reception he would get. He thought he could guess – where his father was concerned, that was. The ringing tone seemed to go on for ages.

"Come on … come on …" he muttered impatiently.

Then he remembered it was the middle of the night. His folks would be sound asleep. His father was a firm believer in the maxim 'early to bed, early to rise' being a vital ingredient in his successful business career. He reflected somewhat resignedly that his old man wasn't just a square – he was a complete cube. But even with all his faults, he was infinitely preferable to live with, than those who ran the sect. Jim's thoughts were interrupted when a click announced the lifting of the receiver at the other end of the line. His mother's voice, fuzzy with sleep, gave the number and asked who was calling.

"Mom? It's Jim here …" He got no further.

"Jim!" squealed his mother, instantly wide awake. Then she rushed on excitedly, "Oh Jim baby, how are you? Are you well? It's been so long since we've heard anything about you. I've been so worried about you, honey. Where are you calling from? … Just a moment, honey …"

Her voice became indistinct and muffled as she spoke away from the mouthpiece to someone. He didn't need any prizes for guessing who she was addressing. He could hear his father's voice in the background, sharp, questioning. Then his mother came back on again briefly.

"Hello honey? You still there? Your father wants to speak to

109

you. Now, don't start arguing with him. You know how it upsets me. Just tell me this, are you coming home, Jim?" His mother sounded tearful already.

"Yes Mom. I'll be home soon," he hastened to reassure her, but offered no further explanation for fear of alarming her. He would explain more fully to his father – if he got the chance.

"Oh, that's marvellous news, honey. You've no idea how happy that makes me ..." There was a muffled interruption, the she went on, "anyway, here's your father now. See you soon, honey. Love you." There was the sound of a kiss being blown down the line.

"Yeah, see you Mom. Love you too. Put dad on, will you?"

He didn't have to ask twice. There was the fumbling sound of the receiver being passed from hand to hand, then his father's irate voice drilled into his right eardrum.

"Is that you, boy? This is a fine time of night to call, I must say. Typical of you, though – always put yourself first, don't you?"

Jim eased the phone a couple of inches away from his ear – his father had the habit of conducting phone conversations as though the person at the other end of the line was going deaf.

"Dad ..." he tried unsuccessfully to get a word in.

"Your mother's been worried sick about you, you know that? But I don't suppose that will have occurred to you, not now you've taken up with this ... this ... charlatan who calls himself a prophet ..." his voice suddenly dropped a decibel as he spoke away from the phone, "... no Muriel, I won't hush. It's about time someone told him the truth about himself ..." Then it resumed again full blast, without a pause, "... are you still there, young man?"

"Dad, listen ..."

"No, young man, you listen for a change. If you're calling to ask for money, forget it! We've heard not a word from you, not even a postcard to set your mother's mind at rest, for six whole months. Ever since you walked out of college and your good home. And now, you have the crass nerve to call at this ungodly hour of the night and ..."

"Dad ... for Chrissake! ... WILL YOU SHUT THE FUCK

UP!!" yelled Jim in sheer frustration. He was rewarded by a startled silence, and immediately took full advantage of it to rush on.

"Dad, listen please. I'm in trouble … real bad trouble. I'm sorry for shouting at you like that but I had t'git you to listen to me. I need your help. If you'll jes' give me a chance to explain, y'kin hang up afterwards if y'still want to. Okay?" His knuckles whitened as he gripped the phone tightly, waiting for his father's response. Then surprisingly, instead of the expected lecture on insolence and the use of foul language, his father's voice sounded concernedly in his ear.

"What was that, Jim? Trouble, did you say? What kind of trouble, son?"

Jim heaved a mental sigh of relief. He had done it. He had actually managed to get through to his father. Something, perhaps the urgency of his son's need for support, had reached out and pierced the shell of his old man's self-righteousness, awakening his parental instincts at the same time. Jim hurried on with his story, while he had the benefit of his father's full attention.

"Dad, I'm on my way back to the city. I'm hitchin' a ride with a trucker. I've run away from the sect, dad – an' that's where the trouble I mentioned comes in. You an' mom were right about them, they're no good." He diplomatically offered the flag of truce by conceding this small victory to his father's sense of 'I told you so …'

"In, fact, they're even worse than you think. I've bin on the run from them all night. They're huntin' for me right now, in fact. The thing is, I need you to meet me with clothes and money, when I git back later this morning – I'll tell you where t'meet me in a minute …"

"Jim, what on earth are you on about?…" his father started, but Jim hurried on.

"Dad, please let me finish. This situation is really serious. Y'see, the thing is, I can't come home while these people are after me. I'll need t'go an' lay up with mom's folks in Pittsburgh for a while. See, they'll come lookin' for me t'make me go back. An' you don't know what they're like, dad … they've got these dogs ... they got my pal Tom ... he didn' make it ... it was terrible ..."

Like earlier, when he had been telling Rocky, his tongue began to trip over the words as it vainly tried to keep pace with his overexcited brain.

"Dogs? What dogs?" His father's voice broke into the torrent of Jim's words. "Take your time, son. You're not making sense. And what's all this nonsense about my meeting you with clothes and money, and your not being able to come home? Of course you're coming home. You've been watching too many spy movies, my lad." His father chuckled, then became serious again.

"Don't you worry, son. If anyone comes here from that ridiculous sect inquiring about you, or daring to suggest that you go back with them, they'll have me to deal with! Now, let's take one thing at a time. Where are you speaking from?"

Jim suppressed a sigh of exasperation. He had known it wouldn't be easy to get his father to appreciate the dangers involved. Not that he could blame him. His old man's Ivy League background did not encompass such things as 17-year old youths being hunted down and eaten by packs of killer dogs. He decided to let it rest until he met him later in the morning. Once he had the chance of an uninterrupted talk with him, he'd be able to explain in detail. Just then, the flashing light and beeping tone of the pay-phone told him he was almost out of time, so he fed his remaining coins into the slot to allow him to finish his call.

"Listen dad, will you please jes' meet me as I asked, an' I'll explain everything. Okay? I'm calling from a phone booth in a gas station. It's a few miles down th'road from Bethlehem House. That's where ... hold on a sec' ..." He paused as the booth door was pulled open from the outside and he felt a sudden draught of cold air on his back.

He half turned, partly covering the mouthpiece with one hand, intending to tell Rocky that he'd be with him in a couple of minutes – and found himself staring straight into the slanted, glittering eyes of Angel One!

Jim shrank back with an incoherent yelp of fear and gasped,

"Archangel Michael!"

The oriental moved like lightning, his open right hand a blur as it smashed viciously down onto the receiver rest. The instrument's base imploded into a V-shape of shattered plastic and crushed wiring.

Before Jim's shocked mind could react, Angel One's hand shot forward again, swift as a striking snake, delivering a rigid three-fingered strike to his solar plexus. A bolt of sickening agony doubled Jim forward, driving the air from his lungs. Already spiralling towards unconsciousness, he barely felt the impact of the vicious axe-hand chop to the joint of his neck and shoulder, which plunged him down into a deep black pit of oblivion.

He was totally unaware of being picked up, thrown over a shoulder like a limp rag doll, and carried away....

12

VIRGIL MILLER STARED, PERPLEXED, AT THE PHONE in his hand. It was giving out the dialling tone. He was sure he'd heard his son cry out just before they'd been cut off. Maybe he was imagining things, though. Secretly he'd been as worried as his wife about the boy, though he'd been damned if he'd been going to show it.

In an attempt to re-establish the broken contact, he reached out and tapped the receiver rest up and down a few times, saying, "Hello? ... Hello? ..." But all he succeeded in obtaining were a succession of staccato clicks in his ear before the dialling tone cut in. Quickly he replaced the receiver to allow Jim to dial through again.

Looking up, he met his wife's eye across the small phone table, which was situated between their twin beds. Her maternal instincts fully aroused from what she'd heard of the one-sided conversation, she asked anxiously, "Anything wrong, dear?

Did you get cut off? What sort of trouble is Jim in? Why can't he come home? Virgil?"

Miller shook his head absently, temporarily preoccupied as his mind rapidly assessed the import of Jim's call and concentrated on recalling all the details. Then it occurred to him that he'd better say something to reassure his wife, in case he communicated his own sense of growing unease to her.

Keeping his tone carefully offhand, he replied, "Oh ... you know Jim, m'dear. The boy always exaggerates everything out of all proportion. If you ask me, the simple fact of the matter is that he's out of funds and having to hitch a lift from wherever he is. He probably thinks we're still mad at him, which is no bad thing, so he's putting on the old Prodigal Son act ... you know ... no doubt hoping I'll relent and coax him back home with the promise of fatted calf and French fries."

As he spoke, he swung his legs out of bed, stepped into his slippers and stood up. Lifting his spectacles from the bedside table, he settled them on his nose and reached for his dressing-gown. He smiled reassuringly at his wife. "It appears, in fact," he continued cheerfully, "that the boy has come to his senses at long last and decided to listen to our advice for a pleasant change. He's left that idiotic outfit he took up with and he's on his way back to us, even as we speak."

"Oh, that's wonderful," his wife Muriel responded brightly. She smiled back at him as she spoke, to convince him his transparent attempt to reassure her was working. Then she added innocently, "Do you think he'll call back? It's annoying he got cut off like that. I wonder what happened?"

"Oh I expect he'll call back all right," he reached across and took her hand reassuringly. "He hadn't finished giving me his sales pitch. As to our getting cut off, no doubt some backwoods operator got the jack-plug caught up in her knitting or something like that." He chuckled at his witticism, then giving her hand a squeeze he added, "Tell you what, m'dear. How about fixing us a cup of chocolate while we're waiting for Jim to call back. Bring mine to the study. I may as well wait down there, now I'm up." His wife bustled from the bedroom, tying on her housecoat as she went, glad to be doing something to occupy herself and keep at bay the nagging feeling that all was not right....

Miller ran a comb through his greying hair to tidy it up and let his mind dwell once more on the substance of his son's disturbing call. The trouble was, the more he thought about, the less he liked it. A worried frown creased his forehead. Events such as Jim had mentioned were far outside the limits of his own experience. In Virgil Miller's neatly ordered, predictable world of steady office hours and quiet suburban home life, such things just didn't happen. People in a normal, sane world didn't get hunted through the night – and by dogs, for heaven's sake!

But at the same time, Virgil Miller was a realist. He believed the evidence of his own ears. He was as sure as he could be that he had heard Jim cry out in alarm a split second before the connection had been broken. It had sounded as though he said something strange, too. What was it ... he concentrated hard, searching his mind ... Wasn't it something biblical? ... Archbishop ... no ... Archangel ... yes, that was it ... Archangel Michael! ... at least, that's what it had sounded like, muffled and indistinct as it had been. It just didn't make sense, though ...

He decided if he had heard nothing more from Jim within half an hour, he'd contact the police and give them the opportunity to earn some of the money he paid in taxes towards their wages. Knotting the ties on the front of his robe, he headed downstairs to his study. When Muriel entered bearing two cups of hot chocolate a few minutes later, he shooed her gently upstairs with hers, promising to tell her the moment any word came from Jim.

"There's no sense in both of us losing our sleep, while we wait for it to occur to him to call us back," he said as convincingly as possible.

"Well, I hope he calls back soon," she replied concernedly, "and doesn't keep you up too long. You've only had half a night's sleep." She paused at the study door, looked back and added wistfully, "Still, it will be nice to have him back with us again, won't it, dear?" When he smiled and nodded, she smiled back, though it was evident the tears were not far away. Then she was gone.

Miller sighed and settled back in his favourite wing-backed chair. He filled and lit his pipe, his movements slow and deliberate, as he waited with as much patience as he could muster for Jim to call again. All the while, he tried to ignore the growing feeling of unease in the back of his mind that all was not as it should be ...

Back at the gas station, the four truckers were grouped round the telephone booth from which Jim had been so unceremoniously removed only minutes earlier. They stared, puzzled, at the mute evidence of the smashed instrument base, the handset dangling from its line and the flattened cup lying on the ground in a puddle of spilled coffee.

Jube was the first to speak, breaking the pregnant silence. "Looks like somethin's happened t'the kid, huh?"

Rocky glared at him from under a raised eyebrow. "You're wastin' y'time drivin' trucks, y'know dat? You sh'd be in da fuckin' FBI!" he commented witheringly.

"Hell Rocky, why git sore at me?" Jube whined. "Jes' cuz ah wuz foolin' with 'im earlier. Ah only said ..."

"I know whatchya said, dummy!" Rocky growled irritably. "I sure as hell didn' think he'd fell in da fuckin' mout'piece, an' bust his way outa da base. Too fuckin' right sumpin's happened to 'im. Da kid said he wuz in trouble. Looks like he meant it. Looks like it caught up wid 'im, too."

He looked angrily round the empty forecourt. "I tell ya one thing, if he's bin grabbed by dem Moonie pricks he wuz tellin' us about, da bastards sure moved fast. He only left us a few minutes ago t'call 'is folks." He shook his head. "Wishta fuck I knew what's happened to 'im. I got a bad feelin' about it."

Red and Jube nodded and muttered their agreement. Chuck, silent all this time, removed the thin cheroot from his mouth and inclined his head towards the pump attendant, clearly visible in the kiosk window.

"How about him?" he asked. His slightly husky voice matched its owner, quiet and serious. "Maybe he saw somethin'? Why not ask 'im, while I check th'road for any signs of these Jesus freaks, in case they're on wheels?"

Rocky followed the direction of his look. "Yeah ... good thinkin', Chuck. Let's do it!" Immediately the big man turned and headed for the kiosk, followed by the others.

They soon discovered that the elderly attendant had been unaware of any unusual activity in the vicinity of the phone booths and being hard of hearing, he had heard nothing either. However, on reflection he then said that he did seem to recall, come to think of it, some kind of vehicle ... a van maybe ... pulling away from out front, some minutes previously.

As Chuck's inspection of the deserted road also proved negative, Rocky decided to call in the police. He felt helpless in the face of the mystery, and at the same time annoyed at himself that he had left the kid on his own, so he wanted to be sure he had done all he could to help him before he left the scene.

No-one argued. Jube and Red in particular felt somewhat shamefaced because of their earlier treatment of Jim, now that it appeared he could be in some sort of real trouble.

Half an hour later, the four truckers were on the road again, burning up the miles on the last lap of their long night haul to the city. Two State Troopers, having noted all the details of the drivers and their story, carried out a perfunctory search of the surrounding area. Later they checked out the highway for a few miles in either direction of the gas station.

To the north, they made the limit of their search pattern the gates of the large fenced-in grounds of the private mental clinic – the one with the biblical sounding name on the notice board outside it. BETHLEHEM HOUSE it read, PSYCHIATRIC CLINIC AND CONVALESCENT HOME. STRICTLY PRIVATE. ADMITTANCE BY APPOINTMENT ONLY.

Without having said as much to the foursome, the two cops were of the opinion that these dumb truckers had been neatly taken for the suckers they undoubtedly were. It looked to them like some double-wide, long haired junkie – if he was long haired, he had to be a junkie – had sold the four a hard luck story, conned them out of a handout of money and free food and had then melted into the night, having first vandalised the phone for good measure. The senior trooper summed up their joint opinion when he remarked scathingly to his partner that it would have served the dumb pricks right, if the junkie had slashed their tyres as well, before lighting out.

Predictably, the troopers turned up nothing on their cursory search, and soon resumed their normal night patrol duties. However, they were conscientious enough to write out an occurrence report later in the morning, before going off duty, accurately setting down all the details supplied to them by the drivers. It was processed in the usual way – a brief description of Jim Miller was issued to crews of cars patrolling the area where he was last seen, and a record of the APB – All Points Bulletin – along with that of the occurrence report, was filed away in the memory banks of the computer in County Police HQ.

Virgil Miller waited a full half hour before phoning the police. He hated being made to look foolish, so he gave Jim as long as possible to call back before taking the irrevocable step of involving the police. Also, he wanted to be sure his wife was asleep before he made the call. There was no need to worry her unnecessarily, he counselled himself, as there would probably turn out to be some perfectly ordinary explanation in the end. When at last it became clear to him that the awaited call from Jim was not going to materialise, he reluctantly he picked up the study phone and dialled the local precinct HQ.

A frustrating quarter of an hour followed as he tried to convey what he felt to be the urgency and importance of the situation, to a polite but obviously unimpressed desk sergeant. From the tone of the conversation, it quickly became obvious that the police would be treating the matter merely as another missing person report.

What made it worse was that he had so few hard facts to give the police to go on. Only the call itself and its middle of the night timing, Jim's remarks about being hunted by people from the sect, something about dogs being used, and a pal named Tom whom these dogs had apparently caught. And finally, his son's frightened cry as the phone had gone dead – the thing which had alarmed him – even that sounded less than convincing when he tried to put his nameless fear into words.

On the other hand, he could give no satisfactory answer to the sergeant's polite but pointed questions about the identity of this religious sect his son was involved with, whether his son had joined them of his own free will. Most important of all, he could not even provide any more specific indication as to where his son had been calling from, other than it had been from a gas station a few miles from a sect property called Bethlehem House, somewhere upstate.

Miller was told there wasn't much the police could do under the circumstances, given the lack of hard facts to go on. The boy had, by his father's admission, joined this religious group of his own free will. He couldn't even give any specific information about the organisation, other than to relate how he had seen his son one day, a few months previously, in the company of some other youngsters on a city street, all wearing coloured robes – a description which could apply to any of a dozen or more sects, from the Hare Krishna Temple downwards.

Finally, he was told, regarding his suspicion of an alleged abduction having taken place earlier at the said unknown gas station, again he was unable to produce any real proof to support this claim either. In the event, the sergeant informed him, a missing person report would be filed, and in the meantime, should any further information come to light which might help them make inquiries, he was advised to get in touch again. A full description of Jim was taken for the record, and that was it.

Fuming with suppressed anger and frustration, Miller slammed the phone down onto its rest. "Damned useless form-fillers!" he muttered furiously. "Small wonder people form vigilante groups and take the law into their own hands." Inwardly he knew he was being unfair. The facts, or lack of them, he'd supplied to the police wouldn't have enable them to find Jim in the upstairs bathroom, let alone somewhere in the entire State of New York.

Over at Precinct HQ, the desk sergeant quickly filled in a missing person report form, then called over one of the office clerks and told him to file it.

The young cop looked uncertainly at the form in his hand, then asked, "You want me to circulate it first, sarge?"

"You'd be better stickin' it in th'fuckin' john, for all th'good it'll do," replied the sergeant sourly. "It's only some rich prick thinks we're a fuckin' child welfare office. Thinks all we gotta do with our time is chase all over the entire State of New York, fer Chrissake, lookin' fer junior, who's fallen out with some religious nuts he took up with. An' if that's not enough, he tells me he thinks junior's paradin' around in some kinda coloured nightie, would y'believe?" He shook his close-cropped head in disbelief. "If y'ask me, dressed like that, junior'll be in California by now with th'rest of the weirdoes down there."

He waved a dismissive hand at his grinning subordinate. "Ah, what's the use, but I suppose you'd better wire it to State HQ in Albany. Then do me a favour – go lose it somewhere in our filing system. An' that sh'd be no trouble, with our filing system! An' hey! ..." he called after the retreating back, "how about some coffee over here ..."

The sergeant shook his head again as his phone began shrilly demanding his attention, as it had done constantly throughout the night. He reached for it wearily. There were more important things to be attended to than runaway rich kids in coloured nighties and they all seemed to happen when he was on shift.

Miller sat for a few more minutes after he'd replaced the phone, thinking hard on his next move. Then a wisp of an idea drifted by on the current of his thoughts. He clutched at it like the proverbial drowning man's straw, and dragged it back into focus. Police inquiries ... missing persons ... detectives ... PRIVATE detectives ... that was the solution he was seeking!

He recalled a recent conversation he'd had with his friend Bob Maynard, during a weekend round of golf. Bob had told him about a private detective he'd employed to find his headstrong teenage daughter who had run off with some penniless chiseller she'd met at college. The detective had successfully traced the girl to a seamy motel somewhere up-state, where she had taken a job as a room-maid, having been abandoned minus her money and her virginity, by her ex-Romeo. The girl was now safely back in the family fold.

At the time, Miller had been pointedly non-committal. He had sensed a loud and rather unsubtle hint was being dropped for him to take the same course of action, in order to trace his own missing offspring. But he had remained stiffly unresponsive, maintaining his entrenched attitude that his son had made his choice against all parental advice to the contrary, so he was certainly not prepared to go chasing after him.

But the circumstances were different now. To hell with the police and their plodding bureaucratic inefficiency – not to mention their damned patronising attitude. Missing person report, indeed! He would contact Bob Maynard first thing in the morning, get the particulars of that private detective from him and engage the man to trace his son. Then, if it turned out he had been abducted by these religious freaks, he'd present the facts to the police and demand that they act to release him and arrest his kidnappers.

Now that he'd decided on this course of action, he felt a lot easier in his mind. He checked his watch and was surprised to find it was almost one-thirty – time to catch up on his sleep. He had a busy day ahead of him. He got up, knocked out his pipe and laid it beside the ashtray on his desk. Pausing at the study door, Miller looked back at the phone for a long moment but it remained obstinately silent. Reluctantly he switched off the light and left the room, pulling the door closed behind him.

Quietly he made his way back upstairs to the bedroom, being careful not to waken his wife. Time enough over breakfast to tell Muriel about Jim's failure to call back and his subsequent decision to hire a private detective. He hated emotional scenes, and he was sure she would take a calmer, more objective view of the night's events in the cold light of morning.

Removing his dressing-gown and slippers, he slid between the sheets of his bed. Within minutes his logical mind, having no further reason for remaining awake, had shut up shop again and he was sound asleep.

He was quite unaware of his wife's muffled sobs as she quietly wept into her pillow. Unknown to her husband, she'd followed his futile call to the police on the bedroom extension and had learned the full frightening truth of Jim's actual words and subsequent unknown fate. She cried herself to sleep.

13

JIM MILLER REGAINED CONSCIOUSNESS LYING FACE down in the rear of the moving van. He surfaced slowly in a sea of pain and despair. The pain was bad enough in itself but the despair was worse. His injured head and battered body seemed to have fused into one huge ache. But they were nothing compared to the sickening realisation of his recapture. That – and the dread of what now lay ahead of him.

Hearing the whine of a gear change and feeling the van slowing to a stop, he pushed himself into a sitting position against one of the sides. It was almost pitch dark, the smoked glass of the rear door windows allowing only a faint trace of moonlight to filter through, but it was enough to let him see he was alone and unguarded.

The simple action of sitting up made his throbbing head swim and he felt he was going to throw up. He held his breath and squeezed his eyes tight shut and in a few seconds the interior of the van stopped spinning round him as the nausea subsided. The attack left him in a cold sweat but his head had cleared a little.

Putting out his hands, he felt about him in the dark and discovered he was imprisoned in what was virtually a locked steel box. The rear doors, when he crawled over to check them, felt discouragingly solid and unyielding and the thought occurred to him that the van had been designed, or converted, to fulfil the very purpose it was serving now. Dully he wondered how many others like him had travelled in it in similar circumstances of despair, during the time the sect had been in existence.

After a couple of quick stops the van picked up speed again, and the soft rasp of gravel under the moving wheels told him they had been negotiating the big double entrance gates of the Bethlehem House estate and were now heading up the driveway. He felt as low as he'd ever been in his life. Especially when he recalled how close he had been to success. He felt in some obscure way that he'd let Tom down too. His failure to carry the escape through to a successful conclusion made it seem as though his friend's terrible death had been entirely in vain.

The van slowed to a stop for the last time and the engine was shut off. The ensuing silence was deafening. He felt like a French aristo whose tumbril had just jerked to a stop at the foot of the guillotine. Fear of what lay ahead crawled through his belly like a fiery snake.

Suddenly there was the sound of a key turning in the lock of the van door and it was jerked open. A flood of bright light blinded him, lancing pain into his injured head and setting it throbbing anew. He cringed back against the side of the van's interior, pressing himself flat to the cold metal as though trying to meld his body into it.

"Out!"

Angel One's sharp command made Jim wince in anticipation of some further violence to his person from his fearsome captor. Nothing of the sort happened. Shading his eyes from the glare of the light, he squinted out from under his hand. Two figures stood flanking the van doorway. Their blurred outlines sharpened as his eyes adjusted to the bright fluorescent lights of the garage, where he now saw they had arrived. On the right stood the black-clad figure of Angel One, on the other side stood a grey tracksuited Apostle.

The oriental jerked his head. "Out!" he repeated curtly.

In obedience to the guttural command, Jim scrambled stiffly and painfully from the van to stand between the two figures of his captors. Involuntarily his body tensed again in anticipation of an assault of some kind. But again nothing happened. Instead,

Angel One jerked his cropped head in the direction of a connecting door a few yards away, set in the garage wall and apparently leading directly into the house.

"Move!" he barked.

On the Oriental's command, the Apostle spun on his heel and led the way, Jim stumbling after him. Angel One followed a few paces behind, effectively sandwiching Jim between them. Prisoner and escort threaded their way past another couple of parked vehicles in the spacious interior of the garage and entered the doorway. This led into a short passageway with a second door at the far end, which in turn admitted them to the entrance hall of the big house. Without pause, the Apostle led the way across the large hallway and through another door on the far side, which Jim knew led down into the basement, although he had never been allowed down into this part of the house until now. Access was strictly forbidden to all members except with special permission and a sign made this clear to all concerned.

Jim now found himself descending a steep flight of stairs. At the bottom a short passageway ran from left to right. To his left he caught a quick glimpse of a grey metal door bearing a sign reading CONTROL – AUTHORISED PERSONNEL ONLY, before he followed the Apostle to the right along the passage, to where it connected with a long corridor, in the form of a T-junction. Turning left into this corridor, they passed several doors to either side of them in the whitewashed brick walls as they walked along its length.

Jim was trying to keep track of his movements and reckoned they were roughly under the centre of the house and making their way somewhere off to the rear. They reached another T-junction and this time turned right. A short distance along this new passage brought them to a dead-end before a blank grey steel door, which effectively barred further progress.

Producing a key, Angel One unlocked the heavy door, and it swung silently open on well-oiled hinges. They passed through the doorway and Jim's heart sank when he saw where they had arrived. They had entered a short, enclosed passage with eight grey steel doors set flush into the walls, four on either side. Each door had a round, glass-covered Judas-hole set at eye level.

Although Jim had never seen this place before, he knew where he was from the descriptions of others who had. These cells – for they were cells – were used as one of the milder forms of punishment in the sect discipline code. Once a member had been encouraged to become hooked on heroin, for example, he then became especially vulnerable to the devastatingly effective punishment of the withholding of his supply. The more serious the breach of the rules, the longer the period of confinement imposed on the defaulter.

It was down here in these cells that the unfortunate addicts suffered their private hell of withdrawal symptoms – sweating and shivering their way through the cramps, the vomiting, the chronic diarrhoea and the other withdrawal symptoms euphemistically referred to as cold turkey. For this reason, these six cells were known as the Turkey Pens. More sinisterly, they were also rumoured to be used as condemned cells, whenever necessary. Jim shuddered as this last unwelcome recollection crawled into his mind.

Angel One unlocked the first door on the left and motioned for Jim to enter. He obeyed and found himself in a bare room, some twelve feet by eight, lit by a fluorescent tube set behind thick glass blocks in the ten foot high ceiling. A thin foam rubber mattress lay to one side of the cell, with three blankets folded neatly on top of it. In the far corner stood a plastic bucket covered by a lid, its function obvious from the toilet roll lying beside it. Protruding from one wall was a single cold water tap, set over a small grating in the concrete floor. Hooked over the tap handle was a white plastic half-pint cup. Any further hope of escape vanished from Jim's mind as he looked round the secure, spartan interior. Apprehensively he wondered what would happen now.

Angel One gave him no further time for contemplation. Jim's shoulder was seized in a painful grip and he was dragged roughly round to face the oriental. The slanted black eyes bored into his and fear constricted Jim's breathing as he gazed into their fathomless depths. Suddenly Angel One released his grip and his harsh voice broke the tense silence.

"Where is the other one?" he demanded.

125

Jim blinked stupidly at him, desperately playing for time by pretending to be still dazed. His brain shifted into top gear and he rapidly decided his only chance was to convince the oriental that Tom was still free and running. If they didn't find his remains for some time, it would prolong his life – at least until they discovered the grim truth. His only hope was to play for time, delaying the inevitable as long as possible, in the faint hope that the miracle of another chance to escape might present itself.

"Where is the other one – your companion? Answer!" Again the question rapped out.

Jim mumbled indistinctly in reply, deliberately slurring his speech as though still dazed. It wasn't difficult. Fear and fatigue had dried up his mouth and throat.

"I … I dunno … " he started.

Suddenly pain exploded in his injured head as Angel One's hard hand slammed into the side of his face. The room spun crazily for a moment and his ears rang with concussion.

"Answer the question! Where is the other one – the boy Sheppard? Why was he not with you?" The glittering eyes lasered into his, seeming to scan the very depths of his mind.

Before answering, Jim shook his head to clear it and also to avert his gaze from the hypnotic grip of the cruel eyes. His mind raced to find a reply which would satisfy his interrogator and prevent a repetition of the blow he had just received.

"I … I dunno know where he is, Archangel Michael … honest … that's the truth." The words tumbled out rapidly, prompted by his fear of the man and his desperate need to convince him of his sincerity. "We split up as soon as we got over the fence. He headed north an' I headed south …" He stopped and held the Oriental's piercing gaze as steadily as he could.

Angel One eyed him coldly for a few pensive seconds. "A strange way for two frightened runaways to act …" he commented drily. Then his voice hardened again. "What was your reason for this. Why did you split up? Why did you not stay together? Answer!"

Jim flinched as the last word whiplashed out, giving him no time to think.

"We ... we thought we'd have a better chance if we went different ways," he replied as convincingly as he could. "We'd planned to do that if we got over the fence."

"Why?" The question shot back at him.

"Well ... we knew you'd be after us, an' we reckoned if we stayed together we'd only be riskin' both of us gittin' caught, if things didn't work out." He warmed to his lie but at the same time was careful not to over elaborate. "See, we reckoned if we split up, it'd give us two chances of gittin' clear away. Besides, it meant you'd have to divide up your search parties too, which'd give us an even better chance of makin' it ..."

Letting his voice tail off, he shrugged resignedly and stood looking at the oriental, shoulders slumped in an attitude of dejection and defeat. He didn't have to play the part, either. It was exactly how he felt! All the time he was praying silently that Angel One would buy his story and continue the fruitless search for Tom throughout the night – and with any luck, throughout the following day as well.

"Who were you phoning?" the oriental demanded.

The sudden change of direction caught Jim completely off guard. "My folks," he replied without thinking, and could have bitten his tongue off immediately the words were out. Desperately he tried to recover the slip. "But I wuz jes' lettin' 'em know I wuz okay. I didn' say nothin' about bein' in trouble ... I only told my father I'd decided to leave. I told 'im I'd no proper clothes an' asked 'im t'meet me with some, when I got back to the city. But I told 'im I wuzn't comin' back to stay with them, cuz I wanted to keep my independence. That wuz okay with him cuz he wuz still mad at me for leavin' home in the first place."

"You didn't ask him to involve the police or to drive out from the city to pick you up on the road?" Angel One's voice was loaded with menace.

"No, Archangel Michael. I wouldn't git my folks in trouble with you by doin' that. I swear it." Jim assured him earnestly.

"And how exactly did you propose to get all the way back to

the city in time for this meeting with your father?" The oriental was still suspicious.

Jim decided at this point to mention the truckers, in a final attempt to get his parents off the hook and free from any reprisals. The four drivers would be well beyond the reach of the sect by this time, so he reckoned it would be safe enough to divert Angel One's attention onto them.

"I'd managed to hitch a ride with a trucker at the gas station, where you caught me," he replied. Then without thinking he added with a touch of defiance, "An' I told 'im an' his three buddies my name, an' how I'd run away."

Angel One's eyes glittered dangerously and Jim hurried on, "See, they were gonna beat me up at first, cuz they said they don't like religious freaks, but when they heard I'd run away, they changed their minds an' decided to help me instead. So they'll prob'ly call in the police now, after findin' the smashed phone, an' me gone."

Angel One shrugged. "The police are of no account apart from their nuisance value," he stated flatly. "Should they make inquiries, they will obtain no satisfaction. You are here of your own choice, remember? And, Miller ..." his harsh voice became vibrant with menace, "if the police do put in an appearance, you will personally assure them of that fact. Do I make myself clear?"

Jim nodded dumbly in response. However, despite the threat implicit in Angel One's words, he felt relief at having achieved his purpose. He had apparently succeeded in diverting attention away from his parents, as he had hoped. So, if nothing else, he had salvaged that much from the wreckage of his abortive escape bid.

His relief increased ten-fold when Angel One abruptly brought the interrogation to an end with the words, "You will remain here until the Prophet returns from the city in a few days' time. He will decide what form your punishment will take."

Before Jim could make any response, the oriental turned and strode from the cell. The door slammed shut and he was on his own. Pouring himself a cup of water, he drank deeply. The water was cold and refreshing, and he splashed some over his face and neck. Peeling off his soiled and torn robe, he dried himself with it, bundled it up and threw it into a corner.

Lowering himself stiffly onto the mattress, he leaned back against the cold concrete wall and closed his eyes to shut out the light and ease his throbbing head. Gingerly he massaged his aching shoulder and stomach, where the oriental had struck him earlier. Soon he began to feel cold, and became aware of an icy draught stirring the cool atmosphere of the cell. Looking up, he traced its source to a ventilation grille high in one corner. Prompted both by the cold and by exhaustion, he unfolded the blankets and rolled himself wearily into them, curling into a foetal ball on the mattress. Almost immediately he felt a soothing wave of sleep wash over him and he sank gratefully into its dreamless depths.

Deep in the woods outside, the bright moonlight filtered down through the tangled branches of the trees to paint a latticework of black and silver on the forest floor. Its pale ghost light eerily lit up a scene of primal savagery, which could have been lifted straight out of some dark corner of Dante's Inferno. The night-black forms of ten amber-eyed demons gnawed on glistening, red-streaked bones, as the Hellhounds completed their grisly nocturnal banquet.

PART III
INVESTI-
GATION

14

LIKE SOME HUGE SURREALISTIC LIGHTHOUSE, THE towering new concrete and glass office block reared thirty floors high out of the surrounding ocean of drab brownstone tenements, that washed against it on every side. It was obvious that the building's designer had given much time and thought to the type of structure best suited to blend in perfectly with the local architectural environment – and had then gone right ahead and designed the exact opposite.

Grandly titled the HARLEM COMMERCIAL CENTRE, the project had been meant to bring badly needed jobs to the local black community, on the fringe of whose ghetto it was situated – and a resultant kickback of badly needed votes to the local Congressman who had conceived the monster and opened it in a blaze of carefully orchestrated publicity. It had failed on both counts.

Inevitably, because of the lack of suitably trained black office workers, the tower block provided only a minimal number of jobs for the local population. Decades of social, economic and educational deprivation made sure of that. As a result, ninety per cent of the building's employees were whites, who commuted to it from all over the city each morning. Equally inevitably, therefore, the locals had scathingly christened the structure 'Honky Tower'.

However, it had one thing going for it, in that it provided the city business community with a source of cheap office accommodation in inflationary times. This in turn meant that it housed a high proportion of detective agencies eager to cut down on overheads and not particularly worried about the lack of a more prestigious business address in the phone book. The firm of Sherman & Grant, Licensed Inquiry Agents Inc., occupied a modest suite of offices on the building's eighth floor.

Brett Grant, the junior half of the partnership, preferred to avoid using the basement car park when he could find a suitable space at the kerbside. That particular morning as he arrived to start his day's work, he found he was in luck. About forty yards short of the tower block, he spotted a gap between two parked cars. Easing his bronze Mustang out of the unending stream of busy morning traffic, he braked smoothly to a halt. The sudden angry blare of a car-horn from behind, announced that he had just beaten another would-be parker to it. He grinned at the gesticulating, red-faced driver slowly cruising past and gave him the finger.

"Up yours too, fella!" he called cheerily and deftly reversed the Mustang into the vacant slot.

Switching off the engine, he leaned back, closing his eyes. He massaged the stiffness out of his neck muscles for a few seconds with his fingertips. His strong-jawed features relaxed as he did so, making him look younger than his thirty-two years. Fatigue gently prickled his closed eyelids and he promised himself – again – that he'd definitely turn in early that night to catch up on his sleep. The trouble was, he reflected, he'd been promising himself that for the past six months since he'd moved in with Pam in her flat. Every time they went to bed, the last thing either of them seemed to have in mind was sleep!

The previous night had been no different from any other in that respect. And that had been despite the lateness of the hour and the fact that they were spending the night in a strange bed in the Curtis's spare room. In fact, the latter factor had only seemed to add spice to their lovemaking in some exciting way. They had arrived at a mutually explosive climax of particular intensity, which had seemed to go on, and on.

Afterwards, lying in each other's arms and slowly floating back to earth together, Pam had murmured sleepily in his ear, "M-m-m, that was good. If that's what visiting your old precinct does for you, you have my permission to go anytime."

He had chuckled and hugged her tightly to him, by way of reply. But neither he nor Curtis had enlightened the two women as to the horrific details of their visit to the morgue when they had returned. As Ben had put it earlier, they had refused to 'talk shop' and so spoil the pleasant atmosphere of their get-together.

Reluctantly Grant dragged his thoughts away from Pam and stretched himself as best he could in the confined space of the Mustang. A frown creased his forehead as he contemplated the morning ahead with a distinct lack of enthusiasm. He hated paperwork – that was the problem. He was essentially a physical person. He much preferred even the tedious leg-work of his job as a private detective, just so long as it kept him out of the office and on the move. He didn't even mind driving for long periods, provided it wasn't a desk he was driving.

But he'd promised Anna, the Agency's efficient, hard-working secretary that he'd spend the forenoon clearing his in-tray and catching up on his backlog of paperwork. Letters to be signed, case-files to be brought up to date, expense accounts to be filled in, progress reports for clients to be dictated, and so on. In fact, all the hundred and one things which had to be committed to paper, and which had to be dealt with regularly to enable a detective agency to function. It was Grant's pet theory that there must be some form of karma which decreed that each day a private eye spent on inquiries had to be counter-balanced by half a ton of paperwork.

His reverie was interrupted by a sharp rap on the window at his left ear. Opening his eyes, he rolled his head sideways on the seatback and found himself looking into a small, grinning black face topped by a mini-Afro haircut, mere inches away through the glass. He grinned back, opened the door, and unfolded his athletic six-foot-two inch frame out of the Mustang and onto the sidewalk. He offered his right hand, palm upwards, to the slim ten year-old black kid he so completely dwarfed.

"Hi Champ. Gimme five."

"Hi Brett." The boy laughed and slapped the outstretched palm. "Watch yo' car fo' yuh, huh?" The big brown eyes looked appealingly up at Grant.

"Oh, is that the reason for the big welcome?" said Grant in

pretended indignation. He reached out and grabbed a fistful of the grinning imp's Afro, and tugged it gently from side to side. "Okay, spill da beans, punk," he growled. "How many mugs ya conned today? Me an' da boys're movin' in on y'racket."

The laughing boy pulled free and skipped back out of reach. "You da fifth ... so far," he replied.

"So far?" snorted Grant in amusement. "Hey man, you better look out, else the Mafia will be movin' in on you."

"No way!" The boy sniffed contemptuously. "Dem Mafia cats won' dare show up roun' dese parts. We got Black Power ... we got da Panthers. Ain' no Mafia honkies gonna face dem!"

"Tell it like it is, Champ," laughed Grant. "Stay lucky. Here, catch ..." He flipped a dollar to the boy, who caught and pocketed it in one swift movement. They slapped palms again, then Grant locked the car, gave the thumbs up to its self-appointed guardian and walked the short distance to the office building.

Climbing the wide concrete steps from the sidewalk, Grant pushed open one of the big plate glass doors. Crossing the tiled floor of the vast echoing entrance hall, he raised a hand in greeting to the uniformed security man in his bullet-proof cubicle under the lit INQUIRIES sign and headed for the bank of elevators.

Grant took one to the eighth floor, where he walked along the brightly lit corridor past the frosted glass doors of other business premises. As he passed each door, his ears picked up the muted office sounds of chattering typewriters, beeping computers and ringing telephones.

Reaching the door of his own office, he glanced briefly at the gilt lettering on its frosted glass panel. SHERMAN & GRANT, LICENSED INQUIRY AGENTS INC., it read. Each time he saw it, he always recalled his senior partner's comment when the signwriter had finished painting it on the door. Harvey Sherman, Harry to his friends, a stocky middle-aged Jew, possessed of the dry wit typical of his people, had remarked, "Sherman an' Grant. How d'ya like that? Makes us sound like a World War Two tank squadron."

A little recollective smile touched Grant's mouth as he opened the door and entered the office reception area. The smile broadened into a cheerful grin as he greeted the secretary busily typing at the desk set against the far wall. She glanced up as he entered and gave him a quick nod of acknowledgement, without breaking her concentration on the dictation feeding into her ear from the clip-on earphone, which was connected to the cassette on her desk. The electric clock on the wall above her head showed the time to be nine-thirty a.m.

Grant crossed to the desk and stood leaning on it with both hands, watching the secretary's nimble fingers flying lightly over the keyboard. She completed the passage of dictation she was working on, unclipped the earphone and leaned back, smiling up at him brightly.

"Good morning, Brett. I hope you have been practising your signature – I have loads of letters for you to sign." She spoke with an attractive foreign accent. Anna was Austrian and had emigrated to the USA with her family some six years previously, when she was eighteen. Despite being Jewish herself, she was as blonde and blue eyed as any legendary Rhine Maiden, much to Harry Sherman's pretended disgust.

"Your Yiddisher momma's bin cheatin' on your poor ol' poppa," he had informed an amused Anna one day. "She's bin entertainin' big blond gentile yoghurt salesmen, while yer ol' man wuz up inna mountains herdin' Edelweiss, or whatever they do fer a livin' out there."

"Hi Anna," Grant returned her greeting, then put on an aggrieved tone as he continued, "Say, what's all this about piles of letters? What've I done to deserve bein' chained to a desk all day?" Placing his hands on her desk, he leaned towards her and whispered furtively, "Listen Warden, do I git time off for good behaviour?"

Anna giggled and pushed him away. "It is your own fault if you have to spend a whole day at your desk. If you would even take some letters home to sign after work, they would not pile up so. Anyway, what about poor me?" she pulled a face at him, "I have to sit at a desk all day, every day."

"Yeah, but I have t'git out an' about – I need the exercise t'keep my legs in shape. You don't ..." he stepped back and

made as though to look under the kneehole of her desk, "...
your legs are in much better shape than mine ... yeah ... much
better!"

Anna blushed and tucked her legs under her chair. "Brett
Grant, behave yourself. What would Pam say if she heard you?"

"Same as she always says ... I'm a sex maniac," he grinned.
"Anyway, stop holdin' me back from my paperwork." He
blandly ignored her expression of amused outrage and asked,
nodding in the direction of the three inner office doors, "Is ol'
Groucho in?"

"Yes," she replied, "Mister Sherman is in – and we have a
client also. They are both in your office."

"My office?" asked Grant, surprised. "Why mine? What's
wrong with his own? He tryin' to save wear on his carpet or
somethin'?"

"No, idiot," she laughed, then became serious again. "This
client, he asks for you by name," she explained in her slightly
stilted English. "Mister Sherman said I was to tell him when
you have arrived, so ..." Putting a finger to her lips to admonish
him to silence, she pressed a button on her desk intercom.

A rasping voice heavily laced with a Brooklyn accent answered
her from the speaker. "Yes, Anna?"

Still looking at Grant, she spoke into the communicator again.
"Mister Grant has arrived, Mister Sherman."

"Thanks, Anna. Be right out." The intercom went dead.

Grant had barely had time to turn away from Anna's desk
when the centre of the three office doors opened and the short,
stocky figure of Harvey Sherman emerged into the reception
area. He pulled the door shut behind him and advanced on
Grant until he was standing chest to chest with his junior partner.
Half a head shorter than the younger man, he nevertheless
glared up at him pugnaciously.

"Well, whaddaya know – here's the night shift comin' in
early. Nice of you t'make the effort. You must've had to rush
y'lunch ..." The rapid-fire Brooklyn accent was also
unmistakably Jewish.

Sherman waved an arm at the wall-clock and rushed on.
"What time is this t'come into work, schmuck?" He spread his

hands in an eloquent gesture of appeal to Anna as he went on, "'I'll be in early tomorrow, Harry', he says. This is early?"

Turning back to the helplessly grinning Grant, he continued, with hardly a pause for breath, "A good job you don't rely on a time-keepin' bonus t'feed you. In two weeks you'd be dead of starvation!"

Sherman paused at last, obviously expecting a reply and Grant said, "C'mon, gimme a break, Harry. It's only nine-thirty. Pam an' me were out last night."

Raising his eyebrows, the older man nodded understandingly. "Aw, I'm sorry, Brett. I never realised." Then his voice took on a cutting edge as he added, "Of course you mustn't let little things like your work interfere with your social life."

He glared up at Grant and emphasised his next words by prodding him in the chest. "Listen dickhead, when you say you're comin' to work early, I assume you mean early, like eight-thirty – same as me – that's an hour ago, in case y'hadn't noticed!"

Grant raised both hands in a gesture of surrender. "Okay … okay … point taken. So I'm a bit late gittin' in. Big deal. What's so special about this mornin' the office can't function without me for a lousy hour?"

Sherman glanced towards the door of Grant's office and continued in a more serious tone, "Because you gotta client in there, that's what. He's only bin here since nine o'clock, waitin' fer y'lordship t'grace us with y'presence. Name of Miller. He smells of money. Smart suit – hand tailored job. Expensive watch. Classy manners. Looks like a bank manager. Talks like one, too."

Grant looked puzzled. "I didn't arrange to see any client this morning …" he began, but Sherman interrupted him.

"He didn' make no appointment. Jes' arrived outa th'blue. He says someone recommended you to 'im. I can't think why! Anyway, it seems his son flew th'coop a while back, an' joined one of those oddball religious mobs we run up against from time to time. Last night th'kid tried t'leave, but these kooks caught 'im an' snatched 'im back in the middle of phonin' his pa fer help. Th'cops ain' interested – no clear evidence of abduction – the usual. So, he wants you t'trace his son an' git 'im back. I didn' disillusion 'im by tellin' 'im you kin hardly find y'way to the office! So, git in there an' sign 'im up fer as long as y'kin squeeze outa him. Like I said, his name's Miller -Virgil Miller, would y'believe? Anyone with a handle like that must have money or he's bin cheated. Go git 'im, tiger ..."

His closing words were spoken as he walked a word-shocked Grant to his office door, propelling him along with a paternal arm round his shoulders. Leaning forward, Sherman opened the door and guided Grant through into the office beyond. Grant found himself facing a tall, distinguished looking man with greying hair, who had risen from his chair and turned to meet him. The clean-shaven face had a decidedly 'bookish' quality. Grant could see why Sherman had said he looked like a bank manager. His own guess would have been either a lawyer or an accountant. The impeccably tailored, dark grey, pinstripe suit spoke of money, again as the eagle-eyed Sherman had noticed, as did the expensive Crombie coat on the stand by the door. Sherman addressed him deferentially.

"Mister Miller, like you t'meet my partner Mister Grant ... my late partner, y'might say ... ha! ... yeah, well ... I'll leave you to get down to business."

As Sherman made to leave, Grant shook hands with Miller and smiled disarmingly. "Pleased to meet you, Mister Miller. Sorry I'm late. On my way here, I decided to check out a line of inquiry on a current case, an' I'm afraid I got side-tracked. That sort of thing happens quite frequently in our line of work." He shrugged apologetically.

From the corner of his eye, he saw Sherman hesitate with his hand on the door handle, arrested by the bare-faced effrontery of the glib lie.

Grant pressed on smoothly. "Would you like a coffee, while we talk? My partner will arrange that, if you wish."

Miller inclined his head and replied, "Thank you, Mister Grant, that would indeed be most acceptable. Provided, of course, I'm not putting you to any trouble." His speech, like his manner and dress, was precise and formal.

"No trouble at all," Grant assured him cheerfully. "How do

you like your coffee?"

"Black please," Miller replied. "With one spoonful of Demerara sugar, if that's possible."

"No problem. Oh, Harry ..." Grant addressed his silently fuming partner in the half open doorway, as though just noticing he was still there, "...be a pal, rustle up two coffees, please. One black, with one spoon of ... uh ... brown sugar. You know how I like mine."

Sherman, restraining himself with an effort, swallowed hard and grated out, "You wouldn' like some sandwiches as well?"

Grant, thoroughly enjoying his turning of the tables on Sherman, appeared to consider this for a moment, then replied straight faced, "No ... it's a bit early for me, Harry. How about you, Mister Miller?"

"Just coffee for me, thanks. I've already breakfasted," replied Miller, quite unaware of the interplay between the two partners.

"Coffees will do fine Harry, thanks," said Grant with a friendly nod of dismissal. He blandly ignored the smouldering glare that Sherman shot at him as he backed from the room, closing the door a little too firmly behind him. Smiling to himself, Grant walked round behind his desk. He switched on his cassette recorder and desk lamp and indicated for Miller to seat himself.

"Well, Mister Miller," Grant began, once he and the client were settled comfortably on either side of the desk. "My partner has given me a very brief outline of the case. As I understand it, your son left home some time ago and joined some kind of religious outfit, that he tried to leave them last night, phoned you, and that you think he was abducted part way through the call. What time was the call, by the way?"

"Oh ... sometime after midnight ... about half past, I think," Miller replied.

"Okay ..." Grant jotted down a note. "And when you called the police with this information, they told you there was insufficient for them to take any action?"

Miller nodded. "That is correct."

"Well, I think we'll kick off with a little background. That's as good a place as any to begin." As Grant spoke, he adjusted the angle of the desk lamp so its soft glow cast a pool of light over his notepad on the desk blotter before him. "Right, we'll start with a description of your son ... Jim, isn't it, or do you call him James?"

"Jim," Miller confirmed. "Christened James, but he prefers Jim."

"Right, Jim it is." Grant noted the name on his pad. "Okay, the sort of things I want are his age, height, build, colour of hair and eyes, any distinguishing marks, that sort of thing. Then onto any reason for his leaving home that you're aware of, and so forth?"

"I'll do my best, Mister Grant." Miller gave a little self-deprecatory smile. "But perhaps I should have brought my wife along for this. Mothers seem to take more notice of these sort of details, I feel. But first, I'd like to say that I've come to you on the recommendation of a friend of mine, a Mister Robert Maynard. You traced his runaway daughter for him after she'd eloped with some disreputable character or other. I think that would have been about ... oh ... six months ago?"

Grant frowned in concentration for a moment, "Maynard ... Maynard," he muttered to himself, then his face cleared. "Oh yes ... I remember the case. Found the girl workin' in a motel upstate. As a matter of fact, I seem to spend a deal of my working time tracing runaways. An' if it's not romance that's tempted them to leave home, it's very often religion. You'd be surprised at how many youngsters git attracted to religious cults, like your son has." He grinned at Miller and added, "In fact you could say the two main reasons for leavin' home are either the lure of the bed or the Bible."

Miller nodded in rueful agreement. "Well, my friend was certainly very satisfied with the result of your work on that occasion and also impressed by your efficiency. He sends his regards, by the way. Now, as for my own runaway offspring ..."

As he spoke, he took a wallet from an inner pocket, opened it and extracted a coloured photograph from one of its compartments. He leaned forward and laid the snap on Grant's desk blotter. "Perhaps a recent snap of Jim would be better than any description I could give you."

Grant examined the photograph while Miller continued to

speak. "That was taken on holiday last August, just over a year ago. He was sixteen then. He hasn't changed much physically since that was taken but I imagine his appearance is considerably more unkempt by now. Judging, that is, from the only time I've seem him since. Him, and some other … members. That was a few months ago, not long after he'd joined this sect."

Grant looked up from examining the snap of a slim, dark haired, blue-eyed youth. The sun-tanned boy was wearing swimming trunks and holding a surfboard, as he smiled self-consciously into the camera. "You've actually seen members of this sect he's joined? Good. That'll be a help. Have you made any contact with them? Who are they, exactly?"

"Yes, I have seen some of these people. But I haven't had any contact with them." He looked embarrassed as he met Grant's questioning look. "I … I was too angry with Jim at that time, to go chasing after him." He shrugged, examined his manicured nails, flicked a speck of dust from his sleeve, then added sourly, "In any case, Jim wouldn't have listened to anything I had to say. We weren't exactly on the same level of communication. In fact, it seemed at times as though we weren't even on the same planet, let alone speaking the same language!"

Miller looked up again and met Grant's level gaze. "I'm sorry if I sound bitter, Mister Grant, but when you've brought up your son to value the important things in life – a good home, a good education, a secure future, social responsibilities, and a proper respect for the laws of God and man – then it comes hard when he rejects it all, in order to follow some hot gospelling charlatan who styles himself a Prophet!" He spat the last word out disgustedly.

Privately, Grant had formed the opinion that perhaps the boy hadn't been rebelling so much against the values his father held, as against his authoritarian manner of forcing them down his throat. But he kept his thoughts to himself. He quietly prompted Miller again as to the identity of this sect his son had joined.

Miller frowned in concentration for a moment, then shook his head. "I must confess I didn't really pay much attention to all the claptrap Jim was spouting at that time. But I do seem to recall it was something which sounded biblical. 'Followers of …'

no, that wasn't it ... 'Disciples of ... something or other ...' something like that."

"'Friends of Jesus' ... that sort of thing?" suggested Grant.

"Yes, something along those lines. It'll come back to me. When it does, I'll let you know," promised Miller.

"It would be a big help when I'm trying to trace them," Grant said. "Now, how did your son come into contact with these people in the first place? Did he say?"

"No, he didn't ever say, but I would assume it would either have been with one of their leaflet dispensing groups they send out to roam the city, or at one of the mobile soup kitchens he said they run," Miller replied. Grant looked up from the notes he was jotting down. "Mobile soup kitchens? Where do these operate? Have you seen them?"

"No," Miller shook his head. "I've only heard Jim mention them. He claimed they dispense soup, coffee and hamburgers to the needy in the poorer areas of the city. Personally, I am of the opinion they only use these so-called charity dispensers to create meeting points, to which they can draw likely members. Then, once they've hooked gullible or impressionable fools like my son, they thereafter brainwash them into blindly accepting their half-baked mishmash of religious hokum."

"You say you actually saw Jim with these people, on one occasion? When was that?" asked Grant. "And how did you know they were sect members he was with?"

"How did I know?" Miller snorted. "Because they parade around in ridiculous coloured robes, that's how. The group I saw Jim with that day ... oh, it must have been about six months ago, just after he'd left home ... were handing out their trashy literature to passers-by, somewhere in the vicinity of the World Trade Centre. I saw them as I passed in my car on my way to a business appointment. If only they could see how ridiculous they look. The attire of the biblical Holy Land is hardly suitable for either the climate or the environment of present day New York." He shook his head disgustedly.

Grant tapped his teeth with his pen and nodded thoughtfully. "You know, I think I've seen some of these kids myself in my travels. So hopefully they shouldn't be too difficult to find."

At this point they were interrupted by the arrival of Anna, bearing two cups of steaming coffee on a tray. Placing the cups on the desk, she darted an amused glance at Grant.

"Mister Sherman's compliments. He says to ring, should you require any further service," she announced primly.

"Thanks, Anna." said Grant, and added straight-faced, "Tell Mister Sherman thanks, but I don't think that'll be necessary. So if he can find something to occupy him for the time being, I'll get back to him if I need anything else, okay?"

Anna retreated, pursing her lips to stifle the laughter she felt welling up inside her, as she imagined Sherman's predictable reaction to this latest verbal thrust from Grant.

Noticing the slightly quizzical look on Miller's face, Grant grinned and explained, "Just poking a little fun at my partner. Keeps him mentally active thinking of swift repartees."

Miller smiled and reached for his coffee. His businesslike mind, having assessed this personable young man on the other side of the desk, instinctively approved of him. He had initially been pleasantly surprised, and somewhat relieved, to find he hadn't at all fitted the image he'd always held of private detectives. Doubtless he had always visualised them as down-at-heel, gum-chewing, wisecracking individuals, who spent their time muck-raking and trying to catch people in bed with the wrong partners. Instead, he found himself being interviewed by an intelligent, smartly dressed young man in a tastefully decorated office. The overriding impression was one of directness and efficiency.

His train of thought was interrupted by Grant's resumption of the interview. Drawn out by the detective's skilful questioning, Miller proceeded to describe Jim's affluent home background, provided by a strict, chartered accountant father and a weak, over indulgent mother. It soon became apparent to Grant that it was a not unusual story. The bored, rich kid, alternately spoiled and over-disciplined by conflicting parental attitudes, rebelling against his lifestyle by deliberately setting out to defy and shock the parents who were stifling his developing character.

Miller obviously failed to recognise that he himself was in

any way to blame for his role in the family conflict. Like so many authoritarian parents, he was unwilling to recognise that his unyielding opposition to his teenage son's points of view and youthful ideals, would only result in driving him towards the very dangers from which he was trying to protect him.

Having filled in the background, Grant then changed tack to concentrate on Jim's phone call of the previous night. "As far as you can recall, Mister Miller, what were Jim's exact words? I'd like to know everything he said, no matter how trivial or insignificant it may have seemed to you at the time."

"Well ..." Miller hesitated briefly, then went on, "... you must understand, he wasn't on the phone long, only a matter of a couple of minutes at the most, before we were cut off. And a great deal of what he did say seemed to be nonsense. I must admit, the thought did cross my mind that he might be ... I think the expression is stoned ... he was so incoherent. Let me see ..."

Miller paused, brow furrowed in concentration, then he began slowly, "The first thing he said was that he was in trouble ..."

Grant looked up from his notes. "Did he say what kind of trouble?"

"Nothing specific, as far as I can remember. When I asked him that same question, all he said was that he had run away from the sect, that he was being chased ... hunted was the word he used ... and that he couldn't come home, because they would come looking for him. He even asked me to meet him with clothes and money. I must admit at that point I did think Jim was exaggerating to gain my sympathy. Especially when he mentioned the dogs ..." At this point he shrugged as though lost for words, and reached for his coffee cup.

"Dogs?" Grant stopped writing and looked up again. "Did he say it as though he meant the real thing? Or could he maybe have been referring to the sect people who were hunting him ... you know, like kids refer to the police as pigs?"

Miller shook his head. "No, I got the definite impression he really meant the four-footed variety, strangely enough. Oh yes ... he also made some mention of a pal who didn't make it, as Jim put it. In fact, what he actually said was that these dogs got his pal. At the time I thought he was talking nonsense, but thinking back on his call after we'd been cut off, he sounded genuinely frightened. That was one of the things which disturbed me about it."

A note of concern had crept into Miller's voice as he spoke and Grant realised there was a human side to the man after all. Underneath the undemonstrative barrier he had erected to prevent his emotions from showing, he obviously loved his son and cared about his well-being.

Grant glanced down at his notes again. "Did Jim give any indication as to where he was calling from?" he asked.

Miller thought about this. "Only that he was calling from a gas station somewhere," he answered slowly. "He also said he'd hitched a ride with a trucker, so I assume he met the man there. But I'm afraid he never gave me an exact location ..." His voice tailed away and a look of intense concentration crossed his face as he searched his memory for something which was eluding him.

Grant, busily taking notes, hadn't noticed. Instead, he repeated the points as he wrote them down. "A trucker ... and a gas station ... right. Anything else said that might help me locate this ..."

"Bethlehem House!"

Grant looked up in surprise as Miller's excited voice interrupted him. Completely oblivious to the fact that Grant had been addressing him, Miller hurried on, "I remember now. Jim said he was calling from a gas station, and that it wasn't far from Bethlehem House."

He held up a hand to stop Grant from saying anything, the look of concentration still etched on his scholarly features. Then he snapped his fingers and exclaimed triumphantly, "Got it! The Children of Bethlehem." Then, catching Grant's quizzical look, he explained with a smile, "That's the name of the sect Jim joined. I knew it would come back to me."

"Okay ..." Grant scribbled busily on his notepad. "Now we're getting somewhere. Any ideas where this Bethlehem House could be situated?"

"Not really," Miller admitted, then added, "Apart from the fact that Jim once told me the sect ran some kind of retreat somewhere upstate. But nothing more specific than that."

"That's okay," Grant assured him. "I think we've enough to give me a good chance of tracking this mob down. Now, before we finish up, did Jim say anything else? Anything at all? It doesn't matter how irrelevant it may have seemed to you at the time. You'd be surprised at how some pieces of seemingly useless information can fit together to build a picture, in the later stages of an investigation."

Miller's brow furrowed, and he looked a little embarrassed. "Well ... there was one other thing ... but I'm not even sure if I heard Jim correctly ..." He hesitated, obviously reluctant to chance making a fool of himself, then took the plunge. "It was just as the phone went dead ... I got the impression he actually said something which sounded like Archangel Michael."

"Archangel Michael?" Grant repeated as he wrote the words on his notepad. "Is this an expression you've ever heard Jim use before?"

"No, definitely not." Miller shook his head. "It's not something I've ever heard him use before. The thing is, Mister Grant, I got the impression that he wasn't using the words merely as an exclamation. On the contrary, he sounded genuinely frightened ... like when he mentioned those dogs earlier in our conversation. I know this sounds strange, but it was rather as though he were actually addressing someone who was right there with him at that moment in time." He shrugged and let his hands fall back into his lap. "Like I say, I know that may sound ridiculous but there it is for what it's worth."

Grant finished writing and sat back. "And of course, Jim hasn't contacted you since being cut off in the middle of his call last night?"

"That's right," Miller agreed.

"So, to sum up," Grant said, "the circumstances of Jim's call, taking into account his apparent fear, the suddenness with which you were cut off, and finally the fact that he has not made any further contact, has given you reason to believe that he may have been forcibly abducted, and is probably now being held against his will by the people who run this sect …" he glanced down at his notes, "… The Children of Bethlehem. And you want me to trace them, confirm that this is the case and if so, and there is still insufficient proof to justify police involvement, you would then want me to take the necessary action, within the bounds of the law, to rescue your son and ensure his safe return home? Right?"

"That sums it up neatly," Miller agreed. Then, glancing at his watch, he added, "Now, if you'll excuse me I must be getting along, if that's all you need from me for now. I have clients of my own to see this morning, I'm afraid. The first one in less than half an hour." He rose and reached for his coat.

"Yes, I think we've covered everything for the time being," replied Grant, also getting to his feet. Walking round the desk, he helped Miller into his coat and opened the door to the outer office for him. "If you'll leave your home and business addresses and telephone numbers with our secretary, I'll be in touch as soon as I come up with anything."

Miller reached for his pocketbook, opened it and extracted two cards. He handed one to Grant. "My card. I'll leave one with your secretary for your records."

"Thanks," said Grant. "And don't hesitate to call us if you remember anything else which might be useful." He grinned reassuringly and added, "And try not to worry too much about Jim. The Canadian Mounties are considering making me an honorary member – I always get my man."

Miller smiled back at him. "Thanks Mister Grant, I'm sure you'll do your best. I certainly feel much easier in my mind, now that I've spoken to you." He held out his hand to Grant and added, "After all my talk of dogs chasing people through the night, I almost feel I should wish you good hunting!" Shaking hands, he turned away and walked through the doorway in the direction of Anna's desk.

15

WHEN GRANT CLOSED THE DOOR ON MILLER'S retreating back, he wasted no time. He returned to his seat and pressed the recorder to rewind. He toyed with his pen as he waited for the machine to click off and ran through the interview in his mind.

What did he have? First, with regard to the sect itself he had the name they went under, a vague location – somewhere upstate – of a retreat or meditation centre of some kind known as Bethlehem House, and lastly the fact that they operated vans dispensing free food and drink to down-and-outs in the poorer areas of the city. From this last fact alone, Grant reckoned they should be relatively easy to track down, as there was a good chance they'd be registered with City Hall as a charity for tax relief purposes.

Second, with regard to tracing the actual location of where the boy was being held – assuming abduction to be the case – the boy had said he was being given a lift back to the city by a truck driver whom he'd met at the gas station from where he'd been calling. From this fact, Grant reasoned that this gas station must be well outwith walking distance from the city – say over twenty miles away – which any healthy determined youngster could be expected to manage in a full night's march.

Third, and perhaps most important, in this trucker he had a confirmed contact the boy had made, if he could only be traced. The boy may also have made other contacts at the same gas station. Furthermore, if the father's suspicions regarding forcible recapture and abduction turned out to be true, then there was always the chance there could have been witnesses to any struggle which took place. So the problem here was to find either the trucker or the gas station. One would lead to the other.

Grant decided to check out this angle with Ben Curtis. If anyone had reported such an incident to their local police, then Curtis could unearth it for him by running a check with all the State forces. It was a long shot but it could pay off, so he decided to play it. He and Ben often swapped information on a basis of mutual trust, born of years of working together, and as friends outside the job.

Fourth and last, there were the boy's references to dogs, and some person(?) he may have addressed as Archangel Michael – possibly a pseudo religious title, Grant guessed shrewdly. He was dealing with one of these crazy religious sects and he knew from previous experience that most of them bestowed grandiose biblical titles of this kind on their leaders. After all, wasn't the leader of this very sect known as The Prophet? The dogs he could only assume were used to track down runaways, in the manner of the old Southern slave plantations.

Having had experience of dealing with this type of outfit on previous assignments of this nature, Grant wasn't surprised at the mention of dogs being used to hunt down fugitives. He'd have to be careful how he approached these so-called Children of Bethlehem when he'd traced them. In the course of relieving them of one disillusioned convert, he had no wish to wind up converted himself – into a corpse!

Having decided on this course of action, he called Curtis at his precinct office and arranged for a check round the County HQ's of the State Police. Any information was requested concerning a missing youth, possible abduction involving common assault, or any other unusual occurrence having taken place at a gas station, probably in a remote area, in the early hours of the morning.

Curtis grumbled a bit at the lack of positive information but agreed to do it as a favour. He told Grant he'd call back in the afternoon with any result, and would leave it with Anna should he be out on inquiries.

Before ringing off, Curtis added, "Hey, remember that hooker in th'morgue last night? Well, Jim Easton jes' called an' told me he analysed scrapin's he took from under her fingernails. He says they appear t'be some kinda black dyed leather. So, it looks like our man wears black leather gloves when he's operatin'. That narrows th'field a lot," he finished positively.

"It does?" asked Grant, dubiously.

"Yeah," Curtis shot back. "Now we know we c'd be lookin' fer an insane dwarf with long arms an' big feet, who wears black leather gloves, dum-dum!" He rang off, leaving Grant chuckling and shaking his head as he replaced the receiver. He settled down to clear his piled in-tray, and had been working steadily for an hour or so, when his office door opened a little way. He looked up and caught Sherman glaring in at him.

Grant grinned at his senior partner. "My turn to go for the coffee, is it?" he asked innocently.

"Very funny," Sherman retorted, entering the room. "Don' worry, I'll git even with you fer this mornin', schmuck. You know us Israelis. We always win in the end ... ask the Arabs! Anyway, how'd it go with Mister Fancy Suit? You sign 'im up?"

Grant confirmed that he had, and the two partners spent the next few minutes discussing various aspects of the interview. Eventually Sherman asked, "You wanna pass on any of your case load to Mike Hammer an' Sam Spade, t'let you concentrate on this fer the next coupla days?" He was referring to the two private detectives employed by the firm, who shared the third office in the premises. They were both still young and keen, and the glamour of the job's image hadn't yet tarnished with them, so an amused Sherman always used these nicknames when referring to them.

Grant thought for a moment and then nodded. "Yeah, good idea Harry. I've a couple of ongoing cases they could take off my hands for the next few days. I want to check with City Hall on this religious outfit the Miller boy's joined, an' I've already got Ben Curtis runnin' a check on the State Forces for me. So, if anythin' breaks, I want to be able to follow it up while it's hot. I don't have much at all to go on at the moment."

"Okay, leave it to me," answered Sherman, rising to go. Half way to the door, he stopped and turned round. "Oh yeah ... by th'way, you owe the petty cash a dollar fifty."

"Huh? How come I owe the petty cash one-fifty?" asked Grant, puzzled.

"Fer the Demerara sugar fer your Fancy-Dan client, that's how come," Sherman retorted smugly. "An' that'll teach ya t'be a smartass with me."

He advanced on Grant, palm outstretched, and the younger man protested half-heartedly, but paid up with a good grace.

Sherman marched to the door, cackling delightedly to himself. He reached for the handle, paused and looked back over his shoulder. "Told ya I'd git ya back," he said. "Jes' remember who it wuz said 'Vengeance is mine'."

"Yeah, the Lord, wasn't it?" Grant replied sourly.

"Nah. Charlton Heston ... dinchya see th'movie?" Sherman closed the door behind him on this parting shot.

Chuckling to himself, Grant got his head down again and continued the task of adding to the growing pile in his out-tray. He aimed to be finished the lot by the time he knocked off for lunch. That way he'd be clear to begin his inquiries, as he began the task of tracing the missing Miller boy.

16

DEEP UNDER BETHLEHEM HOUSE, JIM MILLER PACED restlessly up and down the twelve foot length of his basement cell. His breakfast meal lay half eaten on its tray by the door. He had just had another disturbing interview with Angel One. Disturbing, because although it had been short, it had concerned his fellow escapee who was still missing, and he felt that the oriental was becoming increasingly sceptical of his denials of any knowledge of Tom Sheppard's whereabouts.

He always hated being spoken to by any of the Orientals but of the four, Angel One was the one he dreaded most. When Jim was in his presence, the man seemed to radiate an aura of barely suppressed violence. It hung about him like a chilling mist. His glittering black eyes held the same hypnotic quality for Jim as a snake's for a rabbit. They seemed to strip his mind away, layer by layer, until they had exposed the secret compartment where the truth was concealed.

As he paced back and forth, he gingerly fingered the swelling around the ugly gash on his forehead. His stomach and neck were still tender from the blows the oriental had struck him and the pain reminded him of the shattering moment of his recapture in the phone booth. The phone booth! Of course … he'd almost forgotten … he'd been speaking to his father just before he had been knocked senseless.

For a moment of irrational hope, he wondered whether his old man had made any sense out of his call, and he tried to recall word for word how the conversation had gone. Then his heart sank again as he realised he'd supplied no useful information as to where he'd been calling from. Besides which, he reasoned, even supposing he had been able to supply an exact map reference for the gas station, his unimaginative, law-abiding father would still have been unable to do anything to help him anyway. So, he could expect no help from that quarter.

His only hope, he decided, lay in stalling off the Prophet from punishing him when he returned from his current religious crusade in the city. The only way he could do that was to keep up the pretence that Tom was still at large and liable to bring about unwanted interest from outside. But this ploy would only work provided they didn't find what was left of Tom's savaged body out there in the woods. In the meantime, if he were patient and kept his wits about him, another opportunity for an escape attempt might present itself, unlikely though that now seemed.

As he paced restlessly up and down his cell, his train of thought touched briefly on his encounter with the four truckers at the gas station. He recalled with satisfaction how the chinless redneck named Jube, along with his two asshole allies, had been shut up pretty damn quick by the big heavily built guy, the one called Rocky. He felt a pang of regret when he remembered how close he had been to a ride to freedom and safety with the big guy, just before his recapture.

Never for a moment did he consider the possibility of any further help from that quarter either. Instead, he reckoned the four truckers would probably have assumed they'd been conned out of some free soup and a hand-out. He wasn't aware of how closely this thought mirrored the opinion of the patrolmen who had taken the report of his disappearance in the early hours of that same morning.

Jim finished his bleak appraisal of the night's events by

concluding that he could expect no form of outside help at all. He was on his own.

Angel One stood outside the wire mesh of the kennel compound in the sharp morning cold, listening to the report of the scar-faced Hispanic Apostle in charge of the dog handlers. The oriental had just come from his latest interrogation of the captured runaway in his basement cell. It had been unsatisfactory. Nothing he could put his finger on but he felt instinctively that the boy was lying – or at least that he was being evasive, while at the same time trying to appear co-operative.

However, he knew he still had to allow for the possibility that Miller might just be telling the truth – that the two runaways had in fact split up and that he genuinely did not know of his companion's whereabouts. But ... it just didn't feel right. Angel One trusted his intuition. It had never let him down in matters like this in the past. Why was there absolutely no trace of the second boy? That was what he couldn't accept. After all, they had been on their tracks quickly enough and after Miller had been recaptured, the search for Sheppard had been redoubled using the extra personnel then available.

He decided to shelve the problem for the time being as he concentrated instead on the substance of the Apostle's report. It seemed the dog pack had answered their morning recall on the ultra-sonic whistles promptly enough but had then failed to display either their normal aggressiveness or their usual ravenous interest in their food allocation. Also, they had traces of dried blood on their muzzles.

The evidence of the dried blood was not in itself unusual. Angel One knew the dogs were deliberately kept underfed and half wild, to encourage them to hunt and kill prey, animal or human. But they never refused their sparse morning feed in the kennel compound ... unless they had made a substantial kill during the night. So ... a deer, perhaps? Or an undetected human intruder? Or an escapee?

He knew no deer had been released for the pack to hunt down, as was done from time to time to hone up their hunting instincts. But it occasionally happened that one of the wild forest deer managed to clear the sixteen foot high boundary fence ... to its ultimate cost.

Angel One stared thoughtfully at the dark outline of the woods etched starkly against the slowly lightening dawn sky. A speculative gleam showed briefly in his narrowed eyes, then he nodded curtly to the Apostle now standing silently beside him awaiting orders.

"Come. We will organise an immediate search of the grounds." He swung on his heel and moved off, followed by the young Hispanic.

The two track-suited figures, one grey, one black, strode purposefully towards the house and disappeared inside. Angel One's intuition had told him that the object of his proposed search, the second boy whom they had failed to find during the previous night's hunt, would be discovered somewhere out in the woods. Or rather, what was left of him...

17

AFTER HIS INTERVIEW WITH VIRGIL MILLER, GRANT spent the remainder of the morning determinedly working his way through his paperwork. Shortly before noon, when he had almost finished, his phone rang. He picked it up and spoke into the mouthpiece. "Yeah? Grant here."

"I have Lieutenant Curtis on the line for you, Brett," Anna's voice informed him.

"Okay Anna, put him through please."

A moment later, Curtis's voice rasped in his ear. "Hi Brett. Ben here. Glad I caught ya. Got somethin' on that missin' kidda yours."

"Already?" Grant was pleasantly surprised. "Say, that was quick work. You gettin' super efficient in your old age, or somethin'? Or is this you tryin' to impress me, seein' as how I'm a taxpayer now, helpin' t'pay your salary?"

"That's rich!" Curtis snorted derisively. "Listen, taxpayer, things've changed since you were workin' here. We don' use spy-glasses an' rubber hoses any more. We're computerised now, I'll have y'know. In fact," he added sourly, "we got us a whole fuckin' army of pricks in here, who spend their entire lives runnin' round with little pieces of paper, lookin' fer machines t'feed 'em into."

Over Grant's laughter, Curtis continued, "I kid you not, buddy. An' what's more, mosta these mothers're wearin' uniforms under false pretences too. If y'wuz t'stick any of 'em out on th'street they wouldn' have a clue, unless they'd a computer along with 'em t'tell 'em what t'do.

"An' it's gittin' worse ..." There was no stopping Curtis, now that he was firmly mounted on his favourite hobby-horse. "We hardly use phones t'call other departments any more. We don' need to – the fuckin' machines send messages to other machines now. We don' count any more. I tell ya, th'way things is goin', in a coupla years I'm out of a job. There'll be a fuckin' computer sittin' here instead. An' you won' be able t'pull the ol' pals act with it, taxpayer!"

"Ben, gimme a break. You're breakin' my heart," Grant told him. "Listen, tell you what I'll do for you as an ol' pal. I'll have a word with Harry an' tell 'im we could use an odd-job man around the office – someone t'empty the ashtrays, unblock the toilets – that sorta thing. Nothin' too mentally taxing. Even an ex-Homicide lieutenant should be able to cope. Think y'could handle it?"

"Very funny," growled Curtis. "Anyhow wiseguy, git a loada this fer real efficiency. We got a result on the wire I put out earlier this mornin' on your missin' boy."

"Hey, that's great, Ben." Grant replied warmly.

"Wait'll y'hear it all, before y'start throwin' roses," Curtis put in. "An ol' buddy of mine who's the local sheriff upstate in a place called Rockford, up in Dawson County, called me a few minutes ago. He'd seen my message an' tied it to a routine APB circulated earlier this mornin' by the State Police. Seems jes' after oh-one-hundred, a trucker an' his three mates called out a State Highway Patrol car. They reported an incident at a gas station involvin' a kid who' asked 'em fer help, an' gave his name as one Jim Miller ... you gittin' all this?"

"Yeah Ben, go ahead," replied Grant, the phone trapped between his right ear and shoulder, while he jotted notes on his desk pad.

"Right," Curtis continued. "Well, it seems this trucker an' his buddies were doin' a night run from Montreal to New York, an' stopped off fer a break at this gas station diner a few miles northa Rockford, an' that's where they met the kid. Seems he came in dressed in some kinda red robe, an' told 'em he wuz bein' chased by some religious freaks he'd run away from, accordin' to th'cop's report."

Grant listened eagerly as Curtis went on, "Anyway, seems this guy offered th'kid a lift to the city, an' gave 'im some money t'call 'is folks. Th'kid left to use th'phone at one of th'station's booths out in th'forecourt. A little later, th'guy went to see what wuz keepin' 'im, an' th'kid had gone ... vanished.

"Now, th'trucker prob'ly woulda thought nothin' more about it, but the receiver'd bin smashed an' th'kid had dropped a cuppa coffee he'd given 'im. He thought it wuz worth reportin' to the local law, in case th'kid had been abducted, goin' by what he'd said earlier about bein' chased. The State Trooper filed it as an occurrence report, noted the damage as malicious, an' put out an APB on the kid fer good measure. Cagey bastards, these backwoods cops. They cover their asses all th'time. Prob'ly think they're still fightin' injuns. Well, whaddaya think? Sound like your boy?"

"It sure does," Grant replied. "It not only confirms what his ol' man told me, it also gives me a good lead. What's this trucker's particulars, an' I'll go see him after lunch."

"Get this ... name of Joseph Aloysius O'Rourke. How does that grab ya?"

"Sounds Polish," commented Grant wryly.

Curtis snorted with laughter. "Yeah," he agreed. "With a handle like that, he should be poundin' a beat in th'Bronx, insteada livin' there."

He gave Grant an address in the West Chester district of the

Bronx, then added, "Oh, by th'way, another thing ... that sect you mentioned, The Children of Whatsitsname ... I checked it out while I wuz at it. They're registered as a charity with City Hall. Seems they got permission t'run mobile soup kitchens in various parts of the city. So y'kin follow that up, okay?"

"Thanks, Ben. As a matter of fact, that confirms something else the boy's father mentioned." Grant told him. "He thinks his son may have made his initial contact with these people at one of these vans. He's convinced they use these vans as recruiting stations. He could have a point. I'll follow it up, an' give 'em the once over."

"Jes' watch they don' give you th'once over," Curtis warned him. "I know I don' hafta tell you that some of these religious freaks kin turn nasty if y'tramp on their little patches of holy ground. If this lot think they got the right t'snatch kids who wanna leave 'em, then they ain' exactly gonna put out th'welcome mat fer someone like you, who's tryin' t'snatch 'em back."

"Don't worry, I'll wear garlic an' carry a crucifix," Grant assured him lightly, then asked, "How about this ol' buddy of yours who phoned the info to you – the local sheriff? What's his name, an' I'll look 'im up when I head upstate to find this Bethlehem House pitch?"

"Springfield ... Nate Springfield. He says you're welcome t'call by an' see 'im when you're up that way. He's rock solid. A real useful guy t'have around in case of trouble. Me an' Nate go back a long way."

"Okay Ben, I'll do that. An' thanks again for your help. That's one I owe you," said Grant warmly.

"I'll mark it on th'slate ... along with all the other favours you owe me," Curtis remarked.

"Okay," chuckled Grant, then asked, "Hey, how's your own inquiry goin'? Anythin' turned up yet?"

"Oh, nice of you t'remember I'm in th'middle of a Murder One investigation," growled Curtis. "Nah, nothin' much, exceptin' we've found the bar she wuz in jes' before she met up with her killer. We reckon she musta picked 'im up, on th'streets somewhere, cuz accordin' t'the barman she definitely left on 'er own. An' that wuz aroun' midnight. We've also turned up a guy who thinks he might've passed 'em in th'fog, jes' shortly after that. Didn' git a good look, due to th'conditions, but says he got the impression of a tall, well dressed dude, walkin' with a black girl. Thinks the guy had a white cloth, or maybe a scarf, coverin' 'is mouth. That's what caught the witness's eye. Like I say, not much, but it's the first positive sighting we've had, if it's our man."

"It could be a start," said Grant encouragingly. "You're due a break. Your luck's bound to change sometime."

"Yeah. It'll prob'ly git worse," Curtis replied dolefully. "We've also got a vague description from the ol' wino who found the body. He's bin ravin' about some dark figure who passed 'im in th'fog jes' before he found the corpse in the alley. But accordin' to the ol' soak, he saw a cross between Frankenstein an' King Kong! Anyhow Brett, I gotta go. I've a press conference in ten minutes, an' I still got my will t'finish."

"Your will?" asked Grant, puzzled.

"Yeah, I'm thinkin' of committin' suicide," Curtis shot back at him. "Th'way I figure it, if I give th'press somethin' t'print, that way I git 'em off my back fer a while. See ya." He rang off..

Grant completed his paperwork, gathered it together, and took it out to Anna along with a cassette of dictated letters for her to type up. Depositing the pile on her desk, he stepped back a pace and came smartly to attention, clicking his heels and bowing in the manner of a Prussian officer.

Assuming a mock-German accent, he said, "I haf mein vork completed, Fraulein Strauss. Permission to fall out und shoot meinself, bitte."

Anna smiled tolerantly at him and asked, "Will you be out on inquiries for the rest of the day, Brett?" When he replied that he would, she told him she'd leave the completed letters on his desk for his signature the following morning.

Grant then called in briefly on Sherman and brought him up to date on Curtis's phone call. He informed his partner he'd be out for the remainder of the day following up any leads he got from the trucker O'Rourke, after he'd seen him.

"I want to see if I can find one of these vans they use, just to get a look at their set-up. Then, I'll prob'ly drive up to Rockford to have a look around this gas station where the boy did his disappearing act last night. I'm hoping this Springfield guy might know the location of this Bethlehem House the kid mentioned in his phone call to his old man. It must be somewhere near there."

"You be careful if you do find the place," Sherman cautioned him. "These religious freaks kin be dangerous if they find outsiders pokin' around, as you know from past experience."

"Okay, okay … I know. Ben warned me too. It's a wonder you two ol' mother hens let me out on my own," laughed Grant.

"We're only thinkin' of your welfare." Sherman spread his hands. "They might be cannibals." Sherman's eyes twinkled mischievously. "So, y'might find y'self bein' chopped into liver pate fer spreadin' on their Holy Wafers, or somethin'."

"Oh yeah?" Grant paused in the doorway. "Well I'll tell you one thing, if I do get grabbed by this mob, I just hope this Prophet ain't an ex-rabbi … or I know what'll be gettin' chopped! I'll be comin' back two inches shorter, an' an octave higher!"

Grant slipped through the door and pulled it shut on Sherman's "Since when did you have two inches to lose? You sh'd be so lucky …" With a wave to Anna, he let himself out of the office and headed for the elevators.

18

GRANT GRABBED HIMSELF A QUICK SNACK AT THE local delicatessen lunch counter, then drove across the Washington Bridge into the Bronx. A little over an hour after leaving the office, he found himself seated in a comfortable easy chair in the O'Rourke's living room, clutching an ice-cold can of Budweiser. Seated across from him, an identical can engulfed in a ham-sized fist, was the big trucker Jim Miller knew as Rocky.

After the introductions were over, Grant had declined the offer a meal from Rocky's wife, Kate. A bustling, motherly woman, she had refused to accept that a deli snack was sufficient to sustain a grown man till his next meal. As a result, she had insisted on providing Grant with a plateful of sandwiches that would have choked an elephant, 'in case he felt peckish'.

Rocky had then produced a six-pack of Budweiser, and his wife had shooed the four smallest members of their family of six from the room, the two eldest being elsewhere, and the two men had settled down to talk. Right from the start they were on first name terms, dispensing with formalities by mutual consent.

Grant had taken an instinctive liking to the big, grizzled trucker and his homely wife. His initial impression of them was of decent, salt-of-the-earth folk, who would put themselves out to help anyone in need. Half an hour later, after Rocky had fully described the events of the previous night and his concern over the puzzling and unknown fate of the frightened kid who had appealed for his help, Grant decided his initial judgement of the man had been accurate.

Rocky had just concluded by explaining how his concern had been fuelled by the fact that he had a son of similar age to Jim Miller, when the door burst open and a slim, red haired, teenage version of himself erupted into the room. Clad in a faded sweat shirt, frayed denims, a pair of scuffed sneakers, the freckle-faced youth was carrying a basketball. He skidded to a flustered halt when he saw his father sitting there with a guest. Grant took advantage of the momentary silence to lean forward and switch off the cassette recorder he had positioned on the coffee table between them.

Recovering his composure with the quicksilver reaction of youth, the boy flashed a bright smile in the direction of his parent. "Hi, pop," he greeted him breezily. "Thought you'd still be in bed."

"Obviously," growled Rocky with heavy sarcasm. "If dat's how y'charge round da pitch when y'think I'm sleepin', I'd sure hate t'know what you'd do if y'thought I wuz awake! Why don'cha try openin' da door next time, before y'come through it?"

The boy grinned sheepishly. "Sorry, pop. Didn' mean t'disturb you. I didn' know y'had company ..." he added, glancing in Grant's direction in a naively obvious attempt to change the subject.

His father appeared to take the bait. Turning to Grant, he jerked his head at the boy and said, "Dis herda stampedin' buffalo here's my eldest ... Patrick. Leastways, dat's his Sunday name. Pat t'you." Turning back to the youth, he said, "Pat, say hello t'Mister Grant."

Grant grinned and extended a hand. "Hi, Pat. Pleased t'meet you."

The boy returned his grin and shook hands with the slightly awkward manner of youth trying to be formal. "Pleased to meet you too, sir."

"Mister Grant's a private detective," Rocky informed his son casually. "He's tryin' t'trace a missin' boy I met durin' the night at a gas station up north."

Pat's eyes widened, and mixed feelings of awe and fascination were apparent in his voice when he responded.

"No kiddin'? You a real private eye, Mister Grant?"

Grant nodded amiably at the wide-eyed youngster. He was used by now to this or similar reactions from people, youths and adults alike, raised as they were on a diet of highly glamorised TV versions of his trade. "Sure am," he confirmed. "I'm the gen-u-ine article. Here ..." He reached for his pocketbook and extracted a small slip of white cardboard, which he handed to the boy.

"My card ... keep it." Then, taking out his licence and badge, he flipped the latter open and handed them over for his inspection, too.

"Gee, thanks Mister Grant," said Pat, pocketing the card and scrutinising the licence and badge before handing them back. "Say, do you carry a gun?" he asked, eyes alive with anticipation.

"Don' be so nosy, or he'll sap ya wid 'is blackjack," Rocky put in.

"Wow ... you carry a blackjack too?" asked Pat, completely unabashed.

Rocky raised his eyes to the ceiling and Grant laughed. "I don't carry a gun everywhere I go but I am licensed to carry one when I have to. An' I only carry my blackjack on Sundays. I use it for beatin' up any helpless ol' ladies I find resistin' muggers."

The boy laughed at this and turned to his father. "An' are you really gonna be a witness in one of Mister Grant's cases, pop?" he inquired excitedly.

Rocky nodded. "It sure looks dat way," he confirmed, then added casually, "An' I wuz thinkin' of hirin' 'im t'find out jes' where you think you're goin' wid dat basketball?"

The grin was wiped suddenly from Pat's face. He dropped his eyes and shuffled his feet uncomfortably as his father continued remorselessly, "Correct me if I'm wrong, but I seem to recall y'mother tellin' me somethin' about how y'wuz dyin' widda cold, an' had t'cut college dis mornin'? So ... where's da cold gone? An' what's da basketball for? Or am I mistaken? Is dat some kinda giant pill ... some kinda new miracle cure fer da common cold nobody ain' hearda yet, huh?"

Pat glanced at his father, but was unable to hold his level gaze. Caught off guard by Rocky's ploy of shifting his attention onto Grant, then attacking on his exposed flank, he searched for an answer.

"Well, pop ..." he began. "I had a bit of a cold this mornin', honest. But it's cleared up after half a day in bed. An' ... well ... we got this important league game tonight against East Harlem High ..."

He faltered momentarily under the scrutiny of his father's piercing blue eyes, then rushed on, "... so, I thought I'd nip down to the gym an' put in some shootin' practice. Y'know how I'm our penalty shooter? ..." he finished hopefully, in a transparent appeal to Rocky's parental pride in his son's playing ability.

But Rocky shook his head slowly, his lips pursed disapprovingly. "No way," he growled. "If y'got a cold, y'stay in. No college – no basketball!" he concluded firmly.

"Aw gee, pop ..." protested Pat.

"Don' 'Aw gee pop' me. If y'ain' fit fer college – y'ain' fit fer basketball. Simple!" He spread his big hands and shrugged.

Desperately, the boy tried one more time. "Aw, please pop, don' ground me," he pleaded. "It's real important we win t'night. If we beat East Harlem t'night, an' then Richmond High next week, the title's as good as ours."

Rocky gazed speculatively at his son for a few seconds, as though considering this. Then he seemed to come to a decision. "Tell y'what," he began slowly. "If y'kin prove t'me dat you're fit t'play t'night, I might agree … okay?"

"Sure, pop. You're on!" Pat responded eagerly, swallowing the baited hook unheedingly. Then he paused, a puzzled frown starting to show on his freckled face. "But … what do I have t'do t'prove it?" he asked dubiously.

The twinkle in Rocky's eye belied his rasping voice as he shot back, "Y'spend da next hour washin' da car … an' cleanin' out da inside, an' y'git t'play basketball t'night."

The boy pulled a face as he realised he'd been suckered. But he accepted defeat with good grace, grinning at an amused Grant and shaking his head ruefully as he made for the door. His father's gravel voice stopped him on the threshold. "Ah … one more thing …"

Pat stopped in mid-stride and looked back apprehensively. Rocky continued, "If y'do a good job, dere's a ten-spot in it fer ya, okay?"

The infectious grin reappeared on the freckled face again, wider than ever. "Thanks, pop. You're a pal. Seeya, Mister Grant …" With a cheery wave, he darted through the door, pulling it shut behind him.

Too late, Rocky called after him. "An' don' slam …" The bang of the door cut off his exasperated shout in mid-sentence, "… da door," he finished lamely as it quivered in its frame.

Rocky shrugged at Grant, and shook his head as they exchanged grins. "He's a good kid but I gotta touch da brakes occasionally, jes' t'remind 'im who's drivin' … who's da boss, y'know?" Grant nodded, then laughed as the big man added wryly, "Actually, he ain' rumbled yet – but it's his mother!"

The interview over, Grant pocketed the cassette recorder and rose to go. At the outside door he hesitated for a moment as an idea struck him, then turned to face the big man. "Rocky, do you an' your buddies do the Montreal run regularly?" he asked thoughtfully.

When the big man replied that they did, Grant went on, "Could I ask you to keep an eye open for anythin' strange … y'know, like, out of the ordinary … around the area of the gas station where you met the kid last night? I'm not even sure what I'm askin' you to look out for exactly, just anythin' that might connect to this sect he joined, know what I mean? An' if you or your buddies should see anythin' …" he took out a card and handed it over, "… give me a ring at this number, okay? If I'm not in, leave a message for me."

"No problem," replied Rocky. "I'll pass da word roun' at da depot. An' while we're on da subject, when you do turn anythin' up, an' y'feel y'need any help – you give me a call. I got no time fer dese weirdo religious nuts. Dey cause nuttin' but trouble. In fact, if y'ask me all religions're da same in dat respect. All so busy fightin' an' arguin' amongst demselves, it beats me how dey got any time left fer preachin'!"

On that philosophic note they parted, Grant assuring Rocky he'd call and let him know the results of his search for the missing boy, whatever the outcome. Outside, as he crossed the parking lot, he returned young Pat's wave as the boy paused in his task of washing his old man's big Ford Estate.

"Good luck with the game tonight," Grant called as he climbed into his own Mustang. The boy's cheery "Thanks, Mister Grant," followed him as he eased the car out of the parking lot exit. He waved again from his window in acknowledgement, and accelerated smoothly onto the main highway back towards Manhattan. Now he was ready to begin checking out this sect which had seemingly swallowed up Jim Miller without trace.

19

GRANT'S FIRST STOP WAS AT CITY HALL. WITHIN TEN minutes his check of the register of charitable organisations revealed that one calling itself the Children of Bethlehem was licensed to operate eight mobile food stalls in various poor areas of the city. One of these vans was licensed to operate in the Harlem area. He decided to see if he could track this one down at one of its listed permitted parking sites, as it was on his intended direction of north for his drive to Rockford.

On his way there, he found he was passing close to Harlem Tower, and on impulse he decided to pick up the Champ, if the kid happened to be about. He thought he'd not only give the kid the unexpected treat of a quick run about in the car but he could also use him to watch the car while he was out of it giving the sect van the once over.

As it turned out, this idea turned out to be a winner. The streetwise Champ not only knew of the existence of the sect van but was also able to tell him exactly where it would be parked at that time of the day. It seemed the local kids were among its most frequent customers for free hand-outs. Within ten minutes he'd found it, following the Champ's directions.

It was a long, dark blue van, around the seven ton mark by the look of it, plain gold crosses showing on its side panels and rear door. Almost the entire nearside panel was opened up to reveal a long chest-high counter, the raised flap forming a canopy for the protection of customers against the vagaries of the weather. The van was parked in a Harlem street which could have been used as a film set depicting a suburb of wartime Berlin, just after a Red Army armoured column had passed through.

The van's sombre colour blended in perfectly with its dull surroundings of boarded-up and fire-gutted stores, but the sect personnel in and around it provided a complete contrast. Distributing leaflets to passers-by and moving among the crowd of loungers hanging around, mostly composed of blacks, were four youngsters of about sixteen to eighteen years of age. Three were girls, two black and one white, and the fourth was a bearded white youth. In direct contrast to the drab surroundings of the van's vicinity, their appearance was striking. All four youngsters were wearing loose fitting, brightly coloured, calf-length robes. Two of these were a bright shade of emerald green and two sky blue. As a concession to the November chill, they wore white woollen socks on their sandalled feet and long loose cloaks of the same bright colours as their robes.

Grant drove past the van and parked the Mustang some fifty yards ahead of it, in front of a section of still occupied, undamaged stores. Making a quick purchase of popcorn, a couple of cokes and a selection of chocolate bars in one of the shops, he returned and passed these in the window to the Champ, telling him to wait and watch the car for him.

"Y'gonna talk t'them Jesus freaks, Brett?" asked the urchin, happily ensconced behind the steering wheel with his bag of assorted confectionery.

"I intend to," Grant replied. "But I guess that depends on whether they'll talk to me." He grinned at the youngster and added jokingly, "Maybe they don't talk to honkies hereabouts, eh?"

"Nah, dey'll talk t'anyone," replied the Champ seriously. "Long as yo're prepared t'rap 'bout Jesus an' stuff, dat is. Even give yuh free chow, so's yuh'll listen to 'em."

Amused, Grant studied his diminutive informant. "Is that so? An' just how do you happen t'know so much about them, may I ask?"

"Ah've heard da brothers rappin' 'bout 'em," replied the Champ matter-of-factly. "Folks heahabouts calls 'em da Hallelujah Hamburger Mob." So saying, the youngster popped open a can of coke as though to punctuate this dismissive comment on the sect and its activities.

Leaving the Champ to his picnic, Grant crossed the street to the opposite sidewalk and passed the van on the other side of the street, having a good look at their set-up as he did so.

Walking on for a short distance, he recrossed the road to the same side as the parked van, and headed back towards it. Dressed casually as he was, with a brightly checked car coat hanging loosely from his shoulders, he didn't feel too out of place among the passing Harlem citizenry in their varied styles of clothing.

Approaching the van, he saw there were three more sect personnel on duty within the vehicle itself. Serving behind the counter, on which sat rows of plastic cups flanked by two large, steaming, chrome-plated urns, were two adult women, one white and one black. Both had an air of pleasant efficiency and were clad in green robes of the same style as the four kids handing out leaflets on the sidewalk.

The third occupant was a tall, poker-faced black male, dressed in a close-fitting grey track-suit. Grant recognised the type immediately from his athletic build and air of barely suppressed aggression. He was the muscle – there to take care of any trouble. From what Grant already suspected regarding the possible abduction of his client's son, the thought occurred to him that the big sullen black might also be there to keep the sect members themselves under surveillance.

Grant slowed his pace a little as he reached the fringe of the loosely grouped crowd hanging around the vicinity of the van. Without seeming to, he angled towards the young white girl in the sky-blue robe, allowing her to intercept him with a leaflet. In this way, he succeeded in making it seem as though it was she who had noticed him, instead of the other way about.

He had noticed the girl when he had passed on the other side of the road, but now he chose her intuitively as he approached, as the most likely looking of the four on the sidewalk. She was young, about sixteen or seventeen, he estimated, and vulnerable-looking somehow. Pale faced and thin, her long dark hair was drawn back from her attractive elfin features, and gathered by a blue ribbon at the nape of her neck. Her large brown eyes held a hint of mute appeal in their liquid depths, giving her an almost haunted look.

As he had planned, she spotted him coming, and when they made eye contact, he responded with a little smile of encouragement. She took a half pace to one side to intercept him and, returning his smile brightly, she offered him a leaflet from the bundle clutched to her chest.

"Hi there," she greeted him cheerfully. Her voice was clear

and pleasant. "Please take one. May God bless you and open your eyes to the message contained in His holy words." Despite her long woollen cloak, she looked cold. Grant's smile broadened into a friendly grin as he accepted the leaflet from her. A quick glance at it confirmed that it was a religious tract of some kind, as he had suspected.

"What's this, then?" he asked amiably. "A new soap powder that leaves your whites grey, so the dirt don't show up?"

A little taken aback by his unexpectedly friendly response, the girl only smiled and shook her head, momentarily lost for words. She was more used to negative reactions from passers-by, ranging from at best a grudging acceptance of her leaflets, to open hostility and rejection. Usually the only ones who stopped were the down-and-outs who knew there was free soup, coffee and 'burgers on offer. Occasionally too, someone would try to chat her up, but this one didn't come across like one of those types. She instinctively felt his openness was genuine.

Grant continued putting her at her ease by kidding her gently, pretending to guess what the leaflet was about. "Not a soap powder? No ... don't tell me, let me guess ... ah ... it's a new dog food promotion. This is the brand nine outa ten dogs reject on the TV adverts. No? Okay ... third time pays for all ... I got it! You're standin' for Congress next term. Right?"

The girl laughed, her large brown eyes sparkling with amusement. As she did so, she brought her free hand up before her mouth in a gesture which made her seem even younger. Then, recovering her composure again, she shook her head and replied, "Nope. It's not about any of these things."

"Okay, I give up," he said. "What are you selling?"

"We're not selling anything," she replied, the spark of amusement still dancing in her brown eyes. "On the contrary, we hope we can give people something."

"Oh? Like what?" he prompted.

She pointed at the piece of paper in his hand. "Well," she began, "if you read our leaflet, you'll find it tells you about the work of our church, The Children of Bethlehem ..."

She paused and cleared her throat before continuing, and Grant had the distinct impression that she was concentrating to recall something she'd learned to repeat by rote. This impression was confirmed in Grant's mind, when she resumed her spiel, the words tripping somewhat mechanically off her tongue, in the manner of a child reciting poetry.

"Under the divinely inspired guidance of our leader, the Prophet Martin Bishop, we dispense charity to the poor, in accordance with the teachings of Our Lord and Saviour Jesus Christ, who said ... um ..."

Discomfited by his level gaze, she lost the thread of her spiel and broke off, confused. Instead, she half turned and waved a hand towards the van, using this movement as an excuse to break eye contact. "... If you'd like to accept a coffee, or a cup of soup ... an' a hamburger ... please feel free," she finished haltingly.

"I don't recall readin' that in my Bible," he retorted, his brow furrowed in pretended surprise. "I recall somethin' about Him handin' out loaves an' fishes ... but soup an' hamburgers? That's a new one on me." He grinned at her.

She knew she should have been shocked by his blasphemy, but she found she wasn't. Instead she was amused, and giggled as she turned back to face him. Once again the clear blue eyes held hers, seemingly quite innocently, yet with a disturbing sense of ... probing? Yes, the thought occurred to her, that was it ... probing. Something akin to the feeling Archangel Michael's eyes gave her, only without the accompanying fear she always felt in the presence of that terrifying oriental.

Flustered, she pressed on. "If you can afford it, we'd be grateful for any donation you may feel able to give, no matter how small. But if you can't afford it, then God bless you, and please accept our charity in the name of the Lord. Amen."

"Amen," Grant echoed solemnly. Then he glanced down at the small plastic name-tag pinned to the front of her cloak and read it aloud. "Sister Louise." He raised a questioning eyebrow. "Is that your real name or is it a name the sect gave you when you joined?"

"It's my real name," she nodded.

He inclined his head and smiled down at her. "Pleased t'meet you, Louise. Tell you what ... " he reached for his bill-fold and peeled off a ten, "how about acceptin' this donation in exchange for a holy hamburger an' two gospel coffees?"

"Two coffees?" she asked with a little smile.

He nodded. "Yup ... two," he replied. "I've decided to call a coffee break." Then you can take five, while you try t'convince me you're really happy doin' what you're doin'."

This got an immediate reaction. Her eyes widened, then flicked nervously to either side, as though checking for eavesdroppers. Then she held his questioning look for a long moment, before coming to a decision. To his relief, she nodded and replied calmly, "Okay, if that's what you'd like. I'll be right back ..." and turned away, making for the van.

He watched her slight figure threading its way quickly through the loose throng at the van counter, many of whom were clutching steaming plastic cups and half-eaten hamburgers. Then he turned and moved casually over to a space at the boarded-up window of a fire-gutted store and leaned back against it. He used this ploy of changing position to run his eye over the surrounding loiterers, including those leaning against the boarded-up store-fronts to either side of him. He was checking for anyone who was showing any undue interest in him – anyone who could have been the cause of the girl's nervous reaction, when her eyes had involuntarily flicked to either side. It had been as though she had expected to see someone close by, spying on them.

His quick inspection failed to pick out anyone watching him in an obvious manner but he did spot one likely candidate. This was a young black loitering a few yards away, holding a cup in one hand and apparently engrossed in reading a folded newspaper. He was wearing jeans and a leather jacket, with a purple woollen hat rolled down so as to cover the tops of his ears. The youth seemed innocuous enough at first glance but something about him just didn't feel right to Grant. It was nothing he could have put his finger on. Yet experience had taught him to trust his instincts in such matters and so he mentally marked him down for further attention.

He directed his attention back to Louise over at the van counter. She was in the act of handing over the ten dollar bill and speaking to the white woman in the green robe who was serving her. The woman glanced in his direction when Louise indicated him and seemed to study him for a second or two, before smiling at him and giving him a little nod of thanks. Grant raised a hand in acknowledgement and maintained his air of mild neutral interest in his surroundings.

Seeing Louise weaving her way back towards him carrying two steaming cups and a wrapped hamburger, her sheaf of pamphlets tucked under an arm, he glanced casually past her to the van again. As he did so, he thought he caught the big, grey track-suited black averting his gaze from him. Grant was sure he had been under the speculative scrutiny of those bleak eyes.

When the girl arrived, he accepted the coffee she offered him but declined the hamburger. "Not for me, thanks, Louise. I ordered it for you. You look cold."

She hesitated, then smiled up at him, showing even, white teeth. Thanking him, she said. "Is it so obvious? Do I look as though I'm cold?"

"Some," he replied. "But don't worry about it. I think a red nose suits you … it's very fetching."

"Oh! It's not … is it?" she asked anxiously. Then she caught herself, realising he was teasing her, and laughed. She bit into her 'burger, chewed for a few seconds, then swallowed the mouthful with a sip of coffee. Serious again, she said, "Actually, I'm supposed to be talking to you about our work, you know, and trying to interest you in going along to hear our leader, The Prophet Martin Bishop, tonight at the Washington Centre. Otherwise I could get into trouble for wasting time, when I should be trying to find converts."

"Well, it doesn't look like there's much else in the way of potential customers around at the moment," Grant said, looking round them. "All this bunch seem t'be interested in doin' is fillin' themselves with free soup an' hamburgers, not the Holy Ghost, if you'll pardon my sayin' so." He turned back to her. "But I am interested in hearing your leader speak tonight, as a matter of fact. What time does the meeting start?"

As he'd glanced around them, Grant had noticed that purple hat appeared to have changed his position slightly. He was now a little closer to them than he had been.

"We call it a crusade, not a meeting," Louise corrected him. "The programme starts at eight o'clock, and the Prophet Martin Bishop is scheduled to speak about nine. But I didn't think you'd be the type to be interested," she concluded frankly.

"In that case, it's up to you to convince me of the error of my sinful ways," he retorted, drawing a smile from her. He folded his arms. "Okay … so, convert me."

Louise washed down her last of her 'burger with a mouthful of coffee and regarded him over the rim of her cup, her eyes amused. Lowering the cup, she said, "Somehow I don't think you'd fit in. What I mean by that is, you're not the type to enjoy our way of life.

"What d'you mean I'm not the type?" he demanded in an aggrieved tone. "How d'you know I wouldn't fit in? Life in a hippie commune might just be my thing, for all you know. I'll tell you this …" he leaned towards her and lowered his voice conspiratorially, "… between you an' me, I think I'd be a knockout in one of these cute nighties you all wear."

Louise giggled, once more raising her hand to her mouth in her curiously appealing little-girl gesture. "They're robes, not nighties. An' as for you not fitting in, you're too … well … nice an' normal to be one of us. Oh, I know I'm not explaining myself too well, but you see most of our people come from the streets … or from broken homes, deprived backgrounds … that sorta thing. So, we feel for others in the same predicament … know what I mean?"

She shrugged, searching for the correct words to express herself, then went on, "You see, the sect feeds us an' provides for us. It gives us a home … an identity, even. A sense of … belonging somewhere. An' that's important when you've got no place to go, an' no-one to share with." She looked at him, her face serious now. "You don't look like you need any of these things," she finished quietly.

"Hey … that must be about the lousiest sales pitch I've ever had handed to me," he replied jokingly, trying to lighten her mood again. "In fact, I've a good mind to demand t'see the manager. Is that him up there … the big mean-lookin' cat in the natty grey joggin' suit?" he asked, nodding towards the van and straightening up from the wall, as though intending to put his words into effect.

Her eyes widened in sudden alarm and she reached out a hand to stop him. "Oh no! Please don't ..." she blurted out. Then, realising he was only joking, she tried to recover herself. With a forced smile she continued, "He's got no sense of humour. He wouldn't think it was funny if you made that joke to him ... and ... well, I'd get into trouble."

"Y'know, Louise, that's the second time in a few minutes you've told me you'd get into trouble for something trivial. Y'sure it ain't the Marines you've joined? Come t'think of it, ol' laughin' eyes up there in the van would make a pretty good unarmed combat instructor in the Green Berets, from the looks of him!" He could see from her eyes that he had scored a point with this last remark. Instead of protesting, she confirmed it by shrugging and trying to dismiss the subject.

"Oh, pay me no heed," she said lightly. "It's just my way of putting things." But once again as she spoke, her eyes betrayed her, flicking nervously to either side, obviously checking for eavesdroppers nearby.

Now that he had her on the defensive, Grant decided now was the time to come straight to the point. "Louise," he said quietly, "where and what exactly, is Bethlehem House? An' why, if the sect's as good to homeless kids as you say it is, would they find it necessary to use dogs to hunt down anyone who tries to run away from there?"

Had he slapped her face, he could not have obtained a more shocked reaction. She caught her breath with an audible gasp, her face drained of colour and fear flared in her wide eyes.

"How do you know about ... Bethlehem House?" she asked faintly. "Only sect members know ... oh no! ... you're not? ..." The question hung unfinished on the air between them, which was suddenly electric with her fear.

"Hey, take it easy. It's okay, Louise," Grant reassured her gently. "No, I'm not a member of your sect ... nor am I a spy for this Prophet character, if that's what you're afraid of."

"Then ... if you're not one of them ... of us ... how do you know so much? Who are you and what do you want?" Despite her suspicion, she had begun to relax again, although she was still nervous. Another side-to-side flicker of her eyes betrayed her watchfulness of those around her.

Before answering her, Grant himself glanced casually around. He noted that purple hat had drifted a few feet nearer but was still just out of earshot, provided they spoke quietly. He decided he would take the risk of trusting her. She seemed a genuine kid and her obvious fear of falling foul of the gorilla in the van, for one thing, seemed to suggest she was no longer a starry-eyed devotee of the sect or its leadership, if she ever had been. Nor had the quick recovery of her slip from 'them' to 'us' when referring to the sect personnel, escaped his notice. Turning back to her, he lowered his voice to show her that he too was aware of the danger of being overheard.

"Listen Louise, first let me say this. I'm a friend ... should you ever need one," he assured her earnestly. "Now, if you'll give me two minutes to explain, I'll answer you questions. Then, if you don't like what you hear, I'll walk away. You have my word. Okay?"

She hesitated for a moment then nodded, curiosity overcoming her wariness of him. He pressed on quickly, now that he had her attention.

"As I've already told you, my name's Brett Grant. I'm a private detective. I'm tryin' to trace a boy, name of Jim Miller, who belongs to your sect. It appears he tried to leave this Bethlehem House pitch, sometime last night. He made it to a gas station a few miles from there, an' called his parents. He got cut off, just after tellin' his old man the sect people were huntin' him ... with dogs, he said."

Again fear flickered in Louise's eyes at this last item of information, and Grant paused thinking she might comment. When she said nothing, he hurried on. "The thing is, Louise, his old man thinks his son was caught and taken back by force ... kidnapping, the law calls it. His folks are frantic with worry ... an' I can't say I blame 'em, if that gorilla up there in the van is an example of your church elders!"

She nodded slowly, as though thinking over what he'd said and he was sure her face now showed concern. He decided to finish by driving home his point. "Look, Louise, I don't want to offend you by criticising your sect, or your beliefs for that matter. But kidnapping's a serious crime. Those who commit it are often evil or dangerous. Now, I'm willing to concede maybe your people are just stupid or over-zealous ... misguided, even. But, whichever they are, Louise, it's still wrong! You must see that?"

Her answering nod was more positive this time. "But how do you think I'd be able to help you?" she asked cautiously.

Before replying, Grant glanced round again, smiling as if they were discussing something pleasant and of no great importance. Purple hat was apparently still engrossed in his newspaper – but had again shifted his position to be nearer. There was still enough background talk from the surrounding loiterers to cover their own quiet voices but Grant nonetheless warned Louise of the nearby enemy presence with a quick sideways movement of head and eyes and lowered his voice even further.

"All I want from you is some information, Louise. In return I'll help you in any way I can, if you ever need it. First, tell me about Bethlehem House ... what it is and where it's located? Second, do you know Jim Miller? And would he be telling the truth when he said they were hunting him with dogs? That'll do for now."

To his relief she responded without further hesitation. "Bethlehem House is a sort of meditation centre but its also the place where you spend your first six months training when you join the sect. It's upstate somewhere, I don't know exactly where, but it takes about two hours driving to get there. Oh, wait a moment ... it's just north of a small town ... I've heard its name mentioned, but I can't remember it offhand ..." She frowned in concentration.

"Rockford?" he prompted quietly.

"Yes, that's it!" Her face brightened momentarily, then clouded over again as she continued. "As for the dogs you mentioned, they call them the Hellhounds ... they're a pack of Doberman attack dogs which are released to guard the grounds at night. The Prophet says their purpose is to keep the godless legions of Satan out ..."

"Or maybe to keep the guileless Children of Bethlehem in?" he murmured cynically. Then, realising his pointed interruption had thrown her off her stride, he grinned apologetically. "Sorry, just thinkin' out loud. Go on ... how about the Miller boy?"

"I think I know the boy you mean," she said slowly. "He's a novice, only joined a few months ago, if it's the boy I'm thinking of. But if he did what you say, ran away I mean, then he's in serious trouble. They don't like ..."

She didn't get the chance to finish telling him what they didn't like, because at that moment Grant had glanced up meaning to check if purple hat had moved any closer and instead saw a grey track-suited figure approaching through the crowd and only a few paces away.

He reacted immediately. In a flash of inspiration he adopted a Southern drawl which would have done credit to Detective Tex Turner and suddenly interrupted a surprised Louise, cutting her off in mid-sentence.

"Waal, Ah think th'work you folks're doin' heah is jes' plain wonderful. Only thing is, in my opinion it's a cryin' shame y'have to rely on charity t'do it. Y'all sh'd be able t'claim a gov'ment grant or sumpin' of that sort ..."

The big black had reached them in time to catch most of this. Grant pretended to have just noticed his arrival, turned to him with a beaming smile and greeted him effusively, with hardly a pause for breath.

"Howdy, friend. Ah take it yo're one of th'good people who run this heah charity? Waal, like ah wuz jes' tellin' th'sister heah, I really do admire what yo're doin' fer these pore unfortunates. Real honest t'goodness Christianity at work, that's what ah call it."

The girl was quick on the uptake but she couldn't prevent the spark of fear from leaping into her eyes as she realised who had joined them. Before she could react badly and give the game away, Grant bought her time to recover her composure by continuing his rapid-fire delivery. He stuck out a hand to the newcomer.

"Chester D Calhoun's th'name," he declared expansively. "Ah'm in oil. Jes' grabbin' me some sight-seein' in yore wonderful city between business conferences, when ah came across yore outfit heah. Ah declare we c'd do with a deal more of yore sort in this ol' world. Yes suh! In fact, it'd be no bad thing if y'all wuz t'set up in business right outsida th'Yew-nited Nations ... show all them damn commies that it's soup an' hamburgers th'pore folks of this world're needin', instead of guns an' bullets!"

Louise's face was a picture as a quick succession of emotions flashed across it, first surprise, followed by fear, then suppressed amusement. The big grey-clad Negro smiled tightly back at Grant when briefly accepting his proffered handshake. But the smile didn't reach his eyes.

"Thank you ... Mister Calhoun." His reply was polite enough. His deep voice had a huskiness to it, as though it were rusty with disuse. "I am Brother Mark." He paused, glanced at Louise and continued, "I hope the sister here hasn't been boring you with too many details of our charity work?"

Grant shook his head. "No, not in the least ..." he began but Brother Mark ignored him and instead addressed Louise directly.

"Have you told Mister Calhoun about tonight's Crusade?" he asked.

The girl seemed to shrink into herself a little as she was spoken to. The spark of amusement died in her eyes and she nodded dumbly in reply. Her dread of the big mean-looking black was self-evident. Seeming to sense this, he kept his gaze on her.

Grant answered for her in an attempt to draw the other's attention back to himself. "Oh sure, sure ..." he searched his memory for the name of the place Louise had mentioned to him, "... in the Washington Centre, ain' it? Y'couldn' keep me away from it. Ah've bin t'hear Billy Graham an' Luis Pilau, an' all. Ain' nuthin' ah 'preciate more'n a good ol' fashioned religious meetin', with good hellfire preachin' an' choirs, an' everythin' ..."

On impulse as he spoke, Grant reached into his pocket for his billfold. As he had planned, the movement attracted the black's attention and diverted it away from the girl. Carelessly peeling off five twenty dollar bills, Grant folded them and held them out towards Brother Mark.

"Ah've bin sayin' how much ah admire yore charity work. Waal, Chester D Calhoun's a man who's willin' t'put his money whar his mouth is. Ah'd like yuh t'accept this lil' donation towards yore funds." He pressed the wad of notes into the other's hand as he spoke.

Brother Mark looked genuinely surprised. "Thank you, Mister Calhoun. Most generous of you," he said, accepting the money. "This will be put to good use."

"Ah'm sure it will." Grant beamed at him and, playing the big-talking Texas oilman to the full, he waved a hand in dismissal of such a paltry sum as a hundred dollars. At the same time, he made a mental note to itemise it on his client's expense account … but as something other than a donation to the very people who had enticed his son away from home, or Virgil Miller would definitely not be amused. He thought he'd itemise it under payment for information – which wasn't too far from the truth, all things considered.

"If you'll excuse me," Brother Mark flicked the wad of bills in his hand, "I'll go put this somewhere safe." Nodding to Grant, he made to turn away but paused level with Louise who gazed up at him warily as he towered over her. "Sister …" he began.

At this moment, Grant had another flash of inspiration. He had been trying to think of some excuse for returning to speak to Louise again without arousing suspicion. Right then she was his only positive lead to the sect and Jim Miller. He had also formed the impression that she had grown disillusioned about her life with them. He needed more time to quiz her further on both counts. The cash donation had given him an opening. He followed it up now.

"Say, Brother Mark, I've jes' had me a dilly of an idea!" he exclaimed, with a snap of his fingers. "If it'd be okay with you, that is …"

The big black turned back to him and raised an inquiring eyebrow. Grant pressed on, "I'd sure like our church back in Waco t'start up sumthin' like y'got goin' heah." He waved a hand at the van and its attendant crowd of hangers-on. "Would it be okay fer me t'drop by tomorrow with m'camera, an' git me a few shots of yore set-up heah? It'd give the folks back home an idea of what ah'm talkin' about."

The instant he'd said it, Grant felt he'd made a mistake. Brother Mark's face went suddenly blank but his smoky eyes narrowed with suspicion. Grant hurried to retrieve the situation. Flashing his Texas sunshine smile again, he nodded meaningfully at the folded bills in the other man's fist. "Of course, ah'd be happy t'show my appreciation by makin' another lil' donation to yore funds ... say, five snaps at twenny dollars a shot?"

It worked. The hostility faded from Brother Mark's face at the prospect of another hundred dollars easy pickings from this Texan buffoon. He nodded his assent and this time his tight smile almost reached his cold eyes. Almost ... but not quite.

"Y'got y'self a deal, Mister Calhoun," he replied. "I think that'll be quite in order. An' I hope you enjoy hearing the Prophet Martin Bishop at the Washington Centre tonight." Turning to Louise again, he said, "When you're ready Sister, relieve Sister Martha in the van for a spell. You're due a break too ... we don' want you catchin' flu or anythin' ..."

The message was clear. Don't spend too long with this big-talking, free-spending stranger. Don't get involved. He raised his hand in a parting gesture to Grant and headed back towards the van. Grant watched him go, taking in the coiled spring motion of his walk. There was that indefinable quality in the pantherish tread and in the posture and balance of his body, which suggested to Grant that the man was trained in one of the martial arts, probably karate like himself. He recalled Brother Mark's saying he would go and put the hundred dollars somewhere safe. In Grant's opinion, the safest place for the money would be on Brother Mark's person – he was one mean-looking mother!

In view of the instruction Louise had received to take a spell in the van, and noticing that purple hat had now positioned himself less than six feet away, Grant decided to call it a day. Warning Louise of the enemy presence with a flick of his eyes, he smiled at her and glanced at his watch.

"Waal, ah guess it's time ah wuz gittin' along, Sister Louise," he drawled. "Sure has bin a pleasure talkin' t'you an' Brother

181

Mark. An' ah'm lookin' forward t'hearin' yore leader tonight ..."

He kept up a flow of meaningless chatter as they moved off through the crowd towards its fringe. Louise strolled by his side as though courteously seeing him on his way. When they were again out of earshot of the purple-hatted spy, Grant dropped the phoney accent and lowered his voice again.

"Listen, Louise. You don't need to commit yourself right now. But if you ever decide you want to leave the sect, I'll help you. Just like I intend helpin' Jim Miller. Think about it, okay? I'll see you again tomorrow, an' if you can think of anythin' that might help me get him away – an' any information at all c'd be useful – maybe you'll let me know. Agreed?"

They had stopped at the edge of the crowd and he turned to face her. She nodded solemnly and whispered, "Sure thing, Mister Calhoun. Y'all kin depend on it," in an accurate parody of his phoney Texan accent of a few seconds previously.

He glanced down at her in surprise and saw she was grinning impishly up at him. "I didn't sound as corny as that, did I?" he asked.

"Worse!" she laughed.

She glanced back at the van. "I'll have to go or he will become suspicious of you. I promise I'll think over what you've said but be careful ... please. They don't like any interference from outsiders."

Under the guise of a parting handshake, he gave her small cold hand a quick reassuring squeeze. "Don't worry, when trouble comes lookin' for me, I'm the carefullest guy you ever met," he said lightly. Then as he walked away, he turned and waved back at her. "So long, Sister Louise," he called in his Chester D Calhoun accent. "Till tomorrow."

When he reached the parked Mustang, he shot a quick look back towards the sect van as he opened his driver's door and paused to allow the Champ to scramble over onto the passenger seat. Louise had vanished but he noticed purple hat watching him. Once settled behind the steering wheel, Grant checked his rear-view mirror to see whether anyone was watching him from the driver's compartment of the van. But the mirror effect of the wide, sloping windscreen made it impossible to see anyone behind it.

The Champ looked up at him as they drove off, a knowing look on his small face. "I know now why y'went t'see dem Jesus freaks," he stated confidently.

"Is that a fact?" asked Grant, amused. "Okay, I'll buy it. So, why did I go to see them?"

"Easy," replied the Champ. "Cuz you huntin' fox, is why!"

"Huntin' fox?" Grant burst out laughing.

"Yeah," replied the worldly-wise urchin, grinning hugely from ear to ear. "Y'cain't fool me, man ... you chasin' tail! Ah seen yuh shootin' a line t'the purty lil' blue fox back dere." Then the grin disappeared and the small black face turned serious. "But ah think yo're wastin' y'time, Brett."

"Oh, do you now?" asked Grant, still chuckling. "An' just how d'you make that out?"

"Cuz ah've heard da brothers sayin' as how dem Jesus freaks don' like no-one tryin' t'score with dere chicks ... an' how dey come on real heavy if y'try," the youngster told him solemnly.

Grant's smile became a little strained before it faded from his face altogether, as he digested this last crumb of intelligence. It seemed everyone he met this morning was at pains to drop dark hints and warnings into his path regarding his dealings with the sect. But he wasn't a fatalist, nor a believer in signs and omens. In his opinion, horoscopes were cast by the mentally disturbed for the mentally deluded. Changing the subject, he engaged the Champ in light-hearted banter on the relative merits of the blacks and whites in the Yankees' squad, as he drove back to drop him off in his home area before heading north for Rockford.

His complacency would have been somewhat shaken, had he been able to see behind the blank windscreen of the sect van, as he pulled away from the kerb. He would have seen the grey tracksuited figure of Brother Mark sitting there, having entered the cab through a connecting door from the rear compartment. More to the point, he would also have seen the big black focus a pair of binoculars on the rear licence plate of the Mustang, and note down his number as he drove away ...

183

20

LESS THAN TWO HOURS AFTER DROPPING OFF THE Champ, Grant was introducing himself to Sheriff Nate Springfield in the latter's big, untidy office situated in the building adjacent to the Rockford Courthouse. He found himself shaking hands with a tall lean man in his early fifties, with close-cropped iron grey hair and moustache.

Just as he had done earlier with Rocky O'Rourke, Grant took an immediate liking to the big sheriff. He had an easy-going friendly manner, and the seamed brown skin of his rugged features had the appearance of well tanned leather – an impression which was heightened when he smiled, and it creased into a network of crowsfeet around his faded blue eyes.

"Howdy, Brett. Nate's th'name," he said in reply to Grant's greeting, waving him to a seat at the far side of the big desk which dominated the office. "Y'kin drop the Mister Springfield bit. Any friend o' Ben Curtis is a friend o' mine. I know that might sound a bit cliché, but it also happens t'be true. Now, what's yore poison?"

This last question was flung over his shoulder as he opened a sizeable white painted cabinet affixed to the far wall, marked with a red cross and labelled FIRST AID. It appeared that most of the medication it held seemed to be contained in half a dozen tall bottles, all of which bore the labels of various well-known brands of whisky. Grant eyed the selection on offer.

"Scotch'll do nicely, thanks," he replied.

"Comin' right up," Springfield lifted down the appropriate bottle, along with another of bourbon. "Prefer American m'self," he commented. "I find it smoother on the ol' voice-box."

Producing two half-pint water glasses from one of the desk drawers, he proceeded to splash a good four fingers of neat spirit into each. Handing one to Grant, he set the other on the desk top for himself and replaced the bottle in the cabinet.

"Water?" he asked.

When Grant declined, saying he preferred it neat, Springfield agreed. "Only way fer a man t'drink whisky, I say," he declared approvingly, then asked, "Like a beer t'chase it down?"

Grant nodded his acceptance. "Wouldn't say no."

Springfield strode across to the office door and yanked it open. "Cal!" he bellowed. "Fetch a coupla beers from the cooler, son. An' try not to be all day about it."

The tall sheriff shut the door and recrossed the office. Rounding the big mahogany desk, he settled his spare frame into the high-backed chair there. He cleared a space on its dark, polished surface by sweeping some of the clutter of papers and sundry other objects to one side with a big, gnarled hand. Then he leaned back, swung his feet up to rest his bootheels on the cleared space and crossed his ankles. Reaching into a waistcoat pocket, Springfield pulled out an old curved pipe and a tobacco pouch, and began to fill the blackened bowl. As he tamped down the rough shag with a forefinger, he regarded Grant from under a pair of bushy grey eyebrows.

"Waal Brett, t'save you a heap o' talkin', Ben's already filled me in on the main details o' yore case. An' I've done some checkin' o' my own this mornin' out by the gas station, where the night-shift troopers took the report. From the way things look t'me, I'd say yore client's boy didn' exactly go willin'ly."

Flicking a match into life with his thumbnail, he paused to get his pipe going to his satisfaction, puffing clouds of aromatic smoke into the air around his head. While he was thus engaged, the door opened and a young bearded man entered, his uniform shirt bearing the badge and shoulder-flashes of a deputy sheriff. A couple of inches shorter than Springfield, but of the same lean build, he was carrying two moisture-beaded cans of beer which he stood on the desk top.

Springfield indicated the newcomer with a nod of his head. "My deppity, Calvin Fenton. Cal fer short," he announced to Grant. "Cal ... like you t'meet Brett Grant. He's the private detective from New York I bin expectin'."

Grant and the deputy exchanged nods and Springfield went on, "Used t'be the town drifter, did Cal. Spent his days blowin' dope, bummin' handouts, an' occasionally – very occasionally – doin' odd jobs around th'place. Y'couldn' see 'im fer hair neither, an' the only time he took a bath wuz when he got caught out in the rain lyin' stoned somewhere.

"So I fixed 'im up with a job as deppity t'straighten 'im out," he continued. "Reckoned he wuz in th'jailhouse so damn reg'lar, he'd be better workin' here. He wuz costin' th'community fer 'is keep, anyhow. Still cain't git 'im t'shave off the face fungus entirely," he glared at the grinning Fenton in mock disapproval, "but leastways it's trimmed now … an' he washes more reg'lar, too!"

In the meantime, Fenton had found two clean glasses, into which he now poured the beers. Setting Grant's in front of him, he winked and said, "Waal Brett, as my ol' pappy used t'say, if y'cain't beat 'em, then git 'em t'pay you fer doin' it! Cain't honestly say as how I wuzn't happier doin' nuthin', though." He sighed nostalgically as he said this, as though remembering lost halcyon days of freedom.

Grant chuckled and reached for his glass as Springfield grunted, "Is that so? Well, I cain't say as how I've noticed any remarkable increase in yore work-rate 'tween then an' now. An' speakin' of gittin' paid, how about earnin' some an' fetchin' that report we got this mornin' on that kid that went missin' at the gas station."

"You got it! Colour me gone." Fenton threw him a salute and left the room. He returned almost straight away, laid the report on the table and retired again to the outer office, closing the door behind him.

For the next twenty minutes or so, Grant and Springfield discussed the probable implications of the State Trooper's report, taking into account Virgil Miller's disturbing phone call from his missing son. When the name of Bethlehem House cropped up, Grant briefed Springfield on his earlier meeting with the sect girl Louise and told him about her initial nervous reaction to his questions about the place and its owners.

Springfield listened with growing interest, until Grant concluded, "… so, I'd appreciate it Nate, if you'd give me any information you have on this Bethlehem House pitch. The girl says it's somewhere north of here?" The sheriff leaned forward, heels still on the desk top, and tapped the dead ash from his pipe into the ashtray. Settling back in his chair again, he cleared his throat and pursed his lips thoughtfully before speaking.

"Waal now," he began slowly. "A meditation centre. So that's what that place is. An' them claimin' t'be a psychiatric clinic, too! Always did think there wuz somethin' not quite right about the feel o' that place. One o' them religious communities, is it? Waal, I s'pose that qualifies it t'be described as a nut-house, sure enough." He snorted disgustedly, then added, "Yeah ... that would explain a lot ..." He nodded to himself reflectively.

Grant let the ensuing silence deepen between them, waiting for him to continue. But instead, Springfield suddenly swung his feet to the floor and stood up.

"C'mon, Brett," he said decisively. "I'll take you t'see this Bethlehem House o' yours. It's not far ... only a few miles up the road from here. The gas station's on our route, so we'll drop in there too. We kin talk while we're drivin'."

Walking round the desk, he grabbed his uniform Stetson hat from the top of a filing cabinet and settled it on his head. Grant rose and followed him. The two men passed through the door into the outer office where Fenton was answering a phone at his desk. He looked up as they passed and Springfield told him where they were headed. The bearded deputy waved a hand in acknowledgement as they left.

A few minutes later, the two men were travelling north in Springfield's official car, with its COUNTY SHERIFF markings and badge on the doors and its bank of lights and sirens across the roof. When they had cleared the outskirts of the small township, Springfield picked up the thread of their conversation from where they'd left off in his office.

"Like I wuz sayin', this here Bethlehem House claims t'be a funny farm – Psychiatric Clinic an' Convalescent Home's the fancy title they give themselves. It's one o' them big, ol' fashioned mansion houses, built in the colonial style by some rich industrialist, name o' Bentsen, at the turn o' the century. Prob'ly used it as a kinda glorified shootin' lodge fer himself an' his fat-cat city friends durin' the huntin' season."

He waved a hand at the rolling vista of untamed forest now pressing in on either side of the highway. "Good country fer white tailed deer," he remarked, then continued, "Anyhow, the original family sold out durin' the depression, an' it passed through various hands till World War Two, when the Army requisitioned it as an R an' R home fer wounded officers.

"After the war, the government sold it off an' it became a hotel. But it's purty seasonal round these parts fer the hotel business. Outsida the huntin' season, who wants t'come up here? No-one, that's who! 'Ceptin maybe fer a few businessmen's conferences, an' there ain't enough o' them t'run a hotel on all summer. So it went bust, an' lay vacant again fer a couple o' years, till it got occupied again some five, six years back."

"Have you been inside the place since these latest owners took over?" Grant put in.

"Yeah, as a matter o' fact I have." Springfield nodded. "I called by not long after they'd opened as this private nursin' home they claim t'be, cuz it's my business t'know who's who an' what's where, in this job o' mine. First off, I found I had t'phone fer an appointment though. An' they ain't listed in the local telephone book neither – only way y'kin git their number is by checkin' with City Hall in Albany, where they're registered as a private hospital.

"When I eventually arranged t'call in on 'em, they didn't exactly put out the red carpet. But I cain't say they were downright unfriendly or unco-operative, neither. It wuz jes' a feelin' I got that I wuz … intrudin', somehow. Nothin' I c'd put my finger on, y'understand, but I got the feelin' I wuzn't welcome. Like when y'walk into a roomful o' people an' the conversation stops … know what I mean?"

Grant nodded and asked, "An' what was the place like inside? Did they show you round?"

"Oh yeah," Springfield replied heavily. "Some black dude in a white medical coat gave me a guided tour. The place had all the appearances of a nursin' home. All the things were there you'd expect t'see … patients movin' aroun' in hospital gowns an' slippers, others sittin' out on sun-loungers on the lawns, an' suchlike. They even had what looked t'be nursin' staff in white coats movin' about, an' the ground floor rooms were set up as wards with beds in 'em. Oh yeah, they sure put on a good show for me."

His brow furrowed in concentration for a moment, then he resumed slowly, "Only thing is, now I come t'think of it, everyone seemed like they were actin' a part, somehow. But I didn't figger that out back then. I only knew the whole set-up kinda spooked me. At the time, I think I put that feelin' down to the fact that I thought I wuz bein' shown roun' a nut-house.

"Since that time, they've shown themselves t'be real unsociable too, as far as the local community's concerned, that is. None o' their so-called staff members ever come down to mix in the local bars. I've never known a whole hospital full o' teetotal doctors an' nurses before. Have you? An' they never order nothin' from the local stores neither. All their supplies an stuff must be delivered by their own private transport too, cuz y'never see any tradesmen's vans callin' there. Not even city firms.

"No socialisin' … no trade. Y'hardly ever see 'em at all, in fact. It jes' ain't natural the way they act. But if they're one o' them closed religious sects, that's different. That'd explain all the secretiveness. They're prob'ly all hidin' in there waitin' fer the Lord t'call time-out."

Before Grant could comment, he saw a roadside sign flash past and felt the car begin to slow down as they approached the truck stop it had announced up ahead.

"This here's the gas station yore client's boy made it to last night," Springfield said. Next moment the sheriff was swinging the car into the entranceway and round behind the double rank of pumps. He braked to a smooth halt near the kiosk.

They climbed out of the car and Springfield spoke briefly to the day shift pump attendant, explaining that they were just having a look round in connection with an incident which had taken place during the previous night. The attendant, a bespectacled young man in white coveralls bearing the petrol company logo front and back, said he'd heard about it. He told them the night shift staff were both off duty but to go ahead anyway, and left them to attend to a truck which had just then pulled up at the pumps with a hiss of air-brakes.

"Phone company man's replacin' the busted phone right this minute," he called back over his shoulder as he went, pointing over to the far corner of the forecourt.

They walked across the forecourt towards the phone booths where the repairman could be seen working. The phone company van was parked near to where he was crouched, putting the finishing touches to the installation of a new handset. "Looks like young Pete Warner," commented Springfield as they walked towards the booths.

The repairman looked up at their approach. He was a swarthy, thick-set individual with a heavy black moustache and his eyes registered recognition when he saw Springfield. He straightened up, wiping his hands on a grimy rag, and dropped a screwdriver into the open tool-box at his feet.

"Howdy Sheriff," he said, stuffing the rag into a hip pocket. "What kin I do fer you?"

"Howdy Pete," replied Springfield. He introduced Grant and then explained briefly why they were there. When he'd done so, he asked Warner to show Grant the damaged set he had removed from the booth.

"No problem," The repairman reached into the back of the van and lifted something from an open cardboard box. Turning round, he held the object up for their inspection. In one hand he held a crushed bundle of multi-coloured wiring attached to a base-plate, splintered shards of plastic clinging around it. In his other hand he held the undamaged receiver, which was still attached by its cord to the mangled base. Warner looked from one man to the other without comment.

Springfield pushed his Stetson to the back of his head with a thumb. "Whoever did that sure didn't miss it, did he? Looks like it's bin jumped on," he remarked.

"Hit with somethin', more like ... an' hit hard," Warner grunted in reply. "Jes' one thing puzzles me about it. Usually when a phone gits vandalised, the handset gits it first. It either gits pulled off or smashed. But not this time. This time only the base got it. Nothin' else. No glass broke, no attempt to open th'cash box ... nothin'. Unusual."

"Maybe whoever did it used the handset to smash the base?" suggested Springfield.

"No way!" Warner shook his head. "A blow that heavy would've damaged the handset too. But it ain't even marked."

He held up the receiver to show them its unblemished surface.

Grant glanced from it to the pulverised base in Warner's other hand. As the repairman had said, there was no doubt the latter object had been destroyed by a heavy blow. It certainly seemed to confirm Virgil Miller's suspicion that his son had been forcibly abducted, while in the very act of calling home.

Walking over to the booth, Grant entered it and searched it carefully for any traces of blood or tell-tale scuff marks that would indicate a struggle of some sort had taken place. He found neither. But then, he reasoned, had the boy been surprised by his abductors as seemed likely, there would have been no struggle. Merely a surprise attack and capture – although the absence of blood was no guarantee he hadn't been injured, if the same force had been used on him as had destroyed the phone.

While Warner tidied up his tools preparatory to leaving, Grant mentioned his disquieting thoughts to Springfield. The sheriff listened, nodded, then turned to the repairman. "Pete, I think I'll take possession of that damaged phone. It might be needed later as evidence. I'll give you a receipt fer it."

"Sure thing, Sheriff. Be my guest." Warner handed over the cardboard box. Grant took it and deposited it in the back seat of the Sheriff's car, while Springfield scribbled out a receipt for the repairman. Then, taking their leave of Warner, the two men continued their journey northwards.

The late afternoon twilight was deepening into the early dark of a winter evening, as they covered the few remaining miles to the location of Bethlehem House. When they reached the start of the long boundary fence on the opposite side of the highway, Springfield touched Grant's arm and pointed ahead. At the same time he began to ease off on the gas pedal, lowering the speed of their approach. "Looks like we've struck pay-dirt," he commented. "It ain't often y'catch any o' this lot outside their warren."

Grant peered ahead into the gathering gloom of the opposite verge to see what had attracted Springfield's attention, and saw a pair of shadowy figures standing close against the tall fence. Then, as they cruised slowly past, Grant noticed another four figures on the other side of the fence. All six men were wearing green workmen's coveralls, which blended effectively with the dark background of the woods behind them.

Springfield drove steadily on until they drew level with the big front gates, then he swung the car round in a wide U-turn on the empty highway, and headed back towards the small group. The six men had stopped whatever they had been doing and were watching the approaching car. Under their silent scrutiny, Springfield pulled over onto the hard shoulder and braked to a halt level with them.

Grant now saw the fallen tree leaning at an angle on the fence. A metal tripod and lifting tackle had been assembled on the inner side of the fence, and it was evident the work party were preparing to lift the tree from the sagging wire. Two ladders had also been positioned close together, one on each side of the fence, providing access to either side.

The two men on the outside of the fence were holding pruning shears, which they'd been using to snip off twigs that had thrust through and snagged on the chain-link mesh. Now they and their four companions were standing motionless, their whole attitude a mixture of wariness and hostility.

Grant exchanged a glance with Springfield and the sheriff gave him a wry smile. "They ain't exactly fallin' over themselves t'put out the welcome mat, are they?" he commented drily. "What say we gatecrash th'party?"

"Why not," replied Grant. "Looks like the joint needs livenin' up, if you ask me."

The two men climbed out of the car, pushing the doors shut behind them. Springfield walked round the front of the vehicle to join Grant, setting his Stetson square on his head, the brim tilted slightly forward casting his eyes in shadow. Side by side they trudged the few yards through the long grass and weeds of the verge, towards the motionless, watching group. As they drew near, Grant noticed each pair of coveralls bore a label reading MAINTENANCE CREW on the breast pocket. They stopped facing the pair on their side of the fence and Springfield touched his hat brim in greeting.

"Afternoon, gen'lemen. Havin' some trouble with yore tree-thinnin'?" He nodded in the direction of the fallen tree. "I'd say whoever felled that'un wasn't no lumberjack, from th'looks of it."

The taller of the two young men facing him, fresh faced and sporting a military style crew-cut, suddenly came to life. He gestured towards the fallen tree and replied civilly enough, though his manner was still guarded. "Oh, we didn't fell it, Sheriff ... the wind did. Must've blown it down sometime durin' the night. We jes' had t'cut if free of the stump, so's we kin lift it off the fence."

Springfield eyed the tree and pursed his lips. "Waal, it looks like y'got y'selves a heap o' firewood now. You'll have t'cut an' stack it fer a while, though. Too green t'burn good, till it weathers a bit." Then, without warning he changed tack and inquired casually, "You guys on th'staff here?"

Crew-cut nodded warily and Springfield went on, "That young patient from here musta given th'nursin' staff a good run f'their money last night ... 'fore they caught 'im, that is. He sure raised a few eyebrows at th'truck stop down th'road, when he walked in on 'em wearin' his hospital gown like he did."

The tall sheriff chortled to himself, apparently unaware of the reaction his words had evoked from the two facing him. At his mention of the word patient, crew-cut's eyes flickered with what Grant judged to be alarm. Then he exchanged a quick look with his companion, a sullen young Hispanic with a pockmarked face, before responding to Springfield's remark.

"Patient?" He frowned as though puzzled. "From here?"

"That's what he told the folks at th'truck stop," Springfield assured him. "Then it seems he bummed some money an' called his folks in New York. Only thing is," he allowed a frown of disapproval to cloud his face, "this kid then went an' vandalised th'phone after he'd used it, an' th'truck stop owners reported it to us. Into th'bargain, it seems there were some trucks in th'parkin' lot broken into ..." he slipped in the lie without so much as a blink, "... so, me an' Detective Grant here would like t'have a few words with the youngster."

Detective Grant was having as much difficulty keeping his face carefully blank, as were the men facing Springfield – if for different reasons. The sheriff gave the group no time to gather their thoughts. Hooking his thumbs into his belt, he pressed on remorselessly.

"Of course, if he's under medical care … waal, that jes' might make a difference. But we'll have t'see whoever's responsible fer 'im … doctor in charge of his case … hospital super-intendent … someone like that. Now, who would you suggest we speak to?" He looked inquiringly at the two men before him.

One of the four behind the fence sniggered quietly but crew-cut merely shrugged. "Don' know nothin' myself about any patient gittin' out last night," he replied evasively. "But if y'wanna speak to anyone about it, you'll hafta phone an' arrange an interview. I expect Reception'll let y'know when it'd be convenient t'call. Further'n that I can't help you, Sheriff … we're jes' maintenance crew, as y'kin see, an' got nothin' t'do with the medical staff."

Springfield eyed him for a long moment, then nodded. "Okay. I'll take yore advice an' call Reception to arrange an' interview with someone. Thanks fer y'help. We'll be in touch." He touched the brim of his hat, turned away and stalked off through the long grass. Grant made to move after him, then turned back. He had decided on impulse to let these people know that the boy's identity was known to the police. It might just have the effect of protecting him from any immediate harm, he reasoned. As he faced them, he sensed their hostility towards him and their blank faces only served to heighten the impression.

"Oh … in case you should happen t'mention our visit to anyone …" he let the remark hang on the air between them for a second, before continuing, "… the boy's name is Miller … Jim Miller. Like th'sheriff said, we'll be in touch!" He raised his hand to the unresponsive group and turned away.

Making his way back to the car, Grant noticed that Springfield had not already done so but instead had apparently wandered off at a tangent into the tall grass of the verge, to emerge at a point several yards further along the highway. Reaching the car, Grant climbed in and waited till Springfield rejoined him. When he did so a couple of minutes later, the big man eased his angular frame behind the wheel, started up the engine and put the car in motion without comment.

As the car pulled away, Grant glanced back over his shoulder for a last glimpse of the uncommunicative sect work crew. Through the rear window, he saw crew-cut holding a small dark object up to his mouth. He was as sure as he could be at that distance in the fading light, that the fast receding figure was speaking into a personal radio. Facing forward again, he mentioned this to Springfield.

"Yeah, I noticed." The sheriff nodded towards the rear-view mirror. "Didn't surprise me none. Rum crew, ain't they? Mind you …" he gave a soft laugh, "I sure as hell wiped the deadpan look offa that crop-headed bastard's face, when I mentioned that bit about a patient o' theirs runnin' wild durin' th'night, didn't I?"

"You sure did," Grant agreed with a grin. "An' you nearly wiped the deadpan look off mine too, you ol' fox. Detective Grant, indeed! I hope I never find you givin' evidence against me in court. I'd change my plea to guilty!"

Springfield assumed an air of injured innocence. "I didn' tell th'man a lie now, did I? After all, you are a detective, ain'tcha? I jes' clean forgot t'mention th'word private, that's all." He grinned at Grant. "Sometimes it's not what y'say that confuses folk, but what y'leave unsaid. Brings t'mind a piece o' good advice my ol' pappy once gave me. 'Son,' he said, 'as y'go through life, never pass up a chance t'keep y'mouth shut!' It works too. In yore own experience, think how often you've heard a suspect runnin' off at th'mouth tryin' t'talk himself outa trouble, an' instead only succeedin' in talkin' himself deeper into it."

"That's true," Grant agreed, then added thoughtfully, "An' speakin' of questionin' people reminds me, the sooner I can arrange to interview the Miller kid, the better. That girl Louise I spoke to this afternoon, told me he'll be in big trouble for tryin' to run like he did. In fact, when you went wanderin' off back there, I made a point of droppin' his name to that goon squad, just to prevent anythin' from happenin' to him before I get th'chance to talk to him."

"When I went wanderin' off, as you put it," Springfield retorted, "I wuz followin' tracks leadin' from th'fence to the roadside. I reckon that's th'way yore boy headed ... that is, after he'd shinned up that young tree he'd cut down t'help 'im git over th'fence."

Grant looked at him quizzically. "Y'mean it wasn't blown down, like they said back there?"

"No way!" Springfield shook his head. "When th'wind blows a tree down, it either uproots it an' pushes it over, or else it snaps the trunk like a match stick." He lifted a hand from the steering wheel and snapped his fingers to illustrate his point.

"Now," he continued, "if th'wind pushes a tree over, yo're left with a big clump of earth an' roots, an' a hole in th'ground. But if the tree's bin broke off short, then th'wood splinters, an' yo're left with jagged surfaces on both th'stump an' th'broken off trunk. Right?"

Grant nodded and Springfield went on, "Waal, from what I saw, both ends were clean-cut, stump an' trunk, damn near all th'way through. An' there weren't no splinters layin' around neither, such as there would've bin, s'posin' they'd decided t'waste time an' effort cleanin' up both th'stump an' th'trunk. Nope ..." he concluded, "that tree wuz cut down, all right. Besides which, last night's wind couldn't have blown m'hat off, let alone blow over a strong young tree like that one!"

"Okay, Kit Carson, I'll buy that." Grant grinned at his companion. "I knew I shoulda listened to my ol' pappy's advice, an' stayed in the cub-scouts till I'd got my Junior Frontiersman's badge for fieldcraft." Then turning serious again, he continued, "So, now we know how the boy got out. An' I'm also pretty sure his ol' man's right about them havin' recaptured him. Tomorrow should confirm that, if I get an interview with him. Then my only problem'll be how I'm gonna get him out of there again. These religious sects all have one thing in common – they don't like lettin' people go, once they've joined. I've run up against this sorta thing before, an' it's never easy. So, I'll have t'put my thinkin' cap on, an' work somethin' out ..."

"We'll have t'work somethin' out, y'mean." Springfield put in, with deliberate emphasis on the first word.

"Huh? Come again?" said Grant, surprised.

"I said we'll have t'work somethin' out," repeated Springfield. "An' that's what I meant! Goin' by what you've jes' told me, an' from what I've seen fer myself, I reckon y'might need some help handlin' that lot back there. Besides," he added firmly, "I happen t'be sheriff round these parts, an' I ain't havin' no religious fanatics abductin' minors on my territory!"

"Nate …" Grant searched for the words he wanted. "I appreciate your offer of help, but … look, don't take this the wrong way, but it might be best if you don't get yourself too closely involved at this stage. Since I left the job an' went private, I've had a lotta dealin's with religious nuts like this sect. In my experience it seems like once they get the idea into their heads that they've got some kinda special relationship with the Lord, they start to thinkin' they're above the law! That badge you're wearin' means nothin' to people like them. But you've gotta operate within the bounds of the law, an' rules of procedure. An' it's no use tryin' to fight an opponent if you've gotta stick to Boxin' Board rules, while he's kickin' you in the balls. What I'm tryin' t'say is …"

"I know what yo're tryin' t'say," Springfield interrupted. "An' I agree with you. But what I'm sayin' is, there's times when th'law kin be a handy thing t'have at yore back, no matter how dirty yore opponent wants t'play it. An' I happen t'think we'd make a purty useful combination, you'n'me. I kin hit 'em with th'rule book when it counts, an' if they cut up rough an' you've gotta start kickin' gonads … waal, you've jes' no idea how poor my eyesight kin git at times …" He flashed a grin at Grant. But the faded blue eyes above the smile were flint hard.

"So," he concluded, "first off, I suggest y'leave arrangin' the interview t'me. I'll carry more weight with 'em than you, seein' as how I'm the law round here. Fact is, I think they'll check you out before lettin' you in. An' once they find out you're a private detective, y'wouldn' git t'first base. Worse, they might even let you in an' then rough you up."

Grant warmed to the big, slow-talking sheriff and felt grateful to him. The offer of assistance was welcome, and he got the feeling that Nate Springfield would be a useful ally to have at his back in a tight spot. "Thanks Nate," he said simply. "I appreciate your help."

"Think nothin' of it," Springfield responded. "Truth is, Ben asked me t'take care o' you. He said you owe him a night out, an' he wants me t'make sure you'll still be around t'pay fer it."

Grant laughed at this comment and the mention of Curtis's name switched the conversation onto a lighter vein. The remainder of the drive back to Rockford was taken up by the swapping of anecdotes concerning their mutual friend.

Once back in his office, Springfield immediately dug out the Bethlehem House number from a dog-eared phone book and put through a call to their 'Reception'. The result was much as he'd expected. Announcing himself in his official capacity, he requested an early interview with someone in authority for both himself and a Mister Grant, private detective, regarding serious allegations of abduction and unlawful detention of a minor, namely one James Miller. For good measure, he then threw in the fact that he also wanted to interview the youth concerning allegations of malicious damage to a phone and thefts from parked vehicles, all of which had taken place in the early hours of that morning.

After a delay of several minutes, he was told that no-one of sufficient authority was available right then to consider his request and he was advised to call back the following morning. Springfield assured the person on the other end of the line that he would do just that ... then added blandly, with a wink at Grant, that he was sure everything could be cleared up by a simple interview – and without any need to involve the FBI, on account of the alleged abduction! He hung up on the silence which greeted this parting shot.

The dark of a late winter afternoon had set in by the time Grant climbed into his Mustang for the run back to the city. He had first phoned Pam from Springfield's office to tell her he was on his way, and to get ready for an evening out. "Oh good!" she'd exclaimed. "Where are we going?" When he'd explained, her enthusiasm had instantly evaporated.

"A religious crusade?" She had sounded incredulous. "You're puttin' me on, aren't you? You're not? Now, wait a minute …" She had paused, suspicion and annoyance creeping into her voice. "Brett, is this anything to do with your work?" she demanded. "You know how I feel about you letting your work interfere with our free time together. Before you know it, you'll be getting as bad as your pal Ben – working all hours, like last night."

In the end, he had mollified her with the assurance that this was a one-off and the promise of a meal in one of their favourite restaurants the following week. Replacing the receiver, he'd shrugged resignedly at an amused Springfield.

"I know how y'feel," the sheriff had commiserated with him. "I git th'same durn thing all th'time from mine, too."

Outside, Grant took his leave of Springfield, the latter promising to phone and let him know the arrangements for the interview with the Miller boy. Straightening up from the driver's window, the tall sheriff eyed the sleek lines of the Mustang with grudging admiration.

"Drive careful in that thing," he admonished. "Or it might not be a Prophet you'll be seein' tonight – it might be Saint Peter himself at th'Pearly Gates!"

By way of reply, Grant deliberately gunned away from the kerb with a touch of wheel-spin and a cheery wave to the head-shaking Springfield. Soon the lights of Rockford had disappeared from his mirror and the powerful car was arrowing forward into the swathe of light cast by its own head lamps, effortlessly eating up the miles to the distant city – and his next encounter with the sect.

21

ANGEL ONE WAITED UNTIL HIS THREE FELLOW Orientals had seated themselves. He had summoned them to his private quarters for a meeting. He began by asking for a progress report on the search for the missing boy and was told by Angel Four that results were still negative. Angel Three added that search parties which had completed sweeps of their allocated areas were being redirected to assist those still searching. In this way, they would be assured of having covered the entire grounds by nightfall.

Angel One nodded his approval, then turned to the matter of the reported encounter with the local sheriff by the leader of the work detail. He informed the others that the sheriff had since phoned, requesting that he and a private detective be permitted to interview the Miller boy the following day.

"I propose to grant the sheriff's request , with one important proviso, namely that I myself will be present – as the 'doctor in charge of the patient's case'!" he stated flatly.

He paused to allow them to digest this surprising announcement, then continued, "My only reason for allowing the interview to take place at all, is because the arrival of our next consignment is due any day, and as a result it would be extremely inconvenient to draw any police interest onto ourselves at this time. However, by insisting the interview take place in my presence, I will be able to restrict the subject matter and thus neutralise any threat of what Miller might otherwise have said. At the same time, I will also be able to further convince the sheriff in his belief that this is indeed a mental hospital and so defuse any potential trouble from him in future." He looked round the other three, inviting comment.

Angel Two was the first to break the ensuing brief silence. "I agree with your analysis of the situation," he began carefully. "It is indeed imperative that we avoid any unnecessary confrontation with the police." He hesitated and a frown clouded his smooth features. "But do you think it advisable to permit this private detective to attend the interview? His kind are nothing but legalised bandits. They have caused us inconvenience in the past as you know, with their amateurish attempts at snatching back new recruits from our organisation. With respect, I suggest that you reconsider this one aspect of your plan."

"It is precisely because of his potential nuisance value that I am prepared to allow the private detective to attend," Angel One replied. "If he runs true to type, I am certain he will make some blundering attempt to snoop around on his own ... especially if presented with the opportunity. And then," he concluded grimly, "I will personally discourage him from any thought of future interference in our affairs!"

They considered this in silence for a few moments, then Angel Three spoke. "With respect, I can see another complication arising from this interview, should you proceed with it."

"And that is?" Angel One asked.

"Well, if as a result Miller escapes punishment for his escape, it could encourage other similar attempts and cause us discipline problems."

"And who said that Miller will escape punishment?" Angel One demanded bluntly.

Angel Three looked doubtful. "But now that the police are involved ..."

"The police interest in Miller is only temporary," Angel One interrupted him. "And it is up to us to ensure it stays that way. Then, when it has vanished in a few weeks' time, so too will Miller ... permanently!" He turned to Angel Two. "See to the setting up of the dummy wards by noon tomorrow." His curt order indicated that the subject was now closed.

He now addressed Angel Four. "Have you detailed those who will be on duty with you at the Washington Centre tonight?" he demanded.

Angel Four nodded. "I have instructed six Apostles and twenty Disciples to be ready to leave in ..." he glanced at his watch, "... half an hour."

"Good," said Angel One. Then, turning to Angel Two again, he continued, "I shall be leaving for the city myself within the next hour. I am ordered to report to Dragon Control for a briefing on the forthcoming consignment. You will take charge here while I am gone."

The phone buzzed at his elbow and he picked it up. As he listened to the message from the other end, a cold smile touched his normally impassive face. It was a smile of satisfaction.

"Excellent!" he spoke softly into the receiver. "Tell them to touch nothing. I will come right away." He regarded the others for a long moment, the faint smile still lingering on his face.

"One of our problems has just been solved," he informed them, then added enigmatically, "And I think I can use it to help solve our other one. The meeting is over. Come with me, all of you ..."

PART IV
CONTROL
TO ANGEL
ONE

22

JIM MILLER, THE OTHER PROBLEM THE FOUR
Orientals had been discussing half an hour earlier, was lying flat
on his back on his mattress, eyes closed and hands resting
limply by his sides. Try as he might, he was finding it impossible
to relax his mind and body into a state of restful meditation as
they had been taught to do at instruction classes. His overactive
imagination was the main culprit but his dully throbbing head
wound and aching stomach muscles weren't exactly helping
much either.

The sudden sound of the passage door outside being unlocked
jerked him back to full awareness. He was in the act of climbing
to his feet, when a key turned in the lock of the cell door and
it swung silently open. Angel One stood framed in the entrance,
with one of the grey tracksuited Apostles at his shoulder. Jim
braced himself defensively against the far wall but the oriental
made no move to enter. Instead, he merely gestured towards the
bucket in the corner.

"Pick that up and go with Brother James here," he nodded
at the silent figure behind him. "He will show you where to
empty it. You will be permitted to take a shower while you are
there."

Angel One stood aside to allow Jim to leave the cell carrying
the latrine bucket but made no attempt to follow him as he
padded after his escort. Jim found himself being led back along
the corridor from the section which housed the cells. They
stopped at a door several yards along this corridor and the
Apostle unlocked it and motioned for Jim to enter. He did so

and found himself in a combined washroom and toilet, with a shower cubicle in one corner.

After he had emptied and swilled out his bucket, Jim was handed soap and a towel by the big shaven-headed black Apostle who was acting as his escort. Needing no persuasion, he stripped off and stepped under the steaming spray. For the next ten minutes he indulged himself in the luxury of hot soapy water cascading over his body, as he washed away the last physical traces of the previous night's escapade from his person.

When his injured temple began to sting from the effects of the soap, he turned the shower cold to rinse off. He caught his breath as the freezing water needled down on his upturned face and numbed his chest and shoulders. Without warning, his mind suddenly flashed back to the previous night and for one terrifying instant he was once again lying face down in the icy grip of the stream in the woods, while a few yards away the Hellhounds were ripping and tearing at Tom's bloodied corpse.

The mental flashback might have freaked him out, had not his escort chosen that moment to rap his knuckles on the sliding door of the shower and growl, "Okay, finish off in there," snapping him back to reality. Shivering from more than the effects of the cold shower, Jim turned off the water and stood for several seconds brushing the water from his legs and body with his hands, giving himself time to recover.

When he felt calmer, he stepped out into the dressing half of the cubicle to dry off. There he was surprised to find a fresh robe and underclothing neatly folded alongside the towel. A comb, toothbrush and toothpaste had also been provided. His surprise quickly gave way to suspicion and he wondered why he was being given the kid-glove treatment. However he decided to take full advantage of it and after drying off and dressing, he cleaned his teeth and combed out his long hair. Finished, he felt refreshed for the first time since his recapture, as he followed his taciturn escort back along the corridor.

Re-entering his cell, Jim wrinkled his nose at the stale musty odour which greeted him. He felt embarrassed – he hadn't realised he had smelt quite so bad in his unwashed state – and the thought occurred that pig pen would be a more apt label for his cell than turkey pen. He saw that Angel One had awaited his return and expected the oriental to lock him in immediately. Instead, Angel One followed him into the cell, stopped just inside the door and addressed him.

"Your attention a moment, Miller." The harsh voice halted Jim in his tracks and he turned to face his captor. "It is possible you may have two visitors tomorrow. The local sheriff and a private detective have been making inquiries about you and have requested an interview."

Jim's spirits soared at this startling piece of intelligence. Here was the explanation for the sudden improvement in his treatment, he thought. It seemed his abortive attempt to escape had not been a complete failure after all. His surge of fresh hope flared in his eyes for an instant, before he could hide it.

Angel One watched him with the cold deliberation of a cat toying with a mouse, judging the correct moment to pounce. He allowed Jim his brief flicker of hope, before crushing it out under the impact of his next words.

"However … you can be sure of one thing, Miller. Under no circumstances will you be permitted to leave here! You are only being permitted to speak to these people in order to give you the chance to sort out the trouble you have caused. You will be told exactly what to say – and for your own good, you will obey your instructions to the letter. Understand?"

The black eyes bored menacingly into his, and Jim nodded dumbly in submission. At the same time he mentally crossed his fingers, thinking that when he actually met the sheriff and the private detective, things would be different. Then he'd be able to say what he liked and appeal for their help.

At that moment the big black Apostle re-entered the cell carrying a plastic tray containing his evening meal and this gave Jim the excuse to break off eye contact with Angel One. He felt instant relief as he was released from the unnerving feeling that the oriental was reading his thoughts. He watched the grey-clad figure lay the tray on his mattress, then turn and pad silently from the cell. From the corner of his eye he saw Angel One make as though to follow his subordinate, only to pause in the act of closing the door.

"Miller ..." Jim's head jerked round and he was again held by the compelling power of the slanted eyes. "Think over very carefully what I have said to you. Your co-operation tomorrow could affect your future ... in fact, it could ensure you have a future!" An enigmatic little smile touched the Oriental's lips as he added, almost as an afterthought, "Should you have any doubts, Miller, consider your friend's fate. Perhaps that will help you make up your mind. We will discuss this further in the morning."

The door clicked shut. Stunned, Jim stared at its blank grey surface. Angel One's parting remarks could only mean that they had found Tom's body ... or what was left of it. Then the consoling thought occurred to him that even if they had discovered the truth about Tom, it no longer posed the same threat to his own life. Not now that outside help was at hand, in the form of the local sheriff and a private detective. He wondered how they had come into the picture and decided that his old man must have come up trumps after all – either that or it could have been the big trucker he'd met at the gas station. Whoever it was, he made a mental note to express his heartfelt thanks first chance he got. A bit easier in his mind, he turned away and seated himself cross-legged on his mattress beside his meal tray. He had hardly eaten all day and soon he was hungrily tucking into the sandwiches and milk they'd left him.

He had almost finished eating when a patch of colour caught his eye over in the far corner. Surprised, he glanced up and registered for the first time the objects which had previously been hidden by the angle of the open door, and then latterly lain unnoticed when he was deep in thought. A red plastic basin and bucket were sitting in the corner, the bucket inverted and sitting in the basin. They struck Jim as looking like a cartoon drawing of a Mexican sombrero and the thought amused him, making him smile. On top of the upturned bucket lay a folded towel and on this lay a bar of soap, a toothbrush, toothpaste and a comb. More evidence of his improved treatment since the news of his forthcoming visit, he thought smugly.

Draining the last of his milk, he dropped the empty carton onto the tray and decided to take some exercise. Rising to his feet, he winced as his bruised stomach muscles reminded him sharply of their presence. It occurred to him that the good news about the coming interview had helped him forget his aches and pains for a time. He began to pace up and down the length of the cell, letting his mind dwell on how he would blow the whistle on Angel One at the meeting the following day. The prospect made him feel good.

After only a few turns up and down the cell, something else intruded into his thoughts. The stale, sour smell he had noticed earlier seemed to be getting worse. At the same time, he also became aware of the fact that the air conditioning wasn't working. Another couple of lengths of the cell and he noticed the smell seemed to be stronger at the door end of the cell. Nor was it the odour of stale sweat, as he had first thought. No, it was a ranker smell … and yet, familiar …

Suddenly he halted in mid-stride. He knew what the cloying smell reminded him of. Rotting meat! And he was pretty sure he knew its source, too. He swung round and stared at the upturned bucket where it nestled in the basin over by the door. The hitherto innocuous items of kitchenware filled his vision. No longer amusing, the blood-red sombrero shape had assumed a new, sinister purpose. But his mind rebelled against the unspeakable thought which was hammering at the back door of his consciousness, demanding admittance. It couldn't be that … or could it?

He took a reluctant step forward, then another, forcing himself to approach the red plastic containers in the corner, despite his dread of what he would find there. The smell was definitely worse in their vicinity. Scarcely breathing, he crouched down and carefully removed the towel and toilet articles, as though fearful of disturbing whatever lay underneath. As he laid the articles aside, he noticed that his hands were trembling.

Pausing for a moment to gather his courage, Jim steeled himself to reach out and grasp the bucket firmly in both hands. He lifted it with one swift movement. For a frozen, timeless instant of horror, he stared at what he had uncovered. There, gaping up at him, was the half-eaten, severed head of Tom Sheppard. He knew it was Tom, despite the fact the features were torn and mutilated almost beyond recognition. The flesh of one side of the face had been ripped away, exposing the bared teeth in an obscene grin of death and the eyeless sockets seemed to gaze up at him in blind accusation.

Then the stench of putrefaction hit him and Jim slammed the bucket back down over the abomination with a strangled cry of repugnance. He staggered to his feet and reeled across the cell, making for the latrine bucket. He didn't quite make it – his freshly consumed evening meal beat him to it by a short length, as he threw up violently all over himself, the lidded bucket and the floor.

Outside the cell door, Angel One quietly lowered the flap of the Judas hole. He stood for a few moments longer until the sounds of retching gave way to muffled sobs, then he moved away, a gleam of satisfaction showing in his bleak eyes. The softening-up process was proceeding nicely. By morning, after a whole night in the company of his ghastly cellmate, the boy would be ready to agree to anything.

Half an hour later, Angel One, looking completely different in a conventional dark suit and gleaming white shirt, drove out of the main gates in one of the sect's cars. Of the same sombre blue colour scheme as the rest of the sect vehicles, the only difference was the lack of the gold cross logo on any part of its body work. Turning southwards, he accelerated smoothly away and headed for New York. On this occasion, he had no-one driving him. He was alone.

23

IN HIS OFFICE AT PRECINCT HQ, DETECTIVE LIEUTENant Ben Curtis was slumped low in his padded chair, his legs stretched out under the kneehole of his cluttered desk. He was staring moodily at the sheet of paper he was holding in one hand. His other hand was curled into a loose fist on the arm of his chair, the inevitable cigarette in his nicotine stained fingers sending a lazy spiral of blue smoke towards the ceiling.

The offending sheet of paper which was commanding his attention bore two columns of figures. The column on the left consisted of short groups of Roman numerals, the one on the right, divided into groups, bore the various permutations of their possible equivalents in ordinary figures. The left hand column represented, in chronological order, the sequences of numerals which had been carved into the bodies of all fifteen murdered prostitutes. The final entry, freshly added in Curtis's distinctively rounded figuring, referred to the latest victim – the unfortunate Mary-Lou Evans.

Curtis had been hoping for some lightning bolt of inspiration to strike him – to flood his tired brain with the kind of intuitive brilliance which always seemed to solve the cases of the intrepid sleuths in drawing-room whodunits. His problem was, he reflected irritably, lack of sleep and too many long hours on duty were catching up with him. His concentration was wavering, refusing to maintain its focus on the obscure groups of numbers and their possible meaning. He decided to call it a day, and get himself off home. An early night and hopefully an uninterrupted sleep would help him to see things more clearly tomorrow.

His train of thought was broken by a sharp rap on the door, which opened to admit Detective Lieutenant Donald "Scotty" Cameron from Narcotics. An immigrant at the age of two from his native Scotland with his family some forty-five years earlier, Cameron was a stockily built five-ten with thinning fair hair. Despite his East Side accent and the fact that he was as Scottish in his outlook and thinking as a Big Mac Hamburger, he was still "Scotty" to his buddies on the force.

Curtis liked Scotty. They were on the same wave-length and were firm friends in addition to being colleagues. Now he was doubly pleased to see him because his visit gave him the excuse to break off his futile mental struggle to solve the enigma of the numbers puzzle the killer had set him. Cameron closed the door behind him and advanced into the room.

"Hi Ben. Busy?" he inquired breezily.

"Hi Scotty. I was but I think I'll call it a day." Curtis dropped the offending sheet of paper on the desktop among the clutter of files and other paperwork there and stretched to ease his cramped shoulder muscles. "C'mon in an' park y'butt fer a few minutes. I c'd do with a shoulder t'cry on. Better still, I c'd do with a vacation."

Cameron grinned as he cleared a space on the corner of the desk and rested a hip on it. Pulling out a cigarette pack, he shook one loose and stuck it in his mouth then offered the pack to Curtis. Lighting up, Cameron blew smoke at the ceiling and said, "Okay, shoot. Uncle Scotty's listenin'. I got built-in snot wipers in my shoulder pads. What's buggin' you?"

Curtis exhaled a lungful of smoke and coughed. Leaning forward, he picked up the sheet of figures and passed it to Cameron. "These fuckin' numbers, that's what! That, an' th'fact that we're no nearer nailin' this sonavabitch. I tellya I've stared at these goddam figures till I'm fuckin' near walleyed but all I'm gittin's a migraine. I reckon if we kin decode these, it'll tell us somethin' important about the bastard. If nothin' else, it'll help us build a psychological profile which c'd point us in th'right direction."

Cameron looked up from his examination of the cryptic sheet and cocked an eyebrow in feigned surprise. "Build a what?" He dropped the sheet back onto the desk and spread his hands in a gesture of appeal. "Hey, c'mon man, speak American t'me, willya? I'm only a dumb Narc, not one of your college graduate Homicide types. Did that mouthful by any chance mean y'gotta hunch that crackin' these numbers'll give you an insight into his thinkin', an' from that maybe a motive?"

Cameron's light-hearted mood was infectious and Curtis responded with a wry smile. "Y'got it in one. But right now th'bastard's got us behind the eight ball. All we have are a coupla vague descriptions, an' when I say vague – do I mean vague! Nothin' worth dogshit." He paused and then continued straight-faced, "I tellya, I'm thinkin' of askin' fer a transfer to Narcotics, so I kin take it easy fer a while …"

"Hah, you sh'd be so lucky!" Cameron responded with a laugh. "Outa the fryin' pan into the fire, more like. We got plentya problems of our own right now. As if we didn' have enough trouble with the Colombians an' Jamaicans movin' in on the drugs scene, the streets've bin gittin' flooded with real high grade heroin. Chinese origin, the forensic boys say. Up till now the only information we have on it is that it's part of a big Triad run operation which is bringin' th'stuff in through Canada, an' across the border. The word is it's shipped from Hong Kong to Europe – Hamburg, Amsterdam, Marseilles, take y'pick, then across to the St Lawrence ports of Quebec, Montreal an' Toronto – again y'kin take your pick."

Curtis nodded his understanding. "An' th'border controls are a joke," he commented.

"The border controls are fuckin' non-existent," Cameron snorted. "In any case, the Canadians ain't payin' too much attention to what gits across the border, cuz their cities're gittin' hit with the Chinese smack too. They got a big enough headache tryin' t'keep on top of their own end of the operation. Fact is, although they'd never admit it, the more that crosses the border the better – it's less fer them t'hafta deal with. An' their success rate's no better'n ours. Like us, they've caught the usual clutch of low grade dealers, an' made a few busts, but nothin' important. So, jes' like you with your serial killer, the first lead we git'll be our first real break. See … you ain't the only one with problems, ol' friend."

Curtis nodded his grudging acceptance of this point. "Yeah, I s'pose you're right," he agreed tiredly. "Only it don' help that that prick Elrick's bin pesterin' the Captain fer results, so he kin look good at his next press conference. Says he's gotta have somethin' fer a statement soon." He snorted his disgust. "I thought shootin' a line about nothin' wuz his strong point. Any other time, tryin' t'stop that prick jerkin' off at th'mouth's like tryin' t'plug a sewage outlet with a tampon."

Cameron laughed. "Our super-efficient Deputy Commissioner still gittin' up y'nose, Ben? C'mon now, be reasonable. What would we do if we didn' have him to shield us hard workin' cops from th'spotlight of publicity when we have our successes? The poor guy has his work cut out grabbin' all th'credit an' keepin' his best profile turned towards th'cameras, y'know."

213

"Super-efficient? That fat prick's about as much use as a chocolate jockstrap!" commented Curtis acidly. "An' it's not so much what he does when there's any credit goin' that gets me. It's what he does with all th'shit he collects. He dumps it on th'Captain. An', of course, Devlin jes' holds it long enough t'find out where I am, before unloadin' it all over me. Not that I blame Devlin, mind you," he admitted ruefully. "If I wuz Captain of Detectives, I'd dump all my shit on my lieutenant too."

"Tell y'what," offered Cameron, glancing at his watch and standing up. "How about I buy you a beer before we split."

"Now you're singin' my song. Thought you'd never offer." Curtis pushed himself out of his chair, swept the sheet of figures into a scuffed briefcase along with some other case papers and snapped it shut. He walked round the desk carrying the case and plucked his hat and coat from the wooden hat stand in the corner.

As they headed for the door, Cameron nudged him with an elbow. "Hey, maybe Elrick'll turn out t'be a suspect," he laughed. "Jes' think how you'd enjoy grillin' him."

"Grillin' 'im?" Curtis growled, jamming his hat on his head and shrugging into his coat. "If he didn' sing, I'd plug 'is dick in th'power socket an fry th'fucker!"

24

AS GRANT LET HIMSELF INTO THE FLAT, HE COULD hear Pam singing to herself over the clatter of dishes and the dramatic tones of a TV news reader in the background. He called out, "Hi Pam, it's me," and heard her cheery acknowledgement floating back. Homing in on the sounds of her activity, he found her in the kitchenette, where she was standing over a sinkful of steaming hot water, hands enveloped in rubber gloves, busily engaged in washing some cooking

utensils. There was an appetising aroma of cooking food and
hot coffee coming from the vicinity of the cooker. Suddenly he
felt hungry.

Pam's back was to him and for a long moment he stood
unnoticed by her in the doorway, drinking her in with his eyes,
admiring her tall shapely figure as he did every time he saw her
afresh. He never seemed to tire of looking at her, of watching
her. It didn't seem to matter whether she was moving around,
or sitting still, or just lying asleep beside him, he loved looking
at her and savouring her very presence.

He had known her for a little over a year now, ever since he'd
met her at a dinner party to which they'd been separately invited
by a mutual friend. They'd taken to one another from the moment
they'd been introduced by the hostess, "Pam Mason ... Brett
Grant; Brett, this is Pam. Listen you two, I hope you don't mind
if I rush off and leave you to get to know one another unaided.
Everyone seems to be arriving at once and I've still got some
last-minute things to see to, you know how it is. Brett, be a
darling and keep Pam's glass topped up. Have fun ..." and she
had indeed rushed off, leaving them together.

It turned out when they got talking, that they were both
recovering from unhappy relationships. Brett had found himself
telling her, quite freely, about his stormy short marriage and
subsequent bitter divorce. He'd been mildly surprised at himself
at the time, for it was a subject which still pained him to touch
on, an episode of his life he considered to be a closed book, not
to be reopened – or repeated.

Pam Mason, for her part, had also quite freely and matter-of-
factly told him briefly about her own previous unfortunate
liaison with the man who'd convinced her she'd met her Mister
Right. Until, that is, she'd been confronted one traumatic day
by the man's distraught hysterical wife. The woman had turned
up at the office where Pam had been working as a secretary at
the time and an angry scene had ensued. Quite unjustly accused
of being a husband stealer and a home wrecker, Pam had been
shattered. It transpired her 'fiancé' had been married for some
six years and had two children. Humiliated, and unable to face
her work mates, she'd given up her job. She'd even changed her

home address for good measure, for fear her ex-lover should try to contact her again. After a few weeks of hiding away from everyone to allow her wounded emotions and hurt pride to heal, she'd reemerged into the world and picked up the pieces of her life. With regard to taking the risk of entering into any future close relationships, she had arrived at the same firm intention as Grant – never again!

At the end of the evening however, they'd agreed to meet again – purely on a strictly one-off, let's not get involved basis, of course – and had dated steadily since. Six months later they had decided to set up house together and Brett had moved into Pam's flat as it was more conveniently situated for both their places of work. They had been living together for almost a year now but neither had yet suggested the possibility of marriage, though they each secretly knew it was only a matter of time as the relationship deepened and the bonds of their love strengthened and drew them closer.

As he watched her now, even though she was busily engaged in the unromantic task of washing up dirty pans and dishes, he still felt a stir of desire for her. She was tall for a woman, standing a statuesque five-nine. She could easily have made a living as a model, he reflected not for the first time, having a good figure and terrific legs. Her hair was raven black and she usually wore it neck length like now, framing her attractive face with its pert nose and full-lipped generous mouth. But her large eyes, with their slightly oriental slant, were her best feature. They were that strange mix referred to as hazel and when she laughed, which was often, tiny golden flecks danced in them.

Grant slipped into the small kitchenette and moved directly behind her. Sliding his arms round her waist, he ran his hands lightly up her body to cup her full breasts in his hands. Burying his face into the perfumed softness of her raven hair, he bit her gently on the nape of her neck, then kissed it. "Hi lover," he said. "You smell good."

Responding to his caress, she pressed back into him and moved her hips provocatively against his groin. Instantly, he felt himself growing hard. Arching her head back so her cheek came into contact with his, she murmured, "M-m-m, that's nice. Just put the groceries on the table please, delivery man. My boyfriend'll be home soon …"

Laughing, he straightened up and rested his hands lightly on her hips. "So that's how you pass your time while I'm workin', ya loose hussy!"

"Only if I can fit him in …" she replied airily, "… between entertaining the brush salesman, the telephone repairman an' the telegram boy." She tossed her head coquettishly.

"Wishful thinkin'!" He chuckled and slapped her playfully on the backside. Walking over to the cooker, he sniffed appreciatively at the pans simmering on the hotplates. "Smells nearly as good as the cook. What is it?"

"So I smell like onion soup with croutons, followed by beef bourbignon cooked in wine, with peach sundae to finish, do I?" she asked pertly.

"You could say that," he agreed, then added with a mischievous grin, "But you taste much better."

She laughed. "Brett Grant, don't be crude!"

Pulling off her rubber gloves and untying her apron, Pam walked over and tugged his arm to make him face her. When he did so, she reached up to link her hands loosely behind his neck. Standing on tiptoe, she kissed him lightly on the mouth and said, "Anyway, sometimes I think you only love me for my cooking." Then she ducked away laughing, as he tried to pull her in towards him.

"No you don't," she said, brushing a wisp of stray hair from her temple. "We're going out tonight, remember. And we've got to eat and then get ourselves ready …"

"I'm ready now," he growled, advancing on her and cornering her by the door before she could escape into the other room.

"Brett, now don't you start or we'll never get …" Her half-hearted protest was cut off as he enveloped her in his arms and kissed her. She struggled ineffectually for a moment, trying to push him away. Then she gave in and responded to his kiss, sliding her arms up round his neck again, and relaxing against him. As their tongues teased and explored, he slid his hands down the curve of her back and onto her firm buttocks, then he pulled her hips firmly into his, so she could feel the swelling of his erection pressing against her lower body.

After several seconds, she gently disengaged her lips from his and leaned back in his embrace, her flushed face not entirely caused by the heat in the small kitchen. "This is not exactly the most appropriate way to prepare for a prayer meeting, is it?" she murmured.

"Of course it is," he replied. "Sin first, salvation later." He made to kiss her again, but she stopped him by placing the fingertips of one hand over his mouth.

"No. Not now, sexpot, or we'll never get anywhere tonight … and," she continued warningly, "the dinner'll burn." So saying, she gave a quick twist and this time managed to wriggle free of his grasp. She pointed towards the door. "You run along an' freshen up and I'll finish laying the table."

"Okay," he conceded, with an exaggerated sigh of regret which wasn't altogether false. "What a hard hearted woman I've got," he grumbled as he headed for the bathroom. "She prefers onion soup an' hymns to a good lay."

"Depends on which him you mean," she called after him.

"I heard that," he called back. "Prepare yourself for a heavy interrogation session tonight, witch! I'll stick things into you, until you confess an' give me a name."

"Oh goody! Is that a promise?" her chirpy reply drifted through to the bathroom as he began stripping off. "In that case, I'll try to hold out as long as possible …"

Chuckling to himself, Grant dropped the last of his clothes in a heap, stepped into the shower cubicle, slid the perspex panel shut behind him, and turned on the water.

During the meal, Grant swapped the day's news with Pam. He often did this, discussing his work with her and using her as a sounding board for his ideas and theories. Sometimes she offered the odd pertinent comment or suggestion, having not only an alert mind but also the added advantage of being able to see things from a more detached viewpoint.

When he'd described his meeting with the sect girl Louise,

Pam had asked, "What'll you do if she tells you she wants to leave them, same as the Miller boy? That'll mean you'll have to get both of them away from these people. And have you thought of a safe place for the girl to live? The boy's got parents to look after him but if she's got no-one, like she says, then being taken into care by the State might not be all that different from her point of view. You could be stuck with her."

He'd considered this for a few moments before replying thoughtfully, "Right at this moment, I don't have any idea how I'll go about rescuin' the Miller boy. I'll wait till after I've had a look at their Bethlehem House set-up with Sheriff Springfield, then I'll have a better idea of what I'm up against. But in the girl's case, I've a couple of ideas kickin' around in my head as to how I can get her away from them. She's out in the open … on the street. I reckon they might not be too keen on opposin' a bit of direct action in full view of the public … not to mention maybe even a couple of pressmen pointin' cameras, jes' for good measure."

He had spoken slowly as though he were thinking aloud. Then his eyes had cleared and he had said briskly, "Anyway, I'll cross these bridges when I come to them. I'll work somethin' out. It won't be the first time I've had to deal with this kinda thing. An' another thing," he had narrowed his eyes at her in pretended belligerence, "don't you start tellin' me to be careful, too. I've already got Harry an' Ben fussin' over me like two ol' mother hens. Ben's even arranged for a six foot chaperone with a tin badge, to make sure I don't scrape my knees or get my hair mussed."

Pam had risen and started to gather up the dishes. Pausing beside him, she had leaned down and planted a quick kiss on the side of his mouth. "Maybe it's because if they think a lot of you, like I do, they don't want you to come to any harm."

Grant had looked up at her, a mischievous twinkle in his eye, and started to run his hand up the inside of her leg. "Do you think a lot of me?" he had asked. "Show me how much."

She had laughed and swerved away from him. "Do you never think of anything else?"

Grant had laughed good naturedly and started to gather up

the remainder of the dishes, when Pam called from the kitchen over the sound of running water, "What time are we supposed to be there, anyway?"

"The meeting started at eight," he had answered, walking in and dumping his pile of dishes and cutlery in the soapy water. Glancing at his watch he had added, "It's a quarter past eight now but it'll be time enough if we get there before nine. My main reason for goin' is to get a look at this Prophet Martin Bishop guy, an' that's when he's due to start preachin', apparently. He's the star turn, so' he's got the prime spot ... he's the last act. It'll be interestin' t'see what kinda performance he puts on. It certainly seems to attract plenty of followers."

"Don't be such an ol' cynic," she had admonished lightly. "He may be another Billy Graham, for all you know, an' very sincere in his beliefs."

"An' pigs might fly!" he had scoffed, his voice registering the very scepticism she'd accused him of. "They're all th'same Pam, these holy rollers. They're in it for the money, an' the power they can exercise over other people's minds. An' underneath all the high-gloss pious exteriors, they're all petty little Hitlers at heart. An' goin' by what little I've seen of this one's organisation, I'm willin' t'bet he'll be no different."

Pulling a face at the soap suds, Pam had dropped the subject.

25

WHEN THEY REACHED THE TOWERING NEW EDIFICE of the Washington Centre in downtown Manhattan, Grant slowed the car to a crawl, looking for a parking space, and found himself directed by smartly uniformed Centre attendants to the entry ramp leading down into the cavernous underground parking area beneath the building. Slotting the Mustang into an empty space indicated by another attendant, Grant locked it, paid the required fee, pocketed the ticket he received in return and led Pam to the elevator connecting the parking area to the ground floor foyer.

They stepped from the elevator into the vast entrance hall to be met, not by any of the dark-green uniformed Centre personnel, but instead by one of a group of robed female sect members who had obviously taken over the duties of attendants there for the evening. Some of these sect females were wearing robes of light blue but the majority were dressed in pastel green. One of the green-robed girls moved smilingly to meet them and Grant noticed that she was, like all her companions, young and attractive.

When the girl reached them, she greeted them with a friendly smile and said, "Welcome to our crusade, friends. Unfortunately, you've missed most of the choir singing and early speakers but you're still in good time to hear the Prophet Martin Bishop speak. If you'll come this way, I'll find you seats in the main auditorium. There are a few left, although we've got a pretty full house tonight."

With another cheery smile she turned and led them to the far end of the huge foyer, to one of a row of double swing-doors set into the far wall. She held one of these doors open for them and as they passed through they became aware of the faint sound of choral singing coming through a second set of identical doors facing them a few yards further on. Grant saw they had entered a short, dimly lit passageway between the two sets of doors, evidently designed to prevent noise from filtering into or out of the auditorium beyond.

The girl waited for the first set of doors to hiss gently shut behind them, before ushering her charges through the second set. This time, the opening of the swing-door engulfed them in a wave of sound, as the stirring strains of the Battle Hymn of the Republic swelled around them from the body of the vast auditorium they now found themselves looking down into from their elevated position at its rear.

They had entered near the centremost of five wide aisles which swooped down through the curving tiers of seating. These passageways converged like the ribs of a gigantic fan as they reached the front of the auditorium, the entire width of which was occupied by a broad stage. The stage itself rose in four tiers towards its huge backdrop, which for the occasion was a deep midnight blue spangled with silver stars and bore the message GOD IS LOVE in enormous golden letters. On the ascending tiers of the stage were arrayed the colourful ranks of a massed choir. Colourful, because the choristers were clad in the robes of the sect and arranged so as to form an overall pleasing pattern of pastel blues and greens, interspersed with eye-catching splashes of bright scarlet.

A broad walkway had been erected, leading from a white pillared entrance at the rear of the stage, down through the centre of the choir's ranks, splitting them neatly into two equal sections. This walkway, painted the same gleaming white as the pillars, led to the foot of a raised pulpit at the very front of the stage, from which the Prophet would shortly speak to the waiting audience in the packed auditorium.

And packed it was. As the girl led them about a third of the way down the centre aisle to a row in which she'd spotted a pair of empty seats, Grant looked around him at the sea of humanity filling the vast arena and stretching away on all sides. Glancing up, he saw there were also two massive galleries soaring high above, curving from wall to wall for over half the overhead circumference. These were also filled to capacity, it seemed, to judge from the dimly seen ranks of faces receding upwards to be lost in the gloom.

He and Pam eased themselves past an elderly Negro couple to reach the two vacant seats indicated by their escort and settled themselves into their plush, cushioned embrace. Pam leaned towards him as she slipped out of her coat and whispered, "I never imagined it was going to be like this. There must be a couple of thousand people in here, at least."

"And then some!" he whispered back. "I hear the place holds over three thousand when it's full." Then he added drily, "They'll be kept busy tonight when all the converts start flockin' in – relievin' 'em of their sins, an' their pocketbooks."

"Cynic!" she mouthed at him and gave his arm a nudge.

They settled back to enjoy the proceedings, as the massed choir finished the hymn with a last stirring chorus of 'Glory,

glory, hallelujah!' rising to a harmonic crescendo, then holding and drawing out the maximum effect from the final repeated line, 'His truth is marching on.'

Grant had to admit they sounded well rehearsed and conducted. The audience rustled expectantly as a young black man wearing a green robe appeared and ascended the steps to the pulpit. He adjusted the face-level mike and prepared to read from a bible lying open before him. The robed figure ran his eye briefly over the text, then looked out at the audience.

"Brothers an' sisters, hear the word of the Lord as it is written in Paul's First Epistle to the Corinthians, chapter nine, reading through verses thirteen to nineteen ..." His strong voice came clearly and without any distortion over the auditorium's high quality sound system. Before delivering the reading, he paused and added in tones of quiet sincerity, "An' friends, I'd ask you to pay special heed to these words of holy writ, for they apply jes' as surely today to our beloved teacher, an' latter-day prophet, the Reverend Martin Bishop, as they did then to the Lord's faithful disciple Saint Paul."

Lowering his eyes to the open bible, he began to read aloud, "Do ye not know that they which minister about holy things, live of the things of the temple? And they which wait at the altar are partakers with the altar? Even so hath the Lord ordained that they which preach the gospel should live of the gospel ..."

He continued reading out the short text, which stressed the self discipline laid down by Paul for all holy men called by the Lord to preach the gospel. When he finished the reading, the young preacher looked up again and paused just long enough to ensure their full attention, before concluding to the hushed gathering, "May the Lord bless this reading from His holy word. An' friends, I pray that He might open your hearts to the words of His latter-day prophet, the Reverend Martin Bishop. As Our Lord Himself said, He that hath ears, let him hear."

As the young preacher was speaking, Grant sensed a rising tide of expectation swelling from the rapt audience, as their anticipation of the main event was carefully brought to a peak. The man they'd all come to see and hear was due to appear next. For a moment he fancied he could actually hear their rising excitement as a humming in his inner ear. Then the sound increased in volume and took on a throbbing musical note – and it dawned on him what it was. The massed choir had begun a low rhythmic humming, which was becoming steadily louder to provide a melodic background for the young black's voice, in turn growing in intensity. Grant now recognised the tune the choir was humming and which was now carrying the young preacher's message out over the auditorium on a swelling tide of melody. It was the stirring refrain of the militant Christian hymn Onward, Christian Soldiers! Grant knew the whole thing was being blatantly stage-managed – the subtle manipulation of the audience towards a fever pitch of expectancy – but he grudgingly acknowledged that it was expertly done.

The speaker had now reached the climax of his rousing introduction of the main event of the evening, the star turn they were all waiting for. "We believe," he finally declared in a voice which had risen from a tone of quiet sincerity to take on the ringing clarion call of a declaration of faith, borne on the wings of the hypnotic, thrumming melody of the martial hymn, "that the Reverend Martin Bishop is truly called by God to preach His word. And friends, if you will only open your hearts an' minds to him tonight, we know that you will leave here believing, as we do, that he truly is the Lord's prophet, sent to show us the way of salvation for our immortal souls in these troubled and sinful times."

Someone in the vast auditorium found the build-up of tension too much to contain and called, "Hallelujah!" This triggered an outburst of similar calls. Then, as the young preacher vacated the pulpit and descended the steps, the already subdued lighting dimmed right down. Simultaneously, angled spotlights beamed to form a circle of brilliance centred on the entrance to the walkway at the back of the massive stage.

With perfect timing, the choir burst full-throatedly into the words of the first verse of the hymn they'd been humming, as a startlingly impressive figure appeared suddenly in the centre of the circle of light. The tall silver-haired man who stood there, was clad in a shimmering, ankle-length robe of golden silk, with full sleeves. In one hand he held clasped to his breast a large white bible, the golden cross on its leather-bound surface gleaming in the bright light. It was the man himself. The man about whom Grant had heard so much since Virgil Miller's visit to his office that morning. The man his followers called The Prophet.

His appearance caused a tremor of excitement to run through the packed audience like an electric current and a tide of exultant Hallelujahs! and Praise the Lords! rose from various parts of the auditorium. It was pure showmanship and the audience were loving every extravagant minute of it. The vast majority of them had evidently come ready to be convinced this was indeed a new messiah, bringing to each one a comforting message of hope for a continued spiritual existence, after the awful finality of death.

Even Grant himself felt a stir of response deep within some primitive corner of his being, despite his having long since locked all his secret doubts and fears on the subject in a Pandora's box of scepticism. Irritated at what he saw as evidence of his own gullibility, he quickly suppressed the feeling, reminding himself that he was here in the role of dispassionate observer. His brief was to watch how the magician wove his spells, not to fall under their enchantment.

After a suitable pause of a few seconds, the Prophet moved forward, pacing slowly and with studied dignity, down the gentle slope of the walkway leading to the high pulpit. Someone in the audience began to clap in time with the martial rhythm of the hymn. It was quickly taken up, spreading with infectious enthusiasm, until the full voiced singing of the choir was almost being drowned out by the thunderous accompaniment of thousands of hands beating together in unison. All the while, the tall imposing figure continued his stately progress to the foot of the pulpit steps, which he then ascended in an equally unhurried manner.

The thought flashed through Grant's mind that the Prophet's unhurried movements were perhaps attributable not so much to create an air of dignity, as to prevent its loss, should he stumble on the hem of his ankle-length golden robe. At the same time, he was forced to admit that the man had a definite charisma about him. He was a born showman, if nothing else.

The Prophet finally ascended the short flight of steps to the pulpit and turned to face the packed auditorium, just as the choir completed their rendering of the hymn with a final triumphant crescendo. The rhythmic clapping of the audience gave way to a roar of applause and for a long moment he beamed benevolently at them acknowledging their adulation. Then laying his bible on the padded front ledge, directly under the pulpit mike, he raised both arms high and bowed his head in an attitude of prayer. His silvery hair glinted in the bright glare of the twin spots playing down on him from high overhead, a trick of the light seeming to throw up a shimmering nimbus around his head, creating a halo-like effect.

The applause died away almost as quickly as it had begun and the ensuing silence was deep and total. Seconds ticked by. Then the Prophet straightened up and lowered his arms to rest his hands on the padded ledge before him. His handsome leonine head moved slowly from side to side as he surveyed his hushed and expectant congregation and tilted back as he gazed upwards into the far reaches of the packed galleries.

His hands made a little deprecatory gesture, before falling back onto the pulpit ledge. "My dear friends ... my brothers and sisters in Christ ... my children ... I thank you all from the bottom of my heart for your warm welcome. And it fills my heart with gladness to see so many faithful souls out there tonight. For the more who come to hear the word of the Lord, the less ears there are for Satan to whisper into."

His voice when he spoke was in perfect character with the imposing figure he presented. It was deep and strong, yet somehow mellow despite its vibrant power. Like his personal appearance, indeed like the whole stage-managed build up of the audience reaction, his delivery was also decidedly theatrical. It rang out clearly on the phrase, The Word of the Lord, but allowed the suggestion of a hiss to creep in at the mention of Satan.

"For make no mistake," he continued, after a suitable pause for effect, "despite what the so-called modern day theologians say, Satan is real! He exists! And he is never far away from you.

He is cunning beyond your understanding and uses the voice of sweet reason and logic to seduce you to his evil designs. His is the persuasive voice of false friends who tell you that 'times have changed', or 'today's values are different', in order to lure you into a life of sin and condemn your immortal soul to the nethermost depths of the abyss, to perish in the searing fires of HELL!" His powerful voice rose to a shout on the last word, as the Prophet leaned out over the edge of the pulpit and jabbed an admonitory finger at his spellbound listeners.

This set the theme for the following half hour, as the subject of sin in all its many attractive varieties came under strong verbal attack. During the delivery of the sermon, Grant took the opportunity to study the Reverend Martin Bishop. There was no doubt about it, the man had a strong personality and positively exuded the animal magnetism of the born mob orator.

But taking into account the fact that the man was putting on a public performance, the dramatic gestures and changing cadences of speech were all well rehearsed and executed, the longer the Prophet preached the clearer one thing became, even to Grant's sceptical view – the man actually believed he had been chosen by the Lord to be His prophet. His voice rang with sincerity and his eyes burned with the zeal of his faith in both himself and his holy mission.

Grant's opinion was confirmed when the Prophet finished a thundering denunciation of what was apparently his pet sin – fornication – paused briefly for a few seconds, then declared quietly and with utter conviction, "There will doubtless be some among you who ask by whose authority I am appointed to preach to you." Another pause, then his voice strengthened. "Well, I can answer that charge with the unshakeable confidence of faith. God's authority!" he thundered. "His is the divine authority I claim!"

The burning eyes swept challengingly over the assembly, defying contradiction. None was forthcoming. On the contrary, his ringing declaration of faith was greeted by a chorus of Hallelujahs! Praise the Lords! and Amens! from various parts of the auditorium.

The Prophet seemed satisfied with this response. He laid his

227

clenched fists on his breast in a dramatic gesture and when he spoke, his voice now held a tremor of emotion, "For I had a vision." He glanced upwards as he announced this, to leave his audience in no doubt as to the direction from which it had come. "And in this vision, an angel of the Lord appeared to me clad in shining raiment and holding before me an open bible. And the holy book was open at the blessed words of the Gospel of St Matthew. And certain words on the page glowed as though on fire before my eyes, yet the page was not consumed. Just as the burning bush was not consumed before Moses' eyes, so it was with me. And do you know which passage of the scripture it was that the angel held before me in these letters of holy fire?" He paused, and this time the vocal response from the audience was loud and insistent as they demanded to know the answer.

The Prophet's clenched fists beat gently on his chest as he declared ringingly, "The words which burned before my sight were these ..." now the hands unfolded and his arms extended towards the congregation in an imploring gesture, "Follow me and I will make you fishers of men. Yes, the very words which our blessed Lord spoke to Simon Peter and his brother Andrew, by the shores of Galilee."

"Praise be!" someone shouted. Right on cue, Grant thought, his cynicism undiminished.

As though overcome with humility, the Prophet bowed his head and crossed his hands on his breast. He stood that way for a moment, then without raising his head he went on, "And I replied, 'Lord, I am unworthy.'"

This declaration provoked a sustained outburst of vocal protest from all over the vast auditorium. When he looked up, his eyes were glistening with unshed tears. "Friends," his voice cracked with emotion and he shook his head helplessly, "your faith in me is stronger than mine was at that time." Another pause for effect, then his voice recovered its vitality and rose again in volume. "But then in my vision, the angel of the Lord reached out and touched me and I was filled with the strength of the Holy Ghost and my doubts and fears fell from me. The angel then faded from my sight but my faith did not fade. I have prayed for guidance and the Lord has revealed to me the course

228

I must take in order to spread His truth and bring sinners to repentance and away from the paths of evil ..."

Being more interested in the man himself than in any message he was trying to put across, Grant's interest began to waver as the Prophet expanded on the theme of his divine mission. He stole a glance at Pam, certain she'd be sharing his sceptical view of the proceedings and was momentarily startled to see that she appeared to be gazing spellbound at the golden robed figure out front, as enrapt as any of the people around her.

He inclined his head towards her. "What do you think of ol' Moses up there? Some showman, ain't he?" he whispered, his flippancy intended to break the emotional spell which seemed to have entranced her.

"I think he's dishy," she whispered back, then turned away to hide her amusement at his surprised expression.

Grant for his part accepted her teasing put-down with a good grace and turned back to study the golden-robed figure up front. The Prophet was still in full verbal pursuit of his pet sin.

"... for I tell you, there is no easy path to paradise. The way is narrow and steep and littered with the withered blasted souls of those who have succumbed to the temptations of the flesh and fallen by the wayside."

Shaking his head sorrowfully, he surveyed the vast throng for a long moment. Then he swept up the bible from the pulpit ledge and brandished it aloft. "The Lord's word on this is quite clear," he informed them. "There is no way out. For it is written in the book of Corinthians, chapter six, verse nine, Know ye not that the unrighteous shall not inherit the kingdom of God? Be ye not deceived, neither fornicators, nor idolaters, nor adulterers, nor effeminate, nor abusers of themselves with mankind."

He paused and glared round the auditorium, his eyes afire with zeal, then declared in ringing tones, "I tell you, this is why He has seen fit to visit plague and pestilence upon all those who break His holy commandment, Thou shalt not commit adultery! Plague and pestilence in the form of the so-called 'sexually transmitted diseases', such as syphilis and AIDS. These are the judgement of His righteous wrath upon the fornicator, the adulterer and the sodomite!"

Grant leaned towards Pam and whispered, "That's from the gospel accordin' to Saint Bigot. Sounds like his heaven's gonna be a pretty dull place ... not to mention empty!" She suppressed a giggle and signed for him to be quiet in case he offended anyone in the surrounding seats. She needn't have worried on that score, Grant thought, looking around them. The entire audience seemed to be totally riveted on the golden figure up front as he hurled his dire warnings of hellfire and damnation at them. A line from an old Negro spiritual flashed through Grant's head: Gimme dat ol' time religion ... because that was exactly what he was giving them, and they were evidently loving every fiery word of it. He was responding to their adulation by working himself into a frenzy of denunciation, a sheen of sweat glistening on his face.

"... and we read in the same book of Corinthians, six, fifteen, Know ye not that your bodies are the members of Christ? Shall I then take them members of Christ and make them the members of an HARLOT? God forbid! And in the following verse, six, sixteen, Know ye not that he which is joined to an harlot is one body? For two, saith He shall be one flesh. And finally," he concluded in ringing tones, brandishing the bible at them, "The Lord gives us His judgement on such miserable fallen creatures, when He instructs us in the words of first Corinthians, chapter five, verse five, ... to deliver such a one unto Satan for the destruction of the flesh, that the spirit may be saved in the day of the Lord Jesus."

The burning eyes swept the congregation. "Yes, my friends, that is the terrible and just punishment ordained by God, as it is written in first Corinthians, five, five. Remember it well ... remember it well, I say!"

For a few seconds, he held his dramatic pose, bible held aloft. Suddenly he startled the entire audience as he thundered out, "For the wages of sin is DEATH!" and slammed the book violently down onto the pulpit ledge, causing all those who were hanging on his every word to flinch in surprise. This time, the pregnant silence which followed was unbroken by exultant shouts from his awe-struck listeners.

Taking advantage of the momentary lull caused by the effect

of his performance, the Prophet plucked a silk handkerchief from a pocket in his robe and quickly dabbed at his sweating brow and then at his lips, before continuing. But not before Grant's sharp eyes had noticed the flecks of foamy saliva which had gathered at the corners of his mouth.

This one's straight off a palm tree … he's nuts! Grant thought, and right there and then decided to call it a night. He had seen enough to convince him that there wasn't much to choose between the Reverend Martin Bishop, self-styled Prophet, and other self-ordained religious zealots he'd come across in his time. The only difference seemed to be that in this particular case, if the Prophet's delusions of religious grandeur progressed any further in direct ratio to the regression of his mental stability, then the next logical step would be a bid for the top job – Chairman of the Board. He'd become convinced he was God … or maybe even Napoleon!

Grant was now convinced that Louise's warning of 'bad trouble' ahead for his client's son at the hands of the sect, carried more than a little substance. Especially after having earlier experienced the surly hostility of the sect personnel out at Bethlehem House and now having witnessed first hand the disturbing egotheism of their leader.

It showed not just in his ranting oratory but more in the fanaticism which burned in his eyes. He knew now he had to rescue Jim Miller from the clutches of this fanatic and his followers … Louise too, if she wanted.

He nudged Pam to attract her attention, tapped his watch and jerked his head to suggest they leave early. There wasn't much longer to go anyway, his watch informed him. It was already nine forty-five, and the meeting was scheduled to finish at ten. To his surprise, she shook her head and whispered, "Let's wait till the end. I want to see how many converts he gets. Billy Graham used to get hundreds, they say."

Grant settled back with a sigh of resignation and noticed with relief that the Prophet was building to the climax of his performance, when he would invite members of the audience to come forward and declare themselves for the Lord. In apparent preparation for this, about forty or so robed sect personnel, all apparently drawn from among the more mature 25 – 30 age group, had begun quietly filing out from the wings to form a line along the front of the stage. Once each robed figure was in position, he or she turned to face the audience and stood, hands folded serenely before them, quietly awaiting the nightly harvest of potential converts who had been enmeshed in the emotional net cast by their leader's sermon. And they weren't long in coming.

The Prophet was now all sweet reason and gentle insistent persuasion, in direct contrast to the earlier hectoring tone of his condemnation of sin. The choir had also started up again, providing an added emotional backdrop to his words with the gentle refrain of 'The Old Rugged Cross' being sung softly and tunefully from the darkened stage behind him.

"Come forward now. Declare yourself for Christ tonight. As you can see, the counsellors are awaiting you, ready to help and advise you. Our church runs several retreats in the city, each one an oasis of peace and tranquillity, where you can spend some time if you wish, in order to sort yourself out."

The golden robed figure in the high pulpit was standing with arms outstretched, gesturing for people to come forward, taking full advantage of the emotion-charged atmosphere. "As He hung and suffered on the cross for you, why don't you come forward now and declare yourself for Him? What a glorious opportunity to say 'Thank you, Lord Jesus for your sacrifice'. What better way to say this than to come forward now saying, 'Here I am Lord, a repentant sinner. Wash me clean in your precious blood'?"

From different points in the first few rows of the audience, a few people began to get up and squeeze past the occupants of the other seats, making for the aisles. One, a heavily built negress, was edging past her neighbours only a few rows from where Pam and Grant were sitting. Tears of ecstasy were pouring unheeded down her cheeks and she was sobbing, "Save me, Jesus ... save me, Jesus ..." over and over, as she stumbled along.

Grant felt Pam stirring by his side and when he met her eyes he saw that she looked troubled. Then he felt her hand take his and he squeezed it reassuringly. "Don't worry," he said softly. "They're just shills."

"Shills?" she looked at him, mystified.

"Audience plants. One of the oldest tricks in the business. All the best hucksters use 'em. If you're makin' a sales-pitch, your shills start the biddin', an' then push it along when it looks like flaggin'. It never fails. See for yourself ..." He nodded at the body of the auditorium.

The worried look cleared from her eyes and sure enough, when she turned back to observe the proceedings again, she saw that a dozen or more figures were now on their feet, some crying like the first woman, some dry-eyed, but all nonetheless eager to be 'saved'. Even as she watched, several more began to rise and shuffle sideways along their rows towards the aisles, down which the first few were already stumbling, some needing to be supported by companions or by robed helpers who had appeared among them as though by magic. Once they arrived at the front of the stage, the salvation seekers were delivered into the custody of the waiting counsellors.

The choir had now switched to a soft rendering of 'The Ninety And Nine' to encourage the stray sheep to flock in and the Prophet was using all his considerable powers of persuasion to draw them into the comfort of the sect's fold. "Salvation is the door through which you must pass, and repentance is the only key that will open it. Remember friends, no matter how wicked and sinful you may have been, no matter what burden of guilt and shame you bear, the Lord Himself said that even the eleventh hour is not too late for the sinner to repent.

"Listen!" He cupped his hand to his ear in a theatrical gesture. "Listen ... in the deepest recesses of your hearts and minds ... can't you hear His sweet voice calling to you?" He paused and swept his arm up to point dramatically in the direction of the high, sweeping galleries. "Yes, He's calling to you good people up there, too. Come and join your brothers and sisters down here. Come to Jesus. Listen to Him calling you. Yes, you!" He began to point at various parts of the vast hall, "And you ... and you ... yes, and you up there, too ..."

His exhortations were having an effect, Grant saw, looking

around. Dozens were streaming down the aisles now. There was movement too in the galleries high overhead, as people there began to make their way to the exits leading to the stairways which would take them down to the main body of the auditorium, directed by robed sect members pre-positioned at convenient points.

Suddenly, almost unnoticed amidst all the movement and bustle, a scuffle broke out at the foot of the pulpit from which the Prophet was still calling to the multitude to "come and be washed clean in the blood of the Lamb". The combined noise of the choir, the Prophet's voice, and the general stir of movement within the hall, failed to drown out entirely the sound of a man shouting.

The scuffle and the shouting were quickly suppressed, but not before Grant, who had half risen from his seat, had located its source. He had seen a man standing directly below the elevated pulpit gesturing and shouting up at its occupant. He hadn't caught every word, but heard most of it.

"Where's my daughter? I wan' my daughter back. Where're you holdin' 'er? Give me back my daughter, ya hypocrite! ... Get yer fuckin' hands offa me, ya bastards! ..." This last was addressed angrily to four men, apparently members of the congregation, who had leapt up from nearby seats in the front row, converged on him and overpowered him swiftly and efficiently. Too swiftly and efficiently for mere members of the public, Grant thought. They must be sect members who had been strategically positioned to act as minders for their leader.

The Prophet himself hardly faltered in his verbal outpouring, apart from directing one venomous glare at the man, before recovering his composure and resuming his flow of words. Very few others seemed to have noticed the incident. Those nearest to it were too preoccupied with their own personal anguish, as they stumbled blindly towards the waiting counsellors. To them, the man could just have been one more over-wrought convert, carried away by his emotions.

Grant's professional eye however, had observed that it wasn't hysteria that had overcome the man, but a short, vicious kidney punch, delivered from behind by one of the four men who had overpowered him, followed up by a short-arm jab to the solar plexus by one of those in front. The blows had caused him to collapse into the grasp of two of the others, who immediately caught and supported him by an arm each. Half dragging, half carrying their dazed, gasping victim, the two men on either side of him began to move him swiftly up the aisle in the direction of the rear exits. One of the two remaining escorts positioned himself in front, the fourth man bringing up the rear, forming a tight group. Their actions suggested that the four were a well practised and efficient team.

Grant took an instant decision. "Let's go!" he ordered, rising to his feet and pulling Pam up by the hand. "We're leavin'." She was puzzled at his sudden change of mood but his tone brooked no argument so, pausing only to gather up her coat and bag, she followed him without demur.

They emerged into the aisle just as the hurrying group drew level. The tail-gunner gave them a sharp glance as the tight knot of men swept past. The man in the centre was recovering and beginning to mumble and beginning to mumble dazedly. "Where y'takin' me? Lemme go. I wanna see m'daughter …"

The hoarse protests were cut off in a gasp of agony as the escort on the left used his free hand to grip the man's neck, thumb and fingers clamping down hard on the nerve points behind the ears. Face contorted from the pain, the man allowed himself to be hustled helplessly on up the aisle.

Pam had now become aware of the five men up ahead and of Grant's interest in them. She shrugged into her coat as the group pushed out through a set of swing doors under a lit EXIT sign. Following Grant towards the same set of doors, she asked anxiously, "Brett, is anything wrong? Did that man take ill or something?"

"Not yet," he replied, adding grimly, "An' he won't … not if I've anythin' t'do with it!" and pushed his way through the first set of swing doors, Pam trotting to keep up.

As they entered the short passageway beyond the doors, they suddenly found themselves face to face with the man who'd been acting as rearguard. He had evidently stayed behind either to prevent any pursuit or to delay any inquisitive members of the public, until his comrades had got clear of the foyer area with their victim. Seeing Grant appear accompanied by a female companion, caused him to relax slightly and adopt a less aggressive approach than he might otherwise have used, had Grant been on his own. It proved to be his downfall.

"Excuse me a moment, friends ..." he began, holding up a hand and momentarily off guard.

Grant smiled inquiringly at him ... and kicked him hard in the crotch. The man's agonised grunt as he doubled up was matched by Pam's gasp of alarm. Unheeding, Grant chopped down hard with the edge of his hand on the exposed neck just behind the man's right ear, sending him crumpling to the floor unconscious.

"One down, three to go," remarked Grant cheerfully for Pam's benefit. She had always known his job involved a certain degree of personal danger on occasions, from people who resented having their private affairs investigated and who were liable to resort to violence towards him as a result. However, not only was this her first actual experience of the darker side of his job, it was also a side of Grant she'd never seen before. With her he was always so gentle and considerate, she had never had cause to think of the existence of the violent physical part of his nature.

Her initial shock at the manner of his disposal of the man who had challenged them was quickly replaced by fear for Grant's safety. He had dealt competently enough with this lone sect thug but the thought of his tackling, single-handedly, the other three fit-looking types who had hustled the fifth man past them, caused her a sudden pang of apprehension.

Catching at his sleeve, she blurted out, "Brett ... can't we call the police? Let them deal with it?"

He shook his head. "No way. By the time the police got here, these goons you saw will have taken that poor bastard apart. An' I heard 'im say that all he wants is his daughter back. Just like my client wants his son back. Now, follow me an' stay close. I don' wanna lose those other three gorillas. An' if trouble starts, keep clear of it." With a jerk of his head for her to follow him, he strode forward and pushed his way through the second set of swing doors. After a moment's hesitation and a concerned glance at the unconscious form huddled on the floor behind them, Pam slipped through the slowly closing door in his wake.

26

GRANT EMERGED INTO THE HUGE FOYER AND slowed his pace to allow Pam to come up alongside him. Coloured robes caught his eye and he took in the whole scene at a glance. There were thirty or so young female sect members spread out in a loose cordon across the width of the spacious entrance hall. Each girl was positioned alongside a large, slotted collection box on a stand bearing the appeal PLEASE GIVE AS GENEROUSLY AS YOU CAN TO FURTHER THE LORD'S WORK. THANK YOU AND GOD BLESS YOU. For good measure, each girl was also carrying a collecting can bearing the same message.

"I wondered how this lot put the arm on the faithful," muttered Grant as he surveyed the line of collectors. Some of the girls were looking in the direction of the bank of elevators at the far side of the foyer. Grant followed their gaze and was in time to see one set of doors silently closing on the group of men he had followed from the auditorium.

Steering Pam in that direction, he spoke softly to her from the side of his mouth as they headed for a gap between two of the collectors. "Smile. Loosen up. Look like you enjoyed the meetin'. If this lot think we're tailin' their goon squad, they might raise the alarm an' send for the cavalry."

By now they had almost reached the line and the nearest of the sect girls moved to intercept them. She was a redhead and her green robe both suited her hair colour and matched her eyes. Grant returned her artificially bright smile of greeting and said enthusiastically, "Great meeting. Thoroughly enjoyed it."

He paused briefly, pulled out a twenty dollar bill with a careless flourish, folded it and dropped it into her collecting can. Airily waving away her thanks and blandly ignoring her flustered, transparent attempt to detain them by engaging them in conversation about the meeting, he brushed past her, keeping up a non-stop flow of cheerful talk. "Great preacher too, really socks it to you. Sorry we can't stop to chat, gotta get mobile before the rush starts. Keep up the good work, sister. God bless you."

By now he and Pam had covered the remaining few yards to the elevators. Entering the car next to the one the group had taken, he quickly pushed the button labelled LOW LEVEL CARPARK and the doors slid shut. "Brett, honey ..." Pam began apprehensively, as the car began its smooth descent. "Shouldn't we call the police. I don't want you to get involved ..."

"Pam, listen to me," he interrupted, speaking rapidly. "I am involved. An' I happen to know these people play rough. So, what kinda mess d'you think that poor guy'd be in by the time the law got here? I know what I'm doin', so don't worry. Now, I want you to make straight for the car an' wait for me there. Okay?" He pressed the keys into her reluctant hand, just as the elevator slowed to a stop and the doors slid open.

Grant made to leave, then stopped and stuck a foot against one of the doors to prevent them from closing. He turned to Pam. "Quick," he said, holding out a hand. "Have you got your can of hair spray with you?"

Mystified, she nodded, but spurred on by the urgency in his voice, she didn't waste time asking questions. Flipping open her bag, she quickly removed the aerosol can and placed it into his open hand.

Taking it from her, Grant uncovered the nozzle and dropped the cap back into her bag. He squeezed her hand reassuringly. "I'll be okay, I promise. Just make straight for the car, like I said. Don't hang about."

Kissing her lightly on the lips he slipped out of the elevator car and made for the cover of the nearest rank of parked cars a few yards away. Stopping beside a big Buick, he surveyed the vast concrete-pillared cavern of the subterranean parking area, searching over the sea of car tops for any sign of the men he'd been following.

238

At first glance he saw no signs of any human occupation at all in the poorly lit vastness, not even one of the green uniformed carpark attendants. Then the sound of voices drew his attention to a lighted doorway several yards away and through the angle of the open door he saw some hatless green uniformed figures seated around a table. It seemed the attendants were still gathered in their rest room, waiting for the meeting on the floor above to finish, before moving out to direct the homeward bound traffic.

Grant scanned the huge interior again and this time he caught sight of distant movement across the ranks of gleaming roofs. It was the group he was looking for and they seemed to be heading for the far side of the carpark, well away from the elevators. Looking for a quiet spot where they would stand less chance of being interrupted, Grant reckoned.

Crouching to keep his head level with the car roofs, Grant started out after the men, threading his way swiftly and silently through the ranks of parked vehicles. For a few seconds he made good progress, closing the gap between them. Then, intent as he was on keeping his quarry in sight as he negotiated the maze of cars, he suddenly found himself tripped and pitching headlong to the ground.

His reflexes, kept sharp by his martial arts training, took over even as he fell. He twisted in mid-air, head tucked in, and hit the deck in a judo break-fall. Rolling swiftly over, he regained his feet in a crouch, facing back the way he'd come and ready to defend himself. He found himself looking down on the prone figure of a carpark attendant, sprawled face down, arms outflung on the concrete floor.

Grant examined him quickly. The man was unconscious, his breathing laboured and irregular, but he'd live. An ugly swelling already showed at the jawline beside his ear and he was bleeding from nose and mouth. That, and the uniform cap lying several yards away, were mute evidence of the attack which had answered his attempted interference with the sect thugs Grant was now following. The man must have been on lone patrol duty while his mates were on their break and had been unlucky enough to encounter the group.

Cautiously, Grant raised his head above the roof level of the cars and once more pinpointed signs of distant movement, this time over by the far wall. Ducking down again, he ran at a crouch, weaving his way between the ranks of cars. Now he was moving blind, not daring to raise his head above the level of the car roofs, in case the quarry spotted his approach.

He didn't have to take another sighting on them. As he closed on their estimated position, he heard a muffled cry, quickly choked off, followed by the unmistakable sound of blows. Glancing down, he checked the can of hair lacquer in his left hand to make sure the nozzle was pointing away from him, ready for action. It was as well he did, for when he rounded the last car at a crouching run, he found himself almost on top of the group of men only a few feet from him.

When Grant arrived, the man under attack was being supported between two of the sect goons, while the third administered the beating with clinical thoroughness to face and body. The blows were being delivered with controlled brutality, hard enough to inflict maximum pain without causing permanent damage.

The instant Grant appeared, one of the men holding the feebly struggling victim saw him. His eyes widened in alarm and he shouted a warning to the one who was handing out the beating. Taken by surprise, his companion hesitated fractionally before turning to meet the unexpected threat from his rear. He wasn't fast enough. Grant's right fist, arriving with all his 200 lbs behind it, exploded into his left kidney and he went down as though poleaxed. As the man dropped, Grant followed through and made sure he would stay down by clubbing him behind the left ear with his bunched fist.

Immediately, the other two sect thugs released their semi-conscious victim, who promptly slumped to the ground in a heap alongside the inert form of his former assailant. They lunged at Grant together but without any attempt to co-ordinate their attack. Flinging himself to his left to avoid the flying snap-kick aimed at his midriff by the man on his right, Grant came up hard against the hood of a parked car and triggered the jet of the hair spray straight into the face of the other attacker.

But in order to carry out this manoeuvre, he was unable to avoid completely the throat punch the second man had thrown at him. The bunched knuckles slammed into his right shoulder with paralysing force, spinning him half round and propelling him backwards right over the car's wing. However, even as he cartwheeled over the smooth metal of the wing, Grant had the satisfaction of seeing his opponent stagger back with a scream of pain, clutching his face in his hands as the hair lacquer blinded him.

Grant landed awkwardly on his side and as he rolled over, he caught a glimpse of the second attacker darting round the front of the car towards him. Desperately he tried to push himself off the ground to regain his feet but his numb right arm refused to support his weight and gave way under him. This not only threw him momentarily off balance and at the mercy of his opponent but also, conversely, it saved him from the vicious hip-kick the man launched at his face. Grant's slip caused his attacker to miss his target and the striking heel skidded off the side of the head, instead of connecting squarely with the skull-crushing force intended.

The pain of the glancing blow brought Grant scrambling successfully to his feet at the second attempt. In the same movement, he flattened himself against the car at his back, whipped up his left hand and triggered the spray again. It was more an act of desperation than an attempt to defend himself, but it worked. The aerosol hissed out its blinding mist in a spreading cloud, some four to five feet in front of Grant and his advancing opponent drew up short and threw up an arm to shield his eyes.

But this could only provide a temporary respite and both he and his opponent knew it. The man feinted to attack again but jumped back as the spray hissed venomously at him. His movements were fast and although slim, he looked hard and fit. Another lunge was followed by another retreat from the eye-searing mist. Stand-off!

They were both crouched now, facing one another. Grant was working his numbed shoulder, trying to regain feeling and mobility. Anger and contempt glinted in his opponent's eyes.

Pointing at the can, he bared his teeth in a cold grin and said tauntingly, "That ain't gonna save you, cocksucker. Whatchya gonna do when it runs out ... throw y'nail varnish at me?"

Sweat trickled down Grant's back. With a sinking feeling, he realised the other was right. He knew he wouldn't regain the full use of his aching arm in the little time he had left before the aerosol ran out. He decided to gamble on a surprise attack to gain the initiative and maybe equalise his chances. He suddenly lunged forward, at the same time directing another searing jet at his opponent's face. As he'd expected, the man leapt back, retreating from the blinding threat of the spray.

As Grant launched himself after him, intent on pressing home his attack, an unexpected occurrence took them both completely by surprise. There was a sudden flurry of movement behind the man, then something dark arced through the air above him, and hit him squarely on the back of his head. More shocked than hurt, the man ducked forward reflexively under the force of the blow. Reacting instantly, Grant took full advantage of the surprise intervention and kicked him full in the face.

The sect thug snapped upright, blood spraying from his broken nose, and a second heavy blow landed on his head from behind. Dazed, he staggered forward, straight into Grant's balled fist. The punch, thrown by Grant's numb right arm, hadn't sufficient force behind it to knock the man out but as he went down his head smacked sickeningly off the concrete floor and he lost all further interest in the proceedings.

Panting from his exertions, Grant looked up to see who had come to his aid with such perfect timing. To his amazement, there stood Pam – his lovely, unathletic Pam – handbag swinging from one hand, face flushed, raven hair slightly dishevelled and her eyes sparkling with the light of battle, like some gorgeous latter-day Amazon.

A broad grin spread over Grant's face, and he stepped forward and hugged her. "Well, whaddaya know! All this time I've been livin' with Supergirl, an' you never let on ..." Then, releasing her, he added in a more serious tone, "Thanks honey. You couldn't have timed that better. I had my hands full."

She grinned back at him, pleased by his praise, then a look of concern clouded her eyes when she saw him wince as he worked his stiff shoulder. "Are you okay? Have they hurt you?"

"I'm okay," he reassured her, "but I can't say the same for the guy I rescued from these gorillas. They'd started workin' 'im over before I got here."

He glanced round the carpark, which still showed no other signs of movement. The only sound to be heard was the groaning of the blinded sect hoodlum a few feet away from where they stood. This spurred Grant into action again. "C'mon pardner," he said, turning away. "We'll have t'move our asses outa here before someone upstairs discovers the goon I took out up there."

They rounded the car over which Grant had tumbled a couple of minutes previously and Pam's eyes widened in shocked surprise. Two motionless figures were sprawled a few feet apart, one of these having been Grant's first victim. A third man was kneeling in a crouched position, face buried in his hands, his forehead resting on the concrete floor, groaning from the pain of his tightly screwed-up eyes. This was the one Grant had blinded with Pam's hair spray. It was obvious he'd present no further problem to them.

Grant ignored the two sect goons and walked quickly over to the third man, who was slumped semi-conscious against the wheel of a car. His face was badly swollen, his eyes reduced to slits in the puffy, discoloured flesh surrounding them. Rivulets of scarlet ran down his chin from his swollen nose and bloodied mouth and dripped onto his shirt front.

Crouching over him, Grant raised him into a seated position. Dazed though he was, as soon as the man felt himself being moved, he struck out weakly and tried to struggle free of the supporting arm round his shoulders, obviously expecting a resumption of the attack on his battered person. "Git y'hands offa me, cocksuckers ..." he mumbled indistinctly through split and bleeding lips.

"It's okay ... relax ... we're friends," Grant reassured him. "You're safe now. They won't be beatin' up on anybody for a while. Can you stand? Here ... lean on me ... up y'come ..." Helped by Pam, Grant lifted the man to his feet.

Not quite as tall as Grant but heavier in build, he wasn't too much of a dead weight because he reflexively made the effort to stand as they helped him up. They steadied him between them and the man stood leaning on his rescuers for a moment, shaking his head in an effort to clear it. Momentarily he sagged at the knees as a wave of dizziness threatened to engulf him. But the brief spell of concussion passed, leaving his senses a little clearer, for he suddenly looked at Grant, awareness showing fleetingly in his eyes.

"The bastards worked me over," he stated thickly, then asked, "You a cop?"

"Sort of ... I'm a private detective," Grant told him. "An' I know you got worked over, friend. I got here just in time, like the US Cavalry. Now, let's git th'hell outa here before any more Apaches turn up. Think you can walk? Here ... lean on me ... that's it."

Slipping his shoulders under the man's arm, he took his weight and helped him to take a couple of stumbling steps forward. Unbidden, Pam ducked her shoulders under the man's other arm, so that he was supported on either side. In this manner they made good progress and reached the Mustang without further delay.

Grant propped the man against the side of the car while Pam unlocked and opened the doors. They eased him into the back seat where he leaned back exhaustedly and closed his eyes. Pam climbed in beside him and taking a tissue from her bag, began gently to clean the worst of the blood from his facial injuries. He winced as the eau de cologne she had sprinkled on the tissue stung the cuts and raw abrasions.

Grant had started the car and begun to reverse it out of the parking slot, when he caught a flash of light and movement from the corner of his eye, over by the bank of elevators. As he reversed the Mustang out into the broad passage between the lines of parked cars, he saw two of the elevator cars had arrived and were disgorging a dozen or so young men, all dressed in conventional dark suits. Grant knew instinctively that these were no ordinary members of the public leaving the meeting early but that the first of the enemy reinforcements had arrived on the scene.

His suspicion was confirmed when one of the newcomers pointed at the reversing Mustang and shouted something to the others. The entire group reacted instantly. As though launched from blocks by a starter's gun, they began sprinting flat out towards the Mustang, fanning out as they came weaving their way swiftly through the rows of parked cars. With alarming speed they were too close for Grant to stop reversing and throw the car into forward motion, without the nearest of them being able to reach them and wrench open the doors.

He took the only option open to him to prevent this and put some distance between them and the charging men. Shouting, "Brace yourselves!" to the two in the back, he jammed his foot down hard on the gas, steering one-handed as he twisted round to look through the rear window.

The Mustang bulleted backwards, causing the nearest of the advancing figures to dive aside. Shouting faces blurred past the side windows as the car roared down the centre of the lane. When they reached the nearest of the intersecting lanes which sectioned off the huge parking area, Grant tramped on the brake pedal and swung the wheel hard over. Tortured rubber squealed in protest as the Mustang sank back on its rear axle and went into a controlled skid, which whipped the nose through a ninety degree turn and brought them to a screeching halt facing into one of the side lanes.

The instant the car slewed to a halt, Grant flipped it into forward gear and floored the gas pedal again. The tyres squealed anew as they spun briefly before gripping the concrete. The three occupants were pinned back in their seats as the powerful machine leapt forward. Grant silently thanked his preference for manual gearshift control, having had it fitted in place of the normal automatic system of the Mustang. He preferred the manual system's fractionally quicker response to the gas pedal.

Suddenly, a warning cry from Pam alerted him to the fact that although his quick action had opened a gap of several yards between the car and most of the sprinting figures, the leading pursuer, a young black, had got close enough to lunge forward and grab the passenger door handle. But before he could depress the button to open the door, the force of the car's acceleration tore the handle from his grasp, jerking him off his feet and slamming him into the rear wing. In his mirror, Grant saw the man roll over twice then climb back to his feet. The sect obviously bred them tough! As they sped away, he took the opportunity to correct his previous oversight and flicked the switch to lock the doors.

The intersections in the ranks of parked vehicles seemed to be spaced at roughly forty yard intervals and the next one came up fast. Grant took a fast left into it, then a right at the one following, in order to confuse the pursuit and give himself a chance to find his bearings. He caught glimpses through gaps in the ranks of parked cars of sprinting forms. They now seemed to be fanning out to cover different points of the carpark.

Instead of turning off at the next intersection, Grant shot straight through it doing about fifty. Overhead, one of a number of giant signs suspended from the roof at regular intervals, cautioned: SPEED LIMIT 15 M.P.H. In between each speed limit sign hung other huge signboards, each bearing a large horizontal arrow under the word EXIT. Over their particular lane, these arrowed signs were pointing off to the right.

Making for the last turning in the long lane, Grant dropped his speed, changed down and turned right, following the EXIT arrows. About to accelerate out of the turn, he suddenly hit the brake instead and swung the wheel sharply over, swerving to avoid the inert figure he'd spotted at the last moment, lying directly in their path. It was the first of the three men he'd dealt with earlier when rescuing their injured passenger. Several yards further on, groping his way one-handed along the line of parked cars, his other hand pressed to his streaming eyes, was the figure of the one he'd blinded with the hair spray.

Grant manoeuvred the car slowly past the prone figure, then began to pick up speed again as they passed the stumbling man on their right. At that moment, Pam squealed in alarm as a dark form hurled itself from between the parked cars and landed on the hood.

The daring attacker was a young Hispanic and he spreadeagled himself across the windscreen, effectively blocking Grant's forward vision with his body. Instead of braking to a halt as he was obviously expected to do, Grant did the opposite, in case any of the others were close enough to reach the car and start smashing their way through the windows. Choosing the lesser risk of driving blind for a short distance, he accelerated fiercely for several yards, then slammed on the anchors. The Mustang screeched to a halt and the unwanted passenger was catapulted forward to hit the ground hard several feet further on.

Just then, disaster struck. Grant's left foot slipped from the clutch and the engine bucked once and stalled. Frantically he threw the gearshift into neutral and restarted the engine. But before the car could pick up any speed, the front passenger window suddenly imploded in a shower of glass fragments and a bunched fist rammed through the gap aimed straight at Grant's temple. Pam's scream of terror was deafening in the confines of the car. The fist was followed by a shoulder and head, as the attacker thrust himself part-way through the car window to reach his target.

Honed by twice weekly training sessions on the karate dojo, Grant's reflexes saved him as he flung up his forearm and deflected the blow. But distracted by the attack, he stalled the engine again. Immediately, his assailant made a grab for the ignition keys. Before Grant could react, there was a sudden bellow of "Fuckin' bastard!" from behind him, and a ham-sized fist shot over his shoulder and smacked solidly into the side of the intruder's face, slamming his head against the door frame with stunning force. This unexpected intervention had come from their passenger, who had apparently surfaced from his concussed state to come briefly to his rescuers' aid. However, the effort seemed to drain his meagre reserves of strength, for he immediately slumped back into his stupor again.

Grant took advantage of the enemy's temporary setback to restart the stalled engine and get the car into motion. Not a moment too soon, for as the Mustang pulled away another body threw itself across the hood. But this one overshot on the slick surface and dropped over the nearside wing. The semi-conscious sect thug was still part-way in the window and clinging on desperately, his legs dragging on the ground outside. Leaning across, Grant drove the heel of his hand into the man's face.

There was a satisfying crunch of nose cartilage at the point of impact, and the man gave a strangled cry of pain and disappeared from view.

The Mustang gathered speed but Pam called a warning as more sprinting figures appeared alongside. Fists hammered on glass and the rear offside window starred into an opaque spider's web. It held. But another blow would cave it in.

"So, you wanna play tag, huh?" Grant snarled, and swung the wheel left and right, swerving the car violently from side to side. He was rewarded by dull thumps accompanied by muffled yells of fear and pain and the rear view mirror revealed the satisfying sight of tumbling enemy bodies, as the Mustang sideswiped them away like an angry terrier shaking off rats.

But Grant was given no time to savour victory. Just then another threat presented itself – and a much more serious one at that. A squat dark blue van suddenly swung into their lane from a side turning up ahead and made straight for them. It came on fast, holding the centre of the lane, obviously intent on ramming them head on. Desperately Grant pulled the wheel hard over and skidded the car into a tight right turn at the next junction, barely missing the oncoming van which attempted to ram their rear wing as it barrelled in after them.

Grant gunned the engine and the Mustang surged forward, pulling away from the following vehicle. He took the next left turn fast, tyres squealing in protest and as he did so, Pam's despairing "Oh no!" sounded loud in his ear at the sight which greeted them. A second dark blue van, the twin of the one behind, was heading towards them from up ahead, weaving from side to side as it came. It now became clear that the sole purpose of the original foot soldiers had been to distract them and prevent their escape until the arrival of these vans. It had worked, too.

For the next few minutes a deadly chase ensued. The two sect vans headed Grant off time and again, always combining to block him from a clear run to the exit ramp. The three vehicles engaged in a lethal game of tag – of screeching skidding turns and near misses, in and around the lanes of the huge underground carpark – as the two sect drivers repeatedly tried to ram the

Mustang, with no apparent thought even for their own safety, let alone that of their intended victims. All Grant's driving skills were put to the test as he concentrated grimly on avoiding their kamikaze style attacks.

Then suddenly Lady Luck smiled on him and Grant got the break he'd been praying for. He had narrowly evaded yet another ramming attempt by throwing the Mustang into a gut wrenching, right-angled turn at one of the intersections, when his eye fell on the huge EXIT sign at the far end of the lane. He'd done it! The sect drivers had miscalculated at last, and left him a clear run to the exit ramp. Neither of them were at that moment in a position to cut him off. The powerful car leapt forward as Grant floored the gas pedal.

But his elation was short lived. It turned to dismay when he saw a car up ahead reversing slowly out of the parking line, blocking his route to the exit ramp. The vehicle was being pushed into his path by four of the sect thugs who had originally been harrying them on foot. With a muttered "Shit!", he threw the car into a fast skidding turn at the next junction, and repeated the manoeuvre through a few more intersections in an unsuccessful attempt to shake off the pursuing van at that moment on his tail. The deadly chase was on again – but not for long, as it turned out.

So intent had he been on shaking off his pursuers, he only now noticed that his high speed twistings and turnings through the vast maze of parked cars had caused him to be heading for the entry ramp to the carpark. The huge overhead sign up ahead warned ENTRY RAMP – INCOMING VEHICLES ONLY!

In the same instant that he took in this sign, he also caught sight of the fast moving roof of the second van over the tops of the parked cars off to his right. It was racing in at right angles to cut him off at the next junction, working a pincer movement with its twin, which was now only a few yards behind the Mustang and sticking there as though attached by a rope. They were trapped.

Then the solution hit him in a flash of inspiration, It was so simple, so obvious, he'd overlooked it till now – and obviously so had his pursuers. The ENTRY ramp! If vehicles could enter, they could also leave by the same route! And the risk of collision with some incoming vehicle in the ramp itself would be minimal at this time of night.

However, first there was the more immediate problem of how to avoid a collision with the van speeding in from the right. Grant measured the distance to the fast approaching junction. Making a lightning calculation, he decided to take a desperate gamble to beat the odds. He knew that it was only a matter of time before the sect foot soldiers would have blocked off every clear lane with cars pushed out from the parking lines, now that the idea had occurred to them. If he were to escape to safety with his two passengers, he had to shake off the two pursuing vehicles now, or not at all.

Grant floored the gas pedal, feeding fuel to the powerful engine. The Mustang surged forward in eager response. At the same time, he lightly dabbed the brake pedal a couple of times with his right heel, just hard enough to blink the stop lights without reducing speed. The simple ruse worked like a dream. The following vehicle dropped back slightly, then accelerated again to close the gap. But now the following driver was so intent on watching Grant's tail lights for warning of any sudden braking, he momentarily neglected to check on the position of the other van. The consequences of his neglect were devastating.

As the Mustang cleared the last of the parked cars and shot out across the junction, Grant caught a heart-stopping glimpse of the squat silhouette of the second van rocketing in from the right. Reflected light from glass, chrome and dark blue metal flashed on his peripheral vision, as the looming van seemed to be about to smash in through the offside door. He heard Pam's squeal of panic above the roaring engines. Then they were safely past.

The two sect drivers were not so lucky. Grant bared his teeth in a fierce grin of triumph at the sound of the devastating collision behind them. The loud bang of the initial impact was immediately followed by the screech of tortured metal, as the van which had been following them tipped over onto its side, its forward momentum carrying it skidding onward in a cascade of fiery sparks, till it crashed to a destructive halt against the nearest row of cars.

The second van was thrown into a tyre-squealing spin by the impact. It careered wildly out of control until it in turn ploughed ruinously into the parked cars on the opposite side of the junction, scattering torn metal and shattered glass in all directions.

Grant flung the Mustang into the left hand turn leading to the entry ramp, and in the same instant the angry flare of an exploding fuel tank lit up the huge carpark. The loud thunderclap of the explosion dulled their ears as they raced for the dark square of the tunnel mouth of the entry ramp.

Protruding from the wall of a glassed-in kiosk, a flimsy red and white wooden barrier hung across their path bearing the circular sign NO EXIT. But there was no way Grant was stopping now, especially as he had seen several figures moving quickly from the direction of the elevators nearby. He pressed the gas pedal to the floor and the Mustang roared its contempt as it crashed through the barrier, snapping it off and brushing it aside like so much matchwood. Then they were speeding up the winding spiral of the ramp to the safety of the outside world.

Behind them, several of the newcomers who had poured out from the elevators sprinted after the escaping car in a futile gesture of angry pursuit, which they soon abandoned. Others ran towards the wreckage of the sect vans, one of which was blazing fiercely, to render assistance to their injured comrades.

But one lone figure, an oriental, remained motionless in the midst of all this frantic activity. Angel Four, alerted to the possibility of trouble by the reported discovery of the unconscious Disciple outside the Assembly Hall, had hurried to the basement carpark with reinforcements. Emerging from the elevator, he had witnessed the crash and resultant devastation and now stared, eyes slitted in silent fury, after the escaping bronze Mustang and its three occupants.

When one of the Apostles came hurrying over to give him a complete rundown on the activities in the carpark, he heard him out without interruption. Then, ordering him to take charge of the clearing up operation, the oriental headed for a phone to report the evening's events to his superior, Angel One, at Bethlehem House.

27

ONCE CLEAR OF THE IMMEDIATE VICINITY OF THE Washington Centre, Grant spent several minutes taking evasive action to ensure they were being neither pursued nor tailed. They'd stirred up a such a hornet's nest of violence and fury, he had no doubt that the fanatical sect thugs would have swiftly organised fresh vehicles and would even then be scouring the city for any sign of the bronze Mustang which had caused so much carnage.

A few random left and right turns at successive junctions soon put several blocks between them and the Centre and constant checks in his rear view mirror established that no-one seemed to be in hot pursuit. Pam, though still shaken by the terrifying ordeal of the underground chase, had nevertheless regained much of her natural composure and helped by acting as observer, watching through the rear window for any signs of suspicious vehicles which might be following them. Grant then spent the next few minutes executing some manoeuvres calculated to ensure that anyone trying to tail them to their eventual destination would be shaken off.

Twice he shot lights just as they changed to red, checking each time to see if any other vehicle followed suit. As far as he could tell none did. On impulse he followed the lead of a U-turning yellow cab, backtracked for a couple of blocks, then finally he made a seemingly reckless left turn by cutting across the two inside lanes of traffic, to the accompaniment of angrily protesting horns. Again he checked his rear view. When no other vehicle turned in after them, he was at last satisfied that they weren't being tailed.

Grant also decided against calling at any of the local hospitals in order to obtain treatment for their injured passenger's battered face and body. He had no doubt the sect people would check out such places – he would if he were in their shoes, he explained to Pam. Instead, he headed for their flat, where they could themselves administer first aid to the man, and at least clean up the worst of the mess the sect thugs had made of him. If necessary they could call out their own doctor to attend to him.

After his brief burst of activity earlier, when he'd come so fortuitously to Grant's aid, the man seemed to have lapsed back into a semi-stupor. At first he lay slumped in the back seat, unresponsive and unprotesting, while Pam gently wiped his injured face with cologne soaked tissues. Soon, however, he began to revive under the cool mild sting of the cologne and struggled to sit up, blinking around him and mumbling, "Wha's happenin' … where we goin'?" On being reassured by Pam's soothing touch and voice, he lay back quietly and allowed her to continue her ministrations.

By the time they pulled up outside their apartment block, Pam's patient was still groggy and unsteady on his feet but had recovered sufficiently to be helped from the car and thence into the flat, supported by Grant's steadying hand on his elbow. Once inside, he was helped further along the road to full recovery by a stiff shot of brandy followed by a plentiful supply of sweet black coffee. Then, despite his mumbled protests that they'd done enough for him and he didn't want to put them to any more trouble on his behalf, Pam insisted he strip to the waist so they could properly examine the extent of his injuries.

A couple of inches shorter than Grant, he was a sturdily built man in his late forties or early fifties, his once dark hair beginning to recede and show grey streaks at the temples. Though thickening a little round the waist, his stocky frame was well padded with hard muscle and he obviously kept himself in good physical condition for his age. Looking at him, Grant was reminded a little of Rocky O'Rourke, the big amiable trucker he'd met earlier that day. This guy wasn't as broad in the shoulder as Rocky, nor as deep chested, but they'd easily pass for cousins. In fact, it was probable that the man's strong constitution and powerful build had helped speed his recovery from the worst effects of the heavy beating he'd suffered.

He complained of a throbbing headache and sore ribs but Grant's examination revealed no broken bones. Certainly his face was a mess, his nose and eyes swollen and discoloured, his upper lip puffy and split, but all his injuries appeared to be superficial. Grant strapped up his bruised ribs, while Pam tended his facial injuries more thoroughly, this time aided by the contents of the bathroom medicine cabinet rather than those of her handbag.

"The headache's the after-effects of concussion," Grant informed him. "I should know – I've had the same thing myself a couple of times in the past. You'll have to take things easy for a couple of days. If you'll take my advice, you'll call in on your doctor for a check-up, just t'be on the safe side. You took a pretty bad pasting back there, before I could get to you."

The man paused in the act of buttoning up his shirt and squinted at Grant through the puffy discoloured flesh around his eyes, as though seeing him for the first time that night. "Hey – it was you who jumped those mothers back there! I remember now. Two of 'em were holdin' me, an' the third one wuz givin' me a real goin' over. Yeah ... I remember thinkin' th'fucker wuz tryin' t'kill me ... oh ... 'scuse th'French, lady." This last remark was addressed contritely to Pam, who smiled and waved aside his apology.

To Grant he continued, "Then you arrived jes' in th'nick of time, like the good ol' US Cavalry, an' started fightin' wid 'em. I musta blacked out, cuz th'next thing I remember is bein' in th'back of your car. So, I owe you one, mister. Thanks ..." he stuck out his hand. "Pete Larsen's th'name, by th'way. Who do I have to thank fer comin' to my rescue?"

Grant shook Larsen's proffered hand, then threw him a mock salute. "Cap'n Brett Grant, Seventh US Cavalry at yore service, suh," he replied with a grin. "But I couldn't have done it without th'help of Miss Annie Oakley heah ..." he indicated Pam with a sweep of his hand, "otherwise known as Pam Mason ... when she ain't clubbin' folks unconscious with her handbag, that is."

Larsen smiled at Grant's clowning, recognising that it was Brett's way of accepting his gratitude without making a big deal out of it, and shook hands with Pam in turn. Introductions over, Pam brought in fresh coffee and sandwiches and an ice-pack, improvised from a tea towel and crushed ice cubes, to reduce the swelling around Larsen's eyes. The three of them seated themselves comfortably around the low coffee table and began to exchange their respective versions of the evening's events in a more serious vein.

Grant led off the discussion by explaining that he was a private detective and how his interest in the sect had come about through his having been hired to trace and rescue a client's missing son. He briefly outlined the course of his inquiries that day, including his interview with the sect girl Louise at the mobile soup kitchen, which had prompted him to attend that evening's Crusade. He explained he'd gone along for two reasons, firstly to gain some idea of the numerical strength and organisation of the sect, and secondly to assess the character of their leader, the Prophet, by witnessing his performance first-hand. On both counts, he had been disturbed by his findings.

Lastly, he described how he'd seen Larsen challenging the Prophet, and how when he'd seen him being manhandled out of the meeting by the sect heavies, he had decided on impulse to follow and intervene. The successful outcome of his fight with Larsen's attackers, aided by Pam's timely intervention, followed by the subsequent car chase and its catastrophic result, brought Grant's account to a conclusion.

Then it was Larsen's turn. He lit a cigarette, inserting it gingerly between his swollen lips each time he drew on it. Between equally careful sips of coffee, he told them his story. It transpired that his 16 year old daughter Karen had, like Jim Miller, become a devotee of the Prophet. She had left home to join the Children of Bethlehem some three months previously in open defiance of her parents – almost a carbon copy of the Miller case, in fact.

For the first few weeks after Karen had left home, Larsen and his wife had been frantic with worry. The police had been sympathetic but unhelpful and he had quickly come to accept that they were too busy and understaffed to mount searches for wayward runaways like their daughter. Their missing persons files were crammed to saturation with similar cases. So Larsen had decided to take matters into his own hands. His methods were as direct and physical as himself. He had set out to find and reclaim his daughter by a campaign of direct confrontation with the enemy. To this end he had begun accosting any sect personnel wherever he found them and had caused a few noisy scenes at their mobile soup kitchens.

However, he had soon realised that he was getting no nearer to finding his daughter. All his demands for her return fell on unresponsive ears. It was then he had hit upon the plan of escalating his campaign by taking it right to the top. By confronting the man himself, the Prophet, at every opportunity, he hoped to embarrass him into releasing Karen from the clutches of the sect, or at least into allowing him access to her.

With the blind faith of a loving father, he believed a heart-to-heart talk with Karen would persuade her to return home. He had learned that the Prophet held fortnightly revival meetings in hired halls across the city and a massive Crusade, like the one they'd just attended in the Washington Centre, once every few months. Tonight's confrontation was the third such he had forced at various meetings in the city, over the course of the past six weeks.

As Larsen told it, on the previous two occasions he had disrupted the meetings, just like he had attempted to do earlier that evening, by denouncing the Prophet as a hypocrite and demanding the return of his daughter. On those occasions their response had been merely to manhandle him none to gently from the meetings and warn him off. From tonight's violent reaction towards him, it seemed that he had exhausted their limited patience and that orders had been issued for the 'warning off' to be brutally final on this occasion.

"Ah … I've had worse than this in a bar-room brawl," he concluded dismissively, indicating his battered features and managing a crooked smile. Then he added determinedly, "But I'll be ready for 'em next time. If they wanna stop me tryin' t'git my Karen back, they'll hafta kill me first!"

"They probably will," commented Grant drily. "Especially after all the damage you caused to their vehicles and troops tonight."

"All the damage I caused?" Larsen retorted, feigning an air of injured innocence. "Hah! That's rich, that is! I dunno nothin' about it. I wuz unconscious when it all happened. If I'm asked about it, I'll take th'Fifth Amendment!"

They all laughed, but Larsen bit his off when he found it too painful. He lit a cigarette as Pam poured fresh cups of coffee for everyone. Setting down the coffee pot, she looked up at him, her face serious again.

"All joking aside Pete, Brett's right, you know. From what I saw tonight, these are dangerous people you're dealing with. It's no use going up against them on your own, like you did tonight. Why don't you hire Brett to find where they've got your daughter? Then you could maybe get a court order to get her back legally. After all, he's already trying to trace another youngster who ran away like your Karen did. It'd be like killing two birds with the one stone, so to speak," she concluded brightly.

"Or three ... if their goons get me!" came Grant's swift rejoinder.

"Oh, you! I didn't mean it that way," she replied, flustered, and dug him on the shoulder.

Larsen's lopsided grin was more of a grimace, due to his injured mouth. "I'd sure like t'hire 'im, Pam. But I couldn't afford it. Me an' a coupla other guys own part shares in a breaker's yard, cuttin' up used cars an' suchlike. We make a livin', but th'money I earn don't run to hirin' no private dicks." He squinted at Grant from around the ice-pack he was holding to one of his swollen eyes and asked, "As a matter of interest, how much d'you charge, anyway?"

"A hundred a day, plus expenses. That's the going rate ... but I'd be open to negotiation," he added, mentally wincing as he imagined Harry Sherman's reaction, had his senior partner been present to hear the offer.

"Negotiation!" retorted Larsen. "Thanks for the offer, friend. But with my financial resources, or should I say lack of 'em, I'd need a Philadelphia lawyer t'negotiate for me. An' I couldn' afford one of them either!"

Grant laughed. "Okay," he said, "how about this ... while I'm workin' on my other case, I'll do my best to trace your daughter too, an' persuade her to come home. If I succeed, an' only if, you owe me one day's fee – a hundred dollars flat. If I don't manage to persuade her to come home, you owe me nothin'. In other words, you pay me for results. How does that sound to you?"

Larsen stared at him without speaking for a few seconds, then the lopsided grin touched his bruised mouth again. "Sounds good t'me. Sure is decent of you t'suggest it. I appreciate it, an' I know when m'wife sees the state I'm in, she'll appreciate it even more'n I do. I'll accept ... on one condition."

"And that is? ..." asked Grant.

"If you should need any backup, any muscle, when you go up against these people, you gimme a call. I got friends in th'scrap trade I c'd call on fer help at any time. Y'could say they're guys who like havin' a scrap, not jes' workin' with it! That'd even things up a bit an' make me feel better about acceptin' your offer. Do we have a deal?" Larsen offered his hand.

"We have a deal," replied Grant warmly and shook Larsen's hand. He then gave Larsen one of his cards, and in return took a note of his new client's home and business addresses and telephone numbers, so he could contact him whenever necessary, as agreed.

"I mean it, Brett," Larsen repeated earnestly. "You need any muscle, you call me. I wanna return bout with the bastards who worked me over tonight ... 'scuse th'French again, Pam."

"Oh, that's okay," she reassured him lightly. "After tonight, I think I'm unshockable. More coffee, anyone?"

They talked on for a while and Grant filled Larsen in with more details of the events which had taken place after he'd come to his rescue, as that part of the proceedings were a complete blank to the man. He described how he'd dealt with the first three assailants, and how Pam had come so fortuitously to his aid with the fourth. He then went on to give a blow by blow account of the hectic car chase through the dimly lit maze of the huge underground carpark. When he reached the part about the brief struggle which had taken place in the car itself when it had stalled, this drew a pleased response from a surprised Larsen.

"I hit th'guy? Hah! How'dya like that? I don' even remember bein' there, never mind beltin' anyone. Thing is, did I land 'im a good one?"

Grant assured him he hadn't done too badly at all for someone who didn't even know he was there at the time. "I sure as hell wouldn't like to get in the way of any punches you throw when you're conscious!" he chuckled.

Not long after this, Larsen declared he'd better be getting himself off home to his apartment in South Brooklyn, or his wife Ellen would be worrying about him. "She ain't bin 'erself since Karen left," he explained. "Spends most of 'er time jes' mopin' aroun' th'house. Cries a lot too, fer no apparent reason. Doc' says it's depression. Christ! Wait'll she sees the state I'm in … it'll prob'ly be all she needs t'push 'er over the edge," he concluded bitterly.

They all stood up, Larsen grunting with the effort and wincing from the pain of his bruised muscles. He stood for a moment massaging the stiffness out of his injured ribs.

"How d'you feel?" Grant asked him.

"Lousy," confessed Larsen, adding, "but not as lousy as I would have felt, if you hadn't got to me in time." Carefully he tried a few deep breaths as he rubbed his tender midriff. "Nothin' cracked, I don' think. That's a bonus, I suppose, even though it don' exactly feel like it right now." He glanced at his watch. "Jeez! Lookit th'time. Okay if I use your phone t'call a cab? I don' feel up to drivin' home. Besides, my car's parked somewheres off Broadway. I didn' leave it any closer to th'Centre in case it got damaged."

He stopped suddenly, looked from one to the other and then added in a tone of comical self-reproof, "What'm I sayin'? In case it got damaged, fer Chrissake! I wish t'hell now I'd parked right it in the damn foyer … that way, they mighta left me alone an' attacked the car instead!"

Grant laughingly agreed with him, then said, "Forget the cab Pete, we'll give you a run home an' Pam here'll help to calm your wife. Why don't you give her a quick call an' tell her you're on your way home with a couple of friends you've invited back for a coffee. Then after she's met us an' heard what happened tonight, you can tell her you've hired me, cash on results basis. That way you'll set her mind at rest on two counts. She'll know you're safe from any further risk, and that you've hired professional help to trace Karen."

"Okay thanks, that'd be great," Larsen accepted gratefully.

"I'll git one of my pals t'pick up the car for me tomorrow. Me …
I'm stayin' in bed."

As it turned out, Larsen's wife reacted entirely differently to his
expectations. Ellen was a small woman, a little on the plump
side, with an open, pleasant face which had matured from an
earlier prettiness of youth to a softer attractiveness of middle
age. Once she had got over the initial shock of seeing the
reshaped, rainbow-hued face acquired by her husband, she
showed no sign of her previous mood of depression-induced
lethargy as described by Larsen. Instead, she fussed over him
protectively, insisting that he sit and take things easy, while she
attended to rustling up coffee for their guests.

It seemed that the occupational therapy of looking after the
returned wounded hero was just what she'd been needing to
take her mind off her introspective moping over the fate of her
runaway daughter. She was gripped by a feeling of healthy
anger against the people who'd harmed her husband, and it
swept away the mental cobwebs of depression about her
daughter.

Over coffee, Grant gave her a brief, heavily edited version of
the evening's events, toning down the worst aspects of the
violence and emphasising Larsen's part for her benefit. From
the barely concealed admiration behind the disapproving glances
and sounds she directed at her husband, it obviously worked.
Coffee and explanations over they made their exit, promising
to keep in touch and with the grateful thanks of the Larsens
speeding them on their way.

Driving homeward, the distant myriad lights of the spectacular
Manhattan skyline, dominated by the giant twin towers of the
World Trade Centre, glittered at them like some fantastic
Disneyland creation. As they reached and crossed the Brooklyn
Bridge, the flowing black waters of the East River reflected the
whole effect, its constantly moving surface breaking up the
lights into a twinkling magic fairyland.

Pam stared out at the scene in mesmerised silence. She'd seen
the sight a hundred times before but it never failed to move her.

Grant left her alone with her thoughts, content to re-run the day's events in his own mind. His initial suspicions that the sect people might prove to be dangerous opponents had been confirmed in no uncertain terms by their actions at the Washington Centre.

Their brutal assault on Larsen, followed by the prolonged kamikaze-style attack on the occupants of the Mustang, spoke of the single-minded fanaticism of the zealot. And zealots, whether religious or political, were bad news and always dangerous in Grant's considered opinion. He reflected soberly that maybe the warnings of Sherman and Curtis were worth heeding for the future – if only to ensure he had a future to look forward to!

"Brett?" Pam's voice, sounding strangely subdued, interrupted his train of thought.

"M-m-m?" He glanced at her to show she had his attention. Her face was dark-eyed and serious in the dimness of the car's interior.

"Brett, I've been thinking. Those people tonight … they were just like wild animals. They didn't seem to care if they killed us … or themselves, for that matter …" she paused, searching for the right words to express her troubled thoughts.

"Yeah, I did notice," he commented grimly. "As a matter of fact, I was just thinking along similar lines myself when you spoke. Oh, an' while we're on the subject, thanks for comin' to my aid like you did. You sure pack a mean handbag." He smiled at her as he spoke, trying to lighten her mood.

"It was the only thing I could think of at the time," she confessed. "At first when I followed you, I was petrified. Especially when I heard the sounds of fighting. I crept round a car and saw the two men you'd beaten, then I saw the mess they'd made of poor Mister Larsen and all of a sudden I got so angry … and when I thought they might do the same to you, I got even madder … and I guess I forgot to be frightened any more. So, when I came back round the cars and found myself at that animal's back, I just waited till you forced him back towards me and let him have it!" Her voice held a note of pride as well as anger.

261

Grant reached out in the darkness and squeezed her hand. "Well, I think you were terrific. An' I don't care what you say about forgetting to feel frightened, it was a damn brave thing to do."

They drove on in silence for a bit, then Pam spoke again. "Brett ... you know that young girl you told me about, the one you met at the sect's van earlier today?"

"Louise?" he prompted.

"Yes, Louise. Well ... you know how you said you're going to help her to get away if she wants ... but that if you do you'll have to find her somewhere to stay? Well, why don't you bring her to our place? She could always stay with us until she finds somewhere else."

Grant laughed and shook his head. "You're priceless, y'know that? Earlier tonight you were goin' on about me not gettin' involved, an' why didn't I send for the police. An' now here you are wantin' me to rescue damsels in distress, an' set up a way station for homeless waifs." He reached out and squeezed her hand again. "Of course we'll take her in if she wants to leave the sect an' has noplace to go. Wanna know somethin' else? You're an ol' softie ... an' I love you."

She leaned over and kissed him on the cheek. "I love you too," she replied simply.

"Oh? I thought you'd fallen for ol' Moses in the gold silk nightie, back there tonight," he said teasingly.

PART V
TRIAD
WARS

28

ANGEL ONE HAD LEFT BETHLEHEM HOUSE WELL IN
advance of those sect personnel detailed for duty at the Prophet's
Crusade in the Washington Centre. He made good time to the
city's northern limits but on reaching the Hudson he did not
cross into Manhattan but instead headed on down the New
Jersey side of the river making for the borough of Richmond on
Staten Island, which he entered by the Bayonne Bridge.

Not long after he entered the Island's road network, Angel
One's route began to take a curiously indirect and meandering
course involving frequent changes of direction. His speed varied
erratically too. Three or four times he slowed when approaching
light-controlled crossings, as though undecided on his correct
route, only to accelerate through at the last instant as the lights
changed against him.

After some fifteen minutes of these manoeuvres, the oriental
took one last measure to double check he was not under
surveillance. He chose a long quiet stretch of Richmond Avenue
deep in the Willow district and about half way along its almost
deserted length suddenly turned off into a side road. Immediately,
he swung the car round in a fast U-turn and braked to a halt at
the opposite kerb, facing back towards Richmond Avenue. For
a full five minutes he sat and watched for any signs of undue
interest on the part of any passing driver. Satisfied at last that
he was clean of any tail, he drove off, turning back onto
Richmond Avenue.

Driving fast now, but still checking regularly in his mirrors,
he burned up the miles to the junction with Arthur Kill Road,

where he turned off and was soon headed deep into plush, exclusive suburbs. Ten minutes later he was nearing his destination.

He was now driving past huge turreted and colonnaded mansions built in varying grandiose architectural styles, many of them the typical vulgar progeny of unlimited wealth wed to minimal taste. Each edifice was set in splendid isolation in the midst of its own high-walled and wooded grounds, and reached by its own private road, branching off from the main avenue. Access to each entry was barred by sets of tall barred gates.

Angel One pulled into the entranceway of one such set of gates, braked to a smooth halt a few feet from them and switched off the engine. The metal bars of the spike-topped gates were painted a sombre black. Set in the centre of each barred gate was a metal circle containing gold painted motif of a coiled rearing dragon, with one clawed foot raised to strike.

The car had no sooner halted, than two fit looking young Orientals emerged from the squat stone gatehouse set unobtrusively among the shrubbery to one side of the driveway behind the gates. Each man wore a dark blue, high-necked jacket buttoned to the throat and trousers of the same colour. One approached and stood on the other side of the bars, his companion taking up a position a few yards off to one side, covering him. This ploy would obviously present any would-be assassin with a split target, should an attempt be made to take out both guards at the same time.

The guard nearest the gate waited until Angel One got out of the car and approached to stand facing him on the other side. If either man recognised the other, he gave no sign of it. Instead, the guard inquired politely in English, "Yes, sir? Can I help you?"

"I seek the guardian of the Fragrant Harbour," Angel One replied conversationally as though replying to the man's query. But his reply was made in Chinese.

Without a flicker of surprise at this strange reply, the young guard answered him in the same polite tone and using the same language. "There are several such. Which guardian do you seek?"

"The ninth dragon," Angel One responded.

"How long did his struggle last?" asked the guard.

"Twenty-three suns and moons," replied Angel One.

"The enemy?" the guard probed.

"T'un Hai," riposted Angel One.

"The outcome?" came the final question.

"The dead sleep in safety," Angel One answered.

Apparently satisfied with his examination of the visitor, the guard signalled to the gatehouse. Someone behind its smoked glass window activated a switch and the electronically operated gates swung silently inwards, the gold dragons at their centres glinting as they reflected back the street lighting. Angel One returned to the car, started up and drove past the guards into the New York lair of the Gold Dragon Triad.

The long, gravel-topped driveway curved gently through a shallow S-bend among the neatly planted trees, a method of screening the grounds from prying eyes similar to that used at Bethlehem House. As he steered smoothly through the bends, Angel One's mind dwelt briefly on the meaning behind the cryptic exchange which had just passed between himself and the gate guard. It was based on an ancient Chinese legend that he remembered well from his childhood in the Canton slums.

The legend was of Kow Loon, which means Ninth Dragon, who resided in the ninth of the nine mountain peaks which surround Hong Kong, and who fought T'un Hai, the two-headed Blood Snake of the Dark World who tore the souls of the dead and cast them into the sea. The story told how after an epic battle lasting twenty-three days and nights, Kow Loon defeated T'un Hai and the latter fled to sea, and how Kow Loon still protects the souls of the dead from him to this very day.

He had heard the story often enough at the knee of his maternal grandmother, at a time when such tales helped to take one's mind off the hunger pains of an empty belly. Every time he used the cryptic exchange on his frequent visits to Dragon Control, Angel One's mind flashed back involuntarily to those far-off childhood days of squalor and grinding poverty. These conditions the child, Sung Tang Lee had had to suffer through his inability to change them. But the adult, Angel One had vowed they would never be his lot again, now that he had the ability to control his own destiny.

The van emerged from the trees onto a straight 150 yard stretch leading towards the house, an imposing three-storey edifice in someone's idea of neo-classic, complete with a wide flight of marble steps which climbed to a pillared front terrace extending along the entire frontage. Fifty yards short of this ornamental staircase, the driveway forked left and right, the arms swooping out and round in wide curves to rejoin in front of the building at the foot of the steps. The circular area enclosed by this loop was bounded by a waist-high fence of thick steel posts inter-linked by loops of heavy chain, and contained a kidney-shaped lily-pond edged by grass and low stone benches.

The effect may have been aesthetically pleasing but Angel One knew it was also deadly to an unsuspecting enemy. This final frontal approach to the house was utterly devoid of cover from the moment any vehicle emerged from the outer screen of trees. The occupants would then be completely exposed to the crossfire of the two ever vigilant guards positioned in the top corner windows at either side of the house front. These guards were armed with Armalite rifles fitted with Quick Point sights. The Quick Point sight is designed so that the operator looks into the sight with both eyes, and instead of cross-hairs he sees the target, magnified, with a red dot superimposed on it. Where the dot is – the shot hits. The resultant fast action of the Quick Point sight, allied to the devastating hitting power of the Armalite rifle made a lethal combination.

If any approaching hostile vehicle managed to survive or evade the initial frontal fire directed at it on the straight section of the drive, it would then be exposed to a deadly flank fire when it turned left or right into the loop around the lily pond. Any attempt to avoid this by ploughing straight through the enclosed area, would swiftly come to grief in the five foot depths of the deceptively shallow looking lily-covered pond – if the vehicle first managed to smash its way past the solid steel posts or stone benches, all of which were embedded in solid concrete bases!

Angel One knew he was safe from being considered a target

by either of the two marksmen in the upper windows. They would have been given the 'all clear' signal from the gatehouse guards. But it still gave him an uneasy feeling to know he was probably being used for sighting practice by the two marksmen in their high firing positions as they relieved their boredom and kept their reflexes honed by drawing a bead on him.

He swung round the left curve of the loop and braked to a halt at the foot of the wide marble steps. He glanced up at the tall, ornately carved front door and his eye fell on the large gilt knocker in its centre. Shaped like a dragon, it was identical to the motif depicted on the front gates.

Even as he looked up, the door swung open as though activated by the touch of his glance. Two young Chinese emerged, both wearing the same uniform-like high-collared tunics as the gate guards, the only difference being that the close-fitting tunic jackets of the house guards were white. One of the men remained by the door, while the other descended the steps as Angel One got out of the car. With a polite bow of greeting, acknowledged by a curt nod from Angel One, the guard climbed into the car and drove it away to be parked round the side.

Angel One ran lightly up the steps and the second man stood aside to allow him to enter the house. As he stepped into the spacious entrance hall, he was met by three more white-jacketed house guards, one of whom was older than his two companions, and whose high tunic collar bore two small gold dragon insignia, one on either side of his throat. Even without these visible symbols of his rank, it would have been obvious the elder guard carried authority within the organisation from the way the other two waited in respectful silence while he greeted Angel One, whom he obviously recognised. Nonetheless, despite his apparent recognition of the visitor, the senior house guard proceeded to put Angel One through a strict verbal examination, comprising a question and answer ritual of far greater detail and complexity than the one he had exchanged with the gate guards.

Once satisfied of Angel One's authenticity, the senior guard dismissed his two subordinates and personally escorted him across the entrance hall and up a sweeping, thickly carpeted staircase. From the moment the small party left the front door, Angel One knew that their progress was being monitored by a succession of strategically sited remote control cameras, which tracked them in silent arcs from their various positions in the high ceilings. Reaching the first floor, he was led along a corridor leading into the right wing of the house, until they stopped before one of a number of identical looking doors. The house guard pressed a button on the door frame and waited. Almost immediately a small glass panel set above the button flashed green and a buzzer sounded sharply. An instant later there was a metallic click as the door unlocked electronically.

Holding the door open for him, Angel One's escort bowed politely and motioned for him to enter alone. He did so and had only walked a few paces into the brightly lit room when he sensed the door closing behind him, a fact confirmed by the sound of the electronically controlled lock snapping home again.

The room was large, in proportion with the size of the house itself. But it was made to appear even larger by the fact that it contained only two items of furniture – a delicate, slim-legged, black-lacquered table standing alongside a high-backed, black leather chair – situated in the centre of the room, and facing the far wall. The strong lighting was coming from two small but powerful spotlights sited high in the corners of the back wall at ceiling level and beaming down on the empty chair. Set in the centre of the far wall and focused on the spotlit chair, was the single unblinking eye of a closed-circuit television camera. Below it was the wire mesh grille of a speaker.

For a few seconds, Angel One stood motionless inside the closed door, allowing his eyes to adjust to the glare of the lighting. Then a soft gong sounded from the speaker grille. As the musical note faded, a sibilant male voice addressed him in Chinese from the same source.

"Greetings, Red Sixteen. Please be seated." The Taiwanese accent warned Angel One that the owner of the disembodied voice was the Controller – the official in charge of Dragon Control, as the HQ of the Gold Dragon Triad was known.

As directed, Angel One walked forward to the black leather chair and settled himself comfortably into its contoured padding.

On the small table by his left hand sat a crystal decanter of mineral water and a drinking glass. Lying beside these was a delicate throat-mike, attached to a long thin length of flex, leading down to a connection in the floor under the table. Without needing to be instructed, Angel One fitted the throat-mike round his neck, folded his hands in his lap and waited to be addressed again. He did not have to wait for long.

"You arrived some ten minutes late, Sixteen," the voice continued, its tone deceptively polite. "Did you encounter some problem on your way here, which delayed you?"

"No, Controller." Angel One kept his face carefully impassive as he replied to the thinly veiled rebuke. "I apologise for my late arrival. I was obeying the orders you issued at our last meeting, to be doubly vigilant for anyone attempting to follow me here." As he finished speaking, he added silently to himself, Chew that with your rice, you smooth Taiwanese turd!

Angel One, had been born and raised in the southern Chinese city of Canton, before escaping at the age of seventeen across the border into Hong Kong. Once there, the youthful Sung Tang Lee had soon followed the path of many of his fellow escapees from Communist rule and had joined one of the many branches of the secret society of Hung – known to the West as the Triads. He had never lost his mainlander's distrust of the Taiwanese, regarding them as too Americanised and thus untrustworthy. The antagonism between them was mutual.

For the Controller's part, his dislike of his subordinate was not solely on a personal level. He also regarded Angel One as a serious future contender for his own post, because of the man's dangerous combination of ability and ruthlessness.

Angel One sensed the other's suspicion and dislike, and it served only to increase his contempt for the other. To Angel One the Triad was his home, his family and his life and he could conceive of no personal consideration which should be permitted to supplant that.

"Your apology is accepted," the cultured voice continued smoothly. "I commend you on your caution and so on this occasion I will not regard your lateness as a discourtesy. However, might I suggest that your punctual arrival for future meetings might be assured, if your increased vigilance is coupled to an earlier start on your journey here!"

Angel One hid his irritation at the pettiness of the rebuke and nodded his acceptance of it in the direction of the camera.

The Controller's voice continued without pause. "I want you and your people to continue to be doubly vigilant from now on. We have reports of increased police activity all over the city. It seems that they are becoming increasingly frustrated at their continued failure to score even one significant success against our organisation. To date, not one of our main distribution outlets has been uncovered by them ... and it must remain so!"

A note of contempt crept into the disembodied voice as it went on, "The police of course are being spurred on – even assisted by – our main enemy, the Sicilian gangsters of the so-called Mafia. It seems they too, like their police puppets, are growing increasingly desperate at our success in the competition for the drugs trade, with the resultant loss of revenue this means to them.

"But they cannot compete with us. Compared with our high grade heroin, the quality of the product they distribute is consistent with the current makeup of their organisation – excessively diluted garbage! Their previous monopoly has made them complacent and greedy. So, rather than upgrade their own product in order to compete with us, they are instead attempting through propaganda spread by their tame Congressmen and Senators to change the bogeyman of the American citizen from the Red under his bed, to the Triad in his Chinese Takeaway.

"This, of course, will not be hard to achieve among the majority white American population, who control and wield the political influence in the country. The reason, of course, is simple. Racism. While the white population are prepared to accept and tolerate the Sicilians as an integral part of their mongrel nation, they will never do so where we Chinese are concerned. Quite apart from the obvious ethnic and cultural differences between the Caucasian and oriental races, we also have to contend with the additional prejudice carried over from America's past conflicts with the Japanese, the Koreans and the Vietnamese. The last three generations have been conditioned to hate and distrust Orientals by wartime propaganda."

The Controller's voice paused for a moment before continuing, and when he resumed, his next words were of more direct relevance to Angel One. "Now the Mafia have seemingly decided to escalate their struggle against us. Instead of merely causing us political and police harassment, they have now switched to a policy of more direct attack. Your section has not yet been affected, Sixteen, but these Sicilian barbarians have recently begun a city-wide campaign of violence, obviously aimed at driving our people from the streets.

"It is a crude but increasingly effective attempt to disrupt and ultimately destroy our distribution network at street level. Many of our pushers and low-grade suppliers have recently been waylaid and badly beaten. One or two of our cells have been severely weakened as a result and are having to provide more protection for street dealers.

As you will appreciate, this not only puts a strain on manpower, but it is also bad for business, as prospective customers are being frightened off by the threat of being caught up in violence. So, I would advise you to prepare your section for similar attacks soon from the Sicilian scum in your area. You may have been fortunate until now in having a weaker or less efficient Mafia Family pitted against you, who knows?" the voice concluded disparagingly.

Angel One shrugged. "Or perhaps my section has been protected from such trouble by its strength and good organisation," he replied evenly. Then, before the other could respond, he went on, "I assume we have retaliated to these attacks in support of the affected sections, Controller?"

The fleeting pause which preceded the Controller's reply, told Angel One that his barbed response had struck home. However subtly, he had questioned his superior's competence by the very inference that retaliation might not have been carried out.

"Of course." The curt tone confirmed the other's annoyance at having had a point scored off him. "We have counterattacked whenever possible. However, where the police turn a blind eye to the Sicilians' attacks on us, the same does not apply to the reverse. Nor can we openly challenge this evidence of police bias, for to do so would only result in bringing down upon ourselves an even more unwelcome level of attention from the mass media, spurred on by the political lackeys of the Mafia. Our low public profile, I do not have to remind you, has always been one of our main strengths.

"However, our patience is not inexhaustible. We have let it be known, by spreading the word on the streets, that any further attacks on us will result in full scale war. We have also warned that whereas such a conflict would suit neither of our organisations, they would suffer a far greater degree of damage than us. They are more established in this country than we are, and now own many properties and business enterprises as legal fronts. They seem to forget that while such assets may provide great legal and financial strength in time of peace, they would conversely be extremely vulnerable to attack and would thus be a great weakness in time of war. So, warn your people to increase their vigilance on the streets, Sixteen."

"Of course, Controller," Angel One replied stiffly, irritated by his superior's needless reminder. It implied that he needed advice on how to run his own section. Worse, this latest development made it even more awkward to break his own troublesome news. His anger against Jim Miller grew, for having put him in the intolerable position of losing face, by having to admit to this smug Taiwanese bastard that he had sprung a leak in his previously tightly run ship. The Controller's next words increased his discomfiture.

"Dragon Agent Red Sixteen," the formal use of his full coded title within the organisation warned him that something was afoot. "Today we are honoured by the personal visit of one of the most important executives of our Triad leadership. I refer to the new Director of Operations for North-Eastern United States. You may pay your respects now."

Immediately on hearing these words, Angel One rose to his feet and bowed deeply towards the cold, glittering eye of the camera. As he straightened up again, a new voice spoke.

"Thank you, Dragon Agent Red Sixteen," came the formal acknowledgement from the far side of the room. "Please be seated. I have heard much to your credit, even before coming here. Your section is reportedly the most successful of this Control area. Keep up the good work."

The voice was high pitched and reedy, with a wheezing, breathless quality to it. Mentally Angel One pictured the owner of the voice as a fat man. The Director continued, "I have only recently assumed control of this Directorship, the most important of the four into which the United States is divided, as you know. Previously I was in charge of Northern Europe and before that, Southeast Asia. As any of the personnel who served under me in those areas could tell you, I reward diligence and merit with promotion, when this is deserved."

Although the man was speaking Cantonese – the lingua franca of the organisation – he had a definable Hong Kong accent. Angel One knew, and bore a mainlander's resentment against the fact, that all of the top leadership of the Gold Dragon Triad originated from Taiwan or Hong Kong. They kept it that way as a matter of deliberate policy.

Most of the Triad societies operated a similar policy, no matter which of the three main centres of Chinese population outwith the mainland they originated from – Taiwan, Hong Kong or Singapore. It was made extremely difficult for mainlanders to progress to the inner sanctums of power and control in the Triads, for fear they could be infiltrators, sleeping agents planted by the Communist government in Beijing, to be activated at a time of future take-over of the three territories. As a result of this anti-mainlander prejudice, many former refugees from the Chinese Republic, The Big Circle in Triad parlance, formed their own Triads rather than join the existing ones.

Angel One however, in his earlier persona of the teenaged Sung Tang Lee, fierce individualist and fighter that he was, had made up his mind right from the start that he would join one of the strongest and oldest of the established Triads. And further, he had vowed that he would eventually attain the rank of 489-er, or leader, despite all the odds.

Even as a seventeen year old, his ruthlessness and potential soon came to the notice of the people who mattered in the backstreets and shantytowns of Hong Kong – those with Triad

275

connections – and it wasn't long before he was being approached by the recruiting agents of the various gangs. But he had made his own discreet inquiries, and bided his time till contact was eventually made by agents of the organisation he had chosen.

So it came about that he was initiated as a 49-er – an ordinary member, or foot soldier – into the Gum Lung Hung, or Gold Dragon Triad. True to his inner vow, he progressed steadily through the ranks and within five years his lethal combat skills had ensured his promotion to a 426-er, or fighter, entitling him to the coveted insignia of the Twin Flower Red Broomstick which accompanied that rank. Five years later, he had progressed to the level of a junior ranked 489-er, or Section Leader. This in itself was unusual, as 489-ers were more usually promoted from among the 415-ers, or Negotiators – those who bore the insignia of the White Paper Fan.

The Controller was speaking again. "Sixteen, earlier today I briefed the new Director on our administrative structure, how each designated Control Area within the North-Eastern Directorship has been allocated a code name. Thus, New York City is Dragon Control; New York State is Lotus Control; Chicago, Tiger Control, and so on. Then I dealt with the breakdown of our own Dragon Control's particular sphere of operations. How each of the city boroughs has been assigned a colour coding: Red for Manhattan; Green for The Bronx; Blue for Queen's; White for Brooklyn; and Black for Richmond.

"Lastly, I have described how we have assigned a number to each of our Operatives, with all Area Supervisors or Section Leaders, like yourself, having the figure six included in their assigned numbers. Thus, as Dragon Agent Red Sixteen, you can be identified immediately as Area Supervisor of the Manhattan Borough of New York City.

"Now, I want you to describe briefly your own particular sphere of operations for the Director's benefit, Sixteen. This will give him a complete picture of our set-up, right down to the lower echelons. You may begin."

However, before Angel One could answer, the high pitched, wheezing voice of the Director interposed. "I would also be interested to hear the details of how Agent Red Sixteen set up his operation, considering he built it up from nothing. It could pro-vide a useful role model for the information of future section leaders …"

Despite his other misgivings, Angel One felt flattered by the compliment. He nodded respectfully towards the camera lens. "The Director pays me too much honour, but I shall do as he wishes," he began. "As a cover for my operations, I use a religious sect – one of many such in this neurotic country. It is a perfect front for our operations in two ways. Firstly it provides a secure and secret base, preferable to the more usual one of a restaurant or other business premises. Secondly, it has proved to be a first-class recruiting ground both for street pushers, and also for petty thugs whom we train to act as their minders.

"I joined this sect, which calls itself 'The Children of Bethlehem', some six years ago and quickly set out to make myself indispensable to its founder and leader. He is typical of the megalomaniacs who seem to run these sects, intolerant and existing in an dream world of self delusion. But he holds some strange attraction for the young, rootless, anti-social elements who provide me with such an ideal source of raw material for our purposes.

"I introduced him to some simple Tai Chi meditation disciplines for inclusion in his peculiar religious teachings, after which I began to prompt him subtly into more useful directions of opinion and action – more useful to us, that is. He is so convinced of his infallibility, he is easily manipulated and quickly adopts any attractive idea as his own by a simple process of autosuggestion.

"In order to assume complete control of his organisation from within, I next arranged for the creation of a command structure staffed by our own people. In order to achieve this, it was a simple matter to convince him that he could be in danger from physical attacks by outsiders. I merely allowed one or two incidents to take place at his meetings, where irate parents of some of his converts were not prevented too quickly from abusing him verbally and physically, without any real harm coming to him. This made him amenable to the suggestion that he needed a small but reliable group of personal bodyguards to protect his person.

"Thus I was able to introduce Agents Nine, Fourteen and Twenty-seven. Straight away we four commenced a careful selection process from among the younger sect members and trained them in the rudiments of the martial arts. This elite cadre of personnel are of course answerable to me and my three colleagues and not, as he still fondly imagines, to the preacher. It was then a simple matter to infiltrate a further twenty or so of our own people into positions of minor authority within the sect, to ensure total control of the personnel.

"With regard to the need for a secure base HQ for our further training and operational requirements, I examined the four religious retreats which the preacher had established within the city limits. These are large houses situated in quiet suburban areas, where the wealthier of his followers can attend to relieve their souls of their burden of accumulated guilt ... and their bank accounts of their burden of accumulated wealth. Our tame preacher has a talent for both of these achievements, it seems."

Angel One's cynical observation was rewarded by a wheezing chuckle from his unseen listener and he permitted himself a sardonic smile of acknowledgement before continuing his narrative.

"However, none of these properties was entirely satisfactory for my purposes. In selecting a base from which to operate, security was the paramount consideration. It had to be secluded and remote from the city, to protect against surveillance or attack by any potential enemy ... from either side of the law! At the same time, it had to be reasonably accessible to the city to facilitate movement of personnel and supplies, for distribution of our merchandise.

"Soon, the ideal place was located after discreet inquiries among some of the preacher's wealthier devotees. A former hotel, situated well to the north of the city but within easy driving distance. It also provided a direct link on our Montreal – New York supply route, which was an added bonus. This has meant that it now also serves our Triad as the main reception and distribution depot for all merchandise entering from Canada.

"The building itself commanded its own extensive grounds, with good perimeter security which we have refined and intensified ... although no system is infallible." Reluctantly he added this last qualification, as he suddenly recalled his impending report on the Jim Miller escapade of the previous night.

Once again he felt a stir of cold anger against the boy. The entire summary he was presenting to this powerful personage would have would have been one of untarnished success, but for the necessity of reporting the escape incident. For an instant he considered keeping the whole thing under wraps but just as quickly discarded the idea for two reasons.

Firstly, he was duty bound to report anything – no matter how trivial it seemed – which might in any way interfere with or put at risk the multi-million dollar movement of drugs, especially heroin, via his base on the main Montreal – New York run.

Secondly, he was certain that even if he himself did not mention the incident, and the subsequent police involvement, one of his three fellow 'Angels' would, when making their own individual reports to Dragon Control. The Triad leadership trusted no-one implicitly. Regular safety checks and balances, and inter-agent surveillance, were the order of the day. Which was one reason why they were fast becoming a serious rival to the long-established crime syndicate of the Mafia in the USA and a growing thorn in the flesh of the law enforcement authorities not only in America but also in many other countries, world-wide.

"And that," he concluded, with another respectful nod in the direction of the camera, "is how Dragon Base Red came to be set up, Director."

"Thank you, Sixteen. You have indeed done well," wheezed the Director's voice in reply. "I have only a couple of questions to clarify some points for my own information. This property you have acquired, what is its official cover, should questions ever be asked by the authorities?"

"It is officially known as Bethlehem House, Director," Angel One replied. "It is registered as a private sanatorium for mentally ill patients, run by the religious sect. The preacher himself goes along willingly with this deception but believes it is really a secret base for the training of new converts, which as you now know, is quite close to the truth."

"Good," replied the disembodied voice approvingly. "And how exactly do you use this religious sect to sell drugs on the streets of Manhattan?"

"I have set up distribution outlets using mobile soup kitchens, large vans, run by the sect," Angel One began. "We use only our own carefully selected and trained sect personnel as distribution agents, to supply the drugs from these vans to the pushers on the streets. No outside purchaser of our drugs has any knowledge of where his dealer obtains his supplies. We use a two- and sometimes a three-man cut-out system, by means of which the merchandise is always passed on through at least two separate persons before reaching the pusher.

"Thus, were one of our people to be picked up by the police, the link in the chain of supply would immediately be broken and would lead nowhere. They are all well aware of the dire consequences which will be suffered by anyone foolish enough to talk! In the unlikely event of one of the vans being implicated, the Agent on duty in it would accept full personal responsibility and the preacher's reaction when questioned would be one of shock and innocent outrage, which would be quite genuine on his part, as he has no knowledge of our operation. By the time any police inquiries reached Dragon Base Red at Bethlehem House, it would of course be completely clean. That is a very simple outline of our organisation at street level, Director."

"Excellent ... excellent," wheezed the voice of the unseen executive. "You have displayed commendable imagination and initiative, Agent Red Sixteen, and first class organisational qualities. But have you run into no snags along the way? For instance, is there no danger of this ... preacher ... becoming suspicious of your real activities and perhaps becoming a problem as a result?"

Angel One recognised a scapegoat when one crossed his path

and he grabbed this one gratefully by the horns. "As a matter of fact, Director, he has recently become something of a problem as you suggest, albeit indirectly. In fact, my routine report tonight to the Controller concerns a minor complication which has arisen as a result of the preacher's sometimes erratic behaviour. It necessitates my perhaps having to request a slight delay in the timing of our next shipment, which is due to arrive in the next few days."

"Complication? Delay?" This time it was the Controller's sibilant voice which replied from the speaker. "Such a request would be highly irregular. Unprecedented, in fact!" A cutting edge sharpened the silky tones as he continued, "You know how much money is involved in such a major shipment, Sixteen. Not to mention the inconvenience which would be caused at the Canadian end of our operation. A great deal of inconvenience on this occasion, I might emphasise! Crane Control in Montreal would also be sure to protest against such a requested delay."

The Controller's voice ceased on this disgruntled note. The silence which followed lengthened into almost a minute. Angel One sat immobile, not a muscle moving in his impassive face to betray the anger he felt at having to accept this censure from the smooth Taiwanese turdbrain at the other end of the microphone. His anger was double-edged, directed both against Jim Miller for causing him this humiliation, and also against the Controller for making the most of the opportunity to rub it in.

He sensed an underlying malicious glee in the man's attitude. It manifested itself not so much in his actual tone of voice, but more in the fact that he was so obviously relishing the opportunity of bringing his ambitious subordinate back to earth again in the face of the Director's praise. The Controller's next words confirmed this, when he finally broke the long silence.

"Sixteen, this request for a delay in our arrangements is all the more surprising, in that it originates from your section. Especially as we have just been hearing how it has been run so efficiently … until now!"

Another long pause followed. It deepened and became a void into which Angel One wished he could sink to avoid the embarrassment of further loss of face. Then the Controller suddenly demanded, "Exactly what is this ... minor complication ... you speak of? If of a minor nature only, why does it necessitate a delay in the movement of our next shipment from Montreal? I think you had better make your report now, with a full explanation of this. Go ahead, please!"

Angel One had felt himself beginning to sweat under the silken lash of the Controller's tongue. Now he had arrived at the moment he had been dreading. Again anger stirred within him and he silently vowed to exact retribution from the Miller brat, who had caused him this embarrassment. But he showed none of this outwardly, calming himself with a few deep breaths and a fierce effort of will, until he had his body and mind under iron control once more. When he answered he spoke dispassionately, choosing his words with care, his harsh voice conveying neither defiance nor subservience.

"Certainly, Controller. The problem has arisen like this. You will recall I explained to the Director that the man who nominally runs the sect is a religious fanatic. He is, like others of his kind, mentally unstable to a certain degree. In his case, this manifests itself in his belief that he is a prophet ... a sort of holy man ... of his Christian god. He is encouraged in this self delusion by most of his followers, who regard him as some kind of divinely inspired messenger. To the general public and the mass media he is merely another harmless crank, making a fortune from peddling religion to the masses.

However, he is useful to us in two ways. The media focus their attention upon him and his ridiculous posturing and so he provides us with an ideal front for our drugs operation. Also, his undeniable charisma makes him a rallying point for discontented and rootless teenagers, who in turn provide us with a pool of impressionable raw material. As I have explained, by careful selection and training we are able to encourage and redirect their fanaticism and violence to serve our purposes, quite unknown to him. Undoubtedly our recruiting rate would drop considerably without him.

"That is the credit side. On the debit side, his deteriorating mental state means he periodically undergoes a complete personality change, during which he becomes withdrawn and hostile, exhibiting symptoms of paranoid suspicion towards everyone around him. These periods are occurring with increasing frequency and are resulting in some of the newer recruits becoming quickly disillusioned, when they find their newly discovered god has feet of clay. Discipline has had to be tightened to clamp down on discontent. We have had half a dozen or so attempts to escape from the Base. All of those who have run have been new members, none of them possessing any knowledge which could have posed any real threat to us ..."

"So far!" The Controller's soft voice interjected pointedly. "But," his tone sharpened, "it would seem to me that it must only be a matter of time before this happens ..."

"On the other hand," the Controller was interrupted in turn by the high-pitched, wheezing voice of the Director, "no organisation such as ours is ever completely free from problems. Even the mightiest river can be dammed by the flotsam it disturbs when it is in flood. It is also said that the strength of a tree can only be fully tested by a storm. So, it would seem to me ..." he parodied the Controller's own words, "the reliability, or otherwise, of Agent Red Sixteen's organisation will now be proved by its ability to overcome problems, as and when these arise."

"You are correct, of course, Director," replied the Controller unctuously. "Please continue your report, Sixteen."

Angel One mentally thanked the Director for coming to his aid with the mild rebuke he had issued to the Controller. At the same time, he knew the latter would resent it. Those in positions of authority never like having an underling who is in favour with someone more powerful. Making a mental note to cultivate the Director's support for the future, Angel One continued with his report.

"Two nights ago, another two new members attempted to escape. One failed even to get clear of the grounds. He was caught and killed by our guard dogs. The other was quickly recaptured a few miles from Base, but not before he had managed to reach a phone and call his parents. However, he only had time to tell them he was on his way home, before I silenced him ..."

"Permanently?" inquired the Director.

"No, Director. It was not expedient to do so at the time. There could have been witnesses. It was too public a location. Once back at Base, I interrogated the youth and placed him in close confinement to await execution. This will be carried out once I am satisfied we are clear of any possible outside interference."

"I see. Good. Please continue," the Director's voice instructed.

Angel One took a sip of iced water from the glass by his side, then continued. "The phone call he made did, however, result in the youth's parents becoming worried when he did not arrive home and it seems they hired a private investigator to search for him. This person appeared this afternoon, accompanied by the local county sheriff. They have requested an interview with the youth and have been told they will be given an answer tomorrow forenoon. This interview will be granted and will present no problem. The youth in question will be thoroughly compliant by then. The sheriff is already of the pre-conceived opinion that he will be visiting a mentally disturbed patient in a sanatorium. So, he will present no problem.

"The problem I referred to is the private investigator. From time to time, we have had to discourage other such mercenary snoopers in the past. In the process, we have learned that they are a remarkably tenacious breed of pest, once they scent anything they consider at all suspicious. This one has been astute enough to seek the co-operation and – so he imagines – the protection of the local sheriff. From past experience of his kind, I fully expect he will return to snoop around on his own … which is when he will be dealt with! This, in fact, is the reason for my requesting a delay in the next shipment – of two to three days only – until the private investigator can be eliminated as a future threat. This concludes my report."

A silence of several minutes duration ensued, while the two unseen officials discussed the information they had just received and considered the request. Then the Controller's voice sounded again.

"Very well, Sixteen. Your request for a temporary delay in the Montreal shipment is granted, despite the great inconvenience this will cause to all concerned. However, you should still do your best to remove this problem in time for the shipment to go ahead on schedule, if this is at all possible. You will inform me immediately of all developments."

"Of course, Controller." Angel One nodded stiffly towards the unblinking eye of the camera.

After another short pause, the bland voice of the Controller continued. "You said the youth in question will be thoroughly compliant by the time of the proposed interview with the sheriff and the private investigator. How sure are you of this ... that you can avert their suspicion and thus avoid further serious complications?"

"I can guarantee it," Angel One replied confidently.

"With your life?" The silken tone of the question belied the threat behind the words.

Too late, Angel One saw the trap the Controller had led him into. His relief at having got the awkward part of his report behind him, had made him incautious. Cursing himself for his stupidity, he hesitated only fractionally before replying evenly, "Yes. If necessary ... with my life."

"Oh, make no mistake, Sixteen," the Controller shot back. "If you fail and this results in any interference with the Montreal shipment ... then it will become necessary. You know the price our organisation demands for serious failure."

Before Angel One could react to this, the wheezing voice of the Director put in, "This is true. But, I feel sure that such a drastic penalty will not be necessary in this case. I have every confidence that Agent Red Sixteen will solve his problem, if he continues to act with the same degree of efficiency as he has shown to date in the setting up and running of his section of our organisation."

Once again a timely intervention had come from this unexpected quarter. The possibility occurred to Angel One that perhaps the Director felt the same antipathy towards the suave, self-assured Controller as he did himself. Or maybe it was his way of keeping his assistant executives in check, by seeming to show favour to their subordinates in certain circumstances, so as to indicate subtly that no-one's position was invulnerable.

The Director's voice continued, "However, Agent Red Sixteen, I must point out that the Controller is also correct to display concern over the possibility of anything going wrong, which might adversely affect the coming shipment. You see, the efficiency with which you have run your section to date, has led to a decision being made to channel a double consignment through your base on this occasion. This is due to an unforeseen emergency which has arisen. The Controller will explain ..."

"Certainly, Director." The Controller agreed promptly and took over. "The situation which has arisen is this, Sixteen. Tiger Control have requested our aid in re-routing their next shipment, which was due to arrive and be unloaded in the Chicago Docks, weather permitting, three or four nights from now. However, it seems that a labour dispute has brought the Chicago Docks to a standstill, and this strike looks as though it may take some time to resolve.

"So, Tiger Control have decided it would be expedient to divert their consignment to our arrival port of Montreal, rather than risk it being trapped for an indefinite period in the strikebound Chicago Docks. I did not envisage any difficulty arising from lending our aid and so have already agreed to their request. I have decided that it will be better to move both consignments, theirs and ours, at the same time, even though this will necessitate doubling the capacity of your normal transport arrangements. I consider this will be less risky than moving them separately, within a day or two of each another.

"Now perhaps you understand why your disturbing report, coupled to your request for a delay in delivery, will cause us much inconvenience. Not to mention the loss of face for Dragon Control, should we have to admit that any delay in the movement of millions of dollars worth of merchandise, was due to our inability to deal with the minor problems of a runaway boy and an inquisitive private detective!"

The barbed remark struck home. With an effort of will Angel One managed to hide his anger and maintain an outward calm. It was the Director's voice which broke the ensuing charged silence.

"Before we finish, Agent Red Sixteen, a thought has occurred

to me regarding one of the problems you mentioned earlier …
namely that of the increasing mental instability of this preacher
who fronts the sect. As I understand it, this strange Christian
God he follows, a carpenter by profession I believe, was becoming
something of a thorn in the flesh of the authorities of his day,
which was why they decided to execute him. By all accounts,
up until then this carpenter's following was limited to only a
few thousands in the region now largely occupied by modern
Israel.

"History records that both of these factors were altered
radically by virtue of his death. On the one hand, he was removed
as a threat, both as an heretical innovator of Judaism and also
as a potential revolutionary leader against the Romans. On the
other, his martyrdom gained him untold thousands, then
millions, of converts and eventually ensured his deification as
leader of a world-wide religion.

"Now, it occurs to me that perhaps a parallel could be drawn
here. Let us speculate that if you were to choose the correct
moment and arrange a convenient … accident … then your
preacher would cease to be a problem to you, on the one hand,
while on the other he will attain the status of pseudo martyrdom,
which I feel sure will guarantee the continued influx of converts
for your recruiting material. Many of the youth of this country
seem to be morbidly attracted to dead heroes in the world of
entertainment, so you would be following a trend, rather than
creating a precedent. I would be interested to hear your views
on this little theory of mine, Agent Red Sixteen."

Angel One allowed a slight smile to touch his lips as he nodded
respectfully towards the camera lens.

"I agree with you that getting rid of the preacher would be
beneficial, seeing as how his nuisance value is beginning to
outweigh his usefulness," he began. "I also take your point on
the matter of his death turning him into a martyr in the eyes of
those gullible enough to follow him in the first place. As a
matter of fact, the idea of just such a … martyrdom, as you put
it … has occurred to me recently. So, I shall give your suggestion
serious consideration, Director."

There was a pause, then the Controller's voice said briskly,

"Well, that concludes our business for the time being, Sixteen. You will be informed when the double shipment is ready for transportation from Montreal. The date and time for your rendezvous at the pick-up point will then be arranged as soon as you have eliminated your present problems and have everything under control again. You will inform me immediately you are ready to move."

"Of course, Controller," Angel One replied. He remained seated for a few seconds until he was sure the interview had ended. When nothing further issued from the speaker on the far wall, he rose to await his escort. He turned to face the door but had taken only a single pace towards it when he was drawn up by the Controller's voice sounding again from behind him. Angel One instantly guessed that the Director had already left whichever room they had been in – the Controller's words confirmed it.

"Oh, Sixteen … before you leave … I have arranged a little entertainment in honour of our new Director. A small diversion to amuse him. I should like you to witness it also." Angel One remained motionless, his back to the camera, waiting. The soft voice took on a tone of menace as it continued, "It should prove … educational … to you, as well as entertaining, I think. And be warned … if ever I have to call upon you to redeem your guarantee, then tonight you may also be witnessing your own future!" The speaker went dead.

If the Controller had noticed Angel One's deliberate insult of keeping his back to the camera, he chose to ignore it. The instant he finished speaking, the electronic lock clicked and the door swung silently open to reveal the senior house guard. He left with him and was led back along the first floor gallery, past the head of the wide staircase, to another door on the opposite wing of the house, which the guard signalled to be unlocked. Once again, from the moment the two men left the interview room, they had been silently tracked by the remote-control cameras high in the gallery ceiling. In this lair of the Gold Dragon Triad, security was absolute.

As before, Angel One was politely motioned to enter alone and upon doing so, saw to his surprise that he had entered a narrow viewing gallery, with a triple tier of comfortably padded seats with arm rests, half a dozen seats to a row, facing an outward sloping plate-glass viewing window. The glass was thick, probably armour plate Angel One thought, and tinted a smoky brown to provide a 'one-way' effect.

The gallery looked down on a large empty room, some twelve feet below. The room was about thirty feet square, and the entire surface of the floor was covered by a padded white canvas mat, effectively creating a martial arts combat arena. Angel One's examination of his surroundings were interrupted by the Controller's voice sounding from a speaker set in the wall at the far end of the viewing gallery.

"Be seated, Sixteen. You are about to witness an execution ordered by our Executive Council. As I said earlier, I think you will find it educational as well as entertaining. Especially in view of the guarantee you have given regarding the success of this next shipment – and the price of failure!"

29

ANGEL ONE SHRUGGED OFF THE THINLY DISGUISED threat implicit in the Controller's words, and settled himself in one of the front row seats. In his opinion the man was a fool and he felt nothing but contempt for him. One should always properly assess one's potential enemies, before issuing threats. A strong adversary would only be forewarned of your hostility towards him and be doubly on his guard against you. It may even be counter productive, if he decided to neutralise the threat you posed by attacking first!

Examining the structure and lay-out of the arena spread out before his interested gaze, Angel One observed that the upper levels of its other three sides were occupied by similar large tinted glass viewing windows. This meant that the arena below was overlooked by four separate but identical viewing galleries.

Looking across at the gallery directly opposite, Angel One made out the two indistinct shapes, one slim and one bulky, seated behind the dark angled glass. He assumed these to be the figures of the Controller and Director.

At that moment, the Controller's voice sounded again from the speaker on the rear wall. "The execution you are about to observe, Sixteen, will take the form of a gladiatorial combat ... to the death ... between two condemned men! One of them will inevitably die. The other, if he survives any injuries he may receive, will live ... but only to fight again ... and again ... repeatedly, until he in his turn, is eventually defeated and killed. Appropriate, don't you think?

"But I must confess I borrowed the idea from a British comic opera set in medieval Japan. In it, the leader of Japan, the Mikado, being opposed to capital punishment, devises an ingenious scheme to stop executions. He does this by appointing to the office of Lord High Executioner, the condemned criminal who is next on the list for execution. This of course means the state has an executioner who cannot behead anyone else, until he has first beheaded himself!

"I was intrigued by this amusing concept, and amended it to serve our own purposes. In our scheme of things, both the Executioner and his intended victim are condemned men, as in the original – but the difference is, our Executioner is required to meet his intended victim in mortal combat. Thus, his only chance of prolonging his own life, is to continue defeating each successive opponent in turn. The intended victim, on the other hand, thus becomes a challenger for the post, so the only way he can win it is by killing the Executioner.

"While each successive Executioner survives, he is well fed and treated, and accorded proper training facilities to keep his combat skills honed. However, there is one handicap imposed on him each time he faces an opponent ... namely it is the opponent who is given the choice of weapons suitable for hand-to-hand combat. He may, of course, choose none at all, if he is skilled in kung fu, say, or karate. Tonight, the current Executioner's opponent has chosen the Japanese katana, more popularly known as the samurai sword. It should make for an entertaining spectacle."

As the Controller spoke these final words, two flush-fitting doors opened simultaneously in opposite walls of the combat arena below. Angel One saw two white jacketed house guards enter, each man carrying an unsheathed katana, the two-handed Japanese fighting sword, the weapon of the samurai warriors of a bygone age. Each guard halted a few paces inside the arena, laid the swords on the mat, then turned and left.

Immediately, two new figures entered the arena. One was clad in a black, loose fitting combat suit, of the type worn in judo or karate bouts. Depicted on the back of the jacket, picked out in gold and red silk, was a coiled dragon, spitting flame and rearing to strike. The other wore a plain white combat suit, bearing no motif of any kind. Both were barefoot, and like the guards before them, they were Chinese. In their early twenties, the two were of slim build and looked fit.

The moment the two men entered, the doors closed behind them, locking them securely in the combat arena with grim finality. Watching one another warily, each man stooped and picked up the naked sword at his feet. The razor sharp steel of the long blades glinted wickedly in the bright overhead lighting. Despite his contempt for the Controller's barbaric concept of forcing two men to fight to the death for the entertainment of an unseen audience in the galleries above, Angel One still felt a stir of primitive excitement deep in his gut.

The two combatants advanced slowly and stopped about six feet from one another. The Executioner, in the black suit with the dragon motif, was now seen to be the taller by a couple of inches, which would give him a useful reach advantage over his shorter, white clad opponent. They faced each other, eyes locked, and stood immobile for several seconds. Each man knew he was probably looking Death in the eye, but neither wavered in his level gaze. Then the white clad challenger made a formal half bow to his opponent, who acknowledged by bowing in return.

Suddenly, formalities over, both men snapped into the ready position, one foot advanced, arms raised, elbows bent, the double handed grip aiming the point of the sword high over the right shoulder. It looked an awkward stance, but in reality each swordsman was perfectly balanced – the weapon fusing with the man behind it to form a single killing entity of muscle and steel.

Slowly they began to circle clockwise to the left, cat-footed, each man stepped carefully, watchful for an opening or for a surprise move by his adversary. Suddenly, both men attacked simultaneously in a blur of movement, feinting, slashing, parrying, the flashing blades glittering like silver-blue fire as they whirled and clashed. Then, just as suddenly they disengaged and leapt apart again and resumed their slow circling.

Twice more in quick succession the two combatants engaged each other, their gleaming blades whirling and clanging as each lethal stroke was parried. Twice more they disengaged and continued their slow, circling dance of death.

Then the challenger feinted a sudden thrust at his opponent's throat, but with lightning speed and iron muscled wrist strength, changed the attack to a looping downward slash to the right side of the neck. The black clad Executioner blocked both moves, the tempered steel ringing as the blades met, then equally swiftly, he changed his own parry into a sweeping slash at his opponent's left rib-cage.

But his intended target was no longer there, as the agile white clad figure leapt back outside the deadly arc of ice-cold fire, which was the flashing blade of his opponent. Not quite fast enough, though. Either that, or he had misjudged the other's superior reach, for the tip of the sword sliced neatly through the white material of his loose fitting top. A thin line of scarlet blossomed in the wake of the razor sharp steel, as it gashed the skin across his lower abdomen.

The Executioner's eyes narrowed as he saw the gaping slit in the front of his opponent's jacket, and the blood oozing from the shallow cut to form a spreading red stain on the white material below it. Encouraged, he launched a determined attack using a bewildering variety of strokes and combinations. His long blade moved with eye-blurring speed, as figure-of-eight cuts alternated with downward and upward diagonal slashes and side sweeps in lightning succession. The two ancient blades clashed and rang, singing out their metallic death songs with clear, bell-like notes, as their perfectly tempered steel vibrated and whined like two yard long tuning forks.

The challenger parried each stroke skilfully but he was now definitely on the defensive. A touch of demoralisation seemed to have crept into his demeanour as a result of his opponent's having drawn first blood. The other, for his part, seemed to grow in confidence, sensing victory was his for the taking and pressed home his attacks with increasing ferocity. By now, the faces of both men were glistening with a sheen of sweat as they fought. The gold and scarlet dragon on the Executioner's back writhed with surrogate life on its black ground, as the man's muscular shoulders worked to maintain the smooth sweeping momentum of his whirring blade.

In the viewing gallery above, Angel One tensed in sudden anticipation as the challenger made a potentially fatal error in his desperate defence, a clumsy parry, which momentarily left him open to a downward diagonal stroke to the joint of his neck and left shoulder. The opening was only presented for a split second, but to a swordmaster a split second is all the time that is required – the hair's breadth margin between life and death.

The Japanese katana is primarily a slashing weapon. Its single edged, perfectly balanced blade is mainly wielded in an inward cutting motion, as the long handle is jerked down and inwards towards the wielder's midriff. The swordsman relies on his strength of wrist arm and shoulder as he swings, slashes, sweeps and cuts with his weapon, each stroke flowing smoothly into the next in perfect harmony of movement and co-ordination.

The katana can also be used to thrust straight at an opponent, although the opportunity for doing so does not often occur in the Japanese style of swordplay. It requires perfect timing indeed to execute successfully the suicidal forward thrust, aimed at an opponent who is presenting a flashing steel figure-of-eight at you with a three foot blade in his extended reach. But, it is possible to employ the thrust against a careless or over confident opponent who leaves himself open to its deadly effect. It happened now!

The Executioner saw his adversary's momentary lapse,

recognised the opportunity to despatch him with a right to left diagonal down stroke, and reacted instantly. He let out an involuntary yell of triumph and leapt in for the kill, blade swept high to deliver the death blow.

The challenger reacted with the swiftness of a striking snake. The apparently faulty positioning of his sword was rectified in a flicker of movement. In the same blink of time, he followed through and thrust. His blade became a flash of forked lightning, almost too fast for the eye to follow, as he lunged forward and rammed it straight into his adversary's solar plexus.

The black clad figure of the Executioner stiffened, frozen in mid-movement, his sword still held high, as the deadly blade of his opponent sliced through his intestines and emerged behind him, the gold dragon on his back suddenly pierced by six inches of gleaming steel. The brutal tableau lasted for only a frozen instant, before the victor stepped back and jerked the blade free with a powerful wrench.

The stricken man swayed, the upheld sword slipping from his nerveless fingers to tumble harmlessly to the mat behind him. He sagged to his knees, staring at his nemesis in wide-eyed shock, his teeth bared and his hands clasped to his midriff against the fiery agony in his guts.

True to the ceremonial code of the master swordsman, the victor stepped back and bowed formally to the mortally wounded man in recognition of a worthy opponent. Incredibly, the dying man returned the gesture with a jerky nod of his head, which was all he could physically manage.

Twin rivulets of blood suddenly trickled from the corners of his mouth, and the dying man's eyes turned up in his head as he crashed forward onto his face. The white clad victor glanced down at the prostrate form at his feet, then up at the opaque viewing windows above him, his face flushed with triumph and his defiance clear from the arrogant set of his stance. Angel One guessed that the Controller was the target of the man's defiance. He smiled to himself.

At that moment, the flush-fitting doors in the walls opened again and four white jacketed house guards entered, two from either end of the arena. All were armed with snub-nosed machine pistols. One of the guards gestured with his gun to the victor, who stooped and coolly wiped the sword clean on his dead opponent's jacket, before laying it on the mat alongside his lifeless form.

Straightening up, he strode from the arena followed by the guards. The evening's entertainment was over. A new Executioner had won himself a temporary appointment to the post.

On the long drive back to Bethlehem House, Angel One analysed the evening's accumulation of data in his mind. It was now all too evident to him that he'd have to watch his step very carefully from now on, where his immediate superior, the Controller, was concerned. The man obviously resented his success in setting up and running the Bethlehem House base so efficiently, that it had become the main collection and distribution point for the Triad drugs supply for New York city. The Director's praise of his operation tonight, would serve only to increase that resentment.

In the event, the Controller's trapping him into guaranteeing the coming double shipment with his life, followed by the brutal demonstration in the death arena, had left him in no doubts as to the fate that awaited him should he fail.

So – three problems to be taken care of. First, the Miller boy. Once outside interest in him had waned, he must be liquidated to prevent any possible recurrence. Second, the private investigator who would be present at the interview with the boy. He must be warned off – or he too would have to be liquidated. But if it came to that, care would have to be exercised, as he obviously had police connections. Third, the Prophet. He had outlived his usefulness. Martyrdom, as the Director had put it, would be the best solution. An accident of some kind, perhaps?

He decided to call a policy meeting with his three fellow Orientals at Bethlehem House the following morning, to discuss all these subjects. The most important thing for the moment was the security of the forthcoming drugs shipment. The fact that Tiger Control's consignment was also being routed through Bethlehem House on this occasion, meant that his end of the operation would be under double scrutiny, which made it all the more important that nothing went wrong. He vowed grimly to himself that he would allow nothing, nor anyone, to stand in his way. He had staked his life on the outcome – so too would anyone who tried to interfere.

Strangely, Angel One gave no thought to the possibility of trouble from the Mafia – one of the Controller's main worries – as he drove on his way. Probably because they had, up till then, caused him no direct problems. This situation was to change ... that very night!

30

THE KILLER WAS STALKING THE STREETS OF THE CITY again – for the second consecutive night. His mind was filled once more by the pure flame of his holy mission. A flame fed by the raging furnace of need in his loins. An all-consuming, insatiable need to fulfil his mission – and himself – by cleansing the world of the stain of whoredom.

He could feel the sacred instrument of cleansing, snug in its sheath strapped securely to his left wrist. In his sick mind, it shared his holy mission, as though possessing a will of its own. Soon, it would slake its thirst on the tainted blood of a whore and in so doing would quench the fire of his own need. For a time.

It had never happened to him before so soon after a kill. But it was back as strong as ever – the bloodlust madness, which had overpowered his reason and taken possession of his entire being. And it was a lust for blood, in the most literal sense, which drove him. For his was the most dangerous of psychopathic disorders – his compulsion to kill was sexual. The only way he could free himself from its grip, was through the orgiastic release he attained when cutting the life from his chosen victim.

Tonight it had been the intense, emotion-charged atmosphere at the religious crusade which had triggered him off again, so soon after a cleansing. The exhilarating atmosphere created by the choral singing and the powerful sex-oriented sermon, coupled to the emotional mass hysteria of the audience response, had all combined to overwhelm and sweep aside his weakening hold on reality.

Once again his mind had slipped into the twilight zone of insanity. Like a rabid wolf, the urge to kill was gnawing at his sick brain with increasing ferocity, as he prowled the crowded streets of the city's night life, searching for a victim.

31

CARLA MENOTTI WAS BORED. ON IMPULSE SHE decided to indulge herself in her favourite pastime. She would go out and pick up the first man who attracted her, and bring him back to the apartment for a night of illicit sex. The risk she ran in doing this only served to heighten the pleasure she got.

A tall ash-blonde beauty with green eyes and a marvellous figure, she was that most privileged of whores, a kept woman. She had been a high class call girl, working from an expensive and discreet escort agency when she caught the fancy of Don Bruno Neroni, head of the Mafia Family of the same name who controlled most of the drugs, vice and loan sharking in Manhattan. A few decades earlier, she would have been called a gangster's moll – or in polite society, a mistress.

Neroni had installed her in a sumptuous Park Avenue penthouse apartment, filled with every luxury she could desire. It had the lot – sunken bath like a miniature swimming pool, TVs in every room, well-stocked bar, revolving circular bed, and a kitchen so full of gadgetry it looked like the set of a Star Wars movie.

ANGELS OF DEATH

He indulged her with exotic furs and expensive jewellery. He wined and dined her at New York's finest restaurants. He picked up the tab on all her bills and provided her with a generous monthly allowance most of which she promptly banked in a secret account against the day when she might fall from favour, or perhaps be supplanted by some new playmate. In any case, money was almost unnecessary to her. She had no need for ready cash, except for tipping. She could obtain anything she wanted, from cosmetics and clothing to furniture and food, by means of checking accounts in the top city stores.

All she had to do in return for this life of pampered luxury was to be his exclusive property, available whenever he wanted her. Whether it was to decorate his arm at some Broadway premiere, or to act the vivacious hostess at one of the glittering parties he threw from time to time for visiting Dons, or for sex. Neroni did not make excessive demands on her, in this last respect. In sexual matters he was an old-fashioned romantic. When he wished to share her bed, which he did on average about once a fortnight, she received discreet advance warning of an intended evening visit in the form of a single red rose, delivered by special messenger earlier in the day.

In the early months of their relationship, Carla had been worried by the delicate problem of how she would put him off without causing offence or embarrassment, should one of his proposed visits coincide with her menstrual cycle. It had never happened, though. She had thought of it as just fortunate timing on his part, until the reason had dawned on her. The reason had turned out to be her flat-mate, constant male companion-cum-chaperone and personal bodyguard, Giovanni Furino.

Bruno Neroni was not only old fashioned in matters of romance. He was also an old fashioned Sicilian male where his womenfolk were concerned – extremely possessive and intensely jealous. Anyone foolish or suicidal enough to meddle with Neroni's woman would be a dead man.

But the loss of face, the loss of respect, would be a stain of dishonour no revenge could erase. That would be the worst of it for a Sicilian who had been made to wear horns – who had been made uno becco – a cuckold! Prevention was better than cure in situations like this. To this end, Neroni had carefully chosen a trusted lieutenant from his organisation to act as a combined chaperone and bodyguard.

Furino was no eunuch, but for such a trusted position he was the next best thing. He was a homosexual. He was also one of the Family's top button men. He was only 25 years old, but had 'made his bones' with his first killing, five years before in the most spectacular manner. He had used his initiative, allied to his dark, girlish good looks and slim figure, to take out a caporegime of the rival Tardelli Family and so bring himself to the notice of his Don.

It had come about during one of the periodic short, vicious, inter-Family wars, which erupted from time to time over disputed territories or control over certain areas of crime. The Tardelli Family had started to encroach on Neroni territory in the vice world. Pimps had been beaten up, brothels smashed and closed down, and girls warned off or even taken over – all the usual methods of harassment employed in muscling in on a rival mob's rackets.

The Tardelli caporegime in charge of the take-over operation, one Renato Milanese, had proved a wily and ruthless opponent, and had hit the Neroni Family time and again with seeming impunity. Several of their soldiers had been gunned down, but any counter-strikes the Family attempted were ineffectual. He always kept one jump ahead. So, Don Bruno had put out a contract on Milanese. But he proved a difficult and dangerous target.

Three times, out-of-state 'specialists' were imported to make the hit. On each occasion they disappeared without trace. Finally, when no more outsiders wanted to know, in a fury of frustration Neroni put the word out to the Family hitmen – fifty thousand dollars and advancement in the organisation awaited anyone who killed Milanese.

Young Giovanni Furino had seen his chance to make an early name for himself. He approached Neroni with a devastatingly simple plan which, if successful, would get him within striking distance of the closely guarded Milanese. The Don had heard him out, at first incredulous, then latterly chortling with amusement at the sheer audaciousness of the scheme. He granted permission for the attempt to be made and ordered full support as required by Furino.

The hit was planned to take place in Milanese's favourite eating spot, Fornari's Neapolitan Restaurant in Mott Street, in the heart of the city's Little Italy district. Furino, stunningly attractive in female wig, clothing and make-up, had entered the restaurant on the arm of an unsuspecting young Tardelli hood. He had carefully picked out this stooge in a nearby Tardelli owned bar an hour previously, given him the eye, and then allowed himself to be picked by the young punk. In his shoulder bag, Furino carried two US Army-issue grenades and a .38 short-barrelled, untraceable Saturday Night Special.

Everything had gone like clockwork. After he had been in the restaurant a matter of ten minutes, a car roared past the front of Fornari's and sprayed it with machine-gun fire – causing the entire clientele to dive for cover under their tables. Milanese's table, where he always sat with his ever-present four-man bodyguard, was situated far back in a secluded corner of the restaurant, from which vantage point he could scrutinise everyone who entered. When everyone in the restaurant had dived to the floor, young Furino had quickly drawn the gun and a grenade from his bag. Under cover of the noise of gunfire, screaming, and shattering glass, he calmly shot his escort in the head and, rising to one nylon clad knee, drew the pin from the grenade and lobbed it into Milanese's corner. He had not needed to use the second grenade!

He made his escape by joining the frantic exodus of panic stricken customers and staff from the blazing restaurant and jumping into a waiting getaway car half a block away. Exit Renato Milanese. Enter the rising star of one Giovanni Furino. Because of his known sexual preferences, his fellow members of the Neroni Family referred to him as Gina The Fruit – but never to his face or in his hearing!

He had quickly progressed from that time to become an expert with the knife and the garrotte. He preferred the latter. It was a more personal and sensual way of killing his victim and especially suited to the strong streak of sadism present in his nature.

In one respect, Furino completely justified his Don's trust in him. He would never have dreamt of taking advantage of his position as resident chaperone-cum-bodyguard, by making any physical advances towards his beautiful charge. The prospect of sexual relations with a female held no attraction for him.

Instead, a quite different relationship had grown up between the lonely courtesan and her live-in companion. They had become genuinely fond of one another in a purely platonic way, and an almost sisterly bond had cemented their friendship over the twelve months they had been flatmates.

Carla had eventually confided to Furino that she was bored and frustrated with the sybaritic isolation of her gilded cage. But, she had also added, she did not want to risk losing everything. She wanted the best of both worlds, if it were possible. She was a passionate woman with a healthy sexual appetite and her once a fortnight assignation with Neroni only whetted that appetite.

"Well, don't smoulder at me, cara mia, you're just not my scene at all," he had replied flippantly. Serious again, he had regarded her pensively for a time, then he had asked casually, "You on the pill, Carla?"

When she had admitted that she was, he had raised his eyebrows in exaggerated surprise and drawn her a knowing look. "M-m-m! And you a good Catholic Italian girl, too," he remarked in a tone of mock censure. "So that's what you get up to with that cute little Irish priest in the confessional on Sundays! I know what I'd like to get up to with him ..." He had winked lewdly as she giggled at him.

"Tell you what, prediletta, I'll make a deal with you," he'd continued, serious again. "I like to keep up to date on the Family affairs. You know ... who's moving up, who's out of favour ... that sort of thing. You must hear a lot at those fancy little dinner parties you host so brilliantly. The Dons tend to guard their tongues when little Gina the Fruit's nearby, but they think nothing of speaking freely in front of a beautiful ornament – which is where you come in.

"I intend to get on in the Family, but I don't think your sugar-daddy, our esteemed Don, sees me as anything other than a useful bodyguard for your lovely self these days. The thought of Gina the Fruit as a future caporegime just never occurs to him. In fact, I get the distinct impression that deep in his black, macho Sicilian male heart, he doesn't entirely approve of lil' 'ol me," he had pouted exaggeratedly. "He's an old fashioned Sicilian mafioso, with old fashioned standards of sexual morality. You're his one concession to the fact that he's only human and needs to get his rocks off with someone more attractive than his fat little cow of a wife. As a result, you're his blind spot." He had paused for her comments.

Carla had regarded him shrewdly for a moment, then had said, "Okay, that's my side of the bargain. What's yours?"

"You get to spread your wings, my pretty caged bird ... and your legs!" He had grinned wickedly. "Provided, of course, that you're discreet about it. If we ever got found out, he'd have my balls ... and I do still have a use for them, I assure you. In fact, I'm quite attached to them, you might say, and I intend to stay that way!"

So, the bargain had been struck. Furino got what he wanted – inside information on Family matters, to use as he saw fit towards furthering his future ambitions. And Carla got what she wanted – sex. She would frequent favourite little clubs and night spots that she knew the Don wouldn't be seen dead in, until she picked up a man she fancied. All the time expertly shadowed by her faithful protector.

She would then take her chosen companion back to the penthouse, having explained that her 'husband' was out of town for the night, to prevent any unwelcome attempts to visit her again. Furino would tail them and slip unnoticed into the apartment a few discreet minutes later. Retiring quietly to his own private rooms, he would remain alert and on call should he be needed, until after the client had departed.

So, it transpired that fateful night, that even as Carla Menotti was on the prowl for an acceptable male partner to satisfy the

natural urge of her sexuality, the killer was also on the prowl –
for a suitable female victim to satiate the unnatural compulsion
of his bloodlust.

They met while Carla was hesitating briefly on the sidewalk,
undecided over which of two adjacent night-spots to try first.
She had looked up and suddenly he was there. He was standing
looking straight at her, as though he'd found someone he'd
been looking for. She raised a quizzical eyebrow, slightly taken
aback by the directness of his gaze. He smiled.

She liked what she saw. He was tall and smartly dressed in
heavy black overcoat, black Homburg and gleaming black shoes.
The white silk scarf at his throat gave him a touch of slightly
dated elegance. When he smiled, his strong-jawed face looked
remarkably young in contrast to the silvery grey sideburns
showing under his hat brim. She smiled back.

He knew he had found what he'd been seeking, the moment
he saw her. She was beautiful and expensively dressed, but he
recognised her for what she was. Perhaps it was her posture, the
confident way she carried herself, maybe even the faintest
suggestion of self assured hardness in her. Whatever the
indefinable something was, the moment she had looked at him
and held his gaze, the boldness in her eyes confirmed what he
already knew. The demon in his sick brain whispered it.
"Whore!"

His smile had been quite unconscious, more one of triumph
and anticipation at having found a potential victim, than
anything directed at her in the way of a friendly overture. When
she smiled back at him, he felt a calmness spread over his mind
and flood down through his body, damping down the raging
hellfire which was coursing through his veins to feed the carnal
furnace in his loins. It was the coolness of the hunting predator,
which stills the gnawing hunger in its belly when it scents a prey,
leaving the brain clear and the muscles responsive for the chase
and the kill.

When he spoke, neither his voice nor manner betrayed any
trace of the madness in him. He tipped his hat, slightly inclining
his upper body towards her in a gesture of old world courtesy and
remarked conversationally, "Beautiful night for a stroll, is it

not? Who'd have thought it possible, after the fog of last night?"

She was fascinated by him and felt attracted by the rich, pleasant tone of his voice. At the same time, she was also secretly amused at his old-fashioned manners and speech, and playfully responded in the same mode, but without it being obvious enough to give offence.

"Yes, it is a lovely night. I don't know about strolling, though. It's a pleasure I can't indulge myself in too often ... muggers, you know? I'm afraid unescorted lady pedestrians can't stroll very far in our wonderful city in these enlightened times, without fear of being accosted."

If he sensed her gentle mockery, he took no offence. "Then, please permit me ..." He offered his arm with a courtly little bow. "I'd be honoured if you would pay me the compliment of allowing me to escort you for a short stroll. Let us share our company for a few blocks."

"Thank you, kind sir," she laughed and slipped her arm through his. "I'd be delighted to accompany you. I only seem to see the city through cab windows these days." They set off together, strolling slowly along, chatting about anything and everything, Carla doing most of the talking without realising it.

While they strolled along, seemingly in no particular direction, Carla gradually steered her companion in the direction of Fifth Avenue and her penthouse suite. When they had reached a point only a few blocks away from it, she suddenly expressed surprise and announced the fact that they were almost on her doorstep, so to speak, and invited him up for "a night-cap". At the same time, she gave him the benefit of a full 10,000 volts from her beautiful green eyes.

For his part, he had realised right away with unerring instinct, that he'd been picked up for the purpose of a sexual liaison. The demon stirred within him at the thought and his pulse quickened with unholy anticipation as he accompanied her. All the while, he stifled his irritation at her incessant, inane chatter, forcing himself to be attentive and patient and to play out the tiresome charade for as long as was necessary.

He courteously accepted her offer of a night-cap in the full recognition of what lay behind it. She did not fool him with her airs and graces. He knew with certainty she was only really interested in fornication. She was like a bitch in heat, as were all her kind, he thought with growing anger. Whores all!

These, and similar thoughts, were whispering through his diseased mind, fanning the glowing embers of his righteous wrath into flickering life, as they entered the spacious foyer of the luxury apartment block. By the time he had steered her past a group of chattering, laughing couples who were leaving the building and into the elevator, quite unnoticed by the uniformed security guard, he was silently thanking God for delivering another harlot into his cleansing hands ...

Furino, following Carla at a safe distance as he always did on these occasions, saw her make the pick up. A small frown clouded his thin, handsome face. He had never known her pick someone up in the street before tonight. Usually she did this in the seclusion of a night-spot, having spent some time vetting the available talent, before choosing someone who took her fancy.

Poor kid, he thought. She must have the itch bad tonight. Still, he shrugged mentally, I suppose she knows what she wants. If it turns out the guy can't perform to order, and this one looks a bit on the ripe side to say the least, that's her funeral ...

He tailed them for the next half hour as they strolled arm-in-arm along the quiet, brightly lit sidewalks. He noticed the way she steered the man in the direction of the penthouse. Finally, when the two of them turned into the apartment block entrance, Furino gave them time to get clear of the foyer before following them in.

A party must have broken up in one of the apartments, because a noisy, laughing group of some five or six couples passed him in a gust of alcoholic bonhomie on their way out. He returned their friendly, slurred greetings and stood aside to allow them unrestricted use of the swing doors before entering the foyer himself.

It was his practice on nights such as these to slip into the apartment, unnoticed and unheard and remain on call in his own private suite. On this particular night, Furino saw no need

ANGELS OF DEATH

to hurry. The guy she'd picked up looked like a bank manager more than anything else, he thought. Probably one of these middle-class, once-a-month-with-the-lights-out pricks, who took an hour to progress from the drinks to the first kiss. He smiled to himself and paused to light a cigarette, discovering in the process that his lighter was out of gas. He walked over to the uniformed security guard standing outside his glass-fronted cubicle.

"Evenin', Mister Furino," the greying-haired guard greeted him, touching the peak of his cap respectfully.

"Evenin', Tony," replied Furino. "Gotta light? This damn thing's run dry on me."

The guard supplied Furino with a light and accepted the offer of a cigarette from his monogrammed gold case in return. They stood chatting amiably while they smoked ...

Entering the apartment, Carla led her companion through to her private sitting room and told him to take off his outdoor things and make himself at home. She waved a hand at the well stocked bar over in the corner. "Fix some drinks, there's a dear. Mine's a bourbon on the rocks. You'll find ice in the ice-box behind the bar."

Once again, she turned the full power of her eyes on him, 'smouldering at him', as Gino would have said. Assuming a mock-French accent, she said, "As zey say in all ze best movies ma cherie, I'll go an' slip into somezing more comfortable. Au revoir." She laughed, winked coquettishly at him and disappeared into the bedroom, which opened directly off her private sitting room.

Humming happily to herself, she quickly changed into a easily removed, low cut gown, which emphasised every curve on her firm breasted body. She applied a quick dab of expensive perfume to various strategic points, behind her ears, between her breasts, and on the insides of her wrists, upper arms and thighs. As she prepared herself, a glow of sensual warmth began to suffuse her body, heightening the natural colour of her cheeks and bringing a sparkle to her eyes. She gave a little shudder of pleasure as she

306

brushed her fingers lightly over her erect nipples and ran one hand on down over her firm flat stomach to caress gently between her legs. Feeling herself grow moist in anticipation of the pleasures to come, she stopped before she became too aroused. She made a last few touches to her make up, surveyed herself in the mirror and was pleased with what she saw.

Leaning close to her reflection, she winked, blew a kiss and whispered, "Wish me luck for a real good fuck," as she always did. Then she turned and walked back into the sitting room, carefully poised, saying, "Well, here we are at last. Was I worth waiting for? ..."

She stopped dead in her tracks, her eyes widening and her mouth dropping open in sheer surprise at the sight which greeted her. Her well-bred, distinguished escort of a few minutes previously, was standing in the middle of the room facing her, a strange smile etched on his face. He was stark naked.

Carla gasped. "Well! ... You sure are a fast worker ..." She was about to finish lightly with, "You might at least have waited till we'd had a drink first," – but her attention was diverted elsewhere. Her eyes were drawn involuntarily down his well muscled physique to his enormous erection. Then, they caught the glint of brightly polished, sharpened steel – and she saw the knife he held, point downwards, in his right hand.

The apparition spoke. Or rather, he snarled. One word. "Whore!"

Too late, she realised her danger. She opened her mouth wide to scream. But he took two swift paces forward, his left hand shot out and her throat was seized in a grip of iron.

Carla Menotti did not die easily. She clawed frantically at the hand gripping her throat and then at her attacker's face and eyes. Her senses swam as the blood supply was denied to her brain. Then, as the band of iron tightened round her neck, a shining arc of steel swung forward and plunged deep into her stomach, was immediately withdrawn in a ripping, upward motion, and plunged in again ... and again ... and again ...

Each time the cruel steel shot forward, the same word snarled into her dying consciousness, over and over. "Whore! Whore! Whore! ..."

32

FURINO PASSED FIFTEEN MINUTES SMOKING AND discussing the Yankees' prospects in the next World Series with the guard, an ageing mobster named Antonio Scirea, whom he had pensioned off into this soft number as a favour. As a result, Scirea was his man and totally loyal to him. Furino had made it a policy to dispense quite a few such favours to different people in the Family from time to time, storing up goodwill for the future.

When he considered that sufficient time had elapsed to allow Carla to get settled in with her guest, he consulted his watch and said to Scirea, "Must be gettin' along, Tony. My mistress awaits me, an' all that jazz." He waved a hand and headed for the elevators.

Stepping out on the penthouse floor, he walked noiselessly along the rubberised flooring of the corridor to the door of their apartment. Inserting his key gently into the lock, he eased the door open and slipped inside, closing it soundlessly behind him. He stood in the hallway for a few seconds, listening for any sounds of activity from within the apartment – voices, movement, music. There was nothing. Hadn't he known better, he'd have thought the apartment was empty. Shrugging off the feeling, he started silently across the thick carpet towards his own private suite of rooms.

Suddenly Furino stopped in mid-stride and stood frowning in annoyance. His door was standing partly open. It was an unwritten rule between Carla and himself that they only entered each other's private portions of the apartment by invitation. He knew Carla would never dream of entering his rooms without his permission, so he assumed angrily that it must have been her companion nosing around, perhaps under the pretext of looking for the john. He had all sorts of extremely personal possessions in there, including his photograph albums which contained many intimate and very explicit snaps of him and his closest boyfriends.

As he stood there, working himself into an indignant rage, he caught a flicker of movement from the corner of his eye and his head snapped round. The door leading to Carla's suite stood ajar, a few inches of a gap showing where before it had been firmly closed.

Undecided, he stood there for another few seconds, frowning in puzzlement. He could still hear no sounds of activity from within Carla's rooms, even though the door now stood partly open. A sudden premonition that all was not as it should be prickled the hairs on back of his neck. He decided to make his presence known. If everything was all right, he could then make his excuses and leave. He cleared his throat.

"Carla?" His voice sounded shrill and loud to his own ears in the silence. No answer. Nothing stirred.

"Carla?" Louder. Still nothing. Now the alarm bells were shrilling in his mind. A surge of anger replaced the concern he felt for Carla. Furino knew full well that should anything have happened to her, he was a dead man. The Don would put out the word on him. For the rest of his life, there would be nowhere he could run where he could consider himself safe.

His homosexuality laid him open to crude jibes behind his back from his fellow mobsters about his supposed effeminacy but he was no coward. Advancing to the open door, he slipped his wicked looking, snub-nosed Walther from its shoulder holster and held it at waist level. Stepping out of the line of fire, should anyone try a shot through the door, he set his back against the door frame. He reached out and tapped on the door panel with his knuckles of his left hand.

"Carla? You there?" he called. Nothing.

Bracing himself for action, he pushed the door wide open. He could have been completely alone in the house for all the response this brought. Dropping to a crouch, he peered cautiously round the door frame. The large sumptuously furnished room – Carla called it her 'romper room' – was empty. Still crouching, he suddenly darted three or four paces inside the door, gun extended before him. He swung in a complete circle, sweeping the room simultaneously with his eyes and the gun muzzle and checked behind the angle of the open door. Nothing. The room was empty.

He straightened slowly, his senses hyper alert for the slightest sound or movement. He was now faced with a choice. There were two other doors leading off the room he now stood in. The one straight across from the door he had just entered led to the bedroom, the other off to his right, to Carla's private bathroom. Both doors stood a few inches ajar.

He chose the bedroom. Moving quickly, he strode lightly over the thick pile carpet. A few paces short of the bedroom door he stopped dead in his tracks, staring down at the glistening red stain at his feet. His mind went cold. He crouched, touched it and glanced at the scarlet wetness on his fingertips. It was blood.

A mixture of grief and fury welled within him. Grief for Carla and fury against the bastard who had harmed her. He knew one thing – if his life was forfeit because of his failure to protect his charge, then he would take her assailant with him! Throwing caution to the winds, he covered the remaining distance to the bedroom door at a run. He launched a flying drop kick at it, slamming it violently open with such force that it split down its entire length.

Furino dropped into a crouch again in the doorway, gun and eyes quartering the room beyond. It was as empty of life as the sitting room. He swung round and eyed the bathroom door, his lips drawing back from his even teeth in a grimace of tension and rage. Then he charged recklessly across the room and launched himself into another flying drop kick. Such was the violence of his pent-up fury, that the door was smashed completely off its hinges, to drop away from him into the room beyond. As before, he dropped to a crouch in the open doorway, his eyes sweeping the room over the foresight of his extended gun.

The first thing his eyes registered was the blood. It was splashed and smeared everywhere he looked. Floor, pale green tiled walls, toilet pedestal, bidet, sunken bath ... it was then he saw her ... or what was left of her!

His shocked brain registered the image being passed to it by his eyes, but for a stunned second or two could not comprehend it. He straightened up from his crouch, staring horror-struck down into the bath. He saw her fully then.

Naked, she was lying face up on the bottom of the spacious bath, arms outflung and legs spread wide. Her killer had slit her body open from crotch to throat. But what riveted his eyes was the horrific sight of her ribcage, which had been ripped apart and opened out to either side like two obscene red wings, exposing her entire internal organs. Her once beautiful mouth was stretched wide in a soundless scream and her bulging eyes stared sightlessly at the ceiling.

Shock held him immobile for the space of perhaps four heartbeats. His mind recoiled from the horror of what he saw before him. But a part of his brain remained on the alert and it flashed a frantic warning to him, when it picked up the faint whisper of sound on the carpet behind him. He had momentarily forgotten that Carla's killer was still at large in the house.

He reacted swiftly – but not swiftly enough. He had barely begun to turn to face the danger, when something struck him a heavy blow in the small of his back. He felt a sharp burning pain in the region of his right kidney. The blow knocked him off balance and he stumbled forward. Before he could recover, another blow hit him low in the back ... then another ... and another ... in swift succession. A sudden numbness paralysed his limbs.

He fell then, landing face down in a pool of sticky, congealing blood by the edge of the sunken bath. Instinctively, Furino rolled to one side, trying to get clear of his assailant and regain his feet. But his body refused to respond properly. He felt strangely sluggish, as though he were trying to move underwater.

Falling to one side, he flopped clumsily over onto his back and stared dazedly up at the tall muscular figure of his attacker. The man was stark naked and from his silver-grey hair to his feet, he was liberally splashed with blood. In his right hand he held a long, wicked looking knife. Furino barely recognised him as the man Carla had picked up.

The killer grinned wolfishly down at him, the light of madness glowing in his eyes. Then, Furino remembered his gun. He tried to whip it up and empty the magazine into the madman's belly. But his right arm felt like it was glued to the floor. His muscles refused to obey the desperate commands from his brain.

He tried again, putting all he had into the immense effort, and this time his hand raised the gun a few inches. But it weighed a hundred tons and immediately dropped back to the tiled floor. The grinning killer bent forward and made two swift downward slashes with the knife, one to either side of the supine figure at his feet.

Furino screamed in agony as the gleaming blade sliced cleanly through the muscle and sinew of both forearms, laying them open to the bone. He felt the warm wetness of his own blood coursing down over his nerveless hands. At the same time, he became aware of a similar liquid warmth spreading under his lower back. It was only then he realised what the earlier blows had been – he had been stabbed – probably mortally. He strained to raise his head.

"You fuckin' prick!" he screamed shrilly at the tall, evilly grinning figure. "You know who owns this place? Bruno Neroni, that's who! You're fuckin' dead, you know that? He'll cut your balls off. You're a fuckin' corpse!"

Exhausted, he let his head fall back to the tiles. He began to sob hysterically with pain and frustrated rage, the snot running from his nose down over his mouth and chin. His strength was ebbing fast now ... draining from his tired body and flowing out over the tiles of the floor, to mingle with the widening pool of his life-blood. He felt coldness creeping over him.

His killer spoke then, the fixed grin no longer on his face. He pointed the knife at Furino.

"Sodomite!" he hissed.

Then the wolfish grin spread over his face again, his voice rising to a snarl as he continued, "How dare you threaten me! But in so doing, you have pronounced your own sentence. So be it!"

He stooped forward out of Furino's line of fading vision. Through the fog which was clouding his eyes and dulling his brain, the dying man sensed rather than felt his trouser fly being ripped open. He could do nothing. He felt disassociated, remote, floating ...

A sudden flare of unbearable agony lanced up from his groin, shocking his dying brain back into a last fleeting awareness. His vision cleared long enough for him to register the tall, blood-smeared apparition towering over him. Then the figure blurred again and began to recede. He had to concentrate all his fading will to focus on the dripping objects dangling from the madman's upheld hand. He died while he was still trying to identify them. He was thus spared the final indignity of knowing he had been castrated.

The killer dropped the severed genitals on the floor beside Furino's body. Absently, he caressed the blade of his knife and a little smile of satisfaction touched his mouth, as he surveyed his night's handiwork. The smile only emphasised the smouldering bale-fire of insanity glowing in the pitiless eyes.

After a time, he stirred. Laying the knife carefully on the floor, he walked over, stooped and gripped Furino's body under the arms. With a sudden burst of strength, he heaved the limp form and threw it bodily into the huge sunken bath, where it landed across the legs of the body already in there.

Retrieving the knife, he stepped down into the bath along with the two corpses, and began to cut away Furino's clothing, tossing the scraps out onto the floor behind him. He had a little more work to do, before he was through. His message had to be left for a sinful world ...

Half an hour later, Tony Scirea glanced up from his glass-fronted cubicle and noticed the tall, well-dressed, distinguished looking man striding from the elevators to the big glass swing doors of the entrance. The man saw him watching as he reached the doors, smiled and touched the brim of his hat. Scirea nodded back and acknowledged with a similar gesture.

The big glass doors hissed gently shut again on the empty foyer, as Scirea thought to himself, Nice polite ol' guy. Y'kin always tell a real gent by his classy manners.

Perhaps another ten minutes passed, then one of those trivial coincidences occurred which by a quirk of fate can often have a dramatic influence on other events, to which they have absolutely no connection. One of the elevators opened and two smartly dressed young business executives emerged and strode briskly across the empty foyer. They were leaving after having enjoyed a convivial dinner party in the apartment of an American business client, who had entertained them in the hope of obtaining a lucrative order from their company. They might have gone entirely unremarked by the security guard in his cubicle, but for one factor – they were Japanese.

Scirea was a naturalised American citizen, who had emigrated from his native Italy at a tender age along with his family. He had been drafted into the Marine Corps and had fought proudly as a leatherneck for his adopted country in Vietnam. He had brought back with him from that savage war, an undying hatred and contempt for the slants, as the US soldiers called the Vietnamese of both sides. And in Scirea's opinion, all Orientals were classed as slants. It mattered not a whit to him what nationality any oriental claimed to be. He was quite unequivocal about it – they were all slants!

His jaundiced opinion of the two quite unsuspecting young Japanese businessmen showed in his cold-eyed stare, which followed them across the foyer until they passed from sight through the big swing doors.

"Fuckin' slants!" he muttered contemptuously. Their brief appearance in the foyer that night – quite coincidental as it was – allied to Scirea's prejudice against all Orientals, was to colour his memory the following day and spark off a chain reaction of bloody violence.

33

JIM MILLER HAD HARDLY SLEPT A WINK THROUGH-out the long night. He had dozed fitfully when exhaustion overcame him, but the solace of sleep was denied him by the presence of the waking nightmare in the far corner of his darkened cell.

With the air conditioning switched off, the smell of putrefaction hung heavy so his nose reminded him of the horror lurking by the far wall, even though he could no longer see it. The result was, by the time his light was switched on again early the following morning, Jim would have said or done anything to be spared another night in the company of his ghastly cellmate.

When Angel One unlocked the door and entered the cell, Jim was sitting hunched against the far wall, his forehead resting on his knees, putting as much distance between himself and the thing in the corner as was possible. He looked up, squinting his red-rimmed eyes against the bright light and his heart quailed when he saw the black clad figure in the doorway.

The oriental was alone. Jim met his level gaze, then quickly looked down again, staring at the man's feet. The slanted black eyes were glittering with malice. Then the feet moved swiftly across the floor towards him and Jim cringed back defensively against the wall.

Suddenly his hair was seized painfully by powerful fingers and he was jerked bodily to his feet. His head was slammed back against the concrete wall with stunning force and he was pinned there, helpless, by the scalp-tearing grip. He found himself staring into the cruel, fathomless eyes of Angel One, a few inches away. Jim could feel the suppressed rage in the man. It seemed to pulse from him like an icy aura, enveloping them both in a chilling mist.

"I trust you slept well, Miller? But not as soundly as your companion ... yes?" The words hissed malignantly into the terrified youth's face. The cruel grip tightened on Jim's hair and he could feel roots tearing from his scalp. He let out a sharp cry of pain, screwing his watering eyes shut.

"You lied to me, Miller. Didn't you?"

"Yes, Archangel Michael," Jim croaked.

"Yes, Archangel Michael," the oriental sneered, mimicking him. "Why did you lie? Why did you waste my time, insect?"

Jim, straining upwards on his toes to relieve the pain in his scalp, gasped out, "Because I thought you would kill me if you knew he was dead."

Angel One bared his teeth in a mirthless grin. "Oh no, Miller," he snarled. "You will not be granted the release of death so easily …"

Again he slammed Jim's head sickeningly against the wall, forcing a yelp of pain from him. "Do you know how much trouble and inconvenience you have caused me, worm? Do you?"

"No, Archangel Michael." Jim was sobbing now from pain and fear, hot tears coursing down his face.

"No, Archangel Michael," echoed his tormentor. "Well, I assure you, you have caused me a great deal of trouble. And, I also assure you … you are going to rectify it, aren't you?" Again, he slammed Jim's head viciously into the wall behind him. "Aren't you?"

"Yes, Archangel Michael, yes, yes, yes … anything you say. Please, you're hurting me …"

"Hurting you?" the oriental sneered. "You don't know what real pain is, dogshit. You can't even begin to imagine the pain I shall inflict on you … unless you agree to do exactly as I say." Without warning, he reached up with his free hand and pinched a nerve point under Jim's jaw. The boy screamed as a red wave of agony engulfed his brain.

The pain ebbed again as Angel One released the brief pressure. The grip on his hair also eased sufficiently for him to rest on the soles of his feet. Jim knew with certainty that this terrifying man would kill him without so much as a moment's hesitation, if he thought it expedient. He had to buy himself time, if he were to have any faint hope of escape or rescue. One thing – he didn't have to put on an act to convince the oriental of his fear of him … his terror of him was real and only too evident.

"I'm sorry for the trouble I've caused," he sobbed. "Please don't hurt me. What do you want me to do?"

The oriental was still holding him trapped against the wall, the bleak eyes staring into his from mere inches away. "I will tell you what you will do. But you will not comply merely because I want you to do it. Oh no, Miller, you will do as I say because you yourself will want to do it, I assure you!" he stated confidently.

"When this private detective comes here this afternoon with

the local sheriff, you will tell them you do not wish to leave. When asked why you ran away last night, you will say that you did so because you were emotionally disturbed ... you had an argument with your girlfriend and she said she was finished with you. One of the young female members will confirm this, if necessary. Do you understand?"

"Yes, Archangel Michael," Jim replied through his tears.

"Repeat what you have to say."

"I ... I don' w-wanna leave now ... an' ... an' I only ran away b-because my girlfriend said w-we were through," Jim sobbed.

"Good." Angel One nodded his satisfaction. "See that your memory does not fail you when you meet these people today." The dark eyes glittered with menace.

"And Miller, do not delude yourself with the thought that you may be able to enlist their aid to escape from here. Be in no doubt, should you attempt to do so, they will die ... instantly! But not you, Miller ..." The iron grip tightened again on his hair, reawakening the pain of his tender scalp. "You will not be so fortunate. You will beg for death long before it is granted to you."

His words hissed venomously into Jim's tear-streaked face. "But even then, you will not be allowed to die. When I am finished with you, you will be released into the grounds for the dogs to hunt. And you will not escape them a second time. Not a pleasant way to die. Should you need reminding, look ..."

With a sudden burst of controlled ferocity, Angel One jerked Jim from the wall and hauled him bodily across the cell by the hair of his head. Jim's yell of pain became a scream of horror, as he was forced to his knees in the corner behind the door and Angel One tossed aside the yellow bucket, uncovering the putrid obscenity only inches from his terrified vision.

"Look well!" snarled the oriental over Jim's sobs of protest. "That is the end that awaits you ... if you do not co-operate."

Jim strained frantically back, bracing his hands on the angled walls of the corner. The pain in his scalp meant nothing to him now. All he wanted was to get away from the mangled, eyeless horror before him. The charnel stench made him gag and bile stung the back of his throat. Then a maggot wriggled through one of the eyeless sockets and his empty stomach heaved, as he retched convulsively in an unsuccessful attempt to be sick.

For a few panicky seconds, Jim thought he would suffocate, such were the violence of the spasms which gripped him, then the nausea receded a little and he discovered he was no longer being held down by his tormentor. He scrambled backwards on hands and knees till he fetched up in a state of near collapse, huddled against the far wall, crouched on his foam mattress. He was panting for breath, his face and body drenched in a cold sweat.

Angel One was standing in the centre of the floor, regarding him with a look of pitiless contempt.

"Remember well what I have said, Miller – for your own good, as well as for the safety of these others this afternoon. Your life … and theirs … is in your hands." He turned and walked to the door.

"Archangel Michael?" called Jim haltingly. The man halted in the open doorway, and stood without turning round, waiting.

"Please … if I do as you say … please say you won't kill me … I don't want to die … I promise I won't let you down again …" He was on his knees, sobbing uncontrollably now, his hands stretched out in supplication, all dignity gone, all resistance vanished.

The oriental, his back to Jim, permitted himself a smirk of satisfaction. He had won. But he knew there are times when it is expedient for the victor to make a concession – to leave open a line of retreat for a defeated foe. A cornered rat will fight only when it is denied all means of escape.

He turned slowly to face Jim, his features once more a mask of stony indifference. He decided to play the fish a little longer, so as not to seem to give in too easily.

"I do not bargain with corpses, Miller," he stated coldly. "And your life is forfeit because of your attempt to escape …"

"P-please, Archangel Michael, just give me one more chance … please," Jim pleaded brokenly.

Angel One regarded the supplicant thoughtfully for a few seconds, as though considering his plea. Then he seemed to come to a decision.

"Very well," he conceded reluctantly. "If you do exactly as you have been told ... and only if ..." He held up a hand to stem Jim's rush of tearful thanks. "I promise nothing. But I think I shall, on this occasion, be able to modify your punishment. We shall see. But ..." he added warningly to the weeping boy, who was nodding his pathetic agreement, "it is entirely up to you!"

He turned to leave once more, then paused in the act of closing the door. "I shall leave you in the company of your fellow escapee for a little longer. Should your resolve to co-operate begin to falter, I imagine contemplation of his fate will persuade you to remain firm." The door clicked shut.

Jim immediately scrambled across the cell, retrieved the plastic bucket and replaced it over the ghastly severed head in the corner. Retreating to his mattress, he crawled under a blanket and buried his face in the pillow. Feeling helpless and alone, his tears began once more to flow freely, only this time they were tinged with relief at his hard won reprieve.

As he had done the previous evening, Angel One stood for a few seconds outside the door of the cell, listening to the muffled sounds of sobbing from within. He reflected contemptuously that most people did not require much effort from others to delude them. On the contrary, they deluded themselves!

He was satisfied now that the boy would present no further problem. Next – the sheriff and the private detective remained to be dealt with. Ah yes ... the private detective! His eyes hardened as he recalled the two reports he had received on his return from Dragon Control the previous night.

The first had come from one of the two vans operating in Harlem that day. It concerned a suspicious visitor in the person of a big-talking Texan, calling himself Calhoun, who had put in an appearance during the afternoon. However, the Apostle in charge had not been fully convinced of his authenticity. There had been something not quite right about him, something phoney. He had struck Brother Mark as being something more than the garrulous Texan buffoon he appeared to be on first acquaintance.

Accordingly, he had noted down the licence plate number of the man's car, a bronze Mustang, when he drove away. Through the medium of a City Hall contact, it had been disclosed that the car was registered in the name of one Barrett Telford Grant, occupation – private investigator!

The man had stated his intention of returning the following day under the pretext of obtaining photographs of the van, which in itself had been enough to arouse suspicion. The girl member he had been conversing with, a Neophyte, name of Sister Louise Wyatt, had not reported any attempt by the man to pump her for information regarding the sect or any of its personnel. Brother Mark had astutely decided against questioning her on this point, just in case it turned out that she was unreliable and alerted the man when he returned the following day. The Apostle's report had concluded that he planned to leave the girl on duty the next day – as bait. It was his intention to accost this Calhoun/Grant to find out what he was really after.

While reading this report, Angel One had recalled that the private detective who was calling at Bethlehem House to interview the Miller boy, had also been called Grant by the sheriff who had accompanied him. From this, it could reasonably be assumed that the two Grants were one and the same person.

The second report had been much more serious. It had concerned the running fight and pursuit which had taken place in the underground carpark of the Washington Centre, where the Prophet was conducting his latest crusade.

The incident had started when it had become necessary for a recurring pest named Larsen to be forcibly removed from the meeting. A man, probably aided by a female accomplice, had attacked the sect personnel and rescued Larsen from them, injuring four men in the process.

Following a vehicle chase in the carpark, the intruders had made good their escape, after writing off two of the sect vans and injuring several more personnel, two of whom had to be dragged from the blazing wreckage of their vehicles. The car used by the intruders had been a bronze Mustang!

The fact of both cars in the separate reports being the same make and colour in each case, was too strong to be mere coincidence. It was obvious that this Grant person was proving to be very troublesome and would doubtless prove to be more so – unless stopped.

Angel One decided to issue Brother Mark with specific instructions on how to deal with the man when he called back at the Harlem van, so as to discourage him from further interference in sect business. The Miller boy had responded well to a softening up process. There was no reason why such a course would not prove equally successful a second time, this time with the private detective.

Harlem was, after all, a notoriously tough area and muggings were all too commonplace. It would appear quite a natural occurrence to the police, if a white stranger who had reportedly been flashing money were to be badly beaten up and relieved of his bankroll. Leaving the area of the Turkey Pens, he headed for the Control Room to issue the necessary orders.

PART VI
HUNCH

PART VI

HUNCH

34

THE PHONE RANG ON CURTIS'S DESK. HE GLANCED
at his watch as he reached out and picked up the receiver, a habit
born of his twenty years of police service.

"Homicide. Detective Lieutenant Curtis speakin' ... oh, it's
you Brett. Hell, my watch musta stopped! It says nine forty-five
inna mornin', an' Harry says you don' git up till aroun' noon
sometime ..."

He paused, smiling to himself and lit a cigarette, as he listened
to Grant's response to this sally. Cradling the phone between
neck and shoulder, he continued sorting out and shuffling
through papers, as he carried on his conversation.

"Yeah, yeah, I know I'm a riot at this time inna mornin'." The
cigarette dangling from his mouth bobbed up and down in time
with his words. "Thing is ... some of us hardly ever git th'chance
t'git into a bed, never mind have trouble gittin' outa one! Hah!
Anyway, it must be somethin' real important to have gotten you
up so early. What's on y'mind, pal?"

Twenty minutes later, Curtis replaced the phone and stared at
it for several seconds, deep in thought. He slumped back in his
chair and lit himself a fresh cigarette, turning over in his mind
the conversation he'd just had with Grant.

Something his friend had said had struck a familiar chord in
his memory but whatever it was remained tantalisingly out of
reach of his conscious probing. Curtis had a good memory for
conversations, for actual words spoken – he had to have in his

job, where the slightest discrepancy between what you thought someone had said and what they actually had said, could mean having a case tossed out of court.

Grant had called to bring him up to date on the events of the previous day, especially his visits to the sect van and his experiences at the Washington Centre. He had informed Curtis of his intention to call again at the sect van later that morning to check with the girl Louise, before he headed for Rockford and his interview with the Miller boy. Apparently he had been informed by Nate Springfield just prior to his phone call to Curtis, that the interview was arranged for anytime between 1 p.m. and 2 p.m. that afternoon.

"Hey, you be careful, Brett," Curtis had warned. "After last night's game of tag in the Centre carpark, someone might jes' recognise you at the van. An' there ain't too many citizens roun' Harlem who'd be concerned about some honky gittin' hisself beaten up on th'sidewalk. Fact is, most of 'em would prob'ly join in!"

"Well, if I don't turn up on Nate's doorstep this afternoon by one o'clock at the latest, at least you'll know where to start lookin'. I'll be in touch, ol' buddy. Stay lucky." He had rung off before Curtis could remonstrate further with him.

But that wasn't the part of their conversation which was now niggling at the back of Curtis's mind as he sat smoking, deep in thought, at his cluttered desk. His eyes wandered absently over the piled casefiles and scattered reports, until they came back to rest on the dog-eared sheet of paper directly before him.

It went everywhere with him, folded away in the back of his notebook. At every available opportunity, he would pull it out and study it. He showed it round his colleagues too, hoping one of them might just recognise a pattern in the obscure sequences of numbers listed on its well-fingered surface.

"Fuckin' numbers!" he muttered disgustedly and leaned forward to crush out his cigarette stub in the loaded ashtray. He was in the act of reaching for a fresh cigarette, when suddenly he stopped, his hand resting on the crumpled pack alongside the offending sheet of paper. Numbers! ... something about numbers ... what the hell was it?... something Brett had said ...

Then it came to him. During the call, he had asked Grant what he'd thought of the Prophet, whom he had gone to the crusade to assess. Grant had replied that he thought the guy was as nutty as a fruitcake, but nonetheless dangerous because of the obvious fanaticism which fired him and his followers. He had then gone on to describe briefly to Curtis the sermon and the audience response to it.

"The guy's got this jumbo sized Freudian complex about sex. Fornication he calls it. Makes a good ol' fuck sound like a disease! I think it could have somethin' to do with the fact that he wears a gold silk dress."

"Maybe he's into choirboys," Curtis had responded with a laugh.

"Well he ain't admittin' it if he is," Grant had retorted. "Cuz he even had a quote from the Bible to forbid that too! No kiddin', he was throwin' out quotations like confetti. An' all from the First Book of Corinthians, too ... there, that'll let you know how much he went on about it, if I can remember that. Tell you somethin', these Corinthians must've been a real randy bunch, if they got up to even half the stuff they were warned against!

"Anyhow, like I was tellin' you, he ended up wavin' his Bible at us, an' threatenin' us with hellfire an' damnation if we even so much as thought about havin' a bit on the side." Here he put on a fair imitation of the Prophet's ranting tones of the night before, and continued, "'For it is written in First Corinthians, Five, Five, if you dare to fornicate in anythin' but the missionary position with your eyes closed, you'll be delivered up to Satan to be barbecued in Hellfire, so your soul can be saved on Judgement Day ... remember it well ... First Corinthians, Five, Five!' I tell you, buddy, I won't be able to get to the short strokes from now on, without thinkin' to myself, 'First Corinthians, Five, Five ... First Corinthians, Five, Five!'"

Curtis had laughed at Grant's ridiculing of the Prophet's sermon. But he wasn't laughing now. He pulled the sheet of paper towards him, cigarettes forgotten for the moment. He studied it with a sense of rising excitement.

He ran his eye quickly down the two columns of figures. On

the left, in chronological order, were the sequences of Roman numerals which had been discovered slashed into the bodies of the murdered prostitutes. On the right, in groups, were all the combinations of their possible Arabic equivalents. There were fifteen sets of figures in the left hand column, most of these being repetitions because only three different sequences had been used throughout. They had been used seemingly at random, even though at times the same sequences had been repeated two or three times in succession.

One set had been used only three times. It ran IXXVIVV. The other two sequences had been used six times each. The first of these ran IIVIIIXII; the other IIVIIVV. It had been the two shorter number sequences which had rung the bell in Curtis's mind – the ones ending in the double Roman numerals VV – or five, five!

He chose to concentrate on the last of these sequences – IIVIIVV – not only because it was one of the shorter ones but also because it had been used most recently – on the body of Mary Lou Evans. Eagerly he scanned the sequence of seven numerals. A few times during his countless attempts to decode the killer's messages over the preceding five years, he had wondered whether they could be biblical references, but without a lead there were at least fifteen different possible combinations of numbers which could be taken from this particular sequence alone.

But now he had a lead – or did he? He brushed the doubt aside, he had a good feeling this time. He pulled a fresh sheet of paper towards him and stared at it for a moment. Then he printed V – V and alongside this he printed CHAPTER 5 – VERSE 5?

Now … what if he followed the rest of the quotation Grant had kept repeating? Corinthians was the book he had referred to. From his own sketchy knowledge of the Bible he recalled that this came from the New Testament.

He scored off the two V's from the end of the sequence, then examined the remaining five numerals. He was left with IIVII. Now, if his theory was correct, then this could divide into II for the New Testament – which was the second portion of the

Bible – and VII, which hopefully would refer to the Book of Corinthians – if it were indeed the seventh book in sequence! He rewrote the sequence, dividing it up with dashes, so it read II-VII-V-V, and gazed at it for a long moment. He licked his lips, and found that his mouth had gone dry. Butterflies of tension fluttered in his stomach. He felt as nervous as a kid on his first date. If he was right about this ...

Suddenly, he grabbed up the internal phone and punched the number of the Homicide Detectives' Room. When someone answered, he demanded to speak to Detective Turner right away, then sat tapping his ball-point pen impatiently against his teeth as he waited for him to come to the phone. The seconds seemed to drag past like minutes until the laconic voice of his junior partner came on the line.

"Tex here, Chief," came the familiar drawl.

"Tex, git yer ass in here right away, an' bring a Bible with you ... yeah, a Bible, that's what I said ... What? ..."

He paused as Turner's voice sounded in his ear, then burst out, "Whaddaya mean 'what kinda Bible?' ... a Bible, a BIBLE, fer Chrissake! Whaddaya think I mean, the fuckin' Koran or somethin'?..."

A slightly longer pause ensued, while Curtis listened to Tex's reply with barely restrained patience, before exploding, "Look, asshole, I know there's a Jewish Bible, an' a Catholic Bible, an' a Mormon Bible, an' Christ knows how many others. If I'da wanted any a those, I'da asked fer 'em, right? ..."

He sighed and pinched the bridge of his nose with two fingers, screwing his eyes shut tiredly. "Okay, okay , hold it ..." he gestured to the empty air alongside him with his free hand as he spoke, his voice heavy with reason. "We'll start again. Detective Turner, bring me a copy of the Authorised Version of the Bible, willya? The one otherwise known as the King James Version, as widely used in Protestant churches of Presbyterian, Lutheran, Calvinist or Wesleyan persuasion. Capice?"

Another short pause followed, then Curtis exploded again. "Where? WHERE?" he bellowed. "Where d'ya fuckin' think, ya big Texan lunkhead? Go out an' mug a goddam preacher, for all I fuckin' care! Shoot 'im if y'have to ..." He paused, took a deep breath and continued acidly, "Try the fuckin' Reference Library on the sixth floor, that's where, fer Chrissake! An' don' be all fuckin' day about it, either. I wan' it five minutes ago!"

He slammed down the phone, shaking his head in exasperation. He reached for his crumpled pack and lit up a badly needed cigarette. Now that he was this close to what could be his first real lead on the perverted killer, who had caused him so many sleepless nights since he had been given overall responsibility for leading the city-wide murder hunt for him, he was understandably edgy. Part of him was afraid that the lead would turn out to be a bummer, just like all previous lines of inquiry in this case. Yet, he had a gut feeling about this one ... it felt right, somehow.

To give himself something to do while he waited for Turner to put in an appearance, he drew two lines across a fresh sheet of paper, dividing it into three sections down the page. He headed the first section in the left margin with the sequence he hoped he had cracked – II-VII-V-V. The other two sections he left blank for now. Then, finding the waiting intolerable, and perhaps prompted by the fact that he had sent for a Bible, he glanced up at the ceiling and said aloud, "Hey, Lord ... gimme a break, huh? Lemme be right about this."

As though in answer to his heartfelt plea, the door opened to admit a most unlikely heavenly messenger in the form of the tall figure of Tex Turner. He wore a good-natured grin on his tanned face and clutched a bright red book in one huge hand. Pushing the door shut behind him, he waved the book at Curtis as he advanced on the desk.

"How 'bout this one, Chief? It's one o' them Gideon Bibles. Guy in Reference says it's the only Protestant one they got in stock right now."

"I don' give a shit if it's Saint Peter's own personal one," growled Curtis. "Provided it's what I need. We ain't holdin' a prayer meetin'. Siddown! Listen ..."

He proceeded to explain his theory to the young Texan, who listened with growing enthusiasm for the idea, before saying, "Sounds good t'me, Chief. Right ..." he opened the Bible in the middle, "whar do we start lookin'?"

"Seventh book in the New Testament," replied Curtis.

Turner flipped the pages till he found the index page of the New Testament, then ran his finger down the list of books. "That's First Corinthians," he announced.

"Y'don' say!" A gleam showed in Curtis's eye. "That sounds familiar. That's the one Brett was goin' on about. Okay ... look up chapter five, verse five."

The sound of rustling pages filled the ensuing silence, then stopped. Tex looked up. "Got it!" he announced triumphantly.

"Well, read the fuckin' thing out, dammit!" snarled Curtis. "I ain't fuckin' telepathic."

Turner ducked his head, smothering his grin, before Curtis twigged he was being taken for a ride. Clearing his throat, he read aloud in his soft Texan drawl, "To deliver such a one unto Satan for the destruction of the flesh, that the spirit may be saved in the day of the Lord Jesus."

The lieutenant, busy scribbling down the words Turner was reading out, muttered, "Well, I'll be damned! That ties in roughly with what Brett said, too." He looked up at Turner. "I think we're onto somethin' at last, Tex. Let's see if the others work out ..."

Curtis selected the other sequence which started with two Roman ones – IIVIIIXII – and they began from the assumption that once again it was the seventh book that was referred to. However, the resultant texts of chapter nine, verse two, or alternatively chapter one, verse twelve, just didn't make sense in the context of the type of message they were looking for. So Curtis suggested they try the sixth book, and this time divided the group to read II-VI-II-XII.

The thin pages gave off a crisp rustling sound as Turner flipped back through them. "Sixth book, that's Paul's Epistle to the Romans," stated Turner. "What wuz th'chapter an' verse, again?"

"Chapter two, verse twelve," replied Curtis, his inner tension mounting again like an over wound guitar string. It had to be right this time. Surely the first quotation hadn't just seemed to work out by a cruel coincidence.

"Here it is, Chief ... listen ..." Excitement put an edge on

Turner's slow drawl as he read the words aloud. "For as many as have sinned without law shall perish without law: and as many as have sinned in the law shall be judged by the law." He looked up at Curtis. Their eyes met, full of the unspoken conviction which neither of them yet dared to voice, that they were onto something.

Curtis nodded slowly, as much to himself as to Turner. He spoke quietly. "There's an ol' sayin', Tex, which goes somethin' like, 'once is happenstance; twice is coincidence; but three times is enemy action!' Right, eyes down fer a full house ... let's see what we kin make of the last one ..."

They scanned the final sequence which read IXXVIVV. Having agreed that this quotation must be from the first portion of the Bible, or the Old Testament, the two colleagues proceeded to try various possible divisions of the other numbers, without turning up anything consistent with the two previous quotations. It seemed to have them beaten.

Then Turner had a flash of inspiration.

"How about if this time he's quoted two verses, instead o' one, Chief?"

"Huh, come again?" asked Curtis.

"Well, s'posin' we try it this way ..." he jotted down the sequence, dividing it up to read I-XX-V-IV-V. "That'd be Old Testament, twen'ieth book, chapter five, verses four an' five."

"Could be," Curtis nodded thoughtfully. "Yeah. That could be it. Good thinkin', Batman. Okay, go fer it."

Tex turned the Bible back to the very beginning and ran a big-knuckled finger down the long index of Old Testament books, counting them off. He stopped at the twentieth. "Proverbs," he announced. He flicked through the pages till he reached the required place and scanned the text quickly. He looked up with a grin of triumph.

"Yep, this is it, all right. I think we've cracked it, Chief. Git an earful o' this ... But her end is bitter as wormwood, sharp as a two-edged sword. That's verse four. Verse five says, Her feet go down to death; her steps take hold on hell. Looks like we got ourselves some kinda religious maniac, Chief. Leastways, that's how it seems t'me."

"Yeah, I'd buy that too. An' it might jes' point us in the right direction with a bitta luck, an' some more spadework. Listen Tex, I got another of my little hunches while you were readin'. This latest murder we're investigatin', the Evans case, jes' happened to coincide with a big religious crusade bein' held in the city by this Prophet character Brett's interested in … the one who runs the weird sect I told you about, right? Well, what I wan' you t'do is this …"

While he was speaking, he hunted through the paperwork on his desktop till he found the folder he wanted. Handing it to Turner he went on, "In there's a list of all fifteen killin's we know our man's done. It gives a complete run-down, names, dates, times, locations … the works. Run a check on the dates of all the killin's, cross-referencin' 'em with the dates of any sizeable religious meetin's that were bein' held in the city at those times, okay? While you're doin' that, I'll run a check on all known religious nutters who're known t'have bin in circulation at the relevant times. Okay, git movin'. Meet me back here when you've finished."

"Y'got it." Turner took the folder, got up and headed for the door. His hand on the handle, he looked back at Curtis. "Let's hope we're on th'right track an' we nail this bastard before he imagines he's God an' strikes again," he said.

"Amen to that," responded Curtis with unconscious irony.

In a bloodstained apartment across the city, the savagely butchered corpses of Carla Menotti and her bodyguard bore mute testimony to the fact that the two detectives' new-found optimism was somewhat premature.

35

BLISSFULLY UNAWARE OF THE ACTIVITY HIS PHONE call had sparked off between Curtis and Turner, Grant got his head down for half an hour and cleared up his paperwork. He spent another twenty minutes with one of the firm's other detectives, Sam Ellis, discussing some casework he'd handed over to him. Then, pausing only to inform Anna of his intended schedule for the day, he left the office and headed down to the foyer and out through the big glass doors of the building.

Reaching the sidewalk, he scanned the parked cars at the kerb for his Mustang. For an instant he was puzzled when he failed to see its familiar bronze low-slung shape. Then he spotted the small figure of the Champ roller-skating nimbly on the sidewalk near a dark blue Chevy saloon, and he recalled that he had hired it to replace the Mustang which was in dock having its rear nearside window replaced.

The diminutive black urchin saw him approaching and skated to meet him. Reaching Grant, he swerved expertly round him and fell in alongside, keeping pace with long smooth glides and showing off by pirouetting on every alternate push, his hands clasped behind him.

"Hi Brett." He grinned hugely under the striped woollen ski cap which tightly imprisoned his Afro and covered the tips of his ears.

"Hi Champ," Grant responded, grinning back, both impressed and amused by the showy skill and perfect sense of balance displayed by the diminutive roller skater.

"You goin' anywhere's special dis mawnin', Brett?" The big brown eyes gazed up at him hopefully, belying the studied indifference of his question.

"Could be … why?" asked Grant non-committally.

Aw, no partic'lar reason. Ah wuz jes' wonderin' if you'd be needin' any back-up, is all." The youngster shrugged carelessly and executed a triple turn, arms and legs spread wide. He thus failed to see the strained expression on Grant's face as he quickly turned a snort of laughter into a diplomatic cough.

"Back-up?" Grant repeated. "What kinda back-up had you in mind, exactly?"

"Well … same's yesterday. S'posin' you's goin' fox huntin' again. Ah c'd watch yo' car, or mebbe even take a message fo' yuh." He searched Grant's face anxiously for a response.

Grant eyed the Champ speculatively. He thought of the

previous night's running battle and of the possibility, suggested by Curtis, that he may be recognised if any of the participants in last night's chase happened to be in attendance at the van this morning. It could be an expedient on this occasion to employ an unknown messenger to contact Louise, should he decide this to be necessary.

"Okay," he said to a delighted Champ. "Hop in. We won't be gone too long ... hey, get those roller skates off first ..."

Grant had been observing the van and the constantly changing crowd hanging around it for about twenty minutes. He had managed to find a good vantage point in a parking space between two other cars, about forty yards back from the van, on the opposite side of the road.

He could see Louise quite clearly along with one other blue-robed girl mingling with the passers-by, occasionally handing out a leaflet, which was grudgingly accepted. There weren't many hangers-on at this time in the forenoon. A few down and outs from the local flop-houses hunched protectively over their cups of soup, interspersed with a dozen or so young blacks who were smoking or talking in small groups.

However, Grant thought he could see at least four tough looking citizens who seemed to him to stand out from the rest, although trying to appear part of the general crowd. In his opinion, each one of these four had an air of alertness about him missing from the remainder. If they spoke to anyone, it was only to exchange a few words and not to engage in conversation. One of the four Grant recognised from the day before as Purple Hat.

The Champ was becoming restive. He had been content for about fifteen minutes with the comic books, popcorn and soda Grant had bought him. But now the popcorn and soda were finished and he was of the opinion that his benefactor had chickened out of his intent to chat up the young chick.

Finally, exasperated by his friend's faint-heartedness, he blurted out, "Man, you jes' gonna sit heah all day an' eyeball 'er?"

Grant stirred. He seemed to have heard the Champ's voice without registering the import of the words, because he spoke without answering the question. "Listen Champ, you see those four guys on the outside edges of the crowd over there ... the one with the purple hat like yours ... an' those two in the leather jackets ... there ... an' there ... an' that one in the white baseball boots ... got 'em?"

"Check! I got em'. Mean lookin' mothers," replied the Champ. "You reck'n dey watchin' fo' you ... case yuh try t'steal da chick away from 'em? Tol' yuh what folks say 'bout dat, Brett. Dey don' like it."

Grant nodded abstractedly, happy to let the kid think whatever he liked. He had noticed a few black kids of around the Champ's age and size playing in and around the loose throng of people at the van. Some of these clutched hamburgers or plastic cups, so the sect personnel must give handouts of free food to children as well as to adults. Catch 'em young, he thought cynically.

Seeing the youngsters gave him an idea. He couldn't shake off the feeling he was expected – and not in his persona of Chester D Calhoun either! – so he decided there and then to contact Louise by proxy, using a substitute the sect goons would never suspect.

"Champ, I want you to do something for me," he said. "See that girl in the blue, the one you saw me talkin' to yesterday? Well, d'you think you could manage to speak to her without makin' the four young guys on the outside of the crowd suspicious?"

"Sho' thing, Brett. No sweat. What yuh wan' me t'tell 'er?"

Grant thought for a moment. "Tell her I sent you, an' that I don't think it's safe for me to come over to speak to her. I think they're onto me, so it could cause 'er trouble if I'm seen speakin' to 'er. So tell 'er not to worry, I won't let 'er down, I'll think of some way to contact 'er again soon. Y'got that?"

"Is dat it?" asked the Champ, obviously disappointed.

"It's important that she knows I haven't forgotten 'er or that I won't let 'er down," Grant assured him. "An' listen, don't let those guys see you talkin' to 'er too long," he repeated as the Champ scrambled from the car.

Following Grant's instructions, he left by the rear door behind the driver's seat, climbing over from the front, so that he got out onto the sidewalk shielded by the car from any observer over at the van. He stooped to fasten on his roller skates and Grant addressed him from the window.

"When you've spoken to 'er, go on up the street a bit, before you cross an' head back here, okay?"

The boy finished adjusting his skates and straightened up. He waved a dismissive hand. "Consider it done. An' stop worryin', man," he admonished, as though he were Grant's senior. "Jes' leave everythin' to good ol' Jefferson Brown."

"Jefferson Brown? Who's he?" asked Grant, mystified.

"Me! Dat's who!" The small black face came close to the open window, and the big eyes were round and serious as the boy whispered, "Dat's ma real name. On'y ma very bestest frien's know it. So, don' never go tellin' no-one. Promise?" Grant nodded, dumb struck.

"Cross y'heart an' hope t'die?" demanded the Champ.

"Cross m'heart an' hope t'die," Grant solemnly repeated the dread oath – and the small black face was gone.

Grant watched the slight figure appear on the far sidewalk and glide smoothly along, nimbly swerving round pedestrians as he went, making his progress seem like play. His misgiving at having sent the kid in his place vanished, as he shook his head in amused admiration. The Champ was a natural actor, as were most kids of his age, but he also had a veneer of street cunning overlaying his child's mind, giving him a maturity of outlook far beyond his years.

He watched the Champ approach the loose crowd before the van and saw him stop and speak to Louise. Then some passers-by momentarily obscured his view. When they had passed, the two figures of the girl and boy had gone.

Grant had a sudden surge of panic, and reflexively reached for the door handle, ready to launch himself from the car and start running for the van. He restrained himself long enough to seek out the four sentinels on the outskirts of the crowd. They were all still in position – and paying no particular attention to anything which might be happening in the area of the van.

Then he saw them. A wave of relief washed over him and he snorted with sudden laughter as he saw the diminutive figure of the Champ – "Jefferson Brown to his bestest frien's" – clutching a hamburger in one fist and a plastic cup in the other. Louise was talking to him and smiling.

A moment later, the Champ weaved his way off through the crowd and was gone, leaving the girl on her own again. Grant saw Louise turn her head briefly to watch him go, but she resumed her task of handing out leaflets to passers-by. Grant was satisfied that none of the four he had identified as sentries seemed to have noticed anything amiss.

In a matter of minutes, the Champ was back. Grant reached back and opened the rear door for him and he tumbled excitedly into the car. He was clutching a half-eaten hamburger and a few of Louise's leaflets.

"Well done, Champ," Grant commended him warmly. "You were terrific. Did you give 'er my message? What did she say?"

The urchin nodded, grinning triumphantly from ear to ear. "Yeah, no sweat. Like ah tol' yuh, man, it wuz easy." The small black face turned serious and he lowered his voice conspiratorially. "She agrees it mightn't be safe fo' yuh t'go over t'talk to 'er y'self. She says she thinks dem four cats're watchin' fo' someone, sho'nuff. She don' know who it is or why, but says it'd be best fo' yuh t'take care. Oh yeah … an' she said t'give yuh dese …" he held out the leaflets to Grant. "One of 'em's got a message on it fo' yuh!"

"A message?" exclaimed Grant, surprised. "How in hell did she manage that right under their noses?"

"Easy," replied the Champ, matter-of-factly. "She jes' peeled 'em off the bottom of th'pile, sweet as y'like. Like a Mis'sippi gambler in da movies. Yeah Brett, y'sho' picked y'self a good'un."

Grant chose to ignore this last remark as he shook his head in amused disbelief at the combined resourcefulness of the two youngsters and turned his attention to the thin sheaf of leaflets Louise had given to the Champ. He smoothed them out and flicked through them. There were eight leaflets in all and he found the one he wanted third from the bottom. She had printed her message in between the lines of print, in a neat round hand.

HUNCH

He read: Have thought over your offer of help. The answer is yes. Please take care, they are dangerous if crossed. Re the boy you mentioned, if captured he will be held somewhere in the basement of B/House in the Turkey Pens, where they dry out addicts. One thing you should know – I have no close family. I am an orphan. But I won't impose on you for long. If you find you're unable to help me, thanks anyway. I know you meant it. Regards, Louise.

Grant looked up from the leaflet and stared grimly across at the van. He noticed that a few more people had drifted in to join the loose throng in front of it. However, he knew this would not deter the sect heavies from attacking him if they had orders to do so. He had witnessed enough of their fanaticism and mindless ferocity the previous night to convince him of this. He decided there was nothing to be gained from forcing a direct confrontation at this stage. Besides, as he was on his own, this was one time when discretion definitely had it over valour.

He thought for a moment. He reckoned that a playful child would escape his own attention in the present situation and that the sect heavies would be no different in this respect. Without taking his eyes off the van up ahead, he said, "Champ, d'you think you could take another message to the girl, without these four goons noticin'? Be worth a ten-spot."

"Sho' thing, Brett," the youngster responded eagerly. "What's da message?"

"Tell 'er I'll keep my word to help 'er. Tell 'er to be patient an' not to lose hope. I'll work something out." He turned to look at the Champ. "Okay? Y'got that?"

"Check!" The kid was out of the rear door in a flash. Then something seemed to occur to him and he paused, his face clouding over. Suddenly he turned and leaned in Grant's window. "Brett? ..." he said hesitantly.

"Yeah?" Grant looked into the solemn little face at his shoulder.

"Y'don' have t'give me no money." The Champ spoke sincerely, if a little reluctantly. "You ma frien' ... an' ah like da chick too. Ah'll do it fo' nuthin'."

Grant realised the effort it must have cost the penniless street

339

urchin – one of a large, poor, ghetto family – to speak these words, and so kiss such a windfall good-bye. He regarded the boy with a mixture of admiration and affection.

"That's okay, Champ. But I ain't givin' you the money, man. You're doin' an important job for me ... like carryin' out a mission against the enemy. In fact, you're my undercover man ... Agent Jefferson Brown, code named The Champ. So, y'see, I'm only payin' you your fee for the job."

The small face lit up and the big eyes sparkled with excitement. "No kiddin'? It's that important, huh?" Grant nodded. "Okay Brett, Ah'm gone!"

He flashed away, only to return again minutes later, having once more successfully spoken briefly to Louise without drawing any notice from the four lookouts. They were obviously too preoccupied with watching for his own appearance, to pay much attention to the comings and goings of one of a dozen or so street kids.

When the Champ tumbled into the rear seat for the second time and reported breathlessly, and with comic seriousness, "Mission accomplished, Chief," Grant congratulated him laughingly, started up the car and drove off. He allowed an overtaking truck to come alongside and shield him from the van personnel, as he passed them on the opposite side of the street.

Dropping the Champ off back at the vicinity of the Harlem Tower office block, Grant handed him his well-earned ten dollar fee. "Here y'go, Agent Brown. Y'did a great job back there in enemy territory."

'Agent Brown' accepted the folded bill with a delighted grin, and threw up a salute. Grant returned the salute and then, as he made to drive away, the Champ, looking at the ten dollar bill before stuffing it into a pocket, said, "Man-o-man! ... Ten whole dollars ... whoo-ee!" Then, looking up he shook his head sympathetically and added, "Man, yo' sho' got it bad!" and darted off, leaving Grant gaping after him.

His watch informed him it was almost 11 a.m., so Grant decided to grab a quick snack at the deli counter and head on out to Rockford. He was looking forward to his meeting with

Jim Miller and his abductors. At the same time, he couldn't help but feel thankful that he'd be accompanied by the reassuring presence of Sheriff Nate Springfield.

36

THE BLUE UNIFORMED SECURITY GUARD WATCHED with barely disguised contempt, as the sharply dressed young Mafia hood re-emerged from the elevator in which he had ascended only ten minutes earlier and approached him. He reckoned the punk had seen too many old gangster movies, to judge by the obligatory dark shades he affected under his snap-brim hat. The intended intimidating effect was somewhat spoiled, however, by the single red rose he carried, peeking coyly out from its tissue and cellophane wrapping.

The guard, a burly retired cop in his late fifties, name of Patrick Donahue, had landed his easy job, which comfortably supplemented his police pension, by calling in a couple of favours the Neroni Family owed him from his days on the force. But his opinion of the swaggering Mafia hoods, who were now his fellow employees, was still coloured by his long years of ingrained police thinking.

None of this showed in his carefully expressionless face as he raised a quizzical eyebrow in answer to the peremptory, "Hey you … ring Miss Menotti's apartment. She ain't answerin' th'door," directed at him by the approaching messenger.

"Can't say I blame 'er," replied Donahue shortly. "She's choosy about who she lets in. An' another thing …" he added, pointedly eyeing the single red rose, "she don' encourage Furino to entertain his … ah … friends … at home!"

The young hood coloured up and he took a threatening pace forward. "Who th'fuck d'you think you're talkin' to, asshole?" he demanded angrily. "Watch y'fuckin' mouth or I'll …"

"Or you'll what?" demanded Donahue, thoroughly enjoying

himself. He hadn't baited a young punk like this since his days on the force. He knew the type well. Vicious swaggering killers, all of them. He hated them with a deep contemptuous loathing. In fact, this feeling was born of his secret self-contempt for having spent his police service on the Family payroll ... that and his subsequent acceptance of his sinecure of a job from the Don – the mobster Bruno Neroni.

Donahue knew from long experience just how far he could push punks like the one standing before him now. He had cut his teeth on them in his years as a patrolman on the tough waterfront area of Manhattan's East Side. The angry young mafioso failed to notice that the guard's insolent wide-legged stance, thumbs hooked arrogantly into his leather belt, meant his right hand was resting lightly on his gun holster.

"Or I'll rearrange y'fuckin' face, ya uniformed prick!" he snarled at the guard.

"Careful," warned Donahue, nodding at the rose in the mobster's hand, "or you'll bruise y'pretty flower, an' Gina won' make it with you tonight."

The young hood choked incoherently as his temper snapped. His hand darted under his lapel for the gun in his shoulder holster, intending to pistol-whip the insolent uniformed jerk who had insulted him. But his fingers had barely touched the butt of his automatic, when he found himself staring into the unwavering muzzle of the guard's big Colt .38, two feet from the bridge of his nose. He froze and the tip of his tongue flicked nervously over suddenly dry lips.

"How'd y'like me to blow y'nose, sonny? ... right through th'backa y'fuckin' head! Now, take y'hand outa there! ... slow an' easy ... keep it open, fingers spread ... that's th'way." Donahue's commanding tone, coupled with his cold eyes sighting along the barrel, brooked no defiance.

"Right, we'll start again, shall we? ..." Donahue stepped back and holstered his gun in an easy, practised movement, but retained his grip on the butt. "This time, we'll have a little respect, punk. Now, state y'business."

The mobster swallowed hard, fighting to regain control of himself. His flash of temper had been superseded by fear, when he had been temporarily turned to stone by the black gorgon's eye of the big .38. He glared at Donahue with sullen hatred. "You kin kiss y'job good-bye, mister, when Furino hears about this."

"An' you kin kiss that fuckin' little fruit's ass!" Donahue replied dismissively. "Tell 'im anythin' y'like. I'm employed here by th'Don himself. Now, you were about to ask me somethin' ... politely ... as I recall?"

Taking a deep breath, the mobster grated out from between clenched teeth, "Will you phone Miss Menotti's penthouse t'see if she's at home?"

"No need. She's at home all right," replied Donahue shortly. "I bin on duty since eight this mornin'. The man I relieved didn' mention her or Furino goin' out durin' his tour, an' they ain't gone out while I bin here. I suggest y'lean on th'bell. Maybe they had a rough night up there, playin' hunt th'dildo, or somethin'."

The mobster shook his head, genuine puzzlement on his face. "I rang th'goddam bell so hard no-one could sleep through it. An' I knocked as well. Nah ... if they're in there, they ain' answerin', I tell you. No way could anyone sleep through the racket I kicked up."

Donahue eyed him for a moment longer, then he shrugged, stepped into his cubicle and lifted the phone. He dialled Carla Menotti's number and let it ring for a full two minutes, before cutting it off by depressing the receiver rest with a finger. He dialled again, listened for another couple of minutes, then cut it off again. He called out to the young mobster, who was watching him from the foyer, "We'll check this out. Wait there till I call Toni Scirea. Anythin' wrong up there anytime, he's t'be informed."

This time he dialled Scirea's basement apartment – he was the head security guard and Furino's man into the bargain.

Barely five minutes after Scirea and the young mobster had disappeared into the elevator, the phone buzzed at Donahue's elbow. When he answered it, Toni Scirea's voice sounded tersely in his ear. "Pat? Get up here right away. We got trouble ... big trouble!"

The phone went dead with no further explanation being offered. Donahue dropped the receiver back onto its cradle and strode quickly for the elevators ...

When Donahue arrived at the door of the penthouse apartment, it opened silently before he could reach for the bell-push. Scirea, who must have been waiting behind it, watching for him through the Judas-hole, looked pale and strained. He ushered Donahue in and closed the door before speaking. His voice was hoarse with tension.

"Jeezus, what a fuckin' mess this is ..." he burst out. He drew a deep, shuddering breath before continuing, "They bin wasted. Both of 'em. The Don's gonna go off his fuckin' tree!" He stopped and swallowed hard, his lined grey face working with suppressed emotion.

Donahue, to whom violent death was no stranger after thirty years as a New York cop, was nevertheless taken aback by the shocking news. This particular death was just a mite too close to home for comfort. It affected his employer and thus, indirectly, himself. "Y'sure it ain't suicide?" he asked, with more hope than conviction.

"Suicide?" Scirea nearly choked on the word, then he went on bitterly, "Some fuckin' suicide! It's like a scene from Chainsaw Massacre in there. They both bin worked over with a blade. It ain't pretty t'look at."

"It never is," replied Donahue grimly. "Where are they?"

"Through here ..." Scirea led his colleague into Carla Menotti's sitting room and across to the adjoining bathroom. The young mobster was sitting smoking, white faced, in an easy chair well away from the open bathroom door, and at an angle which ensured he could not see in.

Donahue's lip curled in a sneer of contempt as he eyed him in the passing. "What's wrong, killer? Don't you like admirin' another pro's handiwork?"

"Fuck you!" came the thick reply.

Donahue barked a laugh and Scirea snapped, "Can it, Pat! We got ourselves more'n enough trouble from outside, without fallin' out among ourselves."

Scirea stepped inside the open bathroom door. Donahue followed ... and stopped dead. It was as though they'd walked into a slaughterhouse, but one which the slaughtermen had abruptly vacated, leaving the partially butchered carcasses behind them and without cleaning up the bloody results of their work.

The eviscerated corpse of Carla Menotti had been turned onto its face, and was lying in a huge pool of congealed blood in the bottom of the large sunken bath. She was surrounded by ropes of bluish-pink intestines, which had been roughly pulled from her insides and draped around her.

Seated at the top end of the bath, his widespread legs straddling the dead woman's head, was the body of Giovanni Furino. Like her, he was naked. His head was leaning back, mouth agape, between the gleaming gold faucets, over which his elbows had been hooked to hold him in position.

Donahue whistled softly as he ran his eyes along the woman's cruelly slashed back, till they came to rest on the raw wound between the man's legs, where his genitals had been neatly sliced from his body. Then his gaze travelled on up the naked man's torso, noting that it had also been gouged with gaping slashes.

The only sound in the tiled chamber of horrors was the heavy breathing of the two security guards. Donahue felt the need to break the tense silence. He said the first thing that came into his head. Pointing at Furino's mutilated groin he commented, "Looks like someone stole 'is family jewels."

"They're in his mouth," replied Scirea tersely.

Donahue gave one of his barking laughs. "No kiddin'? That'll make a change for 'im ... suckin' his own dick insteada someone else's!"

"Fuck sake! Is that all y'kin say at a time like this? You're sick, y'know that? Sick in th'fuckin' head!" blazed Scirea, relieving his own tension by venting his spleen on his coarse humoured colleague.

"Is that so?" Donahue eyed him bleakly. "Well maybe that's cuz I work with some pretty sick people. But I'll tell y'somethin'," he turned back and nodded towards the gory duo in the bath.

"I ain't half as sick as whoever it wuz done this!"

Scirea broke the ensuing silence. "How th'fuck do I tell th'Don about ... this?" The unanswerable question hung on the air. Then he said, "Hey Pat ... whaddaya make of them cut-marks on 'em?"

Donahue ran his eye over the series of gaping slashes on the torsos of both corpses. They had been sliced into the flesh so soon after death that thin trickles of blood had oozed from them, running down so as to link some of the cuts together in places, rendering them unrecognisable as Roman numerals. He frowned as he studied the gory result. Suddenly his furrowed brow cleared. He had spotted what he thought was something familiar in the pattern of marks.

"I know this might sound crazy," he began slowly, "but they look t'me like them funny marks the Chinese make fer writin'."

"Them fuckin' slants!" Scirea exploded vehemently. The violence of his response drew a surprised look from Donahue, but he rushed on regardlessly. "I shoulda known somethin' wuz wrong when I saw them animals in a class joint like this."

"Slants? What slants? What y'talkin' about?" demanded Donahue. Like Scirea, he possessed a white supremacist distrust of all Orientals, in his case resulting from his years as a member of the sizeable and elitist Irish-American brotherhood within the NYPD.

Scirea's imagination was fired by the potentially disastrous situation he was in. The Don was still to be told and his reaction would be one of predictable fury. The problem facing him was how to direct that fury away from himself, if possible onto some other target. Donahue's remark about the resemblance of the blood-smeared cuts on the corpses to Chinese ideograms had provided him with that target – the Orientals he had seen the previous night – the slants!

With the eagerness of a drowning man who is suddenly presented with an empty life raft floating past within reach of his desperate grasp, Scirea described the two young Japanese businessmen he had seen leaving the building some time after Furino had left him. In his overheated imagination they now became imbued with sinister significance. "A grand gets you a bent nickel they were two o' them Triads the Family's bin havin' trouble with," he concluded confidently.

Scirea was fast recovering from the paralysis of indecision which had gripped him the instant he had first seen the butchered corpses. "I'll go call Falcone an' arrange to see the Don, so I kin tell 'im personally. Wait here till I git back." With this instruction, he turned to leave.

He had only taken a few paces, when Donahue's voice brought him to a halt. "Before you call the consigliere, I suggest you call the cops. The Don's gonna have enough trouble on his hands without the D.A. gittin' awkward over the late reportin' of a double homicide."

Scirea spun on his heel and faced Donahue again. "You can't forget you were a cop, can you?" he remarked scathingly. "We'll call the law if and when the Don wants us to … an' not before. He's your boss now, not the fuckin' D.A. An' another thing … if the Don decides he don' wan' us to involve the law, the D.A. kin go fuck 'imself! capice?"

Donahue shrugged. "Do it your way. Only thing is, with all this blood around it's jes' possible Homicide c'd turn up prints t'nail a suspect. I expect th'Don'll want t'bring all th'pressure he can on these Triads. That's all I'm sayin'," he said stubbornly.

"So I'll suggest it to 'im," retorted Scirea shortly. "But until we git orders, we do nuthin'." Turning away again, he headed for the phone in the next room to put through his call to consigliere Falcone. As he picked up the receiver, he wiped a sheen of sweat from his forehead and breathed deeply, in an effort to calm the nervous tension which was churning his guts and threatening to loosen his bowels.

37

DON BRUNO NERONI HEARD SCIREA OUT, SEATED behind the big polished oak desk in his spacious office. The security guard finished his report and stood in deferential silence, nervously turning his uniform cap in his hands, waiting for the storm to break. Despite the coolness of the air-conditioned room, he felt sweat dewing his forehead and upper lip and silently cursed himself for his outward display of fear. He felt sure this would be taken for a sign of guilt or complicity.

The silent, hood-eyed figure of the Family *consigliere*, Emilio Falcone, seated in his customary position to one side of the desk, did nothing to soothe Scirea's unease. In fact the circumstances made it worse, for it gave the interview the uncomfortable semblance of a court martial before a panel of two judges.

The Don's only outward reaction to Scirea's shocking news had been a tightening of his thin-lipped mouth and a slight narrowing of his eyes, as he studied the perspiring security guard closely, seeking any hint of a flaw in his story. Now he leaned forward, elbows on the desk, steepling his fingers before him. When he spoke after a moment's pause his voice was calm, betraying no hint of the maelstrom of fury boiling within him.

"You say when Miss Menotti and Furino returned from their walk, Furino stopped to speak with you before he went up to the apartment? Does this mean he let Miss Menotti go up in the elevator unescorted?"

The soft voice did not fool Scirea. The eyes regarding him were grey as stone ... and as cold. He had owed Furino for his job but he reckoned death had cancelled the debt, especially in the dangerous situation he now found himself in. He licked his dry lips and cleared his throat before answering, "Yes Boss ..." He hesitated, then a last shred of loyalty made him add, "but he didn't wait long before he followed her."

An instant later he regretted his words when the Don commented icily, "Long enough ... if someone was waiting for her!"

Scirea shuffled his feet, uncomfortable under the level gaze of the steely grey eyes, and mumbled his agreement. Neroni spoke again, slowly, as though thinking aloud. "You saw these Orientals ... these slants, as you call them ... leaving? But you did not see them enter?"

"No Boss." Scirea shook his head decisively, glad that attention was being diverted away from himself. "They coulda snuck in the service entrance at th'back, or maybe up th'fire escape from the alley."

"You have checked these ways for any signs of unauthorised entry?" the soft voice asked.

"Ah ... no Boss," The Don raised an inquiring eyebrow and Scirea coughed nervously into his hand in an attempt to clear his throat, which felt like it was lined with sandpaper. He spread his hands in eloquent appeal. "I didn' wanna waste any time before I let you know the bad news, see ... an' ... well, I reckoned the cops'd take care of that ... when they come ..." he tailed off.

"You have informed the police?" The Don's voice suddenly hardened to match the twin bores of his eyes.

"Hell no, Boss!" Scirea hastened to reassure him. He blinked nervously as sweat stung his eyes. "I came straight here first. Donahue wanted t'call 'em right away, but I told 'im t'wait until after I'd got orders from you." Triumphantly he thought That's one up your Irish ass Donahue, ya shitmouthed cop bastard! He saw the Don relax again and felt a little better.

Neroni pursed his lips and nodded slowly. "Good ... good. In this you have acted correctly. It will of course be necessary for one of our people to check out the apartment for anything ... embarrassing ... to the Family, before we call in the police. The police ..." His mouth twisted into a sneer, "... yes, they can then investigate how these murderers entered the building. After all, we pay them enough."

He thought for a moment, then seemed to come to a decision. "Very well, Antonio. Thank you for delivering the news personally. I admire a man who does not delegate unpleasant duties to others. It would have been all too easy for you to allow my messenger, young Angelo Capaldi, to report back with the evil tidings."

Relief washed through Scirea, leaving him with a sudden need to empty his bladder. It looked as though he had come safely through his ordeal. Masking his elation, he said deferentially, "I have too much respect for you, Don Bruno, to send another with news which was my responsibility to bring myself."

Then, as the Don inclined his head in acknowledgement,

Scirea decided on impulse to play his lucky streak to the limit and pressed on, "Don Bruno ... I know this is hardly the proper time ... but may I presume to ask if you would consider keeping me on in my job at the apartment building? I know I was employed by Furino, but ..."

"You may have been given the job by Furino but you are on the Family payroll," interrupted Neroni drily. "I will give the matter my consideration. Some degree of reorganisation may be called for. But for the moment I see no reason to change things as they stand."

The Don leaned back in his padded chair. "So ... I want you now to return to the apartment, Antonio, and await further orders. The *consigliere*," he nodded towards the brooding figure of Falcone, "will make the necessary arrangements and inform you when to call in the police. You will tell them how you discovered the crime, adjusting only the time when you entered the flat. This will avoid any awkward questions about the time lapse between the discovery of the crime and your reporting it. That is all. You may leave now and return to your post."

When Scirea had mumbled his thanks and left, the Don at last permitted his pent-up rage to erupt in the sole presence of his silent *consigliere*. Eyes blazing, he slammed his clenched fists down onto the gleaming desk top and spat out his fury, his accented speech thickening and becoming spiced with Italian.

"This is *intollerabile* ... it is an *infamia*! ... These Triad *animales*! Have they no sense of *vergogna* ... of shame? Where is their *onore* to make war on women in such a fashion? They are not human ... they are not even deserving to be named *animales*. They are *rettiles* ... reptiles!"

Emilio Falcone waited patiently till his Don's rage had spent itself. He, better than most men, knew the pattern well. He had lived with it for the best part of twenty years. First, the outburst of fury, followed by a short period of brooding silence, while Neroni composed himself to think rationally again. Don Bruno Neroni never made a decision in anger – which was why he was so successful in his chosen world of organised crime. For a full five minutes or so, Falcone sat in stoical silence while the Don's verbal outpouring of anger washed over him and spent itself.

The brooding silence which followed was almost as impressive as the storm which had preceded it. The fury was still there. It hung over and around the man like a charge of static electricity, but now it was being controlled ... harnessed ... channelled into stimulating the thought processes of his devious and very able mind.

Falcone rose quietly from his chair. Walking over to a bar in the corner, he poured two stiff brandies, returned to place the two large bowl glasses on the desk and resumed his seat.

The seconds ticked past and lengthened into another full five minutes. Then the Don stirred. Picking up the brandy, he swirled it gently, savoured its rich bouquet, sipped and swallowed. When he spoke, his voice was calm again, his emotions once more firmly under control.

"So ... we are dealing with reptiles? Very well, we shall crush them underfoot before they can rear up to strike us higher than our ankles. Call a meeting for tonight of our *caporegimes*. I want the three of them here for eight sharp. Tomorrow we will go to war. A series of co-ordinated strikes on selected targets, where we know these scum to be operating. We have failed to be ruthless enough in our dealings with these rice-eating *banditos*. No longer! They will bitterly regret the day they decided to provoke me by murdering my innocent little Carla."

Falcone jotted down a note on the pad he held on his knee. In his hoarse voice he asked, "And the guard, Scirea? Do we make an example of him to teach others to be more vigilant in future? Is there any chance he could have been got at ... that he could be implicated in what happened?"

The Don considered this for a moment, then with a slight shake of his head he said dismissively, "No. That will not be necessary. I cannot see him conspiring in Furino's death. After all, he was under the impression, as you heard, that he would be losing his job ... and, no doubt, his life ... just as you are thinking now. No, I am satisfied he had nothing to gain by it and everything to lose. He is our man now, not Gino's. And he knows it. But ... we will let him sweat a little, before finally confirming him in his job. It will do no harm and serve to make him doubly vigilant in future."

The Don reached out and took a cigar from an exquisitely carved humidor on the desk and gestured for Falcone to do likewise. Falcone struck a match and lit the Don's cigar before lighting his own. The two men finished their brandies and smoked in silence for a few seconds more, then the Don indicated that the session was at an end by saying, "After you have arranged for someone to check out the apartment, inform Precinct Captain Hegarty ... tell him to ensure any police inquiries are finished as quickly as possible. For all the good they will do. And have some of our people in attendance in and around the building, with orders to discourage any press interest."

Falcone nodded and rose to go. "Oh, one thing more ..." the Don's voice made him pause. "Tell the *caporegimes* to bring with them a list of all Chinese owned properties in their respective territories. Also a list of any known street pushers who are suspected of handling Triad merchandise and where these are known to operate."

The *consigliere* left the room to carry out his instructions and to make the necessary arrangements for the proposed council of war. It did not seem strange or unnatural to him that the man he served had, with a few words, reprieved a man from death – and would, with a few more words that coming evening, condemn many others. Such was the awesome power wielded by this gangster, this dangerous man, who chose to ignore the laws of normal society in favour of his own code.

But even had the thought occurred to Emilio Falcone, he would have accepted it as perfectly natural in the order of things.

38

CURTIS WASHED DOWN THE LAST MOUTHFUL OF HIS lunch – a pastrami and pickle sandwich – with the dregs of his coffee. Grimacing at the taste of the tepid liquid, he wiped his mouth with a paper napkin, then stuffed it and the disposable cup into the paper bag and dropped the lot into his wastepaper basket. He lit a cigarette and continued scrutinising the lengthy list of suspects' names on the computer printout on his desk blotter.

These were the names of known religious cranks who had been convicted of any offences involving violence. After twenty minutes he had ticked off several possibles for questioning. Tapping his teeth with his pencil, he leaned back and ran a critical eye over the short-listed candidates he had selected for his further attention.

He hated to admit it but none of the suspects had the right "feel" about them. He had been a cop in Homicide for too long to delude himself with the popular myth that crimes were often solved by brilliant hunches on the part of the investigating officer. He knew only too well that the drab reality was that most crimes remained unsolved and the ones which were brought to a successful conclusion were usually the result of long, painstaking inquiries. Extracting information from reluctant witnesses could more often than not be likened to a dentist pulling teeth.

Real life detective work consisted mainly of exhaustive door-to-door leg work, interviewing possible eye-witnesses, followed by the long grind of checking and rechecking reams of statements. Even the specialists of the detective branch, the photographic and fingerprint experts and the white-coated scientists of the forensic labs, were only backup teams for the front line infantryman in the never ending war of crime detection – the detective.

However, Curtis's long years of experience had developed his intuition and given him the ability to be pretty accurate in sorting the wheat from the chaff, either when assessing relevant information or probable suspects. But from the condensed histories of the assorted religious cranks on the printout, even although they had all displayed varying degrees of violence, he could find no suggestion of the level of danger potential he was looking for. He sighed resignedly at the unattractive prospect of a long round of tracing and interviewing these pathetic screwballs. Just then he was saved from further self-pity by the timely arrival of Turner, who knocked and entered.

The tall Texan closed the door behind him and waved a couple of sheets of paper at Curtis, an excited grin on his face.

"Chief, I think I jes' might've turned up somethin' that'll interest yuh. Lookit this ..." He advanced across the room and placed the sheets before Curtis, covering the list of names he had been studying.

Despite his ingrained caution, Curtis felt a responsive stir as the younger man's excitement communicated itself to him. He knew Turner to be normally undemonstrative, so his obvious agitation must mean he'd discovered something he considered really important.

Curtis picked up the two sheets of paper, which were covered by short entries in Turner's untidy but legible scrawl. Arranged in chronological order, each of the fifteen paragraphs commenced with a date, a name and a location, and each contained brief details of one of the murders they were investigating. This part of each entry Curtis could have recited by heart, he had been over the details so many times over the preceding five years.

It was the second part of each entry, the fresh information added by Turner, which caught and held his attention. This listed the names of any religious personalities and organisations known to have been particularly active in the city on the relevant dates.

Against eleven of the victims' names there were listed several names of preachers or organisations. Against the remaining four victims, there were only two or three noted down. What riveted Curtis's attention was the fact that there was one entry common to every case – underlined in red by Turner – THE REVEREND MARTIN BISHOP (THE CHILDREN OF BETHLEHEM).

Curtis raised his head and met Turner's eye. He shook his head slowly in stunned disbelief. "How th'fuck did we miss this? Christ, we've checked an' double-checked every possible angle. I tellya, I fed so many facts an' angles into that fuckin' computer, I damn near gave it constipation. But I never thoughta this ..." He slammed his hand down onto the offending sheets of paper on the desktop.

"Don' feel too badly 'bout it Chief," said Turner reassuringly. "After all, it wuz a purty obscure line o' reasonin'. Who'd've thought all these killin's were the work of some crazy Jesus freak?"

"I shoulda thought of it – that's who!" He emphasised his point by thumping himself angrily on the chest with his clenched fist. "What's worse is I actually considered the idea a coupla times, an' tossed it away. The bastard's even bin leavin' a fuckin' great sign pointin' after 'im." He groaned and scrubbed a hand over his face. "I must be gittin' too old fer this," he finished despondently.

"Waal, I think yo're blamin' y'self unfairly," Turner consoled him. "Even the computer couldn't crack those crazy numbers. But you did! Anyhow Chief, lookin' on th' positive side, I reckon we've bought ourselves some time t' follow this up. We know from past experience our man lies low fer a while after every killin'. The shortest gap between cases has bin three months. Right? So, if we git our asses in gear we c'd nail this bastard before he strikes again."

Curtis considered this advice in silence for a few moments. Then he grinned at Turner, pushed back his chair and stood up. "Know somethin' pardner? You're damn right. Insteada me sittin' on my can bellyachin' t' you, we should be chasin' up this lead. Okay, do we know this Bishop character's whereabouts?"

"Sure do," Tex responded positively. "I ran a quick check on 'im. It seems his church rents a floor of that new Eldorado Apartment Block down off Broadway. That's whar he's at right now."

Curtis raised expressive eyebrows. "The Eldorado, is it? Ain't that th' new luxury apartment buildin' they call The Millionaires' Flophouse? The way I hear it, y'gotta be on noddin' terms with the Gettys, Rothschilds an' Kennedys t' be considered fer an apartment there. They say y' don' flash an ID t' git past the security men on the doors, instead y'gotta flash a Swiss bank account number. Seems Christian humility don' figger in th'Reverend Martin Bishop's lifestyle. Anyway, go on, Tex. What else did y'come up with?"

"He's in temp'ry residence there fer now, on accounta he's conductin' a series o' rallies at the Washin'ton Centre. He calls 'em crusades ... what's up, Chief?" Turner paused and looked inquiringly at Curtis, who was staring at him as though he'd seen a ghost.

"Crusades?" Curtis repeated, and continued to stare blankly at Turner for a second. Then suddenly he struck his forehead with the heel of his hand in a gesture of exasperation. "The Children of Bethlehem! Of course!" He exclaimed. "I thought th'name wuz familiar. Christ Tex, this Martin Bishop must be the one Brett wuz on about, the one who calls himself The Prophet. If he is, then accordin' to what Brett tells me, this guy has some real crazy people in his organisation. What's th'bettin' he might jes' turn out t'be the craziest of the lot himself?"

Galvanised into action, he started round the desk. "Right. Let's start from th'top. Run a full check on this Bishop character, then we'll go have a talk with his reverence before anyone else gits sliced up. While you're runnin' your check, I'll ..." He never got the chance to say what he intended to be doing, because halfway to the door, he was interrupted in mid-sentence by the sharp ringing of his phone. He walked back to the desk and snatched up the receiver.

"Homicide, Lieutenant Curtis," he announced, then listened to the voice on the other end.

Turner looked back as he reached the door, and stopped when he saw Curtis signal with his free hand for him to wait. The young detective felt a sudden stab of unease, as he watched the lieutenant's rugged features assume an expression of stunned disbelief followed by one of baffled rage. The import of the call was obviously not good – and Turner had the sinking feeling he knew what it might be. He hoped he was wrong.

Across the room, Curtis grunted a couple of times in acknowledgement of the message he was receiving. Finally he said, "Okay, Jim. I'll be right there. Oh, Jim ... keep this under wraps, okay? Strictly no press, an' tell your men they jes' bin struck dumb. They talk to nobody about this ... an' I mean nobody! Is that clear? Right, we're on our way." Turner watched Curtis slowly replace the receiver and knew with sick certainty that his premonition had been spot on.

When Curtis turned to face his partner, it seemed his lined face had aged ten years in the two minutes of the call's duration. "So much fer us havin' bought ourselves some time before our man made his next move." he said bitterly. "That wuz Jim Carmody from the Flyin' Squad. He's over on 5th Avenue with a murder team. Says he's got two more fer us …"

"Two?" Turner's shocked disbelief mirrored Curtis's of a moment before. "Is he sure they're ours? … I mean …"

"I know what y'mean," growled Curtis, nodding grimly. "Yeah, there's no doubt. They got our special brand marks on 'em, he says. An' git this … one of 'em's only Bruno Neroni's fancy piece … name of Carla Menotti. The other's 'er bodyguard, a little fag name of Giovanni Furino, known as Gina The Fruit. Maybe you've run across 'im?"

Turner shook his head and Curtis continued angrily, "Christ, this is all we needed! An' jes' when it looks like we've got a lead to our man at last, th'crazy fucker goes an' hits two people belongin' to a top syndicate boss. Bruno Neroni, fer fuck sake! That Sicilian suckhole only has half the judges an' politicians in th'fuckin' State in 'is pocket. What's th'bettin' Elrick's phone's red fuckin' hot, right now? This is where th'shit hits th'fan. We'd better be right about friend Bishop, or our asses are in a sling."

"You wan' I should git Connolly t'run the check on Bishop, Chief?" asked Turner. "It'd save us time later."

Curtis thought for a moment. "Yeah. Do that. Tell 'im it's urgent. We'll pick up whatever he's got as soon as we've finished at the murder scene. Then we'll go interview friend Bishop."

He bared his teeth in a grin, his old pugnaciousness reasserting itself. "This cat I gotta see fer myself! Oh … an' on the subject of Bishop," he added as an afterthought, "tell Connolly t'put a surveillance team on the Eldorado Block. Round th'clock. I wan' mug shots of everyone who enters or leaves. An' especially I wanna know every move this Bishop makes. Then meet me in th'car pool."

As the door closed behind Turner, Curtis began to rummage through the files on his desk until he found the one he wanted. He extracted several big glossy black and white prints from the folder, sorted them into two thin piles and then slid them carefully into separate manila envelopes. He put them into separate inside pockets of his jacket. Pausing only to shrug into his coat and jam his hat on his head, he headed for the door.

39

WITHIN TWENTY MINUTES OF RECEIVING THE UN-welcome phone call, Curtis and Turner were standing in the late Carla Menotti's sitting room, amidst the organised chaos of a police murder scene examination in full swing. They were listening intently while Lieutenant Jim Carmody filled them in on the known details. Like all the fifteen preceding cases, these details were gory in the extreme, but unhelpful.

While Carmody's grim report unfolded, Curtis absently watched two forensic men armed with a long tape take measurements from the door of the room to various bloodstains on the carpet and furniture. A sample was then being taken from each bloodstain, smeared onto a glass slide, and sealed in a small plastic bag. A third man was meticulously noting the exact location of their findings on a diagram of the room. Other Squad detectives were carefully examining the room and its contents and dusting for prints.

Just then a short, smartly dressed man wearing horn-rimmed spectacles and carrying a soft hat and small black bag, walked from the bathroom and came towards them. Behind him the doorway he had just come through was repeatedly lit up with eye-dazzling brilliance, as the flashlights of the photographers got to work. Joining the group, the man nodded to them and addressed Carmody.

"I've finished in there, lieutenant," he announced. "You can

move the bodies when you're ready. Messy business, this one."
He gave a slight shake of his head, the expression on his thin
face more one of sadness than disgust.

"Thanks, Doctor Friedman," Carmody replied. Introducing
Curtis and Turner he continued, "Lieutenant Curtis will be
taking over the case from me. He's in charge of a special Homicide
team investigating a series of murders, all of which have certain
common factors present here."

The doctor peered appraisingly at Curtis over the top of his
bifocals. "I don't envy you your task, lieutenant. Speaking for
a moment in my other professional capacity as a psychiatrist,
it is my opinion you're after a very dangerous man here, to
judge from the extent and type of the injuries inflicted on the
two victims in there."

"I don' envy me neither, doctor," replied Curtis with a lopsided
smile. He took out one of the cards he'd had printed giving his
location and telephone number and handed it to the doctor.
"I'd appreciate it if you'd let me have a copy of your autopsy
report as soon as you can, doctor. As far as you kin tell from
your initial examination, c'd y'give me a rough estimate of time
an' cause of death? Strictly off th'record, of course."

The doctor pursed his lips and considered this for a moment
before answering. "In both cases, I'd say death was caused by
multiple stab wounds. In the case of the male deceased, death
would have been hastened by loss of blood resulting from deep
lacerations to the forearms, severing the main brachial arteries
and veins ... and from the fact that he was castrated. The female
deceased has been eviscerated, but I think my autopsy will
show this was inflicted after death."

The doctor's unemotional recital of the horrific details would
do nothing, Curtis knew from long experience, to lessen the
shock of viewing the carnage at first hand. A sudden thought
came to him.

"One more thing, doctor. You say the male deceased has been
castrated?"

Friedman nodded and Curtis went on, "If this killer has run
true to form, then I take it the female's sex organ has also bin
mutilated?"

The doctor nodded again. "My initial examination suggests that this could be the case," he agreed.

"Well," Curtis continued, "I'd be interested to know ... still off the record ... if your opinion as a psychiatrist is that these murders could perhaps be sexually motivated?"

The doctor cocked an eyebrow, and his brown eyes regarded Curtis shrewdly over the rim of his spectacles. "Strictly off the record ... yes. In fact, in my opinion you could very well be looking for a classic sexual sadist. In this case, someone who may achieve orgiastic release only by inflicting pain or damage to his victim's genitalia."

Seeing the mystified look on Carmody's face, Curtis explained for his benefit, "Means the sick way this Section Eight bugscase wastes 'is victims, is how he gits 'is rocks off."

"Graphically, if somewhat idiomatically put, lieutenant," commented Friedman, an amused smile tugging at the corners of his mouth. Then he glanced at his watch. "Well gentlemen, time waits for no man and it positively sprints away from doctors. I'll be in touch. Good day ... and good luck with your investigation." So saying, he raised his hat to them and left the room.

Carmody looked curiously at Curtis. "Okay Sigmund Freud, what's with the sexual motivation bit?" he asked.

"Ah ... jes' a possible angle," Curtis replied vaguely. Then he went on, "But it might be worth followin' up. So do me a favour, tell your team to search for semen stains too. Okay?"

"Whatever you say." Carmody walked over to the forensic boys and passed on Curtis's orders. It was received with raised eyebrows and resigned nods and Carmody rejoined Curtis and Turner.

Without speaking, the three men walked over to the bathroom door and entered the brightly lit room beyond. Stopping just inside the doorway to stay clear of the busy photographers, they viewed the gruesome scene which lay before them. It was as though they had entered a luxuriously appointed slaughter-house. They waited, each wrapped in his own thoughts, until the scenes-of-crime boys had finished their work, packed up their cameras and equipment and left.

Carmody broke the oppressive silence. Pointing at the two mutilated corpses in the sunken bath, he said, "Soon as I saw these cuts, I recalled the special directive you circulated, checked with HQ an' got th'word to contact you." He joined the other two in their silent vigil again for a few more seconds then asked, "Hey Ben, you got a lead yet on the bastard who's doin' this?"

"Could be," replied Curtis shortly. "But I gotta keep it under wraps fer now t'keep th'press off the scent, or next thing y'know we'd have a loada nutcases imitatin' this bastard. Besides, the D.C.'s runnin' scared, cuz he's runnin' fer a second term this Fall. Th'press git winda this, he'll have my balls."

"Huh!" grunted Carmody. "Looks like Furino there must've offended Elrick too, in that case." Then he asked, "What's so special about these cuts all over 'em? Or ain't I supposed to ask that either?"

Curtis fixed his colleague with a hard blue eye. "Fer th'time bein', you don' even see these cuts, Jim," he retorted. Carmody held up his hands in a gesture of surrender. "Okay, okay. I won't be a party pooper. I'll go call the meat wagon an' leave you to it. If you need anythin', holler out. I'll be next door. See ya."

As soon as Carmody had left, Curtis approached the edge of the sunken bath, careful to avoid stepping on patches of sticky, congealed blood. Making sure his coat-tails were clear of the floor, he squatted and examined the slash marks closely. He spoke softly over his shoulder to Turner, "Well, whaddaya know. One of the sequences he's used before but the other's a new one! Take a note of these, Tex …"

Turner pulled a notebook and pencil from a pocket. "Go ahead, Chief."

"Right," said Curtis. "First I'll give you the one I recognise. It's on the female, an' it reads … one-twenty-five-four-five. Got that? That's the fourth time he's used that one." He shifted his position slightly to get a better view, then continued, "Okay, here's the new one he's left for us … it's on the male … it starts with four ones, then there's three X's, then another three ones to finish."

Curtis continued to squat on his heels, staring at the new sequence of numbers slashed into the torso of the male corpse.

"Wonder what the hell this one says?" he mused.

Behind him, Turner examined the same figures on the page of his notebook ... IIIIXXXIII. "Waal, I reckon if we start by eliminatin' the Ol' Testament possibilities first, then that gives us three to start with. Cuz it'd be either the first, second or third book, in that case. Now, if we assume it's the first book, then that could give us ..."

"Hey, Einstein," Curtis's growl interrupted him in full flow. "Before you give y'self a sore head with all the possible permutations, don'chya think it would help if we had a Bible handy to check 'em out as we go?"

"Yeah, right," the younger man agreed. "Only thing is, whar we gonna git one? ..." He frowned for a moment, then his face cleared again. "Hold on, how 'bout I check out the apartment fer one? Mos' folks keep one at home."

"Good thinkin'," Curtis grunted, "Go do it, huh?"

When Turner returned a few minutes later, he was clutching a small white Bible, beautifully bound in soft kid and embossed with a gold cross. Curtis was still squatting deep in thought beside the sunken bath but he glanced round and got to his feet as his partner entered and waved the book at him triumphantly.

With their recently acquired knowledge of how to crack the killer's coded messages, it only took them a matter of minutes to solve this latest one. By a process of elimination, they worked their way through the possibilities. They knew beyond all doubt that they had it, when they reached and checked out the third book of the Old Testament – Leviticus, chapter twenty, verse thirteen – Turner read out, "If a man also lie with mankind, as he lieth with a woman, both of them have committed an abomination: they shall surely be put to death; their blood shall be upon them."

Curtis nodded slowly, as though he had been expecting something of the sort. "Looks like our man thinks he's God's own executioner," he commented. Then, meeting Turner's eye he added softly, "What's the bettin' he thinks he's a prophet too, huh?"

"No takers!" replied Turner.

"Okay, here's what we do now," There was a hard glint in

Curtis's eyes. "We'll leave Carmody to clear up here, while we go talk to our Reverend suspect. Oh, before we go, give Connolly a ring an' see if he's got anythin' for us."

A few minutes later, Turner cradled the phone and shook his head at Curtis. "Connolly says Records got nothin' on any Martin Bishop. He's not on file under that name, anyhow. Says could we git 'im a set of prints? That'll nail 'im if he has a record, an' he's usin' an alias."

Curtis nodded thoughtfully. "I'll see what I kin do. Okay," he added grimly, as they started for the door, "let's go callin' on his Reverence."

Outside the apartment, waiting for the arrival of the elevator, Turner attempted to lighten the mood. "Say Chief, y'know how y'address a Pope as 'Yore Holiness', an' a Cardinal as 'Yore Eminence', an' sechlike? Waal, I wuz jes' thinkin' … how th'hell d'yuh address a Prophet?" He blandly ignored Curtis's long-suffering look and continued, "How 'bout 'Yore Clairvoyance', huh?"

The elevator doors hissed open. "How about you usin' th'stairs?" growled Curtis as he entered the car. Turner chuckled and followed him.

40

"COME THIS WAY PLEASE, GENTLEMEN. THE PROPHET will see you now."

Curtis and Turner rose from the comfortable easy chairs in which they had been sitting and followed the smartly dressed young oriental, who ushered them politely from the tastefully furnished waiting room. The line of snow white shirt collar peeping over the neck of the man's well tailored dark blue suit, showed up starkly against the light ochre tint of his skin.

From his appearance, their escort could have been a young business executive, aide to the chairman of some large company.

The only thing was, they were not about to enter the boardroom or private office of the chairman of General Motors or Texaco. Instead they were being conducted into the private living quarters of the Reverend Martin Bishop, in the eighth floor suite of the plush Eldorado Apartment Building occupied by him and his personal retinue. The man his followers revered to the point of fanaticism. The self-styled Prophet.

It had been almost as difficult to obtain an interview with him too, as it would have been with one of the chairmen of the aforementioned giants of the business world. Indeed, Curtis's initial request for an interview, on flashing his badge and announcing his identity, had been bluntly refused by the first sect member who had confronted them at the door of the suite.

He had been an arrogant young white, flanked by two sullen companions a pace to his rear. Curtis had been coldly informed that the Prophet was meditating and could not be disturbed. Further, he had been informed, interviews were granted by appointment only. The lieutenant had responded by jamming his foot in the closing door and informing the resentful trio that he was conducting a 'murder one' investigation and that any further obstruction would result in everyone, their precious Prophet included, having plenty of extra time to meditate ... in the holding cells of the local precinct HQ!

The few seconds angry confrontation which had ensued had been terminated by the timely arrival of the young oriental business executive type, who had immediately acted to take the heat out of the situation. He had quietly but firmly ordered the door guards to admit the two detectives and had then conducted them to the comfortably furnished waiting room. There, he had politely satisfied himself of their authenticity and the reason for their call. He had then asked them to wait while he arranged for them to see his leader.

The two detectives now found themselves being ushered, still with impeccable courtesy, into a long, split-level room, the upper section separated from the lower by three shallow, wall-to-wall steps. The far wall of the upper section of the room was mostly glass, containing as it did a wide set of French windows, which reached from floor to ceiling and opened onto a balcony garden of flower boxes and potted shrubs.

Both levels of the long room were thick underfoot with expensive fitted carpeting and tastefully furnished in an aesthetic blend of clean-lined modern furniture and complementary decor. Sections of floor-to-ceiling bookshelves filled with matching sets of gold-tooled leather-bound books were set at regular intervals into the two long walls of the rectangular room. The spaces between the bookshelves were occupied by delicate antique tables or glass-fronted cabinet displaying diverse objets d'art in porcelain, bronze or hand-carved wood.

Good quality paintings, individually lit for best advantage, graced the walls. The whole effect was one of elegant affluence.

Someone was seated in an old fashioned wing-backed easy chair, his back to the visitors, looking out through the closed French window panels over a panoramic view of the city lit by the weak rays of a mid-afternoon winter sun. Curtis could see only the right hand of the chair's occupant, resting lightly on the padded armrest.

Their escort halted a few paces inside the door, and announced them in his nasal, heavily accented speech. "Detective Lieutenant Curtis and Detective Officer Turner, Exalted One."

Curtis and Turner exchanged a quick sideways look but remained deadpan as the 'Exalted One' rose from his chair and turned to face them. At first sight his appearance was as startling as his title. Tall, broad shouldered and silver haired, he was clad from neck to sandalled feet in a wide-sleeved, flowing robe of golden silk. Yet, he carried himself with such an air of majestic dignity, it seemed perfectly natural that he should be dressed in this striking biblical style.

The robed figure extended his hands towards them in greeting. "I bid you welcome gentlemen, in the spirit of Christian fellowship. How can I be of help to you?" His voice matched his imposing appearance. It was deep and mellow, giving an impression of strength and reassurance.

Curtis advanced across the deep-pile carpet, trailing Turner and their escort in his wake, till he stood facing the Prophet. Close up to the man, the impression of a powerful physique and latent strength was evident, even behind the deceptive covering of the loose flowing garment he wore.

Without any preamble, Curtis came straight to the point. "I'd like to have a word with you about the murders of some sixteen women, all of 'em prostitutes, and one man, which have occurred over the past five years. The latest two victims were murdered last night. We have uncovered certain evidence which points to these killin's havin' bin the work of someone connected to your organisation."

Curtis was watching the Prophet's strong-jawed face as he hit him with this flat statement, looking for a reaction ... any reaction. He got one. But not the one he wanted.

At first the man merely raised his eyebrows in surprise, while otherwise maintaining his composure. Then he slowly lowered his outstretched arms and his spirit of Christian fellowship evaporated as his lip curled with distaste.

"Prostitutes? Prostitutes, you say?" His deep voice was vibrant with indignation. "I assure you, lieutenant, none of mine would stain their immortal souls by consorting with such vile creatures of Satan. Fornication is a sin and my people are well aware of that."

"How about murder? They aware that's a sin too?" asked Curtis pointedly.

The Prophet gave a derisive snort. "You cannot seriously be suggesting that someone among my followers has murdered sixteen prostitutes?"

"An' one man," Curtis reminded him.

"Lieutenant, this is a very serious allegation indeed to make against my people." The Prophet's derisive tone had disappeared.

"I couldn't agree more," retorted Curtis. "It's a very serious matter. Murder always is."

The Prophet regarded Curtis for a long moment. Then he asked disdainfully, "And just what, may I ask, is this ... certain evidence ... that you claim to possess, which has led you here?"

Before answering, Curtis looked round pointedly at the oriental who was standing silently at his shoulder, then back to the Prophet. "I'd prefer to see you alone, if you don't mind. And then I'd like to interview the members of your staff ... also individually!"

The Prophet opened his mouth to protest but Curtis forestalled him. "It's normal procedure to interview people one at a time, in police inquiries of this seriousness. Besides ..." he held the Prophet's level gaze with his own for a moment, "you may prefer to hear what I've gotta say ... on your own."

For a fleeting instant Curtis imagined he saw a flicker of change in the Prophet's pale blue eyes, an indefinable shifting. He couldn't be sure. He had the craziest notion that had just seen something akin to a swift change of drivers, glimpsed unclearly behind the obscure surface of a vehicle windscreen. Then the moment had passed and the Prophet was replying, sounding irritated at the waste of his time.

"I really can't think why, but ..." He nodded to the oriental and said, "Thank you, Raphael. You may leave us. I shall ring for you when I need you."

There was a fractional hesitation, as though the oriental were reluctant to leave his master alone with his inquisitors, then he gave a curt nod of acknowledgement, turned on his heel and withdrew, closing the door behind him.

As soon as he left the room, Angel Four quickly made his way through the apartment to his own private quarters. Entering, he locked the door and crossed to the phone. He picked up the receiver and punched out the required number. Seconds later he was speaking to Angel One at Bethlehem House. Adopting their native Cantonese, Angel Four briefly reported the arrival of the police at the apartment to interview the Prophet and staff and the stated reason for their visit.

A short silence followed. Then Angel One asked, "What is your opinion? Is it possible he has committed these murders?"

Angel Four thought about that. "It is my opinion that he is certainly unbalanced enough to have committed them," he replied carefully. "You know how obsessed he is with his Christian narrow mindedness about sex. It is unthinkable that he could have been so stupid as to bring such danger upon our organisation ... but it is a possibility that he may have done so. The police seem quite certain of themselves, to my mind."

"I must go now," Angel One put in. "My police snoopers have arrived and are interviewing the Miller pest. Call me back later with a full report. I think it is time to discuss our religious friend more fully ..."

The Prophet faced Curtis squarely. "Now, lieutenant, just what is this evidence you claim to possess, which leads you to suspect that some member of my flock has carried out this veritable crime wave of murder?"

"If you don' mind, I'll ask the questions fer now," replied Curtis firmly.

"But you are making extremely serious allegations here, so I feel ..." the Prophet began to protest.

"Murder is an extremely serious matter, as I've already said," Curtis interrupted bluntly, determined to seize and hold the initiative. His hackles were up. He felt an instinctive dislike of this self-assured holy Joe in his fancy dress get-up. He cautioned himself not to let his personal prejudice influence his professional judgement but his gut feeling was strong. This man had the right 'feel' about him. The sadistic killer he had been hunting for the past five years could be lurking behind the hard blue eyes, the calm exterior. He decided to push hard to see if he could flush him out into the open.

"Lieutenant," the man was saying firmly, "I insist that you owe me at least some explanation if this interview is to proceed any further!"

"Maybe I didn' make myself too clear," Curtis's tone took on a tone of finality which brooked no further argument. "I'm conductin' an investigation into seventeen counts of first degree murder. I don' owe anybody any explanations in order t'make inquiries, or follow up leads."

The Prophet's eyebrows lifted a fraction. "Indeed?" he murmured. "Then perhaps I should have my attorney present, before we continue this conversation? ..."

The two men stood a pace apart, glaring stubbornly at one another, neither prepared to give an inch. To Turner, a silent, forgotten witness at Curtis's shoulder, the space between the two seemed to crackle with the static of their mutual antagonism. Then the lieutenant's head lowered perceptibly, thrusting forward belligerently like a bull preparing to charge.

"Now look," the words rapped out into the charged silence. "For the moment, I'm quite prepared to keep this interview low-key. But for that, I gotta have your co-operation. I'd a thought you'd've preferred, like me, t'git this over as quickly as possible. That way, if it turns out that none of your people is responsible fer th'murders, no harm's bin done ..."

"No harm's been done? ..." the Prophet snorted incredulously.

"That's what I said," Curtis pressed on relentlessly. "Because that way the press don' git t'know, an' you don' git a whole loada bad publicity." He paused to let this point sink in, then continued, "But ... if you decide to insist on a formal interview in the presence of your attorney, then we'll conduct it at precinct headquarters. An' I'll git my attorney t'come along too ... the District Attorney ... an' we'll have us a ball. We'll throw th'book at you an' your people. An' that'll include charges of forcibly abductin' minors an' holdin' 'em against their will ... that's a federal rap, by th'way ... an' assault causin' actual bodily harm. How's that fer starters?"

He grinned mirthlessly into the other man's taut face and concluded baitingly, "An' then you kin quote the fifth amendment back at us. An' the press an' TV boys'll have a field day. They'll jes' lap you up as a prime suspect. You'll push everythin' else off the front pages an' prime time news slots. If you'll pardon the expression, they'll crucify you!"

"A prime suspect?" The Prophet said musingly. He had recovered his composure again. "Is that what you consider me to be, lieutenant?"

"Mister," Curtis replied heavily. "I suspect everyone till I clear 'em. Okay, what's it t'be? The choice is yours. Either I question you an' your staff here an' now, quietly an' with no fuss, or we move downtown an' have us a three ring circus that'll make Barnum an' Bailey's look like a two-bit sideshow!"

Once again the two men stood eye to eye in a contest of will. Curtis felt an almost hypnotic power pouring from the piercing blue eyes boring into his. But the lieutenant was a hard-nosed cop, himself a well practised adept at eyeball confrontations with hostile suspects. He locked mental antlers with his golden robed protagonist and pushed back, refusing to be stared down.

Suddenly, the Prophet shrugged and turned away, abruptly breaking off the brief contest of wills. He flicked a dismissive hand and said condescendingly, "Oh very well, ask your questions. Though you are wasting your time, you will not find the man you are seeking among my people."

Gathering the folds of his robe around him, the Prophet lowered himself into the chair he had been occupying when the detectives had entered and composed himself with studied dignity, folding his hands serenely in his lap. He nodded for the detectives to seat themselves on a long settee a few feet away opposite his chair. Between the two seats stood a long low coffee table. Curtis dropped his hat onto its surface and seated himself, flicking the front of his coat open and pulling out his notebook and pencil as he did so.

Turner, for his part, instead of accepting the invitation to be seated, turned and indicated the long room with a wave of his hand. "Mind if I take a look round, while you an' the lieutenant's talkin' business? Looks like y'got some real fine stuff here."

The Prophet nodded in gracious acknowledgement of the younger detective's apparent appreciation of his not inconsiderable art collection and with an expansive gesture replied, "Not at all, officer. Be my guest." Turning back to the older, belligerent one opposite him, he couldn't resist the opportunity for a put-down. "Your colleague, at least, seems to possess a taste for the finer things of life, lieutenant."

Curtis smiled inwardly to himself. As far as he knew, Tex couldn't tell a Capodimonte porcelain from a Woolworth mug. The request was an excuse for a nose around. But he allowed none of this to show on his face.

"Yeah," he agreed, adding sourly, "Only thing is, on a cop's pay he doesn't often git the opportunity to indulge it." Then with a meaningful glance down the room's opulent length, he went on, "Tell you one thing though, from where I'm sittin' it looks t'me like your method of fightin' sin pays a lot better'n ours!"

A superior little smile played around the Prophet's lips. "Do I detect a note of disapproval, lieutenant?"

"No. Jes' straight envy," Curtis retorted bluntly.

"Oh, come now. Surely not. After all, envy is a sin, so the Good Book tells us," the Prophet chided gently, his deep mellow tones belying the glint of mockery in his eyes.

"So is acquisitiveness, as I recall," Curtis shot back. "The same Good Book's pretty explicit about rich men findin' it difficult t'git through them Pearly Gates."

Part way down the length of the room, Turner smothered a grin as he heard this opening exchange. He recognised the signs. Curtis, he knew, was deliberately setting out to goad the suspect he was about to question. This would have the undoubted effect of creating an atmosphere of hostility. But it would also unsettle the man's complacent self assurance and perhaps produce a verbal slip in the later exchanges of the interview.

The Prophet's eyebrows raised at the unexpected directness of Curtis's rejoinder. "Touché!" he murmured, with a little nod. Then he added, "But let me assure you, lieutenant, that I personally am not rich."

Wordlessly Curtis directed a sceptical look round the room's art treasures and back to the Prophet, who held up an admonitory hand and continued, "These few bits and pieces represent an investment of a considerable amount of my church's funds. Realisable assets acquired as a hedge against inflation. Surely even you must admit it is better that we invest a portion of our capital in a few beautiful objects which give pleasure, rather than in the stock market, say?"

"Wouldn' it be even better, not to say more Christian, to invest it in charity?" asked Curtis acidly. "I'm sure there're quite a few poor folks out there on relief, who'd consider a food parcel a beautiful object. An' it'd give 'em a damn sight more pleasure than all this stuff gives you." He encompassed the room with a wave of his hand.

This time the barb struck home. For a moment the Prophet's face was a mixture of conflicting emotions, anger almost overcoming his self-control before he recovered himself. However, the tight-lipped smile which reappeared failed to reach his eyes, which were now as wintry as two chips of blue ice.

"Lieutenant, I would find your remarks offensive, were it not for the fact that you are so obviously ignorant of the quite considerable charity work we carry out …" he began.

"Like those mobile soup kitchens you operate?" Curtis cut in. "Aw, come on! Y'kin hardly compare a few handouts to bums an' winos with all this …" Another wave of his hand towards the room's art treasures accompanied this scathing comment. Curtis saw the flash of irritation in the eyes of the man opposite and the smile dying on his lips and he knew he was almost there. The man was reacting to his needling like a trout rising to the lure. The abrasive tone of his reply confirmed it.

"Lieutenant, I fail to see how the way we choose to invest or dispose of our financial resources has anything at all to do with the stated purpose of your visit," he commented coldly. "But for your information, the mobile soup kitchens, as you so aptly name them, are not by any means our sole method of dispensing charity to the needy and homeless. We run a rest and meditation centre in each of the city's five boroughs and another in secluded rural surroundings outwith the city."

"The one outwith the city, that'll be Bethlehem House I take it?" Curtis's casual comment was rewarded by an involuntary blink and a flicker of surprise in the Prophet's eyes. An instant later this was replaced by a long, calculating look from these same blue eyes, which were now positively glacial.

After a pause of a few seconds, the Prophet murmured softly, "Well, well! You certainly have been doing your homework, lieutenant."

Curtis bared his teeth in a bright, humourless grin. "Y'could say that," he replied offhandedly. At the same time, he silently thanked Brett Grant for having involved him in his inquiries into the Prophet's organisation and for keeping him briefed. Although his knowledge of the sect was confined only to the few details he had gleaned from Brett, the man sitting opposite him did not know that. Searching his memory, he dredged up another couple of facts from what Brett had told him and carried his bluff a little further to keep his opponent off balance.

"The way I hear it, you run a pretty tight ship in this

organisation of yours," he said. "Once somebody signs on, they're in for the duration, whether they like it or not ... or whether they know it or not! Right?"

All semblance of civility now gone, the Prophet responded heatedly, "How I choose to run my church is entirely a matter between myself and my members. They are fully aware of the commitments of the life they are entering upon. I do not force people to join us. They join of their own free will and accord and agree to dedicate their lives totally to God. They are required to sign a statement to that effect before I will accept them fully into my church."

Curtis snorted dismissively. "Listen, it's me you're talkin' to, not some gullible kid. Those pieces of paper ain' worth shit, an' you know it. If you tried to use 'em to contest a custody suit brought by the parents of any minor presently in your church membership, they'd be laughed outa court. Come to think of it, I'm wrong – they are worth a shit – any judge in th'land would wipe his ass with 'em."

"Your crudity does you no credit, lieutenant," replied the other with lofty disapproval. "The statements I refer to merely prove that no-one is coerced into joining my church. As to my running a tight ship, no doubt you will be aware that the major Christian church, the Church of Rome, does not lightly release their clergy or members of their closed orders from their vows either."

"Yeah. Only difference is, when one of their people decides to leave, even without permission, they don't hunt 'em down with dogs!" Curtis retorted caustically. "What th'hell you runnin' out there anyhow? A rest home or a concentration camp?"

The words hung quivering in the vibrant silence which followed this shot. The Prophet's face drained of colour, his mouth tightened and naked fury blazed in his eyes. Suddenly he surged up out of his chair and for one tense moment Curtis thought the man was actually going to attack him. His muscles tensed in anticipation but the man merely stood with his fists clenched, glaring down at him.

Turner, watching developments from half way down the room,

saw the Prophet raise an arm to point imperiously towards the door.

"You will leave my house sir, right now!" he grated out. "I refuse to listen to any more of this slanderous rubbish." The strong voice shook with the suppressed rage within the man. "I do not believe you have any evidence at all. On the contrary, you have tricked your way into this so-called interview, intent only on insulting and provoking me. I shall be reporting your offensive conduct to your superiors. Now, get out!"

However, far from preparing to leave, Curtis instead leaned back and spread his arms along the low back of the settee. He stared up at the towering figure with studied insolence. Then he slowly shook his head. "I'll leave when I'm good an' ready, an' not before. I'm conductin' a murder inquiry, an' ..."

"You-will-leave-NOW!" thundered the Prophet, incensed with rage. "Or I'll have you thrown out." As he spoke, he leaned forward and made to jab a small bellpush set into the surface of the low table between them.

Curtis's explosive response startled even Turner at the other end of the long room. Without the slightest warning, the lieutenant lashed out with a foot and kicked the low table up into the air. It cartwheeled off to one side and came to rest upside-down several feet away, trailing the broken bell wire, snapped off from its concealed socket in the floor. Without pause, he followed up on the element of surprise his violent action had created, and propelled himself to his feet with a powerful thrust from his outspread arms.

The Prophet had jerked back reflexively as the flying table narrowly missed his face, startled both by this and by Curtis's sudden aggressive surge towards him. Before the man could regain either his balance or his composure, the lieutenant snarled, "Siddown, mister!" and shoved him hard in the chest, slamming him back down into the depths of the throne-like chair.

Curtis leaned forward, rested a hand on either arm of the chair, and thrust his face pugnaciously into his opponent's. "Nobody's goin' anywhere ... least of all you ... till I've finished what I came here to do. Get me?" He emphasised his point by lifting his left hand and prodding the Prophet in the chest.

Suddenly Curtis found his wrist painfully seized in a crushing grip. The face inches from his own was twisted with fury, the eyes bulging. The man was almost incoherent, his deep voice reduced to a malevolent hiss. "How dare you lay hands on me! You have gone too far now. By what right do you presume? ..."

There was a sudden flurry of movement and the Prophet was shocked into silence by Curtis's next action. The lieutenant, certain that his wrist was going to break under the agonising pressure of the vise-like grip, reached swiftly under his coat with his free hand. When it reappeared an instant later, his Police Positive was nestling in his bunched fist. None too gently, he jammed the barrel of the gun against the Prophet's cheekbone, so it angled across the bridge of his nose, the trigger guard an inch below his left eye.

"Let go my arm, mister," he rasped through gritted teeth, "or I'll bust your fuckin' face wide open." He emphasised the point by nudging his adversary's face with the cold metal. The crushing pressure suddenly eased and his arm was released, leaving his wrist throbbing where it had been clenched in the steel-fingered grip.

Flexing his numbed fingers, Curtis gently tapped the gun barrel once against the man's cheekbone and continued, "This is all the right I need with the likes of you, Mister Prophet. An' it's backed up by this ..."

With the still partially numbed fingers of his left hand, he reached into an inside pocket, withdrew his gold shield and flipped it open and held it before the man's face. "Take a good look, mister Prophet. This badge says it all. It says I'm a cop carryin' out an investigation into a series of brutal murders committed by someone who's arguably dangerously insane. Further, it says if I'm attacked durin' these investigations by a potentially dangerous suspect, I kin either pistol-whip ten kindsa shit outa him or blow 'im away, dependin' on how threatened I feel. You git my drift?"

Sitting motionless, except for his eyes flickering between the gun barrel and Curtis's face, the Prophet, almost inarticulate with the rage which was threatening to engulf him and launch him at his tormentor, managed to choke out, "I ... attack ...

you? I attack you?" He drew in a great shuddering breath, which seemed to calm him a little. "And what is this, pray, but police brutality? And without the slightest provocation. Be assured that I shall be preferring charges to that effect, just as soon as ..."

"Detective Turner," Curtis called loudly, cutting across the Prophet's protest. He did not alter his threatening stance, nor break off eye contact with his adversary, as he pushed his bluff to the limit. "Did you witness any police brutality, such as this suspect is makin' false allegations about?"

"Nope. Not me," Tex's laconic drawl sounded calmly in reply. "Never saw any sech thing. Though I do seem to recall the said suspect turnin' violent an' havin' t'be restrained ... uh ... forcibly restrained, I mean."

"You git the message, mister Prophet?" Curtis asked softly. "You ready to answer some questions now?"

The golden robed figure swallowed hard and replied in the same malevolent hiss as before, "Ask your questions ... for all the good it will do you. But know this ..." tiny flecks of spit had appeared at the corners of his mouth, "I will repay you for this some day."

Curtis judged he had pushed the man far enough for his purpose. He was obviously badly rattled. No sense in overdoing it and provoking him into actual violence. There were others in the apartment, after all, who would quickly intervene, and Grant's experience of the fanaticism of this man's followers warned him what to expect if that happened. Abruptly he straightened and stepped back, pocketing the badge and reholstering the gun.

"Heard it all before," he said dismissively. "You'll hafta join the queue. If threats wuz dimes, I'd be a millionaire."

Resuming his seat, he retrieved his notebook and pencil from the settee where he had dropped them when he moved into action. Flipping open the notebook, he laid it on his knee.

Turner, meanwhile, walked quietly up the length of the room and lifted Curtis's hat and the fallen table. Righting the table, he set it down again in its original position between the two men and dropped the hat on the settee beside his boss. He might have been invisible for all the attention paid him by the two men who sat facing one another, the air between them crackling with tension. Silently he retreated once more into the depths of the room.

Curtis poised his pen over a fresh page. "Your full name?" he demanded.

"Martin Daniel Bishop." The Prophet was breathing deeply, his voice more controlled, but the slight tremor of strain was still evident.

"Age?"

"Fifty-five."

"Where domiciled?"

"Here."

Curtis paused and looked up. "This your permanent address?"

"It will suffice, as far as you are concerned," retorted the other.

"Only facts will suffice as far as I'm concerned, mister," snapped Curtis. "Now, where do you reside when you ain't on recruitin' drives in the city ... crusades, I think you call 'em?"

"When I am not conducting crusades," the word was stressed. "I reside at Bethlehem House, our country retreat, which you mentioned earlier."

"That's jes' northa Rockford, ain' it?"

"It is."

"How long you bin a preacher?"

"Over thirty years."

"An' before that?"

"I was ..." The Prophet stopped and gave an exasperated sigh. "Is all this necessary?" he snapped irritably. "Frankly I can't see what slightest interest details of my early life can be to you."

"Background," replied Curtis shortly. "Unnecessary questions I don' ask. Now, what did you do before you took up preachin'?"

"I was at college," The Prophet replied. Then, anticipating Curtis's next question, he added, "Andrew Carnegie College, Lincoln, Nebraska."

Curtis looked up again. "Studyin' theology, I take it? You ordained there?"

The Prophet hesitated for a moment, then replied, "As a matter of fact, I was studying medicine."

"Medicine, eh?" Curtis looked up from his notes. "What happened? Didn' your examiners like your surgical techniques?"

His acid jibe was ignored. "I left college of my own choice when I was called by God to preach His word," he replied stiffly.

"So, you're not ordained?" Curtis pressed him.

"Not by man," came the disdainful reply. "The Lord called me in a vision. He does not issue diplomas to those He chooses to do His work. Was Christ ordained? Was Moses? Or any of His holy prophets for that matter?"

"We live in different times. An' I don' seem to recall any of 'em cuttin' their people off from the rest of the world ... or cuttin' people up, for that matter," Curtis stated flatly.

Observing the scenario unobtrusively from several feet away, Turner thought the Prophet had chosen to ignore this last thrust. His face remained expressionless, only the smouldering blue eyes lasering their hostility at the lieutenant. Then a taunting smile touched his tight mouth.

"You mentioned my crusades earlier. You seem to have made quite a crusade of your own out of this investigation, lieutenant," he said softly. "Almost as though you regard the murders as a direct challenge to you personally, as opposed to the law you purport to represent. I trust you apply yourself with the same commendable zeal to the deaths of ordinary decent people, as you do to these shameless Jezebels of the night."

"Mister, where murder's concerned, there's only one qualification a victim's gotta have to git my undivided attention ... they gotta be dead! Hooker or society hostess, there ain' no difference from my point of view, 'cept one does it fer money, an' so falls foul of the law," Curtis replied evenly.

"Then you are wrong," the Prophet contradicted him heatedly. "Whores are not the same as ordinary decent people. They are the spawn of Satan. The Bible is quite explicit on the subject. The word of God, as given in Leviticus, nineteen, twenty-nine, says, Do not prostitute thy daughter, to cause her to be a whore; lest the land fall to whoredom, and the land become full of wickedness." His voice had regained some of its previous rich timbre as he quoted the words, steadied by his return to familiar territory.

Curtis eyed him steadily. "The Good Book also says, Thou shalt not kill, don' it? An' anyway, I hardly think God's gonna send down an avengin' angel t'go aroun' wastin' all the hookers in th'city with a blade. I thought He went big on the forgiveness bit?" he retorted caustically.

"Tell that to the whores of Babylon, or the sinners of Sodom and Gommorrah!" intoned the Prophet. The taunting smile hovering on his lips had hardened into malice.

"Those were entire corrupt societies," argued Curtis, pushing to see how far his man would go. He was not disappointed.

"So is America today," stated the Prophet confidently. "Her cities are cesspools of vice and sin, run by corrupt politicians in the pay of organised crime syndicates." His voice had begun to assume the ranting tone of the zealot on a favourite hobby-horse.

"For once we're in agreement," nodded Curtis. "But I don' see no fire an' brimstone rainin' down from the clouds." Lowering his eyes to his notes, he added offhandedly, "Nope ... so far, your Boss's score is sixteen defenceless hookers, an' a faggot."

The Prophet bridled at this as Curtis had thought he might. "He makes no distinction between sins or sinners, in His infinite wisdom. Again, it is written, For as many as have sinned without law shall perish without law."

The familiar words glowed across the front of Curtis's mind like a neon sign in the night, and he shot a quick sideways glance in Turner's direction, to see whether he had picked it up too. He had. The younger man was staring hard at him, as though beaming the silent message at his chief, Did you hear what he just said? That's one of the quotations we cracked ... one of the messages that was left on some of the victims!

Curtis felt a surge of satisfaction but kept his face carefully impassive as he faced the Prophet again. "Doesn't that passage also go on to say somethin' about those who've sinned in the law bein' judged by the law?"

The Prophet's surprise wiped the malicious smile from his face and momentarily overlaid the hostility there. He cocked his head to one side. "Well, well. Once again you surprise me with the extent of your knowledge, lieutenant." Then a sneering note crept into his tone, as he continued, "Don't tell me your homework on me included a study of the Bible, too?"

Curtis held his gaze, at the same time reaching into his jacket and slipping out one of the envelopes of photographs he had put there, before leaving the office. "Not so much the Bible, more ... biblical quotations, y'could say."

As he spoke, he withdrew the sheaf of fifteen glossy black and white prints from the envelope and deftly spread them out along the surface of the coffee table between them, like a poker player displaying his hand before an opponent. All the while, his eyes never left the Prophet's face.

"I bin studyin' 'em fer five years now ... since they started appearin' carved into the bodies of murder victims ... these murder victims." He indicated the prints with a sweep of his hand. "You ever seen any of these women before?"

The Prophet lowered his eyes and ran them slowly along the uneven line-up of prints. Each was a blow-up of a standard police records photograph, and each one was a double-take of a female, one snap full face, the other in profile. The faces which stared blankly into the camera lens or off to one side, some pretty, some plain, represented a cross section of New York's racial melting pot; white, black, oriental and Hispanic. All possessed one common characteristic, no matter the ethnic origin of the subject – a definable hardness, which could not wholly be explained away by the harsh, uncomplimentary lighting used by police photographers the world over.

"Well?" Curtis's voice broke the ensuing silence like the crack of a whip. "Do you recognise any of 'em, or don't you?"

The Prophet slowly raised his eyes to meet Curtis's again. The corners of his mouth turned down in disgust. "It is not my habit to associate with creatures such as these." His tone was scathing.

"That don't answer my question, mister," snapped Curtis. "Do you recognise 'em, or don't you?"

Glaring at him, the Prophet replied coldly and with

exaggerated emphasis, "No-I-do-not!"

"You sure about that?" persisted Curtis.

"Very! I repeat, I am not in the habit of associating with harlots." The denial was made loudly and angrily.

"Tigers don' associate with deer … but it don' stop 'em from killin' an' eatin' 'em, every time they git the chance," retorted Curtis.

"What are you accusing me of now? Cannibalism?" sneered the Prophet, his voice dripping with sarcasm.

"No-one's accusin' you of anythin' … yet." Curtis met the other's gaze squarely.

"I'm pleased to hear it." The Prophet looked down at the photographic line up again. "Even to accuse me of association with such as these would be insult enough. You only have to look at them to know them for what they are."

"Oh yeah?" Curtis sounded unimpressed. "Tell me, if you don' associate with 'em, how would you know they wuz whores?"

"Firstly, because you said you are investigating the murders of prostitutes. Secondly, because one does not have to mix with sinners to be able to recognise a sinner," came the scornful reply.

"Oh, I dunno – I find it helps in my line of work," retorted Curtis. Gathering up the prints, he slid them back into their envelope and pocketed it. He plucked the second envelope from his other pocket and carefully slid another thin sheaf of photographs from it.

"Maybe these will jog your memory a little better," he said casually. This time, however, instead of spreading them out face up on the table as he had done with the first lot, he leaned forward and offered the prints to the Prophet, who accepted them automatically.

"These are of the same women," Curtis informed him. "Only, y'could say these ones are more up to date. Recognise 'em now?"

Unhurriedly, the Prophet began to leaf his way through this second batch of prints, dropping each one onto the table as he examined it. This time his gaze lingered briefly on every print, unlike the cursory scan he had given the first lot. Like the first selection these were also double-takes, but this time each contained two full length shots of a naked female corpse, photographed on a mortuary slab. The top half of each print showed the corpse face up, the lower half, the same corpse face down.

Curtis, observing the man closely for any reaction, at first saw only a slight narrowing of the eyes as his adversary ran them over the horrific celluloid gallery of mutilated death. Then he fancied he saw a subtle change come over the otherwise wooden mask of the Prophet's face. For a fleeting instant, there seemed to be a look of ... satisfaction? ... triumph, even? Then it was gone.

However, as the Prophet carelessly dropped the last print onto the table and looked up, meeting Curtis's searching gaze, the lieutenant noticed with a little thrill of excitement that the pupils of the man's eyes were dilated, giving them a dark and slightly unfocused look.

The thought flashed through Curtis's mind – the bastard's turned on by these pictures! – followed by the words of the police doctor in the Menotti apartment an hour earlier: I think you could very well be looking for a classic sexual sadist. He let none of this show on his face.

"Well, mister Prophet?" Curtis demanded provocatively, "You recognise 'em now?"

The other man's eyes cleared. "I find your questions and your attitude grossly offensive, lieutenant ..." he began angrily.

"But not these? ..." Curtis interrupted, indicating the untidy pile of snaps on the table. "You don' seem to find these grossly offensive. Now, I find that very strange."

"I think I remember telling you I was once a medical student," the Prophet countered, sounding bored. "When you have dissected human bodies until the pieces can fit into jars of preserving fluid, then sights such as these ..." he waved a careless hand over the prints, "fail to affect you to any great extent."

"Is that so?" commented Curtis, irked by the man's superior tone. "It occurs to me maybe you bin keepin' your hand in with a bit of part-time pathology on the side."

The Prophet glared at him. "And it occurs to me that you are allowing your blatant prejudice against me to expose your abysmal ignorance, lieutenant. Pathology, for your information, is carried out on the dead, not on the living." His tone was insultingly patient, as though lecturing a retarded child.

"Is that so?" repeated Curtis. Then, he added quietly, "Who said these injuries were inflicted on live bodies?"

The only response this thrust produced from the other man was a derisive snort. "Oh, come on, lieutenant. Not that hoary old detective story chestnut ... 'I didn't shoot him' the suspect protests. 'Who said anything about a gun being used?' the clever detective demands." With exaggerated emphasis, he continued, "I assume these injuries killed your victims. In fact, looking at these photographs, I'd say it was pretty obvious ... even to a non-medically trained person like yourself. So, please don't waste my time or insult my intelligence with your puerile attempts to trap me."

Curtis appeared to be rattled by the sneering tone. "Okay, mister ex-medical student expert. How about the other injuries? The ones on their backs? They coulda bin inflicted after death. An' don' say they couldn't, cuz there's no way you could tell that from a photograph." He flung out the challenge belligerently.

The Prophet felt for the first time since the interview had started that he had taken over the driving seat. He was enjoying his ascendancy in the verbal battle between himself and the ignorant, aggressive baboon opposite. He was on safe ground now, he felt. He could lose this pea-brained cop on medical matters. He glanced down at the pile of prints he had discarded on the table top.

"Oh yes ... the biblical quotations I believe you said you had been studying?" he said condescendingly. "These appear to me to be of too superficial a nature to have caused death."

"Biblical quotations? What biblical quotations?" asked Curtis softly.

The Prophet realised his slip instantly and made an effort to recover it. With a scornful laugh he said, "Come now, lieutenant, we're not still playing childish word games, are we?" Then, once again adopting a condescending tone, he continued, "Very well, let me put the record straight. Let me re-phrase my statement. I assume these marks to be the biblical quotations to which you referred earlier. Does that satisfy you?"

"No it doesn't," stated Curtis flatly. "You assume too damn much, mister. It took us two murders to recognise these marks as Roman numerals, an' fourteen more to work out finally that they were biblical references. Yet, you kin recognise 'em for what they are, jes' like that!" he snapped his fingers. Leaning forward, he reached down and flicked the pile of prints with a fingernail, so that they spilled out along the table top. "Now, s'pose you tell me jes' how you ... assumed ... these were my biblical quotations?" His eyes bored into those of his robed adversary.

The Prophet's brain was moving fast now. He had dangerously underestimated the tough looking, coarse mannered detective, he realised. Playing for time, he gave a sigh of exasperation, reached down and gathered up the prints again. He leafed through them quickly, as though searching for something he already knew to be there. In fact, despite his seeming casualness he was raking each picture with his eyes, searching for one in which the gaping, ragged slashes formed their intended pattern reasonably clearly. Five prints down he found one, then a second, then further into the pile, a third. Relieved, but hiding his feelings, he turned the three prints towards Curtis and displayed them for a few seconds, before replacing the whole pile on the table.

"What else could these Roman numerals have represented but the biblical quotations you mentioned?" he asked matter-of-factly.

"They were pretty obscure t'me," Curtis persisted stubbornly. As he spoke, he leaned forward again and gathered the prints into a neat pile, careful to touch only their edges, then slid them from the table top back into their envelope, which he pocketed.

"That's because you are not a student of the Bible, lieutenant," responded the Prophet, his confidence restored.

"While you are," Curtis nodded. "Yeah, the point hadn't escaped me. In fact, mister Bible student, it also occurs t'me that the person who left these sick little epitaphs musta bin so familiar with the Bible that he wuz able to quote not jes' the books, chapters an' verses he wanted, but the actual numbers of the books in sequence ... in both testaments!"

"Hardly conclusive proof of anything," the other retorted. "I am sure there are many in this great metropolis who can do likewise."

"No doubt," Curtis conceded, then went on, "But I'm willin' t'bet they weren't all holdin' religious meetin's every time one of these murders was committed. But you were! Which brings us to the question of your movements at the relevant times ..."

The Prophet, sensing the trap was closing, gripped the arms of his chair firmly and made to rise. "Enough!" he snapped angrily. "You have gone too far. You are now virtually accusing me of murdering your precious sluts. Do what you please, this interview is at an end ..."

Curtis also moved as though to rise, but threateningly. His big fist shot forward, the pointing finger hovering only a few inches from the other man's face.

"Stay right where you are, mister!" he ordered menacingly, his burly frame hunched and tense. He pinned the other man down with his eyes, daring him to move. "This interview will end when I say, an' not before. Now, don' push me mister, or you're gonna meet with a nasty accident. An' what's more, me an' my partner over there gotta lot more nasty accidents waitin' fer Charlie Chan an' your goon squad, if they try to stop us draggin' your unconscious body outa here ... two Police Positives fulla nasty accidents, to be precise."

After a long tense moment, the Prophet subsided slowly back into his chair, hate smouldering in his eyes. Curtis relaxed slightly but remained poised on the edge of the settee, ready for action.

"Now git this, mister bogus fuckin' preacher man. If you think I suspect you of these murders, then you got it in one." Curtis's anger, fuelled by the years of frustration he'd experienced as he'd hunted the taunting, sadistic killer, threatened to flare out of control. He struggled to keep it damped down but a hint of it crackled in his voice as he went on, "An' git this too ... if as I suspect, you are the man I'm after, then one way or another, I'll have you! Now, you better start convincin' me I'm wrong."

The two men glared at each other with mutual loathing. Watching from the other end of the room, Turner imagined he could almost feel the charged emotions pouring from either man. Observing their few seconds of silent confrontation, Turner became uneasy. He sensed his chief was in danger of losing control. But that wasn't the only thing that made him uneasy. Curtis's anger was strong and barely under control but it was a healthy anger. What troubled Turner more was the look in the unblinking eyes of the robed figure, which was being directed at his chief. The Texan knew that if he'd never before seen murder in a man's eyes, he was seeing it now. There was insanity there too. He was sure of it. Then the Prophet spoke and broke the spell that seemed to be binding all three of them in a timeless suspense.

"Wrong again, lieutenant." His voice was tight with tension. "I don't have to convince anyone of anything. The law says a man is innocent until proved guilty. And such … evidence … as you have produced here today would be thrown out of any court in the land. You don't fool me for one instant with your crude bluff. It certainly wouldn't fool a court of law."

Curtis knew the man was right. He had pushed his bluff to the limit and it had failed to produce anything in the way of a confession of guilt. He also knew he was right about this man and that made him all the more furious with himself. Now the man was warned and would be doubly dangerous as a result – he was sickeningly sure of that too. The lieutenant felt the sour taste of bile in the back of his throat – bitter, like the taste of defeat. He decided to push the interview to a conclusion.

"We'll see," he said grimly. Retrieving his notebook, he poised his pencil over it again. "Now, regardin' your whereabouts an' movements at the times of the murders …"

"Oh, this is ridiculous!" the Prophet burst out angrily. "You said earlier that your investigations span some five years. I don't know what kind of memory you claim to possess but mine certainly will not permit me to describe my movements on any given dates or times over such a period of time. I am sure even someone as unreasonable as you will have to concede that much.

"Okay. So I'll try to be reasonable. Curtis fixed the man with a cold stare. "How about last night? An' the night before that? Your memory go back that far? First, where were you the night before last, between the hours of eleven p.m. and say, one a.m. the followin' mornin'? Second, where were you last night, between midnight and two a.m.? Right, we'll take them one at a time …"

The Prophet made a dismissive gesture. "I can answer both of your questions in one simple word. Here. I was here in my apartment … in this very room. You see, it is my habit to meditate and recharge my spiritual batteries, so to speak, in communion with The Lord for a few hours after each night's meeting when I'm conducting a crusade," he replied smugly.

Curtis gave a snort of disbelief. "Now who's insultin' whose intelligence? You'll hafta come up with somethin' better'n that. Even the Supreme Court ain't figgered a way to subpoena God as a material witness."

"In that case, how about my staff here?" The Prophet suggested smugly. "Do you think your courts will accept their sworn testimony that after arriving back here from the Washington Centre, I did not thereafter leave this apartment at any time over the last two nights? Or will you refuse to accept any evidence which fails to fit your pre-conceived prejudices?"

Ignoring the jibe, Curtis ran his eye quickly round the room's perimeter. "There are no other exits from this room, apart from the door we came in?" he demanded.

"No." The denial was emphatic.

Suddenly, Turner's voice broke into the two-way conversation. "How 'bout that one over there? Maybe you plumb forgot about it, seein' as how it's all covered up, an' all …" So saying, he turned and strode to the far end of the room.

Curtis watched him walk towards a hanging tapestry at the opposite end of the far wall from the door they had entered originally. Reaching the tapestry, Turner drew it aside to expose an identical door to its twin a few yards away, and turned to look back up the length of the room.

"This one heah," he drawled casually.

Curtis turned back and eyed the Prophet bleakly. "Well?" he demanded.

Before answering the lieutenant, the Prophet commented acidly to Turner, "Your inspection of my art collection seems to have been very thorough indeed." Then to Curtis, he went on smoothly, "You asked about exits. That door leads to my bedroom and bathroom. And at the risk of disappointing your overheated imagination, there is no secret helicopter pad leading to the outside ... we are eight floors up, you know."

Curtis pocketed his notebook and pencil. "Let's take a look, shall we?" Standing up, he picked up his hat and indicated for the Prophet to lead the way.

The other man hesitated for a moment, then shrugged and rose. His golden robe swirling around him, he led the way down the length of the room towards the waiting Turner. As they descended the three shallow steps which divided the long room into its upper and lower levels, Curtis glanced down and so missed the Prophet's swift movement, as his right hand darted out to the wall by his side.

Alerted by Turner's involuntary "Hey!", Curtis whipped round, but was too late to prevent the Prophet from pressing the bell-push sited beneath a gilt framed painting. Almost simultaneously came the muffled wail of an alarm sounding from elsewhere in the apartment – an insistent, pulsing note, raising the small hairs on the lieutenant's neck.

The Prophet was regarding him with malicious triumph. "You came here looking for trouble," he snarled. "Well, now you've got more than you can handle!"

41

AS THE PROPHET SPOKE, THE DOOR BURST OPEN AND several fast-moving figures charged into the room. The strident whooping of the alarm filled the room now, along with the running men.

Curtis leapt away from the Prophet and bounded back up the

shallow steps, clearing them in two strides. In the same movement, he whirled round to face the charging figures, drew his gun and dropped into a firing crouch, extending the weapon before him in the classic two-handed grip.

"Freeze!" he bellowed, over the ear-splitting sound of the alarm. "I'll shoot the first fucker who moves!"

The foremost of the attackers skidded to an instant halt under the threat of the levelled gun held by the crouching figure at the top of the steps. A moment's confusion ensued, as those behind cannoned into the backs of the stationary figures in front. Then they spread into a loose group – ten in number, according to Curtis's rapid head-count – and faced him in varying attitudes of readiness to explode into further action at the first opportunity.

Then the Prophet's voice added to the strident whooping of the alarm as he screamed at them, beside himself with rage, "Get him! He's bluffing. He won't shoot. I order you to attack. You will overcome him by force of numbers. Attack him, I say! ..."

Suddenly the alarm cut off and the Prophet's hysterical voice filled the room, as he exhorted the ten excited young sect thugs to attack. Goaded by his fury they edged forward but it quickly became evident that they were reluctant to charge the menacing black muzzle of the small cannon in Curtis's bunched fists and this only served to enrage the Prophet further. It looked for a moment as though the Prophet's hysterical fury was going to make him launch himself physically at Curtis, an action which would undoubtedly trigger his followers to do likewise, engulfing the lieutenant in a suicide attack he would be unable to stop.

The robed figure actually took one pace towards the crouching lieutenant, when the room was filled with the deafening thunder of two gunshots in rapid succession. This was accompanied by the crash of breaking glass, as one of the big floor-to-ceiling windows at the far end of the room exploded outwards in jagged fragments onto the balcony beyond, shattered by the impact of the two heavy slugs from Turner's gun.

The shots took Curtis completely by surprise, just as he'd been wondering how long his bluff would hold. They had an even more profound effect on the other occupants of the room.

The Prophet gave a cry of fear as the bullets blasted past only inches away, so close they fanned his face with the heat of their passage and jerked back to spreadeagle himself against the wall. Three of his followers dived to the floor. The others spun round and found themselves staring down the muzzle of the gun held on them by the grim-faced Turner, crouching low in the same two-handed firing stance as his chief.

"Eat carpet! On yore faces!" Turner dipped the muzzle of his revolver sharply to reinforce his order, and the seven who remained on their feet quickly joined their companions on the floor.

Turner's next order, "Hands behind y'heads!" was obeyed just as promptly.

The two detectives straightened up, keeping their guns trained on the prostrate bodies before them. Curtis glanced over at his young colleague.

"Nice timin', Tex." He nodded his gratitude. "That's one I owe you."

"I'll remind you," Turner quipped, then added with a dubious nod at the scattered figures on the carpet, "What happens now? We takin' this lot in fer questionin'?"

Turner's question was answered in heavily accented English from the direction of the door. "You are leaving this apartment ... and you are leaving unaccompanied by any of our people. That is what happens now."

The two detectives turned to identify the owner of the voice and found themselves facing the oriental who had admitted them earlier. He was standing just inside the open doorway – and he was not alone. Flanking him were two other men. Tall, hard muscled, and cold eyed, they stood silently on either side of the oriental, dwarfing him in size, but not in presence. He was clearly the one in command, despite the fact that his two companions each held a snub-nosed machine pistol, while he himself was unarmed. The guns were covering the two detectives unwaveringly. As though to underline his authority, the oriental barked out an order, upon which the sect thugs scrambled from the floor onto their feet and moved quickly to either side, out of the line of fire.

"Now wait a minute, mister," Curtis began. "You're obstructing police officers in the lawful execution of their duty. I'd advise you to put up those guns for starters."

"Lawful execution of your duty, lieutenant?" the oriental raised a quizzical eyebrow. "Do you have a warrant? I think not. The fact is, when I entered I found you holding our people at gun point. Not content with that, you actually fired at the Reverend Bishop, fortunately missing him but causing damage to property. Be assured that a complaint will be lodged with your superiors. Now if you come this way, I shall personally escort you from the premises to ensure you come to no personal harm."

Before Curtis could move or reply, the Prophet, who seemed to have retreated into shock after having been narrowly missed by Turner's shots, suddenly found his voice.

"They shot at me," he said tremulously. "My God ... they tried to kill me ..." His eyes were vacant and staring in his drawn bloodless face.

"If I'd aimed to kill you, preacher, y'sure wouldn' be standin' there now bellyachin' 'bout it," Turner's soft drawl assured him confidently. Curtis felt thankful that the younger man was keeping his cool in the potentially explosive situation they were in. One panicky move could get them gunned down.

"I tell you, they tried to kill me." The Prophet's voice rose shakily, hysteria threatening.

"You are safe now, Exalted One." The oriental spoke soothingly, as though to a fractious child. "They cannot harm you now that I am here." He signed to two of the members, who immediately crossed to their leader and began to lead him gently, still mumbling about the attempt on his life, towards his chair at the far end of the room.

Curtis decided nothing more was to be gained by continuing the present confrontation, now that things had turned sour. Nodding to Turner to follow his example, he holstered his gun, making his movements deliberate, so as not to spook the cold-eyed gunmen who were still covering them from the doorway.

"Now you are at last showing sense." The oriental gave a

satisfied nod. "If you will come this way, please ..." He indicated the open doorway with an upraised palm.

As the two detectives started for the door, the two gunmen moved out of reach to either side and continued to cover them with the ugly blunt muzzles of their machine pistols. Glancing at them as he passed, Curtis thought the guns looked like modifications of the Israeli Uzi, but whatever they were, they looked lethal and not to be argued with.

When they reached the outside door of the apartment, Curtis stopped on the threshold and turned to face the oriental. "Jes' one thing, before I go," he said. "I'm tellin' you this for your own good. You personally may be uninvolved. But that man in there," he nodded towards the Prophet's private suite which they had just left, "is a prime suspect on a count of seventeen murders. Three of 'em committed over the past two nights. Now, think carefully before you answer this, cuz you could be coverin' fer a very sick an' very dangerous man. To your knowledge, has he left this apartment at any time durin' the past two nights?"

The oriental considered this for a moment, a frown of concentration creasing his smooth brow. Then he slowly shook his head . "No ... not to my knowledge," he replied.

"How about Butch Cassidy an' th'Sundance Kid there?" asked Curtis, nodding at the two silent gunmen who had followed them to the door and still stood, guns levelled, flanking their boss.

"Who?" The oriental stared at him blankly.

"Your two gunslinger friends there. Maybe they saw him go out?"

"Ah!" The Oriental's face cleared and he glanced at each of the men in turn. "Well?" he demanded of them. Each in turn shook his head, unspeaking. The oriental turned back. "There is your answer," he said.

"Could he have gone out without your knowledge?" persisted Curtis.

"No. That would not have been possible," replied the oriental firmly. "Anyone leaving or entering has to pass our door guards and they would inform me. I think you must be mistaken, lieutenant."

Curtis felt that the oriental was telling the truth … or at least, telling the truth as he knew it. But he was equally sure that the Reverend Martin Bishop was his man. So, the oriental must be mistaken, which meant the sect leader was able to sneak out of the apartment undetected somehow. He tried one last throw.

"Is there any other way out of the apartment? A fire-escape, perhaps?" he demanded.

"There is a fire-escape," the oriental confirmed with a nod. "But it leads from the corridor opposite the elevators. You can examine it on your way out of the building," he concluded pointedly and closed the door firmly in Curtis's face.

But the fire-escape in question provided no easy solution to the problem of how Curtis's suspect could have left the apartment without the knowledge of his followers. It was a good twelve feet from the nearest balcony belonging to a window of the apartment they had just left. Too far to reach from a standing jump. There was a nine inch wide ledge running between the balcony and the fire-escape platform. But considering the eight floor drop to the service alley below, only a potential suicide would attempt it.

An icy wind cut the two men to the bone, as they huddled into their overcoats and silently examined the distance between the fire-escape platform and the nearest window balcony. They soon decided to call it a day and get back to headquarters.

"Cain't see 'im goin' that way," Turner remarked as they stepped back into the welcome shelter of the corridor and made for the elevators. "They must be lyin' 'bout 'im not leavin' the place, is all I kin say."

"Nah." Curtis shook his head thoughtfully. "I don' think they were lyin'. I think he slips out somehow without anyone knowin'. Best cover he could have is everyone tellin' what they think is the truth. Too many people lyin' about his movements, an' someone'd slip up sooner or later. The bastard might be insane but he ain't fuckin' stupid." He punched the button for the ground floor and as the door hissed shut, he added, "Tell

you one thing, though – I don' know yet how he does it, and
frankly I don' give a fuck whether he climbs, levitates, or
parachutes down – what I do know is next time he comes out
t'play, we'll be waitin' fer 'im!"

42

BEFORE HEADING BACK TO PRECINCT HQ, CURTIS
checked the stake-out he had ordered on the Eldorado Apartment
Building. There were four on the surveillance team, one each on
the front and rear entrances, one covering the service alley and
the fourth to act as a roving relief or back-up as required. He
warned them to stay alert and to follow Bishop should he leave
the building – especially if he were alone. His final instruction
was that they were to keep him informed of any developments
via their personal radios.

While Turner drove them back to headquarters, Curtis
slumped despondently in the passenger seat, staring out morosely
at the grey overcast day which exactly matched his mood. He
could feel the birth of a headache throbbing dully into life
behind his eyes. Fishing out his crumpled pack, he lit a cigarette.
After only a couple of drags at it, crushed it out savagely in the
ashtray.

"What a fuck up!" he growled. "I had the bastard rattled too.
He wuz startin' t'run off at th'mouth. Christ, what I'd give fer
a session with 'im down at the station house. I'd have 'im singin'
in no time flat – an' it wouldn' be fuckin' hymns!"

Turner deftly negotiated a change of lane, cutting in on the
nose of a furiously honking yellow cab. "Yeah," he remarked
drily. "Either that or y'd both wind up candidates fer
th'nuthouse." He threw a sideways glance at Curtis. "Fer a
while back there, it wuz touch an' go which one of yuh wuz
gonna blow y'stack first, if y'ask me."

Curtis chuckled gruffly, his mood lightening a little. "Some

HUNCH

actor, ain't I? Reckon that wuz worth an Oscar."

"Yeah ... well, that'll compensate yuh fer losin' y'pension when Elrick gives yuh th'bullet, after that lot back there file a complaint about yuh slappin' their boss aroun', an' shootin' th'joint up, an' all," Turner retorted, straight-faced.

"Me shootin' th'joint up? Hah! That's rich that is," Curtis protested in mock indignation. "I thought you wuz auditionin' fer a re-run of the OK Corral. An' jes' when I'd everythin' nicely under control, too. Don' worry though, m'man, I'll stand by you when th'shit hits th'fan at your Inquiry ... jes' so long as we both stick to th'same story ..."

The two men continued their banter for a few more minutes, using it as a way of winding down after the tense situation in which they had just been enmeshed. But the unvoiced thought also lay between them that the situation had been caused by Curtis overplaying his hand. And it was true, Curtis acknowledged to himself, he was becoming too personally involved in the case. He had waited and hunted so long for a real suspect, that when one had finally appeared, he had allowed his judgement to become clouded by his overeagerness to come to grips with him. He had ignored his years of experience and charged in blindly without the one essential to solve a case – enough hard evidence to back up an arrest and arraignment before a court of law.

When they pulled into the basement car pool at Precinct HQ, Curtis sat for a moment after Turner had switched off the ignition. Then he punched the dashboard gently with a clenched fist.

"It's him, Tex," he said seriously. "I know I'm right about that. He's the one. He's got it all ..." He ticked off the points on his fingers. "One – he's a strong bastard. He fuckin' near broke my wrist when he grabbed me. Two – he's tall. Those two points fit Doc' Easton's theory. Three – he's a bigot with a king sized sexual hang-up about whores, which explains the religious quotes he carves on the bodies of his victims. Four – Doc' Friedman said he thinks our killer's a sexual sadist. Well, I wuz watchin' Bishop closely when he wuz goin' through them morgue shots, an' I'm sure he damn near came in his jockey shorts. An'

395

ANGELS OF DEATH

lastly, five – he's funny farm material all right ... he's nuttier than a fruitcake!"

Turner nodded. "I'm with yuh all th'way, Chief. I think he's our man, too. Maybe things'll turn out fer th'best, though. Maybe yuh've riled 'im up so much, yuh'll flush 'im out. He might be so all-fired eager t'git back at yuh, he might go huntin' again sooner, rather than later."

"Yeah ... good thinkin." Curtis nodded in turn. "It might jes' be a good idea t'detail extra cover fer the men on night watch at the Eldorado. We can't have 'im slippin' past us t'go on some revenge mission. That's all we'd need," he concluded grimly.

"Speakin' of the morgue shots ... did y'git his prints on 'em, okay?" inquired Turner blandly.

Curtis grinned at him and lightly tapped his pocket. "You bet! An' I'm headin' fer Fingerprints t'git 'em processed – priority. Then we'll run 'em through the computer t'find out who Mister Prophet Bishop really is. With a bitta luck, he'll have a record heavy enough fer us t'swear out a warrant on 'im, an' then we kin pull th'fucker in. Let's go, pardner ..."

PART VII
MENACE
AND
MAYHEM

43

ANGEL FOUR CLOSED THE DOOR ON THE TROUBLE-
some detective and stood staring at it for a few moments, deep
in thought. Then, abruptly dismissing the two guards, he went
directly to his personal quarters, entered and locked the door
behind him.

Crossing to the phone, the oriental quickly punched out the
number of Bethlehem House and asked to speak to Angel One,
only to be told that he was engaged right then supervising an
interview between the police and the Miller boy. Angel Four
stressed the importance of his call and insisted that the meeting
be interrupted and Angel One requested to come to the phone.

Minutes later, in rapid-fire Cantonese, Angel Four had outlined
to his leader the events which had taken place at the apartment.
He concluded his report by relating his parting exchange with
the detective lieutenant and the policeman's disturbing statement
that the Prophet was strongly suspected of having committed
a series of seventeen murders. A short silence followed this
account, then Angel One's harsh voice sounded in his ear with
flat finality.

"Enough is enough! He has become a liability and as such
will have to be disposed of. When we spoke earlier, you expressed
the opinion that he was mentally unbalanced enough to have
carried out these senseless killings. Now, it seems the police are
of the same opinion. We are already having to deflect police
attention caused by the Miller brat but this report of yours is
much more serious. It threatens us with a major police
investigation which could prove catastrophic." He paused to

consider something, then asked, "How many more nights has his latest crusade to run?"

"Six, including tonight."

"Very well. Let him finish his bookings with the Centre. I will send one of our technicians to install some electronic surveillance devices in his private suite, while he is absent this evening. You will then be able to monitor his every movement and keep track of his whereabouts at all times. It is imperative that he be prevented from leaving the apartment undetected. On the sixth night, when he has completed his current crusade ... kill him! Make it look like an accident. I would suggest a fall from one of the window balconies. It could then be released to the news media that his tragic fall followed a stroke or something of that nature. Understood?"

"Understood," Angel Four affirmed. "I agree we no longer need our revered Prophet. Our organisation is solidly enough based now to be self perpetuating. May I ask how the police interview with Miller is progressing?"

"It is going according to plan. Miller is obeying instructions and sticking to the story I gave him," Angel One replied. "But the private detective is suspicious. He is shrewd ... and a little too knowledgeable for my liking. He may have to be discouraged if he persists in causing us trouble after today. If so, I shall deal with him myself ..."

Angel One replaced the receiver, nodded to the Apostle on duty in Control and left the room. He ascended the stairs from the basement, quickly crossed the large ground floor hallway and turned along a corridor towards the room where he was supervising the interview between the Miller boy and his unwelcome visitors.

Unwelcome as were any outsiders, these particular visitors had also disrupted the entire routine of the house and its community. This was because the appearance of the ground floor – and several of its inhabitants – had had to be altered to fit the pretence of its official designation as a private sanatorium run by the sect.

Gone were the tracksuits and colourful robes. In their place were white coats over conventional clothing for the 'medical staff'; pyjamas and hospital blue dressing gowns for those sect members acting as patients. Two of the larger ground floor rooms had been temporarily converted into wards by the simple expedient of installing beds moved down from the attic dormitories and occupying some of them with patients.

On their arrival, the sheriff and the private detective had been conducted past the open doors of these wards on their way to the interview room. They had even been obliged to pause at the door of the second ward to allow an attractive white-clad nurse to leave, wheeling a gleaming steel trolley loaded with medical equipment. This had afforded them the opportunity for a good look at the set-up.

Then, as the interview with the Miller boy was about to commence, the private detective had sprung the surprise request to be allowed to interview a second member named Karen Larsen on behalf of her parents. Angel One had headed off this awkward request with the lie that she was at present helping to staff one of the meditation centres in the city.

Angel One, his appearance completely altered by a white medical coat with a stethoscope tube dangling from one of his pockets, felt satisfied now that he had finally taken the irrevocable step of pronouncing the Prophet's death sentence. Not only would the decision remove the threat of a police murder investigation which might uncover their drugs operation, but it would also allow him to present the Director with the idea that the execution had been carried out in deference to his suggestion made the previous evening.

Reaching the room where the interview was being conducted, Angel One opened the door and entered. At once his sense of well-being vanished. When called away to answer Angel Four's phone call, he had summoned one of the Apostles, also in medical disguise, to take his place. The white-coated figure of his relief was still present, as were the tall sheriff and the Miller boy – but the private detective was missing!

At once he demanded to know where the man had gone. He was informed that Grant had indicated his need to use a toilet and had been directed to the one situated at the far end of the corridor. This had occurred not long after Angel One's departure. Unable to hide a frown of anger at his subordinate's stupidity in allowing Grant to leave the room without first having summoned an escort for him, he reached for the door handle, intending to go after the meddlesome detective.

"Doctor Sung." The sheriff's quiet voice, addressing him by the assumed title with which he had introduced himself at the start of their visit, arrested him on his way out of the room.

"Yes?" He half turned and looked back at the sheriff, his hand resting lightly on the handle of the open door.

"If you'll pardon my sayin' so, I don' think y'need worry y'self 'bout Mister Grant gittin' lost," Springfield informed him. "After all, he is a detective, so I think he's quite capable of findin' his own way back from the toilet." He smiled to remove any offence from his words.

"Ah, but you could be wrong in that assumption, Sheriff," Angel One replied evenly. "This is an old house, with many inter-connecting corridors. It is very easy to take a wrong turning if you are not familiar with them. So, if you will excuse me for a few minutes, I shall ensure Mister Grant's safe return."

"Safe return?" Springfield's words were accompanied by a quizzical smile. But there was no humour in his clear blue eyes. "Oh, even s'posin' he did take a wrong turnin' like y'say, I'm sure he wouldn' mind riskin' the danger of bein' accosted by some purty young nurse."

Angel One returned his smile, equally humourlessly. "I'm afraid that's not the only danger he would risk, were he to go wandering around unescorted." The sheriff's eyebrows rose at this but the oriental pressed on smoothly, "If I may remind you, we are running a sanatorium for the mentally disturbed and many of our patients are potentially violent. I should have it on my conscience if either of you came to any harm while I am responsible for your safety."

Springfield eyed the white-coated doctor stolidly. He was unable to put a finger on the reason but he felt an instinctive antipathy towards the man. There was something decidedly unmedical about him – a hidden menace. He decided it was time to stop beating about the bush.

"If either of us comes to any harm, Doc', you'd have it on more'n yore conscience. You'd have it on yore record … in the State Pen'!" The sheriff's tone was still casual but the challenge in his words was unmistakable.

"If I didn't know better, I would construe that as a threat, Sheriff." The softly spoken reply showed the challenge had been recognised for what it was … and accepted.

"Nope." Springfield shook his head solemnly. "Jes' plain speakin'. I'm a great believer in it, m'self. Saves a heap o' misunderstandin', I always find."

"Good. Then in that at least we hold the same views, Sheriff. I also shall speak plainly. You and your friend are here because you requested to interview this boy," Angel One nodded at Miller, who was seated pale and silent off to one side, "because of some wild allegations made by his parents. You have no warrant to search these premises. Therefore your friend has no right to go snooping round without permission. If he comes to any harm, he will have gone looking for it. However, unless you delay me further, I intend to prevent any such harm coming to him by ensuring his safe return as quickly as possible. Now, if you will excuse me …" Angel One began to turn away but the sheriff's voice arrested him again.

"How'd it be if I wuz to help you look fer 'im?" Springfield took a step towards the door.

"No thank you, Sheriff. That will be unnecessary," replied Angel One coldly, adding, "Why don't you continue your interview with Miller? It is, after all, why your are here, is it not? I shall ensure Mister Grant returns to join us …"

"Safely, I think you said," Springfield cut in, before the oriental could leave, playing for time. He and Grant had agreed beforehand, with some initial reluctance on the sheriff's part, that if an opportunity presented itself, the private detective would slip off on his own for a scout around. Rubbing a big callused hand thoughtfully over his jaw, Springfield continued, "I sure 'preciate yore concern over Mister Grant's safety. Truth is, I'm a mite concerned 'bout it m'self. Y'see, if we ain' back … safely … in my office in …" he glanced at his watch, "… an hour from now, my deppity's got orders to contact the State Police fer backup t'bust 'is way in here lookin' fer us."

He stared straight-faced at the white-coated figure and shrugged. "It's standard procedure t'provide y'self with backup, y'see. An' my deppity," he shook his head regretfully, "he ain' one fer usin' 'is initiative. He'll take my orders literally, an' act on 'em without delay."

Springfield decided he'd gone as far as he could in delaying the search for Grant, so he added a last reminder to accompany the good doctor on his way. "So, if you'll make sure Mister Grant gits back ... safely ... we'll be on our way. An' that'll save everyone a whole heapa trouble." Again he flashed a bright mirthless smile.

Without another word, but seething inwardly at the sheriff's words, Angel One left the room and pulled the door shut behind him. He made his way swiftly along to the bogus wards, and ordered the sect personnel there to spread out through the house in a comprehensive search pattern to hunt down the interloper. They were instructed, when they found him, to report by phone to Angel One at Control.

The sect members immediately dispersed throughout the maze of corridors and rooms which made up the four floors of the big, rambling house, from basement to attic. Their search pattern spread out like the sensitive filaments of a gigantic web, at the centre of which sat Angel One, like some malignant spider waiting patiently for one of the strands to trigger and send him racing to accost the intruder.

44

RIGHT FROM THE START OF THE VISIT, GRANT HAD been dissatisfied with the way things had gone. First, the denial that Karen Larsen was in Bethlehem House. Then, when Jim Miller was produced, he had not seemed all that eager to see them, contrary to what Grant had expected. The boy had been pale and hesitant, except when Grant had requested that they be allowed to interview him alone. Then he had responded quickly, too quickly in Grant's estimation, to insist that the white-coated Doctor Sung remain in the room with them. The doctor had thereupon intervened to explain that as the boy was currently in a mentally unstable state and looked upon him as a surrogate father figure, his presence provided a feeling of security for him.

The boy had then answered Grant's questions politely enough. His explanation was that his decision to abscond and his subsequent phone call to his parents had been the result of an emotional crisis caused by a row with his girlfriend, another sect member. Grant found this unconvincing. Doubly so because of the involuntary sidelong glances the boy had flicked in the doctor's direction during this explanation, as though checking on his reaction. All Grant's subsequent questions and attempts to stress how concerned his parents were about him, met with a discouragingly negative response.

Finally, Grant had asked him straight out whether he was under any threat or other pressure to deny that he in fact wanted to leave. The boy had sullenly shaken his head and denied that this was so. But he had dropped his eyes as he spoke, unable to hold Grant's steady questioning gaze.

It had been at this point that the doctor had been called away by a phone call and relieved by a younger colleague. Miller had shown no undue agitation at the departure of his 'surrogate father figure', prompting the cynical thought in Grant's mind that they had probably forgotten to rehearse that bit.

Before the new supervisor had the chance to get settled in, Grant had asked him where he could find a toilet, having first signalled his intention to Springfield with a look. Without thinking, the newcomer had replied that there was one a few doors down to the right, at the end of the corridor. Grant had thanked him, excused himself and slipped from the room before the man could protest.

Once outside, he quickly found the toilet and made as though to enter it. A quick check back down the corridor showed him he was unobserved. Immediately, he turned away from the door and walked on to the turn of the corridor and slipped round it out of sight. It was his intention to examine as much of the house interior as he could, before the inevitable pursuit caught up with him.

A new corridor stretched ahead, evidently traversing the entire width of the house. There were doors set at irregular intervals on either side along its length and at its midpoint and far end he could see it was crossed by other corridors. There was no-one about. Grant decided this would be because all sect personnel not detailed to act as staff or patients would have been ordered to stay out of sight, while the outsiders were on the premises.

He quickly checked out the rooms as he progressed, opening the doors just enough to glance in. He was ready, if challenged, to claim he was searching for a toilet and had lost his bearings. It seemed from his inspection that this section of the house served as individual quarters for senior staff. The rooms in this stretch of corridor were comfortably, if similarly furnished, with carpeted floors, neatly made-up beds, armchairs, tables and bookshelves.

The last door he opened before the intersecting corridor at the halfway point turned out to be a spacious linen cupboard, the shelves stacked high with clean sheets and blankets. He had just closed this door, when a white-coated figure turned the corner and almost walked into him.

The tall young black stopped, surprised at meeting one of the visiting strangers wandering about unescorted. If any search for Grant had started, then he was obviously unaware of it as yet. Grant flashed him a friendly grin to put him at his ease. "Hi," he said cheerily. "I'm lookin' for a toilet but I seem to have passed it by. Could you direct me?"

The man relaxed visibly and pointed back the way the stranger had come. "Jes' roun' th'corner, man. Fust door on y'left."

Grant half turned as though to follow the pointing finger. Then pivoting on the balls of his feet he whipped round and punched the man flush on the point of the jaw, his whole weight behind the blow. The young black never knew what hit him and dropped as though his legs had been cut from under him.

Jerking open the linen cupboard door again, Grant quickly dragged the unconscious figure inside its roomy interior. Closing the door, he found and flicked on the light switch. Working fast, he stripped off the man's white coat and donned it himself. Then, grabbing a folded sheet, he shook it out and tore it into strips, which he used to gag his victim and bind his arms and ankles.

Leaving the man curled on his side, Grant stepped back out into the still deserted corridor. On impulse, he turned the corner the man had come round and found himself walking towards a flight of stairs, leading to the upper floors of the house.

Gaining the first floor, he heard voices and caught a glimpse of two more white-coated figures approaching, so he carried straight on up the next flight to the second floor without stopping. There, a quick check on a few rooms told him this level was used mainly as a recreational area.

The rooms were fewer in number and widely spaced along the corridors and much larger than those on the ground floor. In them, taking part in various activities – pool, table tennis, reading, watching TV – were the first robed sect members he had seen since entering Bethlehem House. He noticed that whenever any of them caught sight of his white coated figure, they immediately looked away.

Deciding he had seen enough, he doubled back to the stairs, intending to head for the top floor of the house. It was as well he did because he had barely reached them when he heard voices approaching the junction of the corridors, off to his rear.

Moving as silently as he could, he took the stairs two at a time and emerged under the slope of the roof into a short passage bisecting a long central corridor running the entire width of the attic. On the opposite side of this corridor, the continuation of the short passage ended at the top of a descending staircase leading down, Grant guessed, to the front of the house.

Grant advanced to the junction with the central passage and cautiously peered up and down its length in both directions. It was deserted, so he stepped forward and took a good look around him. Above his head were two large skylight windows, barred on the outside he noted, one set into either slope of the roof's apex. To left and right of him, neat lines of identical doors, set opposite one another in pairs, marched symmetrically off towards either end of the attic.

Walking across to the nearest door, Grant opened it and looked in. It was a compact sleeping cubicle, the spartan interior containing the minimum of creature comforts, compared to the more palatial staff quarters on the ground floor. Two narrow single beds, one on either side of the cubicle, occupied half of the available floorspace. At the head of each bed sat a bedside locker, each holding a table lamp and small transistor radio. The limited space between the beds meant the two lockers were almost touching. A small rug covering the floorspace completed the sparse furnishings. Quick checks behind four more doors revealed almost identical cubicles, all similarly unoccupied. Then, behind the sixth door he struck pay dirt.

The occupant of the cubicle, a girl of seventeen or so, was lying on top of one of the narrow beds, her head supported by a pillow propped against the low headboard. Her eyes were closed, a dreamy smile on her attractive face, as she listened to the pop music pouring through the headphones covering her ears. She lay there quite oblivious to Grant's presence, her fingers slowly beating time to the rhythm of the music.

Grant slipped inside and closed the door behind him. In an attempt to avoid startling her by his unannounced presence, he assumed a friendly smile and tapped her lightly on the foot to attract her attention. To his surprise, instead of the startled reaction he had anticipated, he found himself totally ignored. He tapped her foot again – and got the same negative response. He shook his head in amused disbelief. Surely it was impossible for her to have failed to register his presence unless she was asleep and the movement of her fingers beating time to the music from her headphones belied that. He recalled something Rocky O'Rourke had said about Jim Miller having mentioned that the sect were "into a heavy drugs scene", and guessed she must be high on something.

Moving to the head of the bed, he stood looking down at her. He noticed a small plastic name-tag pinned to the front of her sky-blue robe, similar to the one worn by the girl Louise at the sect van. Sister Carole, it read. He reached down and gently removed the headphones. They dangled from his hand, the music pouring from them sounding tinny and faint in the silence of the cubicle.

"Sister Carole." He spoke her name quietly, keeping his friendly smile in place. It seemed to him that the disappearance of the music, rather than the sound of her name got through to her. The girl opened her eyes and blinked dreamily up at him, her pupils dilated to black pools which almost obscured the brown irises surrounding them. She focused on him with difficulty. Then she smiled and waved an unsteady hand at him.

"Hi man. Grab a cloud," she greeted him. Her hand flopped limply back onto the bed. Then a frown clouded her pretty face. "Hey, where'd th'sounds go?"

Her speech was slow and slurred. From that and the unco-ordinated movement of her hand, Grant knew he was right about her being under the influence of some drug or other, probably an opiate, he guessed.

Just then, Grant heard voices and footsteps in the corridor outside, accompanied by the sound of doors opening and closing. The rooms were evidently being checked out – and he didn't need his detection skills to work out who they were searching for! Taking a chance on the girl's friendly attitude, he placed a finger on his lips in a conspiratorial gesture of silence and jerked his thumb towards the sounds of activity beyond the door.

Despite her fuddled state, the girl caught on quickly enough. Her attractive face crinkled in concentration as she listened to the approaching sounds outside, then she clumsily repeated his gesture of silence and smiled at him. With a friendly wink, Grant returned her smile, stooped and slipped her headphones back in place. Then, moving fast, he dropped to the floor and rolled under the bed out of sight.

Lying with his back pressed to the wall, Grant heard the door open. Breathing as quietly as he could, he watched the searcher's feet move into his line of vision. A pair of brown trainers stopped a scant couple of feet from his face as their owner walked over and stood beside the bed.

There was a sudden clatter as the headphones were

unceremoniously pulled from the girl's head and flung down on the small table. The bedsprings inches above Grant's head bounced, as the man roughly shook the girl on the bed. "Come on ... come on ... snap out of it, ya bitch!" he barked angrily.

The girl whimpered, then gave a sharp cry of pain. "You're hurtin' me," she wailed.

Grant's body tensed in anger as there came the sharp sound of a blow, and the springs creaked briefly from the force of its delivery.

"I'll hurt you good, if y'don' fuckin' straighten out an' answer me," the voice snarled. Another blow. Another cry of pain.

"Leave me alone," the girl whimpered. "I ain' done nothin' wrong."

"Anybody bin in here? Tall guy, stranger?" the man demanded loudly, shaking her again.

"No. I ain' seen no strangers," she protested.

"Oh, sure y'ain't," the man sneered. "Well, this'll remind you to tell us if y'do ..." The bed creaked again as the girl jerked and gave a sharp cry of pain.

Grant's anger overwhelmed his common sense and he braced his back against the wall, intending to thrust his legs straight out and kick the man's feet from under him. At that moment, however, the door opened and another voice called into the room. "C'mon man, quit foolin' around. Y'kin have y'fun some other time. Angel One's waitin' fer results, remember."

The feet moved from the bedside towards the door. As the door closed behind the men, the second voice was saying, "Looks like this floor's clean, but you stand guard at the stairheads, while we go give a hand on the third floor."

Grant slid out from under the bed and scrambled to his feet. The girl was lying on her side, knees drawn up to her chest, her body shaking with silent sobs. He sat on the edge of the bed and gathered her protectively into his arms, holding her close and stroking her hair soothingly. Reaching out, he plucked the headphone jack free of its socket, and the room was filled with the soft sound of music from the radio.

After a moment or two, the girl relaxed and the shuddering sobs died away. Gently, he laid her back onto the pillow and took her hands in his. Her pale, tear-streaked face showed a reddening mark on one cheek where a blow had landed, the eye above it already starting to puff and discolour. She looked up at him, a greater degree of awareness now evident through the mind-fogging effects of whatever drug she was on.

"You okay now?" he asked softly, keeping his voice below the level of the music from the radio. She nodded and gave him a little smile of thanks. "Sorry I brought that on you." He gave her hands an apologetic squeeze. "You've prob'ly guessed I'm the stranger that punk was on about."

She nodded. "Yeah, I kinda guessed that," she agreed. Her voice was soft and pleasant, though her words were still a bit slurred. "We were warned t'keep outa sight, cuz strangers were t'be nosin' aroun'. So, I jes' popped a few pills an' dropped right outa sight." She giggled at this, recovering from her recent experience with the resilience of youth. Then she became serious again. "Listen, Mister Stranger-Man, you'd better drop outa sight too, else y'gonna be in bad trouble when they catch you."

"I can take care of myself," he assured her. Then, intending to question her about Karen Larsen's whereabouts, he started, "Listen, Carole ..."

But before he could go on, she interrupted him. "Not if th'Angels get you ... they'll take care've you, nice Mister Stranger-Man ... 'specially if Archangel Michael gets you ... you'll wind up as dogmeat f'the Hellhounds." She nodded solemnly at him, her big eyes blinking owlishly.

Grant looked at her, half amused. It sounded like drug-induced gibberish, but the mention of the Hellhounds rang a bell – they had been mentioned by Jim Miller when he'd phoned his father on the night he had run. And the boy had also mentioned the name Archangel Michael according to his father.

As these thoughts passed through Grant's mind, Carole's eyelids drooped sleepily and closed. The influence of the drug seemed to be winning again, so before she could slip away from him into her dream world, he released her hands and shook her gently by the shoulders.

"Carole," he said urgently, though still careful to keep his voice low. "Do you know a Sister Karen Larsen? ... Karen

Larsen?" he repeated the name. "Where is she? Where will I find her? Carole? ..."

He was about to give up, thinking he had lost her, when she answered dreamily, "Y'won' see Sister Karen ... she's in th'Turkey Pens ... poor Karen ... poor col' turkey ..." Carole's voice tailed off and a trickle of saliva appeared at the corner of her slack mouth. Grant gently wiped it away with the cuff of his white coat and folded her hands comfortably on her lap. Plugging the jack into its radio socket, he slipped the headphones over her ears, brushed a stray wisp of hair from her face and stood up.

He knew he'd get no more sense out of her, but he'd got what he wanted. He recognised the expression 'Turkey Pens' from Louise's note to him via the Champ earlier that day and she'd also pin-pointed them as being situated 'somewhere in the basement'. He decided that he'd try to locate them to complete his reconnaissance of Bethlehem House, if he could do so before he was discovered. The knowledge would prove useful for any subsequent rescue mission he mounted to free Jim Miller and Karen Larsen from the clutches of the sect.

Stepping quietly to the door he pressed an ear against its edge and listened intently for a moment. Hearing nothing suspicious, he cracked the door open and peered through the narrow slit with one eye. There was no-one within his limited field of vision. Gradually he eased the door further open till he could survey the entire corridor. Its sole occupant was the man who had been left on guard. Five doors away, he was standing with his back to Grant, leaning a shoulder against the corner of the corridor intersection.

Grant slipped out the door, closing it soundlessly behind him so as not to implicate the girl. Flattening himself against the line of the wall, he cat-footed silently up behind the unsuspecting guard. The man was smoking and casually half turning his head from side to side, so as to keep both stairheads under surveillance alternately, for a few seconds at a time.

At the last moment, just as Grant poised himself to deliver a knockout blow to the joint of neck and shoulder, some sixth sense warned the man of danger. He suddenly pushed himself away from the wall and whipped round. But he hesitated, momentary confusion showing on his face as he caught a glimpse of the white coat Grant was wearing. It proved his undoing.

Grant gave him no time to recover from his mistake. Instantly changing his method of attack, he rammed a stiff fingered spear-hand blow into the guard's throat. The man reeled back choking and Grant, following up, grabbed him by the shoulders, spun his sagging body round and drove two vicious punches into his kidneys. A final hard chop to the exposed joint of neck and shoulder put his victim face down on the floor, unconscious.

Dragging the prostrate form into the nearest empty cubicle by the heels, he kicked him none too gently under the bed out of sight. "That's for Carole, ya bastard!" he muttered, as he closed the door behind him.

Choosing the opposite flight of stairs to the one he had come up, Grant began to descend them stealthily, reckoning these would take him down to the front of the house. He paused at the first half-landing and peered cautiously down to the floor below. There was plenty of activity going on, several of the passing figures wearing white coats like his own. He decided to take a chance by relying on his similar appearance to avoid close inspection – always assuming they hadn't yet discovered his first victim in the ground floor linen cupboard, and so realised he had stolen a white coat.

Lowering his head to avoid a full-face confrontation with anyone, he ran lightly down the remaining flights to the ground floor without being challenged. None of the passing searchers on the middle two floors gave his hurrying figure more than a glance, so he congratulated himself on his superficial disguise. It was proving as effective as a recognisable uniform in the enemy stronghold.

Gaining the ground floor, Grant's luck still held. He found he had descended to the big entrance hall at a point opposite the front door, where he and Springfield had been admitted on their arrival. Ahead and to his right were the two open doors leading into the bogus wards which had been set up for their benefit. Immediately on his right was another door. This one was closed and bore a small sign reading, NO ADMITTANCE – EXCEPT

TO AUTHORISED PERSONNEL. Grant wondered if it led to the basement.

Hearing footsteps approaching from the corridor leading to the interview room, his mind was made up for him. Hoping the door was unlocked, Grant depressed the handle and pushed. To his relief, it opened smoothly and he slipped inside, pulling it shut behind him. He found himself standing at the top of a steep flight of concrete stairs. His path to the basement was clear. He had made it. Incredibly, he had completed a virtual circuit of the big house, although it had been by no means a comprehensive examination. He decided to play his lucky streak to the limit and carry on until he was discovered.

Descending the stairs quietly, he emerged at their foot into a brightly lit corridor running off to either side. To his left, it ran for only a few yards before coming to a halt at a grey steel door, on which a white sign bore the message in large red letters, CONTROL – NO UNAUTHORISED ENTRY PERMITTED. In Grant's opinion control rooms were usually manned, so he decided against trying it and instead moved off in the opposite direction.

The corridor, with its whitewashed brick walls, led to another which it joined in a T-junction. There were several solid looking wooden doors set into the walls in either direction of this new passage and Grant chose the arm to his left. As he turned the corner and moved off, he failed to see the figure which emerged from a door at the far end of the stretch of corridor to his rear. The figure watched him try a locked door and move on to the next one, then it withdrew back into the room it had been about to leave.

Blissfully unaware he had been spotted, Grant progressed along the corridor following a zig-zag route, in order to try all the doors on either side as he went along. They were all locked. Then, about half way along, he came upon one that wasn't. It gave under his hand, a crack of light appearing down its opened edge. He heard voices and the sound of activity from within.

Cautiously Grant eased the door open until he could peer into the widening crack with one eye. He saw a section of what appeared to be a long table with a stainless steel surface. He also caught a glimpse of some familiar looking flat plastic objects lying scattered on its surface. Then two movements caught his eye simultaneously.

The first came from within the room, as a white-coated figure crossed his field of vision carrying a large cardboard box. The second movement he caught out of the corner of his eye, as something moved behind him. He sensed rather than saw the danger. But before he could react, Grant felt as though the three floors above him had caved in and hit him behind the left ear. A brief firework display of pain flared in his head then extinguished as he pitched forward into a deep black pit.

45

GRANT STRUGGLED BACK TO CONSCIOUSNESS. Cold ... head feels cold ... The sound of running water seemed to be close to his head. Then his blurred vision registered whiteness. An instant later he was shocked back to full awareness by a deluge of icy water landing on the back of the head and cascading down over his ears and face. Dully he realised that he was being supported face down over a washhand basin, while someone poured freezing cold water over his head.

He tried to raise himself but this was prevented by the two men who had a firm grip of his arms. He ceased his feeble struggling when the numbing draughts of water stopped cascading icily over his head, allowing him to catch his breath. A harsh voice rapped out a command and Grant was hauled round by his two escorts and frog-marched towards the door. Still dazed, he was half carried, half dragged, out of the washroom, his legs stumbling in a vain attempt to keep pace with his upper body.

A few doors further along the corridor, he was bundled into another room and dumped unceremoniously onto a wooden chair. Pain pounded at his temples. It felt like his brain was trying to kick its way out of his skull. He slumped forward, but a hand seized his hair painfully from behind and jerked him upright. His head spun crazily. When his blurred vision cleared, he found himself looking up into a familiar face. Standing before him, regarding him with a mixture of contempt and hostility, was the oriental who had accompanied Jim Miller and introduced himself as Doctor Sung.

Grant raised a hand to his aching neck and massaged it gently. "You guys sure play rough," he said hoarsely, trying out his voice to make sure it still worked. "Remind me not to leave a donation on my way out."

"We can get much rougher," Angel One assured him bluntly. "Especially with troublesome pests who snoop around, cause us a great deal of inconvenience and commit unprovoked assaults on our personnel." The slanted black eyes regarded Grant with reptilian flatness for a moment, then the harsh nasal voice inquired sarcastically, "And on the subject of donations, do you always make them in the name of Chester D Calhoun?"

Grant squinted up at him. "Seems I'm not the only one who's bin snoopin' around," he commented with a wry grimace.

"Did you really imagine your amateurish playacting would fool anyone?" Angel One sneered. "Especially when you drove off afterwards in your own car?"

Grant winced as he continued to massage his neck gingerly, but his discomfort was more mental than physical. Mentally he kicked himself for his carelessness. Underestimating one's adversaries was always a mistake, and against an opponent like this one, such mistakes could prove to be dangerous. With a sinking feeling he recalled he had also used the Mustang in the running battle at the Washington Centre the previous night, which had ended so calamitously for the sect. Almost as though the oriental had read his mind, he spoke again.

"And I can also assure you, Mister Grant, that your interference last night at the Washington Centre, will be the last we will tolerate from you. Like others of your kind who have annoyed us briefly in the past, you are a nuisance ... but in your case, you have become a costly nuisance." He held up a blunt forefinger. "One more such action on your part ..." the finger levelled to point straight at Grant's face, "... and the cost will be to you!"

"Is that a threat?" Grant demanded.

The Oriental's hand jabbed swiftly forward. Blinding pain lanced into Grant's cheek as the rigid finger unerringly found the nerve centre on his left cheekbone. An instant later, the bunched knuckle of the same forefinger rammed into the other nerve centre just under his nose, and Grant couldn't contain the yell that was torn from his throat as incredible agony exploded in the centre of his face. Slowly the red starburst of pain receded and his blurred, watery vision cleared, allowing him to focus on his surroundings again. He flinched reflexively as he saw his assailant lean towards him. "Yes, Mister Grant. That is exactly what it is ... a threat," the oriental hissed malevolently into his face. "A threat ... and a warning. It will be your last!"

"Yeah ... I thought it might be," Grant replied hoarsely, assuming a flippancy he certainly did not feel. Then, mustering his courage he looked up at the menacing oriental and went on defiantly, "There's just one thing you don't seem t'be takin' into account. I ain't the only one who's interested in your activities. The State Police are too. In fact, once Sheriff Springfield and I have reported our findings, they're liable to come bustin' in here to find out exactly how many minors you an' your mob're holdin' against their will. An' they won't buy any phoney hospital set-up, or interviews like the one you've staged downstairs for us."

Angel One regarded Grant with cold calculation. This one was made of sterner stuff than others of his profession, whom he had dealt with in the past. And what he had just said about police interest was confirmed by the presence of the tall sheriff downstairs with Miller. In fact, it was this very factor which was preventing him from dealing with Grant in a much more lethal and terminal fashion. He decided to adopt a new tactic in order to probe for a weakness in his opponent.

"No, Mister Grant. It will not be necessary for me to deal with the police at all," he said matter-of-factly. "On the contrary, you will call them off for me."

"Like hell I will!" Grant retorted vehemently.

"Oh, yes ..." Angel One nodded confidently. "I assure you, you will ... once I have shown you exactly what will be the result, should you ever be so foolish as to incite your police friends to force an entry to this place."

Signalling to the two guards, the oriental spun on his heel, pulled open the door and strode from the room. Grant found himself gripped by the arms, hauled bodily from the chair and bundled through the doorway in his captor's wake. As he stumbled along between his escorts, he concentrated grimly on clearing his spinning head and coaxing strength back into his rubbery legs. The little procession made its way through the corridors of the basement, till they came to a halt before a solid looking grey steel door. The oriental unlocked it and they stepped through into the short passage containing the four cells where Jim Miller had been brought on his recapture.

Angel One turned to face Grant. "When you arrived, you asked me if you could see a girl member named Karen Larsen. I have decided to grant your request ..." Turning away, he unlocked the nearest door, pushed it open and stepped back. Ordering the guards to release Grant, he indicated for him to approach the open door.

When the escorts let go his arms, Grant staggered forward, momentarily off balance. Annoyed with himself for showing weakness, he supported himself with a hand on the door frame. To score a return point, he remarked, "These'll be the Turkey Pens, I take it?"

He was rewarded by a brief look of surprise on the Oriental's face, followed by his soft reply, "I knew I was right about you, Grant. You are too inquisitive for everyone's good ... especially your own!"

Grant reached the open doorway and looked in. He had studied the photographs of Karen Larsen that her father Pete had given him, but for a moment he thought the oriental had deliberately shown him the wrong girl. The pathetic figure curled into a foetal ball in the corner, bleary-eyed, hair disarranged, clutching her knees to her chest in an effort to control the constant shivering of her body, bore no resemblance to the clear eyed smiling youngster in the photographs.

He wrinkled his nose at the fetid odour of vomit, excrement and stale sweat which assailed him. The girl tried to speak when her watery eyes focused on him, but her words at first made no sense because of the violent chattering of her teeth. She seemed unaware, or uncaring, of the dried vomit which encrusted her chin and the front of her soiled robe. Grant doubted whether her own parents would have recognised their daughter in this piteous state.

"Karen? Karen Larsen?" he addressed her gently. Again the girl tried to speak, this time stretching out a trembling hand towards him. There was no real intelligence in the red-rimmed eyes which stared at him, only an awareness that he ... somebody ... was there. He strained to catch the mumbled litany of her reply. Then he made sense of it.

"A fix ... please ... a fix ... please ... a fix ..."

Grant felt a surge of anger course through him, lending him strength. He turned his head and directed a look of contempt at the man by his side. "You despicable bastards!" he grated out "Does this make you feel good? Is this how you get your kicks?"

Angel One glanced at the pathetic figure in the cell. He shrugged. "She is the one who seeks the 'kicks', as you put it. Her habit of taking heroin was acquired before she came to us. But that is beside the point. She is here in that state because of two factors. Your actions of last night ... and those of her father ... another persistent nuisance."

"You're makin' that poor kid suffer like that because of her father's actions ... and mine?" Grant burst out angrily. "On whose orders? Yours? Or that crazy prick I listened to last night, claimin' he's the new Messiah?"

"His, actually," replied Angel One unconcernedly. "But on this occasion, it could be considered an appropriate punishment. After all, doesn't your God order that the sins of the parents have to be paid for by their offspring? A shrewd fellow, your God. He is obviously an expert on human psychology."

"You're a sadistic bastard! You know that?" Grant spat out. "You're as sick as that fuckin' pervert who runs this place. I thought all your kind crawled back under your Shinto shrines after we nuked Hiroshima."

Angel One smiled coldly. "Scratch a white American and you uncover an incurable racialist lurking just beneath the skin." His tone dripped acid contempt. "For your information, I am not Japanese, I am Chinese. And we did not choose this girl's method of self-destruction … she did that herself. But you can inform her father that her future comfort will depend on him. Each time he causes us annoyance from now on, she will spend a week like this." He pointed at the now sobbing girl, who was clutching her stomach and rocking back and forward, vainly trying to ease the painful cramps now afflicting her. "It gets worse," he assured Grant. "Much worse."

Grant had forgotten his own physical weakness in the face of the girl's distress. But now as he felt his fury build against her tormentor, he reminded himself he was neither in the position nor the condition to do anything about it in the present circumstances. Bitterly, for Karen Larsen's sake, he decided to accept defeat … for now.

"If I agree to pass on your message, will you do something for her right now?" he demanded. "Will you give her a shot of whatever she needs to stop … that?"

Angel One permitted himself a small smile of triumph, unobserved by his opponent. So far, so good. It looked like he would succeed in warning this one off. He had correctly guessed the man's weakness – a concern for the suffering of others. He knew now his next intended shock would succeed in removing this man's danger potential for good.

In the meantime, he congratulated himself on having killed two birds with the one stone. This little diversion had also removed the relatively minor nuisance value of the Larsen girl's father from the equation.

One of the guards was dispatched to fetch a fix of heroin for the suffering, pleading girl and quickly returned carrying a disposable syringe filled with a clear liquid. Taking it from the man, Angel One stepped past Grant into the cell and knelt beside the moaning, writhing form. Grasping her upper arm he squeezed it firmly, causing the veins to swell on the inside of her elbow joint. Expertly he slid the needle smoothly into an exposed vein and slowly depressed the plunger. The watching Grant saw the old needle marks clearly now, track marks they called them, on the girl's thin arm and wrist held immobile in the Oriental's strong grip.

Within seconds, the powerful opiate began to take effect, even while the needle was feeding the drug into her system. The transformation was instantaneous. She gave a shuddering sigh and her tense posture relaxed. Her head lolled back against the wall, eyes closed, a euphoric smile spreading over her face, from which the haggard look faded like sand ripples smoothed away by a receding tide. Her filthy condition was blissfully ignored as she sank back into the slack-jawed stupor provided by the drug.

Withdrawing the empty needle, Angel One stood up and handed it back to the guard who had fetched it. He then walked from the cell. Grant did not make to follow as the other passed him in the doorway, but indicated the fetid interior of the aptly named Turkey Pen.

"You're not leaving her in that state, are you?" he protested hotly.

Angel One stopped in the passageway outside and half turned. "Two of our female members will be sent to clean her up," he informed Grant shortly. "She will then be allowed back into circulation in due course and, I remind you, her future welfare will depend on your success in warning off her father."

"You've made your point," replied Grant resentfully. "I've given my word I'll do that much."

"Oh, you will do much more than that," the oriental assured him, a disturbing confidence evident in his manner and voice.

"So you keep telling me," Grant retorted grimly but evoked no reply.

Having locked and left the Turkey Pens, they were once again moving in a tight group, Grant now walking unaided by his escorts, back through the maze of basement corridors. They stopped before another locked metal door. This one was marked in large red lettering: WARNING! HIGH FIRE RISK. SMOKING STRICTLY FORBIDDEN. EXTINGUISH ALL NAKED FLAMES.

The oriental turned to face Grant again. "I told you earlier that you will cease from all further prying into our affairs and also that you will call off the police. You mentioned the possibility of their forcing an entry here." He paused and regarded Grant, who was staring back at him with sullen defiance. "Well, I am now going to show you what would be the consequences of such an ill-advised course of action."

Swinging round, Angel One unlocked the metal door, depressed the heavy handle and drew it slowly open with some effort. Grant saw with some surprise that it was about six inches thick of solid steel. The oriental stood aside and motioned him to look inside.

Grant did so and found another unpleasant surprise awaiting him. The cubicle behind the massive door had been sheathed in steel and converted into a metal walled vault, approximately six feet square and ten feet high. It contained only one large object, set dead in the centre of its concrete floor – a sinister black metal drum, of about twenty gallons capacity. Wires ran from a device attached to its lid, quite obviously a detonator of some sort, to disappear through a hole in the rear wall of the vault. Painted on its side in the same fiery red lettering as the sign on the door, the drum bore the warning: DANGER – HIGHLY INFLAMMABLE

Grant glanced over his shoulder at the oriental. "Very impressive. This is almost as good a mock-up as those bogus wards upstairs," he said scornfully. "You really expect me to believe that you an' all your goons'd commit suicide jes' to avoid a police raid? Nice try, but I don't buy it!"

But his gut feeling didn't share the conviction of his words. Something about this menacing man told him he wouldn't be bluffing. Angel One's next words confirmed this opinion.

"It is no bluff, Grant," the oriental assured him. "Nor do I have the slightest intention of condemning either myself or my staff to such a foolish act of self destruction. In fact, should it ever become necessary to activate this device, I assure you that both I and my staff will be well clear of its effects. No doubt you are disappointed to hear that." An amused smirk fleetingly touched his thin lips.

"Let me put you fully in the picture. There are four of these devices, one positioned at each corner of the building. You may inspect the others if you still think I am lying to you. Each container is filled with the highly incendiary substance known popularly as napalm, and they are primed for detonation. They are set on a time fuse calculated to be sufficient to allow myself and my staff to escape from the building, but not long enough for any attempt to de-activate the devices ... nor to evacuate the other inhabitants."

He then pointed to the ceiling of the small room, directly over the drum and its lethal contents. "You will observe that the ceiling is the only part of this room which is not constructed of metal." Following the direction of the pointing finger, Grant saw that this was indeed the case.

The harsh voice continued relentlessly. "I hardly need tell you the result this will have in directing the full force of the exploding napalm up through the floor above. No doubt you will also have observed the high proportion of wood and other highly combustible materials in the upper levels of this old house, during your uninvited tour of inspection. The initial quadruple explosion will very quickly turn the whole place into an inferno. If you are a betting man, you will be able to calculate the quite considerable odds against there being any survivors."

Grant stared, grim-faced, at the sinister drum with its obscene load of flaming death. He had witnessed firsthand the horrendous effects of its use during his army years, on more occasions than he cared to remember. He knew with sick certainty that the oriental would carry out his threat and would callously condemn the innocent, misguided majority of the sect members to a real-life hellfire, rather than submit to close investigation by the authorities. But why such an apparent over-reaction? There must be more to this than met the eye, if these people were prepared to go to such drastic lengths ...

"Well, Grant?" Angel One's harsh voice cut into his morbid train of thought. "Do you wish to inspect the other three devices, before you rejoin your colleague upstairs?"

Grant shook his head. "That won't be necessary," he conceded hoarsely, his shoulders slumped in defeat. "I'll call off the police investigation." His head was aching intolerably and he felt physically drained. The bitter taste of his defeat was like bile in the back of his throat.

"And you will satisfy the parents of the Miller boy that he no longer wishes to leave ... that he has returned of his own free will?" the Oriental's voice insisted remorselessly.

Grant nodded wordlessly, his eyes fixed on the hypnotic black drum, his flesh crawling from his memories of blackened incinerated bodies and screaming human torches, until its squat menace was hidden from his sight by the oriental closing and locking the door.

"Come, Mister Grant," said Angel One, almost pleasantly, magnanimous in his moment of victory. "A quick wash and drink of water will refresh you for your return upstairs ... and your departure."

It was a silent, pensive Grant who sat beside Springfield on the drive back to Rockford. He had parried the sheriff's inquiry as to the success of his recce, by telling him part of the truth – the part up to and including his capture only. Now he was reflecting on the remainder of his experience and trying to decide how much he could safely tell Springfield, without the latter reacting by regarding the whole thing both as a bluff and an affront to his authority.

On the other hand, Grant knew he would need the sheriff's approval and help, whether official or otherwise, once he'd figured a way to breach the formidable defences of Bethlehem House. A way, that is, that would avoid the catastrophic consequences promised by the maleficent Doctor Sung. On impulse, he decided to place his full confidence in the tall sheriff. After all, he reasoned, Ben Curtis had faith in him. That should be recommendation enough.

Grant turned to his companion, who had driven in silence, leaving him with his thoughts. "Nate, pull over somewhere. I gotta talk to you."

Easing the car to a stop on the verge a little further along, Springfield replied laconically, "Thought there wuz somethin' eatin' you. Y'bin actin' spooked ever since y'reappeared with

Fu Manchu, back there. Y'looked like y'd gone fer a crap in a hayloft, reached out fer a handful o' straw to wipe y'ass, an' found y'd grabbed a rattler b'the tail instead."

Grant smiled grimly. "Actually, that's not a bad description of how I felt. Listen Nate, I didn't tell you what happened after they jumped me. It was like this …"

Ten minutes later, Springfield was in full possession of the facts. When Grant stopped speaking, the sheriff sat for a while in silence while he filled and lit his pipe. Then he spoke quietly, thoughtfully.

"Waal, seems there's nothin' t'be gained by a frontal attack. Nope, nothin' t'be gained, an' everythin' t'lose. So my advice is t'wait 'em out fer a bit, say a couple of weeks or so. Let 'em think they've won. In the meantime, we lay low an' plan our next move real careful. Find some way we kin go in real fast an' take 'em out before they realise what's hit 'em."

Grant looked at the tall, iron grey-haired man. "Are you serious?" he asked incredulously. "You mean you'd put your job on the line to help me?" He shook his head, grinning. "An' here was me sittin' on poison ivy, wonderin' how t'tell you I'd decided t'have a go at 'em whenever I could figure a way, an' expectin' you to chew me out for intent to disturb the peace or somethin'. Thanks, Nate. The most I'd have asked you t'do would've been to look the other way while I made my move."

"No need t'thank me," stated Springfield, knocking out his pipe in the ashtray and tucking it away in a pocket. He started up the car again. "I'll be helpin' cuz I want to. An' fer that matter, I won' be puttin' m'job anywhere. I'm gonna be doin' m'job. An' that'll include closin' down that place back there."

Checking his mirrors, he angled the car back onto the road and pulled smoothly away. "Fact is, I don' take kindly to anyone who terrorises youngsters, like these assholes've done t'that Miller kid. An' especially I don' like assholes who threaten t'slaughter people on my territory."

They drove on in silence until the outskirts of Rockford came into sight, then Grant said dispiritedly, "Right now, it beats me how we're gonna get in there in sufficient force t'get all the kids out, without gettin' 'em all blown t'Glory in the process."

"We'll think o' somethin', Brett," Springfield assured him as they drew up outside the Sheriff's Office. "Right off the top of m'head I'd say we should consider a two or three man strike force, who'd go in first an' take out that Control place you saw. I reckon that's where the fire bombs'll be detonated from, if anywhere. An' we kin have a heavy back-up force, includin' fire fightin' equipment, standin' by t'move in on a given signal."

"Sounds good to me, so far," Grant nodded approvingly. "But, fire fightin' equipment? Hell, Nate, if the alarm got raised an' that place went up, you'd need a whole damn fire brigade to fight it!"

"That's exactly what I'm figgerin' on havin'," Springfield retorted. "Bob Wallace, who runs th'local volunteer fire brigade's a long time buddy o' mine. I'm sure he an' his boys'll 'preciate the chance of some night fire fightin' practice."

Grant searched his companion's leathery face for any sign that he was having his leg pulled, but saw that Springfield was serious. He shook his head and grinned. His aching head and neck felt better already and the sheriff's matter-of-fact approach was making the seemingly impossible of only half an hour before seem possible when subjected to his calm assessment.

"I don't suppose you've decided how you'll get your army in through the gates?" Grant asked with a chuckle. Then he added soberly, "There's two sets of 'em an' they looked pretty substantial to me. They'll take some forcin', short of blowin' 'em open."

Springfield tugged at his lower lip for a few seconds, deep in thought. Then he nodded slowly to himself. "Nope, I wouldn' risk usin' explosives. Too noisy fer one thing, an' they c'd cause the gates t'jam, fer another." He turned to face Grant. "But I seem t'recall you tellin' me the other day of how that trucker frien' o' yours offered t'help in any way he could, right?"

Grant nodded, bemused, and Springfield continued, a mischievous twinkle in his faded blue eyes. "Waal, strikes me as how them big rigs're pretty heavy an' pack plenty o' power. 'Specially in low gear, with the loads they haul. I reckon if one o' them big rigs got itself accidentally tangled up with the outer gates, maybe with a couple o' hooks an' chains an' all, it'd be as easy as bustin' open a chicken coop. An' that'd mean ol' Bob

Wallace's big Dodge fire tender'd have clear run at the inner gates ... an' I wouldn' bet a bent nickel on their chances o' stoppin' that mean ol' ten tonner, neither!"

Shortly afterwards, on his way back to the city, Grant felt reasonably satisfied with the final outcome of the afternoon's events, despite its distinctly unpromising beginning. The interview with Jim Miller had been a non-event. His subsequent recce of the house had been reasonably successful and informative, until it had been brought to an abrupt halt.

Then things had gone from bad to worse. From the pathetic condition of Karen Larsen and the depressing prospect of having to inform her parents, to the final bitter taste of defeat when he had been confronted with the murderous intentions of the sect leadership, in the event of any hostile move by the authorities.

However, the sheriff's solid support and calm review of their chances of bringing off a successful assault, had put things back into a better perspective. They had agreed to muster their respective forces, keeping one another informed of progress by phone until their next meeting, to be arranged for a couple of days hence, when they would review the situation.

His thoughts touched again on the oriental "doctor". The memory of the man's raw menace reawakened a trickle of fear in Grant. But this was quickly supplanted by a growing anger as he recalled the way he had been made to eat crow in the face of the ruthlessness with which the man had discussed the prospect of condemning the entire community of the house to a fiery death. If only there was some way of shaking the arrogant bastard's sense of invincibility, some way to strike back without incurring retaliation on either of the two hostages, Jim Miller or Karen Larsen.

Suddenly he had it – Louise! He could score a minor victory by fulfilling his promise to Louise, of getting her away from the clutches of the sect. If he was successful, it might also serve to draw the Oriental's fire onto him personally and away from Jim and Karen. His mind made up, he set his mind to thinking out a plan of action.

46

LIKE HIS FRIEND GRANT, BEN CURTIS WAS ALSO experiencing feelings of satisfaction at the final outcome of an unpromising series of events. But Curtis's satisfaction was tinged with an echo of lingering anger, resulting from a stormy interview he'd had earlier with Deputy Commissioner Elrick.

About an hour after their return from interviewing the Prophet, he and Turner had been peremptorily summoned. On entering Elrick's office, Curtis had found his Captain of Detectives, Joseph Devlin already in the room, his face wooden with disapproval. Curtis got on well with Devlin on a personal level and his superior had shot him a warning look as he'd entered.

Without further preamble, Curtis and Turner had been curtly informed by the Deputy Commissioner that they were being removed from the case and suspended from duty, pending disciplinary inquiries into serious allegations of assault, unlawful and unreported discharge of firearms and criminal damage to property while questioning an innocent member of the public, namely the Reverend Martin Bishop. At which point, Curtis had exploded.

For the next few minutes, bedlam had reigned. Curtis, hands planted on the desk and physically restrained by Captain Devlin, had given the shocked, white-faced Elrick his character, loudly, colourfully and at some length. He had brought his tirade to a climax by whipping a sheet of paper from his pocket and slamming it down on the desk before the cowering D.C.

"Read this, ya fuckin' useless jerk!" he had yelled. "This is the so-called 'innocent member of the public' you're so hell bent on protectin' from your uncouth officers."

Jabbing the paper with a blunt finger, as though trying to drill holes in the solid wood of the desktop, he had continued at the top of his voice, "The Reverend Martin Bishop, my ass! His prints are on record. But did you have 'im checked out? Did you ask fer my side of the story? Well, fer your information, he's as much a fuckin' Reverend as you are a cop! His real name's

Durbridge, an' he got himself expelled from medical school fer carryin' out an abortion on his girlfriend, after he'd knocked 'er up. She died! An' your upstandin' member of the public served eight years of a five-to-fifteen in the Nebraska State Pen. The only 'upstandin' member' in this case is you, Elrick ... you're a prick!"

At this point, the livid Deputy Commissioner had tried to interrupt in an attempt to regain control of the situation. He would have been as well trying to stop a charging bull by hitting it with a feather duster. Curtis had shouted him down with a few more home truths about fat-butted civilians who got themselves voted into office by virtue of shooting off their big mouths and then went on shooting them off after being elected. Then, lowering his voice to a mere bellow, he had finished, "An' I'll tell you somethin' else fer free ... I know this is our man – the killer we've bin after all this time. With a little backin' from you, instead of opposition, I'll nail the bastard too."

Elrick, never one to admit a mistake on his own part, and with his dignity severely bruised by Curtis's tirade, had stuck to his guns and made one last futile attempt to bluster his way out of it and shift the blame. He had shouted back petulantly that Curtis was trying to cover his ass for having exceeded his authority and had not been in possession of these facts about Bishop/Durbridge when he had committed the alleged offences. Besides, he concluded, this new information did not in fact prove anything, so it changed nothing. Curtis could still consider himself under suspension pending a disciplinary inquiry, which would now also include a charge of verbally abusing a superior officer.

Curtis's response to this had been to roar, "Fuck you an' your disciplinary inquiry! You ain't suspendin' me, mister, cuz I resign – as of now!" And he had ripped his gold shield from his pocket and flung it down onto the desk, from where it had bounced up to hit the startled D.C. on the chest. An instant later, Turner, who had stood silently by all this time, had leaned forward and dropped his shield on the desktop alongside his chief's.

This gesture of support had the effect of damping down Curtis's blazing anger. He looked at Turner. "Tex, you don' have to do this. You were only obeying my orders …" he began.

With a shrug, Turner had retorted simply, "I'm with you, Chief."

Calm now, Curtis had pulled himself free of Captain Devlin's restraining embrace, spun on his heel and strode to the door followed by Turner. Yanking it open, Curtis had allowed Turner to leave, then had turned on the threshold to face the outraged Elrick. "An' one last thing, mister. I'm goin' straight from here to hold my last press conference. Wait'll the story hits the streets of why I quit. I wouldn' bet a bent nickel on your chances of finishin' this term in office, never mind gittin' elected fer another one!"

Elrick had gone purple, leapt to his feet and shouted, "I forbid you to speak to the press. Do you hear me?" He pointed a trembling finger at Curtis, his voice quivering with rage. "I order you to clear your desk and leave this building immediately! Is that clear?"

Curtis's teeth had bared in a ferocious grin. "You don' order me t'do nothin' anymore, mister. I'm a civilian now. An' you better watch how you speak t'me, or I jes' might lodge a complaint against you fer verbal abuse! As fer my speakin' t'the press, if you don' like what I gotta say – sue me. See ya in court!" So saying, he had given the apoplectic D.C. the finger and closed the door on him.

Fifteen minutes later as Curtis, fully committed to his decision, had been in the act of clearing his desk prior to leaving the precinct for the last time, his office door had opened to admit a grim-faced Captain Devlin. Without a word, Devlin had crossed the room, perched on the corner of the desk and tossed Curtis's gold shield onto the cluttered blotter.

"Now listen, Joe …" Curtis had begun to protest, straightening up.

"No, you listen, Ben," Devlin interrupted, his speech still tinged with the soft Galway brogue he had never completely lost in the thirty-odd years since he had left the old country. "You've had your say. Now I'm goin' to have mine. I'll keep it short, because I've only got three points to make. First, you're an eejit. Second, I agree with every word you said in there. An' third, as I told the man himself an' now I'm tellin' you, if you think I'm prepared to stand by an' lose two of the best detectives on me squad without a fight, then you've another think comin'."

Curtis shook his head. "Joe, I've made up my mind," he said stubbornly. "An' besides, there's no way I c'd apologise to that fat prick. I meant every word I said in there."

"Ben, before you can make up your mind, you've gotta have one to make up. So that let's you out on that score," Devlin kidded him gently, as only a long standing acquaintance could. "An' there's no question of your havin' to apologise to Elrick. After you left, I gave 'is Eminence a flea in 'is ear, an' told 'im he had his priorities wrong."

Intrigued, despite his stubborn determination not to go back on his word, Curtis had asked, "What did he have to say to that?"

"He threatened to carpet me for insubordination."

"The hell he did! An' what did you say to that?"

"I put my shield on the desk beside yours," Devlin had replied with an impish grin. "That changed his tune, I can tell you. He soon came round to my way of thinkin' after that, an' agreed to let me square things up with you." Devlin had fixed Curtis with a pair of twinkling blue eyes and demanded, "So, how about it? It's me that's askin' you, not his lordship. Are you still on the team?"

"That ain' fightin' fair," Curtis had protested half-heartedly, his mind already made up to climb down with as good a grace as possible.

"Ach well, as they say back in the ould country, didn't the Marquis of Queensberry take all the fun out of fightin'?" Devlin had retorted with a chuckle. "Sure, the only way to beat a tough opponent is to hit 'im low, an' preferably when he isn't lookin'!"

The two friends had laughed, and Curtis was back on the team. Devlin had then left to find Turner, to relay the good news and return his shield to him.

So Curtis was now feeling satisfied on two accounts, as his anger at Elrick's interference receded into memory. Satisfied with having done something he'd been dying to do for years, namely giving the self-opinionated D.C. a good old-fashioned tongue lashing. And doubly satisfied with having had his hunch about the Prophet proved correct.

The prints he had tricked the man into providing on the photographs of the dead victims had been fed into the computer records. They had come up trumps. The Prophet was on file – but not under his claimed identity of Martin Daniel Bishop.

Curtis glanced down again at the computer printout on the desk before him. Under the respective file numbers of the Federal and State of Nebraska Criminal Records Departments, it identified the owner of the prints as one Milton Bartholomew Durbridge, aged 55, from Omaha, Nebraska. The entry under this heading was concise but informative. It read:

ENROLLED 1952 AS MEDICAL STUDENT AT ANDREW CARNEGIE COLLEGE, LINCOLN, NEBRASKA. EXPELLED 1955. CIRCUMSTANCES OF EXPULSION AS FOLLOWS: PERFORMED ABORTION ON PREGNANT GIRLFRIEND, LAURA JANE DRYSDALE, A FELLOW STUDENT, AS RESULT OF WHICH DRYSDALE DIED. DURBRIDGE WAS ARRAIGNED BEFORE NEBRASKA SUPREME COURT ON A CHARGE OF MURDER ONE. PLED GUILTY TO A REDUCED CHARGE OF MURDER TWO. SENTENCED TO A TERM OF FIVE TO FIFTEEN YEARS. SERVED 8 YEARS, THEN PAROLED 1963.

ADDITIONAL INFO: WHILE IN CUSTODY, DURBRIDGE DEVELOPED A STRONG INTEREST IN RELIGION. COMPLETED A CORRESPONDENCE COURSE IN BIBLE STUDIES AND THEOLOGY RUN BY "PENTECOSTAL CHURCH OF THE SECOND COMING", LOCATED IN LINCOLN, NEBRASKA. ON RELEASE FROM PRISON, HE BECAME A LAY PREACHER WITH THE ABOVE CHURCH. AFTER TWO YEARS, DURBRIDGE DISAPPEARED. AN AUDIT REVEALED THAT TWENTY THOUSAND DOLLARS OF CHURCH FUNDS COULD NOT BE ACCOUNTED FOR. NOTHING COULD BE PROVED, AND

NO CHARGES WERE BROUGHT. HIS PRESENT WHEREABOUTS ARE UNKNOWN.

Twenty minutes of deep thought and two cigarettes later, Curtis reached a decision. He left his office and made his way to the section of the building occupied by the Narcotics Squad. Lieutenant Scotty Cameron was in, as he had hoped, and pleased to see him. The news of Curtis's verbal put-down of the universally disliked Elrick had preceded him on the jungle drum grapevine. Already, the version in circulation was gaining substance and colour with each re-telling, and the popular Curtis had attained the stature of a folk hero inside the space of an hour.

Naturally Cameron wanted the official version straight from the horse's mouth. So Curtis had to spend the next few minutes describing the interview in detail, while the delighted Cameron hooted with laughter and congratulated his colleague on a job well done. Then he offered Curtis a cigarette and asked, "An' what brings one of the Homicide elite to our humble Narcotics ghetto?"

Curtis lit up and expelled smoke from his nostrils. "I'm lookin' fer a favour. It's like this ... since the last time we spoke, I think I've finally got me a red hot suspect. Here, read this ..." He handed Cameron the printout.

Cameron scanned the paper swiftly and gave a low whistle. "You mean this is the Prophet guy Elrick got so all fired up about you slappin' around?"

"The same." Curtis nodded.

"That'll be one less donation to Elrick's campaign fund next time round," Scotty laughed. "Okay, so what's the favour y'want from me?"

"I'll come to that in a minute," Curtis replied. "Let me explain. Remember you told me you suspect the Triads are behind that Chinese heroin that's hittin' the streets?"

Cameron nodded. "It's stronger than suspicion, Ben. I'm pretty sure of it," he confirmed.

"Well, I bin thinkin'," Curtis continued. "It might jes' be coincidence, but when things turned nasty durin' the Durbridge interview today, an' his goons came chargin' in wavin' guns, the guy who took the heat outa the situation wuz an oriental. Coulda bin a chink. The thing is, he wuz obviously a big wheel, cuz they all did what he told 'em, no arguin'. Now, Brett Grant says the sect make drugs freely available to their members, an' also that there are three or four slopes runnin' things at the sect's base someplace upstate. I know it's a long shot but there jes' might be a connection between the Prophet's mob an' the Triads."

"Yeah, could be," Cameron agreed thoughtfully. "The chinks're certainly gettin' stronger at street level. The way we hear it, the Mafia are gettin' worried. They're losin' business to the Triads. It's beginnin' to hurt an' the Mob don' like it." He nodded to Curtis. "Okay, I'll buy it. So, that brings us back to this favour you're after. Shoot!"

"I wan' us to join forces fer a few days, so I kin use some of your men," Curtis replied simply. "See, I need extra manpower to cage this bastard Bishop in, an' to monitor his movements – him an' his mob. Because of the five year duration of our murder investigation, I've had my squad trimmed to eight men. After today's bust up with Elrick, I wouldn' have a snowball's chance in hell of gittin' our numbers increased, 'specially as I'd be wantin' 'em to put the screws on his upstandin'-member-of-the-community friend, the Reverend Martin Bishop!

"Now, the way I see it, if you were to suspect the Orientals in his organisation of bein' Triads, responsible fer large scale drugs dealin', then you'd stake out the Eldorado Apartment buildin' to watch their movements, right? You git my drift?"

"Get your drift?" Cameron laughed. "I'm way ahead of you, ya fuckin' ol' fox. No problem Ben. I'll buy it. You never know, it could even turn out that these chinks you're on about are connected to the Triads. It's worth a shot on that count alone. Okay, when do we move?"

"Right away," replied Curtis. "An' thanks Scotty, I appreciate it."

"Don' mention it." Cameron flapped a dismissive hand. "I got nothin' t'lose ... except my balls, when Elrick finds out I bin helpin' you to nail his pet preacher!" He stood up, walked round the desk and clapped Curtis on the shoulder. "Right, let's go an' get things in motion ... an' yes, I accept your offer of a beer in gratitude for my help."

Curtis grumbled good naturedly about having the arm put on him again, as was expected of him. But this was one beer he didn't mind buying. The badly needed help to mount a full surveillance on his suspect was well worth it. He felt at long last he was getting a long overdue break in his efforts to nail the killer he had been hunting for the past five years.

47

IT WAS A DAY OF INTERVIEWS AND MEETINGS. A little after seven-thirty in the evening, the Neroni Family *caporegimes* began arriving at the palatial and well-guarded Long Island home of their Don. Each arrived accompanied by a second car full of personal bodyguards. A casual observer would have seen only some big wheel from the world of commerce arriving for an important business conference, attended by a retinue of smartly dressed junior executives.

The three mobsters, Paolo Scaglione, short, stocky and square-jawed; Pietro 'Fat Pete' Bonnello, also short, but stout and cherub-faced with thick sensual lips; and Sandro 'Lupo' Lucarelli, tall, lean-featured and swarthy, arrived with their personal retinues within minutes of each other. The *capos* were ushered into the Don's study right away, where they were politely received by the consigliere Emilio Falcone, seated comfortably and given drinks. Their underlings were shown into an outer room to await them and accorded similar hospitality by a couple of the house guards.

At eight sharp, the study door opened and Bruno Neroni entered. Tall, silver haired and elegant, his imposing presence immediately dominated the room. Greeting the three men in turn with an embrace and accepting their respectful condolences on the loss of his mistress, he took his place behind the huge polished desk and waved everyone to resume their seats. Falcone took up his usual position off to one side, the others in a loose semi-circle facing the Don across the desk.

Straight away, they got down to business. Concisely and unemotionally, Neroni outlined the details surrounding the discovery of the murders, the extent of the injuries inflicted on the victims, the supposed 'Chinese ideograms' cut into their corpses and finally, the coincidental sighting of Scirea's 'slants' around the relevant time, pointing to the culprits having been the Triads.

None of the three *capos* wasted time in pretending shock or horror at the grisly details – they had each seen, or done, worse in their rise to positions of power within the Family. The only emotion they expressed was a mutual outrage at the temerity of their hated Triad rivals, in daring to strike at their Don in such a despicable and unmanly way. But then, they agreed, what else could one expect from the Chinese *animales*? They were not men of honour, after all, like themselves!

Neroni then outlined to them his plan of reprisal. This would take the form of a series of co-ordinated strikes against known or suspected Triad-owned properties and hits on all street pushers known or suspected to have any connection to the shadowy rival organisation.

The three were then invited to make their individual suggestions for prospective targets in the territories for which they were responsible, which they did in turn. The merits or problems associated with each suggestion were freely discussed and by a process of selection and rejection, a short-list was eventually drawn up covering what were considered to be the most effective targets and which would inflict the most damage to their enemies.

At the suggestion of Lucarelli – his ruthless ferocity as a former hit-man, allied to his lean vulpine features, had earned him his nickname Lupo, the Wolf – the Golden Lotus restaurant in the very heart of Chinatown itself, which was an area out of bounds to any of the mobs, was selected for a special exemplary strike. It was known to be Triad owned and frequented by their personnel, which qualified it as a prime target. Two other Chinese restaurants were also targeted for known or suspected Triad connections. Otherwise, the remainder of the hits were to be against personnel, the pushers, in an attempt to drive the Chinese organisation off the streets.

The timing of the strikes was to be co-ordinated as far as possible for the early afternoon of the following day, so as to have maximum effect and prevent any resistance being organised. Total surprise would ensure their complete success. The whole planned action was code-named Operation Carla, in memory of the Don's slain mistress. The butchered whore's epitaph would be written in blood, as her death was made the excuse for a long overdue attack on the rival crime organisation. The real reason, as with most wars, was more cynical – greed. Greed for territory and profit.

Two hours passed, then the Don sent for refreshments, and the meeting wound up. Falcone was instructed to ensure that rival Families whose territories bordered those in which operations were being carried out, were informed of the Don's campaign of retribution, so they would not feel threatened by any of the actions. Also, police on the Family payroll in those areas where hits were to be made either on property or personnel, were to be instructed to make themselves scarce at the relevant time.

When his lieutenants had dispersed to make their respective arrangements and carry out his orders, Don Bruno Neroni had an early night and slept contentedly. In ordering the retributive strikes against Angel One's organisation, he did not realise how wrong he was in his actual reason for doing so. Nor, paradoxically, did he realise how close to home he would in fact be hitting because of the actions of the real culprit – the Prophet.

48

LATE THAT NIGHT, ANGEL FOUR PERSONALLY escorted the Prophet back to the apartment from the Washington

Centre, after another successful evening spent collecting souls and cash. He saw the sect leader safely installed back inside his private suite and set two guards on his door, in addition to the regular two on duty on the outside door of the apartment itself. He then inspected and tested the surveillance equipment that had been installed during their absence. Over the headphones he could hear the sounds of movement, as the unsuspecting subject moved about his suite.

Satisfied that his charge was under control for the night, he phoned Bethlehem House and informed Angel One. He also reported the fact that the police seemed to have posted four men on watch outside the building. In return he was told of the successful outcome of the Miller interview, and how the private detective had been warned off. Replacing the receiver, Angel Four decided to take the first two-hour shift on the headphones himself and arranged to be relieved at 2 a.m.

Two hours later, his relief arrived promptly and was shown how to select and tune into the several listening devices positioned throughout the Prophet's private suite. As he handed over, Angel Four passed on the information that the Prophet had eaten, showered, put on tapes of religious music and retired to bed, leaving the music playing softly in the background.

The relief operator, once on his own, phased quickly through the various hidden mikes, but the only sound to be heard was the soft harmony of choral music. He opened the paperback he had brought with him, lit a cigarette and settled himself comfortably in the padded chair. As he read, he absently tapped the book cover with a finger in time to the soothing strains of Abide With Me trickling into his ears through the headphones.

In the poorly lit alley running alongside the towering Eldorado block, Detective Bob Paton was huddled in a service doorway in a vain attempt to shelter from the bitter November wind. Icy gusts disturbed the scattered litter, stirring scraps of paper into brief fluttering life like lost spirits haunting the alleyway, spooking him. Somewhere an abandoned beer can rolled about, its distant metallic clatterings providing the ghostly paper apparitions with a backdrop eerily like the rattling of spectral chains.

Paton glanced at the luminous figures on his wristwatch. Two-forty in the morning. Jesus! Another twenty frigid minutes before he would swap places with one of his more fortunate colleagues, who were still in the comfortable warmth of the unmarked cars watching the other three sides of the gigantic tower block. Who was to relieve him? Oh yes, Stan Kaminsky. The big Polack bastard better not be late or he'd chew him out. Shielding his lighter with a cupped hand, he lit another cigarette. His sixth since he'd taken up post, or was it his seventh? His tongue was furred and his mouth tasted like he'd washed it out with metal polish. He dragged the smoke deeply into his lungs, trying to convince himself it was warming him. Christ, it was cold. That fuckin' wind. It cut you like a knife ... like a knife had cut all them dead hookers ...

The morbid thought interrupted his mood of self pity and reminded him of why he was there. Involuntarily, he glanced up, following the zig-zag of the iron fire-escape as it climbed the side of the building into the darkness above. Nothing moved on it, as far as he could tell. Trouble was, the effort of peering into the cutting wind stung the hell out of his eyes and made them water. He decided to walk up and down for a bit, strictly against orders, which were to remain out of sight.

Fuck orders! He pulled his coat collar up round his ears and jammed his hat down tight on his forehead. Flipping his half-smoked stub away in a Catherine-wheel of sparks, he thrust his hands deep into his pockets, ducked his chin into his collar and began to trudge slowly up and down twenty paces to either side of the fire-escape. Cold and resentful as he was, it never occurred to Paton that his disregard for orders meant that each time he passed under the foot of the iron stairs, he was placing himself in deadly danger for a full twenty paces until he turned to retrace his steps.

Eight floors above, the subject of all the surveillance was preparing once again to prowl the night in search of another luckless victim. This time he was driven not only his increasingly uncontrollable bloodlust, but also by a burning hatred and a desire for revenge – hatred of the bullying detective lieutenant who had questioned him earlier that day and a desire to be avenged for the fear and humiliation the man had inflicted on him.

Silently the Prophet finished dressing in his black outer clothing. Any slight rustling sounds he made were covered by the softly playing music in the background. He had no actual knowledge of the bugging of his suite, of course, but during his time in prison as a young Milton Durbridge he had developed the common paranoid suspicion of many prisoners that bugging was a universal practice of the 'authorities'. Since then, whenever he found himself alone in any room, he automatically conducted himself as though it were bugged. His paranoia served him well now, without his realising it. His preparations were so noiseless that they went entirely undetected by the sect member on duty monitoring the listening devices.

Buttoning his thick coat up to his chin and setting his black Homburg low over his eyes, the Prophet pulled on a pair of thin black leather gloves. Then he carried out the final act of preparation for the night's hunting. Sliding the fingers of his right hand up under his left cuff, he checked that the razor sharp knife was snug in its sheath and strapped firmly to his left forearm. Satisfied, he stepped over to the heavy curtains, parted them and silently eased open the floor-to-ceiling window on its well oiled runners. Slipping through the gap out onto the short balcony, he allowed the curtains to fall together behind him, then he slid the tall glass panel shut again.

The night air felt refreshingly cold on his face as he stood for a few minutes to allow his eyes to adjust to night vision. He sniffed the chill wind like the beast of prey he had now become, and was sure he could taste the promise of snow in its icy bite. He checked the night around him to make sure he was unobserved. Off to his right, rows of similar balconies marched off into the night above and below him on the surface of the tower block. To his left, some twelve feet away, a metal fire-escape zig-zagged its way up and down the building. Directly across the alley from where he stood was an office block and all its windows were dark and untenanted at this time of night.

When his night vision had adjusted sufficiently, he moved into action. Stepping between the boxes of ornamental shrubs lining the balcony rail, he leaned over the waist high metal trellis work. Reaching down, he unclipped an extending ladder from its hidden storage place along the outside base of the railing. The ladder was constructed of a light and very strong alloy and had been painted to match the colour of the balcony rail. Its hooked ends were sheathed in rubber to ensure minimum noise when coming into contact with stone or metal.

Extending the ladder, he carefully reached out and lowered the far end onto the rail of the fire-escape platform twelve feet away – the same platform on which Curtis and Turner had stood a few hours earlier. Drawing the ladder back towards him until the hooked legs of the far end were engaged firmly on the fire-escape rail, he made sure the near end was similarly secured on the balcony rail before him. Then, steadying himself with one black gloved hand on the wall, he vaulted easily up to balance on the rail, before stepping off along the rungs of the ladder, with the ease and confidence of long practice. Not once did he hesitate as he cat-footed over the dizzying drop into the dark chasm under his precarious bridge, despite the keen wind which gusted against him, setting his coat-tails flapping round his knees.

Reaching the fire-escape platform, he stooped, gripped the rail with a hand and swung himself down onto the metal floor with athletic agility. Without pausing, he started down the iron stairs, his thick rubber soles making no noise on the treads. On the platform of the third flight from ground level, in the inky darkness above the poor light cast by the widely spaced alley lamps, he stopped. His black clothing merging perfectly with the night, he peered cautiously over the railing to check if the coast was clear, before completing his descent to ground level … and froze into immobility. There was someone moving in the alley below.

The Prophet's narrowed eyes followed the pacing figure as it moved back and forth under the foot of the fire-escape, effectively blocking his exit route. Swiftly his mind raced through the possibilities. Certainly this was no ordinary citizen lurking in a deserted alley at this time of night. A burglar's accomplice cop-watching? A pimp providing muscle for one of his whores who was turning a trick nearby? Or someone waiting to make a meet and close a drugs deal?

Just then he saw the man glance first at his watch, then up at the iron stairway, seeming to look straight at him, before tucking his chin back down into his collar and continuing his slow trudge up and down. Like someone on sentry duty ... a sentry? A cop! Twin fires of anger glinted in his narrowed eyes. The ignorant scum who had interrogated and abused him earlier today must have posted a police watch on him.

But as he reached this conclusion, another more alarming thought occurred to him. Was it possible they had worked out his secret method of leaving the eighth floor suite? No – they couldn't have, he reasoned, for if they had he would certainly have been arrested and taken into custody by now. Shrewdly he guessed that the watcher was probably part of a surveillance team surrounding the entire building, hoping to block any possible means of exit. His anger and resentment grew, strengthening the red demon of his bloodlust.

Motionless, the Prophet watched the chilled man pacing restlessly beneath him. The minutes ticked past as he considered his options. Then his narrowed eyes gleamed in the darkness as a tempting thought was forged in the raging furnace consuming his sick mind – what better revenge could he wish for, than to slaughter this watcher employed by his hated adversary? What better way to demonstrate his power and superiority? This time though, he would leave no cryptic message carved into the body of his victim. He would leave the lieutenant, what was his name? – Curtis, that was it – no proof, only baffled suspicion.

Reaching under his cuff, the Prophet released the knife and let it slide down halfway out of its sheath till its hilt rested in the fingers of his left hand. It was now ready for instant transfer to his right hand – the killing hand, the cleansing hand – when required.

Slowly, silently, he began to descend the iron stairs. He had taken the first four steps down towards his unsuspecting victim, when his theory that the man was part of a surveillance team was proved correct. He froze into immobility again as a second figure entered the far end of the alley and came towards the pacing man, keeping close to the wall. With a silent snarl of frustration, the Prophet retreated to the platform of the third flight and drew back into the shadows.

Paton saw his relief appear and stopped his restless pacing. He moved over to the door recess he had been occupying before and waited till Kaminsky reached him. "Hi Stan," he greeted the newcomer. "Thank fuck that's my tour over in this fuckin' wind tunnel. You're welcome to it. Hope y'left me some coffee?"

"Hi, Bob," Kaminsky returned his greeting. "Yeah, there's still a coupla flasks in the car. Some sandwiches too." Then his voice took on a tone of reproof as he continued, "Hey man, y'lucky Curtis didn' catch you paradin' up an' down like that. He blew in on the air a while back, so he's in the area prowlin' about. He said t'keep outa sight as much as possible. He wants this mother caught real bad."

"Fuck Curtis! The only thing I'da bin liable t'catch wuz fuckin' pneumonia, if I'da stood in that fuckin' doorway a minute longer," complained Paton. "It's okay for Curtis t'beef about keepin' outa sight. He'll be sittin on his fat butt in a nice warm car, not out here freezin' his fuckin' balls off. I tellya, I got two lumpsa ice where my feet used t'be." He started to move away, still grumbling.

"Ah, quit bellyachin'," Kaminsky said to his colleague's retreating back. "Y'wanna sit on yer ass all day, put in for a transfer to Traffic, an' you'll be guaranteed eight hours of boredom every tour cruisin' about in y'very own squad car."

Paton paused and half turned. "What?" he exclaimed in mock horror. "An' give up the glamour of bein' a detective, an' spendin' my tours freezin' t'fuckin' death in a crummy alley? No way! So long, Nanook." He raised a hand and moved off again, calling back over his shoulder, "Keep a look out for polar bears, it's all you're liable to see here tonight."

Paton's voice grew fainter as he grumbled off up the alley but Kaminsky caught his final comment floating back on the chill night air. "Curtis says this guy's a nutcase ... some nutcase! ... he's layin' up there in a warm bed, an' we're down here gittin' hypothermia ... so, who th'fuck's crazy?"

Kaminsky shook his head, grinning, and watched from his stance within the shadowed doorway until Paton turned the far corner and disappeared from view. Then he inspected the towering fire escape as far up as he could see, which meant only as far a point between the second and third landings. Beyond that, above the dim light cast by the alley lighting, the metal stairs vanished into a stygian darkness, pierced only here and there over the whole surface of the massive tower block by the lights of scattered, uncurtained windows.

It was as he was lowering his gaze to ground level again that he caught a hint of something up there on the fire escape, just above the limits of the poor alley lighting. He had no clear idea what had caught his eye ... a movement? ... a subtle shifting of dark on dark? ... or maybe just a patch of darkness slightly denser than the surrounding night?

Kaminsky stared fixedly upwards, eyes smarting in the cold night wind and beginning to water. He blinked and wiped them quickly with the back of his hand to clear them. Again he fancied he caught a suggestion of something indefinable at the limit of his peripheral vision. A shifting. Black on black. Keeping his gaze fixed in the direction of whatever it was he had seen, he fumbled in his coat for his small flat pocket torch. His other hand crept up to the personal radio clipped to his lapel, ready to key the button and summon instant backup, should it be needed.

With a swift movement, Kaminsky swung the torch up and aimed its narrow beam along his line of vision. Weakly illuminated at that distance, he found himself staring at the railings of the landing between the third and fourth flights. As far as he could tell, the landing was empty. Suddenly a flicker of movement entered the torch beam ... then another ... then several. Snowflakes. It was starting to snow. That was all he needed. Paton would be laughing his cock off in the comfort of the unmarked prowl car.

He switched off the torch and returned it to his pocket, feeling slightly foolish ... and relieved. Huddling down into his collar, he thrust his hands deep into his pockets for warmth and prepared for a long frigid watch. He was surprised to find he was sweating slightly despite the cold and decided to light a cigarette to calm his unease. For a while Kaminsky couldn't shake off the feeling he was being watched, but he put it down to an over-active imagination resulting from his eyes playing tricks on him. After a time, the feeling disappeared.

Kaminsky's vigilance saved his life that night, just as Paton's carelessness had almost cost him his, before the timely arrival of his colleague to relieve him. The Prophet had decided to retreat to the fourth landing for a little, to give the new watcher time to settle and get careless in his turn, like the previous one. The brief conversation between the two men had confirmed his suspicion that they were cops detailed to watch for him by the detective lieutenant named Curtis – the man for whom he had developed such a burning hatred since the events of earlier that day.

He had started to move slowly and silently back up the stairs from the third landing, when he realised the man below had seen him from the way he was staring fixedly in his direction. When he saw the man blink and wipe his eyes in the cold wind, he took a chance, ducked low and mounted the remaining stairs two at a time to the fourth landing, where he crouched out of sight of the man in the alley. Just in time. The landing and stairs below him were dimly lit by torch light. At that moment something cold brushed his cheek and then the flakes drifting down through the faint radiance from below showed it had begun to snow. After several seconds, the torch was switched off and there was no sound of further alarm or movement.

The Prophet straightened up and peered cautiously over the edge of the landing. At first he could see no sign of the new watcher and he raked the alley from end to end with his eyes, searching for him. Then a lighter flared in the deep recess of a doorway directly below, followed by the red glow of a lighted cigarette.

With the patience of the predator he had become, the Prophet settled back to wait for an opportunity to move in for the kill, once the newcomer relaxed his vigil. However, after a long cold hour had crawled slowly by, it became obvious this watcher was not going to drop his guard and become careless like his predecessor. By now too, the steadily dropping night temperature had combined with the lack of action to damp down the furnace of his bloodlust to a smouldering, containable level. He decided to call it a night.

Securing the knife in its sheath again, he silently returned to his eighth floor lair by reversing the procedure he had used to leave it, clipping the ladder back into its place of concealment. In bed, he lay awake for a time and reviewed the situation. He decided he would wait until the last night of the current Crusade. That would give the police watchers time to become bored and careless. Then he would strike. Lulled both by this attractive prospect and the soft background music, he drifted off to sleep.

49

BRETT GRANT WAS ANGRY. SO WAS HIS BUSINESS partner, Harvey Sherman. The two men were standing glaring at each other over the desk in Grant's office. As often happened between the two, both of them strong-willed men, a difference of opinion had escalated to an increasingly heated argument. The friendship they shared outwith their professional relationship allowed them an amount of licence, which would not otherwise have been acceptable to mere business partners. Nevertheless, in the outer office Anna had paused in her typing a couple of times in the course of five minutes to shake her head disapprovingly, as the decibel count of the raised voices soared to fresh heights.

Back inside Grant's office at the scene of the noisy verbal confrontation, the brief angry silence that had punctuated their argument like a stand-off between two battling stags, was broken. Sherman controlled himself with an effort and started again in a normal voice.

"Lemme get this straight. I still can't believe what I'm hearing. This mornin' you told a client that you ain' even prepared to try to rescue his boy from a buncha religious freaks, within a seven day deadline?" Sherman's control slipped and his voice rose again. "Despite the fact that the client offers you a five thousan' dollar bonus! Since when have we been able to afford to turn down that kinda money? That's what I wanna know?"

Grant set his jaw stubbornly and when he answered, his voice was tight and brittle. "I've told the client I'll get his son back … but only when I decide it's safe to do so. I also explained to the client that it'd be too dangerous to try within his suggested seven day limit. He accepted my assessment of the situation, so why the hell can't you?"

"Too dangerous," scoffed Sherman, his voice dripping with sarcasm. "Too dangerous, he says. All because some Bruce Lee lookalike shows you a wired up oil drum an' feeds you a loada crap about blowin' their whole racket sky-high. An' you buy it! Oy veh!" he flapped his hands in a gesture of exasperation. "I tell you, as a bluff, it stinks so bad I kin smell it from here. Do yourself a favour, don' ever play poker. You'd git cleaned out holdin' a full house by some jerk with an ace-high an' a bitta nerve!"

Grant flushed at this jibe. "Are you suggestin' I've lost my nerve? Is that what you're sayin'?" he demanded angrily.

"I'm suggestin' you've lost your judgement." Sherman rasped. "An' in the process, you stand to lose us five thousan' dollars. If you ain' lost your nerve, you've sure as hell lost your marbles, is what I'm sayin'!"

"Five lousy grand. That's all that's botherin' you, isn't it?" Grant's mouth twisted in an angry sneer, his tone scathing. "You'd be prepared to risk the lives of all those kids out there for five lousy grand. Well, I'm not. I've tangled with these nutcases, you haven't. They're fuckin' fanatics. An' as far as I'm concerned that chink bastard wasn't bluffin'. He's an A-1 psychopath. I've met a few, so I know what I'm talkin' about. So Miller can go fuck himself with his bankroll. He doesn't buy me. Nobody buys me!"

"Aw, spare me the Mister Clean routine." Sherman spread his hands and appealed to the ceiling with his upturned eyes. Suddenly he slammed both hands down on the desk top, thrust his face forward pugnaciously and continued heatedly, "Listen schmuck, Elliot Ness an' the Untouchables we ain't! We're runnin' a business. An' in case you hadn't noticed, businesses run on money ... y'know, the green foldin' stuff you don' like dirtyin' y'lilywhite hands on. An' furthermore Snow-white, fer your information our clients do buy us. We charge 'em a hundred a day plus expenses fer our services."

"Our services ... exactly! They pay for our services," Grant shot back stubbornly. "In my book, that doesn't include bribes to induce us to break the law."

"Bribes? BRIBES? Who th'hell mentioned bribes?" yelled Sherman in exasperation. "An' what y'on about, breakin' th'law? You told me yourself y'think th'boy's bein' held against his will, an' his ol' man's worried sick about 'im. So the guy offers us a five grand bonus if we git his kid back in a week – an' all you kin think about is bribes. Know somethin'? You're sick inna head! You're more interested in this Mister Incorruptible image you got of y'self, than you are of anythin' else."

Grant reddened under the lash of his partner's acid tongue. "I said bribes, an' that's exactly what I meant. It's easy for Miller to offer a big fat bribe to me, an' come on strong with the worried parent bit. Where was his concern for the past six fuckin' months his kid's been gone from home with this sect? Do you think he'll back us up in court, if I get hauled up on charges of forcible entry an' assault with firearms ... maybe even a murder rap? Cos' make no mistake, as I told him too, I'll have to go in there real heavy – gun heavy! An' what if they ain't bluffin' an' they blow the fuckin' place sky high, includin' his precious kid? Will Mister Pillar-of-the-Establishment Miller come forward an' admit he hired us to get involved to that extent? Will he fuck!"

Sherman pushed himself upright from the desk, and raised his hands in a placatory gesture. "Hold it ... hold it." With an effort, he lowered his voice and adopted a more reasonable tone. "We're not talkin' here about goin' to war. We're talkin' about a dumb kid bein' held illegally by a buncha religious nuts who parade aroun' in coloured maternity smocks, fer fuck sake! We're talkin' about you havin' a go at snatchin' 'im within a seven day deadline, from a big ramblin' country house owned by these same nuts. Be reasonable, th'guy ain' askin' you to outsmart the KGB an' spring th'kid from the fuckin' Lubyanka. An' he's givin' us five thousan' good reasons fer tryin' to do it. Can you give me one fer not tryin' to do it ... one that ain' based on a paper-thin bluff, that is?"

"How about business ethics – that a good enough reason?" asked Grant stiffly. "I'm not breakin' the law an' endangerin' innocent lives just because some fat cat client waves a chequebook at me. I still got some scruples left, even if you haven't. I was a straight cop, I don' intend bein' a bent shamus. I got principles an' I'm proud of it!" he finished defiantly.

"Principles, schminciples!" roared Sherman, causing the long-suffering Anna in the outer office to wince anew. "Is it breakin' the law to take back stolen property from a thief? An' tell me, can you eat principles? Can you wear scruples instead of clothes? Can you pay off your overdraft with ethics? This winter shall I say to my family, 'It's cold out, be sure to wrap up warm in your scruples'? When they're starving, I should say to them, Eat up your principles, they'll fill your bellies accordin' to my partner? Oh, an' by the way, pack your things, tomorrow we're bein' evicted. The bank's foreclosin' on the mortgage ... they won' accept Brett's business ethics for payment insteada money!"

Had Grant not been angrily standing on his dignity and stubbornly defending his viewpoint, he would have burst out laughing at the unlikely vision of Sherman's well-fleshed wife and daughters 'starving'. Instead, he stuck to his guns. Walking round the desk, he stalked past Sherman to the door. With his hand on the handle, he stopped and looked back.

"Harry, you can save your breath. I'm not doin' it. Subject closed." he said with quiet finality.

"Subject closed, is it? You think so?" Sherman snapped angrily. "Don' forget who's senior partner round here. When it comes to a split decision, I call the shots. So, I'll decide when the subject's closed. If you won' take on this assignment, I'll hire one of our freelances to have a go." If Sherman hoped this would make Grant reconsider, he was disappointed by his response.

"Forget it. He won't get past first base, an' you'll only succeed in gettin' the guy beaten up into the bargain." Grant paused, then added scathingly, "Besides, we ain't so badly off that we need to put people at risk to go after that kinda money." He pulled the door open and walked out.

Sherman went purple. "Whaddaya mean, 'that kinda money'?" he shouted furiously at Grant's retreating back. "Don' you gentiles have a sayin' that clean meat never fattened a pig?"

Grant swung round as he reached the door of the outer office. "Yeah," he retorted. "An' ain't that precisely why your people don' eat pork?"

With this parting sally, he jerked the outer door open and stormed out, slamming it shut behind him. Anna, whose head had been turning from one to the other of the warring partners like a tennis spectator, winced as Grant's parting words were punctuated by the bang of the closing door. A moment later she winced again as an irate Sherman kicked the other door shut in temper.

As the double concussion of the slamming doors died away, the door of the third inner office opened and a young black man stuck his head out and asked, "Hey Anna, what th'hell's goin' down?" It was Sam Ellis, the one nicknamed 'Sam Spade' by Sherman.

Almost in the same moment, the outer door re-opened to admit a slim, olive skinned young man in T-shirt and faded denims. Miguel Perez, the second of the detectives employed by the firm and the other half of the Mike Hammer/Sam Spade duo, raised an eyebrow at the other two, jerked his head towards the corridor and the now departed Grant, and asked, "What's eatin' Brett? He damn near walked over me, like I wasn't there."

Anna shrugged and leaned forward to erase an error on the sheet in her typewriter with correction fluid. "I think Brett and the boss had a disagreement over something," she replied.

"That was a disagreement?" Ellis rolled his eyes exaggeratedly.

"Man, I thought it was World War Three breakin' out. I was gittin' ready t'burn my draft card."

"Yeah, from down the corridor, all that door slammin' sounded like they were takin' pot-shots at each other," Perez said with a chuckle as he headed across the room towards the office he shared with Ellis. As the door closed behind them, Anna plucked the clip-on earphone of the dictating machine from her ear and laid it on the desk beside her typewriter. She depressed a button on the intercom.

"Yeah Anna, what is it?" Sherman's voice rasped from the speaker.

"Will it be all right if I take my lunch break now, Mister Sherman? I have a headache coming on. I think it is caused by concussion on my ears!" she added pointedly.

Sherman's dry chuckle sounded from the speaker. "Ouch! I suppose I deserve that," he conceded. "Okay Anna, run along. Sorry about th'noise. Our business conferences git a bit outa hand sometimes. Are the gruesome twosome in? Mike Hammer an' Sam Spade?"

"Yes, Mister Sherman," she replied. "They are both in."

"Buzz 'em an' tell one of 'em to keep an eye on the outer office while you're gone." Sherman instructed.

"Of course, Mister Sherman. Just like I always do," Anna said reprovingly and released the button.

Deep in thought, Sherman heard the faint sound of the outer door closing behind the secretary a few minutes later. He was sitting in Grant's chair, mentally examining every possibility of earning the five thousand dollar bonus offered by Virgil Miller earlier that morning, for the safe return of his son within seven days. The offer that had been the subject of his acrimonious 'business conference' with his junior partner.

Now, however, it was not just the money that mattered. Grant was right when he said they didn't need it. The firm was financially sound. No, what rankled with Sherman was Grant's remark about having principles. Well, it was now a matter of principle with him too. He felt Brett was being over cautious and also that he was allowing his prickly pride to interfere with his professional judgement, with his old bogey of being offered what he considered to be any form of bribe. The puppy needed a lesson. Business ethics, indeed! Was it not also business ethics to do your best for a client? He'd show his younger partner – after all, he'd been running the agency successfully when Brett had been a stick-toting cop kicking ass on a beat.

Sherman came to a decision. "Solly Levenson," he muttered to himself, thumping the desk gently with a clenched fist. "That's the guy who'll do the job for me. If that ol' fox can't find a way in an' outa that place, no-one can!" With a smile of self-satisfaction, he reached for the phone.

50

WHEN GRANT LEFT THE OFFICE, HE RETURNED HIS hired car, picked up his repaired Mustang and headed across the city to call on Pete Larsen in Brooklyn. He intended to give him a full account of his meeting with Karen, then seek the man's help in his planned rescue of the sect girl Louise, by asking him to recruit some of his pals to provide backup for the snatch attempt. From what he had seen and experienced of the sect's reaction to outside interference, Grant reckoned he'd need as much muscle as Larsen could rustle up. He also intended to fill Larsen in on Springfield's proposed operation against Bethlehem House, knowing he and his buddies would provide willing allies, as Karen's own rescue would be involved.

Unknown to Grant, his planned moves against the sect couldn't have been better timed, thanks to a series of events being set in motion at that very moment elsewhere. War had broken out between the Mafia Neroni Family – and Angel One's section of the Gold Dragon Triad. Operation Carla had begun.

Precisely at noon, the three selected primary targets were hit simultaneously across the city. One in Chinatown, one in Harlem and the third in Lower East Side. Each strike was carried out with clinical efficiency. All three were devastatingly successful.

The Golden Lotus Restaurant in the heart of the city's Chinatown was crowded with diners, many of them oriental businessmen from the surrounding area, when the two big black cars bearing false plates came cruising along, only twenty yards separating them, and eased in towards the kerb as though seeking a parking space outside the ornate frontage of the popular eating place. The dinner-suited Chinese doorman, seeing the two limousines slowing down, and noting they were full of passengers, assumed them to be the arrival of a group booking. He stepped forward to greet the customers in the lead car, his anticipation of a fat tip widening his professional smile of welcome.

In the act of reaching for the passenger door handle, his smile froze into a rictus of terror as his horrified eyes registered the blunt snouts of the sub-machine guns which sprouted suddenly from the nearside windows. It was the last thing he ever saw. An instant later, he was cut in half by the murderous hail of bullets which smashed across the entire front of the restaurant, as the guns opened up with a deafening roar.

The huge plate glass windows and doors of the Golden Lotus disintegrated under the thunderous onslaught of white hot metal, as did the slatted bamboo blinds behind them. Razor sharp shards of glass imploded from the pulverised windows adding to the resulting carnage, blinding and maiming and slashing human flesh to bloody ribbons, as they joined forces with the lethal hail of lead which had created them. Then, as suddenly as it had started, the firing ceased. A rising crescendo of screams from within the shattered restaurant punctuated the cordite laden silence which ensued.

Two figures leapt from the offside doors of the lead car and darted round onto the sidewalk. Coolly, the two mafiosi applied lighter flames to the rags protruding from the necks of the petrol-filled bottles each held. Then, acting in unison, they hurled their deadly missiles through the gaping window frames. The combined blast of the twin explosions and the bright glare of fire which instantly followed, were accompanied by an increased crescendo of screaming. As the two fire-bombers dived back into the already moving lead car, machine guns opened up again, but this time from the back-up car as it raked the now blazing restaurant in its turn, covering the getaway.

The entire incident lasted less than a minute. Less than a minute to kill or maim some forty-five people. Most of those who died perished in the roaring inferno which followed the attack. A scant fourteen people escaped death and the majority were injured, some of them seriously. Only ten of those who died were Triads, members of Angel One's branch of Tiger Control in some capacity, whether as couriers, supervisors or street pushers.

One of those injured was Angel Two, who had been visiting the Golden Lotus to make a routine pick-up of cash deposited by couriers. He was fortunate enough to sustain only superficial cuts from flying glass, his survival instinct having saved him from further injury in the follow-up fire-bomb attack, when he had reacted instantly and hurled himself through the swing doors into the restaurant kitchen and from there out through the service entrance. Thus Angel One had an eye witness account of at least one of the day's attacks.

The attack on the Bamboo Garden in Harlem was more or less a carbon copy of the one on the Golden Lotus. It had been chosen for the dual purpose of not only striking at a known Triad meeting place but also of reminding the ghetto's black drug barons of the Neroni Family's power. Despite the gunfire and fire-bombing, the toll of dead and injured was not so great as that at the Golden Lotus, due to the fact that not many ghetto inhabitants could afford the luxury of lunching out. As in the attack on the Golden Lotus, the actual number of Triad personnel killed in the attack on the Bamboo Garden was minimal – only four in this case, all of them members of the restaurant staff.

The third strike, on Lower East Side's Silver Dragon Restaurant, caused relatively few casualties compared to the other two, and these were confined to the oriental staff. This target had been selected only on suspicion that it was Triad-owned. As it was not actually known to be a regular meeting point of the rival organisation, the attack was kept low-key but nonetheless lethal.

Two carloads of Family soldiers drew up outside and six young mobsters, cradling machine guns and sporting the obligatory shades, leapt from the vehicles and entered the restaurant. A quick burst of automatic fire into the ceiling obtained immediate attention and ensured no resistance.

While two of the hit-team herded the Chinese waiters at gun point into the kitchen beside the cooks and stood guard over them, the other four ordered the customers out, giving them sixty seconds to get clear. The last terrified customer stumbled out onto the sidewalk with a full five seconds of the allotted time to spare. Once outside, no-one hung around. The menace of another two gun-toting hoods made sure of that.

The final act of the attack was brief and brutal. As soon as the last customer had vacated the premises, the attack leader signalled to the two gunmen standing guard over the Chinese staff being held captive in the kitchen. The two gunmen immediately opened up with their automatic weapons and scythed down their human targets with a murderous hail of lead. Then, leaving the bullet-riddled corpses of their unfortunate victims sprawled in pools of blood, the hit-team withdrew, fire-bombing the place on their way out. They roared off in the two getaway cars, leaving a blazing funeral pyre where minutes earlier had existed a busy, crowded restaurant.

Had it been possible for an interested observer to monitor the three synchronised strikes, he or she would have noticed a curious factor common to all three. In each case, no police were in the area, either on foot patrol or in cars – nor did any police arrive on the scene until after Fire Service vehicles and ambulances had already got there, despite the undoubted "major incident" status of each crime.

Further investigation by the hypothetical observer would have discovered that all police patrols in the three areas had been diverted elsewhere to deal with a variety of minor incidents, false alarms, or even in some cases hoax calls. Any attempt to inquire any deeper would have been quietly but effectively blocked and frustrated by officers in key positions in the chain of command – all of whom were in the pay of the Neroni Family and each of whom would later receive a special bonus payment for their co-operation.

Commencing at the same high noon deadline as the three primary strikes, a city-wide series of hits were carried out on the secondary targets – on personnel as opposed to property. Continuing in some areas until the late afternoon, a total of thirty-six street pushers with known or suspected Triad connections were systematically located and executed by various methods. Along with them died another twenty-eight back-up personnel, there for the pushers' protection, who were either brave or foolish enough to try to interfere. It was an orgy of murder spectacular even by the standards of a city plagued by one of the highest crime rates in the world.

The methods of execution employed were direct and in many cases brutal, all intended to spread terror among the rank and file of the rival organisation. The gun, the knife and the garrotte were the most commonly used weapons, according to the personal preferences of the Family hitmen. Where the victims could be picked up and conveyed to less public places than the streets or bars they frequented, they were accorded special treatment. Ten unfortunates who were picked up by Lupo Lucarelli's regime were dismembered bloodily and agonisingly by chainsaws or axes. A few others were subjected to a variety of sickeningly imaginative methods of execution.

In one case, a young Chinese pusher, a promising protégé of Angel One's, who managed to kill one of his captors by breaking his neck with a karate blow before being overpowered, was given special treatment. Specially supervised by The Wolf himself, his body was found in a deserted warehouse that evening by children at play. He had been wired up to a high voltage power feed. To serve as terminals, two six-inch metal bolts had been connected to the mains wires, one to the positive and one to the negative. The negative terminal had been forced into the bound victim's mouth and taped in place – the broken teeth and jawbone mute evidence of his vain resistance to the hammer blows which had smashed it into place. The positive terminal had been jammed into his rectum. Then the power had been switched on.

That night an exultant Bruno Neroni was congratulated by his equally jubilant *caporegimes* over celebratory drinks at the Don's house. From their point of view, Operation Carla had been an almost unqualified success in crippling the Triad street distribution organisation in the Family's territory. Almost. Apart from the loss of the man with the broken neck, one other mafioso had failed to report back to his caporegime at the end of the day's action.

But there was no cause for concern in anyone's estimation. The man in question, a young soldier of Paolo Scaglione's *regime* named Dino Biancomano, had made his bones two years before and since then had killed four more times successfully for the Family. He was considered to be reliable. His assigned target that afternoon had been a young Chinese pusher who operated on the fringe of Chinatown, in the area of Canal Street, where he had begun to lure away regular customers from the Neroni Family's territory of Lower East Side.

A quick check made through a police contact had confirmed the death of the pusher from gunshot wounds. But no trace could be found of any accident having befallen their own man – a hospital check proving negative. He had simply vanished without trace. It was puzzling, but as of yet, no cause for concern …

Had Bruno Neroni and his lieutenants but known, there was every cause for concern. Angel One's organisation had indeed been badly mauled by the day's bloody events. But it was by no means as crippled as the Mafia bosses thought.

True, the strikes had been devastatingly successful, due mainly to the element of surprise. In every incident except one, the assailants had struck, killed and disappeared leaving no trace, nor even the slightest reason for the wholesale slaughter. The one exception was to prove costly – very costly!

The first stage of the hit had gone as planned. Dino Biancomano, mounted on a motor cycle and dressed as a telegram delivery man, had located his target exactly where he'd been told he'd find him, at his regular pitch on the crowded sidewalk. Swooping in to the kerb, he pulled up alongside the pusher and shot him three times at point blank range – twice in the body and once in the head. He had then gunned the bike away from the scene, vainly pursued on foot by his victim's two backup men, who had been there to protect him from attack by rip-off merchants or desperate junkies – an ever-present hazard.

It was then that things had gone badly wrong. Young Biancomano had been pulling effortlessly away from the futile pursuit, when he had noticed a traffic jam up ahead. Acting on impulse, he had made a sharp left turn into a side street. But in so doing he had clipped the kerb with his rear wheel and spilled, parting company with the bike and knocking himself senseless in the process.

A telephone call had summoned a sect van, into which the unconscious assassin had been loaded along with his stalled machine. Accompanied by his two captors, the captive had been transported, along with the injured Angel Two, from the city to the seclusion of Bethlehem House.

In mounting fury, Angel One had been collating the disastrous events of the day as the reports came in. It had soon become evident that his entire street distribution network was under attack. He guessed almost straight away that the unknown enemy must be the Mafia, but it remained to be discovered which of their gangs, or Families, were involved. Then he got the break he was patiently waiting for – the report of the capture of an enemy attacker.

When the van arrived from the city, he firstly received his injured lieutenant's eye-witness account of the attack on the Golden Lotus. Next he listened to the report of the murder of the pusher from Biancomano's captors. Then he turned his attention to the captured prize.

Dino Biancomano regained consciousness to find himself strapped naked to a table, arms and legs spreadeagled. When he saw the bleak-eyed figure of Angel One standing over him and his terrified vision fell on the long gleaming acupuncture needles the oriental held loosely in one hand, he knew he was a dead man.

But death came slowly to Dino Biancomano that long endless night. Slowly and very painfully. Sense of time is relevant. In actual fact he took only a little over an hour to die, from the moment the first needle pierced a testicle. But to Dino Biancomano that hour was eternity. Long before death was granted to him, his adherence to the law of *omerta* – the Mafia code of silence – had vanished along with his manhood, in a red mist of unbearable, screaming agony. By then, Angel One was in full possession of every useful fact known to his tortured victim, concerning the organisation of the Neroni Family and its top command structure, including their identities and movements.

As a result of the knowledge he gained, Angel One immediately ordered a temporary suspension of all street operations till further notice, with the exception of the four mobile soup-kitchens operated by the sect. They had not been harmed, so evidently were unknown to the enemy. He then called a council of war timed for eight o'clock the following morning, Angel Four being summoned to attend from the city.

A plan for a counter-attack already taking shape in his fertile mind, he called Dragon Control and made a full report on the day's catastrophic events, the extent of the casualties they had sustained, and the utterly inexplicable reason he had ascertained for the attack from the tortured mafioso.

He received full permission to proceed with such retaliatory action as he considered necessary. Reinforcements would also be transferred to his section over the course of the next few days to replace its depleted numbers. A further two hours of phone calls followed before Angel One was satisfied he had done everything possible to guard against any further losses, should there be any renewed attacks the following day, before he was ready to strike back.

Around midnight, he received another unwelcome report, although this time it was something completely unconnected to the day's events. A prowler had been captured by a night patrol snooping around the perimeter fence. An initial search of the man's person had revealed him to be a private detective named Levenson. He was being brought in for questioning.

An hour later, Solly Levenson, the freelance private investigator who had been hired by his friend Harry Sherman to look over Bethlehem House and its surrounds in order to sniff out any weak points, had been pumped dry of information. Angel One learned to his satisfaction of Grant's apparent dropping of the case. It seemed his partner, Sherman, would now have to be discouraged in turn. So be it.

Wracked with pain and dazed from the ordeal of his brutally thorough interrogation, Solly Levenson found himself stumbling along the gravel surface of the long curving driveway leading from the house to the outer gates. He could hardly think straight. He was only dimly aware that he had been released after an hour of torment and questions at the hands of the Devil incarnate in human form.

Levenson had been only semi-conscious when thrust roughly out of the front door. Staggering off into the night, he had been unaware of someone standing outside for a few seconds behind him, blowing into a device which only emitted a hissing noise, before retreating quickly back inside and shutting the door. Had he known, and had he recognised the object for what it was – an ultra-sonic dog whistle – he might have felt stirrings of unease. As it was, his numbed mind only knew he had to get away from this place of pain and evil somehow, to warn Harry Sherman that Grant was right. These people were dangerous.

The cold cleared his head a little, enabling him to take stock of his plight and his surroundings. He limped onwards, making for the outer gates. He reckoned if they were locked he could maybe manage to climb over them, as the walk would have given him a chance to recover his strength. The thought occurred then that it was strange how he was not being escorted to make sure of his leaving the grounds as well as the house. Why should this be so? His pain-fogged brain could not think of a reason.

Then he heard the snarls from the darkness off to his right

and the sound of swiftly moving bodies brushing through the undergrowth amongst the trees. He knew the reason then. Dogs! Harry Sherman had mentioned something about guard dogs … Too late the recollection flashed a warning to his dulled comprehension, a split second before he caught the terrifying sight of hurtling dark shapes, amber eyes and white fangs, as the killer pack, Satan in the lead, burst from the woods and fell ravening upon him.

51

THE IMMEDIATE RESULT OF THE CAMPAIGN OF murder and destruction was the cancellation of all police leave and rest days. The streets of the affected areas of the city were given saturation cover by uniformed patrolmen and prowl cars as far as it was possible to do.

Nor was this merely a token gesture to head off the inevitable outcry in the news media. Even those corrupt police bosses who had effectively manipulated the duties that day to allow their Mafia paymasters a free hand, were appalled when the actual extent of the carnage had become known, and had run for cover. The loss of life alone made the infamous St Valentine's Day Massacre carried out by Capone's mob in Chicago look like a rowdy picnic by comparison.

The resultant increase in police patrols meant a fruitless day of frustration for Brett Grant, Pete Larsen and six of Larsen's buddies, who had formed an assault group intent on rescuing the girl Louise from under the very noses of the sect personnel. Grant had enlisted a more than willing Larsen, who was recovering rapidly from his beating, although still showing some of its technicolour effects. The man had not only been willing to help, he had positively insisted, after Grant had broken the news of his daughter's plight.

Larsen had in turn enlisted the equally enthusiastic backup of half a dozen well-muscled drinking buddies, all of whom worked in the scrap metal trade and looked the part. To prevent recognition, with resultant reprisals being taken against his daughter Karen, Larsen and his pals were carrying woollen ski masks which covered the entire features, with holes for the mouth and eyes.

Learning from Grant's recent uncomfortable experience of how easily the sect had traced his Mustang through its number, Larsen had solved the transport problem by providing two untraceable vehicles. This he had done quite simply – and quite illegally – by fixing up two traded-in vehicles which had been scrapped by auto dealerships as unresaleable and subsequently deleted from the City Vehicle Registration Department records.

As a result, Grant and Larsen were parked some distance away from the sect van, in a nondescript dark blue Buick of early-80's vintage. This was to be the getaway car after the snatch had taken place. It looked as though it couldn't have outrun someone giving chase on foot, never mind another vehicle, but in this case appearances were deceptive. One of Larsen's team was a first class mechanic and he had souped up the engine so that the beat-up old Buick would give any pursuing sect vehicle a run for its money.

Larsen's six buddies were parked in a side street not far away in the rear of a former delivery van. They had fitted it out with benches along either side and a table bolted to the centre of the floor, on which they passed the time playing cards, while waiting for the signal from the observation vehicle to move in. This would be communicated by two-way radio, two sets of which had been provided courtesy of Sherman & Grant, Private Investigators – without the knowledge of the senior partner, it must be admitted.

The strategy was simple. When the opportunity presented itself, it had been decided that Grant would snatch the girl to safety, while the other seven, armed with pickaxe handles and baseball bats, would provide the backup and prevent any interference from the sect heavies.

The plan had sounded good, but on the first day of their vigil they had been constantly thwarted each time things looked promising, by the continual appearance of police patrols, either on foot or on wheels. These patrols had come past at irregular intervals, which had made any attempt to time their frequency well nigh impossible.

By the end of that first frustrating day, Grant had feared that the others would be losing their enthusiasm, but found it was not the case. However, he reckoned two days was the limit he could ask them to stay away from their respective jobs, on the sick lines they had all obtained. Accordingly, at the end of that first fruitless day, he had assured them that come hell or high water, they would pick a time immediately after a police patrol had passed and move into action the following day. That day was with them now and Grant was all too aware that it was ticking away minute by inactive minute. He made up his mind to start the action soon, even if it meant risking police interference.

If the extra police presence on the streets was making life difficult for Brett Grant, it was an added bonus as far as Ben Curtis was concerned. It meant he felt able to relax for the first time since he had begun his five year hunt for the killer.

Thanks to the extra manpower provided by Cameron's Narcotics men, not only did he have his man bottled up and under 24 hour surveillance, but he also knew he'd have plenty of backup available if and when the urge to kill drove him out to seek another victim. Then they would move in and take him on the street, once he'd left the protection of his well-guarded lair.

Curtis was determined that the next interrogation session would be conducted on his home territory down at Precinct HQ. Complained to the D.C. that he'd been assaulted, had he? He'd show the murdering sonavabitch the meaning of the term third degree … after he'd read him his rights, of course!

52

THE DAY FOLLOWING OPERATION CARLA, THE DON
initiated phase two of his plan. The Family quietly began to
move in their own pushers to fill the gaps created by the defeat
of their rivals. Every pusher was provided with heavy
protection – a team of at least four men in each case, armed and
well spread out – to prevent any counter attacks. None
materialised. By nightfall a successful day's trading was reported,
with no signs of enemy action to oppose the take-over of their
territories. Although it was too soon to be certain, it seemed
victory was complete.

However, no-one was allowed to become complacent. The
Don issued orders for everyone to be extra vigilant for the
foreseeable future. It had to be assumed that an organisation as
powerful as the Triads would attempt a comeback, if they
detected any weakness or lack of caution in their foes. The
Family must not be caught out in its turn by their own stratagem
of a devastating surprise attack.

Yet, Bruno Neroni would not have been human had he not
permitted himself private feelings of self-satisfaction at his
routing of a dangerous enemy and in having exacted personal
revenge for the death of his mistress. But the peacefulness of
that day was to prove the false calm in the eye of the storm,
before its fury breaks out anew – and in the opposite direction.

By half past eight the following evening, the Don had enjoyed
an excellent dinner prepared in the true old country style of
their native Sicily by his wife. He was comfortably settled in his
study with a decanter of vintage brandy and a good cigar, going
through some business papers. The Family ran several legitimate
businesses, all originally financed by the shrewd investment of
profits from their criminal activities. All these legal businesses
were profitable concerns in their own rights and all were doubly
useful in the laundering of 'hot' money from the same illegal
sources that had provided their initial capital. His satisfaction

increased as he went through the healthy balance sheets and accountants' reports.

The Don looked up as a quiet knock sounded at the door. He recognised Emilio Falcone's quick double tap and called for him to enter. As soon as he saw the *consigliere's* face, Neroni's sense of well-being vanished and a serpent of apprehension uncoiled in his belly. He knew from the pale, drawn face of the normally unflappable Falcone that something was terribly wrong.

When he heard the news that Falcone bore, the reality was worse than he could have imagined. His three *caporegimes,* his trusted and vastly experienced lieutenants who generalled his forces, were dead. All hit within minutes of one another in different locations across the city. In the space of half an hour, his entire top leadership had been wiped out in a shattering triple counterblow by the enemy. In addition, a total of sixteen trusted men, their bodyguards, had died with them.

Falcone had received several calls, all giving fragmented accounts of each disaster. He had waited only until he'd been able to check it all out with a police contact, before presenting the Don with the hard facts. Briefly but succinctly, he related these unpalatable facts as he knew them.

Angel One's counter-attack had begun at seven-thirty that evening. Paolo Scaglione was the first to die. It was his habit to call in at his health club for a relaxing sauna and massage each evening after leaving the offices of the property development company he ran for the Family as his legal cover. The health club was expensive, but this ensured its exclusiveness of clientele. It employed a staff of attractive young males and females expert in administering every possible method of massage and catered for most tastes in physical stimulation and toning up of the human body. You could even have a straight massage, if that was all you wanted! The club was situated in a respectable business area in the Queens.

Shortly before seven-thirty, two young Mafia hoods pushed their way out through the glass swing doors of the club and took up position on either side of the entrance. Quickly and efficiently they scanned the street in all directions. When they satisfied themselves that it was clear, one of them raised his hand in a signal.

Immediately, two cars pulled out from the kerb some distance away down the street and accelerated towards the club entrance, where they drew up with arrogant disregard for parking restrictions. From the rearmost car, two more tough looking hoods quickly emerged and took up position at either end of the cars, so as to aid the first two in covering the street.

There was no lurking danger apparent. Only a few pedestrians were on the move. Among these was a blind man, tapping his way along with a white stick. A few paces behind him was an attractive young woman pushing a pram, its parcel-rack underneath loaded with packages.

The lead car was parked directly in line with the club entrance. The driver climbed out and lounged against the roof of his vehicle, waiting to open the rear door for his boss when he appeared. Satisfied all was as it should be, one of the two flanking the club doorway disappeared back inside to inform Scaglione and his personal bodyguard that it was safe to leave.

The driver of the lead car, still scanning the street like the others, noticed the approaching blind man tap his way carefully to the edge of the kerb a short distance away and stop, obviously prepared to wait until some considerate passer-by escorted him across the road. The girl pushing the pram paused in passing him and offered to help, which he accepted with a nod of thanks. She made to leave her pram unguarded, then appeared to think better of it.

Advancing the few paces to the driver, who was still leaning nonchalantly against the car, she flashed him a cheery smile as she parked the pram alongside the front wing.

"Excuse me," she appealed to him, "Could I trouble you to keep an eye on junior for a moment, till I see this gentleman across the street?"

Embarrassed, the driver glanced round his grinning comrades, then back to the girl. Without waiting for his reply, she was walking back towards the blind man.

"Hey, lady …" he began indignantly, then seeing her reach the blind man's side, take him by the elbow and look back at him, he shrugged and finished lamely, "Ah … be my guest. But y'better be quick, we're jes' leavin'. You ain' back in time, junior's up fer grabs."

She grinned at him. "Oh, just take him with you," she called laughingly. "But I warn you, he probably needs changed." He was rewarded with another disarming smile as the girl stepped off the kerb with the blind man and started to guide him across the street.

The driver was promptly baited by his sniggering companions. "Say, big boy, could y'keep an eye on this for me?" called one suggestively in a falsetto voice. "Watch he don' piss on y'knee when y'changin' his diaper," put in another. "Hey man, whatchya gonna tell th'boss?" called a third. "He'll think y'doin' a sideline in kidnappin' an' he'll wanna piece've the action."

Just then, the short stocky figure of Paolo Scaglione emerged from the club entrance, accompanied by his personal bodyguard, a hulking, 6'4" ex-heavyweight boxer. The young hood who had given the all clear, brought up the rear. The *capo's* eyebrows rose under his hat brim, when he saw the pram parked beside the front wing. Amused, he noticed his driver's confusion as the man darted a look across the street, searching for the blind man and his escort, the pram's owner. The driver caught sight of the couple, as they were about to disappear behind a van parked at the opposite kerb. The girl looked back just as Scaglione addressed his flustered driver.

"Hey Reno, what's all this? Some dame from y'past catch up wit' you, an' leave you holdin' the *bimbo*, eh?" he chuckled. "So, let's see if it looks like its old man," he ribbed the driver and bent over the pram. Reaching in, he gently eased the top cover back to expose the tiny head of the baby … or rather, the head of the lifelike doll which was the pram's only occupant!

The surprise barely had time to register in Paolo Scaglione's brain, before the parcel bomb nestling amongst the other packages under the pram, detonated in his face. The resultant blast hurled his mangled body fully fifty feet beyond his overturned, blazing car. None of his guards survived, scythed down as they were, along with three unfortunate passers-by, by the lethal hail of shrapnel from the bomb along with flying fragments of the disintegrated pram. In addition, several pedestrians and passing motorists were injured in the explosion.

Across the street, the girl and the 'blind man', the latter now minus his dark glasses and white stick, quickly moved from behind the sandbag-packed van, which had been parked there earlier for their protection. It had been bought earlier that day at a second hand car lot and was untraceable. As they hurried from the scene, which by then resembled a war movie set, all flames and screaming victims, the girl paused by a litter bin and dropped into it the small radio transmitter she had used to trigger the bomb. Ten minutes later the two assassins were being driven north to Bethlehem House and safety. Strike one!

Pietro Bonnello was the second target to be hit in Angel One's counter-strike. At 6 p.m. that evening, he had finished a reasonably busy day directing operations at the trucking company he ran for the Family. He had spent the next twenty minutes or so clearing up the paperwork, checking out that day's invoices and the following day's load sheets. Then he had locked up and climbed into his waiting car to be driven home to the plush Richmond suburb where he lived. His bodyguards followed in a second car, as was normal procedure for all three of the Family *caporegimes* and the Don himself.

It was seven-forty when the two cars turned into the quiet, tree-lined avenue in which Bonnello's house was situated. Half way along, a curious thing happened, curious for that secluded area anyway. Up ahead of the cruising mob cars, a motor cycle cop rode out from a side avenue on their left, stopped his bike in the middle of the road and waved them down. As the two cars slowed to a halt, the occupants tensed suspiciously, eyes narrowing and hands reaching for gun butts. Uniformed cops were seldom ever seen in the rarefied surroundings of that moneyed suburb.

Then a hearse glided sedately from the side avenue and turned slowly into the avenue ahead of them. The coffin it bore was piled high with flowers and wreaths. In the rear of the lead car, Bonnello crossed himself superstitiously. The occupants of both cars relaxed and sat back to watch with morbid interest, as the two big black limousines forming the funeral cortege were waved out in their turn by the cop, their smoked glass windows affording their unseen complement of mourners a measure of privacy in their time of grief.

The lead limousine nosed forward as though intending to turn into the avenue in the hearse's wake, then stopped. All eyes watched it, puzzled. Bonnello's driver was the only exception. From up ahead he caught the glow of brake lights on his peripheral vision, and his eyes flicked back to the hearse. He saw it had stopped too. Events happened fast then. Too fast for his warning shout to save anyone.

Before the startled driver's eyes, the rear window and front windscreen of the hearse dropped flat simultaneously, leaving a clear through passage from front to rear of the vehicle. In the same moment of time, the driver and escort dived out to either side of the hearse and crouched on the road alongside, pistols appearing in their hands like magic. Even as these two were flinging themselves from the cab, the mound of wreaths and floral tributes covering the coffin suddenly erupted before the shocked gaze of the now alerted Bonnello and an alarmingly lively 'corpse' rose to a kneeling position in their midst.

But Bonnello's shock was caused not so much by the sudden appearance of the revivified deceased, as by the short metal tube the figure was aiming straight at them from its resting place on his shoulder, one eye pressed to the sight protruding from its side.

Before anyone in Bonnello's car could react to the driver's yell of alarm, the bazooka belched a tongue of flame from its rear, out through the gap left by the flattened windscreen, and launched its deadly missile at them.

The gang boss's car, like those of the other top men in the Neroni Family, had been rendered impervious to attacks by rival mobs by the incorporation of steel plating in its body work and bullet-proof glass in all its windows. But the explosive warhead of the rocket fired at it had been designed to knock out a battle tank, having first penetrated several inches of armour. Its effect was catastrophic. The vehicle erupted into a roaring inferno, the doors, trunk and hood all blowing open as the explosive charge combined with the contents of the fuel tank to convert the interior into a white-hot furnace, instantly incinerating all three occupants, the *capo*, his personal bodyguard and the driver.

No sooner had the initial fireball of the explosion dissipated, than the rear doors of the lead mourners' car were flung open and four figures darted out. Hitting the road at a run, they fanned out as they circled to avoid the blazing wreck and closed on the late mobster's escort car. All had white silk scarves covering their faces below their eyes, and each carried a snub-nosed machine pistol.

The hit team's targets, the four stunned mafiosi bodyguards, never stood a chance, temporarily disoriented as they were by the blast which had reduced Bonnello's car to a gutted shell. The masked gunmen opened up on them and they were raked by a murderous hail of metal, their riddled bodies jerking like marionettes in a dance of death.

The firing ceased as suddenly as it had begun, and the entire group of attackers, including the bogus cop, piled into the two limousines and sped off, leaving the hearse and the motor cycle abandoned – another two untraceable vehicles to occupy the police with fruitless inquiries.

In the spacious interiors of the speeding limousines, now several miles apart and heading for different destinations, the various members of the hit team were busily changing into fresh clothing. Out of the total ten-man team, the four travelling in the first car could now be recognised as members of Bethlehem House's gang of young thugs known as the Apostles. With the exception of the two driving the limousines, their roles had been that of the bogus cop and the driver and escort of the hearse.

However, the four gunmen travelling in the second car, having now unwound the white silk scarves from their faces, were all Chinese. So too was the erstwhile 'corpse' who had handled the anti-tank weapon with such lethal effect. The five were all 426-

ers – fighters – of the Gold Dragon Triad, but of its Hong Kong branch. They had been flown in at the request of Angel One, in line with a long-standing Triad tradition of using imported hitmen to carry out executions of a specialised or particularly heavy nature, in order to thwart subsequent police investigations.

Within two hours of the slaughter of Bonnello and his six henchmen, the five-man Triad hit team were safely dispersed and on separate flights back to their Hong Kong base. Strike two!!

Third and last to die was The Wolf, Sandro Lucarelli. He had been marked down for special treatment by Angel One, after the oriental had learned, via the lurid press descriptions, of the agonising death by electrocution of one of his people. Discreet inquiries had turned up Lucarelli's name in connection with the killing, from a boastful conversation between two drunken young mafiosi in a mob-frequented bar.

That evening Lucarelli, like his two fellow *caporegimes*, saw no reason to alter his normal routine, although he and his men increased their normal level of vigilance. Secretly though, he had an arrogant contempt for the rice-eaters. He felt they were merely upstart opportunists and although he agreed their elimination had been long overdue, at the same time he personally felt the Don had too high a regard for their supposed power. Perhaps a sign that Neroni was getting soft? In the event, Lucarelli's low opinion of the enemy and his resultant refusal to change his routine proved his undoing.

Accordingly, a little before eight that evening, he entered his favourite restaurant, Lombardi's in Broome Street, in the heart of the city's Little Italy district. A widower, Lucarelli dined there regularly, attracted both to its homely old world atmosphere and its Sicilian cuisine. As always, his escort had thoroughly checked the place out prior to his entry and while two remained outside with the cars, the other four accompanied Lucarelli into the premises.

One took a seat in a corner near the door, the others joined their boss at his table in the far corner of the restaurant. In time-honoured fashion, the two junior men sat with their backs to the restaurant entrance, providing their *capo* with a human shield against any surprise attack from that direction. The third man, Lucarelli's personal bodyguard, sat beside his boss, facing out into the main body of the restaurant. Thus secure, Lucarelli ordered up his meal and settled down with drinks all round to await its arrival.

When the waiter re-entered the kitchen with the order, he had time only to register the sight of the entire kitchen staff and most of his fellow waiters lined up against the far wall, under the muzzles of two submachine-guns in the hands of two hooded men, before cold metal touched his temple and a voice hissed in his ear, "Freeze, or you're dead!" He froze.

A shove in the back propelled the terrified waiter across to join the others in the silent, fearful line-up. As he stumbled across the tiled floor, he saw there were more armed, hooded men standing in a group off to one side of the kitchen. His brief glimpse took in the fact that they were all dressed as Lombardi waiters, in cut-away scarlet tail-coats with the letters LR monogrammed in silver on the breast pocket, over spotless white aprons. Then he was ordered, along with the rest of the line-up, to turn and face the wall.

The armed group of bogus waiters now moved into action. Minutes previously they had burst into the kitchen through the rear door from the service alley and quickly subdued the terrified staff. They had then speedily donned spare uniforms taken from the staff dressing room. Now, at a sign from one of their number, all eight of the group removed their hoods. Seven were revealed to be young Latin Americans, all picked from among the sect Disciples, who would easily pass as Italian waiters. The eighth was an oriental. It was Angel One himself.

He signed again. At this, the seven draped white napkins over their right forearms so as to cover the silenced automatics they were holding, picked up a tray each and filed quickly out into the restaurant. Angel One followed in their wake. Silence reigned in the kitchen, as the staff remained facing the far wall, under the menacing guns of the three remaining hooded men, one of whom was positioned just inside the kitchen doorway to collect any other genuine waiters who might enter.

Once out on the floor of the busy restaurant, the eight bogus waiters quickly threaded their way between the tables towards their intended targets. The lighting in Lombardi's was provided by a shaded lamp on each table, creating an atmosphere of discreet intimacy for the customers. Throbbing Italian music played softly from speakers set high on the walls. The general dimness of the lighting thus helped the members of Angel One's assault group to avoid detection, as they weaved smoothly between the pools of soft light cast by the table lamps.

The first person in the place to become aware of anything amiss was the head waiter. He was standing at his customary post not far from the front door, ready to greet incoming diners and direct them to vacant tables. Without warning, he felt something hard jab him in the region of his right kidney and heard a voice hiss in his ear the same message his waiter had been given earlier. "Freeze, or you're dead!" The voice then further enlightened him, "This is Mafia business. Don't get involved. All y'gotta do is act normal, an' keep the customers happy. Do anythin' stupid, you're morgue meat. *Capice?*"

Staring straight ahead, the head waiter nodded, suddenly dry-throated with fear. He was a Sicilian himself. He understood only too well.

Likewise, the young Lucarelli bodyguard at his table near the exit chose to offer no resistance, when he found himself staring into the ugly snout of a silencer. It was poking out at him from under the folded napkin covering the hand of the waiter, who had materialised quietly alongside him. Without needing to be told, he carefully placed his hands flat on the table before him and sat still.

A third sect gunman took up position just inside the front doors of the restaurant, to cover any attempted intervention from outside.

In his secluded corner, Lucarelli glanced up and frowned as four waiters arrived at his table. He knew he hadn't ordered food for his men, they were there to guard him, not to distract themselves by eating. So, why four waiters? Puzzled, but not alarmed, he opened his mouth to make a remark to this effect to the waiter who had stopped beside him, then snapped it shut again, as the man flicked the edge of the napkin back from the blunt barrel of the silencer. The three bodyguards found themselves similarly threatened. No-one moved.

Lucarelli braced himself for the impact of the bullet he knew was surely coming. His mind was in turmoil. Who had ordered the hit? He could only assume that a rival Mafia family was making a move against the Neroni clan, while they were occupied by their street war with the Triads. If so, who had fingered him?

Then a fifth figure stepped into the oasis of lamplight, from the dimness beyond. Lupo Lucarelli, the Wolf, whose savagery was a legend throughout the underworld, looked up into the face of the newcomer – and knew fear. As he met the glittering black eyes of the oriental who stood there, he knew instinctively he had met his match in savagery. Violence emanated from the man like a tangible aura. It reached out like a cold mist and chilled Lucarelli to the bone. And he knew this was no Mafia business.

So paralysed was he, that he failed to react when his personal bodyguard, a thickset brute of a man named Enzo Pertini, made a sudden senseless attempt to go for the gun in his shoulder holster. The silencer at his temple coughed once. Pertini's whole body jerked spasmodically, then he slumped back limply against the wall behind him.

The act was shielded from the floor of the restaurant by the killer's person, and no-one noticed the blood and brain tissue splattered on the flock wallpaper behind his slumped figure. No-one except Lucarelli, that is, who had been sickeningly sprayed with a fine mist of gore from the gaping exit wound, as the fatal bullet blasted its way out through the back of Pertini's skull to bury itself in the wall. The other two Mafia hoods, white faced and visibly shaken, sat rigid, their hands flat on the tablecloth.

The oriental spoke, his harsh voice low and menacing. "Mister Lucarelli, you will convey a personal message from me to your Don. It concerns the death of his late mistress, Miss Menotti. The message is for your ears only and hopefully will prevent the escalation of further mutually damaging hostilities. Come with me please. And do nothing foolish, or I shall be obliged to select another messenger ... from among the living!"

Lucarelli's hopes soared. The unexpected reprieve from imminent death left him feeling light-headed as his fear subsided, releasing him from his unmanly paralysis. He managed, at the second attempt, to rise from his seat and follow Pertini's executioner as indicated, despite the trembling of his legs. As he moved towards the kitchen, the oriental moved in behind him, cutting off any attempt to retreat. His two remaining bodyguards were left behind, sweating under the menacing muzzles of the guns held on them by the two waiters.

Passing through the swing doors, Lucarelli had advanced a few paces into the kitchen, before he took in the hooded gunmen and the line of captive staff facing the far wall. Immediately his fear flooded back. The oriental had implied that he had wanted privacy to pass on his message to the Don. But here were potential eavesdroppers on any confidential conversation. He came to an abrupt halt.

Angel One had anticipated just such a reaction and before Lucarelli could make any move to retreat he punched the mobster hard over the left kidney, dropping him to the floor. Leaning over his gasping victim, the oriental quickly gagged him by stuffing a napkin into his gaping mouth and binding it in place with another. Then he viciously chopped the squirming, whimpering gang boss on each bicep, effectively paralysing his arm muscles.

Signalling to Pertini's executioner to follow suit, Angel One retrieved his hood from a pocket and put it on. Having done so, he ordered the kitchen staff to face about again. He wanted witnesses to his next act, who would ensure the maximum spread of his warning to all future enemies of his organisation.

Walking over to the hotplates, he effortlessly lifted a large steaming pan by its two handles, and carried it back to stand holding it over the helpless Lucarelli. There was a murmur of horrified protest from the assembled staff, as they realised what he was about to do. The protest died stillborn, quelled by a cold look from the glittering eyes of the hooded oriental and each pair of eyes dropped in turn under his challenging stare.

Angel One looked down and met the terrified gaze of Lucarelli.

He addressed him then, his harsh voice ringing out clearly in the silent kitchen. "I have chosen you to convey a special message to your leader, because of what you did to one of my people. The one you electrocuted in such a foul manner. You gave him no dignity in his death. No face. In return, I give you none in yours. And know this before you die, your fellow Sicilian vermin, Scaglione and Bonnello, have both been exterminated within the past half hour. Here is the first part of my message to Neroni ..."

So saying, Angel One tipped the heavy pan over and carefully poured its contents of boiling cooking oil, from head to foot over the wildly threshing figure on the floor. Animal screaming noises gurgled from behind the gag, as the pain-crazed Lucarelli suffered the torment of the damned. There was worse to come.

Angel One stooped and placed the empty pan on the tiled floor. Still crouching, he snapped his fingers and the hooded gunman who had shot Pertini stepped forward and handed him two petrol-soaked rags, which Angel One quickly tied round the calves of the scalded mobster's jerking legs. Then he stood, hauling the purple-faced, blinded, oil soaked Lucarelli with him to his feet in one swift movement.

"And here is the second part of my message," the harsh voice continued remorselessly. "I hope Neroni understands it well ..."

The words were spoken for the benefit of the shocked audience lining the far wall. Lucarelli himself was past understanding anything outwith his private world of pain. As he pronounced sentence, Angel One stooped again and applied a lighter flame briefly to each petrol-soaked rag and as the ruthless Mafia killer was engulfed in the flames which leapt up from his lower limbs, the oriental shot out a hand and propelled him bodily through the swing doors into the restaurant.

Six of the horrified kitchen staff fainted. Most of the others threw up where they stood. Two female dishwashers started screaming in unison, their bunched fists pressed against their mouths. But the sounds of their hysteria were immediately drowned out by the volume of noise from the restaurant outside, as every diner in the premises leapt to their feet in a bedlam of screaming, shouting confusion, when the nightmare figure of the blazing human torch stumbled blindly out among them.

Such was the horrified panic which ensued, that no-one noticed the three waiters who cold-bloodedly dispatched three customers with single head shots, fired from silenced automatics and then darted quickly for the kitchen. The bodies of the four slain Lucarelli bodyguards were only discovered after the police arrived and cleared the restaurant prior to commencing their investigations. Even the still shaken head waiter, normally an observant man, was unable to recall precisely when his armed guard had disappeared. Strike three!!!

All those who had witnessed events in the kitchen, provided the following day's media coverage with graphic accounts of the terrible reprisal, along with verbatim reports of Angel One's message to Neroni. Some among them found themselves in front of the TV cameras and their descriptions became even more highly coloured under the skilful prompting of seasoned interviewers hungry for sensationalism.

No leads could be found to the perpetrators of the crime. Coupled to the hits on Scaglione and Bonnello, the head waiter's account of what had been said to him regarding the affair being 'Mafia business', effectively led the police inquiries up a blind alley at first, precisely as it had been intended to do.

The complete absence of information from the usual underworld sources was puzzling to the detectives on the case. The killers had simply vanished without trace. However, it didn't take long for someone to make the connection between the hits on the Neroni Family and the attacks on the Chinese owned properties earlier in the week. Naturally no confirmation of this was likely to be forthcoming. The case was destined to be filed along with all the other unsolved murders attributable to New York's gang wars.

As Angel One intended, Bruno Neroni got the message and unlike the police, he knew for certain what they could only speculate on. He had wounded the Gold Dragon but failed to kill it. And now it had bitten back – or in Sandro Lucarelli's case, it had breathed fire!

Nor was that the only message the Don got that night. He had retired to bed exhausted at around 2 a.m., after several hours of frantic phone calls and hastily convened meetings. He and Falcone had finally decided upon the appointment of three replacement *caporegimes*, selected on merit from their depleted ranks. They had also ordered a strategic withdrawal from the former Triad territories they had occupied, at least until the situation could be reappraised.

Only one serious problem had remained unsolved – that of how the Triads had obtained the detailed and highly confidential information necessary for the arrangement and timing of the three hits. There were only two possibilities. Either the missing Biancomano had been captured and made to talk, or there was a traitor in the Family. A search for such a weak link would begin the next day.

At 4 a.m. Bruno Neroni was awakened from a fitful sleep by Falcone, who was fast becoming a harbinger of doom. Minutes later in his study, his face still puffy with sleep, the Don was informed by the consigliere that they now had the answer to their two mysteries, the source of the leak and the fate of their missing soldier. They were one and the same.

A short while previously, a motor-cyclist had roared past the outer gates of the house and in passing, had thrown a bulky object over them. The gate guards had dived for cover, thinking it to be a bomb. When no explosion had followed after a tense interval, they had plucked up the courage to investigate the package. It was found to be a wrapped and sealed hat-box, addressed to the Don in person.

Falcone had been informed and had ordered further examination to ensure it was not a parcel-bomb. Accordingly it had been removed to the grounds at a safe distance from the house and carefully opened by one of the men with previous army expertise in such matters. When he had delicately removed the lid, the strong beam of his flashlight had revealed not the lethal mechanism of a bomb, but the severed head of Dino Biancomano, his face frozen in a soundless scream of unbearable agony. Neatly painted in red on the forehead above the sightless staring eyes, was the sign of the Triads!

53

BRETT GRANT DECIDED ON IMPULSE THAT IT WAS now or never. The crowd at the sect van had thinned to around twenty or so, the least it had been since their long vigil had begun the day before. A prowl car had cruised past a couple of minutes earlier, and there was no telling when the next one might appear. He turned to Larsen. "Pete, I think now's about as good a time as we're gonna get," he said quietly. "What d'you think?"

"Okay by me, Brett." Larsen nodded. His ski-mask was sitting on his head like a woollen cap, ready to roll down over his face. Twisting round, he reached over and pulled a baseball bat from under the travelling rug on the rear seat. Holding the bat across his knees, he bared his teeth in a wolfish grin. "I'm ready. Whistle up the boys and let's kick some ass."

Grant raised the radio to his mouth and thumbed the transmit button. "This is the preacher callin'. The prayer meetin's about to start," he spoke the agreed 'go' code into the mike. "Okay troops, move in. Let's do it. Out." As he pushed the radio into the dash compartment and started up the engine, from the corner of his eye Grant saw Larsen pulling down his ski mask to cover his face.

Seconds later, as Grant pulled the car into the kerb a few yards short of the sect van, the Dodge van carrying Larsen's backup team swung out of the side street where it had been parked and headed towards them. Thirty yards short of the sect van, three small objects arced from the Dodge's nearside passenger window onto the sidewalk. The largest of the objects, a small brightly coloured cardboard canister, rebounded from a boarded-up storefront and spun to a stop on the sidewalk a few feet from the two firecrackers which had accompanied it. An instant later, a cloud of thick orange smoke began to billow from the canister and the street was filled with a series of loud bangs as the two firecrackers exploded noisily into life. The heads of all those hanging about the sect van swung round in surprise towards the source of the noise and smoke. Grant nudged Larsen.

"There goes the diversion," he said. "Let's go!"

Grant and Larsen stepped out onto the sidewalk, just as the Dodge drew in behind the Ford and Larsen's six burly mates poured eagerly out to join them. With the sole exception of Grant, who was unmasked and empty-handed, the others presented a fearsome sight, their faces completely covered by their coloured ski-masks and each one clutching either a baseball bat or pickaxe handle. All eight began walking quickly towards the crowd of people at the van, all of whom had their backs to them as their attention was held by the leaping, exploding firecrackers just visible through the acrid, drifting smoke cloud further along the street.

According to plan, a few feet short of the sect van, Larsen and his six mates halted in a loose line. Each eyed the crowd, picking out the ones they thought looked like sect heavies, and who would be liable to cause trouble. Grant had marked Louise's position roughly in the centre of the throng, and walked on alone, quickening his pace. He threaded his way towards her and took her lightly by the upper arm, at the same time speaking quietly into her ear. "Louise, it's me … Brett Grant. I've come for you, like I promised. Come on, let's go. Quickly!"

She looked round surprised, then her eyes widened as she recognised him. This was replaced immediately by a look of alarm and she glanced hurriedly around and then back to him. "Mister Grant," she breathed urgently. "You better leave. They're expecting you. They'll attack you …"

"Don't worry on my account, I've got some backup of my own," he reassured her quickly. "Now come on, before they notice." He pulled her gently but firmly after him as he retreated.

They cleared the last figures on the edge of the crowd and Louise's eyes widened in momentary alarm when she saw the line of masked men and the clubs they held so menacingly. At that moment a shout sounded from behind them. "Hey! What th'fuck! It's that Grant bastard. Stop 'im … he's got the girl."

"Run, Louise!" commanded Grant, sprinting forward and pulling her after him by the arm.

As they dived through the defence line of Larsen and his

mates, Grant heard running feet pounding after them. Then another voice shouted, "Look out! There's more of 'em ..." and the sounds of battle erupted behind. The thud of wood on flesh and the cries of rage and pain announced the enthusiasm and success of Larsen's rearguard in holding off the pursuit.

After the days and hours of planning and waiting, the actual action was all over in less than three minutes. Reaching the getaway car, Grant bundled Louise into the rear seat and told her to lock the doors. He then rejoined the others in case they needed any added muscle, but he needn't have bothered.

The seven-man line was retreating in good order, still facing the scene of the action, each man walking backwards, club held at the ready. Before them lay several bodies, some unconscious, others moaning in pain as they nursed injuries.

Grant counted a dozen or so on the deck and reckoned some of the braver or more foolish members of the crowd had tried to intervene on behalf of the sect personnel, seeing what they would have assumed to be the abduction of a pretty young girl by a gang of club-wielding thugs. Now however, no-one else was volunteering himself to become another wounded hero, having witnessed the painful fate of the others. Satisfied, he turned away, intending to make for the car.

Just then, the rear door of the sect van flew open and a brown-clad figure leapt out, clearing the steps with one bound, and charged straight for Grant. It was the big black Apostle, Brother Mark. He covered the short distance between them in half a dozen running strides then launched himself into a lethal flying hip kick, aimed at his startled victim's head.

One of the retreating line shouted a belated warning but it was too late. The suddenness of the attack gave Grant no chance to defend himself nor even to take avoiding action. He was saved from severe injury only by the split-second reaction of Pete Larsen. Stepping swiftly off the kerb, he swung his baseball bat in a flat arc and smashed it into the flying body of the attacker.

The devastating blow stopped the big black in mid-air and dropped him heavily to the ground, where he lay stunned and gasping for breath. Before he could recover, Larsen swung the solid club up and brought it whistling down again across one of the man's outstretched legs. The clearly audible snap of splintering bone and the resultant scream of agony sounded almost simultaneously with Larsen's snarled, "Kung Fu that, you bastard!"

Seconds later, the eight-man snatch squad had piled into the getaway vehicles and were speeding away from the scene without further incident. After reassuring the still shaken Louise that she really was safe and free now, Grant turned to address Larsen, who had pulled off the mask and was combing his fingers through his rumpled hair. "Thanks for takin' out that big black sonavabitch. I'd have been a gonner if he'd hit me."

"Don' mention it," retorted Larsen with a grin. "I owed you one fer the other night, when you got me away from those goons at the Centre." Then nodding towards Louise, sitting wide-eyed in the rear seat, he commented, "One down, two to go, eh? When do we move in on the funny farm fer my Karen an' your client's boy?"

"Just as soon as I think it's safe, Pete," replied Grant, concentrating on threading his way through the heavy traffic to confuse any possible pursuit, slight though the chance of that was, given the speed and success of their operation. "I'll tell you one thing, though," he added grimly. "When we do, it'll be a damn sight tougher than that little party we've just been to back there!"

Back at Pam's flat, Grant produced a bottle of Jack Daniels and several six-packs of beer and Larsen's team were treated to celebratory drinks. Pam shared in the general euphoria over the success of the mission but her main reaction was one of relief and she went out of her way to make a fuss of a still bemused Louise.

Still high on the adrenalin of their successful venture, the menfolk drank and laughed and swapped individual reminiscences of the short but violent action. As they did so, Pam listened with growing concern, even though they were making light of everything. Her private misgivings about Brett's increasing involvement with the fanatic sect burgeoned into alarm when one of the men mentioned the final incident in the fracas.

"Hey Pete, you sure socked it to that big black martial arts freak who tried t'kick Brett's head in, didn't ya?" The speaker then went on to describe gleefully to an increasingly dismayed Pam, who was doing her best to hide her feelings and look suitably impressed, how Pete Larsen had dealt with Grant's lethal attacker.

But Grant caught the flicker of alarm which crossed Pam's expression during the graphic account, delivered accompanied by actions. He quickly stepped in and tried to make light of it by joking that he'd had the situation well under control, but Larsen had stepped in to show off his batting technique, in the hope there was a Yankee's scout present.

Larsen caught on straight away, recognising Grant's ploy for what it was, and came in right on cue with a pained, "Hey, hold it! What's with this Yankees bit? It's a baseball team I support, not a buncha posers – I'm a Dodgers man."

This had the calculated effect of causing an immediate good-natured argument over the relative abilities and shortcomings of the variously supported baseball teams. A little later, Larsen called time and diplomatically shepherded his mates from the flat, Grant having arranged to let him know when he was ready to move against Bethlehem House. The six others to a man all insisted on being included, a promise Grant willingly gave. When the time came, he suspected he would need all the help he could muster.

When the door closed on Larsen's boisterous squad, Pam place a protective arm round Louise's shoulders. Giving her a quick hug, she guided the girl from the room saying, "Come on, young lady. Let's get you settled into a nice hot bath, while I fix us all something to eat. Then, I think an early night's called for. You've had quite enough excitement for one day, what with all those great hairy men fighting over you … you lucky thing!"

Louise giggled, her eyes shining with happiness at finally being free of the sect and surrounded by normal people, for the first time in ages.

Grant paused in the act of clearing up empty beer cans and threw an amused glance in Pam's direction. "You're only jealous 'cos we weren't fightin' over you," he called after her.

"Is that so? I'll have you know I've had men fighting over me in the past, so there!" Pam flung over her shoulder, tossing her head coquettishly and winking at Louise at the same time.

"Yeah, me an' your ol' man, when I was tryin' t'get the shotgun away from him," Grant came back drily. "Then your mother jumped in an' the two of 'em beat me up an' forced me t'take you off their hands."

"Hah! You should be so lucky," Pam retorted in mock indignation. Then to the amused girl by her side she added, "Just ignore him, Louise honey. He can't help being a chauvinist pig. Maybe he'll go away if we pretend he's not here. C'mon, let's go run that bath …"

54

BY NIGHTFALL OF THE DAY FOLLOWING HIS devastating counterattack, Angel One decided that no retaliatory strike was forthcoming from the Mafia. Despite the undoubted crippling effect of his having wiped out the top leadership of the Neroni Family, he had been expecting some form of counterstrike – even had this only taken the form of a face-saving gesture. After all, there were other Families Neroni could surely approach for help. He had been faintly surprised that nothing of the sort had materialised.

In fact, as it turned out, the short vicious Mafia-Triad war was effectively at an end. Three factors had combined to stop the mutually destructive blood-letting.

The first was the receipt of clear warnings from police sources to Neroni that all protection was suspended and that unless he toed the line and ceased hostilities, pressure would be brought to bear on all the various criminal enterprises of the Family –

and of any other Family which got involved by joining forces with the Neroni clan.

The second, directly resulting from the first, was the delivery of equally clear message from a hastily convened council of the heads of the other New York Families, to the effect that no help would be forthcoming from them, in the event of any further hostilities between the Neroni Family and the Chinese.

The third was a phone call received by Angel One at Bethlehem House. It came from Dragon Control and was short and to the point. The caller, speaking Cantonese, had identified himself by a code word, then continued cryptically, "The Dragon and The Tiger will move tomorrow. Rendezvous at hour of goat. Location number eight. Repeat, please."

Angel One had done so and without further acknowledgement, the caller had hung up. The import of the message was to inform Angel One that the double consignment of heroin was being moved across the Canadian border the following night. Angel One's orders were to meet it and assume full responsibility at the appointed time and place, the latter being an isolated Triad-owned gas station a few miles south of the border.

In the empty conference room at Bethlehem House, the oriental was at that moment sitting deep in thought. During the recently ended meeting he had issued orders for the organisation's street pushers to re-establish themselves discreetly and under heavy guard by backup teams. Invaded territories were to be infiltrated again and retaken, by force if necessary, although wherever possible direct confrontation with Mafia personnel was to be avoided unless resistance was met.

Having set the wheels in motion for the rebuilding of his street distribution network, Angel One was now considering a couple of relatively minor problems. These were loose ends that required to be tied up, before he could concentrate his full attention on the important business of the impending shipment of heroin.

One was the report that the girl member the private detective Grant had spoken to at the Harlem van, sister Louise Wyatt, had been snatched on the street that afternoon by a gang of eight men wielding clubs. They had struck during the confusion caused by the simple diversionary tactic of throwing a smoke canister and firecrackers.

During the ensuing action, six sect personnel had been injured, including the Apostle in charge, Brother Mark. All the attackers had been masked except one, whom the injured Apostle was sure had been Grant himself. This would be investigated and if it turned out to be the case that Grant had indeed interfered again, retribution would be exacted.

The other loose end concerned Grant's partner in the firm of private investigators, the man Sherman. It seemed he too would have to be discouraged from any further attempt to interfere in sect affairs. Angel One considered this matter for a moment. Perhaps a little message should be sent ... a warning ... something which would leave Sherman in no doubt as to the fate of the snooper he had employed.

Courses of action decided for the solution to each problem, he rose to his feet and strode from the room. He intended to halt once and for all the run of ill-fortune that had been troubling his organisation, and at the same time clear the field for the biggest and most important drug consignment he had handled to date. It was equally important for him to gain face with the Director by a display of competence. No-one would be allowed to prevent his success in this.

55

THE FOLLOWING DAY PASSED UNEVENTFULLY FOR most of those concerned. Out at Bethlehem House, Jim Miller spent another long day in the solitary confinement of his basement cell, alternately dozing fitfully or pacing the limits of the four walls, worrying about his eventual fate. All the while, his nemesis, Angel One, completed preparations for the movement of the coming consignment later that night.

On the streets of the city, the crime rate had returned to what the NYPD regarded as normal in the two days since the mutual cessation of hostilities between the rival crime organisations. Curtis's men maintained their cold boring vigil, while for the remainder of the force it was business as usual, as they dealt with the daily crop of murders, rapes, muggings and robberies which kept the crime figures healthy, the courts busy, and the news media happy.

Brett Grant arranged for his current caseload to be covered by Perez and Ellis and took the rest of the day off in order to spend it at home with Pam and Louise. He had reasons for doing so. It would allow him to question Louise in detail about the sect and its organisation, and more importantly, all she knew concerning the layout and security arrangements of Bethlehem House.

Also, it meant he would be on hand to protect both females from any unwelcome visitors, if he had been recognised during the incident at the sect van. He was pretty sure the big black, Brother Mark, had recognised him when he had launched the attack from which Pete Larsen had saved him.

Lastly, he reckoned his absence from the office would have the effect of showing his continuing disapproval of what he still considered to be his senior partner's mercenary attitude in the matter of the bonus offer from Virgil Miller.

For Harry Sherman, the object of Brett Grant's disapproval, the day finished anything but uneventfully. Late in the afternoon he was clearing up the last of his paperwork before calling it a day, when Anna knocked his door and entered. She was wearing her coat and carrying in one hand the day's outgoing letters, which she was in the habit of mailing on her way home. In her other hand she held a small package, neatly wrapped in brown paper and roughly the size of a thick paperback book.

Advancing across the office, she laid the package on the blotter before Sherman. As she did so, she announced in her attractively accented speech, "This came for you a few minutes ago by special delivery, Mister Sherman. There was no sender's name." She glanced at the clock on the wall. "It is just after five o'clock, so if there is nothing else you wish for me to do, I will be off home."

For a moment, Sherman regarded the package with a puzzled frown, then his face cleared. "Ah yes, it'll probably be from Solly Levenson. I've bin expectin' to hear from him. Yes Anna, you run along. There's nothin' else needin' done, thanks." Then, as she turned to go, he added with a mischievous twinkle in his eyes, "An' I won' say anythin' about lockin' the outside door this time, I promise."

Exasperated, Anna looked back, caught the mischief in his eye and relaxed into a smile. "So, perhaps this evening I will forget, as you did not remind me," she rejoined tartly. "Auf wiedersehen." She gave him a little wave and left, drawing the door closed behind her.

Sherman began to unwrap the package Anna had left on his desk, and as he did so he heard the outer office door closing. The firm's other two detectives, Ellis and Perez, had left earlier in the afternoon, so he was alone in the office. Just him ... and the small cigar box lying on the desk blotter in front of him, in its nest of unfolded brown wrapping paper. He reached out to remove the elastic band which was holding the lid closed ... and paused, his hand hovering just above the box.

He felt suddenly reluctant to remove the elastic band and lift the lid. He didn't know why. A premonition? Nonsense! He shrugged the thought away. There were so many cranks around these days, it was natural to be careful, that was all.

Feeling slightly foolish at his hesitation, he picked the box up carefully, nevertheless, and weighed it in one hand. It was light, almost as thought it was empty. Gently he tilted it to one side. Nothing seemed to be loose inside. He tilted it the opposite way, with the same result. He shook it gingerly. Still nothing.

Shaking his head at his own foolishness, Sherman placed the box back on the blotter. Removing the elastic band, he flipped the lid open. The colour drained from his face as he stared down, shocked, at what lay exposed to his horrified gaze. The box contained only two objects, nestling side by side in the tissue paper packing. The room around Sherman ceased to exist as his vision tunnelled in on them.

The first object was a stiff perspex-covered I.D. card. It affirmed that the owner was a licensed private investigator and came complete with a photograph. From the glossy passport-sized snapshot, the face of Solly Levenson stared accusingly up at him. The surface of the perspex cover was smeared with dried blood.

The second object was a human finger. Even had the bloodstained I.D. card not been there, Sherman would have known with horrified certainty that the obscene piece of human debris was the little finger of Levenson's right hand. The ring still encircling it would have told him. It was a gold signet ring with an oval blue face; set into the blue enamel was a tiny gold menorah, the nine-branched candelabrum of Judaism. Sherman wore an identical ring on the little finger of his own right hand.

Time ceased to exist for Sherman and the minutes crawled by unnoticed as he stared unseeingly at the grisly evidence of Levenson's untimely death. His mind accepted without any doubt that Levenson was dead. Worse, Sherman also had to accept that he himself had caused his old friend's demise.

Blindly he reached down and pulled open a drawer of his desk. He lifted out the pint of scotch he kept handy for entertaining clients, followed by an empty glass. Acting like an automaton, he poured and swallowed, poured and swallowed … He hardly tasted the fiery liquor as it seared its way down. He felt its warmth vaguely, but it failed to melt the icy winter of grief which had gripped his soul.

As he drank, he stared mesmerised at the ring on the bloodless grey finger … and remembered. Remembered how there had existed only six of these rings in the entire world. Remembered the six fit and tanned youngsters in their late teens, forced by the tide of history into becoming Haganah freedom fighters in the army of the fledgling State of Israel. Remembered the danger-ous days in a sun-baked land, when comradeship had meant so much in the face of the ever-present threat of violent death.

These six, all close friends, had formed a secret death-squad, sworn to hunt down and kill the Arab terrorists who indiscriminately maimed and killed Jewish civilians in those far off terrible days of mutual genocide, as the new-born Israeli state fought desperately for its very existence against overwhelming odds. They had code named their group The Maccabee Six, after the ancient heroes who delivered ancient Judea from the Syrian persecutions of 175-164 B.C.

As a symbol of their secret covenant, they had commissioned the old Jewish goldsmith in his backstreet Jaffa shop to make them six identical rings, each bearing the menorah design. The menorah device they had adopted because of its association with the Hanukkah, the Feast of Dedication, the eight-day Jewish festival commemorating the Maccabees.

Long after the successful conclusion of the 1948 war, much fighting and killing later, only two of the original six had survived. They had remained close friends, emigrating to the United States together in the late 'fifties, having become sickened by the continuing pattern of terrorist-inspired slaughter, followed inevitably by massive Israeli counterstrike and overkill, which seemed destined to become unending.

The two surviving friends had made their separate ways as naturalised American citizens, eventually ending up in the private investigation business. Levenson had followed Sherman's example in this and they had remained close and valued friends. Levenson had remained freelance, but Sherman, the more enterprising, had established a successful firm and always made sure to put plenty of business his way.

Now, after all the dangers they had shared and survived together, Sherman had sent his old friend to his death, having chosen to ignore Grant's repeated warnings against tangling with these sect fanatics. His eyes blurred with hot tears, which ran unheeded down his lined cheeks to splash onto the surface of the desk blotter. It absorbed them as rapidly as his body was absorbing the neat spirit he was gulping down.

Suddenly the phone rang at his elbow, jerking him out of the alcohol induced self-pity that was gradually replacing his initial genuine grief for his murdered friend. The caller was his wife Miriam, to inquire why he hadn't come home or phoned to give a reason. Getting a grip on himself, Sherman apologised, saying he had been kept late by an unexpected development in an important case and had forgotten how late it was.

When his slightly slurred speech caused Miriam to ask sharply whether the 'important case' contained bottles, he forced a laugh and explained that his contact in this particular business was his old buddy Solly Levenson, so he'd had a few drinks with him. He pressed on before she could object, saying the details of the assignment were still to be completed and they'd do this over a snack at the local deli, then they'd probably wind up rehashing old times over a few more beers, so she needn't wait up for him.

Miriam grumbled a bit about the meal she'd cooked but didn't really object to his announcement of a night on the tiles. He didn't go out often and she knew it would be a welcome break for him. Admonishing him only to "eat well to soak up the booze – an' don't forget the way home – I know you an' Solly when you get to talking over old times," she rang off.

Tipping the bottle over the glass, Sherman saw he had just emptied out the last shot and it had been three-quarters full when he'd started. He tossed it down after the rest. The effect of speaking to his wife had not exactly sobered him up – he was more cold drunk than cold sober – but it had cleared his mind. He had made his excuses to her without really thinking about his reason for doing so. Now he knew why he had done it … had known all along … he was going to carry out one last mission on behalf of the Maccabee Six. For Solly. He would show these murdering bastards what it meant to tangle with old Haganah comrades-in-arms, just as many dead Arab terrorists had found to their cost in the past!

Pushing back his chair, he stood up and walked a little unsteadily over to stand before a replica Constable water-colour on the far wall. Depositing his empty glass on the grey steel filing cabinet to his left, he fumbled with the edge of the painting, then swung it outward on its hinged bracket to reveal a concealed wall safe behind it. Concentrating to combat the effects of the gutful of raw whisky he had consumed, he spun out the combination, swung open the compact door and reached inside. When his hand emerged, it held a snub-nosed Colt .38 revolver nestling snugly in its holster, and wrapped in its thin leather harness.

Slipping off his jacket, he donned the harness. As he adjusted the straps and felt the comforting weight of the gun against his chest, he experienced again the old thrill of battle-fever that used to grip him when preparing to go terrorist hunting, all those years ago in a different world – a different life, it seemed now from this distance in time.

Reaching into the safe again, Sherman lifted out a box of shells and walked over to sit at his desk. Drawing the gun, he broke it open and began to load it. His movements were deliberate and a little clumsy and twice he fumbled and dropped rounds onto the desktop, but eventually he accomplished his task. Snapping the revolver shut, he spun the chamber, thumbed on the safety and reholstered it. Scooping up the remaining loose rounds, he put them into his side pocket where he could reach them easily.

He sat for a moment gazing down at the open cigar box and its grisly contents. This time his eyes did not mist over with the pain of the loss he felt, but instead hardened imperceptibly. Then he reached out, flipped the lid shut and snapped the elastic band over it. Picking up the box, he locked it away in the middle drawer of his desk and drew the phone towards him.

Of necessity, private detectives, like their counterparts in the official police, have to mix with and get to know members of the criminal world. And in the criminal world, as in the straight world, money can buy you anything – and often much cheaper. A five minute phone call later, Sherman had negotiated a purchase and arranged to meet the supplier's agent with the agreed price in used bills, in an East Side bar. Pausing only to take the required sum from the wall-safe, he locked up and left.

Within twenty minutes of leaving the office, he met the contact in a shadowed corner booth of a dimly lit, smoke-filled bar. They nursed their beers long enough to make sure no-one was paying them any undue attention, then Sherman handed over the money and received a small, heavy package in return. The man, small and weasel faced, counted the bills quickly and expertly below the level of the table and slipped them into an inside pocket. He winked at Sherman conspiratorially.

"Enrico says to tell you he didn' know you wuz goin' into da fruit business." He grinned, exposing a mouthful of gold fillings, then in a more serious tone he added quietly, "He says it's none of his business, but if you're usin' dese things y'self, he says t'remember pineapples go boom in a circle. Dey ain' fussy who dey take out, he says."

Sherman stared at him coldly. "Tell Enrico he's right. It ain't none of his goddam business. But fer his information, the client these are for has used 'em more times than Enrico's had spaghetti fer dinner," he replied acidly.

Weasel face spread his hands in a placatory gesture. "Sure, sure ... no offence meant, Mister Sherman. Tell you one thing though," he added, "I'm glad t'be rid of dese fuckin' things. Dey gimme da creeps. So, if y'don' mind, I'll split while I'm still in one piece."

Two hours later, a half empty bag of sandwiches on the seat beside him along with a half empty pint of scotch, Sherman had pulled into a deserted lay-by, well north of the city. Resting on his lap was the compact bulk of the package, which he was in the process of unwrapping. Tearing off the thick brown paper and sticky tape, he revealed a small shoe box of a size that had contained children's shoes. The box was also taped shut.

Bursting the tape with a fingernail, Sherman lifted off the lid to expose the two US Army-issue hand-grenades nestling snugly in their bed of wadded paper. The dim light from the instrument panel glinted dully on their segmented metal casings, and allowed Sherman to check that the release levers were securely held in place by their ring-pull safety-pins.

Absently reaching for the whisky, Sherman unscrewed the cap and took a long pull from the neck of the bottle. Feeling the warmth flooding down his insides, he picked up one of the grenades with his free hand. He hefted it, getting used to the old familiar shape and weight again. Another swallow of whisky, and the memories came flooding back into his inebriated mind, borne on the fumes of the fiery golden liquor. He sat for long minutes, staring unseeing out through the windscreen, his mind's eye flitting from the black frosty night outside, back to the sun-baked Galilee hills, remembering again how it had been ...

Recollecting himself with an effort, Sherman replaced the grenade and slid the box into the dash compartment. Another drink, then the last surviving member of the Maccabee Six recapped the bottle, steered the car back onto the highway and resumed his journey towards Bethlehem House ... and his revenge mission for Solly Levenson.

56

IT WAS AROUND TWO A.M. WHEN SHERMAN, HIS smouldering anger well fuelled by neat whisky, completed his quick survey of the front gates of Bethlehem House and the long stretches of chain link fence to either side of them. The gates and fence were too high for him to climb, so he decided to cut his way through the fence using the wire-cutters from his car toolbox.

Wading through the waist-high grass and scrub of the roadside, he crossed the highway and returned to where he had left the car concealed among denser cover, some forty yards back on the opposite verge. There, the overgrown roadside tangle was chest high in places, and his car was hidden to its roof.

A few minutes later, he was trotting unsteadily back across the blacktop clutching the cutters, his coat pockets weighed down by the bulky shape of the grenades. He had no clear idea of any plan of campaign in his drink-fuddled mind, only a burning resolve to gain entry to the grounds somehow, and exact revenge for the death of his old friend and comrade by killing those responsible.

It was then, just as he regained the cover of the scrub alongside the chain link fence, that he heard the sound of a vehicle engine carried to him on the chill night wind. Staring north up the long straight highway arrowing down through the Catskills from the distant Canadian border, he saw the gleam of headlights in the far distance. Shielding his watering eyes from the biting wind with a raised hand, it soon became evident to him that two vehicles were approaching, travelling close together.

Even half smashed out of his skull as he was, Sherman still retained a shred of the caution instilled in him by his chosen profession. Whether or not the oncoming vehicles belonged to the sect, instinct told him to avoid being seen hanging around suspiciously, and he ducked down out of sight. He had no sooner done so, than the tell-tale whine of descending gears told him that the approaching vehicles were dropping speed with the intention of turning in at the gates.

Keeping low, Sherman moved at a crouching run to within twenty yards of the gates. Beyond that, the grass and scrub had been cut short on either side of the entranceway. Squinting through the latticework of a dense clump of scrub, he watched the approaching vehicles. The one in the lead was compact and squat, roughly the size of a camper. It was dwarfed by the one following, which was a semi and trailer.

Sherman's heart was pounding from a combination of excitement and unaccustomed exercise. For a moment everything blurred dizzily as a wave of nausea shuddered through him, leaving him in a cold sweat. When his vision cleared, the big rig was pulling up in a hiss of air-brakes just short of the gates, but the van was cruising slowly past his hiding place, a small gold cross logo on its side panel glinting in the moonlight.

Turning his head, he watched the van slow to a halt fifty yards or so further on, almost level with where he had concealed his car, then it swung round in a U-turn and cruised slowly back towards the gates. It was obviously checking to make sure the coast was clear for some reason.

Following the van's manoeuvre, it occurred to Sherman that it was strange behaviour for members of a supposed religious cult to be carrying out at dead of night. But his drink-fuelled anger and desire for vengeance pushed his detective's curiosity to the back of his mind for later consideration. Right now, his whole interest in the movements of the sect vehicles was in the possibility of sneaking in through the gates in their wake. Keeping his head well down, Sherman ignored the protests from his stiff joints and long disused leg and back muscles, as he held his crouched posture. He saw the small van pull over and stop this side of the gates and facing the big rig. Suddenly the van's rear door opened and five men scrambled out. All were armed, two with snub-nosed machine guns and the other three with M16 rifles fitted with bulky night scopes. The armed men fanned out swiftly and formed a tight semi-circle, all facing outwards.

As soon as the gunmen were in position, the van flashed its lights at its large companion up ahead. On this signal, the big truck moved forward and turned slowly into the short entranceway leading from the highway, and braked to a halt before the gates. Sherman read the lettering on its side – NATIONAL BIBLE SOCIETY OF AMERICA.

As Sherman watched, the gates began to swing silently open, and the small van edged forward to close the gap between itself and the larger vehicle. Simultaneously, the armed guards began to retreat inwards, tightening their perimeter with well practised efficiency.

At that moment, a sixth figure climbed from the passenger door of the van and surveyed the scene, looking up and down the deserted highway. A pistol dangled loosely from his right hand by his side. In the pale moonlight, Sherman saw that this man, obviously in command, was an oriental. Probably Sung, the bastard who had threatened Brett ... the thought flared through Sherman's alcohol inflamed brain ... and probably the bastard who had killed Solly Levenson!

This conclusion ignited his smouldering anger into a blaze of unreasoning fury and hate directed against the probable murderer of his old comrade-in-arms. He was not aware of removing the two grenades from his pockets. They just seemed to materialise in his hands as, through the red mist of rage which clouded the edges of his vision, he saw the object of his hatred signal to the driver of the rig to move through the gates.

The big sixteen wheeler's engine revved as it rolled forward and the demon in Sherman's brain screamed, "Now!"

Straightening up, he pulled the pin from the first grenade and lobbed it in the direction of the enemy.

"That's fer Solly Levenson, ya murderin' fuckers!" he roared … and ripping the safety pin away, he lobbed the second grenade.

He had a timeless glimpse of six heads jerking round, six pairs of eyes locking onto his dark shape, six gun barrels whipping round to blast him out of existence, then he threw himself flat, covering his ears and pressing himself into the unyielding earth beneath him.

An instant later the two grenades exploded in quick succession and the night erupted in flame and thunder.

The first one bounced off the roof of the van, landed in the road beyond and detonated, scything down all six gunmen, chopping their mangled legs from under them. The second grenade rolled under the moving bulk of the sixteen wheeler before exploding directly behind the cab.

The effect of the twin explosions on the vehicles was devastating. The van was lifted bodily into the air and flung violently into the rear doors of the larger vehicle. The blast of the second grenade under the rig itself, severed the coupling between cab and trailer. The cab, its tyres shredded, swerved into one of the gateposts, and was then crushed almost flat by the huge trailer, which ploughed into its rear.

Miraculously neither vehicle caught fire. But gobbets of burning oil-caked dirt were shaken loose from their undersides, to scatter around in little flaming piles like candles at a wake. This, and the two wrecked vehicles locked together in their death embrace, surrounded by a ring of mutilated, bleeding bodies, was the sight which greeted Sherman when he scrambled to his feet. Pulling the gun from its holster, he surveyed the carnage.

His first reaction was a thrill of savage satisfaction. He moved forward quickly, ears still ringing from the deafening double blast, intending to put a bullet in the brain of the oriental, should he have survived the attack. He was saved the bother. The man was obviously dead. One eye and part of his face was missing, messily sliced away by a whirling chunk of shrapnel.

Suddenly Sherman's drink-induced elation evaporated and he felt sick.

The crumpled victims were not all dead, though. Faintly, but growing in intensity as his ears cleared, Sherman heard the screams of two injured men sprawling in lacerated agony a few yards apart and he decided enough was enough. Help would be arriving very soon. Doubtless the explosions would have been heard from the house itself.

Turning to go, Sherman's eye fell on the gaping rear doors of the rig, evidently forced open under the impact of the van crashing into them ... and on the dozen or so large cardboard cartons which had tumbled from the opening to the ground. One of the cartons had burst open, spilling its contents – books and oblong shaped plastic bags full of white powder.

Alarm bells shrilled in Sherman's head. He stumbled forward and knelt down beside the spilled bags and books. The legend on the side of the damaged carton read BIBLES – COURTESY OF THE NATIONAL BIBLE SOCIETY OF AMERICA, and he saw the scattered books were indeed bibles. But it was the powder filled plastic bags they had been concealing that interested him. Reaching down, he burst open one of the bags with the foresight of his gun.

Even as he dabbed a moistened finger into the powder within, he knew what he would find. It would explain the presence of so many armed men. Sherman recognised the bitter, numbing taste instantly – a knowledge of dangerous drugs was useful in his profession. It was pure heroin!

Swiftly he burst open another of the big cartons lying nearby. His suspicions were confirmed when the double layer of bibles spilled out onto the ground, revealing the tightly packed kilo bags of heroin underneath. A glance into the gaping doors explained why Grant and Levenson had run into so much apparently mindless violence and death. The trailer was packed to the roof with cartons similar to the damaged one, all purporting to contain copies of the Holy Book. At a very rough estimate, he reckoned that he was looking at a heroin shipment with a street value of several hundred million dollars, once it had been cut and distributed.

A sudden premonition of danger struck him, sobering him more effectively than a cold shower. He was very conscious now that he and Brett were up to their necks in a dangerous situation … and involved with very dangerous people. His first priority right then was to get clear before any more of the sect fanatics arrived on the scene. As this thought occurred to him, he snatched up one of the plastic bags and rose stiffly to his feet.

Stepping round the prostrate bodies and closing his ears to the harrowing cries of the two injured men, Sherman reached the edge of the highway and automatically checked in both directions before crossing. To the south it was deserted. But when he glanced north the cold hand of fear clutched at his guts. Far off in the distance, the twin pinpoints of approaching headlights could be seen. And he knew with certainty the oncoming vehicle would belong to the enemy.

Fear galvanised him into motion. Forcing his ageing limbs into a shambling run, he crossed the highway and plunged into the cover of the roadside tangle. Fighting down a feeling of rising panic, he ducked low and ploughed his way through the tall grass to where he had hidden the car. His one intent now was to get away from the scene and present his evidence to Ben Curtis. That way, the whole affair could be passed to the official police. He and Brett were in deep shit way over their heads and he wanted them out – while they still had their heads attached to their bodies!

His fear cleared the cobwebs of alcohol from his mind and drove his tiring limbs to greater efforts, as he fought his way through the snagging underbrush to reach his car. Whatever had happened to Solly Levenson – and the bloodless severed finger they had sent suggested he hadn't exactly been invited to a tea-party – would be nothing compared to what would in store for him, if he were captured by these dangerous people.

His fear was well justified. Nemesis, in the person of Angel One, was at that moment approaching the scene, riding in a third van identical to the one that had been escorting the drugs shipment. It had been following a few minutes behind the other two vehicles, in order to prevent any attempt to tail them.

Sobbing for breath, the muscles of his back and legs burning from the strain of moving in a crouched posture, he reached the car and wrenched open the door. About to duck into the driving seat, he raised his head sufficiently to see over the top of the tall weeds, and glanced back up the road. His heart pounding from a combination of fear and exertion, he saw the squat shape of the newly arrived van pulling up alongside the smoking wreckage of the first two vehicles. Even as he watched, several armed figures poured from the van and quickly spread out to examine the damaged trailer and sprawled bodies.

Sherman watched them for a few seconds, wondering whether they would climb back into their vehicle and head towards his position, in an attempt to pursue whoever had attacked their comrades. However, it quickly became clear they intended to do no such thing, when the one in charge barked out an order and the rest immediately moved to take up defensive positions alongside the damaged vehicles.

He decided to get out while he could. Throwing the plastic bag of heroin onto the passenger seat, he scrambled behind the wheel and pulled the door shut. He reckoned his only chance was to rely on the speed of the big powerful Chevy to outrun any pursuit. The engine started first time, for which he breathed a silent prayer of thanks and he rolled the car forward through the curtain of weeds, angling it towards the highway until it was only inches from the edge of the blacktop.

He shot a quick glance back over his shoulder to make sure nothing was bearing down on him, then he gunned the engine and the car surged powerfully forward, bursting from the roadside tangle onto the road surface. The tyres spun, smoking for an instant as they sought for a grip on the frost-spangled blacktop, then the big car shot forward. Its back end swung sickeningly for a heart-stopping few yards, before straightening up and bearing its sweating hunched driver towards the haven of the distant city.

57

STANDING ON THE ROADWAY OUTSIDE THE GATES
of Bethlehem House, Angel One was in a homicidal fury. He
had arrived minutes behind the drug shipment and its well-
armed escort, making sure no-one was tailing it to its destination,
only to find the devastation wrought by Sherman's lethal surprise
attack. His first priority, he decided, was damage limitation.
Get the shipment safely into the house, in case the attack should
be renewed ... also the dead and injured would have to be
removed inside, as well as the damaged vehicles.

Moving into action, he ordered the five sect heavies who had
arrived with him to take up defensive positions beside the
wrecked vehicles. Once they were in position, covering the road
with their guns and alert for any further attack from the darkness
around them, he contacted Control by radio and summoned
immediate assistance from the house.

One of the wounded gave a sudden shrill cry of pain, and
Angel One glanced over at the scattered broken bodies. He had
noted during his first inspection of the scene that his Triad
subordinate Angel Three was among the dead. With his other
fellow oriental, Angel Two, temporarily out of action and
confined to manning Control by the injuries he had sustained
during the attack on the Golden Lotus, Angel One's top
leadership was now sorely depleted.

Who had carried out this latest attack on his organisation? It
could only be the scum of the hated Mafia enemy. Then he
imagined the gloating reaction of the Controller back at Dragon
HQ, when he heard the news of this latest disaster, and rage
welled up inside him as he stood there in the cold night air.

Suddenly these thoughts were wiped from his mind as
Sherman's car burst from the roadside scrub up ahead and
roared off, tyres screeching and rear end swerving, in the
direction of New York. Its appearance was so unexpected it
took them all by surprise. Not one shot was squeezed off after
it, as it raced off into the darkness. At that same moment however,
blazing head lamps racing down the driveway from the house

heralded the swift arrival of four van loads of reinforcements.

Angel One's rage was instantly supplanted by exaltation. Retribution would be swift on the perpetrators of this latest outrage. And if, as he suspected, it turned out to be the Neroni Family, he vowed to wage all-out war on them. He would exterminate them like the vermin they were, thereby teaching their fellow Mafia families a never-to-be-forgotten lesson that going to war with the Triads was suicidal!

He decided to retain two van loads of personnel to help clear up the damage, but the leading two vans he waved out past the piled up vehicles to draw up alongside him on the highway. Indicating the fast dwindling tail-lights in the distance, he barked out his orders to the occupants of the two vans for the pursuit. The enemy was to be taken alive, if possible ... but wiped out, if for any reason capture proved either impossible or impracticable. The souped-up engines bayed their mechanised empathy with Angel One's fury to the night sky as the two van loads of human hounds took up the chase.

Within minutes, the quarry, grey-faced and sweating as fear drove the alcohol from the pores of his body, knew from the ominous sight of twinned headlights far back in his rear-view mirror that they were after him. Pressing his foot to the floor, he concentrated grimly on holding the road as the needle crept round to the limit of the speedo dial.

As the white lane markings blurred towards him, he prayed for a bit of the same divine assistance which had pulled Moses out of a similar tight spot, when pursued by Pharaoh's army in the exodus from Egypt. Nothing so spectacular as pillars of fire or cloud, was Harvey Sherman's heartfelt plea to the God of Israel that night ... just the gift of a few extra horsepower. But Yahweh must have been having problems with the contentious bunch of His chosen people in the Middle East that night, because the desperate plea of one lone, middle-aged, frightened Jew went unanswered.

Fifteen minutes later, Sherman knew with a growing sense of despair that he wasn't going to make it. Fast though his ageing

Chevy was, the vehicles on his tail were marginally faster. They had steadily overhauled him after they had roared through the sleeping township of Rockford. His faint hopes that their speeding vehicles would be spotted by some zealous Highway Patrol car were diminishing with each unfolding mile of the unending deserted highway, which sped under his wheels in the glare of the head lamps.

His last remaining hope of survival lay in his ability to prevent the pursuing vehicles from drawing alongside, or overtaking him. There were two of them – they would be able to box him in front and rear and force him to a halt. Or they may just pick their spot and ram him off the road at speed. The squat vans were heavier than his car. They would win any trial of strength in a sideswiping contest.

Soon the glare of headlights in his rear-view mirror was threatening to dazzle him and destroy his night vision, as the nearest pursuer inexorably narrowed the gap between them. To prevent this, he reached up a hand knocked the mirror out of alignment. The two pursuing vehicles were almost in overtaking position now … almost within striking distance! The interior of the Chevy was brightly lit by the blaze of the following headlights.

A few seconds later his worst fears were realised when he was jolted back violently in his seat, as the vehicle immediately behind rammed his rear fender. He fought to control the wheel as the back end swung ominously on the frosty road surface. Again the following van smashed into his rear fender … and again! Then the roadway alongside him lit up as his assailant pulled out to overtake.

"Oh no y'don't, ya bastard!" Sherman grated through clenched teeth, and swung the wheel over recklessly. The Chevy swerved in front of the overtaking van and he was rewarded by another crunching jolt, this time from the region of his rear wing. Again he had to fight to control his wildly swerving car, but this time he had the satisfaction of seeing the following lights swinging equally crazily, as the enemy van swerved dangerously on the icy road surface and dropped back.

But the respite was only temporary. This time, after a few

more mutually dangerous collisions, the enemy changed tactics. The entire roadway behind and alongside him lit up as the second van pulled out to run alongside the first, and they came after him abreast on the long straight highway. Now, Sherman knew with a sinking feeling, it would be only a matter of time before one of them managed to overtake, while the other kept him fighting for control of his car by repeatedly ramming him from behind.

Sherman's stomach stirred queasily as they topped a slight rise at speed. He glanced at his speedometer – the needle was hovering on the 120 m.p.h. mark. Then, as his flicked back to the long straight swoop down a gentle decline ahead, hope soared anew in his breast. There, a few hundred yards up front, were the rear lights of what was obviously a large truck, judging by the riding lights on the sides and top corners, in addition to the normal tail-lights, showing its dimensions to following drivers.

Maybe he'd be able to run alongside this big rig for a time, using it as a shield and denying his pursuers the opportunity of killing or capturing him, until he could devise a way of shaking them off. He gambled on their being reluctant to press home their attack before a witness. All truckers carried C.B. radios, and that could mean a call being made to the police.

Closing on the rig, Sherman was given the go ahead to overtake by the driver flicking his tail-lights off and on. He pulled out just in time to prevent the van on his offside rear wing from pulling alongside, in an attempt to box him in. Instead, it was forced to give way and drop back, where it slotted in behind its companion again. Then he was creeping up the seemingly endless length of the towering sixteen-wheeled monster. He eased off on the gas as he did so, deliberately delaying his overtaking, intending to run alongside its roaring bulk for as long as possible.

However, after a couple of minutes of this, the truck driver, irritated by his slowness in overtaking, blared his horn in warning and Sherman heard the hiss of applied air-brakes. The big truck began to slide away behind him, as it slackened speed, the driver evidently assuming the Chevy did not have the power to overtake him quickly enough.

At the same moment, Sherman saw the fast approaching lights of an oncoming vehicle on the opposite carriageway. He had no choice now but to leave the temporary shelter of the big rig, so he pushed his foot to the floor again and felt the old Chevy respond gallantly, surging forward to leave the trailing vehicles well behind.

As the oncoming vehicle, another truck, roared past on the opposite side of the highway leaving the way ahead clear again, Sherman considered staying just ahead of the rig he had overtaken, but quickly abandoned the idea. He decided on reflection that it would not stop the fanatics who were after him from resuming their attack. He had hit them hard and had seen too much. There was no way they would allow him to escape with the dangerous knowledge he now possessed about their drug dealing and other activities. Involving the truck driver, he realised, would only serve to get the guy killed too. These people would stop at nothing. They had proved that with Solly Levenson's murder.

All too soon they were on him again. Through the night they raced, jockeying for position, the vans resuming their determined attempts to ram him off the road or force him to stop. It had developed into a grim contest of nerve, with death awaiting the loser. The lights of the rig were far back in the distance, and the long straight highway ahead showed no signs of any other vehicles. The sect drivers now redoubled their efforts, with increasing recklessness and purpose.

Sherman felt himself tiring, felt his concentration flagging, betrayed from within by the treachery of the bottled ally which had earlier so fortified and encouraged him in his dangerous mission. Hand in hand with his exhaustion, despair began to creep up on him, sapping his will to resist. He couldn't hold out much longer. One lapse on his part, one slip, and they would have him. He felt it would end soon, one way or another. And it did.

He remembered his gun. A surge of irrational hope replaced his despair. His old warrior's mind began to function again. If he let one of the vans draw alongside, he could shoot the driver through the window, before he had the chance to sideswipe the

Chevy off the road. That would leave only one van to deal with, drastically reducing the odds against him.

He rolled down his window. The icy rush of air blew the last cobwebs of alcoholic lethargy from his mind, blasting away the self-defeating fatigue which had been draining his fighting spirit. His anger was rekindled against the evil, murderous organisation who were prepared to kill and kill again, to protect their filthy trade of peddling slow death to the kids on the streets of America.

In his wing mirror he saw the van behind the one on his tail pull out, overtake its twin and keep coming. He knew they would expect him to swing out to block it from overtaking him in turn, but this time he would surprise them by doing the unexpected. He would allow the oncoming vehicle to pull alongside, then he would strike back and seize the initiative. He watched the front of the overtaking van creep into his peripheral vision, and as it did so he released one hand from the wheel, reached for his shoulder holster and drew his gun.

It was at this precise instant, when he was steering one handed and in the act of clearing the gun from its holster, that the following van rammed him again. The wheel jerked out of his grasp, then spun crazily as he lost control of it and the car went into a screeching, tyre-smoking 100 m.p.h. spin.

Frantically Sherman grabbed for the wildly spinning wheel, his gun tumbling unheeded to the floor at his feet. His one chance was to try and steer out of the spin, but before he could even attempt this, the Chevy was rammed again. This time the deliberately timed collision sent the spinning car careering off the road, to smash through a crash barrier like it was made of balsa wood and plunge down a long rock-strewn slope.

The forest had receded from the road at this point, and the trees were sparse and scattered due to the rocky nature of the ground. The Chevy bucked madly in its death throes as it bounced and skidded madly from one rocky outcrop to another, shedding pieces of tortured metal, a door and a tyre as it went.

Inside, Sherman was flung about helplessly like a rag-doll, before being catapulted violently forward over the steering wheel. His forehead met the upper frame of the windscreen with stunning force, his upper body rammed hard into the steering column and agony speared through him as he felt something break inside his chest. Wetness flooded down into his eyes, misting his sight with red and as consciousness faded, he realised it was his own blood that was blinding him. His last thought before blackness swallowed him was to wonder sadly if his Miriam would forgive him for lying to her …

Then the inevitable happened. Still travelling at around 60 m.p.h., the car slewed sideways, hit a large angled slab of rock broadside on, and tipped over. Skidding up the short incline on its side in a shower of sparks and glass fragments, the car sailed over the eight foot drop at the slab's outer edge, as though from the ramp of a ski jump. It barrel-rolled lazily twice in mid-air, before finally plunging to a metal-crunching stop upside down against the base of a big solitary pine tree.

A moment of wheel-spinning silence followed, in which could be clearly heard the chilling sound of petrol trickling from a ruptured tank. Then the car rocked on its flattened roof as it exploded into roaring flames, which engulfed it in seconds.

The dancing light of the blazing furnace into which the car's interior had been instantly converted, showed the shadowy moving figures of the eight sect fanatics, as they bounded and slid their way down the long slope from the roadside where they had parked their vans. Reaching the scene, they stopped short in a loose line some twenty yards away, shielding their faces from the intense heat with upraised arms.

The leader of the group called out, "Can anyone see if the fucker's in there?"

Several of them squatted low and squinted past their upraised arms in a vain attempt to penetrate the curtain of flames belching from the open buckled doors and smashed windows, trying for a glimpse of their victim's charred body in the white-hot interior.

"Nah. Can't see fuck all," called back one of the others, straightening up. "Do you wan' I should go git the extinguishers from the vans?"

The leader shook his head. "Waste of time. By the time y'got back here, it would've burned itself out." He glanced around at the wild, broken landscape to either side of them. "While we're waitin' fer that to happen, spread out an' check to see if maybe the fucker got thrown clear. If he has been, an' he's still alive, Archangel Michael wants him bad. If we don' find him, we wait till the car's burned out, so we kin check what's left of him. One way or the other, we gotta be sure before we report back. Okay, move it!"

Moments later, a shout brought them all together again grouped around the sprawled body of Sherman. He lay at his discoverer's feet, some thirty-odd yards off to the left and back up the slope, where he had been flung from the gap of the missing door, when the car had barrel-rolled off the big angled slab of rock. A quick check revealed he was still breathing, then his examiner straightened up and handed the leader the unconscious man's pocket-book.

Inspecting the contents, the Apostle pulled out the private investigator's licence and I.D. card. His face screwed up as he peered at the typescript in the flickering light of the flames.

"Well, whaddaya know ..." he looked up triumphantly. "We've got us another private dick! But this one's kinda special. This one ..." he spat on Sherman and kicked his defenceless form viciously in the side, "only happens t'be a partner of that bastard Grant that's bin givin' us so much hassle lately."

He grinned evilly down at his unconscious victim and kicked him again. "Archangel Michael's gonna jes' love takin' you apart, asshole ... an' your pal Grant'll be next on the list."

He nodded down at the prostrate form. "Okay ... pick 'im up," he ordered, "an' let's git 'im back to base before he dies on us, so Archangel Michael kin git to work on him."

Four of the sect thugs were in the act of stooping to grasp a limb each, when the whole group was shocked into instant immobility by the sudden roar of a shotgun going off close by and the screaming blast of its lethal discharge whistling overhead. The stunned silence which followed was broken by the menacing sound of a pump-action mechanism being worked to reload. To a man, the entire group spun round to face this unexpected threat – and a drawling voice sounded clearly and unhurriedly from the darkness of the slope above them.

"I hate t'spoil the party, but the first fucker who moves without my permission'll git t'meet a whole passel of archangels ... the gen-u-ine articles!"

As they peered into the darkness searching for the speaker, the quiet voice continued remorselessly. "Now, jes' back up real slow an' easy. I'm awful nervous, an' this baby's got another four shells in her belly an' one up the spout. Anyone who tries t'git smart, gits dead!"

At last the owner of the voice became visible to the group as their eyes adjusted, now that they were facing away from the bright flames. Just beyond the limits of the flickering pool of light cast by the burning car, a tall figure stood, straddle-legged and decidedly unnervous looking, on the slope above them. He had taken up a stance on the outer edge of the big slab of rock over which the car had plunged and the flames reflected red on the black leather jacket and peaked cap he wore. They also glinted on the shortened barrel of the pump-action shotgun, with which he was covering them.

The stranger's stance was firm and commanding, one foot slightly advanced, bracing him against the gun's recoil. His grip on the weapon was also firm, despite the seemingly casual way he cradled it, as they could tell by the unwavering black eye of the muzzle which stared so menacingly down at them.

The threatening figure, clad entirely in black from his boots and denims to the distinctive leather jacket and peaked cap, the latter set squarely over the lean, sallow face with its long sideburns and Burt Reynolds moustache, would have been instantly recognised by Jim Miller. He would have recognised him as one of the four truckers he had met in the roadside truck stop, the night of his abortive escape – the silent one called 'Chuck' by the others.

Chuck – originally christened Carl Beaufort Wood 32 years previously, had been bombing quite contentedly along making good time, perched high in the cab of his big sixteen wheeler, hauling a load of frozen beef down from Canada for the meat markets of New York. As he steered the big roaring monster through the night, he had been combating the boredom of the long night haul by rapping with other truckers on the C.B. airwaves.

Approaching Rockford, he recalled his friend and fellow

trucker, Rocky O'Rourke, telling him of the private detective named Grant, who had been trying to track down the strangely dressed kid they had met in the truck stop the other night. The shamus wanted them to keep an eye open for anything unusual happening around this stretch of road, which could possibly be attributed to the weird religious sect he was convinced were holding the boy against his will.

He had made a point of stopping by the same truck stop as that other night, but this time his three buddies were all either on other routes or on time-off, so he was on his own. Finishing his meal, he had set out again on the final stage of his long haul south, keeping his eyes peeled as promised. But by the time he had cleared Rockford, he had decided nothing untoward was going to happen that night.

Then, in his mirrors, he had seen the three sets of headlights breasting a rise some distance behind him. The two rearmost vehicles seemed to be chasing the one in front, in some crazy game of high speed tag. They had even driven side by side in a two-pronged attempt to force a way past the single vehicle, but it had retaliated by swerving recklessly to thwart each attempt. His attention had been diverted from the C.B. traffic by their antics.

When the lead vehicle, a big Chevrolet, had come within overtaking distance, Chuck had flicked his lights in the universally recognised signal giving the other driver the go-ahead to pull out and pass him. This the driver had started to do, but had then decided to start playing assholes again, running alongside his rig instead of pulling ahead.

Chuck knew his big 20 tonner was in absolutely no danger from any collision with the car, but he had no intention of spending hours being questioned by the police, as to how some stupid jerk had managed to mince himself and his car under his sixteen wheels. So, he had leaned on his horn and touched the brakes to slacken speed, in order to force the other driver to pull ahead. If the Chevy driver had any different ideas, they were quickly dispelled by the lights of the fast approaching vehicle up ahead.

As the Chevy had pulled away, Chuck had caught a quick

glimpse of the driver's hunched form crouched over the wheel and it had conveyed a fleeting impression of desperation rather than of someone enjoying a high spirited race. This impression was strengthened by the determined manner in which the two chasing vehicles gunned past him, cutting in arrogantly so as to cause him to touch the brakes again, before they raced off in pursuit of the distant tail-lights of the Chevy.

The two identical squat vans had taken on a menacing air to Chuck, as he watched them overhaul their quarry ... like wolves running down a prey, he thought. Again he heard Rocky telling them to be on the lookout for any strange events in this area ... so, he tramped down on the gas again and the big rig surged forward, keeping the three vehicles in sight far up ahead.

For the next few miles he had watched the interplay of tail-lights, as the pursuing vans interchanged constantly, still apparently trying to overtake the Chevy. Suddenly Chuck had sucked his breath in sharply around the thin cheroot in his clenched teeth, as the inevitable happened. He had seen the flash of spiralling headlights once, twice, three times, indicating that one of the vehicles had gone into an uncontrollable spin. Then the wildly swinging lights had veered off sharply to the right, and slashed the night in a crazily jerking motion as the vehicle had plunged off the highway.

Seconds later the ugly glare of fire had blossomed far down the slope, clearly seen even from a distance through the thinning trees. From what he had seen of the interplay between the three vehicles, Chuck felt sure that the lone car had been deliberately forced off the road.

Without thinking about what he might be getting into, he eased off his speed preparatory to braking to a stop. At the same time he reached for the mike of his C.B. radio. Keying the button, he had interrupted the casual chatter of the other truckers who were scattered over the state road network.

"This is breaker five-oh-nine cuttin' in with a thirty-three," he announced, letting everyone know the interruption was due to an emergency. Knowing he would have gained their immediate attention, he went on without pause, "Black Knight here again, good buddies. I got me a ten thirty-four, an' it looks like it could be a heavy ten thirty-one ..."

He spoke incisively, using the 'ten code' of the C.B. airwaves, informing his listeners firstly that he had trouble on his hands and needed help urgently, adding that the trouble could even be a serious crime in progress.

He had continued, "My twenty's about five miles south of Rockford, an' I'd sure appreciate it if one of you breakers could airmail me some bears an' a blood wagon. Three hogs jes' blew m'doors off a few minutes back playin' tag, an' two of 'em's jes' forced the third hog off the blacktop. His wagon's like a fourth of July celebration. Sure hope he still ain' inside it, or he's permanently ten-seven. I intend goin' in close to eyeball the situation. Over."

Covering the last few hundred yards, he had seen several shadowy figures leave the two parked vans and go leaping and slithering down the rocky, tree-dotted slope towards the blazing wreck below. As he had slowed to a stop, Chuck had been assured by his fellow truckers over the air that the requested aid would be forthcoming.

Gliding the big truck to an easy stop with a quiet hiss of air brakes, Chuck had reached behind his seat and unclipped the sawn-off pump-action shotgun he kept there for his protection against the ever present threat of hijack merchants. Climbing from the high cab, he jumped the last few feet lightly to the ground. A quick check on the two parked vans twenty yards further on, showed them to be empty.

Stepping through the gap in the broken crash barrier, Chuck had made his way swiftly and surefootedly in the dark by the light of the leaping flames below, down to where eight figures were grouped loosely round a prostrate figure on the ground at their feet. Catfooting up onto the lip of a big sloping rock, he had arrived just in time to see one of the group driving his foot viciously into the unconscious man's side. Then he had heard the assailant order the others to pick up their unconscious victim.

The references to "Archangel Michael" and "Grant" had decided him that these characters were probably members of the weird sect he had been asked to look out for, and that they meant no good by the unfortunate private detective they had captured. From the remark made by the leader of the group, Chuck realised that their victim must be a colleague of the Grant who had contacted Rocky. It was at that point that he had made his presence known and intervened.

Chuck's words hung in the air, the only other sound being the roaring and spitting of the flames which were lighting the scene with a flickering red glow. Then the leader of the eight, a dark-eyed, swarthy Hispanic, stirred. He peered past Chuck up the slope in the direction of the road, obviously checking to see if the trucker had any backup, then back to meet his eyes. He pointed a threatening finger.

"Mister, you don' know what y'gittin' y'self involved in. This don' concern you. Take some advice, if you wanna stay in one piece. Git back into y'truck an' haul y'fuckin' ass outa here. You do that, maybe we forget we saw you … if you're lucky!"

By way of reply, Chuck moved the barrel of the shotgun a fraction, aiming it straight at the speaker's face. "Mister, I'll give you some advice. You don' threaten a man who's got th'drop on you with a pump-action."

His soft voice did not rise in volume but it took on a steely quality as he continued, "An' fer you information, I become concerned when I see someone rammed off the road by a buncha religious weirdoes, who then kick 'im an' announce they're takin' 'im back for the amusement of some nutcase who thinks he's an archangel or somethin'. Oh … an' incidentally … drop the pocketbook."

A hissing intake of breath greeted the reference to the sect and their oriental leader and several of the group exchanged glances. The leader's eyes narrowed, but he did as ordered and dropped the wallet onto Sherman's body. Then he looked pointedly all around, before meeting Chuck's eyes defiantly again.

"Trucker, if I were you, I'd watch my mouth. It could git you dead. There's eight of us an' only one of you. An' there'll be more of us arriving soon. Now, I'm givin' you one last chance t'git y'self out, before y'git in any deeper. Or are you too fuckin' dumb to wanna go on livin'?"

Chuck shook his head. "Wrong again, mister. I ain' alone. I

513

got me all the backup I need." As he spoke, Chuck moved the shotgun barrel slightly to emphasise his point. "An' I kin work the action faster'n you mothers kin come at me. You're welcome to try, if you don' believe me. An' don' threaten me again asshole, or I'll blow your big-talkin' mouth through the back of your fuckin' neck!"

The glint of ice in the shadowed eyes under the short peak of the leather cap matched the frigid tone of the smooth voice. That, and the unwavering black hole of the gun muzzle aimed straight at his face, convinced the leader of the sect thugs that he was only a finger pressure away from a messy death. No-one moved. It was a stand-off. In the flickering light of the now subsiding flames, they saw the black clad figure cock his head on one side in a listening attitude. Then a little smile of satisfaction softened the grim line of his mouth.

"Oh, speakin' of backup," he continued conversationally, "I clean forgot to mention ... I whistled up some reinforcements m'self. Listen ... I do believe they're playin' our tune ..."

Then they all heard it. Faint but clear on the cold night wind, came the far-off high pitched whooping of approaching police cars.

"Fuck you, you stupid interferin' prick!" the leader screamed at him in impotent fury, eyes bulging and fists clenched. "You'll pay fer this ... we'll catch up with you!" Then, heedless of the menacing gun, he swung round on the rest and shouted, "Get th'fuck outa here! Move!"

The whole group burst into instant action, sprinting wide to either side past the rock on which Chuck was standing and scrambling swiftly up the slope towards their vans. Breathing a heartfelt sigh of relief, Chuck turned to watch them go. He saw them reach the vans and pile in, then the faint sound of slamming doors and revving engines reached his ears and the two vehicles pulled away fast, heading off in the opposite direction from that in which the police sirens were approaching.

Turning away, he stooped, placed a hand on the rock's edge and vaulted lightly down to the ground below. Checking that Sherman was still alive, he stood guard over him to await the arrival of the police and ambulance vehicles. He sighed resignedly as he watched the first of them pull up ahead of his truck, lights flashing and sirens dying.

Soon, uniformed figures were scrambling down towards him, torch beams waving and dancing ahead of them as they came. Now came the irksome part of being a good Samaritan in these days of statement-taking, form-filling bureaucracy. It looked like being a long night …

Within minutes of the arrival of the ambulance, Sherman, still deeply unconscious, was stretchered into it. As it sped off for the emergency theatre of the local hospital, preceded by a police escort, he was already being hooked up to a blood plasma drip, administered oxygen and given pre-med preparation by the efficient paramedics in the back of the vehicle.

A couple of miles from the scene, no-one noticed the squat dark blue van which pulled out from its place of concealment by the roadside, as the two official vehicles sped past on their mission of mercy. Keeping well back, it began to tail them to their destination.

While all this activity had been going on, back at Bethlehem House Angel One had supervised the removal of the damaged vehicles, with their valuable cargo, safely inside the grounds. Likewise the casualties, living and dead, had been transported to the house and all evidence of the attack, including the cratered surface of the entranceway cleared up as much as possible.

When everything had been carried out to his satisfaction, Angel One had returned to the house to be informed that Angel Two had requested his attendance at Control as soon as he arrived. There his subordinate had informed him of a radio message, received only minutes earlier, from the Apostle in charge of the pursuit vehicles. He had reported the events of the chase, its partial success and unsatisfactory conclusion, finishing with the news of Sherman's identity and the fact of his removal to Dawson County Hospital.

Angel One had told his subordinate to send a reply instructing the Apostle to remain on watch until further orders and to follow if Sherman was moved again. He had then retired to the privacy of his quarters, where he sat deep in thought for a while, working out a way to silence Sherman permanently. Getting at him wasn't the problem – he had sufficient fanatical followers who would accomplish that. No, the problem was to do it in such a way as to avoid compromising the sect.

After a time a solution occurred to him and a plan formed in his mind. He stirred, picked up the internal phone and called Control. He issued instructions and sat back to wait. A few minutes later, there was a knock at his door and in answer to his summons, a young female member entered the room.

"You sent for me, Archangel Michael?" she asked respectfully.

"Yes." He waved her to a seat. "I have an important task for you, which will be of great benefit to our organisation. This is what you must do …"

58

THE INSISTENT WARBLE OF THE BEDSIDE PHONE prodded Grant into reluctant wakefulness. Fumbling for the switch of the bedside lamp, he clicked it on and squinted blearily against its soft glow to focus on the dial of his wristwatch, lying at its base. It was three-thirty in the morning. Pam stirred in her sleep beside him and he frowned as he lifted the receiver, cutting it off in mid-ring. Who the hell could be calling at this ungodly hour, he thought tiredly, and what was so damned important it couldn't wait till a more respectable time?

"Yeah? Grant here. Who's this?" He spoke quietly to avoid wakening Pam.

"Nate Springfield here, Brett." Something in the sheriff's tone brought Grant fully awake. Something was very wrong. The unflappable Springfield would never call at this time, unless it was some form of emergency. A cold wind of premonition quickly dispelled the last mists of sleep from his mind.

As he listened to what Springfield had to tell him, Grant's face tightened and conflicting emotions crossed his features. First surprise, then a mixture of concern and anger.

When the sheriff had finished, Grant asked, "How is he, Nate?" Grim-faced, he listened to the reply, then said, "I see. Okay Nate, thanks for callin'. I'll be there just as soon as I can make it. Listen, can I ask a favour? Could one of your men stand guard till I arrive?"

The voice at the other end rasped briefly in his ear again, then Grant said, "Thanks Nate. I should've known you'd be one step ahead of me. I sure appreciate it. I'm on my way. I'll be there in just over an hour. See you." He hung up, and slid out from under the bed sheets. As he stood up and reached for his clothes, Pam's sleepy voice asked, "Brett? What time is it?"

"Three thirty in the morning."

"Huh? Three thirty?" Her tousled head lifted from the pillow. "Who was that? Is anything wrong?"

Grant answered her, dressing quickly as he did so. He spoke quietly, but drowsy as she was, she detected a strange tightness in his voice.

"It was Nate Springfield, honey. He was callin' from Dawson County Hospital. It seems good ol' Harry's gone an' done the very thing I warned him against. The ol' fool's bin out tanglin' with Louise's mob, an' got himself hurt in the process …"

"Hurt? Harry? How badly hurt?" Pam was fully awake now. She raised herself on one elbow and was watching his face for any hint of evasion when he replied.

Shrugging on a warm car coat and zipping it up, he hesitated for a moment then met her gaze squarely. He had always been honest with Pam on the occasions she had asked about his work. But when he answered, he kept his tone deliberately neutral in an attempt to avoid frightening her.

"Nate says he's knocked about a bit," he admitted. "Seems his car crashed after a chase. They're operatin' on him right now for head an' chest injuries. I'm headin' out there to check things out. You go back to sleep. It's nothin' for you to worry about."

ANGELS OF DEATH

Pam sat bolt upright in bed, her eyes wide with alarm. "Go back to sleep?" she burst out. "Nothing for me to worry about? Brett, this has gone far enough. It's all very well for you to tell me not to worry but I do worry. I worry about you because I love you. And everyone keeps warning you these people are dangerous ... Christ, I've even seen myself how dangerous they are, remember? So, don't tell me not to worry."

"Pam, honey ..." Grant began.

"No, Brett. Let me finish ..." she said determinedly, cutting off his attempt to interrupt her. "I've never interfered with your work before this, but I don't want you to go out after these people on your own tonight ... not any night ... not any more. Just because Harry Sherman's got himself half killed, I don't see how it'll solve anything if you go and risk getting yourself killed in turn. Why can't you admit they're too powerful and too dangerous and hand the whole thing over to the police?"

She finished and sat looking at him, her sleep-tousled hair framing a face flushed with emotion, eyes bright with unshed tears. Grant's heart filled with love for her. He walked round the foot of the bed and sat on the edge beside her. He took her gently in his arms and hugged her to him reassuringly. Pam clung to him tightly and buried her face in his shoulder. After a few seconds, he eased her away and sat back, still holding her by the shoulders, and looked her straight in the face.

"Pam, I'm not going out after them on my own. Not now. Not anytime," he assured her. "I'm going out to the Dawson County hospital to relieve Nate Springfield. I'm only going to sit with Harry till later this morning, then I'll ring Anna to send Ellis or Perez out to take over from me. I owe Harry that much, I think you'll agree. He'd do it for me. He's not just my partner, he's my friend ... our friend, right?"

He paused, raising his eyebrows at her for confirmation of this point. She nodded reluctantly and he continued. "I agree with you that these people are dangerous. But it's my experience that none of these religious nuts like drawin' too much police attention on themselves. So, my presence in the middle of a busy hospital will prevent them from gettin' any crazy ideas about tryin' to finish the ol' fool off. As soon as possible, I'll get him

518

moved to a safer place in the city, till he recovers. Okay?" He leaned forward and kissed her lightly on the mouth.

Pam blinked back her tears. "Promise me you won't try any hero stuff," she demanded stubbornly.

"I promise," he replied solemnly. Then he grinned impishly and added, "Anyhow, I can't wear my Superman outfit tonight, my tights are in the wash." Kissing her lightly again, he let go her shoulders and made to rise.

But Pam shot out a hand and caught his arm, pulling him back down. Her face was serious, her voice firm. "No, Brett. I'm not joking. It's not a joking matter. Promise me you won't do anything foolish like going after these crazy people on your own. If you love me as I love you, then promise me on your love for me."

He took her hands in his. "Okay ... okay, I promise. I mean it. Honest. I'm only going to sit by Harry for a few hours, that's all. Now, honey, I've got to go. Nate Springfield's waitin' for me to show up."

He kissed her again and this time she responded fiercely, clinging tightly to him as though afraid to let him go. But when she released him and looked up, relief showed in her eyes. "Remember, I only worry about you because I love you, you know," she said.

Grant stood up and walked to the bedroom door. Pausing with his hand on the handle, he looked back. "And because I'm a good meal ticket," he said, and pulled the door open.

"... and because you're a good meal ticket," she echoed, straight-faced. Then she grinned and blew him a kiss. "Hurry back, meal ticket."

He grinned back at her. "Love you," he said softly, closing the door on her answering, "Love you too."

It took Grant the best part of an hour and a half to reach Dawson County Hospital. Entering its clinical, white-tiled environs, his nostrils were immediately assailed by the all-pervading smell of antiseptic so typical of hospitals the world over. It was a smell at once evocative of many things: bustling nurses, white-coated doctors, hushed wards, operating theatres, illness and pain. Especially pain. To Grant's mind, hospitals seemed to be citadels of pain. As though all the suffering of all the patients who had entered their portals, had been absorbed ineradicably into the very stonework of the walls.

Banishing the uncomfortable thought to the back of his mind, Grant announced his identity and the purpose of his visit at the inquiry desk, and was directed to the third floor private room where Sherman had been installed. As he stepped from the elevator and advanced to meet the tall figure of Springfield standing outside the room door, he saw the sheriff was not alone.

Standing talking quietly to Springfield and dwarfed by his tall, spare frame, was a slim young man, dressed in a black overcoat and stiff-brimmed black hat. Despite the neatly trimmed beard and clean shaven upper lip, the man bore a strong resemblance to Harry Sherman. Grant recognised him, although he had only met him once before. He was Isaac, Harry's son.

His sombre attire and style of beard announced his profession to the world at large. To his father's eternal pride, Isaac Sherman had fulfilled his parents' hopes – the secret dream of all Jewish parents – when he had attained the position which represented the pinnacle of achievement in their faith. Isaac Sherman was a rabbi.

The three man greeted each other and Grant offered his condolences to Isaac. Then he inquired of him whether there had been any improvement in his father's condition. Isaac shook his head.

"Not so far, Brett. Mind you, he's not long out of theatre, so we'll have to be patient. As a matter of fact they only brought him here about ten minutes ago."

"Exactly what are the extent of his injuries?" Grant inquired. "Nate here only told me he was pretty badly knocked about when his car went off the road."

"He has a fractured skull, several broken ribs and a broken collar bone. Unfortunately one of the broken ribs pierced his right lung." Isaac recited the grim list matter-of-factly. But Grant could tell that underneath his veneer of composure, the young rabbi was worried.

And no wonder – Grant's own mind was in a turmoil as it took in the seriousness of Sherman's injuries. "How successful were they in fixing him up?" he asked anxiously.

"The operation to relieve the pressure of the depressed fracture of his skull was a success," Isaac assured him. "But the doctor says the rib which pierced his lung has caused the biggest problem. He had bled a lot internally and now they're fighting to prevent post-operative pneumonia in his one working lung, while the other is collapsed to heal. The most the doctors will give him is a fifty-fifty chance of pulling through. But he is strong, my father. And I will pray for him. He will make it, I am quite sure." A sad little smile accompanied these last words, but they were spoken with quiet confidence.

"I'm sure you're right," Grant nodded. Then, to lighten the mood, he continued with a grin, "Don't worry, once he finds out the cost of hospital treatment, they'll need to chain him to his bed to keep him here!" The two younger men chuckled at this humorous reference to Sherman senior's self-professed – and quite mythical – tight-fistedness. Springfield joined in, catching the drift of the joke.

In answer to Grant's next question, Springfield then filled him in on the details of what he'd learned from the trucker who had observed the incident and rescued Sherman from his attackers. Next he told them how he had taken the time to drive out to the vicinity of Bethlehem House to scout around for any signs of unusual activity, before following on to the hospital to stand guard over the injured man until Grant's arrival. It had been a wasted journey. The area round the house had been deserted.

"So," he concluded, "Looks like we can't prove nothin' fer now. We'll have t'wait till Harry recovers, before we find out what happened out there tonight."

The three men chatted quietly for a bit over steaming cups of coffee brought by a pretty, red-haired night nurse. Grant obtained the particulars of the trucker who had saved Sherman's life that night, in order to contact the man and get a first hand account of the night's proceedings. Isaac took a note of the man's particulars too, so he could thank him personally for his action. Then, glancing at his watch, the young rabbi stood up.

"Well gentlemen, if you'll excuse me, I'll be on my way. I've promised to look in on our mother on my way home, to bring her up to date with the news on father's condition. It was the only way I could persuade her not to be out here sitting by his bed." He smiled ruefully, "I don't think the hospital would appreciate being told how they should be doing everything."

Shaking hands with Grant and Springfield and thanking them for their concern over his father's welfare, Sherman took his leave. No sooner had his slim figure passed from sight into the elevator, than Springfield turned to Grant, his face solemn. "I'll need to git goin' m'self, Brett. But before I go, there are a coupla things I didn' mention in front of Isaac. No need fer him t'know everythin', if y'git my drift?"

"You mean it's more serious than you've said up till now?" Grant asked.

"I reckon so," Springfield nodded. "When I told you the road wuz deserted out by Bethlehem House, that wuz the truth. But what I didn' tell you wuz this – I stopped an' had me a scout around. The first thing I noticed were two craters in the entranceway to the gates that'd bin temporarily filled in. Someone had also made an attempt to clean up the entranceway, it'd bin recently washed down, cuz it wuz still damp. Now, ain' that the damnedest thing t'do in the middle of the night? Then I saw the paintwork on one of the gateposts had bin knocked about a bit. Lastly, I took a look in the long grass a little way back from the gates, an' found this …"

Springfield reached into his pocket. When he withdrew his hand and extended it, Grant looked down incredulously at the object lying on the big callused palm. It was the release lever of a hand grenade. Grant looked up, shaking his head slowly, and met the big sheriff's eyes.

"Come on, Nate," he said with an embarrassed laugh. "Are you seriously suggestin' you think Harry's been out there chucking hand grenades around? What d'you think he is? He's an elderly private detective for Chrissake, not John fuckin'

Rambo! Anyway, where would he get hand grenades, an' why would he do a thing like that?"

"S'pose you tell me!" Springfield replied grimly. "All I know is, they chased 'im the best part of thirty miles, before they ran 'im off the road. So, whatever he got up to, he must've riled 'em up real bad, that's fer sure." He shrugged and dropped the release lever back into his pocket. "Like I said, we'll need to wait till Harry can tell us himself what happened out there tonight."

Time was pressing on. Springfield told Grant to phone him later in the day. Then he was gone and Grant was left to his lone vigil.

There was a chair outside the door of Sherman's room, and Grant lowered himself into it, settling back to pass the remaining night hours in the dimly lit silence of the hospital corridor. After only ten minutes, the red-headed nurse reappeared and made to enter the private room to check on Sherman. She hesitated when Grant asked her if he could see the patient, then admonishing him to silence, she relented and nodded for him to follow her.

Entering the room behind her, Grant stood quietly to one side, watching while she efficiently checked the drips, recorded the patient's temperature and finally the reading from the constantly moving blips on the glowing green screen, which were monitoring Sherman's heartbeat and brain wave activity.

Of Sherman himself, he could see practically nothing. His partner was merely an anonymous, heavily bandaged form under the bedcovers. In fact, had the temperature chart on the end of the bed not borne Sherman's name, Grant would not have recognised him at all.

The familiar hooked nose was sunk in the puffy, discoloured flesh surrounding his eyes. The entire top of his head above the level of his eyebrows was swathed in a skullcap of bandages, which also framed his face and jaw. The sunken closed eyes were black from the effect of post-operative bruising. He lay there, pierced by needles and hooked up to tubes, and surrounded by an array of gleaming chrome stands holding the plastic bags of plasma, blood and I.V. drips. Electrodes were taped to his chest and under the bandages of his skull, their thin wires connected to the machines which were quietly monitoring the patterns of his injured body's life rhythms.

The sight of his old friend and business partner lying there helpless, his life dependent on the gleaming apparatus of sophisticated medical technology, dispelled all his irritation at Sherman's stupidity in tangling unaided with the sect. It was replaced by a healthy anger directed against the vicious people who had done this to his friend.

Like a video replay, he saw again in his mind's eye the ranting, golden-robed Prophet, with his Hitlerian style of playing on basic emotions in a cleverly orchestrated atmosphere of mass hysteria; the nightmare chase in the underground carpark of the Washington Centre, and the single-minded ferocity the sect fanatics had shown in pressing home their attack; and lastly, the cold-eyed oriental who had shown him the murderous incendiary device and threatened to condemn several dozen human beings to a terrible death by fire, in event of any attempt by the forces of law and order to enter and investigate Bethlehem House. Grant knew they were thoroughly evil and dangerous, and as he stood silently contemplating Sherman's broken body, he vowed to bring about their destruction somehow ... anyhow.

He was brought back to the present by the smiling nurse ushering him quietly from the room and back to his seat in the corridor. A few minutes later, she returned with a fresh coffee for him and some old magazines from the waiting room. He thanked her and settled down with a month-old issue of Time to keep his lonely, self-appointed vigil.

Half an hour passed peacefully, then Grant glanced up at the sound of footsteps. A nurse was approaching. Not the friendly, red-haired one who had brought him coffee and allowed him to view Sherman. This one was slight of build and dark-haired. Grant felt there was something vaguely familiar about her but thought he had probably seen her earlier at the reception desk downstairs.

As she passed him and made to enter Sherman's room, he

nodded affably to her. She flashed him a professionally bright smile in return and pulled the door quietly shut behind her. It was the smile that did it. The too-bright professional smile of a hopeful salesgirl ... or of a hopeful collector approaching a prospective donor, brandishing her collecting box!

Grant had a good memory for faces and recognition flared in his brain like a Fourth of July firework as he remembered where he had seen the nurse before. His mind flashed back to the foyer of the Washington Centre, the night of the Crusade. She had been the robed sect girl who had tried to delay him and Pam, when they were following the group who had railroaded Larsen.

Instantly he was on his feet, knocking the chair over in his haste and bursting in through the door. Startled, the 'nurse' swung half round, the hypodermic syringe in her hand poised ready for use. Recovering instantly from her surprise, she spun away and thrust her hand towards the bed, aiming the needle at the shape of Sherman's leg under the covers.

Grant lunged forward desperately and his clutching fingers closed on the collar of her uniform. Jerking her backwards with his full strength, he felt the cloth tear but had the satisfaction of sending her light frame staggering clear across the room to slam against the wall beside the open door.

Although winded, she was tougher than she looked. Grant should have realised she'd have qualified for this mission because of her fanaticism and physical ability to carry it out.

Momentarily off balance from the effort of throwing her away from the helpless figure of Sherman on the bed, he was quite unprepared for the speed of her reaction. There was a sudden flurry of movement as she launched herself across the room at him, teeth bared in a grimace of hate and fury, the hypodermic needle driving straight for him like a dagger. It was obvious from the way she was wielding it, that the syringe contained some deadly poison. And as she was now attacking him, it was a safe bet it held a sufficient quantity to kill both him and Sherman, as the latter was the primary target of the sect assassin.

Acting from pure reflex, he threw himself to one side to avoid the stabbing needle. But the girl didn't stop in her forward thrust. Instead, she continued the movement, aiming again for the recumbent figure on the bed. Again Grant lunged desperately to intercept her, this time grasping the driving wrist. Pivoting his body as he dived forward, he used her momentum, judo style, to fling her violently across the room away from both himself and the bed.

They both rolled and regained their feet in one fluid movement, facing one another across the room. Grant had his back to the bed, protecting Sherman with his body. The girl, her dark hair disarranged under her skimpy nurse's cap, her uniform torn at the collar, glared at him. Flecks of foam were visible at the corners of her mouth and the air was hissing through her clenched teeth, although she was by no means out of breath from her exertions. Grant noticed her pupils were shrunk to mere pinpoints. She was obviously hyped up on some barbiturate type drug, which would account for her speed and strength.

Looking at her slight figure poised for action, Grant suddenly felt a little foolish. She looked so frail and feminine compared to his own size and physique. But there was nothing remotely feminine about the way she dropped into a knife fighter's crouch, the deadly gleaming needle held low in her right hand, the other hand spread out to her left to improve her balance.

Grant responded automatically, prompted by his martial arts training, and dropped into a defensive crouch as though facing an opponent on the karate dojo. The sect girl began to inch forward, moving the needle from side to side and feinting to thrust with it as she advanced. She was gathering herself for another lunge and he readied himself for it. He was determined, no matter what, to keep himself between her and Sherman. He watched her eyes for the first hint of the coming attack, all too aware of the deadly gleaming weapon aimed at his midriff. Just then, totally unexpected, a female voice suddenly demanded angrily from the open door, "What the hell's going on here? Get out of here this instant! Both of you!"

The sect girl's attention was momentarily diverted, her eyes flicking in the direction of the red-haired nurse who stood glaring in the doorway, hands on hips. It was the opportunity Grant needed. Before the would-be assassin could recover from her split second's loss of concentration, he leapt forward to the attack. Paying her the dubious compliment of being a worthy and dangerous opponent, he twisted in mid-air, shot out his right leg and hip-kicked her full force in the stomach.

There was a horrified squeal from the nurse at the door as the girl was propelled backwards, to cannon off the wall and crash to a crumpled heap on the floor. She had no sooner landed than she gave a spasmodic jerk and her legs scissored wildly as she fought to regain her feet. But then she seemed to lose her balance and collapsed back onto her face.

Throwing himself bodily across the room Grant landed beside her, ramming his knee into her kidney to drive the air from her lungs and subdue her. Her whole body went rigid, back arched like a bow and she let go a strange bubbling moan of agony. But Grant was in no mood for pity – the bitch had shown none to either the helpless Sherman or himself. Unceremoniously he hauled her over onto her back and seized her right wrist, intent only on relieving her of the lethal hypodermic. He was too late. It was not in her right hand.

Frantically he grabbed for her left wrist, thinking she must have worked a switch. But her left hand was empty too. Then he saw the gleam of metal just above her left hip. It was the barrel of the syringe. The needle was buried in her flesh, where it must have plunged when she had crashed awkwardly to the floor.

Sensing it was already too late, as the girl's rigid body was even now beginning to spasm, he nevertheless plucked the part empty syringe out and held it out to the shocked nurse who was still standing in the doorway.

"Here nurse, take this. An' be careful with it," he cautioned. "I think it contains poison. What kind I don't know, but it's pretty fast acting by the looks of her. This bitch was gonna kill your patient with it, but she's ended up with a dose of her own medicine. You'd better call your emergency team, though I doubt if it'll do her much good."

As he spoke, Grant climbed to his feet and stood looking down at the writhing, moaning figure at his feet. He felt drained, emotionally as well as physically. His would-be executioner looked so young and vulnerable, he knew he should feel pity. But he felt none. His contact with the fanatical sect was dehumanising him, he thought. On the other hand, although she wore the uniform of an angel of mercy, Grant knew full well she had been sent as an angel of death – doubtless by the brutal oriental referred to by Louise Wyatt and Jim Miller as Archangel Michael. The chief death angel of the sect!

The urgency in Grant's voice got through to the young nurse. White faced but composing herself with an effort, she took the proffered syringe, holding it warily as though she had a live scorpion by the tail, and crossed the room quickly to press a bell push on the wall by the bed. The small sign set under it read EMERGENCY in inch high red letters.

Within seconds the room was a hive of activity, as an emergency team of two white-coated doctors and four nurses arrived on the double and began a frantic race against time to save the life of Sherman's assailant. The girl was now purple in the face and choking, her body wracked by agonised convulsions, and her mouth was smeared with bloody foam where her champing teeth had bitten into her lips. One of the doctors sniffed tentatively at the small damp patch of liquid he had squirted from the hypodermic onto a gauze pad. As the faint odour of bitter almonds tainted the air, the doctor spoke only one word to his colleagues, his face grim.

"Cyanide!"

A wheeled trolley had arrived, brought swiftly on the heels of the emergency team by a pair of medical orderlies, and the jerking moaning form was bundled onto it. Working swiftly, one of the doctors cut away the clothing from her side, while the others restrained her and began to strap her onto the trolley. With a fresh scalpel he made a deep incision in her exposed flesh over the site of the tiny puncture wound, in a drastic attempt to drain off some of the poisoned blood. Even while he was doing this, his colleagues had hooked her up to a drip. Then the entire team departed at a run grouped around the trolley.

When the medical team had departed, the red-haired nurse, still shaken from her experience, began to check out her own patient again. Leaving her to it, Grant headed for the door to resume his seat in the corridor outside. Suddenly he was arrested in mid-stride by the sound of Sherman's voice, weak and hoarse and barely above a whisper, speaking his name.

"Brett? … Is that you?"

Grant whirled round and reached the bedside in three strides. He acknowledged with a nod the nurse's hurried admonition not to tire Sherman and spoke quietly, reassuringly, to his seriously injured partner.

"Harry? It's Brett here. Listen ol' friend, you're gonna be all right. But you gotta rest. You're in hospital, an' the doc' says you mustn't talk. You gotta save your strength, okay?" As he spoke, he reached down and gently squeezed Sherman's limp hand where it lay on the cover.

Sherman's blackened, swollen eyes flickered open. For a moment he seemed to have difficulty focusing on Grant's face, a side effect of the painkilling drugs he had been administered, then the brown eyes cleared a little and he spoke again. The words were forced out slowly and with an obvious effort.

"Brett … they … killed … Solly."

The nurse caught Grant's eye and shook her head warningly at him. He nodded back and leaned down closer to Sherman's bruised face. He answered him in a soothing tone.

"Okay, okay … take it easy, Harry. You rest now. We can talk about it tomorrow …"

There was a sudden feeble pressure on Grant's hand. "No … too late!" The words croaked out with surprising strength, cutting off Grant's reply. Then his eyes fluttered shut and his labouring breath could be heard harshly in the quiet of the room. The nurse began busily preparing an injection to send her patient back into a healing sleep, when his eyes flicked open and the weak voice whispered again, the disjointed words faint but clear in the hushed atmosphere.

"Brett … it's drugs … heroin … they killed Solly … proof's in my desk … middle drawer … the bastards … mailed me a finger … my fault … I sent 'im … they tried … t'kill me too … saw too much … stay clear, Brett … it's big … too big for us …"

The voice trailed off into the harsh laboured breathing and the eyes fluttered closed again. This time the nurse took charge firmly, seeing that the strain had taxed her patient's already low reserves of strength almost beyond endurance. She waved Grant back from the bed, felt for Sherman's pulse, lifted one of his eyelids and frowned in concern. From the door, Grant watched her prepare a syringe with practised efficiency, then swab and inject his partner's limp, unresisting arm. He closed the door quietly behind him.

Seated back out in the corridor, Grant's mind was racing. The information Sherman had struggled so hard to give him made everything much clearer. It explained the sect's ruthlessness and total disregard for human life. It explained why they hunted down and recaptured sect members who ran away ... maybe, like Sherman, they had also seen too much! And it would explain why the oriental Doctor Sung – or Archangel Michael, or Angel One, or whatever else he chose to call himself – was prepared to destroy his whole set-up, rather than submit to outside investigation.

Then memory came flooding back. Of course ... it also explained the large room he had looked into in the basement of Bethlehem House, with its long stainless-steel topped table, just before he'd been struck down. And the flat plastic objects lying on its surface, they had been the scrapers bakers use to gather up spilled flour and other fine powders on the smooth surfaces of their working tables. That must be the room where the heroin was cut, using milk, sugar or bicarbonate, and packaged for distribution.

He felt sure Louise knew nothing of such a sizeable operation, or she would have told him about it. Probably she was not long enough in the sect to have been entrusted with such dangerous knowledge. She had certainly mentioned that drugs of all sorts – including heroin – were freely available to sect members as a control device to make them dependent on the leaders for their supplies. On the other hand, it would also make sense if the majority of the rank and file membership were kept in ignorance of the drugs operation, they would then act as a perfect and innocent front against outside scrutiny. He decided to question Louise more closely on the subject that evening, when he had finished his day's work.

Despite all the unavailing efforts of the medical staff to save her life, Sherman's would-be assassin died in terrible agony only minutes after accidentally injecting herself with the cyanide intended for her victim. The death and the cause were reported to the local police, who arrived to take down all the necessary particulars and statements. As a matter of routine, the County Sheriff was informed and so, for the second time that night, Grant found himself chatting over coffee with Nate Springfield. This time the sheriff had his deputy, Cal Fenton, with him.

"If I ain't sleepin' tonight, I don' see why in hell he should be," was the sheriff's comment, adding drily, "Anyhow, it's about time he saw how different things look in the dark."

At which the amiable, bearded young deputy grinned and informed Grant, "What he means is he's gotten too old fer wrestlin' with purty young female felons, so he's brought me along to handle things fer 'im. An' I'm the best there is at handlin' purty young females, when I git the chance!"

The pleasantries over, at Springfield's suggestion Grant phoned Sherman's personal doctor, explained the night's events and asked him to arrange for his patient to be transferred right away to the private clinic he ran in the city. The doctor agreed and said he would attend personally with the clinic's ambulance within the hour.

The sheriff then insisted on Fenton and himself remaining with Grant until the arrival of the ambulance, and thereafter on providing a rearguard escort to prevent either attack or any tailing attempt by any sect vehicles. Grant would go on ahead of the ambulance, acting as leading escort all the way to the eventual destination.

The Dawson County Hospital doctors disapproved strongly of the proposed move, on medical grounds. However, they were soon persuaded by Springfield to accept this risk, as opposed to the greater risk of having their hospital turned into a battleground, in event of any further attempts on Sherman's life that night.

While awaiting the arrival of the ambulance, Grant discussed Sherman's revelations of Levenson's alleged killing and the sect's involvement in the trafficking of heroin. He then expressed the opinion that it would be good if they could hit the sect when it would hurt them most – namely, before they could get rid of the heroin Sherman must have seen. Springfield fell silent for a bit, deep in thought. When he spoke again, he could have been discussing a picnic outing in his slow, placid tones.

"The way I see it is this. After tonight's events, both out at the big house an' in here, I reckon they'll be expectin' some kinda retaliation or police investigation later today. So, for the next twenty-four hours we do nothin'. We let 'em think they've won – that you an' Sherman don' wanna know any more, right? But in the meantime you go ahead an' tell your friends t'be ready fer tomorrow night, an' I'll muster some troops locally too. Cuz tomorrow night, we move in an' hit 'em. An' we hit 'em so hard an' so fast, that Doctor Fu Manchu in there ain' even got time t'light a match, never mind blow the place sky-high! Now, here's how I suggest we go about it ..."

Springfield spoke on in his quiet, matter-of-fact voice for the rest of the time until the arrival of Sherman's doctor with his clinic's ambulance, accompanied by a matronly, white-uniformed nurse. Later, as he drove citywards, escorting his injured friend to safety, Grant felt fiercely exultant. For the first time since his confrontation with the brutal oriental in the bowels of Bethlehem House, he felt hopeful of ultimate victory over the murderous sect, with its evil leaders and fanatical adherents.

Back at Bethlehem House, Angel One received the news of the failure of the attempt on Sherman's life in a mood of mounting frustration. It appeared the attack had been thwarted by the intervention of the target's partner, the private detective Grant. The sect van which had radioed in the report, also relayed their inability to tail the three-vehicle convoy which had whisked Sherman away from the hospital, due to the vigilance of the County Sheriff's car acting as rear escort. He told Control to recall the van, along with the car which had driven the bogus nurse to the hospital.

He paced his spartan quarters in brooding silence, thinking

out his next move. The detective Grant was proving to be a worthy opponent. He was also proving to be a thorn in the flesh and as such would have to be removed. Now there were three counts to be repaid – his interference at the Washington Centre, his abduction of the girl Louise, and now tonight's episode in which his partner Sherman had become involved too. Enough was enough. Grant would have to be neutralised.

However, Angel One's problem was that Grant was too well connected to the forces of law and order. So any action against him would have to stop short of killing him. Then Angel One recalled Grant's reaction when threatened with the immolation of the sect members, in the event of any police raid on Bethlehem House. He stopped pacing and a satisfied smile touched his lips. There was his enemy's weakness – his actions could be controlled by his concern for the safety of others. So be it! A plan of action took form in his fertile mind.

Ten minutes later he had summoned the seven Apostles then in the house to a council of war. He outlined his plan to them, then in his harsh clipped tones he divided them into two groups, one of four and one of three, and issued his orders to each assault team. He then announced he would personally be leading the smaller group and dismissed the meeting.

Within half an hour of the meeting's close, the two teams had been equipped for their respective missions and were speeding south for the distant city in separate vans. In the rear of his van, Angel One stretched out on the padding which had been spread over the floor to ensure a measure of comfort. He was asleep almost instantly. He would only get a couple of hours rest at most but it would be sufficient. In the pursuit of vengeance, a Triad warrior was trained to be tireless.

Through the night the dark shapes of the two vans sped, bringing retribution to Angel One's unsuspecting enemies in the sleeping city. Operation Nemesis was underway.

PART VIII
NEMESIS

59

PAM WOKE TO THE SOUND OF THE TELEPHONE. THE set was at Brett's side of the bed and she reached out sleepily to nudge him awake. He wasn't there, his half of the bed was empty. She came fully awake then, and memory flooded back of an earlier call followed by Brett's departure to be with the injured Harry Sherman. She hoped it would be Brett calling to let her know when he would be home.

She reached across the bed and flicked on the reading lamp and noticed the hands of the alarm clock were standing at seven-thirty. She picked up the receiver, cutting it off in mid-ring.

"Hello?" she inquired hopefully. But she was disappointed when, instead of Brett, an unfamiliar male voice answered her.

"Is that Miss Mason speaking?"

"Yes, this is Miss Mason." Pam replied guardedly. She did not recognise the caller's voice but he sounded civil enough. "Who's calling please?"

"This is Officer Davis of the New York State Highway Patrol, Miss Mason. I'm sorry to disturb you but I need to speak to Mister Grant, please. It's in connection with the traffic accident earlier this morning, involving his partner Mister Sherman."

When Pam replied that Brett was not yet home but could be contacted at Dawson County Hospital, the caller explained that they had already tried there but had been told that he had driven off shortly before, accompanying an ambulance which was carrying Sherman to a private city hospital. The name of this hospital had not been left with the Dawson County medical staff, but it had been hoped Mister Grant may have arrived home by now. He apologised again for disturbing Pam, said he'd appreciate it if she'd ask Grant to call State Police HQ when he arrived, and rang off.

Pam replaced the receiver with a frown of annoyance at herself. She hadn't thought to ask the caller how long ago it had been since Brett had left the hospital. Then her mood lightened as it occurred to her that Brett would be back soon, as Sherman's new hospital admission was somewhere in the city. She decided to have a quick shower and get breakfast started. Swinging her feet to the floor, she stood up and reached for her robe.

Downstairs in the entrance hall of the apartment block, the Apostle who had made the call stepped out of the telephone booth and nodded to his three companions.

"He ain't back yet," he announced triumphantly. "It'll be a pushover."

The four-man team immediately headed for the stairs and climbed swiftly to the fifth floor, where their intended target resided. They did not use the elevator, in order to avoid being seen by anyone.

Arriving at the fifth floor, they quickly located the apartment they wanted. Like all the other doors, this one had a spy-hole at eye level, which enabled the inhabitant to view any caller before opening the door to them. They had come prepared for this. One of the group was dressed in a messenger's uniform, complete with peaked cap and carrying a gift-wrapped package and a receipt book.

This man stood squarely in front of the door, while his three companions positioned themselves to either side, out of view. On receipt of a nod from the group leader, the bogus messenger rang the doorbell and waited. After a few seconds wait, he rang again. This time movement was heard from within and the messenger assumed a pleasant expression as he faced the spy-hole. The other three tensed for action.

Pam heard the doorbell ring just as she was readying things for her shower. She gave a muttered "damn!" of annoyance and her first reaction was to ignore it. Then the doorbell rang again. Her curiosity got the better of her, and she quickly tied her robe about her, pushed her feet into her slippers and headed for the door.

Peering through the spy-hole, Pam saw the uniformed figure holding a gift-wrapped package and a receipt book. Who could have sent a gift this early in the day? ... Then puzzlement gave way to amusement and pleasure ... who else but Brett of course! It must be his way of making up for upsetting her earlier that morning. She felt a warm glow of love for him and she shook her head and smiled.

But, even as she was about to open the door, some shred of caution prompted her to confirm the evidence of her eyes. In the past couple of days, Brett had stirred up a hornets nest of brutality and ruthlessness. Her personal experience of it had taught her it was better to be safe that sorry. She attached the safety chain, cracked open the door and looked round the edge.

"Yes?" she inquired.

"Special delivery for Miss Pamela Mason from ..." the messenger made a show of checking his book, which was folded open, "... a Mister Grant." He looked up at her and raised a friendly eyebrow. "You Miss Mason?" he asked.

"That's me," Pam agreed. "Hold on a second ..." She swung the door to and unhooked the chain.

They came in fast and hard. The partly open door suddenly slammed inwards, propelled by the bogus messenger's kick, catching Pam on the nose and forehead with stunning force. She stumbled back with a cry of fear and pain, lost her footing and tumbled to the floor. She had no time to call out a warning to Louise – not that it would have made any difference.

Events then happened with brutal efficiency and speed. Pam, her head spinning from the painful blow to her face, was dimly aware of figures moving swiftly past her into the apartment, then the door was kicked shut. Then she was hauled roughly to her feet, blood trickling from her bruised nose, and bundled into the living room supported between her two powerful captors. There, a terrified, almost fainting Louise was already in the firm grip of the assailant who had dragged her from her bed.

Still dazed, Pam barely had time to register the sight of Louise's dishevelled figure, when she found herself thrust into a chair by the dining table. Before she could resist, her captors had tied her securely to the chair, using a length of flex ripped from the TV set. As they did so, they pinioned only her right arm to her body, leaving her left arm free. Pam hadn't even begun to wonder why, when she heard Louise give a whimper of pure terror. A fourth figure had just entered the room.

Pam gasped as her hair was seized painfully from behind by one of her captors, forcing her to look up into the face of the newcomer. Her eyes widened in fear as she saw the reason for Louise's terror – the oriental who was standing in the middle of the room, fixing her with a look of savage satisfaction.

She knew without needing to be told, that this was the same man Brett had discussed with Louise, the one who had attacked him in the basement of Bethlehem House. The one Louise had referred to by the curious sect title of Archangel Michael, saying that although he was the second in command to the Prophet, in reality he was the one who ran things.

Looking at the man and feeling the power of his slanting black eyes boring into hers, she thought Lucifer would have been a more appropriate title for him. Brett and Louise had agreed on the one feature of the man, which had left most impression on them. His eyes. Now, as she sat riveted by their glittering malevolence, she felt she had never seen such cold cruelty in a pair of human eyes before.

Suddenly the oriental rapped out an order. Pam felt the painful grip on her hair being released by the man behind her, who then quickly left the room. Although her head was now free, she was unable to tear her gaze from the hypnotic black eyes which seemed to be savouring her terror and mocking her at the same time.

Her head was clearing rapidly from the effect of the blow she had received and she wondered what were her attackers intentions. Her mind was racing as it examined all the possibilities. Rape? If that was their intention, they were going a strange way about it. Robbery? They had made no demands, nor did they seem interested in searching the apartment. What then? Revenge? On Brett? For all the trouble he was causing them? Fear for his safety clutched at her heart. She cleared her throat nervously.

"What do you want with us?" she demanded with as much defiance as she could muster. The oriental did not bother to answer her. He merely continued to fix her with his cold reptilian gaze.

Before she could speak again, her attention was diverted by the return of the man who had left the room in answer to the Oriental's order. In one hand he was holding her large, polished-steel kitchen scissors, with their slim, eight-inch, pointed blades. A nameless fear knotted her stomach when the man handed the scissors to the oriental.

Pam's mouth was dry and she had to moisten her lips with her tongue before she could speak again. "What ... what are you going to do?" she asked tremulously.

By way of reply the oriental pointed the scissors at her and barked, "Gag her!"

Pam heard cloth tearing behind her, and she protested and struggled in vain as a piece of material was forced into her mouth and tightly bound in place with another strip knotted behind her head. The oriental pointed the gleaming scissors again.

"Her hand!"

Despite her desperate attempts to resist, Pam was no match for the combined strength of her two captors. Within seconds they had forced her free hand onto the surface of the table in front of her and pinioned it there firmly. The oriental had then addressed her directly for the first time, his voice harsh and nasal, his speech thickly accented.

"You ask what I am going to do. I am going to teach your friend Grant a lesson. He has already been warned, but it seems he and his friends need to be reminded to keep their noses out of things which do not concern them. You will give Grant a message from me. Tell him if he interferes in any way again, I shall return. But next time I will kill him … and you!"

So saying, he stepped towards her. Pam tried to shrink away from him, and struggled desperately to pull her trapped hand free from the vice-like grip of the two men who held her. Just then the watching Louise overcame her fear of the brutal oriental and she tried to intercede on behalf of her new-found friend.

"No! No … please, Archangel Michael," she blurted out. "Don't hurt her … please, she's done nothing..."

The Oriental's response was swift and violent. He whirled round, took two paces towards the cowering girl and backhanded her hard across the face. As she fell back stunned into her captor's arms, the oriental had gripped her by the throat and hissed into her terrified, tear-streaked face.

"I have not yet decided whether you shall be permitted to live. Watch in silence or there will be worse in store for you … much worse! Do you understand, worm?"

Through her dry sobs of terror, the distraught girl had nodded her submission. She was in a state of near collapse when the oriental released her and she sagged, limp and dull eyed, against the strong hands which held her upper arms from behind.

The oriental returned to his position across the table from Pam. He opened the scissors fully so they formed a cross and took a firm grip on the horizontal blade. The other blade now projected out between the middle fingers of his hand like an eight inch spike. Once more the glittering black eyes held hers.

"Remember, tell your friend Grant this is his last warning," he grated harshly.

So saying, he leaned forward and raised the weapon to shoulder height over her trapped hand. The room lights glinted on the wicked needle point of the polished steel. Frantically Pam began to struggle again, straining to scream against the restricting gag and shaking her head from side to side in mute appeal.

All in vain. The gleaming steel in the Oriental's fist suddenly blurred downwards and Pam's world exploded into red agony, before blackness mercifully engulfed her.

60

HAVING SEEN SHERMAN SAFELY INSTALLED IN THE
private city hospital, Grant and Springfield had parted company.
They had agreed to get in touch that evening to discuss tactics
for their planned assault on Bethlehem House, provisionally
timed for the following night. In the meantime, they would
both start contacting their respective forces that afternoon,
ready for mobilising them on the morrow. Springfield and Larsen
had then made a start on the long drive back to Rockford, while
Grant headed across the city for home.

It was not yet eight a.m. and he considered calling at the office
before Anna and the others arrived, to check out Sherman's
claim about Levenson's death. If what his partner said was true,
and not just a fantasy brought on by the painkilling drugs the
hospital staff had pumped into him, then he'd find the proof of
Levenson's murder in the middle drawer of Harry's desk – proof
in the grisly form of a severed finger.

But he was tired, feeling drained of energy, as his early morning
exertions caught up with him. So he decided to head home first
for a shower and some breakfast to recharge his batteries. Then
he would make his way to the office, bring the other three up
to date on the events of the night and check out the contents of
Sherman's desk. Arriving at his apartment block, he parked the
Mustang and entered the building. He rode the elevator to the
fifth floor, walked along the corridor to his apartment door and
let himself in.

The first thing he noticed was the lack of normal breakfast
time activity. As he hung his car coat in the hall, he cocked his
head in a listening attitude. He was mildly surprised to find that
Pam wasn't yet up and about. She had work to go to and was
usually an early bird. Perhaps having her sleep disturbed by
Springfield's early morning phone call had caused her to sleep
in.

This thought was confirmed when his ears picked up the faint
sound of the shower running. He walked over to the bathroom
door, intending to let her know he was home. However, when

he stuck his head round the door, he was further surprised by
the amount of steam in the room. The shower had obviously
been running for some time – but the frosted glass cubicle was
empty.

Surprise turned to unease. For some unknown reason, he felt
everything wasn't quite as it should be. He crossed to the shower
and turned off the water. Silence fell. Nothing stirred. The
apartment felt empty. Thoroughly alarmed now, he pulled open
the bathroom door and stepped into the hall, intending to head
for the bedroom.

Suddenly he froze in mid-step, the short hairs prickling on the
nape of his neck. He had heard something … a sound … but a
sound which struck a chill into him. It had sounded like a stifled
moan. Then he heard it again. Now there was no doubt about
it, it was the sound of someone in pain but unable to cry out
properly for some reason.

He swung round to face the living room door, from where the
sound had come. It was slightly ajar. Fear for Pam's safety
gripped him. Something was wrong … terribly wrong!

Then his fear was instantly replaced by rage, at the thought
that the sect fanatics had somehow got at Pam and hurt her.
Without any consideration of danger to himself, he whipped
out his gun and launched himself at the door, going in low and
fast.

Bursting into the room, he dived to one side, crouching low
and sweeping the interior with his gun. There was only one
person in the room, and it was all too obvious she presented no
threat to anyone. Grant straightened slowly, numb with shock
at the evidence before him of Angel One's terrible revenge.

Pam was seated at the dining table, slumped forward against
the restraint of the flex which bound her body and right arm to
the chair on which she was sitting. She was gagged with a strip
of cloth, which was tightly bound round her mouth. Her hair
was disarrayed and hanging around her face, not quite obscuring
her bruised forehead or the dried blood around her mouth and
chin, which had trickled from her swollen nose.

All this he registered in his first glance, but what shocked him
most was the sight of her left hand. Stretched out on the table

before her, fingers spread in a pool of congealed blood, it was pinned there by one gleaming blade of an open pair of kitchen scissors. The point of the scissors blade had been rammed in with such force that it had pierced both hand and table top, to protrude a good two inches from the underside of the wood.

Although every instinct screamed at him to go to her aid, Grant's professionalism reasserted itself and warned him this could be a trap to put him at the mercy of a hidden assassin – a trap with Pam as the bait. Even although his shocked immobility had lasted only a couple of seconds, he was even then presenting an easy target to anyone bursting in on him.

Getting a grip on himself with a tremendous effort, he made himself check out the remainder of the flat quickly and thoroughly. There was no sign of the intruders who had wreaked their cruel vengeance on his helpless, innocent Pam. Neither was there any sign of Louise. In the guest room, her bedcovers had been dragged off and flung in a crumpled heap on the floor. She had been snatched back into the clutches of the sect, with what amounted to contemptuous ease.

Curtis arrived at the flat in response to a terse phone call from Grant, to find him cradling an unconscious Pam in his arms, while the paramedics who had given her a knockout shot, carefully hacksawed through the hardened steel of the scissors blade to release her trapped hand.

Much later, after she had been released from the casualty department of the local hospital, a heavily sedated Pam was driven back to the refuge of Curtis's home, by mutual agreement of both men, as a sensible precaution against any repeat attack by the sect personnel. Curtis then poured himself and Grant a stiff shot of scotch, while his wife Ruth attended to making Pam comfortable in the spare room.

Grant then took Curtis through the events of the night, commencing with Springfield's phone call which had summoned him to the hospital. He described the abortive attack on Sherman by the bogus nurse, which had prompted the decision to move him to the security of the private city hospital. He concluded his account with his discovery of the attack on Pam, and related how she had told him of her ordeal, when he had kept her talking to help take her mind off the pain, while they had been awaiting the arrival of the ambulance.

She had passed out after the oriental had driven the scissors blade down through her hand, pinning it to the table top. She had no recollection of her attackers leaving the apartment with Louise. She had drifted in and out of pain-filled consciousness for what had seemed like hours of alternating agony and merciful blackness, until she had become aware of Grant holding her and talking soothingly to her. Then the medics had arrived and given her the magical shot that had dulled the agony and floated her away to welcome oblivion.

Curtis heard Grant out in silence, allowing him the therapy of talking the whole traumatic experience out of his system. But he had then had to use all his powers of persuasion, trying to talk Grant out of launching a suicidal one-man revenge mission that very night. Advising him to wait till the combined attack he was planning with Springfield did no good. Grant was so filled with fury and guilt over what had happened to Pam, he was almost beyond reason.

What finally brought him to his senses, was when Curtis threw up his hands and said, "Ah ... what th'fuck's the use talkin' to you? If you're determined t'git yourself fuckin' wasted, okay ... go ahead ... do it! These people jes' love one-man missions. They jes' eat 'em up. If y'git lucky they'll only half kill you, like they did your partner. If you don't ..." he concluded brutally, "... ask 'em t'mail Pam your dick, why don'chya? It'll give 'er somethin' t'remember you by!"

The two friends stood glaring at one another. Then the anger died in Grant's eyes and he shook his head as though coming awake. He grinned sheepishly at Curtis and raised his hands briefly in a gesture of surrender.

"You're right," he admitted. "I wasn't thinkin' straight. Thanks for talkin' sense to me. An' thanks, too, for puttin' Pam an' me up. You an' Ruth could be at risk if these people find out. That's one I owe you."

"Ah ... forget it," Curtis waved his thanks aside. "It ain't such a big deal. It's one thing for these crazies to attack the home of a private dick – it'd be a whole new ballgame if they did the same to the home of a regular cop. Besides," he added, "the only reason I'm doin' it is cuz you ain't gittin' outa providin' th'booze fer our next git together." He grinned and punched Grant lightly on the shoulder.

Just then Ruth came bustling into the room and announced that breakfast was ready. When Grant said that he didn't feel like eating and that he wanted to get to the office as he had something important to do, she brushed his protests aside.

"Brett Grant, don't give me any nonsense about not bein' hungry. You've been up all night, so you must be. You just don' know it, is all!" she stated with a motherly firmness that brooked no argument. "I never let my Ben leave for a day's work with an empty stomach, an' while you're under my roof you'll be no different!"

Grant appealed half-heartedly to Curtis for support, but his friend grinned and shrugged. "Better do as she says, Brett. I gave up arguin' with her a week after we wuz married. It only took me that long to discover she didn't listen to a word I said."

Later, when Ruth had cleared away the breakfast things and left the two men with a full coffee pot, the talk turned to Sherman's allegations of the sect's involvement in drugs and murder. On the subject of the drugs shipment, they agreed reluctantly that a raid by the state police was out of the question. Even without the danger of Angel One's threat to torch the building, it would be impossible to obtain a warrant on Sherman's word alone. More especially as Bethlehem House was the property of a so-called religious organisation, which meant it would enjoy the even greater protection of the United States constitution.

It was the same with Sherman's alleged evidence of Levenson's probable murder. Again there was only Sherman's word to support the fact that Levenson had gone out to Bethlehem House at all. However, Curtis said he would accompany Grant to the firm's offices, to take possession of Sherman's evidence. It might be able to be used against the sect at some later date, along with any other evidence that turned up.

Just then the phone rang in the hall. Curtis rose from the table and left the room to answer it. When he returned a few minutes later, his expression was serious.

"That wuz the precinct. Tex," he announced tersely.

Grant eyed him apprehensively. "Not more trouble?" he asked.

"You could say that," Curtis replied grimly. He nodded towards Grant's half empty cup. "Don't bother rushin' y'coffee, t'git to the office. Fact is, you ain't got an office to go to. Accordin' to Tex four men called by an hour or so ago, ordered out your staff at gun point, an' firebombed it."

"What?" Grant pushed back his chair and stood up, his whole body tense with anger.

Curtis held up a hand. "That ain't all. Seems they beat up on your two operatives, Ellis an' Perez, when they tried to stop 'em. Tex says they ain't too badly hurt though, jes' knocked about a bit. Your secretary got herself some superficial burns pullin' stuff outa the fire, but she's okay too. Oh ... an' the firebombers left a message. One of 'em said t'tell you it wuz done – so you can't put the finger on anyone!" He shook his head in disgust. "You ask me, you're mixin' with some sick people, my friend."

Grant's eyes were blazing as furiously as the fire that had destroyed his office. "That bastard Sung!" he snarled through clenched teeth. "First Harry, then Pam, now this. I tell you, Ben, that bastard's gonna pay ... in spades!"

"Well, it sure looks like it's only you an' Nate Springfield kin do anythin' to stop 'em right now," Curtis conceded. Then he walked over and gripped Grant's shoulder. "Listen, whatever the two of you got planned fer tomorrow night, jes' be careful, that's all I'm gonna say. Play it cool. A little hate's good to carry with you when you're fightin' a dangerous enemy. But not anger. Too much anger kin blind you to danger an' make you careless. So go in cool, okay?"

Some of Grant's anger evaporated, and he gave Curtis a lopsided grin. "Hey, listen to you comin' on strong with the philosophy bit. You sound like somethin' out of a kung fu movie."

"Yeah, well I know what I'm talkin' about," Curtis retorted.

"All I'm sayin' is ..."

"I know what you're sayin', my friend," Grant interrupted him gently. "Anyhow, you won't have to worry about me," he added lightly. "I'll have your ol' buddy Nate Springfield to keep me in line, if I start to make like Dirty Harry."

"An' he will too," Curtis growled. "Nate an' me think the same way ... we were platoon sergeants in the same company."

"I didn't know that," said Grant, genuinely surprised.

"There's a lot you don't know," Curtis retorted. "An' that won't change if y'don't stay alive long enough to learn! Right, are we gonna stand around here all day jawin', or what?"

Half an hour later, Grant and Curtis were inspecting the gutted offices of Brett's firm, the fire-blackened floors and walls still damp from the firemens' hoses. Standing in the shell of the outer office, Grant wrinkled his nose against the sour stink of charred wood, burned paper and scorched metal, as he listened to Anna's account of the attack, with interjections from Perez and Ellis.

Anna's hands were lightly bandaged, covering the blisters she had received when salvaging files, floppy discs and equipment from the hungry flames. The other two had badly bruised faces, Perez sporting a plaster taped over his broken nose, while Ellis had one eye completely closed and his upper lip painfully swollen and split. In addition, Perez had a plaster cast on his broken left wrist and Ellis had a sling supporting his broken right arm and collar bone.

From their combined account of what had taken place, it seemed the four assailants had burst in through the outer door, minutes after the premises had opened for business at nine o'clock. One of the men had been armed with a silenced automatic and had held the firm's three employees in the outer office at gun point, while his fellow thugs had entered the three inner offices and started wrecking them.

When the gunman had glanced in the direction of one particularly loud crash, Ellis had seized his chance and jumped him, followed a split second later by Perez. However, the man had managed to shout a warning and his three companions had come swiftly to his aid. The two detectives had put up as much resistance as they could, but had been outfought as well as outnumbered, and had been clinically and brutally beaten up. In the confusion, Anna had tried to make a run for the outer door to raise the alarm, but her move had been anticipated and she had been caught and dragged back by the hair.

Once Ellis and Perez had been subdued, the assailants had produced three small fused devices from a satchel, set the timers on them and placed one in each inner office. They had then herded Anna and the other two from the office, and held them at gun point along the corridor at the elevators until the firebombs had exploded a couple of minutes later. The four attackers had then fled down the stairwell, at which point the injured Ellis had run to a nearby office to raise the alarm, while Anna and the less disabled Perez had returned to the burning premises and tried gallantly to salvaged as much as they could before being beaten back by the heat.

The fire service had arrived within minutes, but by that time the flames had taken a good hold and most of the office furniture had been consumed. At this point in her narrative, Anna proudly informed Grant that she and Perez had managed to rescue her computer from the advancing flames. On its hard disc was stored a complete record of all the office files and correspondence, so as soon as they had settled into new premises, it would only be a matter of time before she could print replacement hard copy for their files.

Grant thanked his three colleagues for their efforts on the firm's behalf, and suggested they take the remainder of the day off to begin recovering from the effects of their exertions and various injuries. However, he was touched when all three adamantly refused, stating their intention of remaining to help clear up and move such equipment as they had rescued, to the new temporary furnished premises on the floor above, already arranged by the firm's insurance company.

While this operation got underway, organised by Anna who recruited willing help from surrounding offices, Grant and Curtis closely examined the gutted remains of Sherman's office. The drawers of the metal desk had obviously been forced open before the fire had started, and any contents had been completely incinerated. Not long after this, Curtis took his leave, telling Grant to get in touch with him should anything turn up.

For his part, Grant joined his three colleagues in their new temporary quarters on the sixth floor, where Anna greeted him with hot coffee made in an adjoining office and served up in borrowed cups, but nonetheless welcome. The next hour he spent on the phone.

First off he called Nate Springfield and brought him up to date on the enemy's latest attack on him. They spoke for some time and the sheriff outlined what he thought they would need in the way of manpower, weaponry and equipment for the coming operation against Bethlehem House. The remainder of the hour Grant spent tracing and contacting Rocky O'Rourke and Pete Larsen, and arranging for them to gather their mates and rendezvous at Rockford by 9 p.m. the following night.

When Grant finally rang off, he slumped low in his seat, deep in thought. The events of the past hectic few days ran through his mind, and always the same face hovered at the back of his consciousness, mocking him. It was the face of the oriental he knew to have been behind all the violence perpetrated on himself, Pam and his friends. It was the face of Angel One. But he felt satisfied that he had set the wheels in motion for his enemy's downfall. By tomorrow night his patchwork army would be converging on Rockford, ready to join forces with Springfield's troops. Then the boot would be on the other foot.

61

THE DAY FOLLOWING THE RECAPTURE OF LOUISE Wyatt, Angel One felt he was once again in full control of his destiny. The organisation he had so painstakingly built up had successfully weathered several crises over the past week. Threats to their security from absconding members and interfering snoopers had been dealt with satisfactorily. They had even absorbed and beaten off a full-scale attack on their street distribution structure by a powerful enemy. Later that same enemy had been bloodily counter attacked and neutralised as a threat for the foreseeable future.

The double consignment of heroin had been secured, despite a surprise attack, albeit by one demented man, and Tiger Control in Chicago had taken delivery of their merchandise the previous day. The other four divisions of Dragon Control had received their consignments that day. This success had earned him the approval of the Director. Lastly, he had attended personally to the reprisal attack on Grant's girlfriend and the recapture of the Wyatt girl. The firebombing of the Sherman & Grant office premises had underlined the lesson, while taking care of the possibility that the elder one may have kept the severed finger he had been sent as a warning.

Now only one problem remained to be dealt with. The Prophet. And that was being attended to that very night by his oriental colleague, Angel Four. Yes, things were running smoothly once more. He spent the remainder of the day arranging and supervising the cutting, packaging and distribution of his own section's share of the heroin consignment.

His mind touched briefly on the two defaulters who were awaiting their fate in the basement cells. Miller and Wyatt. But he dismissed them for the time being, having more important matters to be dealt with. Business before pleasure, as the westerners' saying ran.

But Angel One's confidence was misplaced and his self-congratulations premature. Through the darkness of that chill November evening, the patchwork army of Grant and Springfield was mustering. Singly and in groups, in a variety of motorised transport, ranging from thirty-ton sixteen wheelers to private cars, they were converging on their Operations HQ – which just happened to bear a remarkable resemblance to the County Sheriff's office in Rockford!

62

THE EARLY PART OF THE DAY FOLLOWING THE attacks on Pam and the firm's office passed uneventfully for all concerned. But it was the false calm of the eye of the storm – and the storm was to break out anew with renewed fury when darkness fell.

That night, even as Grant's and Springfield's combined troops were mustering in Rockford for their council of war, the Prophet returned to his luxurious city apartment from the final meeting of his latest highly successful and highly profitable crusade. As usual, he was accompanied by his personal retinue of sect heavies. He was still high on the adrenalin generated by the mass hysteria he had whipped up, then fed on, like a vampire sucking the tainted blood of its own unclean offspring.

His euphoria was further fuelled by a delicious anticipation of pleasure still to come. Because tonight he would punish Detective Lieutenant Curtis for daring to offend him. Tonight he would butcher one of his surveillance team. The very thought stirred him sexually and fanned the smouldering coals of his insane bloodlust into flickering life.

Now, in the privacy of the bedroom of his personal suite, swiftly and silently he began to change into the black clothing he wore when prowling the night for victims. As he prepared for murder, he was doing so to the incongruous background of the Mormon Tabernacle Choir's rendering of The Battle Hymn of the Republic. It was a favourite of his because he identified with the third line of its first verse – He hath loosed the fateful lightning of His terrible swift sword. In his sick mind, he was the terrible swift sword of the Lord – chosen by Him to cleanse the world of the sin of whoredom.

As he strapped the cleansing blade to his left arm, a thrill of carnal excitement shuddered through him at the prospect of another kill, as the bloodlust took full possession of him, banishing the last vestiges of sanity from his sick mind. Again he experienced the heightened awareness and sharpening of the senses, which always accompanied his bestial transformation into a primal killer.

He had just completed his preparations – dressed to kill would have been an apt description of his appearance – when suddenly he froze, head cocked in a listening attitude. Below the soft throb of the music, his increased sense of hearing had picked up the quiet click of the outer door to his private suite being closed. Someone had violated the privacy of his lair. Reflexively he flicked off the ceiling light, leaving the room dimly illuminated only by the soft glow of his bedside reading lamp. Like a cornered animal at bay, his eyes swept the bedroom seeking a place of concealment.

Angel Four stood for a moment with his back pressed to the closed door of the Prophet's private suite. He examined the long split-level room stretching away from him to the tall windows at the far end. It was unoccupied, as he had expected it to be. Taking advantage of the cover provided by the soft throbbing music, he glided along the line of the wall until he stood outside the door of the private bedroom.

Pressing his ear to the edge of the door, he listened intently, while a full three minutes ticked past. His ear confirmed what the electronic bug had told him shortly before he had entered the suite, namely that there was no sound of movement from within the bedroom, or its adjacent bathroom.

Satisfied his intended victim was asleep, he gripped the door handle and turned it slowly. He had taken the precaution of oiling its mechanism along with the door hinges earlier that day, so as to avoid any noise that would alert the occupant of the room.

Angel Four eased the door open enough to allow him to slip quickly into the room beyond. He stopped then, staring perplexed at the empty bed. The covers were undisturbed, showing that the bed had not been slept in. His eyes searched the room rapidly, then fell on the door leading to the connecting bathroom. He crossed the floor silently and listened at the closed door. Nothing. Puzzled now, he opened the door quickly.

The room beyond was in darkness. He flicked the light on and the greenish glow reflecting back from the tiled interior showed it to be empty of human occupation.

His puzzlement gave way to a momentary unease, at the possibility that the Prophet may have somehow managed to slip out of the apartment undetected, as the detective lieutenant had suggested. But the thought only lasted a second. He knew it was impossible for the Prophet to have left the apartment. He had set double guards to prevent any such attempt. Then another probability occurred to him. Could his intended victim have somehow guessed, from an unguarded look perhaps, that he had been marked for death? If so, he would try to hide in his panic, never thinking how easily he would be discovered.

Again his eyes quartered the room for the most likely hiding places. There was the bed, of course. He could be cowering under it, or maybe in the spacious built-in wardrobe. He was about to cross to the wardrobe, when his eye caught a slight movement of the heavy floor-length curtains over to his right. A little smile of triumph touched his mouth. Mystery solved.

Crossing the room as though he were heading for the wardrobe, Angel Four suddenly changed direction, took two swift paces to his right, seized the curtains with both hands and jerked them open. As he did so, a black gloved hand shot up through the exposed gap and rammed a razor sharp six-inch blade hilt deep under his ribcage.

Angel Four grunted once in agony as the cruel steel sliced straight up into the pulsing muscle of his heart. His dying brain barely had time to process the fading image of his killer and recognise the black-clad form with the glowing eyes as the Prophet, before its circuits closed down permanently. As he fell, the Oriental's hands were still convulsively gripping the heavy drapes. His dead weight pulled the curtain rail from its mounting and the thick material cascaded down over his corpse, providing it with a ready-made shroud.

63

THE PROPHET STEPPED OUT ONTO THE SHORT balcony and slid the glass door closed behind him. He found the weather had turned foggy again. It was not as thick as it had been on the night Mary Lou Evans had died, but it was still sufficient to reduce visibility to about 30–40 yards. It was ideal for his purpose. An ideal night for murder.

Within minutes he had unclipped and set up his ladder bridge and negotiated the crossing to the fire escape platform with his customary ease. He descended to the fourth floor platform and stopped to scrutinise the dimly lit, fog-shrouded alley below, searching keen-eyed for signs of the hidden watcher he knew would be there.

He quickly located his man in the deep doorway where he had positioned himself, by the intermittent glow of his cigarette. Having done so, he settled himself to wait with the patience of a hunting predator on the stalk, until the prey presented an opportunity for the kill. Motionless, unmindful of the cold or the swirling fog, he watched the man below, waiting for boredom to slacken his concentration and make him careless.

In the end, it was none of these things which gave the Prophet his chance. It was much simpler and more basic. It was the call of nature. He had almost resigned himself to the fact that this cop was too cautious to be caught out like the one he had almost jumped five nights previously, when without warning the man below stepped out from the shelter of the deep doorway.

The Prophet drew back and watched his quarry through the trellis work of the platform at his feet. The cop peered up at the towering fire escape for several seconds, then, satisfied it was deserted, he walked across the alley to the opposite wall. This placed him almost directly under the fire escape's raised bottom platform. The Prophet leaned cautiously over the platform's side rail, and made out the cop's dim figure in the deep shadow cast by the iron staircase. The man was urinating against the alley wall.

Exultation coursed through him in anticipation of an easy

kill. Moving soundlessly on his thick rubber soles, he ghosted swiftly down to the lowest platform. He was now a mere ten feet above the urinating man's head. The cruel blade slid smoothly from its sheath into his right hand. Swinging lightly over the top rail he glanced down, measured the drop to the shoulders of his unsuspecting victim below and stepped into space. As he did so, the silence was shattered by a warning shout from further up the alley.

"Joe, look out! Above you!"

As he dropped towards the startled, dodging man beneath him, the Prophet realised his mistake. There were *two* cops on duty in the alley. For some reason, the watch must have been doubled by his hated enemy Curtis.

In fact the reason was quite simple. Curtis, fully aware that this was the last night of the Prophet's current crusade, had anticipated that he might choose it for a last hunting expedition, before retreating to his lair upstate. Accordingly, he had indeed doubled the surveillance team, detailing two men to each side of the Eldorado apartment block. In addition, the lieutenant himself, accompanied by another three men, was parked not far from the eastern end of the alley, providing an instant backup for any point of action.

In the alley itself, Detective Gary Lomax had been keeping watch on the towering fire escape. He had positioned himself in a narrow doorway, in the vain hope it would provide him with some shelter from the biting cold. Some thirty yards further up the alley, huddled in another doorway nearer to the fire escape, was his partner, a young black detective name of Joe Foster.

As if the cold wasn't enough to put up with, Detective Lomax's disgust and discomfort were increased by the damp clinging fog, which was gradually thickening and reducing visibility. Bored and fed up, he was straining his smarting eyes to pierce the swirling murk to keep the fire escape in view, when his attention was drawn to his colleague moving out from his surveillance position. He watched him move quickly across the alley and make for the patch of deep shadow under the iron stairs. Evidently he was going to empty his bladder and he had chosen to do so in the concealment of the shadow cast by the fire escape, rather than foul up his doorway.

Suddenly Lomax caught a suggestion of movement on the fire escape platform, directly above where Foster was standing straddle-legged facing the alley wall. Then a momentary thinning of the swirling fog revealed to his horrified gaze the alarming sight of the black garbed figure sliding over the platform rail to drop on his unsuspecting colleague. It was at that point Lomax had leapt from the doorway, wrenching out his gun and bellowed his frantic warning.

Foster's nerves had been on edge all through his tour of duty in the alley. Lieutenant Curtis had made it very clear to the surveillance team how mentally unbalanced and dangerous he considered the Prophet to be. He had also warned them that the guy was physically strong and that he had a kink for cutting his victims. It certainly wasn't Foster's idea of an easy tour, lurking in a cold, draughty doorway in a poorly lit service alley, in weather conditions more suited to a horror movie set.

In the event, his nervousness saved him. He was so keyed up, his reaction to Lomax's warning shout was instantaneous. Without thinking, he ducked and started to turn, at the same time snatching for his gun. His speed of reaction was such that instead of his attacker landing square on his back as intended, his half turn meant that the plunging figure crashed into his right shoulder, knocking both men off balance. The downward stab of the razor-sharp blade missed its intended target of the soft hollow at the junction of neck and shoulder and instead sliced his right arm, bone deep, from shoulder to elbow.

Foster screamed in panic as he felt the cruel steel slice his flesh and he threw himself bodily away from his attacker, hitting the ground in a rolling break-fall and spraying himself with his own urine as he did so. He fetched up on his back and forced up his gun hand, ignoring the tearing agony of the slashed muscles of his upper arm. In horrified disbelief he stared at his empty hand. He had dropped his gun! It had tumbled unnoticed from his grasp when his arm had been cut. He was helpless to defend himself against the terrible gleaming weapon in the fist of the menacing black figure looming over him.

The Prophet, having missed his first killing strike, realised he would have to move fast to avoid capture by the trap set for him by his hated enemy. Recovering his balance with uncanny speed, he snarled and launched himself after the still tumbling figure of his intended victim. He could see the whites of the fear-filled eyes in the black face as he leapt at him.

In that same instant, the deafening crash of gunfire filled the narrow confines of the alley. He heard the clang of metal on metal and a ricochet whined viciously past his head. Then a hammer blow struck him below his left shoulder blade, and he was punched violently to the ground by the heavy .38 slug. As he fell, the knife clattered from his grasp.

His brain exploded with fury and he was about to force his numbed body onto its feet again, when his right hand fell on something hard and metallic. It was a gun. With the cunning of the insane, he closed his hand over it, lay still and listened to the footsteps which were approaching at a run. He waited till they slowed to a stop a few feet away and a voice said, "Joe? You okay?" Then he rolled over, pointed the gun at the bulky figure and pulled the trigger twice in rapid succession.

The Prophet's lack of expertise with a gun saved Lomax's life. Jerking the trigger instead of squeezing it with a steady pressure, meant the gun muzzle being pulled slightly down and left for the first shot. As a result, the slug hit Lomax low in his right side, inflicting a painful flesh wound rather than a fatal chest shot. The impact knocked him spinning to the ground. The second shot, fired while the gun was still bucking from the recoil of the first, went wild.

Behind the Prophet, Foster had fumbled out his personal radio with his left hand, his right now refusing to function due to the injured muscles of his upper arm. Keying the transmit button he spoke rapidly, his voice shrill with fear and panic, covered by the noise of the gunfire.

"Foster ... the alley ... it's him ... he's armed ..." Then, remembering the pre-arranged code word, he added hastily, "Armageddon! Armageddon! Get th'fuck in here!"

The Prophet scrambled to his feet. He was hatless, his silver hair awry, his eyes glowing with insane fury. His upper body felt curiously numb but he could feel a burning pain deep within him when he breathed. Swaying on his feet and feeling light-headed, he looked around for his knife – the holy weapon with which he did the Lord's work, cleansing and punishing the fornicating Jezebels of the night, and with which he had punished the sodomite. It had more holy work to do this night. More sinners to dispatch to everlasting hellfire.

Before he could find it, the whoop of fast-approaching sirens filled the night. Next moment the swirling fog in the alley was suddenly lit to a brilliant white by the head lamps of the car which came roaring in at the far end. Animal instinct warned him that the car's appearance meant more enemies that he could handle in his present condition. Baring his teeth in a soundless snarl of frustration and fury, he turned and ran for the opposite end of the alley, away from the oncoming car. The billowing white fog, reflecting back the glaring head lamps, swallowed him up.

64

CURTIS HAD TOLD THE DRIVER TO PARK THE unmarked police car as near as possible to the alley entrance at the rear of the Eldorado apartment block. The driver had found them a parking slot some forty yards distant and there the four man back-up team had begun their long vigil. To pass the time, the conversation had ranged over a variety of topics, from sport to current affairs, then had finally settled after some time on shop-talk – inevitable when any group of cops got together anywhere in the world.

Throughout all this, Curtis contributed least, for the most part staring moodily out of the window. He felt sure in his bones that their man would try something tonight. But he was understandably apprehensive in case anything should go wrong. Twenty years of police service had convinced him that Murphy's law applied especially to police operations – no matter how meticulously they were planned, if it were remotely possible for something to fuck up, then it would!

Not that he would have admitted it to his men. He was aware that their confidence in him was in part based on the myth that he was devoid of any of the normal human weaknesses such as fear or self-doubt. 'Ol' gravel guts' and 'Ol' Stoneballs' were two of the more complimentary nicknames his men attached to him. Curtis knew this and was secretly proud of his image.

It was into this quiet atmosphere of cigarette smoke and casual conversation that the sudden crackle of Foster's radio transmission sounded. The hysteria in their colleague's voice would have been enough by itself to ensure their prompt response but the unmistakable background of gunfire added urgency to the situation.

Even before Curtis's barked order of "Get this fuckin' heap movin'!" the alert driver had already flipped the car into gear and begun to swing into the traffic stream. As they accelerated towards the alley mouth, siren screaming, the lieutenant was calling into his pocket transmitter.

"Curtis to all units … Armageddon … repeat Armageddon … location four … Units One an' Two, seal off west end of alley … Unit Three seal off east end … suspect is armed an' dangerous … move in now!"

They took the corner in a skidding turn and rocketed into the dark mouth of the alley only a few yards ahead of the second police car, which was racing up from the opposite direction. Lights blazing, their car cannoned off the kerb, tyres squealing in protest, then they were roaring along the alley. Curtis, craning forward, left hand braced on the dash, right hand clutching his gun, was straining to see ahead through the swirling fog, with the aid of the car fog lights. Then, they were braking to a skidding halt as the towering framework of the fire escape loomed up out of the mist.

Minutes later the alley was sealed off and thoroughly searched, including the fire escape, thus discovering the Prophet's means of exit from the apartment. From the two wounded men Curtis had the full story of what had happened, but of the Prophet there was no sign. He had obviously managed to make the far end of the alley and slip out under cover of the fog, scant seconds before the other cars had arrived to seal it off.

Fuming with rage and frustration, Curtis called in immediate reinforcements and ordered a full-scale manhunt in the vicinity of the apartment block. He also put out a city-wide A.P.B. on their man, warning that he was armed and dangerous. From Lomax's claim to have hit him, backed up by Foster, he was able to add to the suspect's description the fact that he was reportedly injured by a gunshot wound, probably in the upper body.

Out of the whole mess, Curtis took consolation from two factors – wounded and losing blood, the bastard wouldn't get far on foot. And into the bargain he had lost his knife – already on its way to Forensic, who would doubtless prove it to have been the murder weapon with which he had butchered his victims.

The Prophet sprinted from the alley exit moments before the first of the police cars roared out of the fog and screeched to a halt at the dark gap he had just left. Instinctively he had turned in the opposite direction from the Eldorado block. It would be the first place his enemies would check.

He did not run far. Very quickly he found it increasingly painful to breathe. His left lung felt as though it was on fire. About half way along the block, he dropped thankfully to a walk. Just then a wave of nausea engulfed him and he swayed on his feet like a drunk man. A darkened shop doorway appeared on his left and he ducked into it for a moment till he recovered and regained his breath.

The numbness in his shoulder was beginning to wear off now and he was aware of a sticky warmth on his back, hips and legs, and that the needling pain in his upper back was intensifying. Deep in his sick brain his survival instinct warned him his injury was serious. He had to seek shelter – somewhere to lie up and heal.

From the concealment of the doorway, his feverish eyes examined the street as far as he could see. The lighting was brighter than in the alley and the fog was thinner out here, patchier. Suddenly a coughing fit seized him and a stab of agony lanced through him from back to front. He felt as if something had torn inside him. It had. The upper lobe of his left lung, punctured by Lomax's bullet, had just ruptured under the explosive pressure exerted by his coughing. He spat blood, and a thin trickle painted a red line from the corner of his mouth to his jawline, whence it dripped onto his coat lapel.

He wiped a hand across his mouth, and stared at the scarlet smear on the back of his black glove. Shelter. He had to find shelter. So he could rest up and heal. He must hide from his enemies while he was weak. When he had regained his strength he would go hunting again. Then they would pay for hurting him. In blood!

He pushed away from the wall against which he was leaning and staggered out onto the sidewalk again. As he made his unsteady way along, one or two people glanced curiously at him. They saw what they took to be a wild-eyed drunk, well-dressed and bleeding from a blow on the mouth. Then they saw the gun he was clutching down by his side and they averted their eyes and hurried past. City dwellers, they knew that curiosity didn't only kill the cat like the old proverb said, it could also kill people!

A block and a half from the alley, he saw the solution to his problems. Temporary shelter – and the means of gaining the secure refuge of his lair upstate, Bethlehem House. A bespectacled, smartly dressed man was struggling to open the front passenger door of his parked car, while clutching a large paper bag of purchases from the all-night drug store he had just left. The man succeeded in unlocking and opening the door, then leaned in to deposit his bag on the passenger seat. Having done so, he slammed the door shut, walked round the front of the car, opened the driver's door and began to climb in behind the wheel.

Triumph sent a surge of new strength through the Prophet and he crossed the broad sidewalk at a lurching run, shouldering an indignant passer-by out of his way, jerked open the rear door of the car and half climbed, half fell, onto the back seat. Before the astounded car owner could react, the Prophet had pulled the door shut, reached over the back of the driver's seat and jammed the muzzle of the gun into the man's neck.

"Drive!" he snarled.

The man was petrified with fear. He was a family man and despite being a native New Yorker, he had never been closer to real violence in his whole life than on the TV screen of his comfortable suburban house in Richmond. In his rear-view mirror he could see the glaring eyes and twisted blood-smeared mouth of his assailant and he could feel the pressure of the gun muzzle behind his right ear.

He was acutely conscious of the fact that his life hung on a twitch of his captor's trigger finger. His fear focused his whole concentration on the tiny circle of steel pressed against his flinching neck and on the white-knuckled finger he could imagine curled round the little half moon of metal – the least movement of which would blast him out of existence. Then the gun muzzle prodded him painfully and the order was repeated louder, more insistently.

"I said *drive!*"

Fumbling, leaden-footed, clumsy with fear, he stalled the car twice before succeeding in pulling jerkily away from the kerb. As he did so, he frantically searched his mind for something reassuring to say to the maniac in the back. Something that might save his life. On TV he had heard so-called experts pontificating on how to deal with terrorists in hostage situations – how the hostages should try to establish a rapport with their captors. He gave it a try.

"Listen friend," he began tremulously. "I'll do whatever you want. I won't give you any trouble. I have a wife an' four kids. If it's money you want, I don't have much with me but what I got you're welcome to. Take the car too, if you want ..."

His pleading was cut off by another painful jab of the gun muzzle and by the snarling, thick voice from behind him.

"Shut up and drive! Head north. You hear me? North."

So much for the experts and their fuckin' theories, the driver thought bitterly. He nodded miserably and headed north. Negotiating a turn to accomplish this, his eyes momentarily met the eyes of his captor again in the rear-view mirror. Terror gripped him anew and he tore his eyes away from the insane glare he met there. He began to sweat. He also began to pray.

65

IT DID NOT TAKE LONG FOR CURTIS TO ESTABLISH what had happened. Witnesses were found and coerced or bullied into telling what they had seen, by the simple expedient of sealing off the entire area for blocks around and threatening all-night interrogation sessions, unless information was forthcoming. Within half and hour, Curtis learned his man had been driven off in a green Cadillac by the unfortunate owner of the car, whom he had taken hostage at gun point. An A.P.B. was flashed to all mobile units across the city – with the added instruction that no attempt was to be made to stop the car while the driver's life was being threatened. Instead it was to be tailed and kept under observation, until the arrival of Curtis and his squad.

Curtis was standing beside one of the unmarked Homicide cars parked outside the Eldorado apartment block. Standing alongside him was Turner. While anxiously awaiting the first sighting report of the wanted man, they were watching with some satisfaction the handcuffed members of the Prophet's entourage being bundled none too gently into the waiting paddy wagons by grim-faced uniformed cops.

The body of the murdered oriental had been discovered when the Prophet's private suite had been forcibly entered and searched. A sizeable quantity of drugs, including heroin, had been found and seized also, along with a veritable arsenal of guns and ammunition. It occurred to Curtis that if this was the amount of weaponry the sect maintained in the Prophet's city suite, then Grant could run into some heavy firepower out at Bethlehem House later that night.

A shaft of light suddenly pierced his thoughts ... Bethlehem House ... of course ... that's where the Prophet would be trying to make for, if anywhere. He should have thought of it before. If the wounded fugitive reached the sanctuary of his upstate lair, and if Grant failed in his audacious plan to close it down, then the crazy sonofabitch would be free to kill again ... and again. He would have to be stopped. Curtis came to a decision. He handed Turner the production bag and indicated the prisoners.

"Tex, take over here, willya?" he said. "Get this lot down to the precinct an' throw the book at 'em. I'm takin' this car. Tell Flaherty to relay any sightin' reports to me. I've had one of my famous hunches, an' I'm gonna follow it up. I need you to cover me fer a couple of hours at th'most. If Devlin asks, jes' tell him I'm followin' a hot line of inquiry, okay?"

Turner shot a quizzical look at his chief. "You figure y'know whar' he's headin'?" he asked quietly. When Curtis nodded, the younger man looked troubled. "You goin' after him y'self, Chief?" He was answered by another nod. "You think that's a good idea?"

Curtis met the younger man's eye and held it. Slowly he nodded his head. "That's exactly what I think, Tex. Listen, this bastard's gotta be stopped. But he ain't some two-bit punk on the run after blowin' someone away. Someone y'kin talk into givin' himself up when he finds himself cornered and surrounded by armed cops, an' he gits to feelin' scared an' sorry fer himself.

"We're dealin' here with a fuckin' serial killer, who's too insane to feel fear. An' he's got a hostage. If we corner him, he won't negotiate. The crazy fucker'll blow the poor slob away. So, I reckon I'm the only chance the guy's got of comin' outa this mess alive. Because the moment our man makes a wrong move, I'll take him out! An' I won't git the chance, if we've got half the fuckin' NYPD an' the CBS Newsnight cameras lookin' on."

Turner made to speak, but Curtis held up a hand to stop him. He glanced round to make sure no-one was within earshot, then continued. "Tex, I ain't askin' you to approve. All I'm askin' is that you stall fer a couple of hours. You don' know where I'm at ... or why. I jes' ordered you t'take charge of the prisoners, told you I wuz goin' t'check on somethin', an' took off. Okay? Your ass is covered. Whaddaya say, pardner?"

The younger man nodded his head with obvious reluctance. "Heck, I ain' worried about coverin' my ass. I'm with you all th'way, Chief. Always am, y'know that. But I don' like it. It's yore ass that's on th'line here, not mine. Y'got yore two hours. I jes' hope y'know what you're about."

Curtis reached out and clapped Turner on the shoulder. "Thanks Tex. You're a solid guy. An' you're a good partner t'have, though I hate t'admit it." He grinned fondly at the younger man.

Turner returned the grin. "Flattery'll git y'anywhere."

"That's what I'm countin' on," Curtis retorted as he ducked into the car. He settled himself behind the wheel, pulled the door shut and looked up at Turner through the open window. "Oh, by th'way, I nearly forgot t'mention. I filed a recommendation today fer you t'be promoted to detective sergeant at th'next board. Devlin's backin' it too."

The grin on Turner's face disappeared for a startled moment. Then it returned, extending delightedly from ear to ear. "Hey thanks, Chief ... but I reckon this could be a blatant attempt to influence a police officer in the execution of his duty."

"Too fuckin' right it is!" retorted Curtis and gunned the car away from the kerb.

Turner watched his tail lights disappear round the far corner of the block, his amusement tinged with concern. He liked Curtis and he fully sympathised with his motives in going after the cra d killer on his own. Mad dogs were best put down, not caged in kennels from where there was always the chance they might escape to bite again. He just hoped Curtis would be okay. The Prophet was insane and a remorseless killer. He was also wounded. And wounded animals were always at their most dangerous when cornered. How much more dangerous a wounded mad animal?

Thirty minutes of fast driving, involving quite a few near

collisions in the fog-shrouded streets, had finally brought Curtis's quarry and his unwilling chauffeur clear of the city. Even now they were travelling through sparsely inhabited country as they headed further upstate. The driver knew that the further north they progressed into the wild untamed uplands, the more remote the oases of human habitation would become and the less likely the chance of any assistance in his plight.

Out here the fog bank which hung over the city had thinned to non-existence. A large sign swooped towards them out of the night, its message glowing luminously in the beam of the headlights. LAST CHANCE FILLING STATION 2 MILES UP AHEAD. YOUR LAST CHANCE TO FILL UP FOR 30 MILES it read.

The driver glanced at his fuel gauge. The needle was hovering just over the red. His hopes of a chance to escape soared. He half turned his head and addressed the slumped figure in the back, directly behind him now, the menacing gun held low and pointing straight through the upholstery at the middle of his back.

"We're nearly outa gas. The sign said this fillin' station we're comin' to is the last one for thirty miles. If we've got much further to go, we'd better fill up."

There was a grunt of agony as his captor leaned forward to check the fuel gauge. The driver tapped it nervously with a forefinger to guide the man's eyes to it. Apparently satisfied, the man leaned back, stifling a choking, coughing fit. After a moment of wheezing, bubbling breathing, his voice grated out thickly.

"Very well … stop and fill up. Just remember … one wrong move … and you die!"

The driver nodded. "No tricks. I promise." He decided to try to provide himself with a little more scope for an escape bid. He cleared his throat.

"How about the toilet? You could go with me. I need to go real bad." Although he was hoping to use it to get away from his captor, his bladder was indeed uncomfortably full.

"No!" The barked refusal brought on another bout of painful, quickly stifled coughing. Then, breathlessly, the voice rasped out, "No toilet. Relieve yourself where you sit, if you must. If you attempt to leave the car, I will kill you. I will shoot you in the spine through the back of the seat."

The driver stiffened as he felt the gun muzzle jab him in the small of his back through the upholstery of the seat. His heart sank, his faint hope of creating an opportunity to escape crushed. As he pulled the car off the highway into the gas station forecourt, it occurred to him that his only chance now would be if the pump attendant noticed something amiss and called the police after they'd gone.

He pulled up at the pumps and the attendant, a young black wearing green coveralls and cap bearing the petrol company's logo, approached and leaned down to the open window.

"Fill 'er up?" he inquired.

"Please." The driver nodded jerkily.

"What's y'star sign, m'man?" the young black asked.

"Huh?" The driver was mystified, his mind on other things – specifically on the gun only inches from the base of his spine. At that moment, a warning pressure reminded him of its menacing presence.

"Y'star sign ... y'know ... what grade you wantin'? Don' mind me, it's my li'l joke." The attendant explained with a friendly grin.

"Oh, I see ... uh ... four star please," the driver replied vaguely. He tried to catch the attendant's eye but the man was already turning away and reaching for the nozzle of the pump hose.

The driver sat drumming his fingers nervously on the steering wheel while the attendant busied himself filling the tank, checking the oil and radiator, and wiping the windscreen. All the time, the silence in the car was broken by the harsh, rattling breathing of the occupant in the back seat. When he'd finished, the attendant stuck the chamois leather in his belt with a flourish and leaned down again to the driver's window.

"That'll be fifteen-forty," he announced, presenting his palm for the money. "You wan' Green Stamps?"

The driver shook his head dumbly, as he fumbled out a handful of crumpled bills and loose change from his pocket. His mind was racing now, beads of sweat standing out on his forehead, as he desperately tried to think of some way of alerting the pump attendant to his predicament without endangering them both. Another warning jab of the gun through the seatback made him start, and he dropped a couple of coins at his feet. The attendant looked at him, suddenly curious.

"You okay, m'man?" he asked. "If you'll pardon the expression, you look kinda white." Again a friendly grin split the black face.

The driver mumbled a non-committal reply and thrust a ten and two fives at the attendant. "Here. Keep the change."

As the attendant took the bills with a delighted, "Hey, thanks man," the driver caught his gaze and held it. He flicked his own eyes towards the rear seat, and his heart leapt as the black man's eyes narrowed slightly then glanced at the figure in the back. The driver felt sure the attendant had caught on and hoped he would now walk away without showing it.

The streetwise young black would have done just that, had he been given the chance. He had indeed caught on from the bad vibes the driver had been giving out – the nervousness, the pale sweat-beaded face, the rapid eye movement towards the back seat – that something was bothering the guy. When his eye travelled casually over the man's shoulder, the reason became clear.

He saw the gun first, held against the back of the driver's seat in the extended fist of the hunched dark figure in the rear. Then his startled gaze met the glowing eyes above the white patch of the handkerchief the man was holding at his mouth. Suddenly the pump attendant wanted nothing to do with this. He dropped his gaze from the burning orbs in the dark interior of the big car … and he saw the gun again. It was pointing straight at him now.

It was the last thing he ever saw. The bullet took him right between the eyes, blowing his brains out through the back of his head. His lifeless body sunfished backwards, arms outflung, slammed into a display rack and crashed to the ground in a cascade of oil cans.

When the gun roared deafeningly behind him, the driver felt the heat of the muzzle blast searing the side of his face. He screamed in fear and panic, threw his weight frantically against the door, grabbing for the handle as he did so.

He never made it. In his desperation to escape, he fumbled the lever and the door jammed partly open. The gun roared angrily again and the inoffensive family man slumped sideways against the treacherous door, minus the top of his skull, which had been blasted out through the open side window.

The Prophet sat for a couple of minutes, gathering his strength. Then he opened the rear door and painfully eased himself out to stand, swaying, alongside the car. His back and chest were on fire. He kept his breathing shallow, every breath was agony now, the desire to cough harder to suppress as he bled internally. And each cough that forced its way past his throat brought with it more of the bright frothy blood, which dribbled from the corners of his mouth faster than his red-soaked handkerchief could mop it up. Any normal person would long since have collapsed. Only his raging insanity was keeping him going.

Disjointed thoughts kept floating to the surface of his sick mind from somewhere deep within its murky depths. He had to keep on the move … to Bethlehem House … and safety … from pursuit … from his enemy … from the pain …

The clear image of Curtis's hostile face which flickered on the screen of his inner vision, sent a tide of rage surging through him, lending him strength to overcome the pain. He reached down, gripped the limp corpse of the driver by the blood-sodden collar of its coat, and heaved it clear of the car one-handed. Then he lowered himself into the driving seat, slowly and painfully and pulled the door shut.

Seated again, his back supported, the worst of the agony eased, leaving only the continual pulse of fire deep within his chest with every rasping breath he took. With the choking warm liquid continually bubbling at the back of his throat, it was as though his body was a seething volcano of agony, threatening to erupt and spill a lava flow of his life's blood from the crater of his mouth.

Another racking fit of coughing seized him, doubling him over and ending only when he retched up a gush of phlegm and blood. When the spasm passed, it left him weak and sweating, his chin resting on his chest. After a time he raised his head. He felt curiously calm. His pain had receded a little, as though this latest bout of agony had overloaded some circuits of his brain's pain-response centre. He felt clear headed enough to tackle the remainder of the long journey north.

He reached for the ignition, started up, selected gear and eased away from the pump rack and the sprawled forms of his latest victims. As he pulled out of the gas station exit onto the highway, he drove carefully at first, getting the feel of the big powerful car. Soon he was picking up speed as his confidence increased and, cruising at a steady 80 m.p.h., his whole mind centred on the one burning goal of reaching the sanctuary of the distant Bethlehem House.

66

TEN MINUTES AFTER THE TAIL LIGHTS OF THE STOLEN Cadillac had dwindled to nothingness up the long straight highway, Curtis pulled into the deserted forecourt of the isolated gas station. Deserted – except for the sprawled corpses of the two murdered men, lying where death had struck them down. Death, in the person of the Prophet.

Climbing from his car, Curtis surveyed the carnage wreaked by his enemy – for that was how he regarded the Prophet now – his enemy. He knew he had gone down the road no cop should take, namely that of allowing the pursuit of a criminal to become a personal vendetta. But his initial anger at finding the latest two victims of the insane killer's bloodlust, blazed into an all-consuming hatred of the man who had done it.

A quick glance was sufficient to tell him both victims were beyond all medical help. So Curtis decided his first priority was to resume the chase.

He stared north for a moment, thinking out his next move. It would not be long before some driver would chance on the scene and phone the local police. In the meantime, the slight delay would allow him to run down his quarry. Before the mad bastard killed again.

His decision made, he turned towards his open car door, then paused. He spun on his heel and surveyed the forecourt in the area of the pumps, searching for something he thought he had seen lying there. Spotting what he was after, he walked quickly over to the object and picked it up. It was something he felt might come in very handy. A few minutes of brief activity later, he was on his way again, the needle climbing steadily till it was hovering on the 120 m.p.h. mark.

Less than twenty minutes later, he had sighted the red pin-points of his quarry's tail lights far up ahead. He steadily closed the gap, clawing back the miles between their speeding cars, until only a fast diminishing couple of hundred yards separated them.

Soon the car in front was brightly illuminated by his headlights, and he could see the head and shoulders of the Prophet starkly outlined against the windscreen. Deliberately he kept his lights on full beam as he drew inexorably closer, to dazzle the man and destroy his night vision.

Only thirty yards or so separated them, when Curtis saw the Prophet lift a hand from the steering wheel and knock the rear-view mirror out of alignment to avoid being blinded by the glare. He decided to launch his attack right away, while the other man's night vision was still impaired.

Pressing the gas pedal to the floor, he swung the car out and began to overtake. When he was running alongside, he eased off the gas and matched his speed to that of the other vehicle. He glanced to his right and saw the handsome, leonine profile of the silver-haired killer he had spent the past five years hunting down. In that same instant, the other man turned his head to face him and for a brief moment their eyes met and locked in a bond of mutual hate.

For the space of two heartbeats the two protagonists, hunter and quarry, glared at each other across the intervening gap of a few feet, while hurtling through the night at better than 80 m.p.h. Then the Prophet's lips drew back from his teeth in a soundless snarl of triumph and the next thing Curtis knew, he was staring down the muzzle of the gun the other had levelled at him from point blank range.

Reacting instantly, Curtis jerked the wheel hard over and sideswiped the other car, at the same time jerking his foot from the gas pedal. In the same timeless instant the gun bucked in the Prophet's fist, and Curtis flinched as the passenger window imploded, lashing his right cheek with stinging fragments of glass. He felt the heat of the bullet as it whined angrily past, missing his forehead by a hairsbreadth, and exited via a starred hole in the driver's window by his side.

By the time he regained control of the wildly swerving vehicle, the Prophet's car had drawn some forty yards ahead again. Curtis's hand was reaching into his coat for his own gun, when he paused and made a rapid assessment of the situation. He had to avoid shooting the Prophet, if possible. That could be made to look like abuse of his authority at a subsequent inquiry. He was miles outside his own police area. Out here, he was only Bernard Curtis, citizen, with no authority to chase and apprehend anyone, let alone gun them down. The proper procedure would be to make contact with the local force and turn over the situation to them. Quite apart from the threat of legal proceedings from sect-appointed lawyers, he also had Deputy Commissioner Elrick eagerly awaiting the slightest slip on his part, to pounce and nail his ass to the wall with a disciplinary hearing.

The solution had been in the back of Curtis's mind from the moment he took off in pursuit of the crazed murderer. Finding the bodies in the gas station forecourt had only served to convince him his way would be best for everyone – as well as making the world a safer place. He intended forcing the killer off the road, in such a way as to make it look like he had lost control of his car, overcome by loss of blood from his bullet wound.

But Curtis in his eagerness to catch up with his man, had momentarily overlooked the fact that the Prophet had picked up Foster's gun. This, despite the fact that he had not long seen the evidence of its use with his own eyes, in the shape of the two sprawled corpses at the gas station. His mental blank had almost cost him his life.

He did a rapid calculation. At least five shots had now been fired from Foster's Police Positive, and being a revolver it held six rounds. That left only one shot. If he could make the Prophet fire and miss once more, the gun would be empty … always assuming the man had acquired no further ammunition. It was risky. But it was worth a try.

Determinedly Curtis pressed his foot to the floor, and once more the gap between the two cars narrowed. Then he pulled out and began to overtake again. This time, however, as soon as his front wing was level with the rear wing of the other car, he swung the wheel hard over.

The resultant collision caused both cars to swerve violently, but Curtis was first to recover control of his vehicle, the Prophet being weakened and handicapped by his severe wound. The lieutenant noticed the difficulty his enemy was having in regaining control, from the Cadillac's still swinging rear end. He seized his chance and slammed into its rear wing again. As he did so, Curtis was unaware that the Prophet had twisted half round and was aiming the gun over his shoulder directly at him.

The crunch of the impact between the two wings smothered the crack and whine of the bullet, which drilled through the windscreen before his face. Curtis felt a searing pain lance across the right side of his neck, and saw a small starred hole appear in the glass in front of him. Then his vision blanked out completely, as the whole windscreen went suddenly opaque. Instantly he slackened speed and punched out a sizeable hole in the shattered glass with his clenched fist.

Despite his decreased speed, he had to squint against the onrush of the slipstream buffeting through the ragged hole before him, in order to catch sight of the other car. He was swearing steadily and obscenely as he did so, realising that the windscreen damage inflicted by the near miss would make it well-nigh impossible for him to engage in a high speed chase now.

But his frustration was unfounded. The same collision that had spoiled the Prophet's aim, had also smashed his car out of his one-handed control, much as had happened to Sherman two nights previously. Before Curtis's bleared but exultant vision, the big green Cadillac swerved completely out of control at the end of a hundred yard, rubber-shredding skid, when the front nearside tyre blew out. The car lurched to the right, mounted the grass verge, and ploughed through the safety barrier. Bouncing and bucking down the rough, uneven scrubland of the sloping ground beyond, it finally fetched up hard when it smashed head-on into a rocky outcrop.

Curtis pulled over, doused the lights and parked on the wide verge next to the break in the barrier. Climbing out, he stood for a few seconds to let his eyes adjust to the pale moonlight. Then he stepped through the gap and began to pick his way carefully down the uneven terrain of the slope, towards the crashed car below. Dangling from one hand he carried the object he had brought from the corpse-strewn forecourt of the gas station. As he approached his defeated enemy, he felt no sense of triumph, which surprised him after all the frustrating years of hunting him down. Instead, he felt only a strong desire to bring the whole thing to a finish ... to do what he had come to do, risking life and limb in the process.

Reaching the silent wreck, Curtis walked up to the open driver's door, which was hanging askew on one twisted hinge. He stood for a minute or so gazing down expressionlessly at the pale, bloodless face of the Prophet. Eyes closed, his strong features were peaceful in repose. Starkly outlined against the pale skin of his lower jaw, a thin trickle of blood was running from one corner of his mouth.

Curtis found it hard to believe that he was looking at the killer of at least twenty people. Twenty known victims, that was. How many others he may have slaughtered during his one-man mission to cleanse the city streets of prostitution, God alone knew. The irony was, thought Curtis bitterly, it had all been done in His name.

The Prophet was leaning back, his head cradled on the headrest of the driving seat. He was still alive, as was evident from the harsh rattling breathing, which was forming a bloody froth on his pale lips. The steady trickle of blood from the corner of his mouth was dripping from his chin onto his coat front. Lomax must have scored a lung shot, Curtis observed clinically.

He regarded the mortally wounded man with no pity in his

heart. All too clearly, he remembered the long procession of terribly mutilated corpses, stretched out on cold mortuary slabs over the past five years, in the wake of the man's bloodlust. He hoped the bastard had suffered from Lomax's bullet. He was going to suffer some more before he went!

Just then, Curtis's thoughts were interrupted when the injured killer's eyes flickered open. Dull with pain and shock, they were unfocused for a few seconds. Then they cleared, registered Curtis's presence, and looked up to meet his implacable gaze. The Prophet's bloody lips drew back from his teeth in a silent snarl of hate and he began to speak. The words came haltingly, with frequent pauses for gasping breaths, which rattled in his throat.

"You! ... I knew it was you ... the whore lover ... spawn of the Pit ... you need not think ... that you have defeated me ... the Lord is my strength ... He will bear me up ... in the face of mine enemies ... I am His chosen instrument ... I will return ... when He has healed me ... made me whole again ... I will return ... for you ... I will destroy you ... Curtis-s-s!" The name was spoken with a malevolent hiss, as though he were spitting it from his blood-smeared mouth, so hateful was its foul taste to him.

Curtis held the stare of the glowing, hate-filled eyes. Then he slowly held up the object he had carried from the car – the object he had found in the gas station. It was a gallon can of gasoline. The Prophet's gaze switched to it and his eyes widened as he saw what it was by the light of the moon. Slowly Curtis began to unscrew the cap.

"Mister, if you return from where I'm sendin' you," he said grimly, "they won't call you a Prophet. They'll call you Lazarus!"

Stepping forward, Curtis tipped the can and began to pour its contents over the wounded killer's clothing and into his lap. The stink of gasoline filled the air and the Prophet's eyes widened in shocked disbelief. His expression quickly changed to horror, then fear.

"What are you doing?" he croaked. "No! ... you cannot do this to me ... you are a police officer ... you dare not ... no! ... my God, no! ..."

He struggled ineffectually to extricate himself from behind the wheel, but his maimed body had been pushed beyond its limits of endurance. That, and the steady loss of blood from the massive internal damage inflicted by the passage of Lomax's bullet through ribs, muscle and lung, rendered him too weak to escape the prospect of the horrifying death he now faced.

Impassively, relentlessly, Curtis continued to soak the ranting man's clothing, ignoring his pleas. When the can was half empty, he pulled open the rear door of the car, leaned in and liberally splashed most of the remaining gasoline over the spacious interior. Leaving the door open to create a better fire-draught, he stood again in front of the still babbling, gasping Prophet.

The mortally wounded killer was alternatively pleading and threatening now, his insanity having paradoxically deserted him, in circumstances which would have driven others to the brink of madness. His raving was suddenly choked off in a fit of agonised coughing by the stinging, acrid fumes of the gasoline which cascaded down over his head and shoulders, as Curtis upended the almost empty can and poured the dregs down over him.

Stepping back, Curtis waited till the racking coughing fit ended in a sudden gush of bright red blood, which spilled down over the dying killer's slack lower jaw. Then the Prophet's eyes snapped open again and the pleading was gone. In its place was naked hate once more, and something else – contempt. As though he had suddenly realised that Curtis was bluffing him, frightening him into pleading for mercy in a pathetic attempt to humiliate him – or perhaps to force from him a confession of what the lieutenant claimed were his crimes against the whores he had exterminated. He swallowed to clear his mouth and addressed his enemy scathingly.

"Your bluff has failed … lieutenant … as it did before … you threaten and bluster … but you don't have the guts … to carry it through … like the rest of your breed … you are hidebound by your petty laws … the same laws … which would condemn me … for ridding the world of human filth … the same human filth … you and your kind protect from me … me … the Scourge of God … His Chosen One … The Lord's Anointed …"

"Mister, last time we met you accused me of bluffin'." Curtis's cold voice cut across the demented killer's ranting. "On that occasion you were right. This time you're wrong. This ain't no bluff."

His merciless tone brought a spark of uncertainty back into the eyes of the Prophet. The uncertainty blossomed into fear again, and he cringed before the icy whiplash of Curtis's tongue, as he continued scathingly, "You know somethin' else? You're one lousy prophet, too. You couldn' even prophesy your own death, when it wuz standin' right in front of you. An' I ain't a cop any more after tonight, mister. Wrong again! Soon as I finish here an' git back, I'm turnin' in my shield. This is my last assignment. My swan song, y'could say ... an' yours. An' we're both goin' out in a blaze of glory!"

Before the Prophet's increasingly terrified gaze, Curtis stepped back another few paces and pulled a box of matches from his pocket. He watched in horrified fascination as the lieutenant took out a single match and poised it over the striking strip. A sudden breeze rustled the dried grasses and surrounding scrub. To Curtis's ears it sounded uncannily like the faint clapping of a ghostly audience. He cocked his head towards the sound.

"You hear that, mister?" he demanded. "That's all them poor bastards you cut up, applaudin'. An' this is fer them ..."

He struck the match and applied it to the heads of all the other matches in the partly open box. They flared into hissing, spluttering life, and to the accompaniment of the Prophet's hoarse scream of "No-o-o-o!" he tossed the angrily flaring box onto his gasoline-soaked lap, spun on his heel and walked quickly away in the direction of the road.

As he went, his path was lit by the sudden brilliance of the flames which leapt up in his rear, their hungry roar almost drowning out the agonised shrieks of the writhing human torch in their midst. Almost ... but not quite. Before he had ascended the lengthy slope and reached his parked car, the shrieking had stopped, but the flames were burning fiercer than ever, fuelled as they now were by melting human fat.

Curtis settled himself behind the wheel and laid the empty can on the passenger seat. He fished out his crumpled cigarette pack and lit up. Sucking in a deep lungful of smoke, he looked back at the fiercely blazing funeral pyre for the first time. He felt no satisfaction. He felt no regret. He felt drained ... empty.

He watched impassively, occasionally drawing on his cigarette, until a dull roar and sudden flare announced the explosion of the fuel tank. Then he crushed out his stub, lit a fresh cigarette, and started the engine. U-turning, he drove off in the direction of the distant city, without so much as another backward glance.

About half way back, he made a brief stop and flung the empty gasoline can far into the night.

67

UNAWARE OF THE DEATH OF THE SECT'S FIGUREHEAD leader, Grant, Springfield and their patchwork assembly of troops were preparing to take on the real power behind the throne – the sinister oriental who was using the organisation as a front for his Triad drugs network. As an enemy, he was still very much an unknown quantity to them. The only thing they could be certain of was his propensity for violence. They did not even know his true identity. Known to Grant and Springfield as Doctor Sung, to the sect membership as Archangel Michael, to his fellow sect leaders as Angel One, and to his Triad masters as Agent Red Sixteen, he was truly a shadow warrior of many guises.

However, they were not going in entirely blind against the occupants of Bethlehem House. An earlier phone call to Springfield from Curtis had seen to that, when the lieutenant had passed on his suspicion that the sect could in fact be a front for a Triad drugs operation. He had pointed out that Bethlehem House was conveniently sited to act as a reception point for a trans-border drugs run from Canada. Curtis had ended his call by suggesting that a Triad involvement would explain the apparent fanaticism and brutality displayed by the sect heavies, and warning his old friend to be careful.

At half past midnight, Springfield drew the council of war to a close by pushing back his chair and standing up behind the big desk, where he had been sitting flanked by Grant and Deputy Fenton. The tall sheriff looked round the assembled faces in the crowded office and cleared his throat.

"One last point. I know I've told you this place might be run by these Chinese Triads, but I want everyone t'remember we're dealin' mainly with kids here. These chinks have recruited their so-called Apostles an' Disciples from the streets an' trained 'em to use violence. But Brett here's told you the only ones that'll give any trouble will be the goons wearin' joggin' suits of black, grey or brown. They're the muscle who keep the others in line. We'll refer to these as hostiles, to distinguish 'em from the ordinary members, who all wear them fancy coloured robes an' don't present any threat at all.

"We'll be movin' in fast an' hard once Brett an' Pete take out their Control. Now, when we flush 'em out, I don' want anybody gittin' trigger-happy. We ain't fightin' World War Three here. There won't be no medals for a body count. Return fire if y'come under fire y'self, an' any hostile carryin' a gun will be a legitimate target. But if y'have t'shoot, aim to disable rather than kill, if that's at all possible without puttin' y'self at risk." He settled his Stetson squarely on his head. "Okay, I guess we've covered everythin'. You all know your details, so if nobody's got any questions, I suggest we git our asses in gear an' move out."

The meeting broke up quickly as the other men in the room rose from wherever they had found to sit, some on chairs but most cross-legged on the floor, picked up weapons and equipment, and began to file out. The weapons consisted mainly of shotguns, many sawn off, and the sheriff had issued a plentiful supply of cartridges loaded with birdshot. It had been anticipated they would be operating mainly among the trees surrounding the estate, so the object was to go for maximum noise and shock effect while inflicting the least injuries possible. To this end, Springfield had also issued each man with ten Thunderflash stun grenades, guaranteed to disorientate anyone near whom they detonated, especially at night.

Grant watched them go, chatting amiably and swapping friendly banter as they went, easing their inner tensions as they moved nearer to zero hour. Even though it was true they had come together with a common purpose, he was pleased to see how well they had all mixed.

In answer to Grant's summons, Larsen had turned up accompanied by ten well-muscled companions. Four were the same burly sidekicks who had helped so willingly in the rescue of Louise Wyatt. Having heard the account of her recapture and the sadistic reprisal inflicted on Pam, they were doubly eager to have another go at the sect heavies and had recruited a further six of their own mates and invited them along to the party.

Grant's other ally, Rocky O'Rourke, had also answered the call and enlisted the willing aid of nine other truckers. Three of these were his fellow truckers from the night Jim Miller stumbled into them at the gas station. Rocky introduced them as Carl Wood, Jubal Cantrell and Austen Parker, but Jim Miller would have recognised the latter two as Jube and Red, the pair who had baited him and given him such a hard time before Rocky's intervention had rescued him.

Along with his deputy Cal Fenton, Springfield had mustered the aid of the local Fire Chief, an amiable square-jawed giant of a man named Bob Wallace, along with his entire crew of five fellow volunteer fire-fighters. Big, raw-boned farm hands, they looked to Grant as though they spent their working time wrestling bulls – and winning!

Thirty men in all, by Grant's head count. They would be pitted against the sect's estimated strength, obtained from his questioning of Louise, of the twelve main heavies, known as Apostles, and a further forty to fifty lesser nasties in the bullying hierarchy, who gloried in the title of Disciples. Regardless of their fanciful biblical titles, there was nothing remotely Christian or charitable about them. They were all young, fit and well trained in martial arts by the four Orientals who ran the sect as a front for their Triad drugs ring.

It was also to be assumed the four Orientals themselves would have to be faced, as they had no way of knowing that two of them were already dead, thanks to the actions of Sherman and the Prophet himself. However, when one of the assembled men had suggested that they could have used more men, Springfield had assured them their numbers would be quite sufficient for the job in hand, adding enigmatically that he had a few aces up his sleeve which would reduce the odds against them.

There was one further known obstacle. Louise had also confirmed Jim Miller's assertion that the grounds were guarded by a killer pack of Dobermans, ten in number she said. The pack was released each night after ten o'clock curfew, after which time anyone who disobeyed orders and remained outside the safety of the house, did so at their own peril.

As they filed out of the building onto the sidewalk, Grant eyed the sheriff's broad back and wondered what Springfield was holding back. In addition to the remark about "having a few aces up his sleeve", something else the big sheriff had said was puzzling Grant.

During the meeting, Grant had raised the possibility of the sect's operating an armed outside patrol to circle the perimeter fence, in view of the large drugs shipment Sherman had seen on the night of his suicidal attack. Further, Curtis had informed Grant that the word on the streets was that the recent outbreak of violence and killing had been all about a territorial dispute between rival Triad and Mafia gangs. So it was a fair assumption that their oriental antagonist would be on his guard against any further attacks by the Mob.

Grant had suggested that the first action of the night should be the despatch of two armed groups from the road outside Bethlehem House to circle the perimeter fence in opposite directions. Their purpose would be to seek out and capture any such sect patrol. Springfield, however, had surprised Grant by replying that this would not be necessary as "it had been taken care of." As the big sheriff had volunteered no further explanation, Grant decided to wait and see exactly what Springfield was up to – or more accurately had been up to.

The plan of campaign was to be kept simple and direct. Grant and Larsen would be the first to go into action, their mission to break into the house itself, having penetrated the enemy territory via a gap cut in the fence. Once inside, their objective would be to make directly for the basement as speedily as possible, to seize and hold the Control Room, thus preventing the detonation of the fire bombs.

On the success or failure of this part of the operation would depend the lives of the hundred or more ordinary inmates of the building, because whether or not Control was successfully captured, phase three, an all-out assault by the remainder of Springfield's troops would be launched. This final phase would be triggered either on receipt of a signal from the two inside – or when the house erupted in flames.

Outside the sheriff's office, the men dispersed to the line of assorted vehicles of all shapes and sizes which were parked there. Soon the silence of the sleeping township was temporarily disturbed by the slamming of doors and the revving of engines. Then the line of vehicles pulled away one by one, forming a loose convoy as they moved off along the deserted main street, heading for the edge of town.

In fact, their departure was watched with quiet satisfaction by a surprising number of Rockford residents from behind curtains and various vantage points. News travels fast on the gossip grapevine in any small community, and the watching townsfolk that night thoroughly approved that their sheriff was at last taking steps to deal with the unfriendly and unwelcome strangers who had secluded themselves at 'the ol' Bentsen place up th'road'. As the sound of the engines receded northwards, curtains and shutters twitched shut again and peace descended on the rural town's main street once more.

Heading the seven vehicle convoy was the Sheriff's car, carrying Springfield himself, Fenton who was driving, Grant and Larsen. Next came the three fire-fighting vehicles of the town's volunteer force, two big fire tenders and a turntable ladder. Each vehicle was crewed by two men, with Fire Chief Bob Wallace himself in the cab of the lead one.

Bringing up the rear of the convoy behind the fire tenders were three huge sixteen wheeler trucks driven by Rocky, Chuck, and Red. In the rear of the lead sixteen wheeler rode Jube and the six other truckers who had been recruited by Rocky. Two of the rigs were to provide transport for the ordinary sect members, after their release. The third was to contain the sect heavies, once they had been overpowered and captured. It was crewed by Larsen's ten burly mates.

Within half an hour of leaving Rockford, the convoy had reached its destination and were drawn up on the verge alongside the perimeter fence, just short of the big front gates of Bethlehem House. Standing beside the sheriff's car, Grant eyed the broken cloud cover overhead with mixed feelings. Intermittent intervals of moonlight would mean not having to use flashlights, when he and Larsen entered the enemy's territory. But it could also prove hazardous if they were caught crossing the extensive open ground surrounding the house itself, which he and Springfield had noted on their visit.

Now that their operation had actually started everyone was keyed up and eager to go, and the whole force quickly gathered round the sheriff's car for a final briefing. Springfield held up his hand for silence and the low murmur of talk died away completely. He raised a radio transmitter to his mouth and spoke into it.

"Ranger One to Ranger Two. Are you receivin' me? How's the huntin'? Over?"

As he released the button the receiver hissed into life. "Ranger Two receivin' you loud an' clear, Ranger One." The tinny voice carried to the whole group, despite its low volume. "The huntin's pretty good. Four bucks so far. I kin see your party from our position. Do you want us to join you? Over."

"Roger, Ranger Two. Come right ahead. Out." Springfield slid the aerial down and directed a relieved grin at the quizzical expressions on the faces of his watching companions.

"You'll remember my sayin' I had a few aces up m'sleeve, when we discussed our lack of numbers an' the possibility of these people operatin' outside patrols?" His quiet voice carried clearly to the assembled company. "Well, I reckon it's time to play 'em."

Turning away, he faced across the highway to the north of where they were standing. Following the direction of his gaze, Grant and the others saw movement among the trees there, some fifty yards away. To their surprise several figures, Grant estimated about twenty, filed out from the dark treeline onto the overgrown verge and began to move towards them. The faint moonlight glinted on the barrels of the guns most of them were carrying.

Grant shot an amused glance at Springfield. "Your decks always have that many aces?" he asked.

"Only when the stakes git a little too high fer my likin'," Springfield responded.

From behind them, someone said, "Tell y'one thing – you've played y'last hand o' poker in Rockford, y'ol' fox!" A murmur of quiet laughter greeted this aside.

For his part, Grant felt better about the whole operation. Thanks to the big sheriff's guile, the odds were considerably shorter now. It was now up to Larsen and himself to carry out their part of the night's operation successfully. If they failed, the price would be terrible. For the brutal oriental still held one ace up his sleeve, should they give him the chance to play it. That card was the ace of spades – the death card!

68

AS THE ADVANCING FIGURES CROSSED THE HIGHWAY towards them, it became evident that four of them were unwilling members of the group. This quartet, clothed in black from head to foot in commando-style woollen caps, roll-neck sweaters, trousers and combat boots, had their hands cuffed behind their backs and were being escorted at gun point. It was also evident that they had resisted capture. A couple of them sported bruised faces, and one was limping. A third had a bloodstained rag bound round his forehead like a sweatband, from under which blood was seeping and trickling down the left side of his face.

Their captors were clad in an assortment of gear, army camouflage being predominant. They also sported a variety of headgear, baseball and long peaked golfing caps being favoured, a few wearing ex-army flop-brimmed jungle hats or woollen caps similar to those of their captives. They gave the impression of being a hunting party – not far from the truth, Grant thought, but for the fact that many carried baseball bats and all had their faces heavily smeared with camouflage cream.

The entire party of newcomers came to a halt on the verge facing Springfield's assembled men and the two companies eyed one another in silence for a long moment. Then one of those holding the captives at gun point nodded familiarly to the sheriff.

"Hi, Nate. We're right on schedule. You were right about them operatin' an outside patrol, as y'kin see. We picked up these four ..." the speaker indicated the four sullen captives with a jerk of his hunting rifle, "slinkin' around armed to the teeth." He jerked his head and two of his companions stepped forward and deposited an assortment of weaponry and equipment on the ground in front of Springfield. The sheriff ran his eye over the pile of guns, ammunition pouches and knives, till it came to rest on a radio transmitter. He prodded it with a toe.

"They git a chance to use this?" he inquired of the man who had addressed him.

The other shook his head. "No. We took 'em by surprise," he assured the sheriff. "Oh, they put up a fight when we jumped 'em, but the one with the radio head butted a baseball bat an' called a time-out. It took us five minutes t'bring 'im round again. Ain't that right, sunshine?" He gave a short barking laugh and prodded the bandaged captive with the muzzle of his hunting rifle. 'Sunshine' rewarded him with a look of sullen hatred.

"Okay boys, you've done well." Springfield acknowledged their success with a nod. "I hope the rest of the night goes as smoothly." Then, over his shoulder to Grant and the others of his own company, he continued, "These're some friends o' mine, as you've prob'ly gathered. For their own reasons, they prefer t'remain anonymous, so we won't be usin' names, okay?"

At this, one of the captives spat at Springfield's feet. "That won' do you no good, ya buncha pricks!" he burst out angrily. "You're in deep shit right now. But you go in there, you're way over your fuckin' heads!"

"When I want your opinion I'll ask fer it," Springfield cut coldly across the sneering voice. "Till then, you'd best keep y'mouth shut an' think o' how y'gonna answer charges o' drugs runnin', kidnappin', unlawful imprisonment an' aggravated assault ... maybe even murder!"

"Go fuck y'self! You'll never make any of that crap stick, an' you know it," the sect thug snarled back defiantly. "How about unlawful arrest? Ain't that against the fuckin' law?"

"Unlawful arrest? How about this little lot fer starters?" Springfield nodded at the pile of weaponry. "You gotta licence t'carry firearms?"

"We were guardin' private property," the other replied sullenly.

Springfield jerked a thumb towards the chain-link fence. "In there might be private property. Out here ain't. An' you were caught on this side of the fence," he retorted.

"Fuck you! You're gonna git y'fancy tin badge rammed up your ass before you ever git near a court, muthafucka!" the other burst out heatedly. "You an' th'resta these cop bastards!"

"What cop bastards would that be?" Springfield asked innocently. "I don' see any other cops here, apart from myself an' my deppity."

"Listen lawman, I wuz brought up on the streets. I kin smell pig a mile away, an' these cunts ..." the sect thug indicated his captors with a jerk of his head, "... got the same stink about 'em! An' how d'you explain the bracelets?..." He twisted half round to display the handcuffs on his wrists. "Only cops carry these."

Springfield shrugged. "Don' prove nothin'. Anybody kin mail order these things," he said dismissively. Then, before the other could reply, he turned away and nodded to Fenton. "Cal, lock 'em up."

Fenton moved forward, signalling to four of Larsen's burly mates to accompany him. Taking hold of the captives they dragged them away, struggling and still mouthing threats, in the direction of the "prison" rig. As they watched them go

Grant nudged Springfield and grinned. "Y'know, I think I can smell pig too."

Springfield smiled back. "In your case, I'd say y'nose is too near y'butt!"

Grant laughed, then turned serious again. "I take it these anonymous friends of yours will be stayin' for the rest of the party?"

"Damn right." Springfield nodded. "They'll give us the extra numbers we'll need, when it comes to roundin' up the rest of these Triad Jesus freaks. 'Specially if they manage to fire the place an' have a secret bolthole that comes up outside the line of the fence."

Grant stared at him, surprised. "You mean a tunnel? Are you serious?"

"Sure, why not? The Viet Cong used 'em in 'Nam. Dug hundreds of miles of 'em," Springfield replied seriously. "See, I got to thinkin' about what the chink said when he showed you the firebombs. You told me when you called his bluff 'bout blowin' the place to hell, on the grounds he an' his goons'd burn with it, he said that they wouldn't be there by then. Right?"

"Yeah." Grant's face darkened as his memory flashed back to when he'd stood before the fearsome incendiary device in the basement of Bethlehem House. Again the harsh voice sounded in his inner ear, "... should it ever become necessary to activate this device, I assure you that both I and my staff will be well clear of its effects. No doubt you are disappointed to hear that."

"You're right, Nate." Grant nodded slowly. "An' the bastard even went on to confirm that the bombs are set on time fuses, just sufficient to allow him an' his staff to escape, but not enough to allow them to be de-activated, or to evacuate the ordinary members from the building ... an' most of them are just kids."

"Exactly," Springfield agreed. "Well, like I said, I got t'thinkin' about how our Triad friend would go about gittin' himself an' his goon squad clear, if the buildin' wuz surrounded by a hostile force. That's when the idea of an escape tunnel came to me. I reckoned it'd have t'run' from the house to a point outside the perimeter fence, cuz that'd take 'em clear of anyone who wuz in control of the grounds.

"Next I got to wonderin' where it'd be most likely to come out. I took a trip into Albany an' looked up the architect's plans of the house an' its estate. I discovered an interestin' fact ... namely that the house don't lie dead centre of the estate. It's sited only about a quarter mile from the northern boundary fence. If there is a tunnel, then I reckon it'll come out in the woods somewhere to the north of the fence an' close to it.

"So, I propose to position a cordon at the north-western corner of the boundary fence, while you an' Pete are tryin' to take out their Control. That way, if the worst happens an' they fire the house an' make a run fer it, we'll drive most of 'em back towards the highway, where we'll have a reception committee waitin' to meet 'em! You git my drift?" Springfield looked from Grant to Larsen, and waited for their verdict.

Grant shook his head and laughed. "Nate Springfield, you're an' ol' fox. I can see why you an 'Ben teamed up, you're two of a kind." He turned serious again. "But I think you could be onto something. It's certainly an angle worth coverin', although you'll have your work cut out to round 'em up. Another thing, while all this is goin' on, what about the danger of passin' traffic gettin' caught in crossfire?"

"You let me worry about that part of the operation," Springfield replied. "Anyhow there won't be any passin' traffic. That's bein' diverted till later in the mornin' ... due to road repairs."

Before Grant could respond to this, Springfield glanced at his watch. "Now I suggest we move on to phase two. An' that means you an' Pete are on now ..."

69

IT WAS ZERO HOUR FOR THE WELL-ARMED AND equipped two-man penetration team. Like the captured enemy patrol, Grant and Larsen were dressed from head to foot in dark clothing, only in their case it was less military in style.

They were both bareheaded, but had smeared their faces with camouflage cream and wore dark coloured zip-up windcheaters, denims and trainers.

Each man was armed with a pump-action shotgun with a shortened stock and a sling attachment to allow them free use of their hands, a handgun in a hip holster, and a sheathed knife. Each was also equipped with a Very pistol and two flares, one green one red, a torch with the glass masked by sticky tape to leave only a pencil-thin beam, and a radio transmitter tuned to a master receiver in Springfield's car. In addition, slung across his shoulder, Grant carried a coiled rope knotted every two feet to facilitate climbing. Attached to the rope was a four-pronged metal grapnel.

Springfield and Fenton pulled back the flaps of the cut they had made in the chain-link fence, allowing Grant and Larsen to duck through into hostile territory. The two lawmen wished them luck and with a wave of acknowledgement, Grant and Larsen turned and made their way quickly and silently into the thick woods.

Holding their shotguns at the ready, they threaded their way cautiously through the closely packed trees following the thin beams of their torches. They had travelled only a few yards into the dense timber when the silence of the woods closed in about them, cutting them off from the rest of humanity in a claustrophobic world of towering trunks and patches of thick underbrush. Straining his ears over the slight sounds of their careful progress for any alien noises in the night, Grant found his thoughts increasingly filled with unsettling images of leaping dark shapes and gleaming fangs.

By design they had entered the grounds quite close to the front entrance, and they angled their progress so as to bring them into contact with the main driveway as quickly as possible. To their combined relief, it was not long before the two men arrived at the driveway and stepped cautiously out onto its surface. They began following its twisting route, keeping close to the cover of the trees in case they should meet with any oncoming sect vehicle going to relieve or check up on their outside patrol.

One behind the other, Grant leading, they moved at a fast walk. The only sound in the night was the soft rustling of the trees in the night wind, but to their nervously attuned hearing even that carried a note of underlying menace, especially with the thought of the prowling killer pack uppermost in their minds.

Both men had pocketed their torches to allow them a better grip on their shotguns, and a couple of times they interrupted their progress to stand straining their ears into the whispering darkness around them for any sound of the fearsome dogs. The second time they did this, it suddenly came home to Grant just how terrified Jim Miller and his pal must have been, unarmed and defenceless, the night they had made their escape bid. Here were Larsen and himself, grown men, fully prepared, and yet they were more than a little uneasy at the unwelcome prospect of meeting with the savage beasts.

Then they rounded the last sweeping curve of the driveway and saw the dark bulk of the big house squatting in the near distance, dimly outlined by the fitful moonlight. Grant stopped as soon as the house came in sight and, signalling for Larsen to follow, he moved quickly into the darkness of the trees to their left. Moving away from the driveway they threaded their way through the trees, until they reached the fringe of the woods where they bordered onto the wide expanse of neatly mown lawns, dotted here and there with beds of flowers and shrubbery.

The two men stood side by side a few yards in from the edge of the treeline, examining the layout of the ground between them and the house. They had arrived at a point opposite one corner of the house, but once they left the trees there was no more cover until they reached the broad belt of shrubbery which ran parallel to the side of the building. This shrub bed was a full sixty yards from where they now stood, but just over half that distance from the treeline away over to their left.

Grant checked his watch. It had taken them only ten minutes to reach this far. He tapped Larsen on the arm and pointed off to their left to a spot in the dark encircling woods directly across from the side of the house. He spoke softly. "How about we make our way round there? Less chance of being spotted from the house when we break cover."

Larsen cleared his throat. "Uh ... Brett ... listen. If it's okay with you, I'd rather we wait till the moon goes in again, an' take a chance on crossin' from here ... instead of goin' all the way round there in the trees, I mean. It's these fuckin' dogs. I can't stop thinkin' about the bastards. Fact is, comin' here from the fence I near shit myself each time you stopped. If they do come at us, I'd rather face 'em out in the open. Know what I mean?"

Grant considered for a moment then nodded. "Okay, Pete. We'll go for it. If we do run into the dogs, we'll prob'ly have to use these ..." he raised the barrel of his pump-action, "... so we're as well bein' where we can see to hit 'em."

"Yeah ... an' where we kin see to avoid hittin' each other!" agreed Larsen drily.

Grant plucked the transmitter from his pocket and extended the aerial. He spoke into the set. "Pathfinder One to Rearguard. Do you read me? Over."

The mike hissed softly into life. "Rearguard receivin' you loud an' clear, Pathfinder One." Springfield's reassuring drawl sounded faintly from the tiny speaker. "How's things in the badlands? Over."

"All quiet so far. No signs of enemy activity," Grant reported. "We're about to break cover to head for Fort Apache. Will let you know when we're in position. Out." Grant slid the aerial back into its socket and replaced the little transmitter in his breast pocket. As he did so, it crackled into life again briefly.

"Good luck, Pathfinder One. Rearguard standin' by. Out."

Their eyes scanning the looming dark bulk of the house for any signs of life, the two men moved forward to the edge of the trees. But as they did so, they unknowingly broke the invisible beam linking two electronic eyes set in the surrounding trees. High overhead, its soft hiss merging unnoticed with the night breeze, an ultrasonic whistle triggered into life, beaming its urgent summons to the killer pack.

Blissfully unaware of the impending danger, Grant stood under the outer canopy of the treeline and eyed the cloud cover overhead, in time to see the moon slide out of sight. He turned to Larsen. "Okay, Pete. Let's go!"

Ducking low, their two dark figures sped across the intervening grass at a crouching run, heading for the belt of shrubbery which ran along the south side of the big house. Had they but known, these were the same bushes in which Jim Miller and his pal Tom Sheppard had sheltered at the start of their ill-fated escape bid.

Reaching their goal, the two men crouched panting in the cover of the rustling shrubs, their eyes and ears straining into the darkness for evidence of enemy activity ... two-legged or otherwise! Nothing stirred. Their luck was holding. Now only another thirty yards of lawn separated them from the side wall of the house. Grant's eyes swept up the massive three storied building to the roof. He smiled in satisfaction as he saw what he was looking for, tapped Larsen's arm and pointed upwards.

"There's where I'll hook the grapnel. That big chimney stack. It looks solid enough to take our weight," he murmured.

Larsen licked dry lips and nodded, his eyes returning quickly to their constant sweep of the outer darkness and the encircling black treeline, searching for movement ... for sign of the dogs. In actual fact he had a deep-seated aversion to all dogs, almost amounting to a phobia, which increased in direct proportion to the size of the breed. He hadn't admitted this for fear it would disqualify him from this part of the mission, and anyway he had thought he would feel safe behind the comforting protection of a pump-action.

Now however, crouched out here in the dark rustling bushes, he did not feel at all secure. But he was doing it for his little girl, his Karen, and for her mother, his wife Ruthie.

It was at that precise moment the killer pack picked up their trail back in the woods, having arrived hotfoot in answer to the summons of the ultrasonic whistle. Satan, in his accustomed place in the lead, came to a stop as he picked up the first trace of man-scent. Excited, the dogs spread out, noses questing the surrounding area for more scent clues. Confusingly at first, the trail stretched in two directions, back towards the perimeter fence and in towards the driveway.

Satan ran back and forth on the line a few times, snout quivering as it tasted the delicious scent trace. Quickly his canine smell sense detected that the trail was stronger on the inward line. Seconds later, white fangs glistening with saliva at the prospect of yet another easy kill and of having their lean bellies filled with delicious human flesh, the Hellhounds were hot on the trail of their unsuspecting prey ...

Grant, satisfied that the wide expanse of lawn between them and the dark treeline remained comfortingly deserted, and no light showed in any of the blank windows of the house, slipped the coiled rope from his shoulder. He tapped Larsen on the shoulder to gain his attention and signalled for him to stay hidden while he went forward to hook the grapnel. From his present position, Larsen would be better placed to keep a lookout for trouble and provide backup.

Larsen raised a thumb and nodded in acknowledgement with hardly a pause in his intense surveillance of the surrounding night. Taking a deep breath, Grant darted forward from the concealment of the bushes, keeping as low as possible without actually going on all fours. Immediately he felt nakedly exposed. It seemed impossible he would escape detection, and with each yard he covered he expected the alarm to be raised from within the house. But seconds later he was crouched in the deep shadow under the wall.

Making sure the grapnel was free, he swung it loosely in his right hand, retaining the coiled rope in his left. Standing up, he whirled the triple-pronged metal three times to gain momentum, then let it go on the third upswing. The hooked missile soared aloft, the rope snaking after it as the loose coils flicked rapidly from Grant's left hand.

There was a faint rattle and a metallic clink from high above and Grant sank back into a crouch, waiting with baited breath to see if the slight noise had alerted anyone. A long minute crept by. He straightened up slowly and tugged cautiously on his end of the rope. He had aimed to hook the grapnel round the massive chimney stack at the crown of the gable and it seemed he had succeeded, for the rope went taut as he pulled down on it. He tugged harder, but it was caught fast. It seemed Lady Luck was still smiling on them. He hoped she wouldn't turn fickle when he was half way up the wall.

Placing a foot against the wall, Grant leaned back on the rope. Then he lifted his other foot from the ground and set it firmly on the rough stone surface too. Now his full weight was on the rope, but it held. Bracing himself, he began to walk up the wall, his hands using the knots which were tied at two foot intervals to aid his grip. Half way up he rested for a minute or so to rest his straining arm and shoulder muscles, then continued his exhausting climb.

Grant had always prided himself on his fitness and worked out regularly in his health club gym, but by the time he made it to where the stone coping of the sloping gable joined the chimney stack, he felt as though every muscle of his arms and shoulders were on fire. His fingers were also going numb from the strain of gripping the rope and taking the weight of his body. But he made it. A last burst of effort heaved him over the stone edge of the gable to sprawl thankfully on the slates.

As he lay for a few seconds recovering from his efforts, Grant ran his eye along the expanse of the steeply sloping roof. About half way along its length, he located the barred skylight window he had noted as a possible means of entry, during his recce of the house the day of the interview with Jim Miller. Rolling over, he assumed a sitting position and used his heels to push himself up the slates on his backside until he was seated astride the apex of the roof. From this vantage point he had a panoramic view of the grounds within his field of vision. Nothing was moving.

Leaning over, Grant pointed his torch down in the direction of the black mass of shrubbery where he knew Larsen was crouched, and flashed the pencil beam twice. Immediately a dark form shot from the cover of the bushes and darted quickly towards the house. Grant got the impression that Larsen must have been waiting for his signal, like a sprinter crouched in his blocks waiting for the starter's gun to launch him into motion.

The rope beside Grant went taut and began to give off creaking noises of friction at the point where it disappeared over the edge of the stone coping, as it took the weight of the climbing man below. Just then a ripple of movement far out in the grounds caught the left edge of Grant's vision. He glanced in that direction and stiffened with alarm. Several sinuous black shapes were ghosting swiftly over the grass from the treeline opposite the front of the house. The killer pack was coming.

Noses to the ground, the dogs were coming on at an fast, distance-consuming lope. They were heading straight for the belt of shrubbery where he and Larsen had taken cover. The beasts had obviously picked up their scent and were now following their trail.

The rope was still thrumming and protesting tautly as Larsen hauled himself up its length. Quickly Grant slid down the slates and leaned carefully out round the edge of the massive chimney stack, until he could peer over the coping. Larsen was already a good twenty feet clear of the ground and making steady progress as he inched his way upwards.

At that moment Larsen stopped for a breather, glanced up and caught sight of Grant's head outlined against the night sky. He blew out his cheeks in an exaggerated gesture of effort and grinned, his teeth gleaming whitely against his blackened features in the darkness below.

Grant glanced out beyond the dangling figure. Thirty yards away, the pack were even then thrusting their way in among the strip of bushes. The last thing he wanted to do was panic Larsen, but he had to warn him before the dogs spotted him and gave tongue. That would definitely panic him worse than anything Grant could say. Cupping his hands round his mouth, he called down in a loud whisper.

"Pete, keep movin'. The dogs're comin'. But don't worry, they can't reach you. You're quite safe."

Larsen's reaction was immediate. His head jerked round and he was just in time to see the pack stream out from the bushes only thirty yards away, noses still glued to the invisible trail they were following, and lope swiftly towards the house. When his head jerked back to look up at Grant again, it wasn't his teeth that were gleaming in the dark now, it was the whites of his eyes, wide with fear.

For a sickening moment he swung wildly on the rope and one of his feet slipped a few inches down the wall. Grant's heart leapt into his mouth and he was convinced Larsen was going to lose his nerve, then his grip on the rope, to plummet down to an unthinkable death. But then the other man seemed to regain control of himself, for the next moment he was shinning up the rope as though he had just realised his life depended on it.

Seconds later, Larsen tumbled breathlessly over the edge of the stone coping, helped by a strong one-handed pull on his collar from Grant. As he did so, the dogs reached the end of their scent trail at the foot of the wall and milled around uncertainly, growling their confusion.

"Thanks Brett," Larsen panted, spreadeagled on the slates. "That was too close for comfort. I tellya one thing, I don' give a shit if this turns out t'be Castle fuckin' Dracula, I ain' goin' back down there!"

Before beginning his climb, Larsen had tucked the end of the rope into his belt. So even although the dogs' questing noses sniffed at the scent trail on the wall as high as they could reach on their hind legs, there was no dangling rope to draw their attention upwards to the figures on the roof. But the scent was so fresh, it was obvious the beasts would be unwilling to leave for a while, so Grant decided to ignore them and push on with the next stage of their operation. What it did mean was that the presence of the killer pack effectively cut off that particular escape route if it were needed.

The two men made their way silently along the roof, until they were seated on either side of the skylight looking down into the deserted corridor below. Working quickly now, they took screwdrivers from their pockets and began loosening the screws that secured the steel bars to the window frame. Laying these aside quietly, they then prised up the thin lead sheathing from round the edges of the glass and gouged out the putty holding the pane in place. They were ready to enter now, whenever they chose. Again Grant took out his transmitter and contacted Springfield, keeping his voice barely above a whisper.

"Pathfinder One to Rearguard. High ground taken. Pluto showed up but made no contact. He's still around, so be on guard when you come in. We're about to enter Fort Apache. Deadline ten minutes from now. If no further contact by then, gatecrash the party. Over."

Grant's receiver hissed into life and Springfield's drawl sounded faintly on the night air in reply. "Rearguard here. Message received an' understood, Pathfinder One. Ten minutes to lift-off. Countdown startin' now. Standin' by. Good luck. Out."

70

CAREFULLY REMOVING THE LONG PANE OF GLASS they had loosened from the skylight frame, the two men lifted it clear and Larsen propped it against his knees. Grant ducked his head down through the gap and checked to make sure the corridor below was empty. Then he eased himself through the narrow gap feet first and dropped lightly to the floor. Larsen then passed the window pane down to Grant and lowered himself through in turn.

The men were now standing in the long attic corridor containing the sleeping quarters Grant had visited on his recce of the house. Larsen saw that the skylight through which they had entered was situated at its midpoint, its twin a few feet away on the opposite slope of the roof. Bisecting the corridor at this point was a short passage leading to the two staircases which descended to either side of the house.

Just then, they heard footsteps running lightly up the stairs nearest to them. Quickly they moved out of sight, flattening themselves against the corridor walls to either side of the short passage. Grant unslung the shotgun from around his neck and gripped it firmly across his chest. Larsen did likewise and they waited.

The approaching footsteps ran lightly to the top of the stairs and came towards them. As the figure turned the corner from the stairhead passage into the corridor, Grant drove the shotgun butt hard into his midriff. The grey-tracksuited Apostle, who had come up to make a routine check of the sleeping quarters, doubled over with a grunt of agony. An instant later, the butt of Larsen's gun slammed down on the back of the man's head and he crumpled to the floor in a senseless heap.

Larsen grinned at Grant and made a circle of his thumb and forefinger. "Now that's what I call teamwork," he said. "Like shootin' fish in a barrel."

"Yeah," Grant agreed, then added soberly, "Only thing is, these particular fish happen t'be sharks, an' we won't be able to jump 'em all as easy as this."

Grant listened for a moment for any signs that the slight noise of the brief scuffle had attracted attention from the floor below. When he satisfied himself that it hadn't, he turned to Larsen.

"Okay Pete, you wait here an' cover me," he said quietly. "I'll start wakenin' the kids an' rousin' 'em out."

Leaving Larsen on guard at the head of the stairs, Grant began entering each sleeping cubicle in turn, working his way down one wing of the corridor. Wakening the occupants, he told them to get dressed and wrap up warmly in a blanket. By way of explanation, the bemused kids were told this was a police operation and they were to gather in the corridor and wait quietly for further instructions. A few of the more level-headed ones, obviously relieved at the prospect of imminent rescue from the evil sect which had ensnared them, even joined in and lent a hand. These self-appointed assistants sped swiftly up and down the corridor, wakening their companions and spreading the good news.

Only one factor marred the success of the mission so far. While Grant was wakening the kids, he discovered to his dismay that most of the cubicles held four occupants, sleeping in bunk beds. This meant that the final total of kids to be rescued came to around one hundred and twenty. When they were all sitting cross-legged in the corridor, huddled in their blankets, staring wide-eyed at the two tough-looking armed figures, Grant called in one last time to Springfield.

"Pathfinder One to Rearguard. Do you read me? Over."

"Rearguard receivin' you. Go ahead, Pathfinder One. Over." The sheriff's reply sounded clearly in the hushed corridor, impressing the assembled kids and seeming to confirm Grant's claim to be part of an official police operation – if any needed convincing after seeing one of the feared Apostles being dragged unconscious into an empty cubicle.

"Fort Apache upper level successfully occupied. One hostile taken out. All non-combatants ready for evacuation. Pathfinder Two will stay with them. I'm about to commence the brain surgery." He glanced at his watch. "Commence new countdown. Watch for the fireworks, or gatecrash the party in ten minutes. Over."

This was the code telling Springfield that Grant was about to attempt to take out the basement Control Room. Should they fail to see a green or red flare fired from Larsen's Very pistol within ten minutes, they were to launch the main assault and force their way in. A green light would indicate that the enemy Control had been successfully taken and the detonation of the firebombs prevented. A red light, on the other hand, would mean that something had gone wrong and Bob Wallace's fire-fighters were needed urgently.

"Message received an' understood, Pathfinder One," Springfield's reassuring drawl confirmed. "Stay lucky. Countdown startin' ... now. Rearguard out."

The two men checked their watches and looked up. Taking a deep breath to calm his racing pulse, Grant stuck out his hand on impulse. "Okay Pete, this is it. No matter what happens, you concentrate on gettin' the kids out. See you when it's all over." With an effort he stopped himself from adding, "I hope!"

Larsen's handclasp was brief but firm. "Good luck, Brett," he replied simply. "We make a good team. These assholes ain't gonna break it up. See ya 'round, pardner."

Turning away, Grant walked to the head of the stairs and started down, shotgun held at the ready. Speed was now important. He had to reach the basement and take out the Control in order to ensure the success of the entire operation. Stealthily he slipped down the deserted staircase past the second and third floors without mishap. It was when he reached the ground floor and was only a few paces from the door leading to the basement that things started to go wrong.

He was half way between the foot of the stairs and the door, when he heard voices and footsteps behind him. A sudden exclamation told him he had been spotted. Whipping round, he found himself facing four figures in black military style combat gear and carrying guns and flashlights. They were the relief night patrol on their way to take over from their colleagues, evidently as yet unaware of their capture.

There was a frozen instant of surprised immobility at his startling appearance, before the four reacted. The leader's shout of, "What th'fuck! ..." coincided with the simultaneous upswing of four gun muzzles.

But Grant's reaction was that fraction quicker. He had been keyed up, expecting just such a confrontation, where they had not. In addition, when he had whipped round to face his enemies, his gun was already levelled in their direction. All he had to do was pull the trigger.

The shotgun bucked in his hands and roared deafeningly in the echoing space of the big entrance hall. At such close range, the blast from the shortened barrel took out the entire patrol. The four sect heavies were hurled back, cannoning off the wall at their back, to land on the floor in bloody, twitching heaps.

But as they fell, one of the four convulsively jerked the trigger of his gun. The weapon, a machine pistol, loosed off a short burst, spraying half a dozen rounds in Grant's general direction. Five of the stray bullets bracketed him, whining angrily past to star the wall behind. The sixth hit him high on the inside of his left thigh. He felt as though someone had kicked his leg away from him and he crashed to the floor.

Instantly Grant rolled over and scrambled clumsily to his feet, his left thigh already numb from the tissue shock of his wound. He worked the pump action frantically to eject the spent cartridge and reload. However, he saw there was no need to fire again. The four sprawled figures showed no signs of action. Just then Grant heard shouts and running feet from various parts of the house, converging on the sounds of gunfire.

He would have to get moving before reinforcements arrived.

He felt a sticky wetness on his left leg, glanced down and swore as he saw the bloodstain spreading downwards from around the bullet hole in the denim. But although it felt numb, the leg was still bearing his weight, so he hobbled quickly over to the door leading to the basement, jerked it open and dived through.

As Grant hurried down the narrow concrete stairs, he felt the first warning stab of pain in his torn thigh muscle. Just then the raucous clamour of alarm bells sounded from all over the house and from the basement area ahead of him. Slowed by the blossoming pain in his injured leg, he supported himself with a hand on the rough stone wall and stumbled down the remaining few steps. Reaching the foot of the stairs, he saw movement off to his right along the corridor, but ignored it and launched himself bodily at the door six feet to his left marked CONTROL.

Depressing the handle, he burst through into the room beyond. The black-tracksuited oriental seated before the electronic console glanced round, startled by this intrusion into the forbidden room. On this occasion, the rule of fear they had established over the ordinary sect members worked against the Triad leadership. It was so unthinkable that anyone would dare to enter the Control without permission that Angel Two was momentarily immobilised by his surprise.

Their eyes met for the space of a long heartbeat. Momentarily fooled by the clean white bandage round the man's forehead and the strip of plaster on one bruised cheek, Grant felt a surge of rage as he thought that he was face to face with the brutal oriental who had hurt Pam. In that same instant, Angel Two launched himself out of his chair, the speed of his reaction taking Grant by surprise in turn.

As the oriental lunged for him, one hand shot out aiming a lethal spear-hand nukite blow straight at his windpipe. Had it landed, the blow would have crushed the cartilage and killed him instantly. But in the split second it took Angel Two to cover the few feet between them, Grant reflexively pulled the trigger of the shotgun.

The blast took the oriental in the right shoulder, knocked him off his feet and hurled him clear across the room, where he crashed to a stop with his head and shoulders propped against the far wall. Lying in a widening pool of blood, he stared vacant eyed with shock at his severed right arm lying a few feet from his face, still clothed in its black sleeve.

From the corridor outside someone shouted, alerted by the shot. Spinning on his heel, Grant pumped another round into the breech, pulled the door half open and looked out. It was then he knew for certain that the oriental he had just shot was not the one from whom he had wanted to exact retribution for injuring Pam – because at the other end of the corridor he found himself looking into the glittering black eyes of his hated enemy, Angel One. The man was staring straight at him. To his rear and flanking him were a group of grey-tracksuited figures, armed with lethal looking machine pistols.

"You!" The word hissed from the oriental, his voice sibilant with fury. The black eyes shifted momentarily to take in the mortally wounded Angel Two on the Control Room floor, then back to Grant.

"This time you have overreached yourself. Tonight the Hellhounds will feed on your corpse!" Suddenly he shot out a blunt finger to point straight at Grant and snarled, "Kill him!"

In obedience to Angel One's harsh command, the two Apostles flanking him jerked up their weapons. Grant leapt back behind the cover of the metal sheathed door and as he did so, pulled the trigger of the shotgun, blasting off a wild shot up the length of the corridor. The roar of his shot coincided with the answering crash of gunfire from his enemies' weapons. But their aim was as errant as his own and the hail of bullets ricocheted off the top half of the door to whine viciously into the ceiling of the room, bringing down chunks of plaster in a choking dust cloud. Grant felt the partly open door vibrate against his shoulder as the rounds hammered against the sheet steel of its surface.

Pumping a fresh shell into the breech, Grant waited till the long burst of enemy fire ceased when their magazines emptied. "Sung ... Angel One ... whatever you call yourself ... listen to me," he shouted into the ensuing silence. "I didn't come on my own tonight. I'm part of a major police operation. The entire estate is surrounded. They'll be forcing their way in here in a few minutes. I've taken your Control. So you can forget about burning the house down. Lay down your weapons and surrender. You haven't a chance ..."

His words were drowned out by the roar of automatic fire, as another hail of slugs hammered against the metal sheeting of the door and screamed into the far wall. It was obvious this was the only answer he would get.

This time when the firing stopped, he stuck the shotgun round the door with his right hand and pulled the trigger. The recoil was so violent it almost tore the weapon from his grasp, but he was rewarded by a cry of pain from one of the enemy. Working quickly, he reloaded the chamber of the shotgun with fresh cartridges from his pocket and re-cocked it, feeding a round into the breech.

Cautiously Grant peered round the edge of the open door. Part way down the corridor, one grey-clad figure was sprawled motionless on the floor, while a second was painfully belly-crawling back towards the far end. A head appeared briefly round the corner, then ducked quickly back out of sight as Grant blazed off another shot in its direction. He had to hold the Control at all costs and discourage the enemy from any further attempt to rush his position.

Working the pump action to reload, he stepped into the gap of the open doorway and swung the gun up to cover the empty corridor. As he did so, he heard Angel One's harsh voice shout something unintelligible. Grant was still trying to puzzle out what the man had shouted, when there was a sudden blur of movement at the far end of the corridor and the black-clad oriental leapt out to face him. He was holding one of the machine pistols.

In a split second of surprised immobility, Grant saw the deadly muzzle come to bear on him. Then he unfroze, pulled the trigger of the shotgun and leapt back into cover, all in the same movement. Too late. In that same instant, the oriental fired.

Grant felt a hammer blow strike him on the right breast and a searing pain in his right bicep. Dazed, he staggered back against the console and heard his shotgun clattering to the floor as it slipped from his nerveless fingers. Knowing he had been hit, panic seized him. But when he glanced down at his chest, he saw to his intense relief the smashed casing and circuitry of his radio showing through torn material. The little set had saved his life by deflecting the bullet onto his arm, but it also meant he was now effectively out of contact with Springfield and the reinforcements outside.

Gritting his teeth against the stab of pain from his wounded leg, he dropped to his knees and grabbed frantically for the weapon with his left hand, expecting every moment that the enemy would burst in to finish him off. As his fingers closed round the gun, movement caught the edge of his vision and he heard a harsh bubbling moan from behind him. He jerked his head round and saw something that chilled his blood.

Like some animated corpse in a horror movie, the dying oriental had somehow risen to a kneeling position, blood pumping unchecked from the torn stump of his missing arm. Before Grant's shocked eyes, the nightmare figure fell weakly forward against the far end of the big console, its remaining hand groping over the surface towards a red button.

Now Grant understood the reason for Angel One's seemingly unintelligible shout. It had only sounded that way to his western ears – because the words had been Chinese! Angel One had noticed that his mortally wounded comrade was still conscious. Gambling on the dying man being able to comprehend, he had ordered him to go for the destruct button, while he himself had kept Grant occupied by an exchange of fire.

Still on his knees, Grant raised the shotgun and, ignoring the protest from his injured bicep, worked the cocking mechanism and fired at the nightmarish, clawing figure before him. The gun roared deafeningly in the small room, its lethal discharge taking Angel Two in the ribcage, almost tearing him in half as it punched him back across the room. His mangled body slammed into the far wall, then slumped to the floor, leaving a broad red smear in its wake.

Though momentarily disoriented and deafened by the blast, Grant still felt the floor shake under him and heard the ominous rumble which told him what he dreaded to know. The appalling realisation burst upon him that he had failed. With the fanaticism and blind obedience demanded of a Triad warrior, the dying oriental had sacrificed himself to carry out his brutal superior's final order and had detonated the four firebombs!

71

GRANT SCRAMBLED AWKWARDLY TO HIS FEET, HIS aching chest and right arm joining forces with his throbbing leg wound to make his movements clumsy. A quick check showed the corridor to be empty. Angel One and his followers had made good their escape.

Just then he heard the door at the top of the stairs crash open and feet clattering down the steps. Jumping back, he shouldered the heavy metal door of the Control shut, grabbed up the shotgun and levelled it, ready to fire if anyone entered. But the sound of many pairs of feet charging down the stairs carried on down the corridor without pausing.

Minutes passed till he heard the last racing footsteps fade away, then he cautiously eased the door open and looked round its edge. The corridor was empty of any enemy figures, but more ominously it was now filling rapidly with swirling smoke. Pushing the door closed again, Grant limped over to the dead oriental. Working quickly, he used his knife to cut strips of cloth from the man's clothing.

Lowering his denims to his knees, he winced as the blood soaked cloth pulled free from his wound. Fresh blood immediately began to trickle down his leg, but he was relieved when his examination revealed that the bullet had drilled cleanly through the big muscle of his inner thigh. He had been lucky. The slug had missed the bone and major blood vessels and had not spread during its brief passage, so the exit wound was only slightly larger than the entry wound. Using three of the strips of cloth, he bound his thigh firmly, staunching the flow of blood.

Turning his attention to his arm, he found the deflected bullet had not penetrated it, but had instead sliced its way across the surface of the bicep. He bandaged it with the remaining strip of cloth. When he had finished, he found the pain of both limbs had eased a little with the extra support the strapping provided.

His first-aid completed, he eased the door open again. The corridor was empty of any enemy movement but now the billowing smoke was thick, stinging his throat and making his eyes smart. He thought he could hear the faint whoop of approaching sirens. Springfield's backup must have been summoned by Larsen, either that or they had decided to move in themselves.

Pulling his sweater up over his nose and mouth to filter out the worst of the smoke, he left the Control and made to ascend the stairs. It was his intention to aid Larsen in evacuating the kids from the upper levels, before they became trapped there by the fire. Suddenly he stopped.

Trapped by the fire … the Turkey Pens … Jim Miller and Louise Wyatt would still be locked in them … maybe Karen Larsen too … all condemned to a terrible death … unless he could release them in time …

Moments later, with no thought for his own safety, he was hurrying through the smoke-filled corridors at a limping run. Then he was passing the metal door with the ominous warning sign, and felt a blast of searing heat from its paint-blistered exterior as he did so. Overhead he could now hear the dull roar and crackle of fire, as the hungry flames devoured the old house above him.

He could hardly see now, the increasing smoke and heat choking him and making his eyes water. Stumbling forward blindly, he tried to recall the route the oriental had taken him after his capture on his previous visit. Then he blundered into the turning he wanted, limped down it and came face to face with the blank grey door leading into the four Turkey Pens. At that moment the lights went out.

Grant's hand darted for his torch, but even as his fingers touched it, the floor shook under him and he heard a tremendous rumbling crash in the corridor he had just left. Switching on the torch he swung round in time to see in its thin beam a blast of hot, dust-laden smoke belch past the opening of the short passageway and spill in towards him. Then the angry dancing glare of fire lit up the darkness from further back along the main corridor.

Shielding his eyes against the dust and heat with an upraised arm, he limped back to the corner and peered round. The blast of heat from the wall of flaming rubble he saw some twenty yards away, forced him to jerk his head back and retreat to the door leading to the four cells. Fear and despair gripped him. Even if he shot away the locks and released the captive kids now, they had nowhere to go. The upper floor had collapsed into the basement. They were trapped.

Stunned, he looked down through smoke-bleared eyes at the shotgun in his hands. Maybe that would be the more merciful way for them ... it would certainly be quicker. Tearing the sticky tape from the front of his torch, he directed its increased light onto the grey metal door. Stepping back a couple of paces in the roiling smoke, he aimed the shotgun at the lock and pulled the trigger.

72

WHEN GRANT HAD DISAPPEARED DOWN THE STAIRS to take out the Control, Larsen held up his hands to hush the rising murmur of talk which was starting to swell among the excited kids crowding the corridor.

"Okay, keep the noise down," he told them. "We don' wanna warn the goons who run this place, until our main assault group gits here. It won't be long now."

Obediently the noise level dropped to a whispered exchange, and Larsen ran his eye over the sea of faces packing the long corridor on either side, trying to pick out his daughter Karen. But it was impossible. He suppressed a desire to call out her name. It was better, he decided, that she didn't recognise him for now, disguised as he was. The assembled kids would have more confidence in him if they continued to believe him a cop, rather that just the old man of one of their number chancing his arm.

Suddenly from below came the unmistakable sound of gunfire, the roar of a shotgun sounding along with a short sharp burst of a machine gun. Some of the girls squealed in alarm. Larsen's heart sank. The worst had happened. Brett must have run into trouble. But he made the effort to sound firm and reassuring as he spoke up again to quell any panic among the assembled youngsters.

"Easy there. Everythin's gonna be okay. Jes' sit tight an' follow my orders, an' you'll all be safe."

Swivelling his head left and right like a tennis spectator, Larsen kept watch on both sets of stairs and waited, his gun held ready, barrel pointing towards the ceiling. From below he heard shouting and running feet and from further off came the muffled sound of more gunfire.

Then he felt the floor tremble beneath his feet, and a deep-throated rumble rose from the bowels of the building. Dust floated down from the ceiling and the lights flickered. Several of the youngsters cried out in fright and clung to one another.

The cold hand of dread clutched Larsen's guts. Despite Brett's attempt to prevent it, the firebombs had been detonated. Now it was up to him to get the youngsters out before they were trapped and incinerated. First he had to quell any panic. Raising his voice, he shouted over their rising clamour.

"Okay, can it! I can't hear myself think."

This had the desired effect of quietening them again, and he acted while he still had them under control. Quickly loading the Very pistol with the red cartridge, Larsen aimed it at the open skylight and pulled the trigger. The bulky weapon bucked in his hand and seconds later a brilliant crimson star flared into life high in the night sky overhead. Larsen keyed the transmit button on his radio.

"Pathfinder Two to Rearguard," he barked. "It's red fer go. Repeat red fer go. Send in the cavalry. Over."

Springfield's voice crackled from the receiver in reply, crisp and full of authority now, all trace of the easy-going backwoods sheriff gone. "Rearguard to Pathfinder Two. We read you, an' we see y'red light. We're on our way. Commence evacuation. Out."

Turning his attention back to the sea of faces crowding the corridor on either side of him, he addressed them firmly, injecting his voice with a confidence he didn't feel in order to reassure them. "Okay troops, keep calm. Losin' y'cool won't help none. I want you t'start movin' downstairs. Make fer the front door. Hold hands with the person next to you. Move fast but don't run. Jes' stay cool an' we'll all be outa here in no time. Okay, everybody on their feet, an' let's move it on out!"

Waving a group of the older ones forward, he started them moving first to lead the descent in an orderly manner. He stood his own ground, deciding it would be better to let those at the rear who were awaiting their turn to descend, see his reassuring presence still with them on the upper floor. Besides, he reasoned, they all knew the way to the front door better than he did. It was his job now to maintain order and keep them moving smoothly. As he stood there, waving them past like a cop directing traffic, he kept up a steady monologue of encouragement.

"You're doin' fine … help each other along … don't push there … keep movin' … that's the way … go with th'flow … don't stop till you're outside …"

He kept his voice firm and calm, while the first tendrils of smoke began to rise from below, along with the dull roar and crackle of flames. Things were going well and he saw that less than half of the youngsters were left. Suddenly a passing girl suddenly swerved towards him and threw her arms round his waist. Clinging to him tightly, she buried her face in his chest, her thin shoulders shaking with sobs of relief.

"Daddy, it's you. I thought it was your voice. Oh daddy … I'm so glad you've come …"

Larsen hugged his daughter to him and stroked her hair comfortingly. Swallowing to clear the lump in his throat, he murmured, "It's okay, princess. You're safe now."

Still holding her, he raised his voice again and continued calling into the gathering smoke. "Keep it movin' … that's th'ticket ... jes' stay cool ... everyone's gonna be okay ..."

Then the last of the human tide swept past him and he started down in their wake, guiding Karen with a protective arm round her shoulders. As they stumbled down the stairs, Larsen's heart was full and his watering eyes were not wholly caused by the thickening clouds of stinging smoke billowing up from below.

73

WHILE GRANT AND LARSEN WERE INFILTRATING THE enemy base, Sheriff Springfield organised the main force. Retaining only a dozen men to accompany the vehicles when they entered the grounds, he divided the remainder into two parties and dispatched them to cover the area north of the perimeter fence.

Following his hunch about a probable escape route from the estate, one party entered the woods and followed the line of the perimeter fence to its north-eastern limit. Once in position they were to form a cordon, await his radio command, then beat their way back towards the highway, creating as much disturbance as possible with their flashlights and guns to drive any fugitives ahead of them.

The members of the second party lined the edge of the highway facing the woods, forming a trap into which their colleagues would drive the fleeing sect heavies. Those rounded up in this way would be detained along with the captive patrol in the 'prison' rig.

Once his infantry were in position, Springfield had turned his attention to his motorised troops. Rocky O'Rourke, in the cab of his big sixteen-wheeler, was parked about twenty yards north of the gates. From its rear chassis, two heavy chains were securely attached to the steel bars of the gates. The engine of the big mechanical monster was ticking over with the deep throb of impatient, reined-in horsepower.

Lined up at the roadside on the southern side of the gates, were the three fire tenders with their two-man crews in the cabs. On the other side of the highway the second of the big sixteen-wheelers was parked, engine running and one of Rocky's trucker buddies behind the wheel. The third rig, holding Deputy Fenton's four-man guard detail and their captives, had pulled onto the wide verge ahead of Rocky's vehicle and was now awaiting more prisoners to fill its spacious interior, if all went according to plan.

Springfield himself was standing beside the open door of his car, which he had drawn up on the verge opposite the gates, angled so its headlights were bathing them in a pool of bright luminescence. The watching men saw him duck his head to catch the latest radio transmission from Grant and Larsen. Next moment every head turned to gaze skywards as a brilliant red star flared into life high above Bethlehem House.

The urgent blare of his car horn drew their attention back to the sheriff's tall figure. His arm rose and fell in a chopping motion. He shouted one word across to Rocky.

"Go!"

In answer to Springfield's signal, Rocky's big rig revved up, belched smoke from its overhead exhausts and began to creep forward. The heavy chains lifted, straightened and drew taut, and the stout steel frames of the gates began to buckle outwards. Suddenly they gave under the intolerable strain, ripped free from their mountings and crashed to the ground. Angling his rig onto the verge, Rocky dragged the mangled gates clear of the entrance and off the road surface. As he did so, the three fire tenders roared in through the newly created gap.

The leading vehicle, driven by Fire Chief Bob Wallace, reinforced by short lengths of steel girder welded across its front, lost not a yard of its gathering momentum as it smashed through the inner set of gates, flinging them wide to hang drunkenly from their torn hinges. Then they were through and roaring round the curves of the wide gravel driveway, as they charged towards the enemy stronghold.

Across the highway, the driver of the second rig swung his wheel hard over and accelerated in through the gap in the wake of the three fire tenders. A few seconds later he was followed by Rocky's rig, the chains linking it to the ruined gates having been released from its rear axle by Springfield.

When the small convoy emerged from the wooded-in section of the driveway onto the final sixty yards of straight approach to the house, the reason for the red flare became clear. Both ends of the building were on fire, flames pouring from the end windows of all three floors and licking their way hungrily towards the roof.

As they roared towards the burning building, Bob Wallace hit the siren to let the occupants know help was coming. The two following tenders peeled off to left and right and the three vehicles, sirens whooping, fanned out to cover the entire frontage of the building. They had no sooner skidded to a halt, than the crews had the hoses run out and were training their jets on the leaping flames.

The two rigs bringing up the rear, swung round in a complete circle, and reversed to sit side by side some thirty yards from the front door. This was as near as they dared to approach to avoid the risk of fire damage to the vehicles. Leaping from the cabs, Rocky and his fellow trucker ran to the back of their rigs and threw open the rear doors. From the rear of Rocky's rig, his crew of four armed men jumped down beside him. With their help the loading ramps of both rigs were lowered, then the four men immediately moved off to either side to cover everyone from attack.

They had no sooner done so, than the front door of the house burst open and a flood of blanket-wrapped kids began to pour out. All were in a state of confusion, some near to panic. Waving his arms to attract their attention, Rocky bellowed over the noise of the roaring flames, crying youngsters and throbbing water pumps.

"Dis way you lot ... git aboard ... c'mon, move y'selves ... we ain' got all night ..."

The milling throng immediately surged forward and began to scramble up the ramps into the spacious interiors. Suddenly, somewhere off to the rear, came an yell of alarm and the roar of a shotgun going off, followed by three more blasting off in quick succession. Then someone gave a victory whoop and a voice shouted excitedly, "Didya see th'size o' them bastards? The fuckers were comin' straight for us, too."

Rocky, busy waving his charges on board, glanced over his shoulder in time to see a small group of dark shapes disappearing at a fast lope round the bend of the curving driveway. Four others were scattered motionless on the green turf some thirty yards away.

Satisfied his companions had things well in hand, he turned back to his task of shepherding his quota of stumbling, coughing, bemused refugees into the shelter of the huge container truck. The floors of both vehicles had been thickly lined with straw padding and the grateful kids were settling down on it in reasonable order.

Off to either side, the pumps continued to play their hissing jets into the rooms within the limits of the hungry flames, in an attempt to delay their spread. But they were losing the battle.

Remarkably quickly, however, the last of the human tide ran from the house entrance and up the ramps of the rigs, which were now almost packed full. Smoke was now pouring thickly from the doorway and it had just occurred to Rocky that no enemy personnel had as yet put in an appearance, when Larsen came stumbling out, eyes streaming, one arm hugging his daughter protectively, shotgun dangling from his free hand.

"Hey Pete, keep comin' straight ahead," Rocky yelled at him, waving to catch his attention. As Larsen reached him, Rocky asked, "You da last?"

Larsen coughed to clear his lungs, hawked and spat. "Yeah," he rasped hoarsely, labouring for breath. "I sent 'em all down ahead of me."

"Okay, let's git dis lot outa here fast, before da roof goes." So saying, Rocky called in the four man crew who helped the driver of the other rig to raise his ramp and close the doors. Then they clambered aboard Rocky's rig, and Larsen gave him a hand to heave the ramp up into place and swing the rear doors shut on his full load of human cargo.

When he, Larsen and Karen had settled into the high cab, the girl in the middle, Rocky selected first gear and started them rolling slowly forward, following the other rig away from the roaring inferno behind them. As he did so, he leaned on the horn for a long blast, to let the others know he was clear. Without delay, the fire-fighters gave up the unequal struggle to contain the leaping flames. Shutting down their pumps, they began hastily reeling in their hoses, preparing to pull back in their turn.

"Dis y'gal?" Rocky nodded down at the girl between them.

Larsen looked down fondly at the gaunt soot-smeared features of the hollow-eyed girl and nodded back. "Sure is," he replied. "This is Karen. Karen, meet Rocky."

The girl smiled shyly up at the big man behind the wheel and got a friendly grin in return. "Pleased t'meetchya Karen," he said. "Yer old man an' his sidekick done real well goin' in an' gittin' you out. Hope you appreciate it, gal."

She nodded her agreement and glanced up proudly at her father. But he was not looking at her. Instead he was staring wildly at Rocky over the top of her head.

"Jeezus Rocky!" he burst out. "Brett ... where's Brett? You see 'im come out?"

The big truck shuddered to a halt, spraying gravel from under its locked wheels, as Rocky tramped down hard on the brakes.

"Hell no, I ain' seen 'im." His eyes and voice mirrored Larsen's alarm. "Christ! He must still be in dere ..."

Next moment, both men were out of the cab and sprinting back towards the blazing house. The other rig, unaware of anything wrong, kept going and disappeared from view along the driveway. The fire tenders were pulling away from the doomed building as the two men pounded towards them, waving them down. The three vehicles jerked to a stop in line abreast and the two panting men halted alongside the one driven by Bob Wallace, the Fire Chief.

"What's up?" he called down to them.

"Brett ... you seen Brett?" The question was flung at each vehicle crew in turn. Heads shook, negative responses were shouted back.

"Oh shit!" groaned Larsen. "He's still in there. I'm goin' in after him." And he began running wildly towards the smoke-belching front doorway.

"Pete, don' be a fool. You'll never make it," roared Rocky and took off after him with surprising speed for one of his size and bulk. His years in the ring had left him the legacy of being quick on his feet and he caught Larsen some twenty yards short of the door. He seized the demented man round the shoulders and began to drag him back to safety.

At this distance, the heat from the rapidly spreading flames was almost unbearable. Using his superior strength, Rocky dragged and wrestled the struggling Larsen another twenty yards back, doubling the distance between them and the blazing building.

Suddenly the issue was resolved with terrible finality for them both, as the inner floors gave way and crashed down in flaming ruin. The flames which belched from every opening caused the two struggling men to fling themselves flat on the ground to escape their scorching blast.

Scrambling to their feet, they stumbled to safety, back to where their comrades had left their vehicles and gathered in a group, staring grim-faced at the roaring inferno. After a few minutes, someone broke the silence in an attempt to offer a glimmer of hope.

"Hey, you know somethin'? We ain't seen any of them crazy sect bastards Sheriff Springfield warned us to look out fer neither. Maybe they left by the tunnel he was on about ... well, maybe Brett coulda gotten out that way too ..." The speaker tailed off lamely.

No-one answered him. The faint hope he had offered shrivelled and died in the heat of the hungry, leaping flames. Then the roof caved in, throwing up a huge column of fire and glowing sparks to the night sky.

One by one the watching men turned away and made their way silently to their vehicles. Last to leave were Rocky and Larsen.

74

WHEN THE FIRE FIGHTING AND RESCUE DETAIL HAD regrouped outside the main gates, Wallace, Rocky and Larsen gave Springfield a brief account of their successful operation. Only two questions remained unanswered – the puzzling absence of any sect heavies and Grant's worrying non-return. The big sheriff considered their report in silence for a long moment. He lifted his uniform Stetson, ran his fingers through his iron grey hair and resettled the hat firmly on his head before replying.

"You've done well, all o' you," he started. "Gittin' the kids out after those crazy bastards had fired the place, took priority over everythin' else. Regardin' the non-appearance of the chinks or any of their goon squad, I reckon that confirms my theory 'bout 'em havin' an escape route. Way I see it, Brett's prob'ly followed 'em an' used the same way out." He paused, then added quietly, "… leastways, I hope that's what he's done."

There was a murmur of agreement from the assembled men, then Springfield asked about the burst of gunfire he'd heard not long after they'd entered the grounds. He was told this had been to drive off an attack by the dog pack.

"We got four of 'em," one of the men commented. "Big bastards they were, too. The rest got th'message an' fucked off. Didn' bother us again."

Springfield nodded. "Yeah, that's cuz they come out th'gates an' hightailed it up the road. Big mean lookin' brutes, right enough. They turned off into the woods where th'fence ends. I heard more shootin' right after that, so I reckon it jes' ain' bin their night."

At the mention of shooting, as though right on cue the faint sound of gunfire erupted on the night wind. Although muted by distance and intervening trees, it clearly came from deep in the woods to the north-east.

"Reckon we're startin' Phase Four." Springfield's quiet voice drew their attention back to him. Lifting his radio to his mouth, he keyed the transmit button. "Rearguard to Blue Leader. What's the action? Over."

They waited impatiently for a reply but none seemed to be forthcoming. The distant gunfire was now interspersed by the faint sound of police whistles and the loud thump of thunderflashes. Springfield was about to repeat his call, when the receiver crackled into life.

"Blue Leader to Rearguard. We got us some good huntin' here, sheriff." A few paces away, Rocky raised an amused eyebrow as he recognised the unruffled drawl of his trucker buddy Chuck. The disembodied voice continued, amidst a clearly transmitted background of gunfire, explosions, whistles and excited war-whoops. "So far the bag is two dogs an' some hostiles. Unfortunately, only the dogs're permanently ten-seven. We've taken some minor casualties of our own, but nothin' to worry about, they're all walkin' wounded. The woods're full of hostiles, an' we're drivin' 'em towards the road, accordin' t'plan. Hope y'ready for 'em. Over."

"Rearguard to Blue Leader. Reception committee's in place'n ready for ;em. Keep 'em comin'. Good huntin'. Out." Springfield returned the radio to his pocket and turned to the others, who were already checking magazine loads. He addressed the Fire Chief.

"Bob, you stay here with your fire crew an' guard the vehicles. The rest of you come with me."

Minutes later they had joined the long cordon of armed men, strung out at five yard intervals on the grass verge opposite the woods, from which the sounds of gunfire, explosions, whistle blowing and yelling were now appreciably closer. Fenton moved his big prison rig closer too, in anticipation of a fresh intake of captives. These were not long in arriving.

Soon the first tracksuited figures stumbled from the trees into the waiting dragnet. As soon as they broke cover, they were immediately dazzled by powerful flashlight beams, then loudly challenged at gun point to drop any weapons they were carrying, and to surrender.

Most of them gave up right away, realising they had been caught in the jaws of a carefully laid trap. Many were already suffering from pellet wounds inflicted by the shotguns of Chuck's hunters and the last dregs of their resistance crumbled before the menacing line of armed men.

Only a few tried to be heroes. Those who did were swiftly cut down, peppered with birdshot, as they raised their guns to fire. Eventually the flow dried up and a head-count revealed a total of thirty-two, including the original four-man patrol, when the last captive had been locked in the back of the prison rig.

Springfield's satisfaction with the success of the night's operation, was somewhat tempered by the fact that only three of those captured were from the upper echelon of grey tracksuited heavies, the Apostles. All the others were from the sect hierarchy's lesser rank of Disciples. He supposed it was only to be expected. With the exception of their mentors, the black-clad Orientals, the Apostles would be the best trained and therefore the most resourceful members of the sect's command structure. It was also possible, he reasoned, that some of their number were either away in the city, or casualties of the house assault. Of the four Orientals themselves, not one had been seen or accounted for.

After the last captive had been secured, the cordon remained in place to bag any stragglers, waiting until their colleagues who had been doing the sweep through the woods arrived to join up with them again. The gunfire and noise in the woods had been lessening as it drew nearer and the targets became fewer. Soon an uneven line of bobbing flashlights were seen approaching through the trees, and then the two cordons met up in a noisy reunion of mutual backslapping and congratulation.

The 'walking wounded' mentioned in the earlier exchange of radio messages, turned out to be seven in number. Six had minor gunshot wounds, the seventh had tripped over a fallen tree and broken an arm. All were given first-aid and patched up until they could receive proper medical attention later.

Springfield organised a quick roll-call to check if anyone was missing, deputing the leaders of each group to count his own comrades. Rocky had accounted for all his truckers, with the exception of his three buddies, Chuck, Jube and Red. He was still trying to find them among the milling blackened faces, when a sudden shout drew everyone's attention to a flicker of torch light weaving through the trees towards the highway. Minutes later, a small group of six figures emerged from the woods.

The two in front were shivering teenagers dressed in thin cotton calf-length robes, a long-haired youth and a thin elfin-faced girl. The youth was holding a flashlight and had his arm comfortingly round the girl, who was sobbing quietly, her cheeks wet with tears. Bringing up the rear were Rocky's three buddies, Chuck, Jube and Red. Between them they were carrying the sixth figure – the limp, white-faced form of Brett Grant.

Jube had his feet, the other two were cradling his upper body between them, his head lolling back against their linked arms. The small group halted as Springfield and the other ran up and formed a loose throng around them.

Nodding down at their silent, unmoving burden, Chuck answered their unspoken question. "We got him away from the Chink. I think we were too late. I can't feel his pulse." Chuck sounded tired. He looked round the circle of faces, his eyes coming to rest on Springfield's. "I think he's dead."

The stricken silence which followed this statement was broken only by the sound of Louise's quiet sobs.

75

IT TOOK TWO SHOTS TO BLAST THE LOCK OFF THE stout, metal-sheathed door. Dragging it open, Grant stepped quickly through into the clear air beyond and pulled the heavy door shut behind him, blotting out the smoke and heat. He swept the torch beam round the short passage and saw the two cell doors on his left were ajar.

Fearing the worst, he stepped forward and reluctantly pushed the first door wide open, fully expecting to see a sprawled, lifeless body. But the cell was empty, except for some crumpled bedding and odd items scattered around. The second cell was the same. The two cell doors on the other side of the passage were locked, but a quick check through the Judas holes showed these were also unoccupied. It looked like the escaping oriental had collected the two captives and taken them with him, as he led his followers to safety.

This puzzled Grant. Angel One had shown no concern for the safety of all the other sect members upstairs, so why had he seen fit to save these two? Hostages? Bargaining counters? Yes, that could be it. But how had they got out? He had seen no-one on his way here. The question hung unanswered in his mind. It was academic anyway, for just then another ominous rumble of collapsing masonry shook the foundations, peppering him with flakes of plaster from the ceiling and driving home the fact that he was trapped, with no means of escape.

Suddenly Grant felt drained and aware once more of the increasing ache in his injured arm and leg. Walking to the far end of the cells passage, he lowered himself to the floor until he was sitting with his back to the wall facing the door with its broken lock hanging askew. He stared dully at the hole he had blasted with his shotgun, and saw the red flicker of flames beyond the door. Now smoke was beginning to filter through the hole and round the edges of the door itself. The heat was building up too, as the fast spreading fire neared the other side of this temporary barrier. Even as he watched, the paint on the metal surface of the door began to blister.

Grant's eyes and throat were stinging from the thickening smoke, so he decided there was nothing for it but to check the mechanism of his shotgun. Grimly he worked the pump action to eject the load, closing his mind to the thought of the wall and ceiling smeared with his brain matter, when he put the muzzle in his mouth and pulled the trigger.

He leaned forward to retrieve one of the ejected cartridges now scattered on the tiled floor around his feet. As he did so, his eye fell on a small brass-rimmed slot barely half an inch long, set into the floor next to the fallen cartridge. It looked for all the world like a keyhole. He examined it closer, and it was only then he noticed the faint crack which ran between the edges of the tiles.

A spark of hope was rekindled in him, as his eye traced the faint line and saw it formed a two-foot square. He was certain he had found a cleverly concealed trapdoor. If he was right, and he sent up a silent prayer that he was, it could be he had stumbled on Angel One's secret escape route.

His tiredness and despair vanished as though they had never been. Scrambling to his feet, he tested the floor at his feet by stamping with the heel of his uninjured leg. He was sure there was a hollowness within the two-foot square, compared to the area around it.

Grabbing a handful of fresh cartridges he began to reload the shotgun, fumbling a couple of times in his new-found haste. He was further hampered by sweat stinging his eyes, as the heat and smoke built to an intolerable level in the confined space of the small passage. Then he was aiming the gun down at the brass slot. In his eagerness to escape the encroaching flames, he worked the action and fired three times in rapid succession.

The acrid stink of cordite filled his nostrils, a dull pain throbbed in his blast deafened ears, and a trickle of wetness on his mouth and chin told him his nose was bleeding. But the discomfort was all worth it. Blasted through the tiles at his feet was a ragged hole, six inches in diameter.

Inserting his left hand, Grant took a firm grip and heaved upwards. The solid trapdoor lifted and crashed over onto the tiled floor, and his heart soared as the torch light revealed the wooden rungs of a ladder descending into the darkness below. A cool breath of stale dank air assailed his nostrils, but to Grant it smelled sweetly of life and freedom. Good old Nate Springfield had been right about the existence of a tunnel after all.

Stepping onto the first rung, Grant began to descend the ladder into the shaft below. Not a moment too soon. His upper body was still above floor level, when a tongue of fire licked through the broken lock, and next instant the entire inner surface of the door was a sheet of flames as the blistered paint caught. Grant quickly descended below ground, pulling the trapdoor shut over his head as he did so.

When he reached the foot of the ladder, he turned and directed the torch light down the length of the tunnel in which he now found himself. To his surprise, he could see no sign of its other end, despite the considerable reach of the powerful beam. He saw that the floor, walls and roof of the tunnel were lined with rough concrete slabs fitted closely together without mortar. A dull rumble from above shook loose drops of water from between the joints in the roofing slabs, which sparkled briefly in the torch beam.

Realising that this section of tunnel might cave in under the weight of the collapsing building overhead, Grant started forward. The roof was about six foot high, which meant he had to stoop slightly to accommodate his extra two inches of height as he moved along. After he had walked a little distance, he noticed that the concrete slabs underfoot were glistening damply in the torch light from the constant dripping of moisture seeping through the joints in the roof from the earth above. From this he reckoned the underground passage was now clear of the house foundations and heading out towards the outer fence.

Grant shivered as the cold dank air chilled him and he quickened his pace. Then, up ahead, he saw what he thought was the tunnel's end. However, when he neared the blank concrete wall, he saw an opening to his right and found he had merely reached a ninety degree turn, round which the tunnel still stretched as far as his torch beam could reach. Assuming the Turkey Pens had been situated at the rear of the house, he reckoned he was now heading for the outer fence somewhere off to the north side of the grounds.

Minutes later, when Grant estimated he must have covered a good quarter of a mile, he again saw a grey wall barring his passage in the torch beam up ahead. This time it proved to be the tunnel's end and as he drew nearer he saw the shadowy outline of a ladder etched against the concrete.

Arriving at the foot of the ladder, Grant's feet crunched in a sprinkling of fresh soil underfoot. Looking up, he found he was standing under a short vertical shaft, at the top of which was another trapdoor. Wincing at the protesting ache from his injured leg, he climbed the rungs until his head was touching the underside of the smooth wooden planking. Switching off the torch, he pocketed it to leave his hands clear for handling his gun.

In the pitch dark, he ducked his head, mounted another rung of the ladder and pressed his shoulders against the underside of the trapdoor. A breath of cold, fresh air wafted over his face, as the heavy wooden square eased up a few inches. At the same time, the sound of distant gunfire, explosions and shouting came to him on the night breeze, somewhere off his right and muffled by the intervening trees.

Raising the trapdoor a little more so he could see out, he cautiously pushed out the barrel of the shotgun and checked for any sign of enemy personnel, as best as he could in his limited field of vision. In the patchy moonlight filtering down through the latticework of branches above, he could see no lurking figures.

He knew if someone was standing in the blind spot directly behind him, he was in trouble. But there was nothing he could about it. So he decided to waste no more time, and thrust the trapdoor up and back with his shoulders. It was heavy, being covered by a thick layer of turf, and as soon as he could he checked over his shoulder to satisfy himself the area was entirely clear, before climbing stiffly all the way out and dropping the trapdoor shut again.

He stood for a moment, gun held loosely at waist level, trying to get his bearings. He was surrounded by dark woods, he could see no sign of the boundary fence under which the tunnel had brought him. The distant gunfire and commotion was moving further off to his right. He realised this would be Springfield's cordon of beaters driving the escaping sect heavies towards the highway and he moved off in that direction himself.

The fitful moonlight was bright enough to see by, so he didn't bother to use his torch as he threaded his way forward through the trees. He had only gone a short distance, when he found himself stepping into a small moonlit clearing, some twenty yards across. A sudden movement among the trees on the opposite side of the clearing caused him to stop. He dropped into a defensive crouch and swung the muzzle of his shotgun up. As he did so, he was all too aware of the ache and stiffness in his injured arm and leg, threatening to handicap him in any confrontation with an enemy.

He was also cursing his luck at being caught out in the open, when three figures stepped forward into the moonlight and stopped facing him across the intervening space. The two figures in front of the small group were robed sect members. They were standing side by side and ahead of the third figure, who was positioned directly behind them.

In the clear moonlight, Grant recognised all three. The two in front were Jim Miller and Louise Wyatt. The third figure, standing behind them with a hand gripping each of their necks, was the black clad oriental, Angel One.

76

TIME STOOD STILL AS THE TWO MEN LOCKED EYES across the eerily moonlit space. The sporadic gunfire, explosions and shouting in the depths of the forest, seemed to belong to a different world. Which in a way was true – their enmity was a personal element within the events of the wider conflict.

Grant had to suppress the trickle of fear which ran through him, tightening his solar plexus and quickening his pulse, as he faced this dangerous man. Fear debilitated, and he would need all his wits and ability at his command, if he was to survive this encounter.

Angel One, for his part, sensed the fear in Grant and knew he had this hated enemy in his power ... once he had disarmed him. This he would achieve by forcing him into discarding his weapons. Know your enemy was a prime rule of combat. Angel One applied this precept now. From experience he knew Grant had a weakness he could exploit – his concern for the safety of others – and it was a flaw which would now prove fatal.

Grant forced himself to hold the challenging stare of the

glittering black eyes for what seemed an age, but what was in fact only a few seconds. Then the tense silence was broken by a frightened whimper from Louise, held helpless as she was by the paralysing steel-fingered grip on her neck. The tiny sound of distress broke the spell and spurred Grant into action. He took an involuntary pace forward and raised the shotgun to point straight at Angel One's face.

The oriental did not flinch but merely drew the two youngsters close together in front of him, effectively shielding himself by placing them between himself and the killing arc of the shotgun's blast. Then his harsh voice cut across the moonlit silence of the clearing.

"I think it is time to trade, Grant."

Slowly Grant lowered the shotgun to waist level. He had no choice other than to negotiate the release of the youngsters. He was certain the brutal oriental intended to kill them no matter what assurances he might give to the contrary, because of the trouble each had caused him. Their only chance lay in the strength of the Oriental's desire to kill him instead. He moistened dry lips with the tip of his tongue before replying.

"Okay, I'll make you a deal." He made an effort to sound positive, trying to seize the initiative. "Release them an' you can go. I give you my word no-one will try to …"

"You are in no position to offer me any deals," Angel One interrupted coldly. "I will dictate the terms … and they are not open to negotiation. Throw away your weapons and face me in combat, and I will release these two. Refuse, and I will snap their necks and be gone before you can pull that trigger. Those are my terms. Do you accept or not?"

Grant eyed his enemy bleakly. "So that's why you waited for me to show up!" he commented grimly.

Angel One gave a derisive snort. "You flatter yourself, Grant. I was merely waiting until your police friends finished their clumsy sweep through the woods."

He cocked his head, listening to the receding noises, then continued, "I brought these two as hostages to guarantee my freedom, should I run into any enemy forces." The faces of the two youngsters were screwed in pain up against the pressure of his cruel grip on their necks. "But now I can use them for a different trade."

Grant's mind was in a whirl as he sought desperately for a way out. He had noticed straight away that Angel One was unarmed, having obviously discarded the gun he had fired in the corridor earlier. But that made no difference – he knew he stood no chance against the oriental in single combat. Maybe if he could delay a little longer, Springfield would discover his sweep had failed to capture the ringleader and send men in to flush him out.

"How do I know you'll keep your word and release them, if I agree and disarm myself?" he demanded. "Why should I trust you?"

"Because I am Chinese," Angel One replied simply. "To us a man who breaks his word loses all honour. But enough time wasting. Either you accept my terms and face me in combat, or I will leave you here with your weapons … and two corpses!"

"You've got a strange sense of honour," Grant riposted bitterly. "You lose face if you break your word, but not if you use defenceless kids as hostages to force an injured opponent into fighting you!" As soon as he had spoken, Grant could have bitten his tongue off, realising his words displayed weakness.

The oriental glanced at Grant's bandaged arm and shrugged. "Very well, you may keep your knife, if that will encourage you to accept my challenge." There was undisguised contempt in his voice.

Realising this was the only concession he would be likely to get, Grant nodded his acceptance. The knife did not tip the scales much to his advantage, but even a slim chance was better than none.

"Good. We will begin the exchange," Angel One told him. "The pistol first. Then I will release the girl."

Aiming the shotgun as steadily as he could with his right hand despite the throbbing pain of his wounded bicep, Grant reached down and across his body with his left. Awkwardly he unclipped the flap of the holster on his right hip and withdrew the pistol, holding the butt between thumb and fingers.

"Throw it well away from you," ordered Angel One.

Grant obeyed, flinging the pistol off to one side with a sweep of his arm. As the weapon spun off into the darkness, Angel One released his grip on Louise and shoved her stumbling off to one side, at the same time drawing Jim Miller square in front of him to maintain his human shield.

"Now the shotgun," he commanded, his glittering black eyes never leaving Grant's.

Grant hesitated momentarily, reluctant to discard the main weapon in his arsenal. He now knew Angel One would keep his side of the bargain and release the youth. But he also knew the moment he threw away the shotgun, he was also throwing away his last hope of survival. Even fully fit he would have stood little chance against the oriental, who was an expert in martial arts combat. With a wounded arm and leg, he stood no chance at all.

But his purpose was to save Jim Miller's life, not his own. With a sudden swift movement, he seized the shotgun with his left hand and sent it whirling off into the night after the pistol.

As the weapon crashed into the underbrush among the trees somewhere off to his left, Grant saw the oriental shove Jim Miller away from him and step forward. Gritting his teeth against the pain, he made a grab with his right hand and ripped the knife from its sheath. As he transferred the blade clumsily to his left hand, he knew he wouldn't make it. He had already witnessed the incredible speed of his lethal opponent, and also of his fellow oriental whom he had shot and killed in the Control Room. So, he was surprised when he succeeded in drawing the knife and felt its comforting weight in his left fist, before his enemy had managed to reach him.

Then he saw why. Angel One had not moved. The man was toying with him and treating him with contempt, by showing just how little he rated him as an opponent. It was clearly intended to gain a crushing psychological advantage, before a blow had been struck.

Paradoxically, it had the opposite effect on Grant. His humiliation and fear were washed away by a tide of anger, at this open display of contempt. Then a flicker of movement caught his eye off to one side of the clearing and he saw the two youngsters were still hovering there uncertainly.

"You two get the hell outa here!" he yelled at them. "Make for the road. Go on ... move!"

The anger in him made his voice sharper than he intended. But it had the desired effect of snapping them out of their indecision and galvanising them into action. Grant saw Jim Miller grab Louise by the hand and turn away, pulling her after him. Next moment their wraithlike figures had darted out of sight among the trees like two startled deer.

Now Grant was alone in the night with his fearsome adversary. Only a few yards of moonlit turf separated them. He dropped into a defensive crouch, the knife held defensively before him. The moonlight glinted on the razor edged blade, boosting his morale, even though he knew the weapon gave him only the slightest of chances against the lethal human killing machine facing him.

As a last resort he decided to take a leaf out of the Oriental's book, by using psychological warfare against him. Making a beckoning motion with the outheld knife, Grant flung out a verbal challenge to Angel One, trying to goad him.

"Come on then, what y'waitin' for? I'm the one who's fucked up your entire operation. I hope I've cost you plenty. You drug dealers are the scum of the earth. An' I bet your Triad bosses won't be too pleased with you, either. I hear they don't like failure. An' I'm the one who's made you fail ..."

Grant had no idea how close he'd come to the truth, as he taunted his enemy. Angel One, who was all too aware of the probable consequences when he reported the calamitous events of the night, became irritated despite himself. Smoothly, menacingly, he dropped into the *zingi-tu'ii*, the Kung Fu fighting stance, perfectly balanced on the balls of his feet, his hands held open in the double-axe position.

Grant sensed he had succeeded in needling his opponent and tensed himself in readiness. Even so, he was still almost caught out when Angel One launched his attack, by the eye-blurring speed of its execution. His own martial arts training had honed his reactions, and these came to his aid now. Throwing himself to his right, he only just avoided the murderous flying dragon-stamp kick aimed at his face. As he did so, he struck out reflexively with his knife at the outstretched leg of the flying figure, and had the satisfaction of feeling the blade strike home.

In the same instant, however, Grant was caught a numbing blow on his left shoulder, as Angel One reacted to his move with uncanny speed, chopping down at him as he hurtled past and over him. The painful blow was hard enough to knock him off balance and he tucked in his right shoulder, hitting the ground in a flying break-fall. The stab of fiery agony from his injured arm forced a gasp of pain from his throat, even as he completed the rolling movement to regain his feet.

Instantly he whirled to face his enemy, knife held ready before him. Now his left shoulder was aching from the lightning fast, iron-handed blow he had taken. He expected to have to face an immediate follow-up attack, but nothing of the sort happened. Angel One had firm control of himself again, after his uncharacteristic loss of self-control. He had been surprised at the speed of Grant's reaction and had received a painful, though superficial flesh wound in his left thigh from the knife thrust.

Holding the crouched, double-axe-hand attack position, Angel One consciously slowed his breathing. He drew in a deep *kapalabhati* breath, concentrating his mind on the renewal of his *ch'i*, the inner energy which increases strength and speed of reflexes, and imparts greater pliability. When he attacked, he would move with the speed of the striking snake, the power of the charging buffalo, and the ferocity of the hungry tiger.

Grant watched Angel One closely, waiting for the attack to be launched. He poised himself, blade weaving defensively before him, ready to take instant evasive action. Yet, when the oriental came at him, the man moved so swiftly that he was once again almost taken by surprise.

One moment Angel One had been crouched motionless as a carved statue, the next he seemed to have been transposed several feet nearer in the blink of an eye, like a faulty sequence in some badly cut movie. Grant flung himself to one side ... but this time he was just a split second too late. The vicious front snap-kick caught him caught him just above his right hip, instead of square in the groin, but its force knocked him spinning to the ground. Pain flared in his thigh wound as he landed heavily on his injured leg.

Frantically he rolled clear of any follow-up attack, and as he did so he felt something hard and bulky dig painfully into the small of his back. For an instant he thought he had rolled over a stone protruding from the turf of the clearing, then he realised what it was and his heart leapt. It was the Very Pistol. He had completely forgotten about it, not having considered it as a weapon. As he scrambled awkwardly to his feet, he switched the knife to his right hand and clawed behind him with his left for the pistol's butt.

Angel One had realised that Grant was lame in one leg and knew also that his partly landed kick had further slowed him. He was poising himself to launch a final attack on Grant, intending to finish him off at his leisure. Suddenly he saw his hated enemy reach behind him. Next moment Grant's hand reappeared holding a blunt, wide-mouthed pistol. He had time only to recognise it for what it was – a signal flare gun – before it belched a tongue of green flame at him.

Angel One was saved only by his superb reflexes, honed by years of martial arts training. He reacted instantly, throwing himself sideways into a diving break-fall. Even so, the hissing flare passed so close to his face in its fiery trajectory, it scorched his left cheek. Overshooting its intended target, the flare cartridge smashed into the bole of a tree on the far edge of the clearing, burst into blazing life and dropped sputtering to the ground, giving off clouds of acrid green smoke.

The entire clearing was now lit up as brightly as at mid-day, with an eerie green glow. Momentarily blinded by the eye-searing blaze of the ignited flare, Grant sensed the avenging form of his adversary closing on him once more. In desperation he whipped the knife back to his good left hand and lunged forward with the blade extended before him. A second later he yelled in agony, as the twin bones of his left forearm snapped like boxwood against the rigid bar of Angel One's downward forearm block.

The knife dropped from Grant's nerveless fingers and he staggered back, throwing up his right arm to shield his face.

Next instant his world exploded into rib-splintering agony, as Angel One drove a crushing *seiken* fist-blow into his chest. Grant had time only to register the knowledge that he had lost the unequal contest, and with it his life, before the final *hiraken* knuckle-blow landed, breaking his nose and cheekbones, and smashing him into bloody oblivion.

He was entirely unaware of Angel One advancing to stand over him. The oriental gazed down at the broken body of his defeated enemy. He permitted himself a few seconds to savour his revenge, before delivering the coup de grace with a *heti'i* power-kick, which would snap Grant's neck like a dried stick.

77

WHEN GRANT'S SHOUT HAD SPURRED HIM INTO action, Jim Miller had seized Louise's hand and pulled her after him, as he bolted to safety among the trees. Safety from Angel One, whom he felt sure had intended to kill them, had it not been for Grant's timely arrival.

The oriental had released them from their cells a short time before and ordered them to precede him down through an open trapdoor into a secret escape tunnel. There they had joined a large group of sect heavies, many of whom were armed. The whole company had then made their way along the considerable length of the dripping tunnel by torch light, until they had exited at its other end into the moonlit woods outside the perimeter fence.

The others had been ordered to split up into small groups and make good their escape as best they could and, if successful, to report to pre-arranged meeting places in the city. All the sect heavies had thereupon melted into the dark gaps among the trees. Jim and Louise however, had been forced to remain with their captor alongside the open trapdoor, until he had satisfied himself the coast was completely clear.

His caution had proved right when a short time later the sounds of gunfire, explosions, shouting and crashing pursuit had erupted in the woods, coming from the direction in which most of the escaping sect heavies had headed. Immediately the two youngsters had been forced to descend back down into the tunnel. There they had clung together shivering in the dark while Angel One had stood on the ladder, watching through the slit of the partly open trapdoor until the advancing enemy cordon had safely passed, driving the fugitive sect heavies before them.

Re-emerging from the tunnel, Jim and Louise had been gripped firmly by their necks and forced to advance through the trees in silence. They had not gone far when they had stepped into a small clearing. Their captor had instantly pulled them to a stop, his grip tightening painfully on their necks.

The reason was immediately apparent. There, some twenty paces away across the moonlit clearing, was a crouched figure pointing a shotgun straight at them. It was not until the oriental had addressed the armed newcomer with the blackened face, that the two youngsters had recognised him as the private detective Brett Grant.

Now, stumbling through the close packed trees in the patchy moonlight, Louise panted, "Jim ... what are we going to do? ... we can't just leave Brett back there with that monster."

"Damn right we can't!" Jim replied breathlessly, without slackening the pace. "We're headin' for the guys who're doin' all the shootin' up ahead ... the ones we hid from in the tunnel back there ... they must be friends of his ... maybe cops or somethin' ... if Angel One didn't want them to find us ..."

"Hold it right there!" The sudden loud command brought them skidding to a halt, speared by the beam of a powerful flashlight. They made out a shadowy form in front of them, by shielding their eyes against the blinding glare. Then the figure spoke again and Jim's heart leapt like he would never have thought possible a few nights earlier, as he recognised the nasal drawl of the red-neck trucker called Jube.

"Waal, lookie heah ... if it ain't lil' Miss Nightin'gown again. Y'know, flower child, we're gonna hafta stop meetin' like this, or folks'll start talkin' ..."

"Jube!" Jim burst out excitedly, hurrying forward to him with Louise in tow. "Jube, Brett Grant's in trouble. He got us away from this chink that runs the sect. But he's injured an' won't stand a chance. That slant-eyed bastard'll kill 'im. Y'gotta help 'im. Hurry, please."

The urgency in Jim's voice got through to Jube. He lowered the flashlight. "No sweat, boy. Jes' you lead me to 'im."

Turning his head, he bawled over his shoulder for his companions to follow him and was answered by muffled shouts from deeper in the woods. Then they set off at a run, Jim and Louise leading the way, Jube pounding along behind them. The two youngsters found the going much easier this time, with the way ahead lit up by the bobbing light of their new-found ally's powerful flashlight. Suddenly a bright green glow pulsed through the trees up ahead.

They arrived at the edge of the trees just in time to see Angel One advance to stand over the sprawled figure of Brett Grant. Jube had witnessed – and taken part in – sufficient bar-room brawls in his life as a trucker to know that a sure-fire way of making certain a felled opponent stayed down, was to heel-stomp him. He guessed, correctly, that this was the oriental's intention.

Aiming high for a body shot, so he would avoid hitting the prostrate Grant, he squeezed the trigger. The click of the misfire, as the hammer snapped home on the dud cartridge, was all the warning Angel One needed. He whirled round, saw the danger and reacted instantly. In a sudden blur of motion, he leapt away from Grant and sprinted for the cover of the trees.

In the split second it took the cursing Jube to work the action and fire, his target was no longer there. Tracking the swiftly moving oriental with the muzzle, Jube worked the action and fired twice more in rapid succession. He might as well have tried to hit a flitting moonshadow. Before the thunderclap echo of the last shot had died away, the clearing was empty, except for Grant's motionless body.

At that point, Jube's two fellow truckers, Chuck and Red, burst into the clearing, guns at the ready. While Jube stood guard over Grant and the two youngsters, the other two truckers spent a fruitless few minutes checking to see whether the dangerous oriental was lurking in the immediate vicinity. When they found no sign of him, they returned to regroup in the clearing.

It was then that Chuck had carried out a quick examination of the unconscious Grant, to ascertain the extent of his injuries. He had not liked what he found. He quickly diagnosed broken ribs and a bad arm break. The pale, badly bruised face and thin trickle of blood from one ear, suggested a skull fracture too.

Equally serious, his trucker's rudimentary knowledge of first-aid led him to suspect that the pink frothy blood evident around the badly swollen nose and mouth could mean a punctured lung. He had seen similar symptoms before on road accident victims. But what worried him most was the apparent lack of breathing or pulse. Rising from his kneeling position, Chuck met the anxious eyes of the others grouped around him.

"I don' like the look of him, that's the truth," he announced quietly. "Fact is, I think we're too late. But the least we kin do is git 'im to a doctor quick as possible."

At his words, Louise began to sob quietly into her hands. Jim blinked back tears of his own, swallowed the ache in his throat and put a comforting arm round her shoulders.

"Here boy, you take this an' lead the way," Red instructed him, handing over his flashlight. "Head for the road. We'll follow you an' carry Brett between us. If we come across any o' them sect goons, holler out an' drop flat on y'faces, so we kin git a clear shot at 'em. Understand?" Jim nodded.

Slinging their guns over their shoulders ready for use at a moment's notice, the three truckers picked Grant up, Jube and Red linking arms under his shoulders, and Chuck taking his feet.

"Okay, let's move it." On Chuck's order, the makeshift stretcher party set off with the two youngsters leading the way, Jim supporting the quietly sobbing Louise and lighting the way for those behind.

When Angel One raced from the clearing, narrowly evading the lethal hail of screaming metal shot, he avoided the subsequent search with contemptuous ease. When the two truckers gave up their cursory attempt to find him and rejoined their companions, he advanced to the edge of the clearing to keep them under observation. As he stood there, his glittering black eyes were the only feature that identified him as a living creature, and not a darker patch of shadow in the benighted forest.

From his vantage point he watched their examination of Grant and their subsequent departure with his limp form. He briefly considered following and attacking them. But his coldly analytical mind dismissed the idea. He had meted out vengeance to his chief enemy, Grant, so any further attack upon mere pawns would be unnecessary, therefore illogical. He watched them go with quiet satisfaction.

78

SPRINGFIELD LOOKED UP FROM HIS EXAMINATION of Grant's inert form, a more thorough examination than Chuck had been able to give him earlier. Gathered loosely around him on the roadside verge, the two youngsters and the three truckers had been joined by Rocky and Larsen. They were all waiting in grim silence for his verdict.

Climbing to his feet, the tall sheriff pocketed the small hand-mirror he had been holding to Grant's lips. When he spoke, his matter-of-fact tone did more to reassure everyone than the actual words of hope that he spoke. "I kin feel a pulse. It's weak an' it's irregular, but it's there all right. An' there's mistin' on the mirror, so he's still breathin'. Least that's somethin' …"

He broke off as Jim Miller let go a Indian whoop of relief and delighted grins spread across the faces of everyone in the group. He raised his voice slightly, cutting short their premature celebration. Gone was the slow-talking, up-state sheriff. Instead they caught a glimpse of the real sharpness and authority that lay underneath.

"Now hold on there. Ain't no cause fer partyin' yet awhile.

He's in a bad way. He might be hangin' on, but it won't be fer long if we don't git 'im to Dawson County Hospital PDQ. Pete ..." he addressed Larsen directly, "go git m'car, an' tell my deppity I need him here fast."

Larsen was sprinting away almost before Springfield had finished speaking. The fatigue of the long traumatic night fell away from him, as though by magic. The faint hope offered by Springfield's diagnosis of Brett's condition lent wings to his heels as he raced off down the road towards the vehicles parked at the front gates under Fenton's care.

Minutes later, Deputy Sheriff Cal Fenton found himself in charge of winding up the night's operations, and responsible for getting the whole shooting match back to Rockford. There, temporary accom-modation had been arranged for the rescued sect personnel in the local church hall and community centre, and for the captured heavies in the town jailhouse.

While this was being organised, the sheriff's car, Springfield at the wheel, was speeding through the night towards Rockford and beyond, heading for Dawson County Hospital. In the back, the deeply unconscious Grant was lying across the rear seat, his head cradled in Larsen's lap.

Springfield knew the flame of Grant's life was flickering dangerously low and that time was short. He could almost hear the flapping of spectral wings, as the Grim Reaper himself pursued the car and the badly injured man they were trying to snatch from his clutches.

"Okay mister," he thought defiantly. "If it's a race y'want, it's a race y'got!" Pressing his foot to the floor, Nate Springfield drove as he'd never driven before...

79

ANGEL ONE STOOD MOTIONLESS, WAITING UNTIL the bobbing lights of the makeshift stretcher party had disappeared from view and the faint sounds of their progress had receded into the distance. Then, satisfied he was alone in the night, he moved into action.

Raising his tracksuit top, he tore a strip from the exposed white T-shirt underneath. Lowering his tracksuit bottom, the left leg of which was sticky with drying blood, he quickly bound the already clotting wound in his left thigh inflicted by Grant's knife thrust. His first aid completed, he made a last check around to make sure he was still alone and unobserved then moved off, heading deeper into the forest away from the highway.

Keeping the perimeter fence a few yards away on his left, Angel One loped silently along until he reached its north western limit. Swinging left then, he began following the fence's long sweep to the south. He was now heading back in the direction of New York City, by circling the perimeter of the vast estate. Through gaps in the forest canopy high overhead, he could see the night sky was tinted crimson, telling him Bethlehem House was still burning.

Breathing deeply and evenly, he jogged steadily along through the rustling darkness of the forest, enjoying the exertion and allowing the exercise to wash away the pressures of the past night. Of necessity, he followed a twisting route through the trees in order to avoid patches of thick underbrush, all the while making sure he never strayed too far from the guiding line of the perimeter fence on his left.

Once he had passed the southern limit of the fence, Angel One planned to angle his run in towards the highway. He reckoned that he would by then have far outflanked any cordon thrown up by his enemies, and could safely make for a phone. From there, he would be able to summon transport from Dragon Control in the city.

As he ran, his senses remained alert to the night around him, to ensure he did not blunder into any other hunting parties like the one that had intervened when he was dealing with Grant. It was this radar-like scanning of the night around him, which warned him of a new impending danger. But the hunting party that was on his trail now, was unlike anything he could have anticipated.

The instinctive warning came to him a few minutes after he had cleared a small brook in an easy leap and resumed the even rhythm of his distance-eating stride. Perhaps some subtle imbalance or irregularity in the whispering, rustling night sounds of the surrounding forest, allied to his ultra-sensitive survival instinct. Whatever it was that had triggered his mental alarm system, it set the adrenalin pumping into his bloodstream, and snapped his mind and body into a state of combat readiness.

He began turning his head from side to side as he ran, to locate the source of the unknown danger. There ... he had it ... whatever it was, it was coming from behind him. Then his ears picked up the soft pattering of multiple animal feet, and the sound of undergrowth being brushed lightly aside by swiftly moving bodies. Wolves? Unlikely – they rarely attacked man – but he took no chances. He increased his speed until he was running flat out, buying a few seconds of precious time to allow him to find a good defence position.

Next moment, he emerged into one of the many small clearings scattered about the forest. Sprinting across it, he reached a particularly thick-trunked tree at the farther edge. Instantly he whipped round and dropped reflexively into the *zingi tu'ii* kung-fu fighting stance. In that same instant he saw the menace he faced.

Bursting from the trees ahead of him, three black shapes came hurtling towards him over the pine needle floor of the clearing. He didn't need the sound of their attack snarls, or the sight of their glowing amber eyes and gleaming white fangs, to know that the survivors of the killer pack – the Hellhounds – were on him.

80

WHEN THE FIRE FIGHTING AND RESCUE TEAM HAD crashed the gates and raced into the grounds, the killer pack had not been far away. They had only a short time before followed the tantalising fresh scent-trail laid by Grant and Larsen, which they had then lost at the foot of the house wall.

After casting about in vain for several minutes to pick up their quarry's lost line, their frustration had abated into impatience and Satan had led the pack off in the direction of the tree-line to the westward. Suddenly the night had erupted into a confusion of fire, noise and light, as first the house had erupted in flames and then five heavy vehicles had come roaring up the twisting driveway, headlights blazing.

Startled, the pack had run for the shelter of the trees, where they had milled about uncertainly. But then they had seen a number of man-things leap from the line of vehicles in front of the blazing building, and spread out in a loose line. Kill-fever had gripped their trembling bodies and incensed their savage brains at the sight of so many strange man-things waiting to be torn to pieces. The bloodlust had even overcome their primitive fear of fire. And Satan had led them to the attack.

It was then that things had gone badly wrong. One of the man-things had seen them coming and shouted a warning. The others had spun round, and the short sticks they were holding had belched terrifying thunderclaps and flashes of bright flame. Worse, a screaming hail of invisible death had scythed down Shiva, Moloch, Ahriman and Loki in bloody, twitching death. None of the others had escaped unscathed either, each of them being lashed in varying degrees with myriad points of searing pain.

It had been too much even for their savage canine courage to take. The six survivors, led by Satan, turned tail and fled, instinctively following the twisting route of the driveway in the direction of the main gates. Half way along the driveway, however, they lost another of their number.

Nemesis had been wounded more severely than the others. Blinded in one eye and losing blood rapidly from a punctured artery in her neck, she dropped back unnoticed by the others. Instinct told her to find somewhere to lie up, so she turned unsteadily into the shelter of the trees. With the last of her failing strength, she dragged herself into a patch of undergrowth before collapsing. Within minutes she had bled to death.

The five remaining dogs had raced on down the driveway, past the gaping ruin of the buckled gates, and out onto the highway beyond. Exiting from the outer gates, Satan saw another man-thing – in this case the tall figure of Nate Springfield – and swerved left to lead his decimated pack away from any further fire-and-thunder attacks, such as they had just painfully experienced. The dogs had followed the line of the fence until it ended abruptly, whereupon they had glimpsed many more man-things up ahead. Instinctively they had again swung left and plunged into the familiar shelter of the woods.

Dropping to a steady lope, the pack had run on deep into the forest. There they had just begun to feel safe again, when they had scented more of the hated man-things lurking among the trees. Satan had swerved sharply to pass between them and the fence. Not quickly enough however, and once again the night was split by flame and thunder as fire-sticks had roared terrifyingly close to them. Kali and Hades had been plucked from their midst as though by a giant hand and flung several feet away, almost cut in half by the point-blank blast of sawn-off twelve-bores.

Mindless with fear and panic, the last three Hellhounds had bolted again in headlong flight. Deep into the safety of the forest they ran, intent only on putting as much distance as possible between themselves and the death-dealing humans.

The three dogs had run of for some distance, before slowing again to a steady lope. Then Satan scented water off to the left and swung in that direction. Soon the three were gratefully lapping up cold, life-restoring liquid from a small stream, before settling down to lick the small pellet wounds in their steaming flanks. With the loss of Kali and Hades, now only Baal and Set remained to accompany the big, black lead dog, Satan. But even this last remnant of the once ten-strong killer pack would prove a deadly threat to anyone unfortunate enough to cross their path.

The three big Dobermans lay up, licking their wounds and

nuzzling their flanks with their teeth to pick out small pellets embedded there. Now and then the long-muzzled heads would lift, pointed ears erect, at the muffled sound of distant gunshots. But these were receding and soon ceased altogether, after a burst of three in rapid succession. Soon they dozed beside the gurgling brook, muzzles resting on outstretched forelegs, recovering their strength after their earlier exertions. The minutes crept silently past.

Suddenly Satan's head snapped up, ears erect. Something was moving in the night, and not too far from where they lay. In a flash he was on his feet, followed instantly by Baal and Set. The three sleek heads swung to point unerringly towards the sound that had disturbed their rest.

Nostrils dilated and quivering wetly, they winded the night air for a scent trace. Even this far from the house, the air was permeated with the acrid stink of burning, but soon their sensitive canine smell-sense picked up the telltale odour of a man-thing. Their acute hearing had already informed them that only one set of feet was running in the night, the light footfalls vibrating to them through the drum-like quality of the primeval forest floor.

Now the erect pointed ears scanned for further clues as to the quarry's line of movement. And soon the telltale night wind, whispering through the trees, brought them the information they sought. Excitement rose in them, hardening muscles and quivering their sleek flanks in anticipation of the hunt.

Then Satan's upper lip lifted, exposing the big gleaming incisors, as a growl rumbled deep in his chest, and the three big Dobermans leapt forward in unison. They cleared the stream in one lithe bound and took up the chase. Already the painfully acquired experience from the traumatic events of the night was fading, overridden by the kill-fever which was gripping them, taking over their entire beings.

Swiftly they closed on the running prey up ahead, the scent growing stronger in their nostrils, heightening the bloodlust of the chase. Then they sighted their quarry. The man-thing was alone. And he was carrying no thunder-and-fire stick to inflict pain on them.

The savage hatred Satan felt for mankind had been reinforced by the events of the night. Fury filled his canine brain and coursed through his powerfully muscled body. Giving tongue to his raging bloodlust with a ferocious snarl, he bulleted forward at full speed. His battle cry was echoed by Baal and Set, as they hurtled forward in his wake.

It was at that moment their quarry became aware of them and increased his own speed sharply, sprinting flat out across a small clearing. The three killer dogs burst from the trees in hot pursuit, their gleaming white fangs bared for the attack.

Suddenly, as they arrowed in for the kill, the man-thing did something they had never experienced before in any hunted victim. One instant he had been running flat out, the next he had stopped, whipped round to face them and dropped into a defensive crouch. His unexpected action momentarily surprised them, but their canine brains instantly readjusted speed and timing of strike, as they arrowed in for the kill.

81

THE INSTANT ANGEL ONE SIGHTED HIS ATTACKERS he knew static defence would be well-nigh impossible against such opponents. Part of his speed-of-reflex training as a kung-fu master had been to evade, or divert with forearm blocks, spears flung at him by other trainees in the martial arts school.

But the spears had come at him one at a time, inanimate projectiles unable to change direction, speed or purpose once thrown. The three ravening bolts of fury launching themselves at him now, presented an entirely more complex problem. They were animate, versatile, and extremely fast. And they were coming at him in a concerted three-pronged attack.

In that first split-second, Angel One decided his only chance of survival lay not in defence, but in attack. Had he been facing any of the big cat family, with their formidable armoury of fang, claw, power and speed, for all his martial arts training, he would have been in with very little chance of survival, let alone victory. But pitted against the solely fanged attack of dogs, no matter how ferocious, his own superbly trained body possessed superior weapons in the form of brain, hands and feet.

The dogs' initial surprise at Angel One's turning to face them was further compounded by his screaming kung-fu attack cry and his sudden leap high to his right. The momentary confusion it caused in their reaction, meant that Satan and Baal missed their swiftly moving target by inches, as they found themselves snapping at empty air in mid-leap.

In Set's case, his confusion was fatal. One instant he had been in mid-spring, forelegs extended and jaws agape, aiming himself at the crouching man-thing before them, the next, the target had moved with blurring speed, rising swiftly to meet him head-on. Or, to be more accurate, foot-to-head-on. Because Set's existence ended in a brief moment of agony, as he took the full force of Angel One's flying hip-kick on his open upper jaw. The Oriental's heel rammed the Doberman's head back, snapping his neck instantly.

Angel One landed lightly alongside the still twitching body of his victim and immediately re-aligned his fighting stance, facing in the opposite direction to meet the next attack. It came without pause, as the two remaining dogs recovered swiftly from their missed strike and hurled themselves at him again.

They charged in, converging on him from about six feet apart, like a white-fanged arrowhead. But in the fraction of time it took for the dogs to renew their attack, Angel One's combat-trained eye registered something vital. One of the oncoming dogs was slightly nearer to him than the other, and was leaping high for his throat. The other, only a couple of feet further off, was boring in low, aiming for the region of his groin.

In that fleeting instant of time, he decided to block the high attack, and counter-attack the lower. Throwing his left arm high, he presented his rigid forearm to the open jaws of the leaping Satan, offering it as an alternative target to the beast's intended throat-rip.

Satan took the bait and fastened his teeth reflexively on the blocking forearm. Even as he did so, Angel One was already shifting his weight onto his left foot, in preparation for his counter-attack on his second assailant. This took the form of a lightning-fast front snap-kick, which met the charging Baal squarely on the chest.

The hammer-blow force of the lethal *chungdan ap-chagi* foot-strike, catapulted Baal's body up and over in a backward flip, his rib-cage crushed and imploded into his ruptured lungs. Crashing to the floor, the mortally wounded Doberman's jaws champed open and shut in a bloody froth, as he convulsed in his death throes.

Instantly switching targets, Angel One drove a quick punch at Satan's flank as the dog fell back, his attack having been deflected by the forearm block. The blow struck only partly home because Satan was already twisting in mid-air, trying for another bite as he dropped away. In this, the big dog was partly successful, managing to inflict a painful gash in the back of Angel One's striking hand.

A brief stand-off ensued now, with Angel One crouched in his fighting stance, pivoting slowly in the centre of the clearing, while Satan circled him snarling and seeking an opening to attack. The oriental concentrated on keeping the big amber-eyed beast squarely to his fore, banishing from his mind the pain of his badly bitten hand and forearm, as well as his wounded leg.

Waiting for the dog to launch its attack, Angel One was acutely aware that other surviving members of the killer pack might arrive at any moment to join the attack on him. There was also the chance that the commotion of the brief struggle might have attracted other human enemies, who might even then be closing in on him. Accordingly, he decided to bring the contest to a speedy conclusion.

To break the impasse, he made a sudden threatening move forward. It had the desired effect. Satan stopped circling and swung to face him, head low, teeth bared, his volcanic anger rumbling deep in his throat. At this, Angel One taunted him, baring his own teeth and imitating the big dog's snarl.

It worked. Provoked beyond control, Satan bayed in fury and

launched himself at his tormentor's face. Unknowingly the big Doberman had reacted in exactly the way his devious human opponent had wanted.

Angel One took one swift pace forward to meet the oncoming Satan, and his blood-smeared right hand pistoned forward, fingers extended and ramrod stiff. The lethal *nukite* finger-strike rammed straight between the gaping jaws of the leaping dog with terrible force, smashed through the upper palate and pulverised its brain into instant oblivion.

Disengaging his bleeding hand, Angel One wiped it on the quivering hide of his latest victim. Retreating to the edge of the clearing, he stood for a full five minutes, listening intently to the night sounds for anything out of place. When he was satisfied no fresh threat was about to manifest itself from the darkness, he moved off back the way he had come, retracing his steps until he reached the shallow stream he had leapt a short time before.

Pausing again to ensure he was still alone and unobserved in the night, Angel One quickly peeled off his tracksuit top and T-shirt. After washing his wounded forearm and hand in the clear cold water, he tore the T-shirt into strips and bandaged the injuries, as he had done earlier with the knife wound in his leg.

Refreshed by a drink, he donned the tracksuit top and set off once more on his interrupted journey south. When he re-crossed the clearing, he barely spared a glance at the three lifeless black shapes scattered there as he sped past.

Stretched out where they had fallen, the last three members of the once invincible Hellhounds killer pack stared sightlessly after their executioner – a far more efficient and dangerous killer than Nature had ever equipped them to be at the height of their savage power.

The light footfalls of their human destroyer faded into the night and the silence of the brooding trees closed in like a shroud over the scene of his latest carnage.

82

GRANT WAS MOVING STEADILY DOWN A LONG gentle slope. He seemed to have been moving for an immeasurable time. He had the impression of being enveloped in a faintly luminous mist, like some high-flying bird drifting through a summer cloud. He knew he must be dreaming.

All around him too, he sensed music. But it was like no music he had ever experienced before. It was soothing and restful and seemed to be urging him gently onward in some mysterious fashion. Dreamily he tried to concentrate on it, to classify it, but it defied his effort. It had no identifiable melody, it was just beautifully melodic, rising and falling gently as it carried him along. He sensed, rather than heard it, as if it and the all-pervading light were one and the same.

Ahead and around him as he drifted forward, the melodic light was increasing gradually, growing stronger and brighter as though he were heading for the source. He was conscious of a growing feeling of peace and well-being as he drew nearer – like a weary traveller returning home after a long and tiring journey.

Then he heard the voice.

The melodious sound and the forward motion ceased, and he was floating in a hazy limbo of silence, listening intently. But listening for what? The voice or the music.

Then he heard the voice again.

It was faint and far off, but insistent – and it was calling his name over and over. The voice seemed familiar and he felt he should recognise it, but at first he felt it only as a persuasive force tugging at him, trying to draw him back from the comfort and welcome of the light.

He tried to resist the voice – to shut it out from his mind – to will himself towards his destination again – towards the light. He had succeeded in drifting forward and downward again, when the voice drew him to a stop once more. It was pleading with him now, calling him back. Back? Back where? He felt confused, lost. Then recognition dawned.

It was Pam's voice.

Though faint and far off, her words suddenly became clear to him and he could understand their meaning. "Brett ... I love you, sweetheart ... please come back to me ... please don't leave me ... I love you so much ... I don't want to lose you ... please, Brett honey, come back to me ... don't give up ... don't die ..."

"... don't give up? ... don't die? ..." He examined the thought curiously, dispassionately. Was that what was happening to him? For a long moment, Grant looked at the brightness ahead. It was not calling to him as Pam was, but nevertheless it promised welcome, no pain, peace ...

Reluctantly, he willed himself to turn and go back ... back up the long slope, towards the sound of his beloved Pam's voice which was still calling to him incessantly. As he did so, he felt a great sadness, an acute sense of loss, filling his entire being. The feeling faded with the dwindling light, as he moved away from its source.

Soon the ascent grew steeper and he began to tire. Pam's voice still urged him onward, encouraging him, but as he struggled upwards towards it, the darkness was closing in thickly around him, making it progressively harder to see or breathe. He became aware that his heartbeat was growing stronger – until soon it was pounding in his chest, each pulse bringing with it a stab of increasing pain. Had it not been for Pam's voice cajoling him onward and upward, he would have given up the struggle.

At last, faint and far off in the total blackness which now surrounded him, he saw another gleam of light. Unlike the previous soft glow, this new light had a sharpness about it, and it beckoned him upward like the guiding beam of a lighthouse in a dark stormy sea. Slowly, painfully, he forced himself upwards to reach it. The ascent had now become so steep, it seemed as though he were now swimming up through the darkness, which was thickening and growing viscous. It was exhausting him.

The light was directly above him now, increasing in intensity and hurting his eyes. Not that it mattered. His whole body seemed to be one total ache now. But as he drove himself into a last titanic effort to surface into the light, the pain began to divide and concentrate itself in separate areas of his body; his head, his right arm and his chest. He felt exhausted, as though he had just run a marathon.

Then a face swam into view above him, filling his blurred vision, as he regained consciousness. It was Pam. She was smiling at him, although her eyes were bright with unshed tears. He tried to smile back and winced as his stiff and swollen upper lip objected agonisingly.

"Hi, lover," she said, her lips trembling as she fought back the urge to weep with happiness at his recovery. "Welcome back."

"Hi," he mumbled back, his bruised, swollen mouth making his speech thick. "Heard y'callin' me. Came as quick as I could." It was all he could think of to say, at that confused moment of re-awakening. His voice was hoarse and weak, as though rusty from disuse. He felt groggy and disorientated. Pam's face was slipping in and out of focus. His head and chest were pounding intolerably.

"Is the pain bad, honey?" he heard Pam's anxious voice from far off.

"Yeah," he managed to mumble. "Rough."

"I'll ring for the doctor. He'll fix you up ..." Pam's voice faded.

Then he became aware of new faces floating high above him. Strange faces. One was thin and bespectacled, a man's face. The other was a female face, topped by a little white cap.

The man was speaking to him. He knew this because he could see his lips moving. But he could hear nothing except a dull roaring in his ears. Then he felt a tiny prick in his arm and the pain, the faces, the roaring, all began to recede, and he floated away into a warm, restful darkness.

83

WHEN GRANT REGAINED CONSCIOUSNESS AGAIN, the pain was still with him, but now it was at a bearable level.

He discovered quickly that he could lessen his discomfort by lying still and keeping his breathing shallow. He learned this the hard way, when he tried to move his head. The resultant sharp pain made him suck in his breath, which in turn caused a burning stab of agony in his chest.

He lay still until the pain had subsided again to a dull ache, then let his eyes examine his surroundings as far as was possible without moving his head. His field of vision was restricted by padding taped over his nose and cheekbones. But from what he could see, he was in a private room in some hospital, to judge from the clinically white decor and the chrome steel stand by the bedside, holding the drip bottle which was attached to his left arm by a tube. Just like Harry Sherman, the night of the attack by the bogus nurse, the thought occurred to him.

Why am I here? was his next thought. For a moment his mind was blank, then it all came flooding back. The events of the past week raced past his mind's eye in a matter of seconds, the mental images flickering before him in rapid succession like a movie trailer. Virgil Miller in his office; meeting Louise at the sect van; the ranting, golden-robed Prophet at the Crusade; the nightmare chase in the bowels of the Washington Centre; the confrontation with Angel One after the Jim Miller interview; Louise's rescue; Pam's hand impaled to the table; Harry Sherman's bandaged form and the fight with the bogus nurse in the hospital room; his capture of the Bethlehem House Control and the gunfight in the basement corridor; the escape from the fire through the underground tunnel; and lastly the fight with Angel One in the clearing ... the fight ... he couldn't recall anything after being hit in the chest ...

He knew he must have been knocked out and he wondered just how much damage the oriental had done to him. His left arm was attached to the drip, so he gingerly raised his stiff right arm, which was heavily strapped from shoulder to wrist and began to explore the extent of his body and head injuries as best he could. Suddenly he heard the room door open and a brisk female voice addressed him as footsteps approached the bed.

"Aha, so we've decided to waken up, have we? Hand down please, Mister Grant. You might hurt youself." His arm was grasped gently but firmly and pushed back down on the bed cover. The owner of the voice came into his field of vision. Grant found himself looking up at an attractive dark-haired nurse. She smiled down at him as she smoothed the bedclothes and began checking him over.

Pushing a thermometer gently into the corner of his swollen mouth, she continued chattering away brightly. "You've collected a few broken bones and they're newly set. So if you go poking and prodding about, you may dislodge something and hurt yourself. You're also on a drip, as you can see. You could pull that loose too, so you'll just have to be patient and lie still for now. How do you feel?" This last question was apparently directed to her watch, which she was studying as she checked his pulse.

"Hungry," he replied indistinctly round the thermometer. His swollen upper lip felt enormous and stiff, as though he were recovering from a dental injection. The two factors combined to make speech difficult. The slim tube feeding into his bandaged nose didn't help either.

"That's a good sign," she told the clipboard on which she was entering the details of his pulse rate. Moving round to the other side of the bed, the nurse proceeded to change the bottle on the drip. "Are you in any pain?" she asked the bottle.

"Some," Grant replied round the glass tube in his mouth, just in case the question was really intended for him.

The nurse plucked the thermometer out of his mouth. She checked its reading and entered another note on the clipboard.

"I'll fetch the doctor and he'll give you something to make you comfortable. He'll want to see you anyway, now that you've regained consciousness."

She paused and glanced towards the door, through which Grant heard the sound of footsteps entering, and smiled. "Ah there you are, Miss Mason. You'll be pleased to know our patient has decided to waken up and grace us with his company, at long last."

The nurse moved away from the bed and out of Grant's vision, to be replaced immediately by a shining-eyed Pam, relief and concern vying for control of her features. She leaned over him and kissed him gently on the corner of his mouth. "Hi sweetheart," she said. "Welcome back. How do you feel?"

"Deprived," he mumbled through swollen lips.

"Deprived? How deprived?" she asked, mystified.

"Wanna prop'r kiss, tha's why," he replied thickly.

She laughed. "Is that so? Well, you can't have one just now. Your mouth's too swollen, and I don't want to hurt you."

"If I don' get a kiss, I'll be hurt worse," he persisted.

"Clown!" she laughed, shaking her head. But she leaned down and placed her soft lips gently on his bruised mouth. A butterfly would have exerted more pressure alighting on a flower petal. Grant inhaled her perfume, felt the feather-light warmth of her lips on his, and closed his eyes contentedly.

After a few seconds, Pam straightened up, seated herself on the chair beside the bed and took his right hand gently in her own. The action jogged Grant's memory. "Hey, how's th'hand?" he inquired.

"Fine thanks, sweetheart. See," she held it up for his inspection. Only the tips of her fingers were visible above the bandaging, which extended to her wrist. "Anyway, I've been so concerned about you, I clean forgot to feel sorry for myself. But don't worry, I'll make up for it when I get you home. You can sit by my bed for five days, and pamper me, for a change."

"Five days? I've been out for five days?" he demanded incredulously.

She nodded. "You passed the crisis yesterday evening. We thought ... we thought we'd lost you. You seemed to be sinking lower and lower. Almost as if you were losing the will to live, the doctor said. I watched that damned green dot bouncing lower and lower, until it almost hypnotised me." She nodded her head at the cardiac monitor over against the far wall.

"Finally, the doctor said there was nothing more they could do. Then I remembered how sometimes people in a coma can be reached by the voices of their favourite pop stars, or someone they loved. So, I started talking to you ... asking you to come back to me ... not to leave me. And it worked. You did. You came back to me."

She paused for a moment, choked with emotion and dabbed

her brimming eyes with a tissue. Then she sniffed, smiled at him and continued. "You regained consciousness about half an hour after I started talking to you. Oh ... that reminds me ... when you came round, you mumbled something about having heard me calling you. Did you? Can you remember?"

He nodded slowly once. He had a throbbing headache building, centred behind his nose and eyes. But he didn't want to say because he knew if he did, Pam would insist on leaving him to rest. To please her, he briefly outlined his dream-like experience, his speech slurring due to the awkwardness of his stiff, swollen mouth. He was rewarded by the happiness which showed in Pam's eyes, when he told her he was quite sure she had indeed called him back from the brink of death. He was further rewarded when she leaned forward and kissed him gently again on his bruised mouth.

"Okay you two, break it up! Nate, go git a bucket of cold water an' throw it over 'em," Curtis's voice rasped from the door.

Pam sat up, her face flushed with happiness and an almost girlish embarrassment, and grinned at the two men who had just entered. They crossed the room to stand at the other side of the bed. Curtis turned to Springfield. "Whaddaya think, Sheriff?" he said. "Should I book 'em on a charge of indecent behaviour in a public place ... or should I jes' book 'em into a motel an' let 'em git on with it?"

"Waal now ..." Springfield rubbed his jaw thoughtfully, "... it's a mite difficult t'say. 'Specially seein' as how yore bookin' days're over now ..."

"Damn! So they are, I forgot. I'd like to have bust 'im on one last rap before I finished, too." Curtis sighed with regret, then grinned down at Grant and Pam. "We dropped by t'see how the invalids were, but I kin see you're both well on the way to recovery. I guess I'll jes' hafta eat these damn grapes myself." He waved a bulging brown paper bag he was carrying in one hand. "Anyway, how're y'both feelin' ... or hadn't y'got that far yet?"

Pam flushed again and laughed. "Ben Curtis, don't be crude."

"Who's crude?" He spread his hands in appeal. "I'm jealous,

is all. If it wuz me lyin' there, my Ruthie'd be ransackin' the house lookin' fer the insurance policies, t'check they wuz payed up t'date. An' why're you lookin' at me like that? Y'look like either you got constipation, or y'got somethin' t'say." This last remark was addressed to Grant, who was indeed waiting for a break in Curtis's verbal flow, in order to get a word in.

But at that moment the nurse returned accompanied by a white-coated bespectacled young doctor, who frowned when he saw Curtis and Springfield.

"I hope you're not over-taxing the patient." His voice, like his features, was sharp with disapproval. "He'll be weak and easily tired at this stage, having just recovered consciousness."

Pam and the others moved aside to allow the doctor and the nurse to check Grant out, and Curtis pulled a face at the doctor's back, making Pam stifle a giggle.

"We jes' dropped in t'cheer 'im up, doc'," Curtis said to the white-coated back, as the doctor prepared a syringe and slid the needle expertly into a vein in Grant's arm. Finished, the doctor laid the syringe on the nurse's tray and turned to leave.

"Well, I should prefer you to leave your visiting until the patient is stronger," he told Curtis. "But you're here now, so you may have a few more minutes with him, until the drug I have just administered takes effect. Mister Grant has a long way to go before he will fully recover from his injuries. Rest and quiet are what he needs most, right now. So, please make your stay short."

At the door, he turned and addressed Pam. "You may stay if you wish, Miss Mason. But I'd advise you to get some rest yourself. Mister Grant has passed the crisis point now and you've been denying yourself proper amounts of sleep for the past five days. Having you collapse from nervous exhaustion isn't going to speed his recovery any." He nodded to them all, and swept from the room.

The nurse was still hovering about the bed, patting the pillow, tucking in blankets and generally fussing over her patient. Curtis moved over to the bedside again. He looked down at Grant. "Well ol' buddy, we'll push off. Someone's gotta work, while others lie around gittin' pampered by pretty females." He winked. "Some folk have all the luck, eh?"

Grant felt a gentle lethargy creeping over him and the aches and pains of his battered body began to ebb away as the drug started to take effect. But his head cleared as the pain receded and he remembered what he had been going to ask Curtis.

"What did Nate mean, your bookin' days're over?" He spoke slowly to avoid hurting his bruised mouth. "Y'haven't chucked th'job, have you?"

"Sure have," Curtis admitted happily. "When I saw all th'trouble you caused ol' Nate here, I decided y'weren't gonna come out t'start on my patch when y'recovered. So, I decided to resign an' come an' join you instead. After all, someone's gotta run th'show, while you an' Harry lay aroun' playin' the wounded heroes, an' gittin' bed-baths from pretty nurses."

Grant hoped he had heard his friend correctly. "Y'mean you're actually runnin' th'firm till me an' Harry git back?"

"Whaddaya mean 'till you git back'? I'm runnin' th'firm … period!" Curtis shot back. "Didn' Pam tell you? … Oh no, I forgot, you two were too busy fer talkin' when me an' Nate came in. Okay, it's like this. Remember you once offered me a job? Well, I decided t'take you up on it. I had a word with Harry, an' I'm buyin' in as a junior partner … always providin' you've no objections, that is. If y'have, there'll be no hard feelin's. I'll jes' tie a knot in y'drip-feed, an' embezzle all th'funds."

Grant felt light-headed, but he could not tell whether it was due to the drug taking effect, or the happiness he felt at this news. He looked from Curtis to Nate to Pam.

"Is he on th'level?" he asked weakly.

Springfield and Pam both smilingly nodded their confirmation, knowing how pleased he would be at learning the news that he and his old friend and colleague would be teaming up again.

"I'm afraid it's true, Brett" Springfield said in mock sympathy. "An' the NYPD won' take 'im back, so you're stuck with 'im."

Pam laughed. "Yes, it's true sweetheart," she added her confirmation. "Harry agreed for his part, like Ben said. He's a lot better, by the way. He says it's up to you to confirm the decision with your agreement."

"Well, partner?" Curtis grinned down at him. "I mean,

th'champagne an' caviar kin wait fer now. Jes' a grateful 'welcome aboard, an' thanks fer steppin' into th'breach Ben, ol' pal', will do. Well, whaddaya say, partner?" He spread his hands, the bag of grapes clutched in one, his hat flapping from the other.

The room started to fade, as Grant's mind succumbed to the strong sedative the doctor had administered. The faces around him were the last to go, standing out with startling clarity against the sleepy darkness that was closing in. He felt happier than he had for a long time. Just before he went under, he made a last effort. He tried to return Curtis's grin, despite his stiff, swollen lips, and managed his exit line with commendable clearness.

"You're fired!"

As he slipped into contented oblivion, Grant was rewarded by the burst of laughter which greeted his rejoinder.

84

SPRINGFIELD WALKED CURTIS AND PAM TO THE hospital carpark, where they stood chatting by Curtis's car. Understandably, the conversation turned to the events of the past couple of weeks, in which they had all been involved. Curtis remarked to Springfield that he must have seen more action in Rockford in the space of a few days, than he had done in the previous few years.

"S'pose y'could say that," Springfield replied. "But thankfully it looks like things'll be gittin' back to normal again round these parts. It's bin a mite hectic while it lasted, but it wuz worth it jes' t'smoke out that nest of rattlers that wuz runnin' Bethlehem House. Y'kin bet yore bottom dollar I'll be keepin' tabs on the sect's new set-up from now on," he commented grimly.

"You mean you're letting them stay?" asked Pam, surprised. "After all the trouble they've caused?"

"Fair comment, I s'pose," Springfield began slowly. "But it's like this … their church owns the property, an' it turned out there's a heap o' genuine folk in the city end of the organisation, who'd no idea what wuz goin' on out here. They didn't know their church had bin taken over an' wuz bein' used by the Triads as a front fer a major drugs operation.

"Any who were inclined to doubt it, an' there were a few, finally got th'message when Ben here got the soup kitchen vans busted, an' the Narcs proved they'd bin the main drugs distribution points fer supplyin' the street pushers, usin' the charity food handouts to the city down-an'-outs as a cover. Anyhow, they've re-organised themselves an' found a new preacher t'lead 'em to glory. This one's sane," he added drily.

"They gonna rebuild the house?" asked Curtis.

Springfield nodded. "Seems they intend to, but it'll take 'em some time. In the meantime, all the genuine members who've stayed on are livin' in the tented village they've set up in the grounds, around the burned out house. It's like an injun encampment, all that's missin' are the totem poles an' feathers.

"There's a coupla hundred of 'em altogether, most of 'em homeless kids with noplace else t'go. We've told 'em they've t'keep the place open to inspection fer health an' sanitation, so there'll be no recurrence of any take-overs from outside, like happened before." He paused and scratched his chin reflectively. "Only one thing still bugs me, though …"

"What's that?" Curtis squinted up at the sheriff through the curling smoke of the cigarette he had just lit.

"That chink who damn near killed Brett … the one the kids called Archangel Michael, or Angel One, or whatever." Springfield's faded blue eyes had gone flint hard as he spoke. "I'd sure like t'have pulled him in that night. Dangerous bastard, that one. An' we now know he wuz the Triad connection, the one who took over the sect an' corrupted it."

"Yeah," Curtis nodded, then added bitterly, "an' used that crazy Prophet bastard as his front man."

"Looks that way," agreed Springfield. "But wasn't it ironic that the preacher wuz the one who eventually blew everythin' wide open, an' led you to the chink's drugs operation?"

"Poetic justice," Curtis agreed. "Added to my brilliant detective work, of course," he added with a grin.

"Oh yeah … five years worth!" said Springfield, and all three laughed. Then the big sheriff became serious again. "Anyway, like I wuz sayin', this Angel One character's still on th'loose. Ain't showed up anywhere. We're keepin' an A.P.B. on 'im, though. An' he's the reason I'll be keepin' a twenty-four hour guard on Brett, till he's fit t'be moved to the same clinic as Harry in the city."

"Better safe than sorry," Curtis nodded. "But personally I think he's split, now his organisation's blown apart. Besides, it could be you're over-ratin' this guy, Nate. Oh, I know he's good, an' he gave Brett one helluva beatin', but that don' mean he's some kinda superman. After all, don' forget Brett wuz handicapped by bein' injured before they fought that night."

Springfield made as though to answer, then checked himself with a quick glance in Pam's direction. Curtis was quick to notice this.

"Okay, Nate Springfield, give! Somethin's buggin' you. What d'you know that you ain't told us?"

Pam had also caught Springfield's glance and his subsequent reluctance to speak, and put in spiritedly, "Nate, don't hold anything back on my account. After what that evil bastard did to me, you couldn't possibly tell me anything about him that would make me more frightened of him than I already am."

Springfield shrugged. "Okay, then here it is … I don' happen t'think I'm over-ratin' this chink, Ben. Reason bein', we did a complete sweep of the whole area outside the perimeter of the grounds, jes' in case our man wuz lyin' up in the vicinity. We didn' find him, but we sure as hell found where he'd bin. See, we found the last three of the ten dogs of that killer pack the sect kept. The other seven had bin shot by our men durin' the course of the night. But it's how these three were killed that bothers me." He paused, searching for words.

"Whaddaya mean, how they were killed," prompted Curtis. "Don't y'know?"

"Oh yeah, we know all right." Springfield nodded slowly. "An' that's what bothers me. I got the local vet t'run an autopsy on the carcasses. Know what he came up with? One had its ribs kicked in through its lungs ... leastways that wuz his opinion of how it prob'ly happened. The second one had its neck an' jaw broke – again by a kick, he reckons. An' the third one's brain had bin pulverised – by a blow delivered through the roof of its mouth! He found traces of human skin on its teeth, so I think we kin safely assume the damage wuz inflicted by some kinda karate blow. "Nope," he finished, "I don' think I'm over-ratin' our Chinese Angel friend one bit. Which is why I'm keepin' a guard on Brett, in case this one-man demolition squad decides to have another go at takin' him out."

"Point taken," replied Curtis, starting up the car. "Okay Nate, thanks fer everythin'. We'll be gittin' along ... an' I'll be keepin' an eye on this young lady here, fer the same reason. I'll be in touch ..."

They drove in silence for some time, before Pam spoke. She sounded troubled. "Ben ... do you think there's any chance of that man ... that Angel One ... being caught? I know that Jim Miller's parents have hired protection for the time being, until they decide they're safe from reprisals. And all because that terrible man got away that night, after he'd nearly killed Brett. And look what Nate says he did to those poor dogs too ..."

"Poor dogs! Hah! That's rich, that is," chuckled Curtis, trying to lighten her mood, even although the subject was anything but funny. "Listen honey, these poor dogs were big vicious Dobermans, trained as man-killers. They ate people, fer Chrissake! They prob'ly saw that Angel One guy as a Chinese takeaway meal ... a kinda Karate Chop Suey ... hah! How d'ya like that? Boy, I'll bet they gotta surprise when their lunch turned round an' kicked 'em all over the forest."

But Pam wasn't in the mood for levity. "Ben, I'm sorry, but I don't think it's funny," she persisted. "You might think I'm being silly, but I feel he'll blame Brett for everything that's gone wrong for him, and come back looking for revenge."

She half turned to look at Curtis, raised her heavily bandaged hand and shuddered as she added, "I get nightmares now, just thinking about that man and what he did to me." She sounded tense and close to tears.

"Curtis reached out and squeezed her arm reassuringly. "Don't you worry your pretty head about the chink. An' no way do I think you're bein' silly. Fact is, I think you've got a whole lotta guts, 'specially after what he put you through. You tell me you're scared he might come back at Brett? Yet you've sat by his bed fer damn near the whole of the past five days'n'nights. I call that pretty brave."

She smiled wanly and gave him a quick sidelong glance. "I wasn't really all that brave. I had Brett's gun in my purse all the time I was sitting by him ... just in case."

Curtis threw back his head and roared with laughter. "Well I'll be damned ... whaddaya know, Annie Oakley rides again," he spluttered, when he had recovered his breath. He reached out again and hugged her to him briefly. "You're priceless, y'know that! Brett's lucky to have you. I jes' hope he appreciates you. Anytime he doesn't, you let me know an' I'll bust his nose fer 'im again."

Then, serious again, he continued soberly, "Anyway, as I wuz sayin', I don't think we've anythin' to worry about as far as this Angel One fella's concerned. He don't know where either you or Brett is fer now. An' my guess is he'll be layin' low fer a while, tryin' t'save his own hide. Tell you one thing, though, if he puts in an appearance at the office, it'll be the biggest mistake of his life ... an' his last one!"

He patted the bulge under his armpit as he continued, "Me, I don' go in fer all this kung-fu stuff. I'm like you, Brighteyes. I got me a surefire, old-fashioned American way of dealin' with all them Bruce Lee fanatics. It's called a Saturday Night Special, an' it's more effective than anythin' them martial arts freaks kin dream up."

Pam smiled contentedly at him and settled back in her seat, reassured by Curtis's confidence, and the fact that he'd be part of the firm now. She felt that Brett – and she – would be safer with the added strength and shrewdness of Curtis on the team at Sherman & Grant ... or would that now be Sherman, Grant & Curtis, she wondered.

After a few minutes, her eyes began to close as the lack of sleep caught up with her, and she began to doze off. She was vaguely aware of Curtis covering her with a travelling rug, then she was fast asleep, lulled by the steady drone of the engine and the comfortable warmth of the car's interior.

Curtis, for his part, wished he felt as confident as he had tried to sound. He couldn't admit it to Pam, but he was more than a little disturbed by the fact that the Triad enforcer had escaped Springfield's dragnet, after having almost killed Grant. And that latest piece of information, that he had then brutally destroyed the three big killer Dobermans, only served to emphasise how lethally dangerous the man was. Curtis recalled that it had only been the resourcefulness of the two kids and the fortunate intervention of the trucker Jube, that had saved his friend that night. That and nothing else!

He just hoped the chink had a good dose of the fatalism that seemed to be a part of the oriental make-up, accepted his defeat, and kept his path from crossing theirs again. Only time would tell.

85

AT THE VERY MOMENT HE WAS BEING DISCUSSED BY Pam and Curtis, Angel One was standing in the combat arena in the Triad HQ of Dragon Control. Barefoot, he was wearing the white combat suit of the challenger and holding a gleaming katana – the sword of the Samurai warriors of ancient Japan.

Facing him on the other side of the arena was the current Executioner, whom Angel One had watched fighting and killing the previous holder of the office barely a week before. Clad in the black combat suit with the gold and scarlet dragon motif emblazoned on its back, he too was barefoot and armed with a fearsome looking katana, its razor sharp blade reflecting back the bright overhead lighting.

The armed guards who had escorted the combatants into the arena retreated through the flush-fitting doors, which they closed and locked behind them. The two men, Executioner and challenger, stood motionless for a few seconds, each weighing up the opponent he would now face in a fight to the death. Only one would be permitted to leave alive.

The black-clad Executioner was first to move. Stepping forward, he advanced to the centre of the arena, where he stopped and saluted Angel One with a half bow. As Angel One advanced in turn and returned the formal pre-combat courtesy, he was acutely aware of the fact that they were being observed from the spectators' gallery above. Behind the blank blue glass sat the Controller and Director, and Angel One knew that the former was there to gloat over his recent downfall, and hoped-for death, at the hands of the Executioner.

When Angel One had reported back to Dragon Control early on the day following the destruction of his Bethlehem House base, the Controller had been unable to keep the malicious satisfaction out of his voice when he had berated him for his ignominious failure, as he put it, in allowing his entire organisation to be destroyed by unforeseen enemy action.

Angel One had argued in vain that the actual heroin loss involved was negligible, most of it having been moved on, and that the setting up of a new base was only a matter of time and resourcefulness. But his argument had been rejected as unacceptable. The Controller had countered by pointing out that the loss of the street trade alone in the Manhattan area, until control and distribution could be re-established, would cost them millions in lost revenue.

Even the Director's attempted intervention on his behalf, citing his past record of success, had on this occasion been over-ruled. This the Controller had been fully entitled to do, of course. The rules of the Gold Dragon Triad being that he had the unquestionable right, as Controller of the New York area of operations, to sentence any of his subordinates to be executed for a serious failure or breach of discipline.

Further, in this particular case, not only had the Controller seen fit to over-rule his Director, but had only permitted a mere four days recuperation period to allow his fallen agent to recover from his injuries. This all-too brief period was over, and now on the fifth day after his return, the only partly healed Angel One was standing in the death arena, sword in hand, preparing to fight for his life.

But Angel One was determined to thwart his vindictive superior, if at all possible. To this end he had formulated a plan of action in his devious mind. The first move had been in his choice of the katana as the weapon of combat. On the face of it, this choice seemed suicidal. Although Angel One had been trained in kendo, the ancient art of Japanese swordsmanship, as part of his overall mastery of martial arts, he knew from having witnessed his opponent in action, that the man was more skilled than he with the katana. So, it seemed from his choice of weapon that he had handed the advantage to his opponent, before a blow had been struck.

In fact, Angel One was counting on this factor making his opponent confident of defeating him. But what the man did not know was that Angel One had also encompassed a darker facet in his mastery of the martial arts, namely a knowledge of ninjutsu, the deadly art of the ancient Japanese assassins from the Clan of Death – the Ninja.

The Ninja complied with no code of honour in combat situations. Their sole purpose was to kill, by any means, provided the end result was the death of the chosen victim. They were expert assassins, and murder was their trade. Accordingly, Angel One had drawn on his ninjutsu training when preparing himself for the arena, with the purpose of springing a nasty surprise on his twin enemies – the Executioner and the Controller – should the opportunity present itself before he was himself killed.

The formalities over, each combatant adopted the ready position, sword extended towards the opponent. Angel One's T'ai Chi mind disciplines had enabled him to subjugate the pain and stiffness of his physical injuries sufficiently for his body to operate at near maximum efficiency. At least for the short period of time he expected the combat to last.

Feet astride, knees flexed, bodies perfectly balanced, the two began circling slowly, eyes locked, watchful. Suddenly the

Executioner attacked without warning, his sword blade a glittering arc, as he slashed right and left with expert twists of his powerful wrists. Each whirring stroke of the razor-edged steel would have sliced clean through a human limb with almost as much ease as it cut the air.

Angel One leapt back, parrying expertly enough, but knowing that his opponent was merely testing his defences, seeking out any weakness. The long blades clashed and rang, their movement too fast for the eye to follow with certainty. As suddenly as they had begun, the two men disengaged, as though some unspoken signal had passed between them, and resumed their wary circling.

Now it was Angel One who attacked with no hint of warning. Once more the long gleaming blades clanged together, the clear bell-like notes of their joyous battle song sounding loud in the high-walled arena of death. Now it was the Executioner's turn to give ground, but he parried the blurring strokes of his adversary with almost contemptuous ease.

This was exactly what Angel One wanted. For his plan to succeed, he needed to create over-confidence in his opponent. He had to tempt his man to go on the offensive and close with him, sure of his superior speed and skill, because his intended surprise attack would have only the one chance of success. If it failed, there would be no mercy shown him by the enraged Executioner. The only outcome then would be his own death under the sword of his more skilful opponent.

Once again they broke apart. Again they circled slowly, eyes locked, alert. The Executioner was sure of victory now. But he was too expert a swordsman to make the fatal error of becoming careless, despite the knowledge that he had the measure of his opponent. He decided, there and then, to finish it quickly.

He feinted twice in rapid succession, right and left, his blade flickering menacingly like the tongue of a venomous snake preparing to strike. Then he used a trick from his swordmaster's repertoire. As he leapt to the attack again, he uttered a hoarse, nerve-shattering scream, the purpose of which was to startle his opponent momentarily and distract him for a fatal fraction of time. Enough time to deliver a killing blow.

But the Executioner's attack scream turned to a shriek of

agony, as Angel One seized his chance and launched his own surprise counter. Using an ancient Ninja fighting technique for disabling an adversary, he spat a tiny steel dart from between his teeth with deadly accuracy into the man's right eye.

Blinded, the Executioner stumbled back, thrusting his sword out before him in a reflexive but vain posture of defence. Angel One leapt after him, merciless as a tiger springing on a tethered goat. The long blade sang its death song, as it whirled in a gleaming figure-of-eight.

The first looping slash sliced neatly through the Executioner's raised forearms, and his sword dropped to the floor, his severed hands still clutching its hilt. The backhand slash completing the figure-of-eight sped unerringly for the doomed man's neck, and an instant later his severed head somersaulted high in the air, to bounce and roll to a stop on the mat several feet away. The headless trunk stood for a long second, the blood fountaining in a gush of scarlet from the raw stump of its neck, before collapsing bonelessly to the mat.

Immediately, the arena doors opened to admit the four armed guards. Silently they indicated to Angel One to lay down his sword, which he did. Then they formed up around him to escort him from the arena. Angel One nodded curtly to his opponent's decapitated body, completing the time-honoured ritual of combat formalities, spun on his heel and marched jauntily from the arena in their midst. Savouring the sweet taste of his victory, he did not even acknowledge the Controller's presence by so much as a glance in his direction. He calculated he would insult him more by ignoring him.

86

IN THE VIEWING GALLERY OVERLOOKING THE arena, the Controller had leapt to his feet, his face contorted with fury. "Did you see that?" he demanded, his face twisted with rage. "He cheated! He used a filthy trick to defeat the Executioner. He will face his next opponent unarmed. I will see to it …"

"No! I forbid it!" The Director's voice cut sharply across the Controller's tirade. Gone was the wheezing, genial tone he normally adopted. Instead, the authority in the fat man's voice and manner were unmistakable now. Even so, the Controller's anger made him incautious.

"But Director, he has flouted the rules of the Combat Arena," he protested vehemently. "As his Controller, I have the right to decide what form his punishment …"

"*Enough!*" The Director exploded angrily. This time the Controller got the message and fell into sullen silence. "He may have contravened the rules you devised, for your admittedly entertaining method of execution by single combat. But that is not important."

He eyed the Controller coldly and the younger man quailed visibly as his superior continued, his tone now dripping with acid, "What is important however, is that Agent Red Sixteen is most resourceful and extremely ruthless. Qualities which are very useful to our organisation."

Sensing that his victim was going to escape him, the Controller switched tactics. Swallowing his anger, although the effort nearly choked him, he modified his tone and manner to one of quiet reason and said, "But Director, with respect, surely his total failure must be punished as an example to others?…"

"His failure was not total," the Director interrupted impatiently. "The actual loss of merchandise was not so much as to be catastrophic. Mainly what the sect vans were carrying when they were raided by the police. And in any case, the circumstances were exceptional. No-one could have foreseen an attack from such an unexpected source. When his organisation came under attack from the Mafia gangsters, he did not fail, did he? His response on that occasion was brilliant, both in planning and execution. It was so effective, it will be a long time before any of the Sicilians dare to attack us again, if ever!"

The Director paused and watched the scene below for a few

thoughtful seconds, as a squad of house servants bagged and carried out the human remains, and began stripping off the blood-soaked canvas cover from the padded squares underneath, removing it for cleaning. Then he addressed the Controller again.

"A word of advice. You are undoubtedly a good administrator, but you are in danger of allowing your judgement to become warped by your obvious dislike of Agent Red Sixteen. In any organisation, one often has to work with subordinates – and superiors – whom one does not like. But a good leader should never allow his professional judgement to be coloured by his personal antipathies."

He paused to allow his words to sink in, before continuing briskly, "Now, I have come to this decision ... as far as I am concerned, Agent Red Sixteen has been punished sufficiently by having faced an opponent in the Death Arena. I am therefore rescinding the sentence of death you pronounced, and shall re-assign him in a capacity which will make full use of his special abilities. He will be given the task of hunting down and destroying external enemies who are posing a threat to the Gold Dragon Hung. He will also be used to seek out and excise weak links within our organisation, as these can be even more dangerous than external enemies. I think the Americans use the term 'troubleshooter' for such a one. In all of this, he will be directly responsible to me. Is this clear?"

"Yes, Director." The Controller nodded his assent. Then he rose, faced his superior and bowed deeply. "And I apologise for my stupidity," he said humbly. "Thank you for your advice. I assure you I will strive to be of more worth to the Gold Dragon Hung.

Inwardly he was seething at the slight to his authority, but under the eagle-eyed scrutiny of his superior in the dreaded society, he carefully kept his features blank. He knew he would have to tread very warily from now on. His erstwhile subordinate had been raised to a position of considerable power now, and he would no doubt recall how little mercy he had been shown by his former Controller. Yes, he would have to pay attention to the Director's thinly veiled warning, and be careful not to become a 'weak link'....

The Director signed his acceptance of the apology. "Consider the matter closed. Now, please have Red Sixteen sent for, so that I may inform him of my decision."

The Controller hastened to obey, dispatching one of the guards to fetch the Director's new Troubleshooter. Unspeaking, they awaited the return of the guard with Angel One, till the Director's wheezing voice broke the silence to rub salt in his subordinate's wounded pride with gentle sarcasm.

"Look on the positive side, Controller. You will be able to enjoy the spectacle of two fresh claimants fighting for the privilege of occupying the coveted post of Executioner. I have probably saved you from years of frustration, waiting and hoping for someone good enough to come along and kill the one I have taken from you." His chins and belly shook with silent laughter, as he delivered this aside.

The Controller's acknowledging smile was as brittle as frosted glass.

EPILOGUE

AS HE RELAXED IN THE STEAMING WATER OF HIS POST-combat bath, Angel One reviewed the events of the past chaotic two weeks, and reflected on the capriciousness of fate. In such a short space of time, he had plunged from the pinnacle of success to the depths of defeat. Then he had been reprieved from an open-ended sentence of death by combat, and raised to a position of great prestige and power which also promised a life of action and danger well suited to his special talents.

But despite his subsequent Phoenix-like rise from the ashes of defeat, he reflected that his fall from grace had been mainly due to the persistent interference of the private detective Grant. He recalled the final outcome of the short fight in the forest clearing and wondered if his final power-punch to the face had killed him.

Perhaps once he had time to spare from his new duties, he would check up. What if he discovered that Grant had survived? Should he kill him? Or would that not be defying fate? … the same fate that had reversed his own fortunes that very night? The thought of revenge was tempting, though …

Angel One sank deeper into the luxurious heat of the steaming water. He felt it easing his injured limbs and revitalising the tired sinews of his hard-muscled body. His mind rebelled against further decision-making. Perhaps he should continue to follow his karma and allow Grant, if he were still alive, to follow his. Should fate ever cause their paths to cross again, that would be time enough for decisions.

The End